PRAISE F...

The Weight...

National Jewish Book Award winner
An Amazon "Best Book of the Year"
A *Ms.* "Bookmark"
One of the *Jewish Exponent*'s "2017's Top Reads"

"An amazing feat . . . A great literary and intellectual mystery . . . you feel as if you're sifting through these letters yourself . . . A very immersive summer read."
—Megan Marshall, *Radio Boston*, "Authors on Authors"

"This astonishing third novel from Kadish introduces readers to the seventeenth-century Anglo-Jewish world with not only excellent scholarship but also fine storytelling. The riveting narrative and well-honed characters will earn a place in readers' hearts."
—*Library Journal*, starred review

"*The Weight of Ink* hooked me so deeply . . . Kadish, with storytelling genius, mirrors events and eureka moments across the centuries, binding the characters to one another. And an enormously satisfying ending wraps everything up while leaving enough rough edges to mimic the loose ends of real life."
—Adrian Liang, *Amazon Book Review*

"Rachel Kadish's *The Weight of Ink* is like A. S. Byatt's *Possession*, but with more seventeenth-century Judaism . . . A deeply moving novel."
—*New Republic*

"A richly textured, addictive novel . . . Kadish has fashioned a suspenseful literary tale that serves as a compelling tribute to women across the centuries committed to living, breathing, and celebrating the life of the mind."
—*Booklist*

"A superb and wonderfully imaginative reconstruction of the intellectual life of a Jewish woman in London during the time of the Great Plague."
— *Times Higher Education*

"An impressive achievement . . . The book offers a surprisingly taut and gripping storyline . . . *The Weight of Ink* has the brains of a scholar, the drive of a sleuth, and the soul of a lover."
— *Historical Novel Society*

"Deeply satisfying to anyone who enjoyed Geraldine Brooks's *People of the Book* . . . [*The Weight of Ink* is a] historical epic that transports readers back to the days of Shakespeare, Spinoza, and the Great Plague, uncovering some rich details of Jewish life in the 1600s along the way."
— *Jewish World News*

"So many historical novels play with the 'across worlds and centuries trope,' but this one really delivers, tying characters and manuscripts together with deep assurance. A book to get lost in."
— Bethanne Patrick, *Literary Hub*

"*The Weight of Ink* is my top Jewish feminist literary pick. Kadish's novel weaves a web of connections between Ester Velasquez, a Portuguese Jewish female scribe and philosopher living in London in the 1660s, and Helen Watt, a present-day aging historian who's trying to preserve Ester's voice even as she revisits her own repressed romantic plot. Both Ester and Helen are part of a long literary line of what writer Rebecca Goldstein has termed 'mind-proud women.'"
— *Lilith*

"From Shakespeare's Dark Lady to Spinoza's philosophical heresies, Kadish leaves no stone unturned in this moving historical epic. Chock-full of rich detail and literary intrigue."
— *Kirkus Reviews*

"Kadish knows how to create a propulsive plot peopled with distinctive characters. *The Weight of Ink* has enough mysteries to keep readers turning pages, and a fair amount of thematic and intellectual heft . . . Rewarding."
— *Forward*

"Like A. S. Byatt's *Possession* and Tom Stoppard's *Arcadia*, this emotionally rewarding novel follows [...] present-day academics trying to make sense of a mystery from the past ... Vivid and memorable."
— *Publishers Weekly*

"A page-turner ... [Kadish] knows how to generate suspense — and sympathy for her large cast of characters ... Packed with fascinating details ... *The Weight of Ink* belongs to its women ... Kadish's most impressive achievement, it seems to me, lies in getting readers to think that maybe, just maybe, a woman like Ester could have existed in the Jewish diaspora circa 1660."
— *Jerusalem Post*

"*The Weight of Ink* is the best kind of quest novel — full of suspense, surprises and characters we care passionately about ... A beautiful, intelligent and utterly absorbing novel."
— Margot Livesey, author of *Mercury*

"Kadish draws us deep inside the vivid, rarely seen world of seventeenth-century Jewish London, conjuring the life and legacy of an extraordinary woman with an insatiable hunger for knowledge and education. A vital testament to the importance of books and ideas, *The Weight of Ink* unfolds like a revelation."
— Kate Manning, author of *My Notorious Life*

"Kadish has fashioned a literary mystery spanning centuries, continents, and languages; a mystery of great moral stakes and elemental human desires."
— Leah Hager Cohen, author of *No Book but the World*

"*The Weight of Ink* tells of the struggle and the triumph of a woman trying to do justice to the largeness of her intellect and ambition. As audacious in its conception as it is brilliant in its execution."
— Rebecca Newberger Goldstein, author of *Plato at the Googleplex: Why Philosophy Won't Go Away*

"A gifted writer, astonishingly adept at nuance, narration, and the politics of passion."
— Toni Morrison

"Rarely have I read a contemporary novel that so immersed me in its world and drew me so deeply into the lives of its characters. Rachel Kadish is a brilliant storyteller, with a mystery writer's instinct for pacing and a willingness to take on the largest human questions. *The Weight of Ink* is astonishing."

—Carol Gilligan, author of *In a Different Voice*

The
Weight
of Ink

Books by Rachel Kadish

The Weight of Ink
Tolstoy Lied: A Love Story
From a Sealed Room

The Weight of Ink

RACHEL KADISH

Mariner Books
Houghton Mifflin Harcourt
BOSTON   NEW YORK

First Mariner Books edition 2018
Copyright © 2017 by Rachel Kadish
Reading Group Guide copyright © 2018 by Houghton Mifflin Harcourt
Publishing Company
Q&A with author copyright © 2018 by Rachel Kadish

For information about permission to reproduce selections from this book,
write to trade.permissions@hmhco.com or to Permissions,
Houghton Mifflin Harcourt Publishing Company, 3 Park Avenue,
19th Floor, New York, New York 10016.

hmhco.com

Library of Congress Cataloging-in-Publication Data
Names: Kadish, Rachel, author.
Title: The weight of ink / Rachel Kadish.
Description: Boston : Houghton Mifflin Harcourt, 2017. |
Description based on print version record and CIP data provided by
publisher; resource not viewed.
Identifiers: LCCN 2017003440 (print) | LCCN 2017010659 (ebook) |
ISBN 9780544866676 (ebook) | ISBN 9780544866461 (hardback) |
ISBN 9781328915788 (paperback)
Subjects: LCSH: Women historians — Fiction. | Jewish women — Fiction. |
Jewish fiction. | BISAC: FICTION / General. | FICTION / Literary. |
FICTION / Historical. | FICTION / Jewish. | GSAFD: Historical fiction.
Classification: LCC PS3561.A358 (ebook) | LCC PS3561.A358 W45 2017 (print) |
DDC 813/.54 — dc23
LC record available at https://lccn.loc.gov/2017003440

Book design by Rachel Newborn

Printed in the United States of America
DOC 10 9 8 7 6 5 4 3
4500716902

for Talia and Jacob

Nay, if you read this line, remember not
The hand that writ it

—William Shakespeare, Sonnet 71

L ET ME BEGIN AFRESH. PERHAPS, this time, to tell the truth. For in the biting hush of ink on paper, where truth ought raise its head and speak without fear, I have long lied.

I have naught to defend my actions. Yet though my heart feels no remorse, my deeds would confess themselves to paper now, as the least of tributes to him whom I once betrayed.

In this silenced house, quill and ink do not resist the press of my hand, and paper does not flinch. Let these pages compass, at last, the truth, though none read them.

Part 1

November 2, 2000

London

S HE SAT AT HER DESK.

It was a fine afternoon, but the cold sunshine beyond her office window oppressed her. In younger days, she might have ventured out, hoping against reason for warmth.

Hope against reason: an opiate she'd long abandoned.

Slowly she sifted the volumes on her desk. A dusty bilingual edition of Usque's *Consolação* lay open. She ran the pad of one finger down a page, before carefully shutting the book.

Half past one — and the American hadn't so much as telephoned. A lack of professionalism incompatible with a finding of this magnitude. Yet Darcy had said the American was his most talented postgraduate — and Darcy, perhaps alone among her colleagues, was to be trusted.

"Levy can help with the documents," Darcy had said over the phone. "Glad to lend him to you for a bit. He's amusingly ambitious, in the American sort of way. Thinks history can change the world. But even you should be able to tolerate it for three days."

Recalling, Helen almost chuckled. *Even you.* Good for Darcy. He, evidently, still thought Helen someone worth standing up to.

Three days, of course, was nowhere near the time required to make a true assessment. But it was something — far more time, in fact, than Helen had any right to. Only the Eastons' ignorance of the usual protocols had prevented them from laughing her out of their house when she'd announced that she required further access to the documents. She'd dared ask no more, sitting there at the dark wooden table opposite Ian and Bridgette Easton — the sun from the windows lying heavily aslant the couple's manicured hands, the towering mullioned windows casting bars of shadow and diamonds of light . . . and Helen's own thoughts tumbling from what she'd just glimpsed.

Consultations like yesterday's weren't unheard of, naturally; people sometimes turned up old papers in their attics or at the bottom of handed-down trunks, and if they didn't think to call an antiquities council they contacted the university and asked for the history faculty. Yesterday's caller, though, had asked specifically for Helen Watt. Ian Easton: the name had meant nothing to Helen, though he said he'd been her student once, years ago.

"My wife, you see, inherited a property." Easton's manner over the telephone was apologetic; Helen might not recall how she'd graded his efforts as a student, but evidently he did. "The house, which belonged to my wife's aunt, dates from the late seventeenth century. Our plan all along has been to renovate, then open a gallery in the house. Of course it's all my wife's idea—she's the one with the aesthetic sense, not me, and she understood right away what could be done by juxtaposing high modern art with those seventeenth-century rooms. Unfortunately, though"—Easton paused, then continued carefully—"there have been delays. Two years' worth, in fact. Consent to renovate a listed building is hard to come by in the best of cases"—an uncomfortable chuckle as he hastened not to offend—"not that the local planning authority's caution is inappropriate. The conservation officers are only doing their job. But, rather inconveniently, it seems my wife's late aunt spent decades offending members of every historical preservation group in the vicinity. Now that we've finally obtained all the requisite permissions, we've had an electrician open a space under the old carved staircase to put in wiring. And the fellow quit work after fifteen minutes. Called me over to say he'd found a stash of papers in Arabic and the building ought to be checked for hideaway imams or maybe terrorists, all the same to him, in any case he'd be off to another job till I sorted it. Seems he didn't notice that the papers he found are dated more than three hundred years ago. I had a look, and I think the lettering might in fact be Hebrew—there's something, I think it's Spanish, addressed to a rabbi. So . . ." Ian Easton's voice trailed off awkwardly. "So," he added, "I'm calling."

Telephone cradled to her cheek, Helen had let the pause lengthen. She considered the file open on her computer, the cursor blinking endlessly as it had the past hour, midway through a paragraph she'd no taste for. She couldn't remember ever feeling dull about her work. But this was how it was lately: things that had once felt vibrant were draining from her—and, now and then, other sparks had begun appearing in her mind as though thrown up by hammer blows. Flashes of memory, riveting—the soft thump of a shed door closing in the desert heat, smells filling her nostrils for a dizzying instant. Sparks extinguishing, thank heaven, before they could catch.

She'd straightened a low stack of books. "Perhaps Monday," she said.

"Thing is"—Ian Easton's voice attained a slightly more anxious pitch—"I wonder if you might come today. We've had quite a time getting this electrician, and we don't want him to take another job. And the papers seem fragile, I've felt I shouldn't move them."

In truth, she knew she could afford a few hours. She'd barely progressed in her writing all day, and this paper she was writing was mere cleanup work, something she'd promised herself to finish before retirement. A summation of the sparse facts known about the dispersal of the London Jewish community during the 1665–66 plague—their imported rabbi fleeing England the moment the pestilence set in; wealthy congregants escaping to the countryside; then little trace of London's Jews in the city's records until the community re-formed a few years later under new leadership. She'd not be sorry to leave the work behind for an afternoon.

Still she'd hesitated, interrogating Ian Easton for further details of the history of the house. When at last she acquiesced to his request, it was in a tone certain not to encourage romantic fantasies regarding some collection of old papers under his stair.

A brief drive to Richmond to check out some papers, then. She'd undertaken it with a dim sense that this was the sort of thing she ought to be doing: getting herself out and about on a clear day, while she still could.

As she'd settled into the car, her keys had rattled so wildly in her hand that she'd had to tame the keyring with both fists before singling out the right key. Forcing it into the ignition took three tries. Today was a bad day, then. She'd need to bear that in mind.

Twenty minutes later she'd parked her car in Richmond and was walking up a half-sunken stone path, her steps slowing as she caught her first sight of the house. Ian Easton had said over the phone that the building was from the late seventeenth century, yes, but Helen had until this moment thought the claim unlikely—there were few original seventeenth-century houses in this area, most fastidiously preserved and documented down to the last weathered brick.

But there could be no doubt that this house was of that era. Looming in the chill afternoon light, it was so unlike its neighbors it seemed huddled in silent conversation with itself. The ornamented eaves, the inset stone carvings midway up the façade of soft-cornered bricks, even the small rounded stones of the path to its heavy front door—all were unmistakable. This house's design was an obvious echo of the few remaining seventeenth-century manor houses of the area, though not on their palatial scale. Still, here was a structure clearly built in that same age by someone with considerable wealth and social aspirations. It was easy to see, too, why this building lacked the status and renown of some of its contemporaries. Whatever grandeur it had possessed in the seventeenth century, the house had clearly been brought half to its knees by neglect—and, worse, by bits of slapdash modernization: an incongruous addition to the left of the main entry, more Victorian than English Baroque; a length of degraded aluminum gutter laid amid the slate, presumably to manage a long-ago leak; telephone and power wires blizzarding the house, slicing across the strict lines of the mullioned windows.

She approached the door, her cane slipping on the irregular stones. Her breath was uneven from the unaccustomed exertion—she slowed to calm it. On a narrow window beside the door, a reflection of her own bent figure. As she leaned closer, it rippled as though on the dark surface of a stream: a pale, aging professor in her outdated suit. Tilted to one side, leaning on her cane.

She set one hand, tentatively, on the cool brick beside the window. Like a common housebreaker, then, Helen Watt leaned in. Her breath fogged the glass, but as it cleared she was able to make out the dim atrium, at first faintly but then in greater detail. She drew a sharp breath. Wooden cherubs lined the lintel above an interior doorway. More like them wreathed the top of the great room's dim hearth. The very same cherubs adorned half the seventeenth-century manors and palaces still extant in Surrey, though the name of the master carver whose calling card they'd been was lost to history.

Straightening, she took the cold iron knocker in her hand. Both —the smooth weighty metal and her thin quaking hand—were impervious to the sunlight that fell profligate over everything: the door, the marble threshold, the sleeves of her wool coat. The knocker's blows reverberated dully through the thick door and died. And in the silence —the unmistakable silence of an old house—she felt, for just an instant, the old feeling: the impossible ache of standing so close to a piece of history. A feeling like something dropping endlessly inside her—like being in the presence of a long-ago lover who had once known her every inch, but now refused to acknowledge her.

A tall, well-coiffed blond man opened the door. "Professor Watt. We appreciate this more than we can express, truly"—Ian Easton's strained greeting echoed in the dim cavernous entry as he gestured her inside, but she hardly heard him. Heavy wood carvings, a towering ceiling framed by a balcony that looked down from the house's third story, rows of boxed artwork resting on the stone floor. The smell of fresh paint.

Ian was talking, his brow furrowed. "I was your student ages ago, naturally you won't remember me." He was at least well-mannered enough to spare her the necessity of saying as much. He led her forward into the atrium, slowing his gait to match hers. "I'm so sorry we've had to trouble you, surely you have more important things to do with your time."

She stopped walking. Above her the broad lintel loomed, the carved cherubs arrayed like sentinels.

Ian stopped beside her, though after a respectful pause he continued his explanation. Of course when he'd seen what he thought was Hebrew lettering he'd recalled her expertise in the area. Really, if she could offer some suggestion as to what to do with the papers he'd be tremendously grateful, because—

Even under a thin coating of dust, the cherubs' smooth faces shone with expressions of childish wisdom.

Ian was speaking, but the house was speaking louder—the house was nearly deafening her. It struck Helen that there was a chance it might matter very much indeed how she got along with her former student.

She forced herself to bring her attention to bear on the casually but carefully dressed man stooping to address her as though still anxious to earn his professor's approval.

"The thing is," he was saying, "we've already had such a hard time getting permits. At this point, any further delay . . ."

Under Helen's sudden scrutiny, Ian faltered. Leaving the rest unspoken, he led her toward the grand staircase. She had time to take in an abundance of burnished wood, the heavy banisters and side panels ornamented at every step, and more elaborate carvings ascending the walls where the staircase turned and rose toward the second floor—but Ian led her past the stair, around its base, to a plain paneled area facing away from the entrance.

There, on a small card table beside the window, was a single cracked leather-bound volume. Beside it lay the two pages Ian had told her about over the phone: the first items his electrician had removed from under the staircase upon discovering the documents.

For an instant she allowed herself to stare at the pages, taking in the thick textured paper she dared not touch; then at the counterpoint of two alphabets on the page—the Portuguese lettering that led from left to right, interrupted by scattered Hebrew phrases that ran in the reverse direction.

Slowly she read, and reread.

Ian's voice, coming from just behind her. "Over there," he said, and pointed.

She lifted her eyes. There, in a dim corner at the base of the staircase, untouched by the blinding light of the landing's windows, was a small panel that had been forced open.

Ignoring Ian's tentative offer of help, Helen approached the opening. Lowering herself slowly to the floor, her cane trembling heavily under her weight, she knelt before it like a penitent.

She stayed that way for a long time, her hands pressed to the cool floor, and a great heaviness nearly overcame her, as though all her years had suddenly taken on physical weight. For a long while she simply stared at the crammed shelves, breathing very quietly. Then finally, knowing she should not, she lifted a quaking hand to remove a single page.

A moment only. The page, astonishingly, rested unharmed on her two outspread palms, like a bird that had agreed, for just this moment, to alight there.

"You're here!" said a ringing voice. A tall, slim woman clicked across the stone floor.

"My wife, Bridgette," Ian said.

Helen forced herself to rise and shake the smooth ringed hand Bridgette Easton offered.

They led her from the staircase to a small high-ceilinged room off the house's drafty entryway, Ian disappearing momentarily and returning with a teapot. They settled across from her at a thick wooden table beneath the room's three sun-struck windows — each nearly as tall as a man, with ancient uneven glass that turned the shallow walled yard beyond into a bright impressionist landscape, dazzling Helen's vision.

"Of course," Ian began, "we want to do the right thing."

Slowly Helen nodded.

"But we hadn't counted on this obstacle. Not after all those we've already tolerated."

There was a brief and uncomfortable silence — long enough for Helen to study the Eastons in earnest. Ian and Bridgette. Two heads of blond hair, the wife's combed and falling in a straight line to her shoulders, the husband's thinning and fine. Ian and Bridgette Easton: dressed in chic professional attire, thirty-something, faint lines about their still-young mouths and eyes. Blinking at the smells of fresh paint and sawdust, their backs to the doorway through which the dark carved staircase was just barely visible.

"When do you think you'll be able to remove the genutza?" Bridgette pressed.

"Genizah," Helen said. "And as I explained to Ian over the phone, we don't yet know that's what this is. All we know is that the documents include some that are in Hebrew. And" — she drew a deep breath, forced her voice to assume an indifferent tone — "some correspondence between seventeenth-century rabbis."

Bridgette laughed prettily. "It's a fact that there were Jews in the building's early history — my aunt always said so, and the records confirm it. But *rabbis*?"

Bridgette had the long, tensile body of a dancer and, Helen noted, the habit of arranging herself in her seat rather than sitting in it.

"We don't know yet," Helen said very slowly, "whether any rabbis lived here. The papers could have been moved from another location. As for when we can relocate the documents to allow for your renovations, that depends on the condition of the papers. They need to be assessed before they can be safely moved."

Bridgette shook her head tersely: this was unacceptable. "The Richmond Preservation Council hasn't forgotten, you understand, that my aunt refused their invitation to make her home part of their annual walking tour. We've been ready to do these renovations for over a year, but the council has made things impossible at every turn. Delays of months for the simplest approvals. It's not as though we want to change anything major"—Bridgette waved her fingers dismissively—"but apparently they're still hysterical over Orleans House getting bulldozed in the 1920s."

"Of course, their concern is understandable," Ian interjected. "We all value the local history."

Bridgette, her white blouse crisp, a sheer green scarf knotted at her neck, pursed her lips and leaned forward to pour tea. The amber liquid was loud in the silent room. "My aunt lived here alone, and she never added so much as a coat of paint to the place. There's been a preposterous amount of labor involved in making this house presentable. Any additional delay at this stage would be"—Bridgette stopped stirring her tea for just an instant. Her narrow wrist, with its delicate bottle-green bracelets, was flexed, the small spoon poised midair as though she were trying to choose the precise words with which to warn Helen against any further attempt to thwart her.

"Quite regrettable, really," Ian finished for her.

Bridgette, displeased, gave her husband a significant look.

And now Helen remembered Ian Easton: a boyish student trying to fit his lanky body at a seminar table that would never suit him. One of those affable young men from a mildly wealthy family, well-liked and serviceable on a rugby field, smart enough to suffice in secondary school but not university. Still, she recalled, he'd labored hard in her class despite his clear lack of talent.

On shelves behind the Eastons were piles of sun-faded leather spines: books that might have been valuable if only they'd received proper care, here and there topped by sloppily stacked design magazines with covers featuring monochromatic furniture and jarring abstract art. One long stretch of shelving was littered with worn paperbacks, doubtless dating from the aunt's tenure in the house — soon to be discarded, Helen guessed. Helen's upbringing among her parents' circle might have been one relentless tutorial in how to categorize strangers in a heartbeat — but she couldn't deny there were moments when the training was useful. Already she'd taken the measure of Bridgette's fading old-money family — who, Helen guessed, approved of everything about Ian, except, not that they mentioned it except when drinking, his undeniably middle-class upbringing. They'd be the sort of family that was quite liberal in word, but in deed was unlikely to stray far from its privileged roots. And gallery plans notwithstanding, Bridgette herself didn't strike Helen as the sort inclined to make sacrifices for art. Perhaps Bridgette was merely keen on the imprimatur of sophistication — or even the income — a seventeenth-century showplace would bring. Somehow, though, Helen doubted that even establishing a successful gallery would quell Bridgette Easton's restlessness.

Was it the towering height of the windows or simply Helen's own weariness that made them seem so like children to her? Ian and Bridgette Easton, seated at the narrow table in the downstairs room of their long-awaited inheritance. Unaware that the real treasure in the house might well be the very papers they were so eager to be rid of.

"I'll begin," Helen said, "with just one of the many possible explanations for what your electrician uncovered behind that staircase panel." Bridgette's face tightened. No matter; pedantry, in this case, might be to Helen's advantage. She began at the beginning. She explained how the biblical third commandment — yes, the one about *name of the Lord in vain* — had been interpreted in Jewish communities from antiquity to mean that any document that contained the name of God could not be thrown out, but instead had to be buried as a person would be buried (the Eastons' eyes glazing over at the word *antiquity,* but Helen was accustomed to this). How synagogues and religious communities, from *antiquity* onward, stored these document troves, called genizahs, until such time as burial could be arranged. How the richest of these troves contained not only worn-out prayer books and drafts of sermons, but nonreligious material: letters, business ledgers ... any document at all could qualify, given the traditional Jewish practice of opening all correspondence with the phrase *With the help of God.*

"The tea," said Bridgette. "It's too hot?"

Without raising a hand from her lap, Helen offered a narrow smile. "Soon enough," she said. As though it were the temperature of the tea that kept her from lifting the delicate cup to her lips, rather than her certainty that the sight of her trembling, tea-spilling hands would give everything away . . . that somehow the Eastons would see in that tremor not only Helen's ill health but her very heart, beating inside her as it hadn't in years.

Raising her voice just enough to be commanding, she pressed on, and Bridgette subsided warily. Had the Eastons heard of the Cairo genizah, with its evidence of daily Jewish life going back more than a thousand years, its findings still being sorted by shamelessly possessive scholars though the genizah had been opened in 1896? (The Eastons shook their heads, two reluctant schoolchildren accepting a scolding.) She'd continued, her words rapid, aware she was gaining the upper hand, aware she mustn't falter. She impressed on them the astonishing good fortune of finding these documents, be they a genizah or some other manner of collection, in the center of the house, rather than in the fluctuating humidity of a basement or the heat of an attic. Explained the durability of flax-based paper, unlike modern wood-pulp paper, with its fatally acidic lignin.

The Eastons exchanged subtle glances as they assessed her: the gray-haired, blue-eyed scholar they'd conjured—perhaps unwisely?—from the university, lecturing them about document conservation while sitting unnervingly still at their table. Hands pressed into her lap, tea untouched.

It was Ian who asked the question Helen had been waiting for, though she hadn't known in what guise it would arrive. Setting his teacup in its saucer, he lifted his eyebrows slightly as though the question were of no importance to him.

"Will you take the papers to your community, then?" They watched her.

"I'm not Jewish," she said flatly.

Their relief was so obvious, it made them seem foolish to her: the easing of those fine lines around the mouth, the hands relaxing on the wooden table, Bridgette's long torso arrayed more languidly against the seatback. Nor did she blame them. Clearly they'd assumed that her work in Jewish history meant she herself was a Jew. And now it was plain what had been behind Bridgette's warning glances to her husband. Helen could guess that in the hour since Ian had phoned her, the Eastons had had time to rue what they might have set in motion. Probably they'd been advised that the Jewish community, if it got wind of this, would make their lives impossible. She imagined the sequence of the Eastons' worries: ogling Jewish-American tourists knocking on their door, heaven forbid. Or worse, the Israelis, who didn't waste time ogling but had simply ripped those murals by that murdered Jewish writer, Bruno Schultz, out of a wall in Ukraine to smuggle them to Israel. The Richmond Preservation people might be irksome, but at least they had a sense of procedure.

Not, of course, that Jews didn't.

Helen said nothing, waiting it out. Sure enough, as the seconds passed the Eastons' relief gave way to the puzzlement that she'd come, over the course of her career, to expect. The new question dawned as plain on their faces as if they'd spoken it aloud: What was she doing here across the table from them, then? What had drawn a non-Jewish woman of her generation to this obscure life as a specialist in Jewish studies?

"Perhaps we ought to leave it to *them* to handle the papers?" Ian said carefully. "The Jews," he added.

"No!" The single word shot out before Helen could stop it—and in the silence that followed, the rest rang unspoken: *the papers are mine.*

Instinctively she rose from the table, as though to escape the shame of what they must think she'd meant—the academic pettiness, the Christian arrogance, the sheer desire to possess.

The Eastons stood with her.

"What I mean," she said, "is that these papers are yours and they're mine—the papers are all of ours, they're England's history. They belong at a major research university."

Words none could refute.

"I'll alert the head of my department immediately, and start the acquisition process. You'll hear from our librarian." Then she added, "You'll be paid, of course."

The Eastons' faces went neutral, but Bridgette's had gained a faint flush. Her husband might be too conscientiously genteel to care about the money; Bridgette wanted to know how much.

Ian's eyes met Helen's—and she saw that despite his stylish clothing and well-cared-for hands he was a straightforward man. "The main thing is to do what's right," he said. "And to get the papers out of here so we can continue with our renovations."

Helen nodded—and proceeded as though her next request were mere common sense. "To strengthen the argument for the university to purchase the documents," she said, "I'm going to ask you for three days to make a basic assessment. I'll have to do it here. I don't want to risk moving fragile papers; that's a job for trained conservators."

Bridgette looked nettled.

"You have my promise that I won't remove anything from the premises without your permission."

Bridgette glanced at Ian as though warning him not to respond.

Helen worded the next carefully. "If the university is interested, they'll ask you to bring in an outside evaluator—Sotheby's, perhaps —to estimate a price."

Bridgette's eyebrows rose. Sotheby's.

"Given your circumstances, I'm sure they can be persuaded to move quickly," Helen said. "Our archives feature a large collection from the Interregnum, and the fact that your papers seem to date from that period may be enough to persuade the librarian to make the purchase." Turning to Ian, she assembled her face into a mask of mild professorial impatience. "I *will* warn you," she said, "that inviting hobbyist collectors to come pick through the papers for second opinions is likely to not only damage the documents, but scare off serious interest." She turned from Ian to his wife, and lingered on Bridgette's clear, unblinking gaze.

"Understood," Ian said. He took his wife's hand, his large palm enveloping hers, and after a brief hesitation Bridgette pressed it with a small smile. Ian's face broke into a grin of relief. "Just a short delay until the papers go. Looks like we'll have our gallery, then?" He kissed the top of Bridgette's golden head and after a moment her smile turned genuine.

Under the blinding patterned light of the windows, the Eastons had sealed the agreement with a few final niceties. Helen could read their relief. They didn't care, in truth, whether the university or the British Library or even the chief rabbinate of Israel ended up with the documents. They'd be able to tell their friends they'd done the right thing. The Eastons had passed their own test, remaining fair-minded as their beloved gallery-in-the-making was threatened by two crammed shelves of strange Semitic lettering. They'd now be rewarded with a worthy story to relate over drinks, proof of the quixotic personality of their demanding old house. What's more, like virtuous characters in a fairy tale, they'd be granted a bag of gold as well as the fulfillment of a pressing need: to have these foreign-tongued remnants, someone else's long-dead hopes or prayers or sorrows left orphaned under their staircase, gone.

But the papers. Leaving the Eastons at their door, Helen had closed herself into her car, shut her eyes, and allowed the image to fill her vision: two shallow shelves of papers, visible through the rectangular space the electrician had opened in the side of the staircase. As perfectly packed as the contents of a small library. Folded letters, more than three hundred years old, with broken wax seals, aligned with unbound quires and faded leather-bound spines. And slumping into a gap where the electrician had removed a bound volume, one loose off-white page. Kneeling on the cold floor in the shadowy corner beneath the stair, Helen had reached out, and touched, as if her own wish to touch were still the most natural thing. A thirst that merited slaking.

A single inked page, resting on the quaking bed of her palms. The writing hand graceful and light, the ink a faded brown. The Portuguese and Hebrew words had been finished here and there with high, distinctive arches that sloped backward over the letters they adorned: the roofs of the Portuguese letters sloping to the left, those of the occasional Hebrew verse to the right, the long unbroken lines proceeding down the page like successive rows of cresting waves approaching a shore, one after another, dizzying.

IN THE HOLLOW SILENCE OF her office now, she caught her reflection on the glass face of the clock on her desk. Even blurred, there was no masking the sharp vertical lines that caged her mouth, or the taut line of her chin, or the ropy tendons of her neck that betrayed her habit of skipping or rushing through meals. The cheeks, sloping steeply from high, round cheekbones, were colorless, feathered with wrinkles. She saw her face, for just an instant, as her younger colleagues might. Leaning closer, she breathed evenly, and watched a faint fog cloud the glass.

It had, long ago, been a face that had attracted attention, if not for its beauty then for another quality.

The most truthful face I've ever seen, Dror had once said.

But sometimes truth hurt.

She turned away from the reflection; she would not indulge the fallacy of wondering what her life would have been, had she been born to a different face.

A knock on the door. "Come," she said.

He was young, tall. He stepped into the office, took off his ski cap, and folded it into the pocket of his jeans. He wore a T-shirt and a wool overshirt: casual enough to raise eyebrows, even among those history faculty who fancied themselves too modern for such concerns.

"Professor Watt?" he said.

The old combativeness reared in her. She'd long intimidated her peers as a matter of course, before the effort of interacting with them at all had become too much trouble. "You're late," she said, "Mr. Levy."

She watched Aaron Levy register her rebuke. He didn't seem perturbed by it. He had a lean body and handsome face, but that American softness about the mouth. The effect was a confident friendliness that might at any moment become a smirk.

"I'm sorry," he said. "There was a delay on the bus line."

He spoke with a slight lilt. She hadn't expected him to be so Jewish. It was going to cause problems. But it wasn't this, but something else, that disturbed her. Another errant spark of memory. Dror.

She said, "You might have telephoned."

He studied her. "I'm sorry," he said evenly. A countermove rather than an apology.

She was staring, she realized. She corralled her focus. She wouldn't let the excitement of one day turn her into a fool. Yes, Aaron Levy bore a physical resemblance to someone—someone she'd cared for very much. And what of it? People, on occasion, resembled one another.

She spoke sharply. "Do you understand, Mr. Levy, the professionalism that will be required of you?"

Surprise and indignation pinked his cheeks. Then, a heartbeat later, she watched him accomplish a willed descent into leisure. He relaxed visibly, his thin frame angling back to lean against the wall. His eyes crinkled at the corners, his face went quick with mischief. He was, she saw, a man used to getting around women through flirtation.

"I tend to like a challenge," he said.

No, she told herself—he was nothing like Dror.

"Required by these papers," she enunciated. "By the documents that have been found in Richmond. Or did Darcy not explain the situation sufficiently?"

She had his attention. Something in those eyes flickered and engaged her gaze, this time seriously—as though the smooth Aaron Levy had yawned and exited the party, leaving someone else in his wake. "Andrew Darcy said that the last discovery of an untouched genizah of this age has to have been more than five decades ago."

"Six," she corrected. "And we won't know for certain whether it's a genizah until we examine the documents."

"He said you might need someone who can translate Hebrew and Portuguese."

"I am perfectly capable of translating those languages."

He folded his arms.

"If you're to join this effort," she said, "you'll devote the next three days to following my instructions. Based on what I've already reported to Jonathan Martin"—the head of the History Department, whose cozy relationship with the vice chancellor and cherished goal of outshining rival UCL might at last be working in Helen's favor—"the acquisition process is soon to be underway. And assuming the evaluation of the documents goes well, the university will attempt to purchase them. If it succeeds, which I believe it will . . . and *if* your skills are sufficient, which I've yet to see"—she let the words linger—"I might be able to offer you the opportunity to work on these papers going forward."

He said nothing.

"Of course, that would mean delaying your dissertation. I understand you've been laboring on that for quite some time?" She waited, the provocation deliberate, though she was surprised at her own sharpness. There was no reason for the sensation flaring inside her, as if he were a threat she must at all cost repel. He was a postgraduate student, that was all—and, from the sound of things, one on a rather ill-chosen mis-

sion. Darcy had said Aaron Levy was investigating possible connections
between members of Shakespeare's circle and Inquisition-refugee Jews
of Elizabethan London. To Helen, the topic sounded better suited to
a department of English, but evidently Aaron had campaigned for his
chosen topic until Darcy had acceded. Specifically, young Mr. Levy was
looking for proof that Shakespeare's Shylock wasn't modeled solely on
the infamous Doctor Lopez—the Jewish physician of Queen Elizabeth
who was executed for allegedly plotting her murder—but also drew on
interactions with other hidden Jews of Shakespeare's acquaintance. An
ambitious and probably arrogant choice for a dissertation.

Had Aaron Levy chosen to study Shakespeare's Catholic roots, it
would have been different; that field had been blessed relatively recently
with the astonishing gift of fresh evidence—a religious pamphlet
found in the attic of Shakespeare's father. That single document had upended and revitalized that arena of Shakespeare studies, leaving young
historians room to work productively for years to come. Shakespeare as
a hidden Catholic, Shakespeare as a Catholic escape artist sneaking in
subtle commentary under the eye of a Protestant monarchy—*there* was
fresh terrain.

The territory of Shakespeare and the Jews, in contrast, was well
scoured. Other than *Merchant of Venice* and some fleeting or dubious
references elsewhere, the plays offered no mention of Jews . . . and beyond the plays there was almost no direct evidence to examine. One
might speculate about anything, of course: the identity of Shakespeare's
alleged Dark Lady or Fair Youth, or for that matter what the Bard
might have favored for his breakfast. But without evidence, claims of
any watermark of Jewish presence in Shakespeare's work were no more
than theories—and Shapiro and Katz and Green, among others, had
covered those theories exhaustively. If the reigning lords of the field had
been unable to find anything more solid, what was the likelihood that
an American postgraduate would be able to do so? According to Darcy,
the young man, for all his promise, was struggling.

Aaron's expression betrayed nothing. He offered a slow, neutral nod.

"The documents are in Richmond," Helen said, briskly now. "In a
seventeenth-century house currently owned by a couple named Easton,
who inherited the house from an aunt. The records I've seen thus far
show that the residence was built in 1661—by Portuguese Jews, in fact.

The house then changed hands in 1698, then again in 1704 and 1723. One wing was torn down and replaced in the nineteenth century, and the house was purchased in 1910 by the aunt's family—who then allowed it to deteriorate.

"It seems that I was Mr. Easton's tutor over a decade ago for a class in seventeenth-century history, during the course of which I evidently made some mention of the fact that I'd written several articles about the Marrano Jews of Inquisition Europe. Making me the only scholar of Jewish history he'd encountered in his life—and hence, all these years later, the recipient of his telephone call upon the discovery of some Hebrew writing in a space under the stair." She felt a wry smile form on her lips. "I myself had no recollection of Mr. Easton. Apparently I found him unimpressive. But I am now"—she said—"sufficiently impressed."

Two or three of her colleagues were passing down the hall. The commotion of their footsteps rose and subsided, the drafty Victorian hallways magnifying their transit to heroic dimensions. She set a hand on her desk, as though to steady something—but the pale light from the window struck Aaron Levy's brown eyes and conferred on them a gentleness that mocked her: Helen Watt, sixty-four years old. Guardian of well-worn opinions and disappointments. The paths of her mind like the treads of an old staircase, concave from the passage of long-gone feet. She felt it ripple through the solidity of her book-lined sanctuary: only the slightest tremor of memory, yet it halted her. A scent of bruised herbs, of dust. And an iron dread, suddenly, in her soft belly. Yes, Dror had had those same tight curls, those almond eyes. But how different. For just an instant, then, Dror's face was before her: his sun-browned skin, his jaw, his lips speaking, unhesitating and unsparing. *Helen. That's not true. You know it isn't.*

She shook off the assault. In its wake, a reverberating emptiness.

It was clear, wasn't it, that seeing the papers had undone her. Why else this return of long-dead things?

The soft ticking of the electric heater. A postgraduate she'd never met, perhaps forty years her junior, stood opposite her desk. He was watching her, and his concentration was complete, as though he were hearing everything: all that she'd told, and all that she hadn't.

She had not yet invited Aaron Levy to sit, she realized. "The Interregnum period," she said, in answer to the question he hadn't asked. Her voice came out more weakly than intended. She gathered herself and continued. "The first document I saw dates from the autumn of 1657."

He gave a hum of recognition. 1657. The early days of the readmission of Jews to England, after nearly four centuries of official expulsion.

"The university's ability to acquire the papers," she said, "will depend on the whim of the vice chancellor, the disposition of the university librarian, and of course on the Eastons' cooperation. It's the Eastons I'm least certain of. While a rabbi's letters hiding out under their staircase will certainly be a curiosity the Eastons will enjoy recounting over wine, that isn't the history they're interested in *juxtaposing* in this gallery of theirs. They're being polite about it, to be sure. But I've seen their sort of cooperation before. It doesn't last. And—"

"What's in the documents?" he cut in.

"The documents, as I've said, are from the period of—"

"Yes," he said, suddenly animated, "but what have you *read*?"

"It appears to me," she said, slowing her speech to underscore his interruptions, "that one Rabbi HaCoen Mendes, apparently elderly, came here from Amsterdam and set up housekeeping with a small retinue in London in 1657. As far as what I have *read*, Mr. Levy, it's a copy of a letter this Rabbi HaCoen Mendes sent to Menasseh ben Israel." She paused to let the name sink in, and was gratified to see Aaron straighten in surprise. "A remarkable letter," she continued. "Written just before Menasseh's death. Also, a leather-bound prayer book, printed in Amsterdam in Portuguese and Hebrew in 1650." She hesitated. "I can already say it's significant material. The letter alone, even if it proves to be the only legible document in the entire set, addresses Menasseh in quite personal terms, not to mention confirming several things about the reestablishment of the English Jewish community that have been the province of sheer speculation. I believe this to be a most fortunate discovery."

His arched eyebrows said *Understatement*.

She pushed on. "This finding is to be kept confidential until the university has finalized the acquisition. I've let the appropriate people know in no uncertain terms that they ought to do this and do it quickly." Though it had meant asking Jonathan Martin's help—then standing by silently as he verbally preened his feathers about the funds and political capital at his disposal. "Provided the acquisition is successful," she said, "the university's conservation lab will work on the documents, after which we should be able to study them through the library."

"So," he said slowly, "we don't have access to the papers until they're acquired and processed by the lab?"

"On the contrary." She breathed. "It seems I've obtained permission for a three-day review of the documents in situ, before they're removed to be assessed."

He looked at her curiously. Slowly, then, his gaze moved past her, to the hearth. Then above it, to the framed sketch that hung there, its lines hasty but clear: the profile of a flat-topped mountain standing alone in a rock-strewn desert.

It was a silhouette her colleagues on the history faculty didn't comment on—to them, surely, it was merely an anonymous mesa in some anonymous desert. But a Jew—an American Jew who'd no doubt been to Israel on one of those self-consciously solemn tours of heroism and martyrdom—would recognize Masada. And would assume that any non-Jewish British professor who cared to put the silhouette of Masada over the hearth was guilty of a romanticized philo-Semitism—or, worse, the barbed sentimentality of those who poeticized the martyrdom of the Jews.

When Aaron turned back to her there was amusement in his expression. Let him believe what he would, she told herself. Even were she to explain every last piece of it, he'd never understand why someone like Helen might keep a sketch of Masada across from her desk where she was forced to face it every day . . . a framed reminder to chasten her, should she indulge the notion that she might have embraced a different life. And a reminder too of the sole faith that still offered her a semblance of comfort, so long after she'd stopped believing in comfort —the faith that history, soulless god though it was, never failed to offer what must be understood.

And because history cared not at all if the negligent left its missives unread, she insisted on caring. She, Helen Watt, picked up each piece of evidence—she'd devoted her life to picking up each piece of evidence, retrieving the neglected minutiae of long-ago lives. Reconstituting a vessel shattered by a violent hand.

Still, an unpleasant sensation lingered, as if she'd just given something intimate over to Aaron Levy—as if he could somehow sense all that the sudden appearance of these documents seemed to have shaken loose in her. She kicked the feeling away. She was not such a fool—not yet, at any rate—as to be so easily unseated by a resemblance . . . nor to think it gave a stranger the power to sully what mustn't be sullied.

"Do you follow what it is that I require?" she said. "I'm in need of an assistant capable of working efficiently and to high standards."

She braced for the obvious question: what was her rush? Even a postgraduate would know that three days' time was too little for real scholarship—and that ultimately it was Sotheby's opinion, not theirs, that would persuade the university to purchase the papers. Nor could a scholar of Helen's age, less than a year from mandatory retirement, plausibly have illusions about altering the course of her career by pushing for rogue access to documents that hadn't yet been catalogued. She readied her rebuttal: it was the documents and the documents alone that mattered—and it was for the documents' sake that Helen Watt had demanded these three days. Manuscripts had lain undisturbed more than three hundred years. They awaited the touch of human hands. Now that the discovery had been made, delay was unconscionable.

Unconscionable. A clear, rational word.

Behind it, though, floated another truth. Uneasily, she forced herself to acknowledge it: the only real urgency here derived from an unwell woman's need to avoid delay. From this ominous feeling that had begun in her the instant she'd first seen the documents: the astonishing sensation that her mind—her one refuge amid all the world's tired clamor —was tinder.

To her surprise, though, Aaron seemed to have decided not to challenge her motives. "I'll do it," he said. His head tilted, he gave another lofty smile, adding, "I believe I can free up the next three days."

She almost laughed, so evident was his need to declare his importance.

Slowly she set her two hands on her desktop. Her right hand, for the moment, was still. *Enemy hands*—she let the phrase ring loud in her mind.

She rose. His eyes fell to her cane, which she reached for with intentional vigor: nor was her failing health his concern.

When his eyes met hers again, she felt his deliberate indifference.

She let him pass, then closed the door firmly behind them. He walked toward the street and didn't slow to accommodate her. Her cane sounded a hollow rhythm as she followed him, his step light, his tall frame taking possession of the hall.

They would work together in pursuit of whatever it was their lot to discover. He didn't like her. But neither did he pity her. At least there was that.

2

November 15, 1657
9 Kislev, 5418
London
With the help of G-d

To the learned Menasseh ben Israel,

It is with a quaking heart for the death of your son that I write. Word that he had been gathered to his forefathers reached me only after my arrival here in London. I am told I arrived only a scant number of days after your departure from this teeming city to bear your son's body back to Holland. I am told, also, that you are not well in body, and that your quarrel with the community here was fierce in the end.

It is my hope that as you accompany his body to its rest, you yourself will find comfort, and also renewed health.

As I am unable to speak with you in direct and intimate counsel, therefore I speak now on paper with the aid of one who sets down these words for me. I ask no reverence for my counsel, for surely you have better advisors than one so infirm as I. Yet, my esteemed friend, I have known you since you were a child at the knee of my friend your father. I pray, therefore, that you will consider my voice in this matter.

I write now to ease your heart as much as words on paper may. It is said in London that you believed your mission here to have failed. Yet it is my belief that in your days here in London you have

planted a hardy sapling. This land will yet provide a safe home for the
persecuted of our people, not in my days and perhaps not in yours,
but surely in the lives of those now borne in their mothers' arms. *So
said the old man: As a boy I gathered fruit from the trees planted by my
forebears. Am I not, then, required to plant the trees that will sustain my
grandchildren?*

I come now in hope to the very London you rebuke. I departed
Amsterdam not because I was forced to, for I was blessed in Amsterdam even in my infirmity to be supported by our community
and aided by my students, so that my poverty was no burden in that
city. Yet I chose to accept my nephew's summons and to spend my
remaining days here in London—yes, in this very community that
refused your great hopes.

Your hopes were great indeed, my friend. There is no higher
labor than that which you undertook, and the pledges you were
able to secure for the Jews of this land surpass those any before you
achieved. Yet no man can bring the Messiah unaided, no matter how
his groans and the groans of our people rack the earth.

I beg you, then, to cease your bitter regrets, which give your soul
no rest.

Your father, blessed be his memory, may perhaps never have
told you that he and I suffered side by side under the cruelty of the
Inquisition in Spain. Together we endured and witnessed what I
shall not describe, your father being summoned thrice to torture and
I twice, the second time resulting in the loss of my sight. Yet my ears
remained undamaged, and I, alongside your father, heard daily the
cries of those burning on the pyre. Do not think that all their words
were holy.

Do not condemn, then, those who heed the call of fear.

May the names of the martyrs be blessed.

If my words cut, then let them cut as the physick's knife, to
restore health. And let my own imperfections, numerous as grains of
sand, not mar my message.

My ship, with the help of G-d, proceeded through untroubled
seas to London, and my nephew Diego da Costa Mendes has
secured for my household a small residence on Creechurch Lane. I
shall spend my remaining days offering my learning to these Jews

who step so slowly in the direction of all you have envisioned for them. They have invited my meager scholarship, my dear Menasseh, because they are not ready for the force of yours. So you must know that your tenderest message of hope has indeed entered their spirits.

We are four: myself, my housekeeper, and the two orphans that I have taken with me, son and daughter of the Velasquez family of Amsterdam, both brother and sister being of good ability although the young man is lax in his studies, and it is with difficulty that I recall him to them. I venture out but little, for I have no yearning for the wonders of a city my eyes cannot see, but desire only to labor here until such day as the community may merit a greater leader such as yourself. I pray that you preserve yourself in good health until that day. I speak in the belief that anguish of the soul and of the body are but the two sides of one leaf, and I will say plainly that I fear for your well-being, which while G-d safeguards, he yet requires that we also shepherd.

My friend, I urge you. Do not succumb to darkness. Lack of hope, as I learned long ago, is a deadly affliction. And in one so highly regarded as you, it is not merely a blight on one precious soul, but a contagion that may leave many in darkness. Recall that the light you bear, though it may flicker, yet illuminates the path for our people. Bear it. For in this world there is no alternative.

If I could but offer to you the patience of the blind.

May G-d comfort you along with all the mourners of Zion and Jerusalem.

R. Moseh HaCoen Mendes

א

3

November 2, 2000

London

SHE — THE PROFESSOR, HELEN WATT — drove silently and without so much as a glance in Aaron's direction. In fact, in the twenty-minute drive from her office Aaron's questions had brought only perfunctory replies — as if she'd rethought her decision to include him in her project, and was stonewalling until such time as she could conveniently eject him from her car.

Well, if she was regretting her choice, she wasn't the only one. The farther they drove, the more it seemed to Aaron that he'd made a mistake in accepting Darcy's offer — *a small holiday, if you're so inclined, doing a spot of work for one of my colleagues in need of temporary assistance.* The request had been impossible to refuse, delivered as it was in Darcy's perennial air of wry cheer — a demeanor Aaron was certain was tattooed onto the English genome, right beside wry despair.

Though perhaps the cheer part was something one attained only after completing a Ph.D. Asking English postgraduates *How's your work?*, Aaron had discovered, elicited only some variation on *Bloody torture.* Nor was this followed, as it would have been in the United States, by an invitation to confide about his own struggles, or perhaps even go for a commiserative drink or run in the park. If there was camaraderie on offer here in London, Aaron didn't know how to access it. Or perhaps the English postgraduates simply didn't like him. In fact the absolute freedom of being a postgrad here — no classes or exams, just acres of time in which to research and write — had swiftly revealed itself to be a glorified form of orphanhood. Which was why he'd been startled to be hailed in the hall by Darcy, even if all Darcy wanted to discuss was the possibility of a favor for a colleague with *some intriguing papers to sort*. The whole exchange had taken perhaps a minute; upon obtaining Aaron's assent, Darcy had clapped him mildly on the shoulder—*Good man*—then turned to greet a passing colleague, dismissing Aaron. Was the conversation, Aaron wondered only later, a test? Did Darcy suspect just how far Aaron was from any sort of meaningful progress in his own work—and if Darcy did, was this invitation to take up a temporary project in fact the English version of dissertation euthanasia? He should have refused.

Now, as the afternoon traffic bore them out of the parts of London he knew and into genteel suburbs, Aaron couldn't escape the feeling of being trapped, carried against his will away from a duty he desperately needed to fulfill. Or was it a sickbed he needed to attend to? There, back in the part of London they'd now left in their wake, was the hidden corner of the library he'd haunted nearly every waking moment for the past fourteen months. Shakespeare and the Marrano Jews: the research that yielded nothing coherent, just tantalizing bits of information that resisted his every effort to shape them into an argument . . . and that would, in the space of even this brief absence, be cooling into unmalleable rock.

Helen Watt's car, a spare navy-blue Volkswagen, had an unprotected feel that derived somehow from the absence of either amenities or clutter. No food wrappers, no envelopes with directions scribbled on the back. No tape or CD player, just a simple radio. When he cranked his window, the flimsy passenger-side handle had the stiffness of disuse.

"The documents," Aaron said. "Are they primarily in Portuguese or in Hebrew?"

She tooted her horn at a sluggish sedan and completed a broad right turn before answering. "Unknown."

"And the house where the documents are," Aaron said. "When did you say it was—"

"1661."

He didn't do himself the indignity of persisting. In fact his desire to ask questions, the thickening of his pulse that had accompanied her description of the documents in her staid book-lined office, had died on the slow walk from her office to her car. A substantial walk, at such a pace. She did not use a disabled parking space, nor did she have the license plates, though he was certain she'd qualify. She soldiered along in slacks and blouse and unbuttoned coat, satchel on one shoulder. Unadorned, save the thin gold chain securing the dark-rimmed bifocals that swayed at her prominent breastbone; apparently oblivious to the wind that gripped the exposed back of Aaron's neck. One foot, in its ordinary brown oxford, dragging, as though reluctant to follow the course she had commanded.

He had only the vaguest idea where Richmond upon Thames was —upon the Thames, he presumed—but understood he'd further erode his position with Helen by asking. So he merely watched from the window as the stores thinned through Chiswick and gave way to homes. Those shops that still cropped up here and there had turned resoundingly upscale. This part of London seemed to be built entirely of brick, in colors ranging from deep red-brown to pale orange. A row of stately houses slid past Aaron's window, each fronted by a brick wall topped with winter-dulled moss. Pebbled drives led through the walls, inside which Aaron glimpsed ivy and climbing tree-vines, and yards paved in patterns of more moss-speckled brick. Bordering the side streets were strict lines of those bizarre English trees, pruned so the ends of their naked limbs looked like balled fists ready to take a swing at the clouded sky, should it encroach.

Helen piloted up a long, curving street lined by boutiques and small restaurants and one arty-looking movie theater; then into a maze of narrow residential streets that hugged the slope of a hill. Somewhere below, Aaron noted, obscured by ivy and the occasional tree and more brick walls, was the river.

The street where Helen finally slowed was more modest than some they'd passed, and was lined with homes—some sizable, others small —all undeniably old and all with well-tended yards enclosed in brick and ironwork. There were no pedestrians—evidently those residents who were not at work or school had found livelier attractions elsewhere. On one side of the street, incongruously, two storefronts punctuated the line of houses. One was a narrow grocery that didn't look up to par with what Aaron had glimpsed elsewhere in the town. The other was a pub named Prospero's, a small establishment with a faded black-and-mauve façade. It looked empty, despite the lights on inside—a business, Aaron thought, that could clearly use an infusion of hip.

And you *would be able to tell them how to be hip?* He imagined Marisa's bracing laughter, and it warmed him, and at the same time tightened some ratchet inside him so that he grimaced.

The wrench of the parking brake cut the silence.

Helen reached behind him and drew her cane from the backseat.

The house she led him toward was far larger than the others on the street, a fact initially obscured by the tangle of trees in the garden and the stone wall's heavy coating of moss, which felt not like a mark of distinction, but of neglect. As Helen Watt struggled with the gate's heavy latch, Aaron turned to survey the scene: a lifeless neighborhood, a dead-end street where Aaron had been sent on a dead-end mission in support of someone else's work. This whole enterprise was going to be a disaster, a distraction he ought to extract himself from at the earliest convenience. He let the wash of his mood carry him as far as it would.

Trailing Helen at length through the gate, he glanced back one final time at the pub across the way. Prospero's. How fitting. The one play of Shakespeare's he'd never understood.

He followed her up the path, her cane leaving small depressions in the withered grass.

The building was made of faded red brick—but now that Aaron looked closely, he could see what hadn't been obvious from the street: the chipped bricks revealed startling variegations, yellows and pale oranges coming through, patches of green moss or dark brown staining. The façade, three towering stories, was mottled with age. It was clear this building was older than the venerable houses to either side—and that it had once been grand. Side walls, topped here and there, with large round pieces of ornamental stonework that looked like nothing so much as upside-down pineapples, extended from either side of the house as though opening to embrace an abundant property; but the walls were truncated at the neighbors' fences on either side, giving them a forlorn, unrequited look.

Beneath Aaron's feet, a path had emerged: small unmatched stones of different shapes and shades, black and brown and gray, square and round, mortared together and so smooth with age they would have given away the building's antiquity even if it weren't for the windows that now loomed before Aaron. What was the word for that shape? Like the spade on a deck of cards, the tall narrow windows swooped in at the top and pointed sharply upward. They were tightly divided in that crisscross diamond pattern that so frustrated the view—Aaron had been inside such historic buildings, had tried peering out through such heavily sectioned glass, only to get the feeling he was trying to see out of a prison. It was something he could never get used to in England: here, sandwiched between other houses on a residential street, sat a building so obviously old he wanted to gawk. In the United States a building like this would have been preserved as a museum. He didn't wonder that someone wanted to turn it into an art gallery—though he wouldn't bet a penny on its success. The whole neighborhood seemed sunk in a hundred-year sleep.

Helen banged the knocker heavily on the arched door. It was answered a moment later by an attractive blond woman dressed in stylish charcoal gray, her smooth, shiny hair in a bun and her narrow hips accented by a mauve belt.

Perhaps the street wasn't as lifeless as he'd thought.

She shook Helen's hand with a polite nod. "Bridgette Easton," she said when she saw Aaron, and he extended a hand with an appreciative smile.

The building was cooler than he'd expected, and smelled of old ash. A free-standing heater ticked quietly from across the entryway, whatever heat it generated vanishing into the gallery above. Aaron caught a dim impression of the third story—a carved balcony ringing the entryway, wide doorways hinting at spacious rooms beyond.

"I'm glad you've come," Bridgette said. She led them swiftly across the entrance hall, past boxed artwork and a card table bearing an open laptop, deeper into the house. "I need to leave just now, but do make yourselves comfortable." There was something about her manner—a hungry energy beneath the upper-crust polish. She turned and bestowed on Aaron an appraising smile. He watched the two thoughts cross her face: That he was good-looking. And that he was Jewish.

He smiled at her again, this time openly flirtatious. She blushed slightly, and he felt amused and then dulled, as though he'd scored a victory that did not interest him.

"Coffee is in the kitchen," Bridgette said. "Please help yourselves."

Aaron followed Helen past a capacious stone hearth set in a long wall of decorative paneling, some sections adorned with simple fluted borders, others carved with intricate wooden wreaths. Their footsteps echoed in the unfurnished room. He trailed her through a large doorway to the left, on the other side of which rose a broad wooden staircase.

And there he stopped. Nothing of the building's exterior—not even the stone walls, with their once-giant wingspan—had prepared him for this. The staircase was opulence written in wood. The broad treads ascended between dark carved panels featuring roses and vines and abundant fruit baskets; gazing down from high walls, their faces full of sad, sweet equanimity, were more carved angels. And halfway up the stairs, two arched windows let in a white light so blinding and tremulous, Aaron could swear it had weight. Windows to bow down before, their wrought-iron levers and mullions casting a mesmerizing grid across the carved wood: light and shadow and light again.

Helen had lifted her cane and was pointing.

He turned away from the windows, into the nook alongside the base of the staircase, and saw the gap opened in the paneling.

It was easy to see what had happened. The electrician had simply identified the easiest way to access the space beneath the stair, and had worked open a locked panel—a small and modestly decorated section of the staircase's side wall, with a small keyhole cut into its corner. The panel, now slid to one side, was still partly visible—and to judge by the sawdust speckling its surface, its keyhole had received an enthusiastic working over by whatever tool the electrician had used to prize open the lock.

Inside, in the dim cavity, he could see papers.

"Wow." He expelled a long breath. "Nobody discovered this till now?"

Helen's voice sounded almost reverent. "This house is almost three hundred and fifty years old. It must have a half dozen hidden cupboards, jib doors in the paneling to hide the passageways the servants used, heaven knows what else."

Aaron nodded. A plain panel tucked in a shadowed corner, eclipsed by the front entrance and the distracting grandeur of the staircase, wasn't likely to capture anyone's attention.

"Apparently the aunt kept a side table positioned in front of it"— Helen indicated a small antique-looking end table standing beneath the nook's small window—"and for all we know, her own parents or even grandparents had placed it there."

"Still," said Aaron, "three hundred and fifty years, and no one thought to jimmy the lock?"

Her voice sharpened. "How closely do *you* look at what's right in front of you?"

He waited a moment. In the silence the accusation dissipated, and he shrugged it off. Something about him, it was true, did seem to make certain people angry. Certain women. He generally found it amusing.

In truth, he saw how the panel could have remained unopened by the house's various owners — how a few halfhearted attempts to pry open a locked panel could subside easily into *That's the panel that doesn't open.* If no one had the key . . . if no one had any reason to believe there was anything inside . . . ? Time and history might march on, but human nature didn't change.

Aaron knelt in front of the opening, which measured roughly one foot by two feet. Through it two shelves were visible, packed with obvious care. An archive in miniature: leather-bound spines lined up meticulously alongside the brittle edges of loose documents.

He leaned closer.

Heavily lettered parchment bindings flush with stab-sewn quires. Here and there glimpses of broken and crumbled wax seals in faded browns and reds. Had he ever dreamt this? He felt certain he had. It was as though someone had reached through the centuries with a message: *Here it is. I left this for you.* As though an ancient library had breached the border into now, into the life of Aaron Levy, who had not until this moment understood how powerfully he needed something like this.

He extended his fingertips.

"Wash your hands," Helen snapped from behind him.

He could not bring himself to look at her. He found a narrow green-painted washroom behind a paneled door. When he returned, Helen had made no move toward the documents.

There was a single loose page in the gap on the shelf. She nodded him forward, as though toward a skittish animal.

"Take it," she said.

He couldn't understand why she didn't simply reach for it herself. A test? If she thought he'd tolerate having to prove himself at every turn, there would be a confrontation in the near future. For an instant he met Helen Watt's eyes. Cornflower blue. The even features and pale com-

plexion of a privileged English face, blanched of anything he recognized
as emotion.

Reaching a hand cautiously into the stairwell, he stopped abruptly.
He checked his balance, one palm against the solid wall to his left. He'd
felt, for just an instant, alarmed by the fearsome weight of his own body
—as though he might stumble forward and crush the fragile documents, the image like snuffing out a life.

A heartbeat later, though, he'd shaken the feeling—and reflexively began to compose how he would describe the sight before him to
Marisa.

The shelves were perfectly packed, he'd write. *Like a gift someone had
prepared for us.* He moved his hand toward the shelf, and as he did so
he told himself, *Mine is the first human hand in more than 350 years.* He
touched the loose page. The paper was raspy but pliable between his
fingers. Pulling it gently from the shelf, he saw it was a letter, in Portuguese. He read the Hebrew date, *Heshvan 5420,* and he calculated the
English date: October 1657. The salutation read *To the esteemed Menasseh
ben Israel.* The handwriting was eloquent—elegant and decisive on the
cream-colored page.

It was signed by the same HaCoen Mendes who had written the
letter Helen Watt had described.

At Helen's direction, Aaron set it down on a small table positioned
beneath the nook's narrow mullioned window, modest cousin to the
mighty windows on the landing above. But as Aaron pulled up one of
the Eastons' rickety-looking ancient chairs, Helen turned him back.

"That book too," she said.

He returned to the stairwell. Reaching in again, he withdrew the stiff
leather-bound book that was next on the shelf. It was a thin volume,
the edges of the pages marbled in dull purple and black, and well worn.

The last person to hold it: dead three centuries.

He stepped toward Helen, conscious of the radiating warmth of his
own body, the thrum of his pulse in his temples. For a moment, he lingered beside the table. Then slowly, ceremoniously, set the book down.

She flicked on the small lamp, its glow weak beside the stark diamonds of light shed by the window.

The cover of the book was embossed in Portuguese. *Livro-razao,* it
said. Ledger. He opened it. Abruptly, a flurry of brown ash assaulted

him—in his face, his hair, a bitter sediment on his tongue. "Jesus!" he spat.

"Careful!" she snapped at the same time.

A fine dust clung to his lashes. His fingers, still holding the ledger half open, were coated as well—dark with the remains of now irretrievable words. Something living had just died at his hands. Tears of shame prickled at his eyelids and he shook his head as though against the dust. Then shook it again, as his revulsion with himself rebounded in an instant toward Helen. Straightening, he glared at her.

Her eyes were on the book. "Iron gall ink," she said after a moment.

Following her gaze, he understood that the damage had been done before he ever touched the ledger. The pages were like Swiss cheese. Letters and words excised at random, holes eaten through the page over the centuries by the ink itself. What remained, blurred brown ink on thick paper, appeared to be a detailed accounting of a household's expenses, the pockmarked entries clustered in Portuguese and Spanish and Hebrew, the handwriting varied. He didn't dare touch the page. Moving as gently as he could, he closed the book; perhaps something could be salvaged in a more controlled environment. He spat the dust quietly into his sleeve.

"The letter." Her voice was tense.

His words rang with petulance, surprising even him: "Maybe *you* ought to handle this one."

Her gray hair had fallen into her eyes. There was a silence, long enough for him to feel the first sting of shame. Then, her face impassive, she raised one hand in the air.

Dumbly he watched Helen Watt's palm and saw it waver incomprehensibly—the thick fingers working the air as though to spell words in some obscure sign language.

A few seconds more. Then she lowered her hand.

"The later pages of the ledger may be in better shape," she said, turning away from him, "but we'll let them determine that in the conservation lab."

So this was why she needed him. She couldn't trust herself to touch fragile documents. Was that his role then? To be her robotic arm?

She was reading the letter. Reflexively, his eyes followed hers to the aged paper. Its textured surface drew him, and without looking to her

for permission he touched a corner of the page—and felt the fine grid
of ridges and troughs, delicate and intimate as the lines of his thumb-
print. Held to the light, it would reveal the pattern of the paper mill's
screen and perhaps a watermark that might indicate, with a little research, where the paper had been purchased.

The letter was in good condition, only a faint brown haze around
each word, a penumbra of age.

They read in silence.

After a moment she turned to look at him. Without a word, he nodded: he knew it too. Not seven feet from them were two packed shelves
—and if the rest of that material had been selected by the same source
who had seen fit to preserve this letter, and if even a quarter of those
pages were readable, this could be a monumental find.

In the hush that filled the house, a new landscape opened to Aaron
Levy.

Gingerly, he collected more loose pages from the shelf: three letters
and a copy of a sermon, all in Portuguese; a half page of Latin jottings
that looked like someone's reading notes on a theological topic; something in Hebrew—a list of ritual items to be prepared for a Passover
seder. He laid the pages on the table, then pulled up a second chair
and studied the document before him, lingering over the archaic Portuguese. Beside him, Helen took even longer with the page in front of
her.

Moving very slowly from one document to the next, they surveyed
the lot.

At length she straightened, removed her glasses, and lowered them,
suspended on their thin chain, to her breastbone.

"I hadn't heard of HaCoen Mendes," he said.

Her voice was husky. "I've seen one or two references to him in
seventeenth-century sources, as one of the early teachers of the Jewish
community here after they came out of hiding. He was blinded by the
Inquisition in Lisbon in his youth, taught pupils in Amsterdam into
old age, then came to London near the end of his life. Apparently only
one work of his was ever published, and posthumously—an argument
against Sabbateanism. I've never read it. I don't even know if copies still
exist."

Aaron paused, rereading. One line drew him, his eyes tracing the elegant, looping lines of the Portuguese words. *Unlike me, you are not yet an old man. May I then offer my counsel, that your able body and spirit might make use of it?*

An inexplicable longing tightened Aaron's throat. "I like him," he said quietly, and regretted it immediately: the unguarded tone of his voice, the naïveté of his words. He waited for her to say the obvious: it wasn't his business to like or dislike a subject. But she said nothing, only turned back to the documents.

"Of course," she said after a moment, "he didn't write these himself. You note the initial of the scribe?"

"Scribe?"

"Scribe, scrivener, copyist, whatever term you use for it. As I said, HaCoen Mendes was blind."

She stood and walked through a doorway to a side room, returning a moment later with another page. She'd laid it atop a tea tray and carried it carefully, as if handling fine china. "This is the one I read yesterday."

As she passed it to him, he noted that her hand shook less dramatically now—evidently the tremor was variable.

He read the letter slowly, its antiquated phrasings difficult to decipher. When he'd finished, he looked at the other pages spread before him. There it was, at the bottom right corner of each letter: the faint spidery mark that he'd taken for a few small test-strokes of the quill. Now he saw it was the Hebrew letter aleph.

"The copyist was probably one of his students," she said. "We might eventually be able to work out who. It was a minuscule community." She paused. "HaCoen Mendes's practice of keeping copies of letters he sent does imply that he knew he was doing something significant in aiding the reestablishment of an official Jewish community in England. Perhaps he felt his records would be important to someone." She looked at her watch, and what she read there seemed to distress her. "We'll meet here tomorrow," she said. "Seven o'clock in the morning, until six. I've arranged it with the Eastons. That will be the schedule the following day as well. And that's all we have."

Aaron stood. With regret he lifted his eyes from the page.

She pulled two plastic sleeves from her satchel and handed them to him, indicating with a wave that he was to insert the letters. As he set to

work she stood, leaning on her cane, looming over him. *Like a gargoyle.*
The thought amused him and he felt suddenly buoyant.

"So our scribe is aleph," he said.

"Presumably."

"Avraham?" he mused, sliding one page into its holder with deliberate slowness. "Asher? Aryeh? Aaron?"

"We know nothing more than aleph."

"Aleph the faithful scrivener?" He grinned abruptly at her. "Doesn't
have much of a ring to it. Lacks pizzazz, don't you think?" This was how
he would save his sanity working for this woman. Because he *was* going
to work for her.

He could admit to himself only now how the panic had grown in
him these months—quietly, steadily, soft and choking like silt. How
anxiously he'd wished for an excuse to flee his chosen subject. Shakespeare, where the best and brightest went to test their mettle. Shakespeare, where Aaron Levy had launched his mission to hypothesize
and prove, applauded by every mentor who had ever said he had great
promise. Shakespeare, where Aaron had lately begun to understand that
while he was terribly good at promise, he seemed to have promised
more than he could deliver.

But this find was something entirely different. Every historian
dreamt of this sort of mother lode. No one would question why he'd
turn his attention away from Shakespeare for a little while. And if this
cache of documents fulfilled even half of what Helen Watt seemed to
expect of it, then—it wasn't too far-fetched to imagine this, though
of course it would be premature to speak of it—some fragment of its
riches might become a dissertation. A solid, unassailable dissertation.
Maybe even a dazzling one, fulfilling every bit of promise Aaron had
ever issued.

A fresh chance.

He would survive working with Helen Watt—even as the thought
occurred to him, he recognized it as a stroke of genius—by pretending
she was a different sort of person. He would act as though she were a
woman with a sense of humor.

She was looking down at him, her jaw tight.

"Joke," he said. "Ha ha."

THAT NIGHT, OVER TEA IN the chill of his flat, the heater ticking quietly by the legs of his desk chair, he wrote an e-mail to Marisa.

Hey there Marisa.

The cursor blinked at him, impassive, a virtual sphinx.

"Hey there." The acceptable territory between the risky "Dear" and the too-chilly "Hi."

How goes life on the kibbutz? Have you repented of your foolishness yet, and booked a ticket back to London to enjoy rain and greasy chips? & how goes the Hebrew? You know I can't help with modern usage, but if you ever run across a falafel vendor speaking ancient Aramaic or biblical Hebrew, I'm your man.

"I'm your man." He stared at the words, wondering how she might hear them.

Marisa. Too often he'd relived it when he should have been dissecting Shakespeare: The slow tease of her black tank-top lifting over her head. The shock of her eyes as she turned. Her hands, her every motion, as direct as a drumbeat.

Therefore my mistress' eyes are raven black. If Shakespeare had a Dark Lady to yearn for and despair over until her image wore a path in his thoughts, couldn't he? Or was something about Aaron too petty to qualify for such poetic heights of passion—was he, despite every accomplishment and award, too mundane?

Sometimes the twin thoughts pinioned him, tackling him as the water thrummed against his chest in the shower or as he loaded his dinner tray in the college's hall: that he'd only fancied himself good enough to be her lover. Just as he'd fancied himself a true scholar of Shakespeare's world.

He typed with a fresh burst of energy.

Here, an unexpected turn of events. Are you sitting? Sit. Shakespeare will have to wait, I'm afraid. There's been a trove of old documents found, from the seventeenth century. It's been hiding under a stairwell in a dormitory suburb of London through who knows how

many owners, and only now did someone think to open up the space
for renovations. And presto: History Unearthed.

The trouble is that the prof who's looking into this is an utter
bitch, a Brit of the ice-in-her-veins variety. She's invited me to be her
assistant and I can't resist the temptation, though it's going to be hell
working with her, so will you kindly remind me to keep my sense of
humor?

The first interesting thing about these papers—and the thing
that gives us a good guess at which group of English Jews left them
—is that they aren't only in Hebrew and English and Latin, but
also in Castilian and Portuguese. That probably doesn't make a bit
of sense to someone who isn't wasting her youth researching seventeenth-century Jewish history . . .

Dared he risk boring her? He could lose the tenuous intimacy that
stretched between them. One wrong move, he felt, would snap it. And
sharing the strange excitement he felt over these two shelves of documents would be like standing before her naked.

But wasn't that the point?

Hesitantly he worked the keyboard, and as he did it seized him: if
he could only bring her into his excitement, pick her up with his two
typing hands and carry her into the world as he saw it, she would know
him.

And no one had ever known him.

He laid this thought before him, examined it for self-pity, found
stores of it, and declared it true nonetheless. Who, in fact, understood
him? None of his many ex-girlfriends. Not his chatty mother, his doe-
eyed sister, nor even his rabbi father, with his rigidly benign religion. If
Aaron could persuade Marisa to feel what he'd felt today in front of that
staircase in Richmond, it would be like having her in his arms—unspooling his life and respooling it in her presence. Marisa beside him, as
he cringed in the pew through sermons that earned his father effusive
praise; beside him at the newly sponged kitchen table Sunday mornings, as he moved from the newspaper to hardcover tomes taken from
his father's immaculate library—cracking the spines of history books
his father had never opened, to learn of the deaths of entire worlds, the
sowing or defeat of ideas, millions of lives rising and falling in the surf

of time . . . all filling Aaron with awe and fear, and a kind of excitement
he knew not to admit to the high school classmates who admired his
cool mastery of all he encountered.

Today, when he'd peered under that staircase, it was as though what
he'd starved for all these lifeless months of dissertation research had
been restored to him. History, reaching out and caressing his face once
more, the way it had years ago as he sat reading at his parents' kitchen
table. The gentle, insistent touch of something like a conscience, stilling
him. Waking him to a lucid new purpose.

And to something else he preferred not to dwell on. At the sight of
those shelves beneath the stair, his bones had balked at supporting his
weight. He'd felt them waver, almost fail as he caught his balance—as
though they understood already, decades ahead of Aaron, about death.

Even the recollection made him shudder.

He took his hands off the computer keyboard, stretched his arms
high over his head until he felt a satisfying crack somewhere in the
middle of his back, then sipped the bitter tea he'd made on the hot plate.

He didn't care if Marisa was right for him. What did it even mean,
for one human to be right for another? The correct match of life goals to
ensure a few decades of life-cycle events and platitudes? He didn't care
what Marisa's toughness portended, or whether her free spirit would
scoff at domestication—he didn't care, in short, whether a man could
make a life with such a woman. He wanted to be good enough for her.
He craved the compact grace of her body, the sharp line of her cropped
hair, the soft skin of her upper arms sliding down his shoulders. The
onslaught of her laughter.

Desire moved his hands across the desert of his keyboard. To weave a
web for her. To lure her with intelligence, humor. To pique her curiosity
until she couldn't refuse it.

Are you ready for the lecture, Marisa? I promise I'll be as brief as I
can, and you'll be committing the magnanimous act of humoring
an irrationally exuberant postgraduate who needs to think through
a new discovery. Think of this as your charitable donation to seventeenth-century scholarship.

So here are a few things most people don't know. Ready? The
Jews were booted out of England in 1290 (see under: tribulations,

massacres, betrayals, the usual). And were officially gone for nearly four hundred years—although yes, of course, a few came and went disguised as Christians.

Jump ahead a couple centuries to the height of the Inquisition, and now the Jews of Spain and Portugal are fleeing those countries however they can. And some of these Spanish-and-Portuguese-speaking Inquisition refugees find a new home in Amsterdam, where lo & behold the Dutch—the practical, business-minded Dutch—offer these amazingly tolerant laws regarding the presence of religious minorities. Of course Jews in Amsterdam still can't intermarry or socialize with Christians, but hey, they're allowed to be Jews, so long as they don't try to convert anybody or foment heresy . . . and for the 1600s that's a goddamn picnic.

So these Inquisition refugees move in, call Amsterdam their "New Jerusalem," and get busy trying to revive Judaism. And this turns out to be no simple task, because under the Inquisition they've now spent generations as Marranos—meaning secret Jews in Inquisition times, who practiced only vestigial bits of the religion, and even then at risk of death. ("Marrano" was the Spanish word for "pig." Pretty much sums up Catholic Spain's view of Jews.) But now that they're safe in Amsterdam, these until recently secret Jews are so intent on being Good Jews—that is, practicing their faith and reeducating everybody and not making waves with the local populace—that they not only prioritize Jewish education, but suppress dissent, impose rigid social order . . . and give the young Spinoza, who grew up in their ranks, their biggest, most badass excommunication. Never mind the temporary excommunications they usually meted out to troublemakers. These Jewish leaders in Amsterdam banned Spinoza for life and forbade all Jews to have any contact with him, just to make sure nobody would think Amsterdam's Jews were encouraging religious upheaval.

They were, the record shows, just a wee bit intense.

And also kind of messed up in a predictably tragic way. I'll skip the details of all the pleasant things the Inquisition did in those days. But in Amsterdam these traumatized Spanish and Portuguese Inquisition refugees now looked down on the eastern European Jews they met—Polish Jews fleeing pogroms—and wouldn't let them marry into their community or even be buried in their cemetery. Not only that, the Spanish and Portuguese Jews still considered Iberian languages and culture to be the gold standard for sophistication ... which goes to show how the Stockholm Syndrome works. They might have spoken Dutch with non-Jews, but they used Portuguese for daily life and Castilian (medieval Spanish) for anything more formal.

And that's where I'm lucky ... because in addition to the far-too-many years of Hebrew and Latin under my belt, I happen to have a solid reading knowledge of Portuguese, helped along by a semester I spent bumming around Brazil, and I can get by in Castilian.

Am I boring you yet?

You know, some women find pompous son-of-a-bitches a turn-on.

(You will note I don't hold that comment against you. Though I should.)

A comment she might not even remember making, so little he meant to her. While his thoughts bent irresistibly. Her jet-black cropped hair, her tank-top lifting over her head, the muscles of her back lengthening as her arms reached for the ceiling—he hadn't guessed a woman's back could be so beautiful, could humble him with its strength. And had Shakespeare at least had the pleasure of a substantial affair with his Dark Lady, if there ever even was such a woman—or had he, too, wasted sweat and ink and solitary hours in a dark bedroom on a woman he'd slept with only once?

So if you're even still reading, if you haven't yet deleted me from your inbox for the length of this thing, you might guess that the people who wrote those papers found under the stairwell were Portuguese Jews, and from Amsterdam. And the thing is, they also knew Menasseh ben Israel. He was one of the most famous of the Portuguese Jewish rabbis in Amsterdam. The guy was respected not only among the Jews, but by Christians too—he was in with both Rembrandt and the queen of Sweden, a big deal for a Jew.

Now imagine this: Menasseh's day is a big time for all kinds of desperate messianic thinking. Plenty of eyes are peeled for the Messiah—even Christian scholars have definitively declared that 1666 is going to be the year the big one comes back. And famous, well-connected Menasseh ben Israel is sitting there in Amsterdam in the 1650s and thinking about bringing the Messiah, and also thinking about all the tortured Jews in Spain and Portugal and even the tortured Jews in Poland and Russia who need safe haven. And he hears a rumor that the lost tribe of Israel has been found in Brazil: Jews! In the Americas! And he remembers the prophecy that Jews have to be present in all corners of the world in order for the messiah to come.

And in all the known world of that time, guess which country is the only one with officially no Jews?

Bingo. Now you can guess where all this is heading.

So old Menasseh approaches Oliver Cromwell, who's now won the English Civil War. And he tells Cromwell it's time to bring the Messiah by letting the Jews into England. And despite difficulties I won't go into because your eyes are surely already glazing over, Cromwell decides he likes the idea. At this point it's an open secret that there already are Jews in London, about twenty families of extremely successful merchants—they claim to be Catholics but keep a rudimentary Jewish practice in secret. So whether it's because Cromwell just wants his England to benefit by welcoming prosperous merchants, or because he thinks he might use his Jews with their ships and their connections in Europe's ports to collect intelligence . . . or else maybe because he honestly does believe it's going to hasten the messianic age . . . Cromwell agrees to let Jews live in England. He can't do it officially—try though he may, he can't get Parliament to agree to welcome the Jews. But he does it sort of semi-officially.

Of course, public opinion immediately turns ugly. The local English merchants raise a fuss at the prospect of competition from some imagined Jewish influx, and the usual anti-Semitic rumors circulate: the Jews are buying St. Paul's Cathedral for the sum of one million pounds . . . the Jews are coming to use the blood of Christian children in their Passover feasts. Poems were circulating about how Cromwell, before executing Charles I, had befriended the Jews because it was only natural that someone who wanted to crucify his king would want to take lessons from those who crucified the savior.

So now, politically speaking, Cromwell can't approve any substantial Jewish immigration. But he gets as far as letting the hidden Jews who are already in London be officially and openly Jewish . . . as long as they're not too blatant about it, and don't invite hundreds of their Jewish cousins to join them in London.

Given that the last time we Hebes had been in England, the locals had taken to massacring us as calisthenics to warm up for the Third Crusade, stepping out as Jews must have seemed a dubious proposition. But bit by bit these London Jews start being more public about their religion. Meanwhile, though, Menasseh ben Israel has a big falling out with them. He doesn't think the Jews are being bold enough about outing themselves, and he keeps trying to push Cromwell for fuller official acceptance. But the Jews of London don't want him to do it—the Inquisition is still going on, remember, and even though London's Jews are themselves safely out of Spain or Portugal, plenty of them lost family members to the Inquisition. They know just how bad things can be. And they've been living under cover in London just fine, thank you. Sure, they're grateful to Menasseh that they've now got permission to be openly Jewish, but they don't want to take instructions from some naive rabbi who spent most of his life in tolerant Amsterdam. They want him to stop pushing before he brings trouble down on their heads.

Menasseh ben Israel insists, he tries to get Cromwell to press forward, and he can't get anyone to budge. For all his effort, no expanding English Jewry, no Messiah, nada. Failure.

Then Menasseh ben Israel's son, who had traveled to London with him, dies. Menasseh goes back to the Netherlands. And then he himself dies there a couple months later, at the age of fifty-three.

Oh yeah—and Cromwell up and dies right after this. So much for any guarantees of safety. At which point the gears start turning for the monarchy to return, and things start to look dicier again for the Jews.

So now here's why I've recited this whole interminable history, Marisa (and no, it's not just because I had to memorize this stuff for my undergrad comps). Today, this afternoon, I literally had my hands on two letters sent from an obscure rabbi to old Menasseh ben Israel himself, reporting on the London community's progress and urging Menasseh not to give up hope. And they're not just dry stuff, Marisa.

I read one and I have to say, I felt I was in the room with the guy who wrote it. I liked him.

So there's the history. But there's another complicating factor: the documents are written in iron gall ink. This ink is such a fucking headache, Marisa. It's the kind everybody used after they moved over to the soot-based stuff. Some varieties stay stable for centuries, and some batches eat through paper — and nobody knows why, because nobody knows exactly how iron gall ink was made. But the effect is bizarre and totally unpredictable. Say a man 300 years ago sat down to write a letter, and let's say the ink that happened to be in his ink-bottle when he started was a good batch . . . now, 300 years later, what he wrote on the first page of the letter is readable, maybe just a bit blurred. But when he got to page two of the letter, let's say he started a new bottle of ink, and this one was a bad one. So 300 years later half of the words written in that ink will have eaten through the paper. Single letters can get spliced out of the paper. Entire words or phrases can just dissolve themselves out of the letter, especially where the writer maybe lingered over a word (dripping extra ink) or wrote with a heavier hand to place added emphasis. If he let a blot form on a word . . . 300 years later the acids may have excised that word and only that word.

I opened a ledger this afternoon, not knowing it was completely deteriorated inside, and the whole thing blew up in my face. I had paper ash in my eyelashes. Professor Ice Queen looked like she was going to behead me with her fountain pen.

He stopped and reread by the faint light of the screen. His e-mail showed nothing of where he had hesitated — not where the clock had ticked as his hands lingered on the keyboard, not the unaccustomed indecision that made him drag his mouse back over entire blocks of text and click them into oblivion. His incapacitating, shameful yearning ate through nothing that was visible.

So there you have it: we dive into the papers beginning tomorrow. A side trip into the late seventeenth century, a little breather from the Shakespeare work, which will probably enrich my approach to the dissertation when I return to it. Darcy, my advisor, seems pleased.

Now write back and tell me all the clever and naughty things you've been up to, far from dusty libraries and nasty old English-women, out there in the Promised Land where the men and women are bold and brave, and even shitty airline food, traffic jams, and taxes are good for the Jews.

—A.

He pressed Send, and regretted it.

4

November 22, 1657
16 Kislev, 5418
London
With the help of G-d

To the esteemed Menasseh ben Israel,

Word reaches us here in London that you have traveled as far as
Middleburg but are unwell.

In the days that remain to me I shall not attain your level of
scholarship. I am unable to open for myself the doors of holy books,
but must wait for a student to read their precious words aloud. Yet I
will presume to speak to you once more. I have not told you, nor shall
I, of all your father endured at the hands of the Inquisitors in Lisbon.
You do not need to be told, for you have ever understood, and willingly labor on behalf of our people. Yet it is not required of you to
bear on your own shoulders the burden of hastening the Messiah's
arrival, when we will throng to greet him with tears in our eyes.

Unlike me, you are not yet an old man. May I then offer my
counsel, that your able body and spirit might make use of it? The
spark of your learning is still needed by the people. And, my son, if it
is extinguished, even the blind will feel the darkness deepen.

I beg of you to rest, to seek healing of the spirit and healing of
the body.

Our life is a walk in the night, we know not how great the

distance to the dawn that awaits us. And the path is strewn with
stumbling blocks and our bodies are grown tyrannous with weeping
yet we lift our feet. We lift our feet.

   With the help of G-d,
   R. Moseh HaCoen Mendes

א

5

November 3, 2000
London

A BRITTLE LIGHT STRETCHED ACROSS THE dark tabletop, across the manuscripts before him. Seated under the tall
windows of the shelf-lined room the Eastons had turned over
to them—the house's old library, by the look of it—Aaron rubbed his
hands together for warmth. The Eastons hadn't provided a heater, and
the house's great hearths were in other, grander rooms. No wonder people had died young in the seventeenth century, he thought. Shivered to
death, probably, in drafty rooms like this.

Outside, a dusting of snow.

Helen Watt sat opposite him, a separate set of documents laid before
her, writing in pencil on a notepad. Upon Aaron's arrival, nearly on time
despite the sluggish bus, she'd greeted him with only a pointed glance at
her wristwatch—and, as he'd spread notebook and papers around him,
a cluster of facts: the records Helen had tracked down so far showed
that the HaLevy family, to whom the house had belonged for a period
of thirty-seven years, were Portuguese Jews who had arrived in London
around 1620. The family also seemed to have owned a substantial house
back inside the walled city of London. Possibly they'd used the Richmond house as a country residence—in those days London was defined
by the City walls and Richmond was the countryside, a half day's ride by
coach or a slow trip up the Thames.

Other than that update and rapid instructions regarding which
documents to start with (evidently she'd decided to trust his skills as a
translator for the moment), Helen Watt had said not a word to Aaron
in more than an hour—nor had she inquired whether he himself had

troubled to do any outside research. Well, if she wanted to underestimate him, let her; he'd intended to tell her straightaway about the connection he'd discovered, but maybe he'd pick his own time to raise the subject.

He surveyed the pages before him now. He'd chosen the best preserved of the first batch to begin with, and had made quick work of six documents, one each in Hebrew and English and four in Portuguese. Quick consultations with online resources had aided him past a few rough spots in the translations, and he was pleased with his progress, despite the stern looks Helen shot every time he turned to his computer. Bridgette had breezed by to set up a web connection for him, leaning past him at the table, her wrist brushing his as she typed in her password. He'd felt Helen Watt watching keenly then, too, and had laughed inside at the iron weight of her gaze.

The document Aaron had just begun translating was a sermon, recorded in the same elegant sloping hand, the same aleph scratched at the bottom. He was beginning to feel a camaraderie with this Aleph —who had probably been trapped day after day in some chilly room like this one at the rabbi's household inside the City walls—working hours on end, inked quill in his cramped hand. Slaving away to do the boss's will.

He chuckled aloud, and pretended not to notice when Helen's head jerked up from her work.

Opening a new file on his laptop, he began the translation. *Upon the Death of the Learned Menasseh ben Israel,* the sermon was titled. Below that: *by Rabbi Moseh HaCoen Mendes, to be read aloud to the congregation.* The sermon was several pages long, and where some words had been crossed out and rewritten the ink damage was heavy. Nonetheless, Aaron found he could make his way through the text. *The people of Israel gather in sorrow today . . . God will comfort the mourners . . .* Slowly he typed the words into his computer, platitudes he recognized from his own father's sermons. There was more substance here, of course, including a heartfelt tribute to Menasseh: *The learned Menasseh ben Israel was a man who carried in his soul the knowledge of his father's torment in Lisbon at the hands of the wicked . . .*

Following this prelude, the sermon turned from praise to careful persuasion—true to the form, Aaron noted. He'd heard enough ser-

mons in his life to consider himself a bit of a specialist in the genre. As a
boy he'd even whispered made-up bits of sermons before the bathroom
mirror, emulating his father's measured delivery and envisioning the day
when he'd surprise his father with the information that he too (in Aaron's youthful imaginings he'd be grown, a university student, magically
transformed, every awkwardness vanquished) was going to take a pulpit.
That vision had lasted until one Sunday morning when Aaron had come
upon his father sitting at the breakfast table, already clean-shaven and
reading the news—a sight Aaron had seen every week of his life, yet
this time he understood it in a sudden fever of adolescent indignation:
his father, shaking the spread newspaper into amiable submission before
reaching for his coffee, wasn't sifting the day's news for any fresh truth,
but simply for material that confirmed his own stance. The congregation
—suburban, Reform—expected sermons that sampled the world and
revealed threats worthy of a frisson—worthy perhaps of an uptick in
charitable giving, perhaps a few evenings' volunteer work. But not panic.
Sermons that revealed the world as perhaps arduous, but never without
mercy.

Read the newspaper, Aaron's father liked to say, *you'll grow to be an educated man.* Aaron had taken the advice to heart. And had read enough,
by age fourteen, to see that his father's safe sermons bore no resemblance to the sheer bloody courage the world required.

Neither, to be honest, did Aaron's own petty teenage cowardice; his
tendency to split hairs when what was required was action; his tendency
to inflate personal slights—in the classroom, on the playing field, with
the girls he dazzled and then bewildered. Not that any of that seemed
to hinder him: he was the high school smartass goading teachers while
his classmates guffawed. He was the college freshman who didn't miss
a beat when his Modern American History TA took him aside with the
air of one delivering a painful but necessary blow: *I understand no one
offered to partner with you for your research project. It might help, Aaron, if
you'd "get rid of that smirk"*—the TA making air-quotes on pronouncing
the last words, to show Aaron that he was only repeating a complaint
made by fellow students. (It might have helped, Aaron had thought, if
he'd actually *wanted* a partner.) An ex-girlfriend, in a bitter outburst she
obviously hoped would wound Aaron, had even called him Teflon Man.

But sometimes when he talked about history his voice cracked.

He gave himself credit for not waging war in his father's home—if only because his father's cheerleading brand of Judaism never seemed worth the melodrama of a fight. Instead he'd quietly turned his back on the version of manhood he'd been groomed for. And in the place of religion and all that went with it—community, party line, family —he'd set history: the one thing that struck Aaron Levy as worth being humble for.

He made his way slowly now through the dense Portuguese of Rabbi HaCoen Mendes's sermon. As he translated, he could feel the words attempting to corral the listeners into considering their own priorities.

> The labor Menasseh ben Israel gave his life to, as surely as the
> martyrs still give their lives in the flames of the Inquisition, is of
> a breadth and depth that will sustain the most weary soul. Do
> not consider then, however learned you are, that your knowledge
> is complete. For learning is the river of G-d and we drink of it
> throughout our lives.

Though the vocabulary and substance could not have been further from the sermons Aaron's own father delivered, this one was clearly heading for a familiar destination. Educate your children. Join the Temple Brotherhood. Donate.

> Ignorance is now your great enemy, and I do none any favor by
> flattering you that you are not ignorant.

Now there was a sentence Aaron's own father would never have dared speak to his own self-satisfied congregants.

> Being Jews now in the light of day, you may wish a rapid remedy for
> your ignorance. Glimpsing the void in your souls, you will by nature
> wish for that which will fill it at once. It is from this wish that you
> must be on your guard, and discern the light of true learning from
> the false. There will be those who would sell you false knowledge and
> promise ready redemption. Yet it is only G-d who chooses the time
> of His revelations, and when He brings us to the world to come it
> will be sudden and not of our planning. It is not G-d's will, nor was

it that of Menasseh ben Israel, may his memory be a blessing, that
Jews should wager on the Messiah as dicers will, but rather that we
labor steadily and humbly all our days.

The sermon ended there. No phrases to soften the message, no consolation. Only this stark warning.

Aaron reread, impressed. Was HaCoen Mendes trying to inoculate
his listeners, as early as 1657, against the quickening spread of false-messiah hysteria? At that date Sabbatai Zevi, the most devastating of the
messiah-imposters, whose delusional claims would roil Jewish communities throughout Europe, had yet to build his enormous following. But
perhaps HaCoen Mendes had already heard rumor of Sabbatai Zevi's
rise and was beginning to develop the counterarguments that he'd later
lay out in more sophisticated form.

It would interest the scholarly community, this one.

He saved the file in which he'd translated the sermon and turned
to the next document in his pile. The ink damage was heavy, the English handwriting halting, with some strike-outs where the writer had
reconsidered his spelling. At the bottom of the last page, the initial
aleph. Clearly Aleph was less comfortable in English. Stood to reason,
if Aleph, like the rabbi, had arrived in England only a few months before writing this.

Aaron began reading from the beginning.

Upon the Death of the Learned Menasseh ben Israel, it began. He read
the first lines and saw that it was merely a translation of the Portuguese
sermon. Good—he could compare it to his own translation later, see
how his Portuguese scored against Aleph's English. *Me and you, Aleph,*
he thought. A friendly translation-smackdown across three and a half
centuries. Relieved and suddenly hungry, he stood, pushed his chair far
from the table, and stretched for the ceiling with an ostentatious yawn.

Helen looked up.

"Lunch break," he said. He took his sandwich from his bag and settled on a chair in a corner, away from the table where the documents
were spread.

Dropping her glasses to her breastbone, Helen blew out a long
breath.

"What did you find?" she said.

He unwrapped his sandwich. "First, two letters in Portuguese, addressed to HaCoen Mendes. One regarding books he'd asked to have sent to him from a bookseller in Amsterdam. The other telling HaCoen Mendes about a student who will be coming to study with him and proposing a weekly fee. After that, something in English, a bill for a purchase of candles." He bit into his sandwich and chewed.

"What books did HaCoen Mendes order?"

"*The Path of Knowledge,* which seems to have been a commentary on the Midrash. And Montaigne. *Essais.* In French."

Helen raised her brows.

"Then there was a bill for some volumes of Talmud from the Hebrew press in Amsterdam, and then a small ledger for the rabbi's household in London, this one in decent condition, containing records for about a fifteen-month period — 1657 to 1659. Food, sea coal and firewood, writing supplies — sounds like the rabbi ran a small household with fairly modest expenses, other than the books."

She nodded thoughtfully.

"Quite a contrast with a house like this." Aaron paused, craning his neck for a moment to look at the paneled ceiling. "I wonder what it's like upstairs. How many bedrooms, how luxurious. It might help to learn a bit about how the HaLevy family lived." Setting aside his sandwich, he stood. "I'll just run up and see how many rooms they have up there."

She didn't budge. "You can't go up without the Eastons' permission," she said.

How could she sit and not move a muscle, when her curiosity must be piqued? A simple look upstairs would at least give them a sense of how spacious the rooms might have been, how the people who stored away these papers might have lived. Yet Helen Watt's posture was rigid, her hands planted firmly beside her dark slacks on the wooden seat.

Have it her way, then. He'd go upstairs on his own some other time, when he could get her out of his hair.

She was looking at him suspiciously. "Those are the rules," she said.

Goddamn Brits.

"And of course, the rooms probably look nothing like they did in the seventeenth century."

He didn't respond. Let her try to penetrate *his* silence for a change. He returned to his seat and made a show of imperturbability.

"Anything else of note in the ledger?" she said.

He let her wait a long moment. "What surprises me," he said, "is how vague it is about the income of HaCoen Mendes's Creechurch Lane household, given how meticulously it records expenses. There's no list of the names or the tuition payments of his students. There's a category for 'contributions'—I'm guessing that could be the income from HaCoen Mendes's teaching—but it feels almost deliberately obscure. Given that Cromwell had made the Jewish community's presence officially legal, I'd think they might have started to let go of their caution."

She was shaking her head. "Then you haven't been paying attention."

He let out a short, irritable laugh.

"You're American," she said simply. "You think straightforwardness is a virtue."

A muttered curse escaped him, but she spoke steadily over it. "I don't mean that as an insult, Mr. Levy. It's merely a fact. English people usually make the same mistake. Truth-telling is a luxury for those whose lives aren't at risk. For Inquisition-era Jews, to even *know* the truth of one's Jewish identity could be fatal. Someone detects Jewishness in the way you dress, in your posture, in your fleeting expression when a certain name is mentioned—well, even if there's nothing they can do to you in England except perhaps expel you from the country, still, months later your relatives back in Spain and Portugal might be arrested and die gruesome deaths." She'd stiffened. It occurred to Aaron that she was angry, but not at him. "The Anglo-American idea of noble honesty, Mr. Levy"—she stopped herself, then fell silent, as if performing some inner calculation. Evidently he wasn't worth the risk of whatever she'd thought to say next.

"What else?" she said.

She'd just stayed her hand from something. He didn't know what. He decided he didn't care. "There's a sermon," he said. "HaCoen Mendes wrote it for someone else to deliver, on the death of Menasseh. It contains an argument against false messiahs."

She sat forward in her chair.

"But before I tell you about the sermon," Aaron said, savoring the sudden sharpening of Helen Watt's focus, "I should tell you that just this morning I happened to do some of my own research on Rabbi HaCoen Mendes." He continued, his voice nonchalant. "As you know, despite being an influential teacher HaCoen Mendes was limited enough by his blindness that he published only that one text of his own —his pamphlet titled *Against Falsehood*, printed posthumously in London by an admirer." He'd begun his delivery slowly—but as he went on his excitement carried him. "It took a little work to track down the actual text online, but I did. And actually, it's quite something." In fact, HaCoen Mendes's pamphlet was probably the best contemporary reasoning Aaron had read against mass hysterias of the late seventeenth century. The argument was lucid, solidly constructed, even poetic at times in its warning against the temptations of false messiahs. The entire text of it had been appended to the brief article Aaron had found after a long search—the only scholarly article that seemed to exist about HaCoen Mendes. The article, written decades ago by an obscure scholar, had touched on HaCoen Mendes's tribulations under the Inquisition, praising *Against Falsehood* and comparing it favorably to less forceful anti-Sabbatean arguments of its day. It was surprising, the scholar noted parenthetically, that a writer of that caliber should have produced no other published works.

But it was the pamphlet's dedication that had leapt out at Aaron.

"That pamphlet HaCoen Mendes wrote?" he said to Helen Watt now. "It was dedicated to Benjamin HaLevy."

She said nothing.

"The same Benjamin HaLevy," he persisted, "who once owned this house."

Her eyebrows rose: was he under the impression she'd failed to catch that connection?

But he could see her thinking. And he could see *what* she was thinking: now they knew how the documents had most likely gotten here. Benjamin HaLevy must have been a patron of the rabbi's, and would naturally wish to collect and preserve his papers.

Helen gave a thoughtful nod. "And what's in this sermon you just read, on the occasion of Menasseh's death?"

"It is not God's will," Aaron quoted, *"that Jews should wager on the Messiah as dicers will."*

She actually smiled, a gossamer smile so innocent, a person could imagine she had once been nicer. "That's a real find. So HaCoen Mendes was already cautioning against false messiahs in *1657*. How long is the sermon?"

"Four pages," Aaron said. "And then there's another copy of it in English—maybe they translated it for the younger generation growing up in London."

"Make sure to read through all of the English," she said.

"Sure, but it's just a translation."

She sat straighter. "Didn't you hear what I said about these people? They might have written different things in Portuguese than they did in English."

You and me, Aleph, he thought. *Except your boss wasn't a witch.*

He took a large bite. He chewed, enjoying it. Clearly his sandwich made her cross.

"When is Sotheby's coming?" he asked. Sotheby's made her cross.

"Tomorrow," she said.

They sat: he chewing, she waiting for him to finish. A parody of a companionable lunch hour. "So tell me," he said, his affect neutral. "How did you come to history?"

She wasn't fooled by his attempt to soften her. Still, she sat in silent consideration as though the question had been sincere. Facing the window, she sucked in her cheeks, a gesture he'd noticed she made when thinking. Calculating, again, whether he was worth a response.

A bitter humor took over her face. She said, "I was forced to it."

October 2, 1657
15 Heshvan, 5418
The English Channel

H OW BRILLIANT THE MOON. Its sharp disk shedding a halo against the high black sky. A moon so bright it seemed impossible it made no sound.

Every weathered board of the deck plain in the marble light. Every wavetop aglitter. Every trough bottomless, rushing with the truth of the unthinkable chill below. The sails bellying overhead, their severe shadows rocking with the motion of the ship. Black, white, black. The shadows crossing and recrossing her slim fingers as they lay still on the rail.

A night waiting for someone but to pronounce what was already evident.

Swathed in blankets on a low bench beside the rail, the still form of the rabbi seemed to float like the foam on the sliding waves, his white beard and pale face rising and falling on each breath of the ocean.

Beyond them, nearly lost in the shadows near the ship's prow, her brother stood silent. Not a word to her since their departure from Amsterdam. As though he had determined to leave some last shred of softness behind, and a mere glance at her face could undo his resolve.

The water clapped hollow against the prow and the vessel slipped under the fine pricking of the stars, toward a dark solidity on the horizon.

England.

A sickening hope, like a gall in her stomach.

November 4, 2000
London

H ELEN WAS STIFF WITH CHILL. The thick sweater she pulled tighter around her shoulders was little help, and the small heater she'd brought with her didn't seem to reach this side of the library. But the tall windows here provided the best light.

All afternoon, Bridgette had made it her business to pass by the room in her high-heeled boots and a multi-hued green scarf of dizzying intensity, inquiring yet again into their progress or enunciating solicitously over the phone words Helen was clearly meant to hear: "I'm *awfully* sorry I had to change the plan, but the schedule has gone into someone else's hands. I sincerely hope this delay doesn't make a mess of the whole project." Ian might have been cowed by Helen's insistence on three days' reading to persuade the university to make the purchase; not so Bridgette. Today was to be Helen's final day with the papers, and Bridgette had made known that it would end early: Sotheby's was due at the Eastons' in late afternoon to begin assessing the manuscripts.

That morning, before leaving for Richmond, Helen had called Jonathan Martin's office once more to check on his progress. Notably, he had gotten on the phone himself rather than relay a message through his secretary, to tell Helen that he'd spoken personally with Ian Easton, and that Ian had struck him as "an affable fellow"—which Helen understood to mean "pliable": Jonathan Martin's favorite sort of person. Martin, meanwhile, was planning to discuss the question of purchasing the documents with the vice chancellor over lunch.

The possibility almost made her laugh aloud: for once, after all these years, might Jonathan Martin's ability to silk his way around the system work in her favor? Until this week, she'd felt assured of finishing out her remaining months with minimal contact with the man. She'd stopped attending his lectures and receptions years ago—let the junior faculty show up to flatter, she'd no interest in competing over office-space allocations. She'd be long retired, thank goodness, before the department's move to the renovated wing Jonathan Martin had been so delightedly raising funds for these past years: *connectivity, convenience, creative development of space*—nothing, that is, to do with the real work of history, and everything to do with Martin's wish to once and for all declare superiority to the rival department over at UCL.

Yet now this was the man on whom her fate seemed to depend: Jonathan Martin, who, when she'd told him about the documents earlier that week, had sat silent a full seventy seconds. She knew; she'd watched the clock in his office. In fact, she wouldn't have put it past him to watch it himself. Seventy seconds: enough time to make the uninitiated squirm. But she was well acquainted with the man's ostentatious deliberations.

"Helen, this is a major find," he'd said—still staring out the window. Posing for Rodin, she supposed.

If it was childish to indulge her distaste for him by keeping up a withering internal monologue as yet another of Martin's silences ticked by, at least it kept her from rising from her chair and pounding her bony fist on his hardwood desk for him to stop curating his own image—Jonathan Martin, with his well-groomed graying hair and impeccable shave—and start doing what any head of a history department in his right mind ought to do.

At last he turned back to her. "An extraordinary find to conclude a career with, I must say." Behind the words she could read his regret that the one to make such a find had been Helen Watt—a dried-up scholar, inconveniently unphotogenic, on the cusp of a mandatory retirement no one but her would rue. How much better if one of Martin's bright young hires had made the discovery! Someone who could be relied on to hitch a ride on the publicity that might come from this, become an academic star, and accrue years of benefit to the university.

She watched Jonathan Martin flick aside his displeasure. For the moment. And reach for his telephone and, in his basso profundo voice, instruct his assistant to connect him—immediately!—to the university librarian. It so happened, he confided to Helen as he waited for the connection, that he had some funds available for just such a purchase, from a longtime donor eager to help raise the profile of the department. If that's what it took to get the papers before *some other university* made news by acquiring them, he'd be glad to have the History Department contribute a portion of the expense . . . though for that contribution he'd naturally expect a certain consideration.

Which meant, Helen knew, that he'd lean on the librarian to give his scholars preferential access to the documents. A violation of the Freedom of Information Act, but of course there were ways around that for a political creature like Jonathan Martin.

"Afternoon," Bridgette breathed as she entered the room, this time wearing a black wool coat and carrying an armload of magazines. Aaron looked up as though startled by her entry—as though he could possibly have missed the staccato footsteps approaching him. He gave Bridgette that smile, the one that involved only one side of his mouth. Helen couldn't help but watch. The princely, cocky tilt of his head. The smooth olive planes of his face, the heavy lashes, the dark almond-shaped eyes. Only a boy who'd been raised in luxury could carry his good looks that way.

Dror. Even his good looks hadn't belonged to himself alone.

Bridgette seemed about to stop—then regained stride, deposited her magazines on a shelf of the library, and returned to the entryway. Aaron stood at the table, watching her go, looking entertained.

Slowly, magisterially, he turned his head in Helen's direction.

The outer door shut, making her jump.

Aaron had turned back to his document. Adjusting the gloves around his narrow, sinewy wrists, he emitted a grunt of annoyance.

She'd required that he wear gloves, of course. At the store, the clerk had given her a choice between latex surgeon's gloves or a pair of prim white dainties left over from another century's afternoon tea: the opportunity to make Aaron look like a forensics hero while handling the documents, or like a nineteenth-century fop. As the clerk rang up her purchase she'd chided herself for her own satisfaction.

He peeled off the thin cotton gloves, dropping them inside out on the tabletop, and sat, pulling his laptop toward him. "Don't worry," he said without looking up. "I'm not checking my e-mail." He typed for a few seconds, then waited, eyes on the screen.

With a vexation she didn't fully understand, Helen turned back to the letter before her. It was addressed to HaCoen Mendes. Fragments of the old red wax seal remained where the recipient had pulled the folded page open. The ink had faded to a dull brown but was legible, the paper torn at one end but otherwise intact.

> February 17, 1658
> 13 Shvat, 5418
> Amsterdam

To the learned R. HaCoen Mendes,

News of your praiseworthy labors reaches us here in Amsterdam, as David Rodrigues brings report of your work to welcome the children of our English brothers under the tent of the Torah and to further the work begun by Menasseh ben Israel of blessed memory, as it is written, *It is not incumbent upon you to complete the labor, nor are you free to desist from it.* In these days when our hearts recoil from further ill news of our people's suffering in Portugal, it is our prayer that your labors will succeed and find favor with G-d. He will bring peace and redemption within our days, and we are assured that it will be so.

We will send the books that you require by the end of the month, and are pleased that you aspire to find among the Jews of London candidates for the study of such texts.

There is one matter that remains of concern to us. Rodrigues noted with sorrow your tidings of the Velasquez boy, who surely walked in the shadow of the great curse with which G-d afflicted his family in the form of the fire that consumed the parents' lives, the understanding of which is G-d's alone, as it is written, *The ways of G-d are a pure light wrapped in darkness.* Rodrigues was disturbed, however, by the presence of the young man's sister in your house of Torah.

We understand well that learned scribes are few among the London community. It is a wilderness of ignorance that you tame, pupil by pupil, and it may be that no Jewish family of London has a son learned in the necessary languages. Yet the Velasquez girl is at an age when she must seek marriage, and it is therefore only a reasonable kindness to her that she not be burdened with duties and thoughts beyond her realm. Although there be differences among our kahal on the principle of female learning, and we recognize that the girl's own father was known to favor such indulgence while he lived, still even he would surely disapprove a long continuance of such labor for a daughter. I myself trust in the words of Rabbi Eliezer of the Talmud, *For the word of the Torah should be burnt rather than taught to women.* I remind you that the girl has no dowry, and I am told that even the Dotar is not eager to provide her one, due to the ill reputation of her late mother. We advise you to consider that continuance of her labors as your scribe will deny her any remaining prospect of marriage.

With understanding that it is ever difficult to find a learned scribe who is obedient to your needs, we will take care to select an appropriate student and will send him to your care at the first opportunity, should you but send word that you are unable to find a suitable young man in London.

Although I made only brief acquaintance with the Velasquez family before the parents were gathered to G-d, yet I write with great respect and tenderness for the fate of all the sons and also the daughters of our suffering people.

In perfect faith in the coming Redemption,

Yacob de Souza

The certainty hit with a thump of adrenaline. With effort Helen resisted it. She closed her eyes, then opened them and reread. She checked her translations. The Portuguese was archaic but clear. Sliding her notebook close, she studied the dates of the documents they'd so far discovered that had been signed by the same scribe—one, a brief note requesting two volumes from an Amsterdam bookseller, directly predating the letter Helen had just read.

She sat back in her chair. And was startled by an unfamiliar sensation in her chest: the flurry of her own heart, like something long silent abruptly waking to argue its innocence.

"Mr. Levy," she said.

He didn't seem to hear.

"Aleph was a woman," she said, testing the words.

He raised his eyes from his computer screen as though dragging himself from a great depth, and regarded her without focus. He looked, for the first time, vulnerable.

8

November 12, 1657
6 Kislev, 5418
London

A SHUDDERING BOOM.

Rolling echoes up and down the quay.

Damp wood, damp thatch, damped footsteps staggering on rotting boards — the men with ropes taut on their shoulders straining the crate away now from the stone wall it had collided with. Swinging dangerous from a high pulley, the crate sank — the men cursing it lower and lower onto a waiting barge, which took the weight and pressed deeper into the choppy water.

A scattering of seagulls against a white glower of sky.

She shielded her eyes.

The skirts she wore were miserably thin, and the wet London air carried a blunt cold she couldn't outpace. Her shoes, too, now proved paltry, though they'd been adequate to Amsterdam's smoother streets. She'd slipped on waste-slicked cobbles all the way down the narrow alleys to the river, and the soles of her feet ached past endurance. All about her, a tumult of English faces: sharp, incomprehensible features, shaped by words equally sharp and foreign. Were she to speak the softer language pent inside her, her utterances would go unrecognized — sound shorn of meaning.

How quickly, with the first touch of her foot on English shores, she'd become a thing without words. The ugliness of her life pooled inside her. Long ago she might have let it turn to tears.

The rabbi had sent her for her brother. Three days now since Isaac had last set foot in their household — three days that the rabbi had no scribe to set down his thoughts.

She hadn't yet glimpsed her brother among the dockworkers, but knew to look twice. Isaac was ever thus. In Amsterdam, when their father had taken him about the port to educate him in the ways of the city's trade, he'd been a quick student as well. Then only a boy of ten, he'd slipped easily into the tableau of sailors, much to the discomfort of the well-shod merchants and investors surveying the scene. In their father's bemused telling, the boy had all but leapt in to help the laborers break open crates, tugging to the best of his small ability on chests of cargo, until the laborers could no longer dislike the boy for his kinship with the watchful Jewish merchants in their black cloaks and broad feathered hats.

Ignoring the stares of the laborers preparing to heave a second crate, she moved cautiously along the riverside. She slid carefully around an old, bleary-looking man tarring the hull of a small boat—but his fingers grasped at her hem as she passed. She yanked the fabric away, and he winked into her face and raised thick palms as though to say *Age permits me*. She turned away, flushed, and here he was: her brother, standing among the English dockworkers as though he'd been born to this place.

She'd known she'd find him here—she'd told the rabbi so. Why then did it sting to see him so at his ease amid strangers?

"Isaac," she said.

He raised his eyebrows in that new way he had, neither acknowledging nor denying her.

Her throat seized. She'd never possessed Isaac's ease with people. She'd been, always, a peculiarity: Isaac's peaked, quiet elder sister with her constant apologies, her inability to make her voice heard in a crowd, her strange devotion to the bookish labors most girls were glad to be spared. Until now, though, her brother's talent to befriend had been hers to share. All his life Isaac had gathered goodwill easily, and shared its harvest with his sister—friends, jokes, treats from vendors in the market. But here in England, though they slept under the same roof his ways were unknown to her.

"Isaac," she repeated. She stood opposite him, her hands useless at her sides. In Amsterdam she'd have reached up and tugged his straight hair, not hard enough to hurt but enough to say she knew his tricks, even if he was a man now and half a head taller.

Two of his companions had turned. Both were thicker set and far older than Isaac—men old enough to have families, perhaps to have deserted them. The shorter had a wide pockmarked face and staring blue eyes; the taller had thinning tufts of hair and features thickly veined from weather or drink—his eyes seemed buried in his florid face.

She turned to Isaac, her imp who was no longer impish, his blue eyes and gold-wheat hair . . . still her brother? It was weeks now since he'd shaved off his beard, but his naked jaw still made her uneasy—a reminder that he'd cast off the last remains of home. She feared she was not exempt from that purging.

"The rabbi needs you," she said quietly.

At the sound of her Portuguese, she felt the workers' attention thicken around her: another foreigner?

"He's composed letters, Isaac," she continued in a near-whisper. "In his mind. He requires your hand to set them down on paper."

A shifting of the workers' bodies—their growing awareness of their power over her. She stepped closer to Isaac. But he didn't notice the men's attention, or feigned not to. He pursed his mouth and then said something to her, in English, too fast—as though he'd forgotten that, unlike him, she'd had no opportunity to learn the spoken language, confined by household duties as she was. What good, here on these clanging docks, was the English she'd once gleaned from the printed page— the single volume of mysterious and confounding English poetry that she'd studied in secret in her mother's room in Amsterdam, so long ago?

With a shake of his head, Isaac laughed a hollow laugh. He said, in Portuguese, "I left my scribing hand across the channel." His eyes, averted, said the rest: *and my allegiance to you as well.*

She couldn't hold her voice steady. "Isaac—"

"Tell the rabbi I'm occupied," he said. "Tell him I've let a room and won't be returning to his household."

The words left her mouth thickly. "You ask me to spit on the one man who's aided us."

There was no change in his expression, yet her words had struck him. An instant's hesitation. In it, she saw her brother as he'd once been. His straight golden hair, the perfect grace in his compact body, the salt-and-butter smell of him snugged in her arms those long-ago afternoons in Amsterdam when he'd been left in her charge. Mischievous Isaac, unscathed by endless scolding from the house servants, or by teachers whose voices rose with the fury of betrayed admirers. Untouchable by any discipline but their father's mild remonstrances. In the wake of their father's quiet disappointment Isaac would turn to Ester, his determined expression suddenly vague, the spark of a request in his blue eyes—if not for approval, then for forgiveness. She had granted it, always. She'd scooped the blond fringe from his eyes. Helped him hide the broken glass of the nursemaid's mirror until he'd replaced it with another, taken from their mother's dressing table.

And yes, she'd tied herself to the ballooning sail of his mischief— why pretend she hadn't? She'd relished the freedom Isaac claimed in boyhood, freedom she herself was denied. Once she'd found him leaning from an upper window of their house, pelting the street with rotted apples he'd picked from the kitchen refuse, and she'd grabbed the linen of his shirt and twisted her fingers in it, round and round, until the shirt was tight around his middle. He'd tried to shrug her off. But instead of pulling him away from the window as they both expected she'd do, she'd knelt behind him and looked down to the street, at the cowed form of a man she recognized in a heartbeat—the synagogue beadle who had called her an unnatural girl, after the maid let out word that Ester had used up the household's supply of candles for nighttime reading. The beadle had said it after Sabbath prayers, and repeated it gladly and often when he saw the approval the observation garnered. *The girl has her mother's beauty and must be overseen strictly—for with the mother's blood so visible in her, the girl's obedient ways might yet crack to reveal the same unruliness of spirit.*

Without a word to Ester, as though understanding her heart and knowing she wouldn't stop him, Isaac had taken aim again. She'd dug her fingers deeper into her brother's shirt and felt his warm small body, all strength and purpose, and she'd leaned on him, her fingers tight in his shirt, and they'd breathed together as he reached back and heaved, and the brown apple smashed against the man's temple and banished him, retching threats, down the road toward the synagogue.

The neighbors had been scandalized, of course. But as their mother looked at Isaac that evening, something in her expression flexed and was satisfied. It had been their father who'd taken Isaac to the synagogue to apologize to the man. From the window Ester had watched them go, and on their return had stolen to Isaac's bed and left there on his pillow the small, clumsy figure she'd sewn—a dog of sorts, stuffed with bits of cloth she'd taken from the housekeeper's sewing basket. A plaything to soothe his spirit.

He stood before her now, a grown man. It was true that his face had hardened long before coming to London. Yet here, in these few weeks since their arrival, something further had settled in it—something new and stringent—as though he'd undertaken the final stretch of a journey he'd set upon after their parents' deaths. Without the short blond crop of his beard, his jaw was naked, tense. There had never before been a single thing unnatural in Isaac, nor a single thing unfree—yet now his face, which had ever been whole, seemed composed of parts. There were, she now noticed, lines on either side of his mouth, and when he spoke he seemed to her like a wooden puppet with hinged jaw.

"Scribing is for a different sort of youth," he said. "For *you*, if you'd been born a boy. Never for me. Even *before.*"

Before the fire. Isaac had barely spoken of it these two years.

But his voice, which had been so eerily aloof, was now rising, snapping. "So the rabbi would have me pen interpretations of verses? Beautiful tributes to martyrs perishing in the Inquisition?" At the core of the spiraling words, a crying loneliness. "The rabbi wants my hand to set his holy thoughts to paper? Tell him I'm devoting myself instead to living up to my reputation as a murderer. Tell him what he knows: in my hand, his words would turn traitor. Tell him, won't you"—he gestured to his face—"that the beard is gone. That I no longer even look a Jew."

The workers had stood these minutes in silence, watching theater in a language they didn't comprehend. Now one let out a chuckle: a lover's quarrel, was it?

Isaac's words flew at her. "I'll wager you haven't told him about my beard. I'll wager you let him think I'm still what he wishes." He tilted his head. "Tell him, if you like, that I'm lost and you couldn't find me. Perhaps he'll mourn me for dead." Isaac smiled grimly.

"Isaac, please—"

The shorter of the men was laughing, saying something in English. He stepped forward. A leer, a gesture toward Ester: *Is she yours?*

Slowly, Isaac shook his head.

Like a shawl unwinding from her shoulders, she felt her brother fall away from her.

In an instant the shorter man was upon her—his thick hand gripping her cheek, fingers pinching hard as though testing the merchandise. And just as swiftly she was shoved back—she saw only Isaac's shoulder closing down, hard, with the swing of his fist into the man's belly. For a moment the two stumbled at close quarters. Then the man fell and lay clutching his middle, gasping. The taller man, lunging forward—to join the fight, or stop it?—set his hands roughly on Isaac's shoulders, and was pushing Isaac back—Ester could see now that the shove was a warning, not an attack. But before any of them could draw breath, Isaac had swung again, and the second man stumbled and fell against a crate, his head hitting the wooden slats with a dull knock.

The man moaned. Ester watched him rouse himself, slowly, carefully. And his glare of newborn malice, aimed at Isaac.

She turned and strode back the way she'd come, the pain in her feet reeling her along the cobbles, the shops along the narrow street looming dark before her.

Footfalls, and Isaac caught her mutely by the arm.

"Come home," she told him, her head down. Beneath her aching feet, the stones of a city she'd no desire to know. All about them the slams and cries and raucous laughter of strangers. So this was to be her London: a city disfigured in advance by the stain they carried to it. She was crying, her face hot—why now? She'd hardly wept in the years since the fire. Even at their parents' burial, where her failure to weep was seen by the gossips as further sign of an unnatural spirit—even then she hadn't, for the burning in her chest had eradicated any tears before they could escape. But now some weakness assaulted her and she'd no defense.

"Come home with me," she murmured again.

Isaac's words carried no venom this time, only weariness. "The rabbi's house isn't our home." He'd no quarrel with the rabbi, she knew. His enmity was aimed at life itself, and there was nothing she could do to ease it. "Or perhaps," he said, "perhaps *you* can make it home. Ester. You can . . . marry. Have sons and daughters." She raised her face, but he wasn't looking at her. He stared into the white sky and spoke softly, as though constructing a pleasing tale for children. "You can. *Ester*. You're still . . ." He glanced down at her, and there it was: that glimmer she hadn't seen in so long, the light that said he knew her. "You're made differently." He spoke quietly but for a moment his voice had its old sturdiness. "You're like a coin made out of stone instead of metal. Or a house made out of honeycombs or feathers or maybe glass—something no one else in all the world would think to make a house of, Ester —something strange, but sound too. You've been like that always. But no matter all that, you're still a woman. A woman can recover. Women aren't"—he hesitated—"they're not *set*. Not like a man is. A man has to be a hero or a . . . villain." He gripped her arm tighter. "This is what I want to tell you, Ester. This is the only thing I have to tell you." His body tensed and she saw him glance toward the river, as though the labor awaiting him there could absorb all the violence mounting in him.

Then he breathed and let go her arm, forcing himself still. She felt the effort it cost him to quell the wish to move, strike out, do something to release all that was pent in his body. Instead he spoke, quietly. "A man comes into the world to perform one function, Ester. Maybe it's good. Maybe it's evil. But starting that fire, you see, was my function. That makes me evil." He looked at her squarely. His face was naked as she'd not seen it since he'd been a boy. But it held no request for forgiveness.

"On my way out of this world, I'll do something. Something good. Like *Samson*." His lips held the grim echo of a smile. "I'll bring down some wicked house. *Down!*" On the word he slammed a fist into his open palm with such ferocity she cried out. "Right down on my head," he said, simply. He breathed. "Or I'll save someone. A boy, maybe." The thought, for an instant, seemed to choke him. "I'll climb onto the deck of the boy's ship, just before the ship's engulfed by fire. And before I'm burned, before I die, I'll *shove—him—off*." In each expelled word, a dizzying hatred.

He would strike and strike, she understood, until he'd struck himself down.

He turned and strode toward the docks.

She walked back on the cobbles as though they were made of glass.

THE RABBI WAS WHERE SHE'D left him. He raised his face to her, but waited until she'd hung her shawl.

"Your brother's not with you," he said quietly.

"No."

The chill rain that had begun during her walk streaked white beyond the large room's high windows. The fire was loud with sap. Rivka must have stoked it high before leaving on her errands. Ester could picture her: her thick arms straining the wool of her dress, and every gesture enunciating her determination to defy the winter in the rabbi's aged body. In Rivka's absence the snapping fire, loud and sudden enough to break thoughts in half, continued her vigilant tending.

Rabbi HaCoen Mendes sat close to the hearth. His form was slight in the high-backed chair. His cheekbones were pale knobs, his beard a yellowed white. Below his thick gray brows, the welded skin of the scars appeared tight, poreless as a child's.

She pulled a chair near to the fire and sat. The rapid lick of the flames wrested shadows to and fro across the floor. She raised one foot, crossed it carefully over the opposite knee, unbuckled her shoe. The sole of her foot throbbed through her stocking and she felt it gingerly. Just a moment's respite. Then she'd go back to the kitchen, where Rivka would have left ample work for her. How she'd have loved to be asked, like Isaac, to work with quill and ink.

Instead she spent her waking hours kneading thick, dry dough under Rivka's direction, stirring stews heavy with potatoes and the occasional slice of salted beef shipped from the Jewish butcher in Amsterdam. Day after day she prepared Rivka's spiceless Polish food, which bore no resemblance to the Portuguese dishes she'd been accustomed to in her parents' home. At Rivka's direction she prodded these ingredients into meals, which she carried in to the rabbi and his occasional students ... only to return them, barely touched, to Rivka — the rabbi's because he had no appetite, the students' because even they, raised on heavy English fare, knew better. But Ester had neither strength nor skill to propose any fare more pleasing.

Even after her parents' deaths in Amsterdam, when Ester had labored in others' homes for her keep, she'd still been treated as a daughter of the Portuguese community — set to sewing and other lighter tasks while the heavier labors were accomplished in back rooms by Dutch or Tudesco servants. Only here in London did she at last see the truth: a household was a creature of bottomless hungers. It ravened for wood and coal and white starch, for sailcloth and bread and ale; for breath and sinew, and life itself, which wreathed away invisibly beneath the press of daily labor like the wax of a lit candle. When the kitchen or the eternally waning fires didn't demand Ester's attention, she was sent to polish brass and pewter jugs with mare's-tail, scour pots and floor, turn the beds, haul linens to the attic in buck-baskets. Daily, she beat drapes and furnishings to remove the soot of the cheap sea coal that heated the household; only the rabbi's fire was made up with wood, as Rivka insisted that soot harmed the rabbi's frail constitution, and Rivka would not under any circumstance have him breathe the coal-warmed air that drifted through the rest of the house.

Through these labors, Rivka offered Ester little by way of talk, though when tasks proved difficult she was patient with Ester's clumsiness. Now and again Rivka offered a brief smile, or a squeeze of her thick hand on Ester's arm to release Ester from some too-taxing chore, which Rivka then bent to herself. But these gestures never blossomed into greater warmth. Ester knew Rivka wished her comfort. But it was plain Rivka felt the distance between them to be unbridgeable, and their fellowship inevitably transient: the daughter of a Sephardic family, even an orphaned one, would marry and have a household of her own. Rivka, her hair thinned and colorless, her body as thick as her accent, seemed never to have entertained such dreams, even in her own long-ago youth. Wringing dry the heaviest feather coverlet for the rabbi, the next for Isaac, and then Ester, and the thinnest for herself, Rivka kept her own counsel—expending few words beyond her occasional incomprehensible Tudesco mutterings, which seemed to Ester more expressive than anything Rivka ventured in her terse Portuguese.

Sometimes, mending with her cramped stitches, Ester stole a moment's reprieve to listen to the rabbi and his students in the room at the foot of the stair. *Moshe kibel torah m'sinai . . .* Words she herself had learned from the rabbi. She'd been still a girl when her father had first brought the rabbi to their house in Amsterdam. She'd known him by sight long before, of course: Rabbi HaCoen Mendes, seated at the edge of the men's section in the Talmud Torah sanctuary, his lips moving to prayers he knew by heart. In Amsterdam, students had been brought to HaCoen Mendes when the other rabbis were unavailable or unwilling to teach them. To the younger boys he would tell quiet tales that left them rapt: Daniel and the lion, Akiva and his devoted wife, Bar Kochba and the saplings. The older boys he tasked with reading passages of

Mishneh Torah, then dug for their opinions until they lit up with comprehension or became bored. Some took advantage of his blindness, making frivolous alterations to the content of the passages they read aloud, or circulating mocking verse while the rabbi spoke: pranks whispered of with righteous anger in the women's balcony at the synagogue. Yet Ester had heard her father say that the other rabbis took advantage of HaCoen Mendes's tolerance as well, sending him their most troublesome pupils. HaCoen Mendes never complained. When the congregation's most disobedient student of all—Miguel de Spinoza's son, a pupil determined to upend all tradition for the sake of his own self-regarding logic—was excommunicated for his hubris, HaCoen Mendes even had himself escorted to the synagogue to voice his objection to the severity of the punishment—to no avail.

She wished now obscurely, as the rain splashed on the London cobbles outside the window, that the rabbi could plead thus to some court on her behalf. But for what reprieve? The life she'd known in Amsterdam had vanished. The very table where she'd once pored over the rabbi's lessons was now ash. So, it seemed, was her spirit, which had risen to greet each text she'd studied with the rabbi. In that too-brief time of her studies, a tide of words and reasoning had lifted her and rushed her far past the stagnant canals that hemmed the Jewish neighborhood, toward some bright distant horizon. She'd wanted that horizon so much, it dizzied her.

Yet now she touched books only in the basest sense. The rich library they'd brought with them from Amsterdam to London required tending like all else in the house, for coal soot found its way even behind the curtain that protected the long shelf of books. The first time Ester had been assigned the task of dusting the rabbi's treasures, she'd drawn back the curtain and stood breathing in wonder at the leather-and-gilt spines. The library, a gift from the congregation in Amsterdam to support the rabbi's undertaking in London, was a gauntlet of expensive tomes thrown down by Amsterdam's Jews. The titles embossed on the spines were astonishing: *Pirkei Avot,* yes, and *Moreh Nevuchim* and *Ketubim,* of course, but also works of philosophy. Standing flush with Menasseh ben Israel's *De la Fragilidad Humana* was a volume of Aristotle's writings—as though the Amsterdam Jews who had donated these books assumed that England's Jews had become such boors in their separation from the community that they now required not only reeducation in Jewish teachings, but an introduction to the rudiments of thought itself. Slowly Ester slid books from their perches. Frontispieces, framed by calligraphers, were inscribed with the signatures of the Amsterdam merchants who'd had these extravagant gifts bound for their London brethren—without, Ester felt sure, ever reading the books' contents themselves. She opened a supple leather binding to discover a work by the Englishman Francis Bacon, translated into Castilian. What use had the givers of this lavish volume felt the Castilian would be to a Jew of England? And was it envy that made her think the men who had given these books valued the bindings more than the words they bound?

But Rivka, seeing Ester stilled and dreaming at the task of dusting, had issued a grunt of disapproval and sent Ester to wring linens.

Not two months since their arrival from Amsterdam—yet the brief flare of hope Ester had carried with her had deadened in these damp stone rooms. Considered slight before her arrival in London, she'd grown thinner still. Some afternoons her exertions darkened the air and she had to sit on the floor while the room swooned about her. Once, as she crouched waiting for the swooning to cease, with the shelf of magisterial volumes above her as unreachable as the moon, it seemed to her that the stone floor she clung to was an isle on which she'd been exiled from the last remains of all she'd once loved. It came to her to wonder whether the banished young de Spinoza too had felt his rebellious mind darkened in his own exile by the labor of earning his keep. Had his thoughts, rumored the worst sort of heresy, also been smothered, as the rabbis surely hoped?

Questions that floated away in the silt of the dim, rocking room.

Nights, when Rivka's snores resounded, Ester lay silent under the cover, willing herself toward the sweet sleep she now craved more than almost all else. *The death of each day's life.* End it, she thought. End this day's life if the world holds mercy. Her long-ago studies were mere shadows—she could not recall what had made her think them worthy. Here and again, as she lay in the dark, a thought might rise murky out of the fatigue, and—she couldn't help herself—she'd hold it tender as a newborn lest it slip from her hands, caressing it, trying to shield it against oblivion. Until finally it slipped, a spark extinguished by sleep.

A dream, buried in the night like a seed of light in the dark: her father's hand, atop the polished wooden table — patting it once, twice. Protection, safety. Gone.

The rabbi's face was turned toward the livid flames.

"Since your brother chooses not to return," he said, "I'll ask to employ your hand the remainder of today."

She stood. With tentative steps, she made her way to the table. Lowered herself into the wooden seat, hesitated, then selected a goose quill from the jar.

Its smooth shaft, rolling between her fingers, was foreign. Had it been two years since she'd held a quill? More?

"Begin a letter to Amsterdam," the rabbi said quietly. "Sixth of Kislev."

The paper was before Ester. Her hands were clumsy.

She wrote,

>   6 Kislev, 5418
>   With the help of G-d

"To the honored Samuel Moses," the rabbi said.

She dipped the quill and wrote the words, her lettering cramped. The wet blue-black letters shone on the thick paper.

"We have received with great thanks your shipment of two volumes," he continued. "The number of our pupils grows with the help of God, though slowly."

She dipped the quill, and in her haste to return it to the paper, tipped the bottle. A satin puddle glistened on the page she'd begun. A stain blossomed on the back of her left hand.

The fire crackled in the silence.

"What's happened?" the rabbi asked.

"The ink bottle," she whispered.

He nodded. Then bent his head until his beard touched his chest. After a moment she realized he was waiting for her to clean the spill and begin again.

She looked at her hand. Rivulets of ink had spread into the creases between her fingers, settling into the frail pathways of her skin like a map of all that was ruined. Didn't the rabbi understand that the quick pupil he'd tutored at her father's house was lost? Was it his sealed eyelids

—the perfect, blanched skin of his scars—that permitted him to imagine her as she'd once been?

But of course, he wasn't asking her to scribe because he thought her a worthy instrument. It was, rather, that he had no choice.

She stood. "Isaac will be back," she told the rabbi, careful to keep the wretchedness out of her voice. "He'll write for you."

"Your brother will not return," the rabbi said softly. "He never harbored any love of the labor of ink and paper. And now"—he gestured gently with the tips of his fingers: Now that that fire has occurred. Now that Isaac is damned in his own eyes.

A welling silence.

"I brought Isaac to London," the rabbi said, "in the hope that he might have a different life, free of what trailed him in Amsterdam. For the mercy of the Almighty can release us"—he paused, as though bracing to bear his own words—"from all bonds of slavery. And cause even the blind to see."

She could not quiet her thoughts. How could he speak of seeing? Did faith so sustain him that he felt his stolen faculties restored? She'd no such faith. Even in girlhood, the comforts of the Hebrew prayers in synagogue had failed to attach to her, leaving her perplexed among the chanting believers. Yet she could almost believe Rabbi HaCoen Mendes's words, for how else did he endure blindness with such serenity, if not for some inner vision—some vista of consolation available behind his sealed lids?

Rabbi HaCoen Mendes sat with his fingertips pressed together. "Isaac does not accept the life I offer him," he said. "I must trust him to the hands of the Almighty. But I fear, Ester, that he won't rest in that embrace." The rabbi turned his face toward her. "Your brother places himself at the mercy of rougher hands."

It was true. There was no worth in pretending any longer. Isaac would not be back.

"Write," said the rabbi. "Please."

She didn't move. Her clumsy hand shamed her.

"I spoke too quickly," he said, "and caused you too great haste. The spill was my doing."

She righted the bottle with her stained hand, cleaned the mess with

a cloth, and, taking a fresh page, dipped her quill in the small reserve of
ink that remained.

"To the learned Yacob de Souza," the rabbi dictated.

She wrote.

Your kind inquiries after my health are more than I merit. I am well
tended to in my household, and remain whole in spirit and body.

She finished the line, and waited. The air above the wood fire was
alive with pirouetting waves of heat. Even at this distance from the
hearth, she felt the heat echo on her face. Beside her feet, under the finely
finished writing table, a small stove awaited lighting, to dry the ink of
the rabbi's words more rapidly. Rabbi HaCoen Mendes's nephew, who
despite his own indifference to Jewish learning had acquired and furnished this house for them, had spared no expense in remaking this
damp residence into a proper house of study for the aged man.

In the silence now, something kindled in her. The writing table
seemed abruptly to be a vast expanse—a plateau where some small remaining freedom might be possible. A tidy stack of paper, a wide glass
jar of quills, a pen knife. A stick of red sealing wax. The smooth grain of
the tabletop. She felt her body rush with quick heat, as though every bit
of her, every plain and hidden part, were waking.

The rabbi was speaking again, his blind eyes turned to her. The words
he spoke streamed through her hand, leaving a bright black wake on
the page.

Your concern for my position here is further evidence of your generous nature. Yet I urge you to put your mind at rest, dear Yacob, and
devote your efforts to those in greater need. The rumors that have
reached you are correct. The community here does not hunger to
learn. Yet this does not shake my faith in the rightness of my labors.
I, for my part, accept the very things you rue. Menasseh ben Israel,
it's said, heard indifference in the community's failure to embrace
him. I hear, instead, fear. I sit among them in the synagogue and I
hear their hands sliding on their woolen cloaks that they've laid on
the benches beside them. How tightly they hold to these garments,

as though loath to be parted from them should they need to leave
in haste. I listen to them shift each time the synagogue door opens:
they must turn their heads to learn who has arrived or departed before they may reenter holy prayer. I say this now without rebuke, but
in the hope my words will aid: it is all too easy to speak, when one is
at leisure in Amsterdam, of the glory of martyrs. Those rabbis who
do so, I suggest humbly, are not those who themselves endured the
Inquisition, but those who learned of it from afar . . . and perhaps, if
I may say, do not understand fully the nature of what they speak of.
Some of them argue that we must shun those who conformed with
the Christian church — that we must abhor as saint-suckers those
who chose, rather than the pyre, another night in their safe beds.

The Almighty created man in his image. He created not only our
endurance and our infrequent wisdom, but also our fear. Man has no
desire to be persecuted, and this impulse too must be the doing of
G-d. Some will disagree with me. So let them tend another congregation, one whose Jews are not so fear-pricked as mine. I will tend to
this flock that does not love my presence, for the invalid that spurns
physick requires it no less than the one who welcomes it.

The last of the rabbi's words, freshly inked, glimmered before her.
He sighed. "Copy the letter for me," he said, "and sign it."

She took a second sheet of paper from the stack and began, the
words spooling onto the page under her hand. As she worked, the rain
needling quietly against the window, she felt the writing lift her out of
her weary body, so she could almost look down on her self from the low
ceiling: A young woman bent over a table. A young woman scribing in
the chair that should be her brother's.

Slowly, steadily, her hand repeated its passage across the page.

Once, twice, then again.

Isaac.

He'd been a boy still, on the verge of manhood, but a softness yet in
his cheeks. He'd stepped away from some nighttime escapade to fetch
her, flinging stone chips at the window beneath which she slept. She'd
risen, found her shoes in the dark, and descended the stair to the flaring of the lantern in her brother's hand — a blackened over-large thing
taken from some unlocked storeroom, with something uneven about

its light so that the shadows shrank and grew wildly inside the house. In the swinging lantern-light her mother's tapestries from Lisbon—dark mythic scenes shimmering with gold thread—loomed and extinguished. Bright and dark forms materialized, fled along the walls. In the seasick light her brother was a boy, a man, a boy . . . a feverish-faced stranger in this world of mahogany and silver plate.

And then he was her brother once more, gesturing her impatiently toward the street. "You won't forgive yourself if you miss this," he said. "It's at a far dock, but if we go fast you'll see. Someone smashed three barrels of fish, and the birds—Ester, you have to see, it's ten thousand wings like—"

She never saw it. Did he stumble as he turned, his shoe knocking the heavy doorstop? Did the lantern grow too heavy in his hands, had its handle grown so hot he had to shift his grip? Whatever the cause, the flame had tipped out of the lantern without a sound, spilling over the lip of the metal like liquid gold, touching the curtain by the parlor window, and instantly beginning a desperate climb to the heavens. Before Ester could move another step on the stair, the door was framed with fire. The tapestry a roaring scene of black curling figures.

And then Grietgen was shoving her in the back, she was cursing Ester down the stairs, shrieking: *To the street, to the street,* naar buiten, *children!* Steps from the door, Ester glimpsed her father, halfway down the stairs, stumble, stop—then turn to climb back up to their mother's chamber, racing upward alongside the flames.

Then Ester was on the street, the night air cold on her face. In the flaring, crashing dark, the neighbors. Futile pails of water: steam ribboning off windowpanes. Inside, timber and fabric raging untouched. The street's cobbles dark with wasted water, reflecting licks of light. And then, the tip of the roof aglow. Brighter, brighter, the rooftop a jailed star in the night.

The fire shot into the sky.

A single rending shriek. She'd never known whose it was.

Her brother had been gone before the roof had fallen. Toward dawn, he was found curled asleep on the deck of a ship set to depart that morning. He was led to shore and to the synagogue, mute and soot-stained, by the ship's navigator—who surveyed the Jews chanting mourning prayers in rent clothes, then rubbed the thick silver cross dangling from his own neck and, producing Isaac, said in Dutch thick with shyness and regret, "This one isn't old enough yet to throw his troubled self into the sea."

But now he was.

Rabbi HaCoen Mendes's voice. "I wish you to scribe for me every day," he said. "Tell Rivka, please, to hire a girl to fulfill your household labors."

She was unable to form an answer. She stared instead at the rivulets of ink sunk into her skin, and for an instant heard her brother's voice in her head: Isaac, as he had been before the fire, ruddy and alight with plans. *Now thank your brother for your good fortune! Though if you'd only step out of your shuttered rooms, Esti, you'd love the fresh winds better than a life of books.*

She bent her head and whispered a prayer she'd no faith in: "May it please the Almighty to guide Isaac's feet to safety." The words were hollow. Here she sat, in his seat, while somewhere in London he was negotiating a price for his own death.

DAYS, A WEEK, A FORTNIGHT — it took no longer. Wash day: Rivka, who'd silently doubled her own labors rather than expend the rabbi's money to hire a girl, had risen before dawn and spent the morning with her broad back bent over the buck-baskets, thick reddened hands wringing. At midday Ester left the rabbi's side to help haul the water-heavy linens to the attic. Then Rivka went out into the chilly afternoon to purchase a new clothesline.

Ester was laboring over a page of *Pirkei Avot,* reading and reread-ing to the rabbi at his request, inking the last of an interpretation he wished her to record and send to a student in Amsterdam, when the door opened softly, then closed behind Rivka.

She stood before Ester without removing her cloak. Had Rivka ever stood before Ester thus — face to face, hands stilled at her sides? Her words to Ester were always sidelong, directions meted out in passing as Rivka moved from task to task. Yet now Rivka's gaze glimmered, as though the cover on a well had been lifted.

Ester rose from her seat.

"I looked for him where he labored." Rivka's brown eyes, small in her thick, lined face, turned fierce as though to repel her own message. "At the docks."

"Isaac?" Ester whispered.

"A man tried to tell me in German, but he didn't know enough words. And in English"—Rivka shook her head like a mule tormented by a fly. "Maybe two days ago. The man said it was someone he'd—" Rivka broke off with a gesture: someone Isaac had angered. "The man said they attacked Isaac, from behind. A knife. He didn't see them come."

Silence. For an instant, Rivka's hand floated toward Ester's shoulder. But at Ester's flinch Rivka lowered her hand, nodding as though she understood and even agreed: neither of them could bear consolation.

Ester whispered, "Where . . ."

Rivka's face buckled. "They threw him in the river."

She departed for the kitchen, closing the door behind her. A moment later Ester heard a racked, terrifying sound. Then a low Tudesco chanting.

"Ester," said the rabbi.

But she couldn't answer. Strange sensations filled her. A loud silence in her ears, her body cold stone. She needed something to warm her. She needed Isaac's head nested beneath her chin. A confusion of pictures in her mind: His small boyish body. His grim squint at the London skies, as he predicted his own death. He'd dreamt of saving someone. Now he'd gone without redeeming anything.

She turned at a whispering from beside the fire. The rabbi sat, arms wrapped around his thin chest, his head shaking slowly from side to side. His lips were moving in prayer.

Softly she said, "Does God console you now?"

She'd spoken the words thinking they were a question. But as they rang in the hushed room, she understood they were an accusation. An apology rose in her, reflexive. She let it dissolve unspoken.

There was a long silence. "And you," the rabbi said softly. "Though it may be a dreadful and long time before we feel His consolation."

From the fireside and the kitchen, prayer and weeping. She tried to imagine dropping into grief. She pictured it, like letting go of a rope. To crumple with sorrow, fall at someone's feet, beg mercy? But these things required belief that mercy existed in the world.

She was nineteen years of age and could no longer bend her mind to believe in the comforts embraced by others. The fire had forged them both—she and her brother—into brittle instruments. Should she bend, she would break.

She struck the tears away with the backs of her hands.

No star remained now to navigate by. Isaac had been her last.

A frenzy of words filled her—all she'd confess now, if he were only with her. With what gladness she'd have trusted him with every thought of hers, every bewilderment—every secret save one she'd carried in silence all these years, for it would have wounded him.

Instead his clenched voice rose now in her memory. *A man comes into the world to perform one function.*

What function remained for Ester? Father, mother, brother, gone.

She stared at the chair she'd risen from: Isaac's chair. Then, a terrifying, grief-stricken freedom flooding her, she lowered herself into it.

Only a single desire remained to her: To be amid these books. To hear the quiet scratch of quill on paper. To find, amid these consolations, some slim filament that had once been hers, and follow it to its unseen destination.

She picked up the quill, stained with ink, and dipped it. The thought came to her, unwelcome: *ink purchased with blood.*

The price of her freedom.

Slowly she began to copy out the rabbi's interpretation.

At the sound of the quill he turned to her, his face taut with concentration.

She shaped the Portuguese and Hebrew words carefully. It took a long while. At length, long after the sounds of Rivka's praying had faded and the house settled into deep silence, she finished the copy.

She signed her own initial, and watched the black ink settle into the page.

א

9

November 4, 2000
London

H E SAID HE WOULDN'T, and then he did. He positioned
himself next to the towering window, his shoulder brushing
the lowest panes. Outside, snow flurried like ash. Keeping his
profile to Helen Watt and his laptop angled so as to obscure the screen
from her view, he checked the translations of two Portuguese words on
an online *dicionário*, then turned off the sound on his laptop and opened
his e-mail.

There in his inbox was a reply from Marisa. The subject line: "Professor."

Professor Levy:
   Thanks for the lecture, I'd been missing my 3-hour college semi-
nars.
   But seriously, thank you for being a pompous son-of-a-bitch. I
learned something, which is more than I can say for most of the conversations I've had lately. I'm stuck here in kibbutz-ulpan with two
potheads and a right-wing fanatic for roommates, and so far spend
almost no time with the kibbutz's actual Israelis — the only saving
grace being that ulpan is kicking my ass. That's what I'm here for: I
aim to come out fluent in Hebrew if it kills me. Otherwise the kibbutz thing is dull for a city girl. The evening breeze in the orchard is
lovely, yes, but the smell from the cow barn gets old fast. There's a su-
pervisor here who thinks the foreign students are his chance to play
drill sergeant. On our cases for the least little thing when we're not in
class, nothing better to do with his time than try to rake me over the

coals for smoking a cigarette for five minutes when he wants me to
be clearing rocks off a field. He had me down as a soft American, so
he was in for a bit of a shock yesterday when he muttered something
nasty to me under his breath in Hungarian and I let loose on him in
the same. Poor man, how was he to know my grandmother taught
me how to say "I'll put your balls in the laundry wringer" in her na-
tive language? The other students had no idea what was happening.
But he laughed, and this morning he passed me a cigarette on the sly
and said he thinks I'll make it in this country.

The ESL teaching job I've lined up in Tel Aviv doesn't start till
spring, so till then it's more grammar tests and more field work—the
real kind, not the sort you professor types do.

Keep me posted, please, on the drama with the documents, and
on Professor Ice Queen. I hope the papers turn up enough surprises
to rattle her out of her bitchiness. And enough to keep Aaron Levy
happy. That's a good thing.

Marisa

Her black cropped hair. The long muscles of her back. The single
afternoon they'd been together.

She'd sat across the room from him every Monday and Wednesday
afternoon through the damp London spring. Fourteen weeks of Advanced Classical Hebrew, a class Aaron took seriously, leaning against
the back wall of the room and half-raising his hand to pose questions
about archaic verb constructions that left the professor and the two other
postgrad students nodding with enthusiasm, and the undergraduates
looking mildly terrorized. Only Marisa seemed amused when Aaron
spoke, though he wasn't entirely certain he was in on the joke.

Midway through the term, when she'd approached Professor Ludman after class, Aaron had lingered over his open notebook to listen.
Marisa was, from what Aaron could hear, requesting an alternate as-
signment, one more relevant to her situation. She was a visiting student,
here from the United States for only these few months in London before moving on to Israel. She couldn't care less, she told Ludman flatly,
about her grade—no offense, but she'd earned this scholarship to London before she'd settled on her Israel plan, and she was now reshaping
her studies around that, and what she really needed was modern lan-

guage—not classical Hebrew. Suppressing a laugh, Aaron had waited
for Ludman to suggest drily to Marisa that she try something on the
World Wide Web.

Instead, Professor Anatol Ludman—a middle-aged scholar known
for his rigorous pedagogy—smiled an almost fatherly smile that said
he was pleased by Marisa's spunk. Aaron listened, stunned, as Ludman
offered to lend her some modern Hebrew materials at the next class.

The next week Aaron left class at the same time as Marisa.

"You're going with a student program?" he asked, as they turned into
the corridor.

She slowed long enough to study him, that same amused expression
on her face.

"To Israel, I mean." He raised an eyebrow. "I mean, I don't suppose
it's one of those Encounter Israel bus tours?" He meant to be funny, he
supposed, though he couldn't have said exactly what the joke was.

She looked at him with her gray-green eyes. Then she laughed easily, in a way that said she knew exactly what the joke was, and it wasn't
what Aaron thought. "Nope," she said. "Not one of those Encounter
Israel bus tours."

And she walked away.

At a student Holocaust Memorial Day vigil later that spring, he'd
seen her from across the small gathering outside the library. He'd pretended not to watch her . . . though how could he fail to watch Marisa,
standing alert amid the crowd? Even motionless, she was decisive. A
different manner of creature from the silent, reverent group surrounding her. A fuse waiting to light. He was puzzled by her position near the
front of the gathering, and still more puzzled by her brief conference
with the Jewish Society leaders as they prepared to begin the ceremony.
She hardly seemed the sort to hang out with the bubbly, over-earnest
Jewish Soc types. Not until she was on the stone steps with the somber
student leaders—not until she was speaking the names of relatives and
holding a candle—did he understand: Marisa was the granddaughter
of Holocaust survivors. He'd missed it entirely—missed it because she
was nothing like the survivors' granddaughters he'd met at his own college Hillel or his father's synagogue. Those were mostly dutiful girls,
many bearing the names of lost cousins or aunts whose ashes had been
blown all over Europe; perpetual A students who repeated the stories of

their families verbatim, lest a detail be lost. He had no quarrel with such girls, nor did he ever wish to touch one.

He watched, riveted, as Marisa lit a candle, then looked over the heads of the small assembled crowd as though she preferred to make this tribute without the intrusion of their input.

One September evening, still disheartened by the murky and insufficiently air-conditioned summer, Aaron had left the library and ducked into the visual arts building. He aimed to treat himself to a free dinner at a post-lecture reception: a postgraduate's tithe from the fields of academia, sustenance for the hours ahead. The thought of yet another evening's dogged bargaining with an indifferent Shakespeare made panic blossom in his gut. As he firmed his grip on the rail and climbed faster, he indulged a faint, rote hope of running into Marisa, whom he'd twice spotted from a distance in the café, downing her coffee with two or three of the art students. But the stairwell was deserted.

At the second-floor landing he swung left as usual, then stopped short, his shoes squeaking to a halt on the linoleum floor. Through the partially open door of the painting studio to the right he'd glimpsed something he was certain he'd imagined. He walked to the door nonetheless. He pushed it fully open. There was Marisa painted on the canvas, naked. Her skin peach and white against the black velvet drape she lay on, the planes of her body seeming to vibrate with life—small, firm breasts, nipples like drops of dark honey. Her figure lay still on the canvas but there was a warm mocking light to her eyes under her raised black eyebrows, as though the painter had caught her saying *Yes, you.*

Behind the canvas was the cot where she must have posed. The velvet drape was bunched over the arm of a nearby chair.

The pungent smell of drying paint. He let it fill his lungs.

The painter had signed his work. The name, Rodney Keller, was familiar to Aaron—a talented art postgraduate. At the art students' opening last spring—another set of hors d'oeuvres Aaron had raided —Rodney's intensely pigmented portraits had been on exhibit: people more vivid than life, their colors too sharp, their gazes so cutting and direct that the portraits were suffused with the hyper-real intimacy of a camera too close to its subject. Aaron had found himself taking an uncomfortable step back from those canvases. But this painting was different. Rodney Keller had painted Marisa not with the mannered exaggerations of those other portraits, but instead in the quiet, straight-forward boldness of her beauty.

As Aaron stood before her image, elated and stricken, an unheroic question grew in him. He tried to resist it, and failed: Had Marisa slept with Rodney Keller?

Or, was Rodney Keller gay? He seemed gay to Aaron. Seemed it, but Aaron couldn't be sure.

He backed out of the studio.

Nearly a month later, he'd found her after a lecture by an Israeli journalist, titled "Our Side of the Story: An Israeli Perspective." It was anything but coincidence—Anatol Ludman had announced the lecture to his class before the end of last term, and Aaron watched Marisa make note of the date and time—he even heard her tell a classmate that the event was only days before she was due in Israel.

The journalist's weary lecture had been so thinly attended, Aaron couldn't help wonder whether Jewish Studies had deliberately under-publicized it to minimize the inevitable protests an Israeli speaker would draw. But the small audience made for a deeper-than-usual question-and-answer period, which continued until only the journalist and a small knot of audience members stood at the front of the hall—among them Marisa, separated from Aaron by only three undergraduates, then two. Finally, at a broad hint by a portly professor Aaron recognized from the Classics Department, they all drifted outside, past the lone protester lofting a sign that read *Zionists = Nazis,* and into a nearby pub.

He waited until Marisa was on her second beer—he kept track from a distance, chatting with an undergraduate whose name he didn't bother to learn, biding his time. When he approached her at last, his own un-touched beer dangling casually in his hand, she grinned into his face. "I've been watching you," she said, before he had a chance to say more than hello. "You're more complicated than you seem."

Surprised, he matched her grin, the afternoon turning suddenly weightless. "Is that so?" He leaned against the bar and raised his beer. "How do I seem?"

She took a swig from her beer. "You seem like a pompous son-of-a-bitch."

He swallowed. He could smell the beer on her breath. "But now you've discovered . . . ?"

"I get the feeling there's more to you." For a moment she sounded utterly serious.

He could make out the shape of her breasts through her T-shirt. "Tell me," he said, pleased that he sounded both gracious and smooth.

She leaned in and gave his cheek a light, stinging slap. "Tell you about *yourself*? No, thank you."

He felt himself flush, but recovered quickly. "Then tell me about Israel. And don't walk away this time."

She sipped her beer once, twice, before seeming to forgive him enough to answer. She was going to do a few months on a kibbutz, she said, an intense language course combined with volunteer work to help her make the leap into life as a new Israeli citizen. Was sick of American Jewish culture, of *American* culture altogether—and by the way, the English could take a flying leap as well. As she spoke she watched Aaron, a challenge in her expression. She said, "I want to be with people who know what they care about and aren't afraid to say so."

For once he kept his mouth shut. He didn't try to prove to her that he knew what he cared about. He couldn't. Had he opened his mouth, he might have confessed that all he cared about right now was not making a fool of himself any more than he already had, not watching her recede out the door, across the courtyard, past the man packing up his *Zionists* = *Nazis* poster outside the windows, and away into the city —the last glimpse of her he'd ever catch.

He said—had he ever said this to a woman, and was it as much of a cliché as he feared it was?— *"Tell me more."* And then listened, or tried to. When she turned her sharp, teasing questions on him, he answered as carefully as though he'd been wired to a polygraph machine. Because he knew, somehow, that to be glib with Marisa would bring an end to the conversation once and for all.

An hour later they were in her room, their bodies a slow, winding tangle on the sheets.

It was impossible for him to pinpoint, after, what was different. He looked at her body, and at his own, and his chest caught as though on a hook. Something in the room had changed. The floor of her dormitory room was still strewn with items yet to be added to her half-packed suitcases—but the light from the small window above her bed had melded with the glow of her skin and the golden sounds of the sliding sheets and the bright heart-pounding world outside, as though some unspeakably precious substance were being fused, and the only words that came to him — words like *holy*, like *sacred* — belonged to things he didn't believe in.

Their bodies were at an angle: her muscled calves cantilevered on Aaron's long shins, her body reclining against the wall in an echo he couldn't resist, and he confessed, "I saw your portrait."

Marisa laughed. Her face was to the ceiling; he saw it in profile.

"Did it turn you on?" she asked. "People say that."

He didn't trust himself to speak. He prepared an enigmatic smile, which she did not turn her head to see.

People.

How many people?

"Rodney's the man," she said. And yawned, and kicked her legs into the air and rocked her trim body forward, hopping off the bed in a smooth motion and crossing to the bathroom.

The man. He almost laughed at the unfairness of the expression, an expression that, from her, could mean anything. And did *people* mean women, too? It seemed possible, anything seemed possible. Or did *people* simply mean besotted fools like him . . . a guy who thought the earth had moved even though Marisa apparently had not been left weak-kneed by what they'd just done on her gold-lit, rumpled bed? Maybe it meant fools whose dissertation topics weren't invitations to disaster, who didn't tighten their pecs when naked in front of her — in short, who were possibly (was it possible?) not intimidated by Marisa.

She returned with two glasses of tap water.

How was it that no gesture of hers could be servile? That she could bring him water naked, after they'd made love on her blanketless bed in her half-packed dormitory room, and he'd accept it from her knowing that he, and only he, was the barefoot supplicant.

Before they'd parted, while they still sat naked side by side on the bed, she'd set her water glass on the floor and taken his chin in her palm.

He met her gaze and tried not to blink.

"When I fall for someone," she said, "it's absolute and immediate." Her gaze wasn't ungentle — but neither did she seem worried about his feelings. She looked at him with the directness of someone making an inner calculus over which he was to have no influence. "Or else I know, absolutely and immediately, that I have no interest."

He didn't allow himself to duck her eyes.

"With you I'm not sure." She released his chin but didn't drop her gaze. "There's something about you that makes me hesitate."

A moment passed. Then Marisa's expression eased, and she offered him a smile of unexpected softness. "I'm not used to hesitating," she said.

HE SAT NOW AT THE TABLE, hunched against the cold, his screen blanched in the window's light. Then he looked at the header on Marisa's e-mail and saw that she had written it only eleven minutes before—early evening, Israel time. If he hurried he might catch her.

Thanks for your note, Marisa, he typed. *I'm glad my lecture didn't make you run for the hills.*

The taste of beer came back to him, the smell of the dimly lit pub, the feel of her slap on his cheek. With a focus that had eluded him at the time, he now recalled bits of their conversation at the bar. Marisa seated, her sandaled feet tucked behind a rung of the high stool; he standing, beer in hand. There had been an instant—hadn't there?—when something shifted. He was almost certain now that he remembered it. Just before Marisa straightened and took his hand, and led him away from the pub to her bedroom. There'd been some kind of segue—a story Marisa related about her gay brother, before shaking her adamant mood with a laugh—but Aaron didn't rack his memory for its details now because the arrow of memory had already carried him beyond it and straight to what he needed. Why hadn't he recalled this part of their discussion before? Marisa saying something disparaging about American Jews, and Aaron asking what Marisa had against them, given that she was one. And then Marisa had looked right at him, her forehead furrowing—and then, in a conspiratorial flash, she'd seemed to decide that something about Aaron might be worth taking a flyer. "No offense," she mock-whispered. She rested one hand lightly on his forearm; he felt its warmth through his rolled sleeve. "American Jews are naive. They don't want memory, or history that might make them uncomfortable, they just want to be liked. Being liked is their . . . *sugar rush*." She sat back, lifting away her hand. The ghost of its warmth remained on Aaron's skin. "American Jews are addicted to sugar," she pronounced, "*and* to being liked." Aaron could only laugh at the beery neatness of this declaration, but Marisa's eyes tightened as though his amusement displeased her. "It's a serious thing," she said. "I'll probably be the most left-wing person in all of Israel, but at least I'll be arguing with people who deal with reality instead of living in a bubble."

Marisa, granddaughter of Holocaust survivors. Her fierce words about memory felt like the key to something important they might have in common.

He typed:

I think about this a great deal: If we looked through the eyes of history, we'd live differently. We'd live right.
—A

He pressed Send. Then, unwilling to close his laptop, he pretended to engage his mind with other things that would please Helen, looking up definitions of archaic Portuguese words he already knew while his e-mail window remained open on his screen.

Three minutes, four, five.

His screen blinked. A reply from Marisa. He opened it. The e-mail was one line long.

If I looked through the eyes of history, I wouldn't want to live.

Helen Watt was talking to him. He looked up but did not comprehend.

"For the third time," she said. Her expression was keen with something that looked like anger. "I think Aleph was female."

He stared at her.

"Evidently you don't realize what a significant development this may be."

He offered, more weakly than he wished, "I do."

She shook her head skeptically. "She'd have to have an education beyond what a girl would usually receive," Helen said. "She'd have been in a situation quite unusual for—"

"What's the evidence?" he interrupted.

Pressing her lips together, she indicated the letter.

He donned the hateful gloves, pulled the letter toward him, and read it through. When he'd finished, he pushed it away carefully across the tabletop. "Fascinating, sure." He knew he oughtn't be so brusque, but for the moment he didn't care. "They probably married her off the next week, though—sent some young man from Amsterdam to scribe for the rabbi just like they said they would. I doubt there's much of a trail to follow."

Helen Watt pursed her lips and seemed to keep a thought to herself.

He sat back at his computer. His mind rang with defenses, vindications, excuses. He wanted to open his e-mail and type *What I meant was.*

Instead he opened the file he should have been working on all along. The busywork would right him. And then, when he'd settled himself down, he would know—he would work out—how to answer Marisa.

Cursing his gloves, he rifled the stack and pulled out the English version of HaCoen Mendes's sermon. The spellings were worse than the usual seventeenth-century fare, the writer either poorly educated or new to English. "Use a dictionary, Aleph," he muttered, though of course there had been few dictionaries in those days. He began the mindless labor of comparing this version with the translation he'd already prepared from the Portuguese version. The work was slow and, despite his effort to resist, his path through it was riddled with self-recrimination. Why had he e-mailed Marisa without first thinking it through? In his haste, had he offended her? Failed a test?

Well, Marisa, he thought, *you have my full attention.* Something no other woman had yet achieved. It was perhaps not so great an honor as he'd thought.

He forced himself to concentrate. Quickly he read through the remainder of the lecture. The Portuguese and English versions were identical—though Aaron's English sounded like English, and Aleph's grammar was upside down even by seventeenth-century standards. *But rather that labor we steady and humble in our day—*

Beside him, Helen was absorbed in her work.

"I'm going out to get lunch," he said.

She nodded without looking up.

"Would you like anything from the shop across the way?" An olive branch. Some grad students fetched coffee, some dog-sat for the professors they worked with; Aaron as a rule did nothing of the sort.

She shook her head.

"Don't you eat?"

Helen lifted her head from her work.

He'd meant it as a joke, the old tactic of establishing familiarity by assuming it, but the words had come out tinged with antagonism.

She was silent for a moment. Then she said, "I eat."

She went back to her work.

Where was the button he could press to erase the past fifteen minutes? He had no business being nasty to the only professor likely to save him from Shakespeare. He wanted to apologize, but Helen didn't look up. And he couldn't bring himself to call for her attention when he didn't know what words ought to follow.

He put on his coat and left the building. The air was colder than he'd expected. He walked quickly through the thin scrim of snow to stave off a faint, unfamiliar nausea of self-doubt. He bought himself a sandwich from the grocery next to Prospero's and doubled back to the house to eat it.

Helen was nowhere to be seen.

They had only another hour before the Sotheby's representative was due. He ought to translate at least one more document. He hung his coat on the rack in the entryway and set his food on the table in the library—he'd eat quickly and keep working. He sat, began to unwrap his sandwich, then stopped.

He told himself he could use it as a bargaining chip. He'd have information Helen might someday want, and if she didn't kill him, she'd thank him. They still didn't know, after all, the exact nature of the relationship between Rabbi HaCoen Mendes and the Benjamin HaLevy who'd owned this great house. Maybe knowing something about how HaLevy's family had lived, how extravagant his house had been, would prove essential.

Of course, she'd told him not to.

Exactly.

He felt himself smile, and when he stood, though no one was there to see, he walked with a deliberately confident step.

The staircase was wide, the risers low, the climb an ascent of infinite shallow steps. His shoes thumped softly on thick wooden treads—the solidest construction he'd ever seen. No wonder the thing had lasted centuries. He passed the second floor, catching a quick glimpse of hallways leading to a series of side rooms—he'd explore there later if time allowed.

On the topmost floor the staircase ended in a wide landing, its cream-colored walls punctuated by large rectangular shadows—spots where portraits had once presumably hung in more extravagant days. A broad doorway led off the landing into a wide, dark-paneled balcony, its railing topped with elaborate carved flowers. Four partially open doors led off the balcony and several more were closed. Crossing to the nearest open door, Aaron swung it wide. It glided on silent hinges to reveal a small room. Furnished with desk, computer, and bookcases, it could have passed for a modern study if not for the narrow mullioned window and the carved wreath on the ceiling. Back to the balcony. The second door Aaron opened—a narrow jib door barely distinguishable from the wall's paneling—revealed a twisting servants' stair—a steep, dim descent that had once led, presumably, to the necessary rooms at the root of the house: kitchen, scullery, wine cellar. But the third door revealed a broad and more elegant chamber, brightly lit, with high windows and its own large hearth. The hearth was empty, the floor strewn with boxes. Evidently the Eastons hadn't yet fully unpacked. Aaron could see that an open door beyond the sea of boxes led from the back of this room to a second large chamber, also filled with boxes, beyond which he could glimpse a doorway to a third. The suite of rooms, now impassable due to clutter, had obviously been designed in the style of the apartment of a nobleman or noblewoman: an anteroom, followed by what would have been a bedroom, followed by the closet, the most private of domestic spaces, a room for Shakespearean intrigue—Hamlet killing Polonius through the arras, Lady Macbeth sleepwalking. Whoever had built this house, Aaron thought, had either held high social station or aspired to it. If he guessed right, there would be another matching apartment opposite it—the lady would have had her own set of rooms, the lord his.

And sure enough, the fourth door off the landing revealed the largest space yet. This anteroom, clearly now in service as the Eastons' sitting room, was topped with carvings that matched those in the first anteroom Aaron had seen, and was lit by three grand windows. In the center of the high-ceilinged room were a sofa, a few chairs, and a low table scattered with magazines and used dishes. Beyond it, a wide, open doorway led to a room containing a casually made bed and, everywhere, traces of Bridgette: a scarf dangling from the dresser top, two pairs of high-heeled shoes askew on the floor. Set in the far wall of this second room was a closed door—presumably the entrance to the inner sanctum—another elaborately carved closet, Aaron guessed, if it hadn't already been converted into a modern master bathroom.

The door in the far wall opened. "Oh," said Bridgette.

She wore a bathrobe. Her loose hair was bright against the green silk. For a moment she stood, disoriented, the centers of her blue eyes dark. A woman unguarded and afloat, unsure whose life she was waking to.

Then, swiftly, her expression tightened and turned wry. "Aren't you supposed to be working downstairs?"

The house was silent. He had no idea whether Helen had returned from wherever she'd disappeared to. Before him, Bridgette stood, her composure restored, one hand set on her hip.

"Apologies," Aaron said, keeping his expression neutral. He couldn't help noticing the flow of the silk down Bridgette's body. The places where it clung.

"Are you looking for something?" Suspicion warred with something kittenish in Bridgette's voice.

He told her the truth. "I was checking the number of rooms."

"Why?" she countered, a smile forming on her lips.

"We're interested in what sort of household hid those documents. How wealthy, how large." The *we* was a mistake, Aaron realized; she'd assume he'd snooped at Helen's request and would surely mention it to Helen. "Actually," he added with a small smile of his own, "*I'm* the one who wanted to know. I think getting the basic layout of the house may be helpful. I didn't think anyone was home." He lowered his voice. "I hope you'll forgive me?"

She pursed her lips as though considering this. "Sotheby's is coming," she said softly. "You'll have to wrestle with your curiosity someplace else. Outside of my bedroom."

He was grateful that he didn't blush easily. "Of course."

Her blue eyes were wide set, the elegant planes of her face lovely. He could make out her nipples under the robe.

"You do seem extremely curious," she added, a lilt in her voice.

The power was his to claim or forfeit. He remembered himself, returned her stare, and waited until their eyes had been locked for several seconds. He said, "I am."

He turned and left the room. And crossed the landing with the sensation of waking from the trance he'd been in since receiving Marisa's second e-mail. *This,* he thought, was who he was. A man who knew when to leave a woman to absorb his words.

He was fairly certain that he had no particular interest in Bridgette beyond playing the game. But he sure as hell could play.

He descended the staircase at an unhurried pace. Whatever repercussion he might face for going upstairs, he'd keep his cool. It was a commitment. A religion. Aaron Levy, high priest of chill. He took the steps deliberately, savoring the steady working of his leg muscles, and he determined to answer Marisa's e-mail with dry wit—after waiting at least one day.

Downstairs, Helen was at the table. As he entered she looked up distractedly, seeming not to notice that his footsteps had come from the wrong direction. The papers before her were in disarray, as though she'd abruptly discarded caution and shuffled them with her own hands. He glanced at his watch. The assessor from Sotheby's would be here in forty-five minutes.

Helen's face was taut. She addressed Aaron as though they'd been in the middle of a conversation, and it was a moment before he could follow her meaning. "The next eleven documents are all dated in the six months after the Yacob de Souza letter. And each one is in her handwriting and bears her initial." With wavering fingers, Helen gestured at the pages fanned across the table. The motion was clumsy, and he resisted an urge to snatch the fragile papers away. "Letters," she indicated. "Lists. Another sermon. Two orders for books. So Aleph didn't stop scribing for the rabbi, if I'm understanding this correctly. They *didn't* replace her, at least not in the half year after that letter from Amsterdam. But now look at this." She waved him toward a page covered heavily in a broad and unfamiliar handwriting.

It was a letter from an Amsterdam scholar he'd never heard of, dated only by the Hebrew *5 Shvat, 5424,* and written in an elaborate, scholarly Hebrew. Aaron skimmed, understanding half of what he read. The subject was a disputation about the nature of time in the Torah. Evidently some third party had asserted that the Torah's chronology contradicted itself, and the writer was launching what promised to be a lengthy elaboration on the meaning of phrases such as *thousands of years.*

Helen was waving impatiently.

"I'm reading as fast as I can," Aaron protested.

"Skip to the fourth paragraph."

He started the paragraph, near the bottom of the page. *For G-d is not bound by nature but is its creator and alters it at will, so the understanding of the sun's movements and the cycling of the seasons rests beyond man's* — Aaron puzzled over the next words, something about either understanding or wisdom.

"The margin!" Helen commanded.

There, in the margin alongside the third paragraph, written in the same elegant handwriting Aaron had been reading for three days, were the words *Deus sive Natura.*

He stared at the page: the blockish Hebrew of the Amsterdam rabbi; the small sloping letters added by Aleph in the margin. And the Latin: one of Spinoza's catchphrases. He recognized it from a philosophy course he'd taken his senior year in college. *Deus sive Natura: God or Nature.* The phrase encompassed Spinoza's radical notion that God and nature might be one and the same. It was the springing-off point for Spinoza's mind-bending contentions about extension, determinism, and more.

"This makes no sense," Aaron declared.

Helen waited.

"Where the hell does a seventeenth-century Jew — let alone a seventeenth-century *woman,* if Aleph is even really a woman — get off making a reference to Spinoza? Spinoza was banned. Plus this is Latin, and there's no reason a Jewish woman would study Latin, let alone have any involvement with philosophy." Yet there was no denying that Aleph's margin note was a direct comment on the part of the letter that referred to God as separate from nature. A *contradiction* of it. He thought a moment. "This letter is what, 1660?" he said. "Spinoza hadn't even published his major works then, had he? Who would even know about his theories at that point?"

Helen's answer came low and compressed. "Maybe someone from the community that excommunicated him. The Portuguese Jewish community of Amsterdam."

Aaron raised his head. "Do you think HaCoen Mendes or his scribe might have crossed paths with Spinoza?"

"It wasn't a large community."

There was a sharp knock on the great carved door. It echoed in the entryway.

Neither Helen nor Aaron moved. Then, abruptly, Helen pulled several more pages to her and began scanning them.

The door's knocker sounded again, heavily. Then again.

There was a rustle from above, followed by Bridgette's step on the stairs. "Coming . . . ," she called. She was dressed now, wearing slacks and a powder-blue wrap and heels. She didn't look at Aaron as she passed.

Helen still hadn't raised her eyes. Aaron heard a man's voice, and Bridgette's teasing response: "You're early. You scholars are an eager lot."

A flirtation meant for Aaron's ears, or the unseen stranger's? Aaron was too preoccupied by what he'd just read to care. But the portly figure that accompanied Bridgette across the entryway provided the answer. The assessor, a short, middle-aged man, grasped two satchels in his right hand. A stack of large polyester-film document sleeves refused to stay tucked under his left arm, causing him to pause midway across the room to adjust them; as soon as he resumed walking, they slid immediately out of place once again. It would have been comical, Aaron thought, in another situation. Everything about the man said bookworm. Everything about him said cozy, likable, unthreatening, and Aaron hated him immediately. Any notion they'd had of what these documents might be had been sent flurrying by three words of Latin: Aleph might or might not have been a woman; might or might not have been copying down opinions she didn't understand; might or might not have been championing Spinoza's notions. The mystery, Aaron felt instinctively, should rightly be Helen's and his to solve—but now the documents were being impounded. And if the assessor spotted the Spinoza reference, there was no guarantee that the whole trove wouldn't be snatched by another institution that could limit Aaron's access—the papers might even be locked away by a private collector, if England didn't have strong enough patrimony laws against that sort of thing.

Bridgette led the assessor into the nook beside the stair; without a word, Helen and Aaron stood and rounded the corner, in time to see the man bend before the open panel under the stair.

There was a long silence.

"Oh my," the man said.

Aaron followed his gaze to the open space: the top shelf that Helen and Aaron had only partially succeeded in emptying, the untouched shelf of documents below.

The assessor straightened with a grunt of effort, his eyes still fixed on the cupboard beneath the stair. The soft smile that broke on his face hurt Aaron's stomach.

Helen's voice behind Aaron nearly made him jump. "Good afternoon."

The assessor turned, still smiling. "You're the historian Mrs. Easton has told me about, I trust?"

"Yes," said Helen. "A pleasure to meet you." She turned from the assessor to Bridgette—who pressed her lips together in a way that said *Now that that's done with.*

In fact, something in Bridgette's tight expression surprised Aaron. He hadn't spotted it until now—but Helen had gotten under Bridgette's skin. He'd no idea why. He decided not to care.

He braced, instead, for the launch of Helen's argument: they needed more time with the manuscripts. Another hour or even half-hour would do.

"Well then," Helen said to Bridgette. "Thank you for your toleration of our little endeavor here. We'll be on our way."

Helen turned for the library.

Aaron followed her only as far as the doorway. There he stopped, confused. Helen was gathering her things with the slow, careful motions of a woman who could not, after all, get worked up over something as trivial as having these papers taken out of their hands for what, with luck, might be only a period of weeks or months.

He turned back to look at the open stairwell. There, beyond Bridgette pattering about her renovation plans and the assessor fussing with his

satchels, lay a set of documents that had traveled mutely through centuries to arrive here, fragile and mysterious as a newborn. Aaron Levy,
unworthy, had cradled them for just a moment in his hands. And all he
wanted was to hold them again.

"Mr. Levy?" Helen Watt stood with her satchel, her coat folded
across her arm.

Did the woman reserve her strength strictly for bullying subordi-
nates? Was she incapable of mustering to do battle when it was important?

In the silence, the assessor let a pile of transparent sleeves slither
onto a chair. As the man knelt laboriously to remove a first document
from the shelves, Bridgette gave Aaron an amused smile.

He met it with a flat stare, then turned for the library. He stacked his
notes, packed away his laptop, threw on his coat, and followed Helen
out the front door. Someone—Bridgette, he presumed—shut it behind them.

Outside on the path he confronted Helen. "So you're just going to
walk away? Wait for someone else to decide whether we ever get another shot at those papers?"

It had stopped snowing. A light coating covered the ground, and the
black branches of two trees overhanging the yard clicked against each
other in a brief wind.

"I didn't wish to argue for more time," Helen said quietly, "or draw
attention to what we found in the margin. The assessor might not notice
it. Not every specialist in antiquities, not even one from Sotheby's, is
going to know the difference between a catch phrase of Spinoza's and
three random Latin words."

Gathering her coat collar tighter to her throat, she looked up at the
house. "Both of us did," she said.

She was complimenting him, he realized belatedly.

"If Sotheby's spots the Spinoza reference," she continued, "and if
they think it's evidence that someone in the London Jewish community
might have been debating Spinoza's ideas even before Spinoza published them, the availability of these papers is going to be hard to keep
mum. The price of the documents might rise out of our reach. Jonathan
Martin may be able to jolly the vice chancellor into a moderate expen-
diture, but there are limits."

The stonework of the house was bluish in the falling light, the frigid afternoon rapidly darkening. Inside, the assessor would now be beginning his work in earnest. The thought of the papers being carted away from this hulking edifice — the stairwell that had housed them left hollow — filled Aaron with an irrational loneliness.

He was surprised to note that Helen was, for once, looking at him in a way that was almost sympathetic.

"Well," Aaron said, momentarily disoriented. He buttoned his coat and tried to sound chipper, though he'd no stomach for it. "At least we've got a head start on other scholars who might hear about the papers."

He expected a lecture about the universal benefits of collaborative scholarship, which would have restored him to a comfortable irritability. Instead Helen smiled grimly, as though she appreciated his competitive spirit.

Darkness had begun to blur the roof and the out-flung walls of the large weathered house. Aaron crammed his fists into his pockets and looked, dumbly, at his feet. The snow-covered dirt he stood on had been trod more than three hundred years ago by the occupants of the great house. He wished obscurely now for the company of those people — as though knowing them could warm him, change him in some necessary way he couldn't manage on his own.

"It doesn't make sense," he said softly, though he wasn't even sure what he was referring to. All of it, maybe: Marisa's e-mail, the assessor's satisfied smile, the papers. His own strange, abrupt grief.

Helen started down the path, her cane leaving small black circles in the thin snow.

He walked beside her, matching her slow pace. "Why," he said, his voice strengthening, "would *any* Jew in a religious community risk taking Spinoza seriously — let alone write down his words? All contact with Spinoza and his ideas was forbidden. If I'm remembering right, it was forbidden in the most severe, threatening terms the rabbis could muster."

Helen stopped walking. She leaned on her cane. At first Aaron thought she was resting, but then he saw her eyes. Their cornflower blue was shockingly keen, her face alive in the lowering sun. She didn't look like the colorless harridan he'd suffered under for the past three days.

She wore an expression of complete attentiveness, at once mournful and reckless.

Knowing when not to speak was a talent that visited Aaron rarely. But as it settled on him now with its feathery grace, he knew to be grateful.

She said to him then, crisply, "Never underestimate the passion of a lonely mind."

She lifted her cane and continued ahead of him down the path.

Part 2

10

October 2, 1659
15 Tishrei, 5420
London

My love is as a fever, longing still
For that which longer nurseth the disease.

She fitted her hands to the rippled glass of two diamond-shaped panes.

On the street below a thin, distorted stream of strangers passed — none bracing his gaze against the white sky to glance up at her window.

What might she possibly be longing for?

She pulled herself away from the window. Rubbed her hands together to warm them. The failure of the Lord Protector's son was rippling through London; she'd heard shopkeepers say change was everywhere. In the wake of the younger Cromwell's abdication, gambling and theater were springing back already. Motes of life rising, defying the morbid sobriety of the Puritans. Soon, perhaps, there would be a final end to Puritan apparel, a return to bright fabrics, ribbons. Even, perhaps, the return of a king.

And if there were? What had she to do with London even now, and what sense wishing for change?

The figures below her window wavered in the thick glass of the bottom panes. They stretched, their somber colors braided — then seemed to loft, curving into the air before snapping out of view — angels or devils climbing their own ladders, wending toward their business in a world beyond her reach.

There remained only one flame still lit in her life. It glimmered in the room below, in the rabbi's mercifully quiet library.

She descended the stair.

From the library, the rabbi's voice dipped and rose. After a hesitation, his soft chant was taken up by the bleary voices of his two pupils.

"Moshe kibel torah m'sinai" . . . How many times had she heard Isaac repeat the words of this lesson at the rabbi's patient insistence? And how Isaac would have laughed at the spectacle that greeted her now as she reached the bottom of the stair: the HaLevy brothers—two young men with beards already sprouted on their chins—reciting phrases that should be the province of boys fresh from their first haircuts.

For an instant, Isaac's boyish chanting voice broke the surface of her memory. She pressed her fingertips into the hard wood of the handrail until they whitened.

She would constrict the world to a pinhole.

Pushing off from the handrail, she walked across the room, toward the light still available to her. She settled at her table, ignoring the curious glances of the HaLevy brothers. She took up a quill and began to copy the letter she'd written for the rabbi that morning. Across the room, the rabbi was passing the next phrase to the brothers, tipping each syllable gently from his lips: *"U'masrah l'Yehoshua, v'Yehoshua la'zkenim."* The younger of the two mumbled after him; the older had fallen silent.

The rabbi paused, waiting for his second pupil to repeat the words.

"I didn't hear," the older brother said, in a voice that made no attempt to mask his lack of interest.

Did he think the rabbi too blind to comprehend rudeness?

But Rabbi HaCoen Mendes merely offered the line once more, and the elder brother repeated it in an indifferent tone. His younger brother's voice swiftly joined, as though in apology for the elder's inattention.

The two dark-haired sons of the merchant Benjamin HaLevy: according to Rivka they'd been sent to study with the rabbi only because their father wished to please the rabbi's rich nephew, Diego da Costa Mendes, with whom he'd invested heavily in a trade venture in the New World. Ester lifted her face from her work for just a moment now to regard them. The younger was slightly built, with a pale, oval face and a nervous air. His eyes rested on the rabbi only briefly; then returned, troubled, to his older brother; then ventured toward Ester, almost reaching her before fleeing back to his brother, as though seeking the next cue as to how he ought conduct himself.

As for the elder brother, Ester had free rein to watch him now. He'd leaned back in his cushioned seat with his eyes closed, bored.

"*V'zkenim li'nvi'im,*" the rabbi continued.

The next time Ester looked up from her work, she saw that the older brother had sat forward and was watching her, his eyes a keen adamantine color—green and brown that made her think of dirty brass. He was taller and more thickly built than his younger brother; the set of his jaw said he was accustomed to the fulfillment of his wishes.

"Coffee," he called, his voice booming across the rabbi's in the quiet room.

She'd started in her seat. It took her a moment to realize he was issuing a command, and another to realize it wasn't addressed to her, but to Rivka in the kitchen.

There was a silence, interrupted only by the sound of the fire. Then he smiled at Ester, just slightly. *Here we are, looking at one another,* his smile said, *and the blind rabbi doesn't know.* An idle invitation, issued perhaps only to amuse himself. Nothing in his demeanor said he thought her worth more.

Still, she felt herself straighten, her indignation twinned with curiosity.

The rabbi continued. "The sages would say three things," he said. "'Be temperate in judgment. Take many pupils. Make a fence around the Torah.'"

The elder brother's eyes still held hers—a lazy dare. He was sprawled in his seat, as though its confines, too, bored him. He lifted his chin.

Beside him, the younger brother turned from him to Ester, uncertain.

Alvaro HaLevy—that was the younger one's name. And the elder was Manuel. She met Manuel's stare with a stony one of her own. His brows rose: he was amused by her defiance. Together they ignored his smooth-cheeked brother.

"Make a fence around the Torah," she pronounced, without dropping her gaze. "Meaning, establish further requirements beyond the perimeter of God's laws. This shows the sages' eagerness to follow God's word, and their wish that even those who stumble fulfilling the details of these additional laws won't risk violating God's will."

The rabbi turned his face and spoke mildly. "I trust, Ester, that Manuel and Alvaro are capable of interpreting the passage without your aid."

She flushed, but brushed aside the rebuke—and along with it, some dim hunger Manuel's stare had woken in her. At least she'd made her mind clear to Manuel, she told herself, on the matter of his rudeness. It served nothing for the rabbi to tolerate such behavior. In this she and Rivka were in agreement.

As if summoned by this last thought, rather than Manuel's command, Rivka emerged from the kitchen. She served the rabbi first, then set a small bowl before each brother. It pained Rivka, Ester knew, to dispense the sooty coffee to the rabbi's students—she was in the habit of grinding the precious beans only as a medicinal for the rabbi. Although the rabbi's nephew had thus far paid them a handsome upkeep, Rivka still treated each month's payment as though it might be the last, and counted each coin with a suspicion that made the delivery boy mutter about *the hag Jewess*. But even Rivka understood that the HaLevy boys' money and family connection must be respected. If they required coffee, she'd serve it.

Only later, rinsing the grounds from the bowl in the kitchen, would Rivka mutter her verdict: *uma papa santos*. A saint-sucker. Her rounded shoulders rolling in rhythm as she worked bread dough with the heels of her hands, she'd break her laboring silence to say abruptly to Ester, *They've traded faith—for—gold*. In truth, it seemed to Ester that Rivka's condemnation encompassed any Portuguese Jew who'd succeeded in evading death, whether through true conversion or merely by donning a thin mask of Catholicism here in London. Only those who'd confessed to the Inquisition and been killed—or nearly killed, such as the rabbi —seemed to merit Rivka's respect. Her thick back twisting to one side, then the other, her hair escaping her cap in limp strands, Rivka hove into the dough with the single-mindedness of one who knew death to arrive in the form of flying hooves and clubs—never in the form of a choice. The Inquisition, in her view, offered all of Sephardic Jewry a gift denied to her and the other Tudesco Jews: the opportunity to *choose* death, rather than having it descend unannounced. Death, for Rivka and her Polish kin, was a pogrom scouring all in its path—not an iron-wielding priest offering a small window to freedom that might possibly be unlatched by disavowing one's Judaism. Once, wringing linens in the attic, she had said, *In my village, they died without even a moment to pray. That's how it was: The men with clubs came. The village died.* Though Ester waited, there was no more. Rivka bent over the buck-basket in the dim attic. A sudden splatter of heavy droplets raining into the wash water.

But if Manuel HaLevy knew that the woman who now served him coffee considered him a saint-sucker, he was indifferent to the charge. He raised his bowl in one hand and drained it at once. "More," he said.

Rivka removed the bowl.

A knock at the door.

Rivka, bowl in hand, opened it. The change in her expression was instant: the quick snuffing of a candle.

"Well?" A voice like a curled ribbon, high and pretty—and familiar, though Ester was surprised to hear it at the rabbi's threshold. "You did receive our letter saying we'd call?"

Ester had long been struck by Rivka's ability to make herself impenetrable in the face of Amsterdam's wealthy, offering no detectable response in face or body to their scoldings as she tended their needs. Now Rivka, impassive, swung the door wide to admit Mary da Costa Mendes, the daughter of the rabbi's nephew. Entering behind her daughter, Catherine da Costa Mendes chided in a fainter voice, "Mary, didn't you know better . . . than to have my note delivered to a Tudesco?" Overriding Mary's murmured excuse, her mother's voice continued in bursts: "Next time, Mary . . . have the message boy deliver the letter to . . . someone who can read."

For the barest instant, Ester saw the ripple where the arrow went in —but by the time the two women had stepped into the house, Rivka's face had closed and locked once more.

They entered, mother and daughter, elegant dark skirts swaying fore and aft like bells as they walked. Mary's dress was laced tight, placing her abundant bosom and the white flesh of her upper arms on full display. Her plump face was framed by immaculate black ringlets. She peered about the room with hungry fascination. Catherine da Costa Mendes handed Rivka her fox-fur tippet; then allowed Rivka to ease the cloak from her shoulders, revealing a broad farthingale and heavy skirt, each thickly embroidered with silver thread. Unbidden, Isaac's name for such women rang teasingly in Ester's memory: *tapecaria andadoria: walking tapestry.* But Catherine da Costa Mendes's labored inhalations, audible from across the room, made Ester doubt she was in robust enough health to bear the weight of her attire about London.

"Coffee," the woman breathed at Rivka.

Rivka disappeared into the kitchen.

In austere silence, Catherine da Costa Mendes surveyed the rabbi's study. Beyond offering a generous nod of greeting in the street or the synagogue, she'd not concerned herself with the doings of the household her husband supported. Even within London's small constellation of Portuguese Jews, the da Costa Mendes family was set apart. Alone among the synagogue's matrons, Catherine seemed uninterested in gossip—more than once Ester had seen her summon Mary from an avidly whispering cluster with a disapproving glance. Nor did the family come and go from the synagogue by foot, as did even the wealthiest of the other Jews. It was common to see the trio alight from a fine black coach, even on the Sabbath: deep-voiced, silver-haired Diego with a vigorous step, pattens protecting his fine shoes from the street's muck; Catherine more slowly and with the air of one much older, as though the years had spun faster for her than for her husband. And, stepping onto the cobbles delicately—toe, then heel, as though confident of being watched, pausing with a white hand laid as if casually on the coach's well-shined black veneer—their one daughter, sole surviving child of whatever number Catherine had birthed.

The rabbi spoke—for a moment Ester had forgotten his presence. "Whom do I have the honor of welcoming in my home?"

Catherine da Costa Mendes turned her head regally to gaze at the rabbi. She was not, it was apparent, accustomed to explaining herself. Broadening her gaze to include the HaLevy brothers, she summoned Manuel with a slight nod.

The brothers rose—the younger with a quick and nervous smile, Manuel at his leisure but with respect.

"Catherine da Costa Mendes," said Manuel in a deep and formal voice. "And her lovely daughter, Mary."

Had something—amusement, perhaps?—flickered below those last words of his? Ester noted the color rising in Mary's face.

"Greetings to you, Uncle," said the matron in Portuguese.

The rabbi stood. It seemed to take him a long time, and longer before

Catherine da Costa Mendes understood what was required and stepped forward and laid her gloved hand in his, not unkindly, for him to kiss.

The rabbi sat. "Welcome to this home your family so graciously provides us."

Catherine, standing above him, replied with a nod, and opened her mouth to speak. But Mary spoke first—not to the rabbi, but to Ester. "We're here to see you!" Mary said, as though the announcement were a gift.

None had asked to visit with Ester since her arrival in London—she couldn't fathom what Mary might wish with her. Dumbly she gestured at the quill and paper on the table. "I've yet to finish," she said. "It's for the rabbi . . ."

But a lift of the rabbi's head in Ester's direction said she'd find no shelter in this excuse.

She stood, straightened her skirt, and followed the two women to the small side room where Rivka was setting two bowls of coffee—not hot enough to steam, Ester noticed—on a small table between two seats. The room was cold, having no hearth, and musty from disuse. Until now, Rivka had kept the door shut, to prevent this chamber from stealing heat from the larger room.

Catherine claimed the larger chair beside the window. Mary plumped down on the smaller seat, the fabric of her skirt covering most of the cushion and leaving only a narrow space beside her. "Sit," Mary said to Ester.

Ester lowered herself into the space.

Mary looked at her mother with evident satisfaction, as though Ester's obedience proved a point in an argument Ester hadn't been privy to. Then, sitting so close that the abundant layers of her dress overwhelmed Ester's paltry muslin skirt, Mary turned to face Ester full on. Ester found herself edging away until her leg pressed against the hard wooden railing of the seat.

From the doorway, where she stood with her back to the closed door and her arms tucked behind her in a pose of compliance, Rivka spoke flatly. "Is the coffee to your liking?"

Her tone invited no answer and the women gave none.

"What's your age?" Mary said abruptly.

It took Ester a moment to muster an answer. "Twenty-one."

"Only?" said Mary, disbelieving.

Catherine cast a glance at her daughter: *I told you.*

A pout flickered across Mary's lips; evidently she'd thought Ester older. "But the hair," she said. As Ester's hand floated to her hair, Mary let out a ripple of eager laughter. "See her hair, Mother! A half silver and a half sable. Like a woman thrice her years, except her brows are black. She might as well don a periwig and be a proper Royalist gentleman." She tugged a loose lock of Ester's hair. "Or perhaps it *is* a periwig, you seditious girl." Mary's face shone with pleasure at her own daring. Then, as though Ester were a pet newly adopted, she tucked Ester's arm under her own. "Well," she said. "Lost color may be had again. We'll turn it black soon, or whatever color suits."

Catherine frowned at her daughter, then addressed Ester. "How do you amuse yourself?"

There was a silence. At last Ester echoed, "Amuse myself?"

Catherine gestured loosely, impatient to be understood. "What are your amusements?"

"I've none."

Catherine lifted her eyebrows. "Good," she said.

Ester withdrew her arm carefully from Mary's. "I don't understand the nature of this visit."

"Well, then." Catherine drew herself up. "Here's the nature." She waited through two shallow breaths before continuing. "All London is eager for folly. I don't call it wrong. The city has been overfed with strictures, and now clamors to shake off Puritan ways. New entertainments now begin. And our Mary is enamored of every one that's dreamt of —whether or not it be madness." For a moment Catherine gazed at the wall as though it were a window. But this dignified show of distraction was, Ester sensed, only a way to rest from the taxing act of speech. Even through carefully applied powder, Catherine's face showed marks of long and heavy strain. Ester was surprised at an impulse to stand, loosen the woman's stays, rub her broad back. The desire tightened her own chest. It was a feeling she hadn't known she still possessed: the wish to tend to a mother.

"Mary is overfond," Catherine continued at length, "of being at the fore of every new fashion. Nonetheless, a young woman wishing to marry well requires to be seen in society. Within certain limits." There was little tenderness on Catherine's face as she spoke, Ester noted, but rather a weary fear that seemed to have long ago vanquished all other maternal feeling. "My daughter," she said, "is in need of a companion. And as perhaps is evident, I am hardly in constitution to accompany Mary on foolish errands through London." Catherine fixed Ester with a stare. "Breathing," she said faintly, "no longer seems to agree with me." She turned away. "The country air improves it, but my husband requires his household and business here in London."

She seemed to have finished.

In the silence, Mary's soft, cautious breaths mingled with Ester's own. Ester shut her eyes to savor the sound. In memory it merged with the steady long-ago sound of her brother's breathing. A foolish thought welled in Ester: what might it be to have a sister?

She spoke swiftly to counter such indulgent visions. "I can't serve as Mary's companion," she said. "The rabbi requires my presence."

"The rabbi," said Catherine, "will release you as we require." Her gesture took in the furnishings, the small room, the house. She said drily, "I'm certain he'll feel he owes us at least that thanks."

Mary had turned once more and was surveying Ester. "She'll need to learn the English manner of dress."

Without warning Rivka spoke from her station by the wall, her voice harsh. "We shame them," she said. She was addressing Ester, and the direct force of her small brown eyes was shocking, wrenching Ester from what remained of her reverie.

When Catherine answered, her eyebrows lofted slightly, she addressed her words only to Ester, as though it were a matter of good taste to ignore such unaccountable rudeness. "It's no matter of vanity," Catherine said levelly. "Though you may look on us and think it so. You are still foreign and unaccustomed to London ways. *We*"—a slow sweep of her hand—"we dress and speak as Englishwomen do. You sail here from Amsterdam, make house in the place provided by my husband, and proceed to walk about the parish dressed in such manner that a placard saying *Jewess* might as well be hung on your back. It's your choice to do so, I've maintained—though other women of the community have disagreed with me. But if you're to accompany my daughter about London, then it becomes very much my concern how you dress."

"It concerns *me*, Mother," Mary interrupted. Her voice had turned both prettier and harder-edged. She seemed both affronted and puzzled by Ester's disinclination to follow her about London. "I agree with the others. These two *do* shame us. Now that all London knows there are Jews about, do you wish the ladies promenading on St. James to be whispering about Jewesses who dress like"—she hesitated, then gestured at Rivka in her cap and work dress; then more vaguely at Ester, who flushed in sudden awareness of how she'd allowed the quality of her own dress to degrade—"like *nightsoil* men?" Mary let the merry question hang for a moment, her high, round cheeks and rosy lips sweet under black brows and bright black eyes—but Ester noted that Mary's flickering gaze landed near but not quite on her mother's face.

Then, seeming to tire of defiance, Mary twisted to search out something in a soft cloth pouch she'd set beside her. Straightening, she reached over without warning and her finger slid hard across Ester's lips, spreading something slick.

As Ester recoiled, Mary laughed. "Rose madder," she said. "Here." She thrust a small wood-framed glass into Ester's hand, just large enough to nestle in her palm.

A face looked back from the glass wavering in her hand—the lips gleaming a soft, dark red. For a vertiginous instant it was not Ester's own, but her mother's: cascading hair, eyes black and dangerous.

Since she'd last looked in a glass, her face had changed, thinning in such a way that the resemblance to her mother was sharper. She'd known from stray hairs in her comb that the years since the fire had marked her. Yet a true storm of silver had begun in Ester's hair—she touched it. It was as Mary said. Only her arched brows remained pure black. The face was young, but its crown old. Small wonder Mary hadn't been able to guess her age. Wobbling in the glass, her own face fractured and assailed her. Her father's large and solemn eyes warring with her mother's ample, mocking mouth.

"Some young man will beg to kiss you now," Mary lilted.

Ester wiped hard at her mouth with the sides of her fingers. She wished to rebuke Mary but could summon no words.

"But why dash it away?" Mary cried.

Catherine's reprimand bore down on Mary. "Because, Mary, this one is wiser than her own mother."

Shouldn't Ester have guessed that her mother's ill reputation would follow her from Amsterdam? Constantina, trapped within her own fury. Beauty and spite entwined. Ester tore away from the image.

Yet Catherine, head tilted and scrutinizing Ester's stiff posture, seemed to see something that eased her. "No," she said slowly. "This daughter won't mimic that mother, though she does possess some beauty of her own."

Mary's coquettish tones had faded to impatience. "She can serve as my companion then?"

Slowly, pensively, Catherine's fingertips circled in the air: something still troubled her.

"What else now, Mother?" Mary cut in, querulous. "Is it the brother?"

As Catherine hesitated, anger leapt in Ester's belly. She rose, brushing aside Mary's staying hand. How dare this woman in fine fabrics deign, in a single shallow breath, to judge Isaac's life and death?

But before Ester was fully on her feet, Catherine nodded decisively. "I'll permit it," Catherine said.

"No!" Ester's thin hands had balled into fists, her nails biting at the flesh of her own palms.

"Ester?" The haughtiness was gone from Mary's expression—she looked lost. Her bewilderment stilled Ester.

"I can't," Ester managed.

For a moment, then, Catherine's eyes touched Ester's as though recognizing something there that she respected. "But you can," said Catherine slowly. "My daughter, it happens, has a nature that requires supervision by one without foolish vanities of her own. You, it happens, have no foolish vanities. Nor do you have prospects. It's a suitable task for you. And more than that, it will improve your chances." *Of a good marriage.* Catherine raised her eyebrows, awaiting acknowledgment of the wisdom of this. "You're young," she continued after a moment. Her voice was not ungentle, and Ester found herself wondering how many daughters Catherine had buried. "Fate might yet shelter you."

Turning at a small sound of protest from Mary, Ester saw that a vague envy suffused her face, as though she'd just watched something inaccessible pass between her mother and Ester.

Catherine closed her eyes a moment, then nodded: the matter was decided. "You'll go to the dressmaker immediately, and acquire a dress suitable for society." Bending forward stiffly, Catherine gestured: she wished the servant's help to stand.

So fully had Rivka retreated into silence since her outburst that Ester had nearly forgotten her presence; but now she stepped forward. Whatever further opinions she held were writ on her in an obscure language. She helped Catherine to her feet.

For a moment Catherine stood opposite Ester, her rigid bodice straining at each inhalation. Under her thick face-powder, her expression flickered—the faintest hint of conspiracy, even humor?—then faded. Her face slackening now with fatigue, she turned away, listing on Rivka's arm.

Matching her mother's slow pace, Mary stepped out toward the waiting coach, pausing once to gaze with dull apprehension at the cinder-gritted wall blocking one end of the street, the balconies crowding overhead, the pale gray smoke from the tanneries draping the narrow strip of visible sky.

IN HIS STUDY, THE RABBI was still seated beside the fire, opposite the HaLevy brothers, reciting. "*The world is balanced upon three pillars: The study of Torah. The worship of God. Acts of kindness.*"

The last word was lost to a reverberating slam. Manuel HaLevy had dropped a book on the stone floor. Slowly he bent and retrieved it.

"My apologies," he said flatly.

There was a brief silence. "That concludes our lesson," said the rabbi. If he suspected Manuel had dropped the book deliberately, his face didn't betray it.

As the brothers gathered their cloaks, the rabbi called to Ester. Yet instead of asking the nature of Mary and Catherine's visit, or protesting any claim the da Costa Mendes women might make on her as Ester half hoped he would, he said only, "The commentaries were bound two weeks ago. It's time to retrieve them, Ester."

This was the third such set of books he'd ordered from Amsterdam: tomes of scholarship suitable for pupils more advanced than any here in London. In truth, the rabbi's folly in this matter puzzled Ester: who else but they might conceivably study such volumes? Still, if he wished to conduct himself as though a crop of scholarly youths was ready to sprout through the cobbled streets at any moment, it was to her own benefit.

"I thought Rivka—" Ester began.

But the rabbi shook his head, almost sternly—as though the da Costa Mendes women's visit had prompted him at last to acknowledge what they both knew: that Ester hid from London. Days passed when she ventured no farther than their door, shying from the city that had swallowed her brother. She'd become a creature Isaac would have scorned, cringing from daylight. The pallor she'd just glimpsed in Mary's glass proved it.

"Ester," the rabbi said. With his long fingers he indicated a high shelf behind him.

She counted as he instructed her, taking the silver coins from the narrow brimming box and dropping them into a pouch. With trembling fingers, she fixed the clasps of her cloak. Then set out, hurrying, her shoulders tightening against the unexpected cold.

The street was nearly empty, blocked at one end by an age-darkened stone wall. Above her, the tiered houses cast their shadows on the cobbles, each level of a building jutting farther than the one it sat upon as though competing to darken the street. Between the topmost balconies, which threatened to touch overhead, the hazy sky promised nothing.

The bindery the rabbi had named was somewhere in Southwark. She knew how to reach the river, but that was all. She hesitated. Then, deciding, hurried out of the street and to the next wider one, as though speed could prevent the city from touching her.

The edges of the cobblestones were slicked with waste, every few steps a new odor assaulted—how to breathe without breathing? The city tilted at her, dangerous—the foul streets in which she'd lost Isaac. By now the HaLevy sons would have turned into the alleys past the Clothworkers' Hall. She quickened her step to catch them—for as much as she distrusted the elder brother, still she'd rather ask directions in Portuguese than in English.

Rounding the corner, she spied Manuel and Alvaro HaLevy strolling ahead of her. Here on the street, they appeared less foolish than in the rabbi's study. More powerful.

At the sound of her steps, the younger brother turned. Shyly he smiled, and laid a hand on his brother's sleeve, stopping him.

Manuel took in Ester's presence on the street with an expression of mild surprise: he hadn't suspected she'd be so bold as to seek him out. He folded his arms, looking amused.

She addressed them bluntly in Portuguese. "Where's Chamberlain's bindery?"

"Across the river," Alvaro said in his English-accented Portuguese. "Just beyond the bridge." He gestured at the road, in the direction they'd been walking. "It's the second turn to the left off the main road. Beside a bread bakery."

She gave a curt nod.

"Be careful," Alvaro added, staying her as she started past. "Mind you don't miss the closing of the gate, you'll be caught outside the walls." His voice dropping to an earnest near whisper, he continued in a mix of Portuguese and English. "Last I was there," he said, "a boy came swinging a spar." As he spoke he flushed, his slight figure inclining toward her as though he were in need of comfort. "He swung it hard, so my head felt its wind. He and his companions said Jews excel at murder. That we helped slice off the head of their last king."

Manuel was watching Ester closely.

She addressed Alvaro in Portuguese. "*Obrigada.* For the warning."

Alvaro's flush flowered into full red. He nodded and looked to his well-stitched black shoes, strapped into matching pattens.

But Manuel was smiling softly at Ester now, as though he'd just heard a pleasing joke. "They wanted him to drop his breeches," he said in English, not bothering to translate, "so they could see what a Jew looked like."

Alvaro paled.

"I ran," Alvaro said simply, and Ester saw he'd long been resigned to the pleasure his older brother took in shaming him.

"*Obrigada,*" she said to Alvaro again. "You're good to warn me."

"He ran like a puppy," sang Manuel.

Alvaro *was* a puppy. She held back from nodding. And his elder brother was a cur too free with his bite. "And *you* wouldn't run?" she challenged Manuel. She let a small, teasing smile form on her lips.

Hadn't she sworn to herself all her life never to act in this manner? She looked at Manuel HaLevy and it didn't matter. She wanted to see—wanted Alvaro to see—that smirk swept from the elder brother's face.

"Perhaps you *should* stay and lower your breeches for them," she said. "I'd wager that if you did"—she let her gaze slide to his waist, then below, then rise to meet his inscrutable eyes—"you'd look no different from the English."

He let out a sound of surprise. Then his brass eyes fastened strangely on hers. She matched his gaze, no flush of heat marring her composure: a skill gleaned from her mother, though Ester had never before felt compelled to use it. It hardly mattered whether she'd guessed correctly that the London community didn't yet submit its sons to the rite; Manuel's expression had turned like something fermenting—as though he were assessing Ester anew. He looked as though he wanted to wound her for shaming him as a Jew, and he looked as though he wanted her eyes to travel the same route down his body once more.

Abruptly the recollection of her mother's red-lipped visage, reflected in the mirror in her own palm, unraveled her resolve. She turned and began walking away.

"I heard about your brother," Manuel said from behind her. "Not a very committed son of Israel himself, was he? Running off from the rabbi's house to brawl like an animal among the dockworkers?"

She walked on without a glance back.

The streets narrowed, then widened abruptly and thickened with people. A boy swung out of a doorway and trotted down the street, carrying a roll of cloth. Neatly dressed maids with parcels walked ahead, whitsters hefting baskets of soiled linens. A horse and coach in the street, passing her so narrowly her cheek felt the heat off the animal's flank. Sudden laughter in the doorway of a tavern, from its dark windows an oily smell that at once warmed Ester and turned her stomach.

Why now would she embrace her mother's ways, when she'd so long and so fiercely guarded against them? Even a girl like Mary, petty and vain, knew the dangers of risking her reputation.

As though taking a cautious sip of strongest liquor, she permitted herself a single image. Her mother's green dress. And her voice: a burning draught. *Ester. You're just like me.*

She'd insulted Manuel HaLevy today because he angered her—yet, she admitted, also to pique him. For though Ester disliked him, still her body had woken to his challenge—just as every caged part of her, her thoughts, her breath, her pulse, seemed to wake now to this city from which she'd hidden herself. London, which had consumed her brother; London of her mother's drunken, eviscerating whispers. The very language spoken on these streets fired Ester strangely—as if a thing long shuttered in her spirit had, quietly and all at once, quickened.

With the quickening, memory. How could one love such a mother —and how not long for her? Those in the synagogue who'd claimed they wished nothing to do with Constantina had ever lied, for didn't they savor their gossip of Constantina's famed tempers? Didn't they gladly visit the home of Samuel Velasquez—and not only because of his standing as a merchant, but because of the opportunity to admire Constantina's lush beauty in the elegance of her home, and be present for those moments of delight and danger when her spirits lifted? For when Constantina Velasquez's face and figure lit with happiness —when she laughed and played delicate melodies on the parlor spinet as her own mother had taught her, or sang a sinuous verse in her rare, light, throaty voice—then she no longer seemed ill-suited to the world but instead was the very heart of it, so that to turn away was impossible. And if it was true that Constantina's temper sometimes plunged, or that she mocked those who should not be mocked; if it was true that her disobedience sometimes took the form of coquetry—dancing when the mood took her, lifting her skirts to a shocking height, even setting a hand lightly on a man's chest, as if for emphasis, as she spoke to him, and continuing to converse with a faint smile as though she didn't notice the man coloring—still, most took their cue from Samuel's silence and said nothing until they'd left the house.

The most famed example of Constantina's rebelliousness Ester herself recalled, though she herself had been but a child: eight days after giving birth to Isaac, Constantina had barred the door of the bedchamber with splayed arms and refused to allow the infant to be circumcised. Women were sent to persuade Constantina: naturally in Portugal they'd lacked the freedom to circumcise their sons, yes. And now indeed there was strangeness in rejudaizing the young—but wasn't circumcision the mark of their new safety? Constantina merely turned her dark eyes on them and laughed in their earnest faces. More than one of the women cried with bewilderment upon leaving the Velasquez house, and had to recompose herself before returning home to make prim report of a mind distressed by the rigors of childbirth.

Only the *herem* issued by the Mahamad, barring members of the Velasquez family from setting foot in the synagogue until the deed had been done, ended the matter. Samuel Velasquez took his infant son bodily from his wife. He left for the synagogue disheveled from their struggle, Constantina's fury pursuing him down the stairs: "Naturally you agree with the Mahamad! Now that you cling to Judaism like a babe to a teat you're not half the man you were — you should never have let them do it to you either!" While the door's slam still reverberated, Constantina seized paper and quill. In swift, sharp strokes she penned her letter, and moments later dispatched the wary maid to the synagogue with instructions to deliver it to the most dignified-looking rabbi she could find, and watch his face while he read it. "And make certain my husband sees," Constantina cried as the maid exited.

Nonetheless, the boy was circumcised and returned to the house within the hour, crying lustily and refusing to be soothed by the drops of wine fed to him. Right on the parlor table Constantina swaddled her son, and before turning him over to the nursemaid and seeking her own comfort in a wine bottle, she'd rocked him for a time with a tender grief, as if she held in her arms her own unsoothable spirit. Ester had witnessed all from the top of the stair — squeezing her eyes shut even after her mother had gone, so that she might continue imagining that she herself were the wailing infant held so tight.

And when Ester's father first brought Rabbi HaCoen Mendes to their home, Constantina's voice tore the air over Ester's head. "I gave no permission for that man to come into my house."

"That man," said Samuel Velasquez slowly, "is a rabbi. He's going to tutor the children."

Her father. His thick brown hair and neatly trimmed beard only starting to gray. Broad palms smelling faintly of aniseed oil, coffee, and the barrels of spice he inspected at the docks; his fine white blouse and breeches pressed, his mild brown eyes wide with fatigue.

ALL THROUGH THAT FIRST HOUR Ester had spent with the rabbi, her father had lingered on the perimeter of the room as though to protect them from the storm he knew was coming. In the hush of the parlor, the blind rabbi's face lifting in her direction like a plant slowly turning toward the sun, Ester had answered Rabbi HaCoen Mendes's gentle questions—what did she know of Hebrew, which works had she read in Castilian and which in Portuguese? She'd read aloud from the volume the rabbi had brought, whispering apologies for her every hesitation or stumble.

Immediately upon the rabbi's departure, the quiet shattered.

"*Don't* speak to me as though I'm simple!" Constantina's voice, breaking, tightened Ester's own throat.

In her green gown with its deep bosom, Constantina closed her delicate hands on the carved back of Ester's chair. "He's a rabbi, yes! A poor, miserable creature who lost his eyesight for the priests' satisfaction—and now he and all the rest of them want us to lock away our senses. No attending plays we like, or eating what food we wish, or heaven forbid letting our legs be glimpsed during a dance if it pleases us!"

The maid entered, head down, and closed the windows—although the thin glass could hardly keep such fury from the eager ears of neighbors.

"I'll no longer discuss the matter of attending Spanish comedies," Samuel said. "The Mahamad is against it."

"The Mahamad," she enunciated from behind Ester, "exists only to wallow in its own holy muck."

"Constantina!"

"No! When my mother and I ran from Lisbon, we ran to save our lives. Not our *Jewish* lives. Our *lives*. We ran because even if we never said a prayer, even if my mother and aunts went to the dance hall after their Friday feast"—swiftly she stepped to her husband and jabbed her finger into his chest—"even so, the priests wanted to drag us into their torture rooms." As her father edged back from the onslaught, Ester understood that Constantina had been drinking. He said nothing, but Ester felt him shut like a heavy door, leaving the room colder.

"You brought me to this place as a bride," Constantina continued, at an even higher pitch, "and you decided we would be *pious*. But no one is pious in every single thought—no one, except *you*." Constantina said the word with a glad viciousness.

Forearms on the table, face averted, Ester had closed her eyes. What, she asked herself, did the rabbi see behind his sealed lids? And what, she pressed silently, was the true meaning of the verse the rabbi had recited from *Pirkei Avot*? The rabbi's lesson turned in her mind, pieces of a puzzle seeking their match. Something in them troubled her. She could not get the notions to align.

"You were content," her father said, "when I arranged to educate our children in French and our son in Latin, as befits our standing. Yet you want me to shun our own people's learning. Your grandfather didn't die, Constantina, for us to shun it." Her father's voice too had risen. Ester cringed at what it might unleash. Yet she couldn't help clinging to the sound of his words. "In Amsterdam, even a girl may study the faith. And if Ester may learn, then she ought. I'm in disagreement with many on this matter, I know. But Rabbi HaCoen Mendes is willing to teach a girl. And"—he pronounced the words softly but firmly—"as the master of this house, I have requested that he do so. I do not make it my habit to insist with you, Constantina, though some call me a fool for the degree to which I tolerate your whims."

In the long silence that ensued, Ester shut her eyes. Behind closed lids, she forced her mind to the rabbi's words. *The saving of a life is equal in merit to the saving of the world. So it is said, he who saves one life saves a world.* Yet if this was so, then what exactly was meant by *world*? Were there worlds of different size and merit? Or was the world of one soul as capacious as the world that contained all of creation—infinite, even? Was Ester's world, peopled by her parents and her brother, equal to all the others God had created?

Yet if all worlds were equal, then each world the Jesuits murdered was equal to all God's others. How then could one be certain God's power was greater than that of the Jesuits?

The thought rang frighteningly, forcing her eyes open: Had she trod near the notions of heretics? Even in her studies, was she taking up her mother's ways?

Her father was speaking. His voice was low but firm. "I need not remind you what could become of you in Portugal, Constantina. This

Amsterdam congregation you hate, despite your rage against its rulings, is your protection."

Constantina stood motionless. It seemed the fury was draining from her, hopelessness entering in its wake. "You trap me in a box full of Jews," she said quietly.

Her father's face was weighted with fatigue, yet instantly a tender sympathy rose there, and Ester saw that his love for Constantina was untouched, and should his wife but permit it he'd take her in his arms to comfort her. He said, gently, "It was not I who decided it should be a trap."

A moment's equipoise. Then Constantina's face clouded. She waved vaguely at the open book in front of Ester. Then briskly. "Leave that nonsense."

Ester didn't move.

"I said leave it!"

Slowly, as though looking up from underwater, Ester met her mother's dark eyes.

"Well," Constantina said. A strange loneliness rippled in her voice. But she stood soldier-straight as she continued, braving whatever bewilderment had seized her. "You may indeed be a Jewess, Ester," she said. Yet though the words were addressed to her daughter, all Constantina's attention was on her husband. "But you, Ester, are a Jewess with Iberian blood and a coat of arms in your family."

Samuel's posture sagged, as though a melody he'd listened for had vanished. "It serves little," he said quietly, "to put stock in purity of blood. Or in titles purchased by great-great-grandfathers that nonetheless failed to purchase safety."

Whatever had stayed Constantina's hand, it was gone. With a small smile, as though delivering a fatal blow, she said, "Perhaps I'll tell her, why don't I, that her mother's bloodline also traces to a fine Christian Englishman?"

Samuel spoke quickly. "I should like to protect my family from your legacy of shame, as I protected you when I married you." Without another word, he stepped around the table and toward the door. Before he reached it, Constantina was there. Ester heard her mother's slap on her father's face. Then Constantina's sobs, receding up the stair. The slam of a heavy door, something smashing on the floor—then her mother's sharp "Jesus Christo!" followed by a sob of drunken laughter.

When Ester next looked up, her father had left.

"I'm sorry," she whispered to the empty air.

The house vibrated with quiet. The rabbi's texts lay before Ester in the light from the window—the books he'd given her to study. She lowered herself into them, line by line—at first holding her breath so as not to dispel her fragile understanding. Then, gingerly, breathing.

SHE HURRIED DOWN THE NARROW London streets now, remembering: days of luxuriant study at the polished wood table of their home in Amsterdam, while her mother clipped past without acknowledging Ester's presence and the maid Grietgen cleaned gently around her. Rising from the rabbi's texts, Ester might pore over her father's copy of a French treatise about the soul and matter, and the extension of matter in space. The contrast riveted her: the difference between the thinking of Christians and the increasingly complex rabbinic texts Rabbi HaCoen Mendes brought for her to study. The Christians, it seemed to Ester, wished to fathom the mechanism of the soul: by which levers did it pull the body into motion, and by which was it pulled by the divine? Yet the rabbis had little concern for such deliberation. What, they wished to know, were the minute instructions for doing God's will? How must the economy of devotion be paid in laws of kashrut, in decorations of house and body, in the number of repetitions of a prayer . . . how were laws for behavior to be observed under this and that specific circumstance?

The difference between the two manners of thought seemed to hold the key to something she couldn't name. Must the two—the Christian and the Hebrew, the soul and the measurable, tangible world—remain disconnected? Or was there some middle terrain where a person—even someone like Ester's own too-thin self, with her always-cold hands, her ribcage that felt too narrow to contain all the air she needed to gulp— might understand the purpose of life more readily? And what of the arguments of the apostates—why did the rabbis ban such speech, rather than welcome it in order to refute it?

And how to answer the older maid's soft huff of disappointment: "Didn't your mother teach you what to do with the stained cloths? Or is she too busy with that bottle of hers to notice her daughter's a woman?" The sheen of blood on her fingers, the smell of it—a confused humiliation suffusing all. To forget the maid's words, she pulled the text closer and followed the rivulets of the rabbi's teachings into fresh streams of argument that promised to carry her past the Herengracht, past the torpid waterways of the city toward some conclusion of such brightness it made her reel. At times she could barely speak in response to the rabbi's questions. Other times she could hardly find enough breath for all the words she needed to utter, though the rabbi listened with great patience. On those days the new thoughts so brimmed in her that she felt the white plaster ceiling and the timbers and the brickwork walls couldn't contain her—should she raise her head to speak once more, she'd shake the house down.

But at last Constantina realized what the maids had known for months. And even Samuel Velasquez couldn't deny Constantina's logic: Ester being now of an age sufficient for marriage, her education ought be ended.

The teeming bright world, shuttered. The rabbi, along with the French and Latin tutors, came to the house now to teach only Isaac —and though Ester endeavored to listen as she did her embroidery and the other tasks now assigned her, these lessons served mainly to remind her of what was lost. Isaac's attention roved the room so that the long-suffering instructors had to teach the simplest texts and grammars over and again. Ester entered sometimes with an offer of tea or ale, or even stood at the threshold, waving her hands silently to wake her brother to attention—but Isaac ignored these signals with a sleepy shrug. The books Ester had studied were returned to the synagogue, and on the occasions when she was able to seize a few moments to read her brother's simpler ones, she was distracted by every footfall, fearful the very act of studying the smooth lines of Hebrew letters, or even her brother's prescribed doses of French or Latin, might ignite the ever more fragile mood of the house. For Ester's womanhood seemed to have stung her mother, and Constantina regarded Ester now with a gaze full of obscure meaning. And when Samuel Velasquez, with the aim to cure Isaac of his waywardness, took the youth on a trade voyage, Constantina found at last, in the emptied house and a swift-emptying bottle of wine, the freedom to disburden herself.

Shall I tell you, Ester, the truth about love?

Listen now to what I learned from my own mother about the unmaking of her heart. And the making, Ester, of mine.

That summer a silence settled in Ester's mind, brittle and expectant —it stretched for days, weeks, begging to be broken.

Then, as though summoned by that silence: a burgeoning roar.

The night, the glowing roof. The fire's brilliant leap from the tip of their house into the black sky. As if the flames had at last gained their freedom, the sky pulling them into its embrace.

Up, and up.

A year, more. Hollow, wishless months of needle-pricked fingers and a dull pain in the center of her chest, her voice stoppered. Isaac's face shuttered and locked. The words *I'm sorry,* which spilled from her so steadily while her mother was alive, were now unutterable, though she knew her failure to make apology for her presence stiffened the backs of the synagogue matrons who housed and fed them. With each week those matrons' whispers gained volume: *What now?* What of the blond-haired son who had carried the fatal lantern—surely it was the judgment of God that acted through his young hands, yet what to do with a youth with such a curse upon his head? He might be a capable dock laborer, but dock work was for Christians or Tudesco Jews, not the son of a Portuguese family. And what of the girl—see her there, mending with her dreadful tight stitches, gone from being the indulged daughter of a respected man to a burden on the community. Why doesn't she cry over at least her father—poor man, to live and die alongside such a wife?

How great was the matrons' relief, then, when Rabbi HaCoen Mendes sent word through his Tudesco housekeeper that he'd take in the orphans. And how much greater when the blind rabbi—himself a burden on the community, unseemly though it was to say so—declared his willingness to accept Menasseh ben Israel's call to carry the light of learning to London. Though Menasseh's plan was of course unlikely to succeed, all would benefit should London indeed become a refuge for Jews. What's more, a welcoming London might even draw off the ill-bred Tudescos, whose vulgar ways lately threatened all that the Portuguese congregation had built in Amsterdam.

So the beadle had announced prayers for Rabbi HaCoen Mendes's success, the wealthy men of the synagogue had donated elaborately bound books for his mission—and the rabbi, like the orphans in his trust, was removed from the community's care.

So much expiated in one ship's plashing departure.

SHE WALKED. OLD MANURE BLANKETED the London cobblestones. She passed soot-darkened brickwork, cats hale and lame, a stone edifice carved with a chipped angel. A hoof-marked yard tangled with withered vines, a fire-damaged house. Each step, a move deeper under the skin of the city. Walking, she recalled herself as she'd once been: the soft long layerings of her skirts, the wide winged collars parting at the small bones of her throat. The girl she was in Amsterdam before the fire seemed to her a figure in a framed portrait: downcast eyes fleeing the timid gaze of a neighbor boy with a shyness that now struck Ester as the most repellent of foolishnesses. She was ash now—that girl her father had escorted to synagogue and released with pride into the decorous crowd. Samuel Velasquez's dignified tread, the smell of his wool cloak —the recollections a heavy pain in her throat.

Ash: the girl who had once existed, with her vague moralities, her posture bent in apology, her desperate trust that virtue might guarantee safety. And her desperate hope too that all within her that was unruly, raging, sensuous—all that terrified and drew her—could be quashed.

Along the narrow street, youths hauled sacks of sand, an ink vendor cried his wares, saltpeter men hauled stained sacks through a stable door. A girl leading a milch-ass knocked on a door and, when there was no answer, leaned her forehead to the door with a bleary call for any with babes in need of milk. Above the street, signboards mutely announced their wares—one carved in the shape of a mortar and pestle, another in the shape of a barrel of ale, another painted with a picture of crockery, that the unlettered might know where to enter with their coin. And now the road sloped downward beneath her shoes—first the slightest dip, barely perceptible. Then a steeper slope, as though not only her feet but the whole city were rushing toward the river. As she neared the water, something in the air seemed to loosen. Elsewhere in the city the Puritans' grip might be easing slowly; here, by the river, the impatience for release seemed to pulse faster. A crane loomed over the heavy chop; a skiff discharged its passengers at a stair; in the long, commanding calls of the river men and the gulls, a barely restrained defiance. Here and again between buildings, the river now appeared, gray and leaden and powerful.

The foot traffic thickened suddenly, and as it did, the way before Ester narrowed. She was in a crowd, passing alongside strangers into a corridor of stone, and without warning she was jostled and swept onto the great looming bridge—or rather, into a dark, narrow passage that became a tunnel. The bridge was lined with solid walls of shops on either side, and the merchants' homes, stacked above, jutted and met to form a roof over the thoroughfare of the bridge. The crowd slowed as it pressed deeper into the dim corridor between lamp-lit shops. She could neither hear nor sense the river beneath her feet. There were men and women within a hand's breadth, jostling her with silent familiarity. She shrank from them—she'd not been touched by so many people, she was sure, in all her life. Yet there was nowhere to retreat—and there was something, too, that astonished her, something dangerous and free in the touch of this crowd. She might have been a flea, so little was she noted. A flea—not a Jewess. Not the survivor of a fire that was whispered of throughout Amsterdam.

Ahead now a horse went wild, kicking its rear legs high. There was a man's warning shout and a burst of alarmed cries before it was subdued. A lath-thin woman, her strawberry-gray head balding, pressed her shoulder hard into Ester's; a man with tousled blond hair seemed not to notice how he knocked Ester with his elbow; on her other side two women carrying babes gossiped as they shuffled, not minding how intimately they brushed against her.

When Ester had seen London's bridge from a distance, she'd imagined a wide clearing, a vantage point from which one could grasp the view of the city. But the bridge offered no vista; instead it was the artery through which all of London pulsed, stopping terrifyingly now and again—the crowd around Ester thickening rapidly in the lull—only to continue. Pressed forward, Ester kept pace to avoid falling. She was in a crush of English strangers and her breath came quick with fear—but their unfamiliar smells and rough fabrics and stout limbs carried her, and the heat of their bodies warmed her.

A clearing between two shop buildings formed a brief window, and through this the river came into sight, and all of London on either side of the bridge—spilling past the city walls, piled along the banks as far as she could see. For a moment the heavy pounding water wheels below the bridge sounded clearly, and she saw the gray river, half dammed by the bridge, swirling high against the pilings on her right. Opposite, on the bridge's downriver side where the water poured out of the narrow arches through which it had been forced, the level of the river was lower by a grown man's height. So hard did the water rush, furrows of swift furious glass, it seemed impossible that this bridge—a city to itself—was not swept downriver.

Pressed once more by the crowd, she walked on, but no sooner had her eyes reaccustomed themselves to the dim passageway than a pale white glow appeared ahead—the end of the bridge.

All about her, men and women were strangely marked by the growing light—their faces half shadowed and half lit, sculpted and beautiful. It seemed to Ester that inside this dark tunnel of a bridge they'd shaken off the wariness that had cribbed the city. They thronged about her, their passions and hopes plain to see, their lives and their deaths patent. In that instant she forgave them fully for each thing that had made her fear them and their city. A strange tenderness seized her. For a heartbeat she was certain the bridge was in motion, shuddering as it prepared to tear away from its moorings and carry them all out, far beyond this city. But it was only the vibration of the rushing water, and the summoning din from the riverbank. She could hear the cries, once again, of gulls and boatmen, the clanging and thud of river commerce. She could smell the cool rolling road of water sluicing beneath all of them.

For the first time, she felt it: this was the freedom her brother had sought.

There was life in London. There was life in her. And desire. A flame leapt in her, defiant of the bounds in which she'd prisoned it.

How could desire be wrong—the question seized her—if each living being contained it? Each creature was born with the unthinking need to draw each next breath, find each next meal. Mustn't desire then be integral—a set of essential guideposts on the map of life's purpose? And mightn't its very denial then be a desecration?

The thoughts were heretical, and they were her own. A frightening, alluring hunger surged in her, she knew not even for what—a fever for truth, for the touch of truth, the touch of warm bodies, the crush of unknown arms. She wanted to press her mouth to the mouths of the strangers beside her—to learn from their mouths the language they spoke. Somewhere across this bridge, beckoning her, were books that would be hers to explore and question—and yes, *argue* against—for in her new daring now nothing seemed impossible, and she allowed herself to admit even this: that she thought the sages scant in their exploration of what she most wished to understand—the will that set the world in motion and governed it. Shutting her eyes, letting the crowd steer her, she saw behind closed lids the books that awaited her, the thinkers' collected voices inked onto each crowded page. An ecstasy of ink, every paragraph laboring to outline the shape of the world. The yellow light of a lamp on leaves of paper, the ivory-black impress of words reasoning, line by line. Yet in the confused picture in her mind, the hands caressing and turning those lamp-lit pages were not her own, but a stranger's. She didn't know which she wanted more: the words or the hands, the touch to her spirit or to her skin.

And then, pale daylight. She was across, the sound of the water behind her, the clatter of stone and hooves and wheels ahead.

Glancing back at the gate through which she had emerged, she saw a spectacle she could not at first comprehend. Above her, set on black pikes atop the bridge's gate, were objects that might easily have been rocks, stumps, some natural decaying thing. As understanding assailed her, she stumbled to a halt. The hair tarred back, slack cheeks shiny and corroded like charred paper. Blackened heads, preserved in tar: traitors to the government. She'd heard rumor of this—the English government's reminder to all of the price to be paid for disloyalty—yet now her stomach heaved and she could not look away, nor pass beneath them.

One had a mouth agape. Void eyes open as wide—wider—than a man's eyes could ever open in life. Wide enough, at the last, to see the cost of his most treasured beliefs.

But the living bodies about her swept her forward. All about her, their will focused on gaining the river's margin, the English seemed for this moment to fear nothing—not the unlatched eyes high above them, not even a change of governance that could soon mean different heads lofted in punishment for the telling of different truths. She wanted to breathe the warning into all their ears: *never let your true thought be known, for it is by truth that you are noosed and for truth burnt.*

And even in the same instant, she wanted to beg the secret of their boldness.

But they were already departing from her. Amid the churn of the crowd, she left behind the blackened heads that shuddered, now, in a biting wind. On the cobbled street beyond the bridge, the crowd thinned and dissolved. She stood, released, on the south side of the river, her skin afire with the touch of English strangers who had borne her across. A hundred hands, living and dead.

11

December 1, 2000
London

THE RARE MANUSCRIPTS ROOM WAS HUSHED. Solitary postgraduates sat at tables here and there, looking sleep-deprived. There was a fraught, reverent silence, broken by the occasional ripple of pages turning. The soft scratch of a pencil. The sound of knuckles cracking. A single long sniff.

Helen sat alone at a large table. A slim volume from the Eastons' house lay on the brown cushion before her, its pages held open with weighted strings. The news that this first batch of documents was ready had reached her yesterday evening, in the form of a terse telephone message from the librarian, Patricia Starling-Haight. Helen had arrived this morning at the precise moment Patricia Starling-Haight unlocked the heavy door of the manuscripts room, and she'd moved through the usual protocols under the librarian's owlish gaze — relinquishing all writing instruments, securing her bag in a locker, silencing her mobile phone — all before the librarian would budge to produce the first documents. She'd been here since, and had read through three letters already. Aaron had made similar progress — his document was arrayed on a cushion farther down the table, though Aaron himself was currently nowhere to be seen. With luck they would get through another few before closing.

Once more the librarian floated past. When she'd gone, Helen leaned forward surreptitiously and breathed in. This volume — a small book of liturgical poetry — had a dark, smoldering smell like something burnt long ago, the fire extinguished but the danger still detectible.

She sat back a moment to savor the notion of the entire collection of papers being prepared in the conservation lab upstairs — to savor, in its entirety, the string of fortuitous events that had led to this day, starting with the fact that the purchase price of the documents had been steep but not prohibitively so. The assessor's remark about the documents' time span (*the dates spanning Interregnum and Restoration leave open the possibility of some as-yet-undiscovered material of value to historians of these periods*) had possibly pushed up the price a thousand pounds. But Jonathan Martin, with his eternal ambition of outshining UCL, had stepped forward with money from some Department of History cache. And that money, coupled with a phone call from the vice chancellor, had sufficed to persuade the librarian to authorize the purchase. All of it might have been derailed, of course, had the assessor recognized the Spinoza reference—it had been a gamble, and by no means a certain one, for Helen to walk away from the documents that afternoon in Richmond, rather than demand more time as she'd longed to. But assessors, like document conservationists, were rarely scholars. They saw the documents as physical artifacts. It was the historians who cared about their meaning.

And it was librarians who adjudicated crime and punishment, where paper was concerned. In fact Helen understood why Patricia Starling-Haight, with whom Helen had exchanged only brief conversations over the decades, was looking particularly severe today. In her position, Helen would have been livid. It was bad enough for a librarian to be strong-armed by a man like Jonathan Martin into purchasing documents with a dubious connection to the existing collections (Interregnum papers being more readily found at National Archives). But then, once the library had purchased the Richmond documents, Martin had insisted that the documents be placed at the front of the queue in the conservation lab. The head conservationist—a woman named Patricia Smith, whose fiefdom was the conservation laboratory two floors up from the rare manuscripts room—had been moved to march to Martin's office herself to inform him that commandeering her laboratory was outrageous, and his precious seventeenth-century trove could bloody well wait for its turn after the four estates' worth of documents already on schedule to occupy her through August.

Helen could imagine the two Patricias' responses when Martin not only refused to relent, but made it clear that—although each document was to be made available to Helen the moment it was ready—the conservation lab and the rare manuscripts room were to inform all inquiring parties (Martin having already spoken with the usual journalists about a *possibly significant seventeenth-century find*) that while of course, in keeping with the law, these documents would be made available to the public *the very moment* they were ready, the whole collection was currently quite fragile and was still being prepared by the laboratory.

So turned the wheels of power at the hand of an ambitious chairman, freedom of information laws be damned. But this time—this time, for once—those wheels were turning on Helen's behalf.

The irony of being Martin's new favorite cause was something she should have enjoyed. In truth, though, it rested uneasily.

With both reigning Patricias in high temper, the hush in the rare manuscripts room was more fraught than usual. That the Patricias distrusted historians was nothing new; Helen had overheard enough whispered complaints over the decades she'd been visiting this room to know the essentials: historians saw rare documents merely as sources of information, rather than as objects of inherent value; historians didn't care about the original documents once they'd stripped them of information. Patricia Starling-Haight had seen a history postgraduate chewing *gum* over a sixteenth-century illuminated manuscript. Patricia Smith had worked on fifteenth-century manuscripts that would have been salvageable if not for the irreversible damage a historian had wrought by *Sellotaping* two fragments together. Helen had once seen Patricia Smith ride the lift down from her laboratory to berate a history student who had accidentally punctured a document through some inexplicable pencil-point accident. Pausing before she bore the document out on its cushion like a patient on its pallet, the conservationist had practically hissed in the student's stricken face. "That's hours of labor to repair, and I'll turn my hand to it when I'm good and ready." Seeing the student's gaze drift despairingly to the document, she'd added, with the ferocity of an animal protecting its young, "I suppose your dissertation will have to wait, then, won't it?"

Helen didn't mind the Patricias' strictness—she felt an unspoken affinity with these women whose life of commitment seemed to parallel her own, though she knew only a little about them. Patricia Starling-Haight, Helen had heard, had been raised by an older sister during the war while their mother worked for the code-breaking operation at Bletchley Park. Patricia Smith had a daughter struggling to make a ca-

reer in dance, and a son on the dole who long ago had to be banned
from napping in the library. As for what the Patricias might know of
her, Helen had no idea.

Today, though, it was apparent that Helen was the enemy.

At an echoing noise, Helen started. A tall spectacled student entering the rare manuscripts room had let the door bang behind him. He
stood frozen a few paces past the door, half-turned, his hand extended
as though to grab back the sound: an animal caught in the headlights
of Patricia Starling-Haight's glare. With a bemused shake of her head,
Helen returned to the book on the cushion before her. The date of the
edition was 1658; the original Hebrew had been translated into Portuguese by one Simion de Herrera. *Contented are they who dwell in Thy
house . . . Contented are they who follow the Lord . . .* The cover was stiff,
concave, bound in dark red leather. Gilt edged the pages. Other than
brown shadows where the front and back pages had lain in contact with
the leather covers, the paper was healthy. Ink damage was moderate,
each page bearing only a faint brown burn-through of the text on its
opposite side: a ghostly echo of the verse from the page just turned, as
though the words had not been left behind but rang softly through all
else that might be said.

Once more, she forced her eyes to focus on the lines before her. It
was not that the text was difficult. The poems were mainly alphabetic
acrostics, many familiar to her, though she hadn't read these particular translations. Yet Helen couldn't shed the sense of something awry.
She found it difficult to articulate the problem precisely. The logistical
arrangements for her work were as smooth as could be hoped: thus
far, she had every reason to believe she and Aaron would have exclu-
sive access to the documents for the rest of the term. But there was
something about reading these documents singly, catalogued by number
rather than by the logic of their arrangement on the shelves under the
staircase, that felt wrong. To Helen, the arrangement of the documents
in the stairwell had seemed deliberate, as though the unknown hand
that had placed them there had intended the order as a message in itself.
Now that message had been eradicated. Here in the rare manuscripts
room she felt as though she were peering through a narrow aperture at
a picture whose larger contours she couldn't see. It reminded her of the
way people Aaron's age read the news, framed on a computer screen

with only a few lines visible—a pressured, stymied vision of things, instead of the daily grasp of the broad sheaf of newsprint that was an adult's true contact with the world.

"Fifteen minutes to closing," Patricia Starling-Haight said, startlingly close to Helen.

"Page, please," Helen countered.

Looking somewhat mollified, Patricia positioned herself beside the book, lifted the string weights, turned a page, and resettled the weights. This was Helen's self-imposed rule: she'd avoided touching rare documents for years, ever since her tremor reached a level where she feared it could do damage. With a nod of approval, Patricia Starling-Haight retreated.

Aaron was approaching the table. He'd left the room without a word to Helen forty minutes prior. Now he returned as though unexplained forty-minute breaks were one of those inalienable American rights. He pulled up his chair a few vacant seats away from Helen and slid his own cushion into place, a handwritten letter centered on it.

"Fifteen minutes to closing," Helen said to him.

From his pocket he withdrew a pen, held it just under the table, and clicked it with a mischievous grin that made it clear he was impressing himself. This was Aaron's way in the rare manuscripts room. He sucked hard candies when the Patricias' backs were turned. Earlier that afternoon, just after the librarian walked past, he'd actually lifted a document himself and moved it from its cushion to one that evidently pleased him better.

Let the Patricias make a meal of him. Helen returned her gaze to the left-hand page of poetry and made another note in her spiral-bound notebook. Her scrawl was ranging wide this afternoon—she could write only on every second line and was consuming pages like a schoolgirl. She gripped the pencil stub more tightly. It was maddening to her, how sluggishly she was thinking today. It wasn't the levodopa; she'd stopped taking that weeks ago against Dr. Hammond's advice, and had no regrets—the medicine had left long, dark spaces between her thoughts, each thought an island in a sea of nothing, the islands few and far between. The feeling had not been unpleasant, and that was the problem. Waking in the middle of the night to an inky peace that stretched on and on with no break, she'd become frantic. She could not recognize her own mind. The quiet in her head was the silence of defeat. She'd spent the night shivering in her thin nightdress, terrified. Unable to lie down lest she lose what remained of herself as she slept, her hands climbing at her throat, her temples. She'd told a skeptical Hammond she'd rather keep her tremor.

Yet now her mind felt almost equally blank. What was wrong with her today? She'd have stood and paced the room to rouse herself, would the Patricias not have descended upon her for conduct threatening to paper fibers. The cruelest of ironies came to her: now that the papers had found her, it would be too late—because she lacked the stamina. Because in recent weeks she'd stopped fighting the fatigue—she elected to go without some small trifle she'd left in the next room, rather than stand up with her cane to fetch it; to let the toner cartridge on her printer gradually drain, rather than drive herself to the store to purchase a replacement. She was too infirm—she tested the thought for the first time—to put together the pieces of this puzzle. To do the documents justice.

Aaron's mobile phone rang, loud.

"Christ," muttered Helen. Both Patricias converged from opposite sides of the room in a silent ballet: rare-manuscript Valkyries, simultaneously pointing to the sign on the wall that forbade mobile phones.

Aaron eyed his phone's display, then switched it off and pocketed it with a sheepish shrug to the Patricias, as though he'd forgotten he had it on him.

The Patricias glared and withdrew.

Helen rose carefully from her chair and walked over to Aaron, who still looked amused. She peered at the manuscript in front of him: a list of books pertaining to Passover observance. "That wasn't written by Aleph," she said.

Aaron nodded. "Probably it's written by her replacement. I expect she stopped writing."

"No," Helen said, more firmly than she intended. "Aleph might have lost her scribing position, but she wouldn't have stopped writing."

Aaron looked up. It was clear he was going to take the contradiction personally. "How do you know?"

"You saw the Spinoza reference, didn't you?" She struggled for the words to articulate her meaning: if a woman had risked as much as was necessary to write three words by a banned philosopher on a rabbi's letter in 1658, she wouldn't stop there. "She simply isn't going to stop writing."

Aaron looked unconvinced. Helen knew her own reasoning was absurd—even self-interested. A thousand things might have stopped Aleph from writing, and it was the height of folly for Helen to impose her own wishes on a female scribe.

"All we know," Aaron said, "is that for at least a few months a woman might have worked as a scribe, which is an unusual and interesting fact. But we've got nothing more. I mean—you're treating that Spinoza reference as though it meant she was some sort of rebel herself . . . rather than just someone whose job it was to faithfully copy down the words dictated to her. But for all we know, the rabbi she scribed for said, 'I hear Spinoza has been cooking up some idea about *Deus sive Natura,* I must remember to write a sermon condemning it, please make a note of it.' And she wrote it on the only paper at hand."

He was right, of course. Still. There was something about Aaron— some tiny, dismaying thing he awoke in her—that made it impossible to concede even this to him. With a jolt of confusion it came back to her that she'd aimed to sack him after those three days at the Eastons'. No matter that his work was good—she could easily find a more compliant assistant. Why hadn't she done so? She couldn't now recall.

"I believe," she said, "the Americans call this thinking outside the box."

He shrugged in a way that said *Not this American.*

"Closing time." Without further warning, Librarian Patricia swept one document-bearing cushion, then another, off the table, and left Helen and Aaron to pack their things.

IN HELEN'S OFFICE, AARON WAS pulling his day's translations off her shuddering printer when there was a knock at the door. Helen opened it to find Jonathan Martin's secretary, Penelope Babcock—an indeterminately middle-aged, attractive woman who exuded a perennial doe-eyed charm.

"I thought I'd stop by," Penelope said, a polite half-smile on her el-

egantly lipsticked mouth, "to let you know that Jonathan will be grant-
ing access to Brian Wilton's group to view the Richmond documents."

Helen gripped the doorknob. "Sorry?"

"Brian Wilton," Penelope enunciated, "will be allowed access in the
rare manuscripts room alongside you."

Helen let out a sound.

"He'll begin work next week," Penelope said. Her smile had thickened. "His presence won't interfere with your labors there, I'm sure."

At Helen's ongoing silence, Penelope's arched eyebrows rose higher.
"As you know, Brian is a former student of Jonathan's. Jonathan has
always kept a door open to his former students, as a matter of courtesy."

Penelope, presumably, had taken up this mission of mercy on her
own initiative, after scolding Jonathan Martin about not giving Helen
notice of his planned move. Penelope was scrupulous about her likabil-
ity in the department—Helen had always suspected it was Penelope's
defense against the eternal rumors about herself and Jonathan Martin,
and Helen couldn't fault the tactic.

Whatever the motivations behind Penelope's mission of mercy,
though, it was Helen's role to thank Penelope politely, nod as if Jonathan's consideration toward his former student were the height of chiv-
alry, and shut the door. There was no defensible basis for doing otherwise. For doing what she now did: Stand mute, unable to bring herself
to thank Penelope Babcock. Then shut the door slowly, without a word,
on Penelope's lovely face.

She pressed her forehead to the door. A shiver of betrayal, like the
soft fringes of some warming, life-restoring garment being slipped
from her skin. For just a moment, she indulged the memory of standing
before the Eastons' open stairwell: before a silent chorus of documents,
stilled voices trapped beneath the treads of a once-grand house. Documents waiting patiently all these centuries for someone—for her!—to
read and decipher them. Was it folly to feel that those pages, remnants
of a long-lost community of Jews, were written expressly for Helen's
very eyes, to soothe her heart now, after all these years? Was it too grandiose to say that in exchange for such a find she'd tendered her life?

Perhaps it was. Perhaps she was simply desperate for this last illusion
that her prospects were not all long spent.

Aaron stood at her desk, papers in hand. She braced for him to say something, but he didn't.

She sat. She opened a notebook and stared, disoriented, at a page of her own childishly wide scrawl.

As if he knew she needed a moment to compose herself, Aaron knelt over the shoulder bag he'd set on the floor, and began sorting papers.

His silence endured as she turned several pages of the notebook.

She heard herself speak. "I suppose that wasn't lost on you," she said.

From that position, he looked up at her with a mildness that took her aback. "We'll be fine," he said. "This is yours. We've got a head start. Besides, there's no substitute for having seen the documents in situ."

She considered him. He was actually reassuring. For a moment he could have been someone's trusted friend or older brother, offering a boost from the sidelines.

Straightening, he handed her two sheets of paper. In silence she scanned them. Translations of two more letters, both from a Jewish press in Amsterdam and both addressed to Rabbi HaCoen Mendes—one asking for clarification of the number of prayer books required by the London congregation, the other confirming the shipment of said books.

While she read, Aaron faced away from her desk.

She finished and set down the papers. "That will do for today," she said.

He seemed in no hurry to leave. He bent his neck, wound his scarf slowly, buttoned his coat. Stood a moment. Then gestured toward the frame over the hearth. "So," he said, "why Masada?"

She lifted her eyes to the portrait of the mountaintop. It was suddenly evident, as it had somehow not been before, how badly the sketch had faded over the years. She'd never known the name of the artist—a soldier off duty; Helen had spied him leaning on the hood of a jeep and filling pages of his sketchbook. It hadn't been hard to persuade him to part with one of his profiles of Masada. She had been a good-looking young woman in 1954. And the soldier, pockmarked and skinnier than he'd appeared from afar, had seen only the curve of her skirt over her hips; only the smoothness of her face and not the iron there.

That shy soldier in whose callused hand she'd placed a few coins would be a grandfather now, or dead. Years of that quantity had passed.

And here she sat. Still facing down the mountain's silhouette from across her desk.

Aaron was studying the sketch up close, his cropped curls now blocking her view. There was something softer about him today, she was sure of it. As though he were angling toward some question he wanted to ask, despite himself. "I mean," he said slowly, "I know it's a dramatic landscape."

Her voice was sharp. "Why do you ask?"

Aaron turned to her, and she was startled by the hesitation on his face. "I have a friend there," he said. "Well, farther north. She's staying on a kibbutz, actually."

She didn't believe for a moment that it was a friend. Aaron wasn't the sort to have female friends. He was the sort to have girlfriends or bitter exes.

Something was troubling him, some topic he could neither mention nor walk away from. It was as though he were trying to motion her to pick up some conversational lead.

"I was a tourist there," she said. The lie stiffened her shoulders, and she felt a twinge of regret.

He gave her an odd look, as though he disbelieved that she'd ever been a tourist: a person who did a thing merely for pleasure.

She gestured at the papers on her desktop. "You can go now," she said.

He hesitated, then left, closing the door behind him.

She picked up a pen, set its point gently on the desktop, and with the slightest pressure of one finger held it vertical. It stood, then gave way as a small, invisible tremor passed through her.

Why not tell him?

It was a crazy question, but she followed it ruthlessly. She had seen early in life that there was none in this world to audit one's soul. A man could deform himself into the most miserable of creatures, and no holy hand would descend from the clouds and cry *Halt.* And if there was no auditor, then one must audit one's own soul, tenaciously and without mercy. So she'd done at every significant turn in her life—and so she would now once again be her own pitiless interrogator, even if it meant mocking herself in terms that did violence to the few tender feelings she still had.

Why not tell him, indeed, if only to ensure that some piece of it lived on—some spark of who Helen Watt had once been? Or did she fear resurrecting a time in her life when she'd made a decision she dared not question—for if she did, and found herself wrong after all these years, what was there to do?

She couldn't remember the last time she'd been tempted to speak of it. The story that had once singed and flared in her had long since receded, as her habit of silence turned, over the decades, into law. Did she mean to take it to the grave with her, then? Plainly, that was what she was going to do. She was going to take it to the grave. And it would end there.

Dust.

How many times had each cell in her body changed over since those days? It made no difference. She could still feel it: the dry press of the heat on the concrete roofs of the army base, the jeeps, the dusty khaki uniforms. The too-blunt knives that slipped off the furrowed skin of cucumbers and the bickering between the cooks in the kitchen and the endless work dicing tomatoes that stung every nick on Helen's clumsy hands, and the leben, the leben, the fledgling Jewish state was afflicted with leben, the same menu over and again until a tank driver stood on a chair in the dining hall and recited a poem about flatulence, and one cook flung a soapy dishrag at his head and the other stormed out in tears, and Gevatron on the radio singing "Finjan" again and people crying out in the night—eleven years after liberation and the end of the war, they still cried out from their bunkbeds on the army base for gassed brothers, mothers shot and piled in a pit; a single such cry would leave Helen staring for hours at the dark ceiling long after the girl with the black eyes and eternally tight jaw from the intelligence detail exploded from her bunk with a ragged "Quiet already!" And the bunks subsided gradually into snores. Only Helen rising to stare out the windows, or step out the door under the sentry's silent gaze to walk the perimeter of the base under thick, brilliant stars.

But when the sun blared across the desert rubble and hid the stars, the night's solitary cries were drowned in the din of *we*. *We* building the Jewish nation. *We* making the desert bloom. *We* was the strongest, most death-defying word, the feats of *we* were stunning and true and brimmed with love. And the Arabs who walked alongside the dusty roads averted their eyes or stared hard into the dirt their own feet trod, while her own fair English complexion burned in the sun and the smells of the desert filled her nose, and she witnessed all that strove and sang and clashed around her and she counseled herself against seduction.

Helen's fellow volunteers—one Englishman, one Canadian, five Americans, and one Italian—were all Jews. All had signed up for work on a kibbutz—yet they never passed the kibbutz gate. For forty minutes they sat in the sweltering bus in the southern desert, gazing at a distant palm orchard rising from chalk-bright earth while laughter and cigarette smoke rose from a shifting cluster of sandaled Israelis outside the bus. Finally an English-speaking kibbutz member mounted the bus steps to announce their new destination. A mistake had been made— the kibbutz currently had a glut of volunteers and no beds. But someone knew of an army base nearby that was short-handed, and the kibbutz had taken a quick vote and decided to volunteer their volunteers. Scattered applause. "Put us wherever we can do the most good," a tall Canadian named Walter intoned, as the bus rumbled back onto the main road in the noon glare.

Dror, the officer tasked with managing the volunteers' adaptation to the army base, was displeased. At a hastily arranged meeting that night, held on the rock-strewn ground as the sunset glowed orange and pink above them, he paced in his dusty khaki uniform, his own carriage taut though he'd commanded them to stand at ease. "Look around you," he said. He addressed them in accented English, then repeated the instruction in Hebrew.

Dutifully the volunteers turned, taking in their surroundings: a few dozen low buildings, a radio tower and a water tower, a row of tanks parked beyond.

Dror pointed to the east, into the dusky hills. In a low voice, switching languages and scanning their faces to make sure he was understood, he continued. "Over there, that line of dark rock: Jordan." He swiveled, pointing south, then west. "There, Saudi Arabia. There, Egypt. Drive a half day to the north: Lebanon, Syria." He turned back, surveying the group. "There's been war on this spot where you're standing. There will be more."

With his tight black curls, high forehead, and handsome, angular face, he looked to Helen like something out of an illustrated Old Testament—noble and severe.

"We're a small base," he said, "but everything is on our shoulders. If you spend your six months here, you'll understand what that means. If you came for a vacation, go home. In the places you're from, they care about rank and dignity. Here the work you'll be asked to do might insult you. If it's going to insult you, leave now. Someone has to clean the toilets. Someone has to do laundry. In the places you're from, they've forgotten one person can make a difference. But here you'll find everything you do matters. Every single thing is handmade. Every building you paint or walkway you pave is pulling the yoke." The kibbutz member who had accompanied them to the base stepped forward and addressed them in English. "I'll be back at the kibbutz, but don't worry. We'll make sure the educational outings you were promised by the volunteer office will still take place. And despite how fierce Dror sounds, he'll let me talk him into letting you off duty." He clapped Dror on the shoulder. "You can join our outings as our security detail, my friend—we'll be *your* vacation."

Dror replied with a disapproving shake of his head; then a swift, relenting smile. He seized his friend in a mock headlock that ended with the two men's arms slung over each other's shoulders. Helen watched them turn for the mess hall, brothers.

In the base's kitchen Helen diced tomatoes and washed crate after crate of peaches trucked down from a northern kibbutz, and the thick white fuzz of the fruit made her skin bloom into a red prickly rash, from her hands to her upper arms. Dror, making rounds of the new volunteers, took one glance at her miserable attempts to avoid the fuzz-laden spray as she worked the nozzle over the peaches.

"Nurit," he called.

Nurit, the cook, set down a pot of steaming beets. At a motion of Dror's head, she moved Helen to cucumbers, steering her by the shoulders to the counter and placing the handle of a knife into Helen's fist with an expression of forbearance, as though Helen were yet another new appliance found to be unfit for real labor.

"Our English flower," Dror laughed, as with his boot he slid a mop bucket to a corner where no one would trip on it, then exited the kitchen.

Pressing her lips tight, Helen sliced with slow, wretched care.

The volunteers were housed with the soldiers. In the bunk above Helen slept Muriel, who'd survived the war as a child in hiding in Romania and refused to undress in front of the other girl soldiers for a reason no one asked. Muriel's face had the compact vividness Helen had seen only in central Europeans — a piercing intensity, as though life must be kept burning against endless odds. Most of the female soldiers had responded with indifference to the information that Helen wasn't Jewish; some even nodded appreciation. Only Muriel had looked as though the fact were a violation, and upon learning Helen was her bunkmate, swore audibly. Seated on her mattress, Muriel spilled water from her canteen, swinging her legs in silence as drops rained down onto Helen's bed below. She cut her own hair sitting on Helen's bunk and refused to clean the leavings. At night the sharp ends, scattered on Helen's pillow and sheets, pricked Helen's skin like an accusation — as if Muriel could somehow see the cream-colored bedroom with the cream-colored bedcover beneath which Helen had slept for nineteen years . . . or hear Helen's mother's exclamation, breaking the hush of a breakfast of marmalade toast, "This isn't about Notting Hill again, is it?" Helen's decision to go to Israel *had* been about the riots, of course — just as it had been about singing the last resonating notes of "Blessed Are Those That Be Undefiled" in the lush wooden chapel at her school's winter concert, the echoes of the words silenced by polite applause. It had been about the girlhood friend who broke up with Helen, accusing her — "When you have a feeling you just act on it" — simply because Helen departed abruptly from a party she found dull; it had been about hiding an airline ticket and Hebrew dictionary in her bureau and knowing neither parent would commit the loving impropriety of snooping; it had been about a thousand other things Helen reviled even if she couldn't name them.

Mornings, while the girls waited for Muriel to finish changing her clothing in the bathroom stall, Helen looked at her own wan reflection in the dented metal mirror above the trough sink and tried to imagine it purged of something irredeemably English: the part of her that, despite her unflinching intentions, knew to applaud politely and stay above the fray.

Weeks passed; she was rotated from kitchen duty to collect spent shell casings on the firing range. Next she was sent to clear a field where a landing strip was to be built, joining others in gathering rocks and pitching them onto the bed of a slowly rolling pickup truck. Through the sun-shot days she listened to the other girls chatter and daily understood more of their Hebrew, though she didn't attempt to intrude on their sharp, hopeful talk. At the firing range she took instruction from Dror alongside the other volunteers. The kick of the Mauser was surprising, but she was a good shot, as she knew she'd be: she hit the man-shaped target in the chest and then the head, and Dror noted it with a nod and turned away from her to coach the others.

A half kilometer from the base, she and a few of the other girl soldiers hand-mixed and poured the concrete floor of a shed in the middle of the desert, for what purpose they weren't told. They laid the floor and were sent on to other tasks; weeks passed. Only Dror seemed frustrated by the supply officer's lack of haste in providing materials for walls and roof. After a third week Dror instructed the girls to paint the floor. They were dropped off once more with brushes and paint and water and one gun for their protection. A floor in the middle of the desert, surrounded by nothing but rocks and a single dusty track. The girls painted half of the floor white and then sat on the shadeless earth. The sun was high and Helen sweated in her uniform and cap. Mid-morning Dror arrived with a pale green melon, which he sectioned with a knife on the hood of his jeep. It dripped and the girls ate the slices with their hands. Dror spoke to no one. He sat on the fender and smoked while they ate, then collected the rinds in a plastic bag.

"Drink," he commanded them, seeing the still-full bladder of water beside the half-painted floor.

Dutifully, Helen and a few of the others filled their canteens.

"That water tastes like camel piss," Muriel said.

Dror laughed despite himself, as at a saucy younger sister. "Drink the camel piss, then."

Muriel lifted her chin in a way that made the other girls fall silent. "It's bad for our gorgeous complexions."

He tossed the bag of rinds into the jeep. "So is going thirsty in the desert."

"We'll drink if we're thirsty," retorted Muriel.

"Drink," Dror repeated, his tone weary and firm, like a father ending an argument.

But Muriel's face tightened, and Helen saw that she resented Dror and was in love with him. And Helen could see, in the slow way he settled into his driver's seat, that Dror chose not to know this.

"Drink," he said. He started the jeep. "By the time your body feels thirst you're already dehydrated. This is the desert. Don't be a fool. In the desert, fools die." The notion of fools dying seemed to anger him and he did not speak gently. He started away, turning in a tight arc to head back toward the base.

"Heil Hitler!" Muriel called as he gained speed.

For an instant the jeep's pace faltered. Then, his face inscrutable, Dror lurched past.

"*You* live two years under enemy guns," Muriel screamed after the receding jeep. "Then I'll listen to *your* opinion."

The pale dust of Dror's passage hung on the horizon.

"What's your problem?" the girl beside Muriel said quietly. "He lost his mother and sister."

Muriel's face showed that she hadn't known. But she gave a hard laugh. Taking her neighbor's canteen, she slowly drizzled a dark pattern of water on the rocky ground.

Helen watched the water evaporate.

When it was gone, the other girl reclaimed her canteen and capped it with a relenting shrug. "He's so good looking. It's too bad he's a prick."

That night Muriel cried softly in the bunk above Helen's.

Her father wrote a letter. *Your mother tells me that you have not yet set a definitive date for your return. This adventure of yours has lasted long enough and it's time you ended it. There's a path in life, and one cannot step off it for long without consequences. Your mother and I ask you to book return passage now and we look forward to your arrival.*

ONE EVENING IN THE MESS HALL, when she'd been on the base two months, shouts rose over the clang of metal trays. A tank soldier was leaning over a counter to argue with a red-haired dishwasher: something about a stack of trays slipping, hot soup. The dishwasher looked unimpressed, even when the tank soldier's voice rose to a bellow.

Helen filled her plate with diced cucumbers and tomatoes and proceeded to the volunteers' table. "What's the trouble?" she ventured as she sat.

The Jewish student from Canada with the thick black-rimmed glasses shrugged knowledgeably. "That one"—he pointed at the soldier—"was a kid in one of the camps. They didn't survive if they didn't scrap over everything." With a glance at Helen, he added, "What do you expect?"

Would there be some final bar she might one day clear, proving that she too could understand? She watched the Jewish volunteers eat their food.

The shouting had stopped; the soldier made his way slowly between the tables and sat near the rear of the hall. But the dishwasher hadn't finished; a moment later he leaned out over the counter, waited for enough heads to turn his way, then with a pointed gaze at the tank soldier silently tapped a finger to his temple: *something's broken in there.*

Instantly the soldier sprang up, a metal pitcher like a blunt weapon in his hand, and Helen felt a slide in her gut as he ran past their table and vaulted the counter. The dishwasher swore and evaded the soldier, shutting the kitchen door against him. An enormous sound: the soldier slammed his empty pitcher into the door. Then, instead of entering the kitchen's other door, which still hung open, he slammed the dented metal into the wall again, then again. Did he mean to frighten the dishwasher? To demolish the door, or himself? The pitcher's metal bent, then tore jaggedly. Blood spattered—the tank soldier's own. And then Dror was running and then he'd slid over the counter and was tackling him.

The two fell hard on the painted cement floor.

A moment later Dror stood, dusted his shirt painfully with one hand. With the barest gesture, as though not to shame the other man, Dror motioned for him to stand.

Helen expected the tank soldier to spit in Dror's face, so contorted with rage had his expression been at the instant when Dror's shoulders hit his waist and the two fell. But as he rose opposite Dror, his eyes cleared. He lowered his head, and raised it, and stood silent, as Dror slipped the mangled pitcher from his hands with a gesture of tender respect. Then Dror wrapped a kitchen towel around the tank soldier's cut wrist and led him swiftly out the server's door through the front entrance of the mess hall, toward the commander's office.

After dinner she gathered her cleaning supplies from the shed behind the kitchen, working by the light from a lamppost—a solitary bulb blazing over its patch of dirt. Roaches big as her thumbs ran past her sandals, their black shells glinting.

When she entered the rear door of the kitchen to finish her cleanup duty, Dror was standing there alone, cradling his forearm against his chest. He looked distracted, as though he'd come to this temple of empty metal countertops and drying plastic containers to work something through, only to be stranded without a clear thought.

Her sandals slapped the painted cement floor. She stooped to lift the bucket of dark water beside the sink, dumped it, and refilled it, the cold faucet flow ringing into the metal. She looked up to see Dror watching her as though shocked to find another breathing soul in his vicinity. Or perhaps he was merely vague with pain from the arm he petted absently like a child that might be soothed into silence. She'd never seen him unfocused—she was accustomed to seeing him stride sternly toward his purpose, and she was uncertain now how to behave.

She kept her eyes on the mop, sank it into the cold water, wrung the heavy gray strands, and let their weight splay on the floor, erasing spatterings of blood. He watched with concentration, as though her actions were the key to something he needed to understand.

When she neared his feet, she stopped and looked at him squarely.

He said, with an expression of relief as though the words cleared his mind, "You have the most truthful face I've ever seen."

The next night his forearm was in a cast. The soldiers were smoking and playing music at the outdoor canteen. Helen sat to the side, sipping from a can of peach nectar. Within earshot of the canteen's record player, a half dozen soldiers moved through the steps of a folk dance on the bare ground. Lagging a beat behind the soldiers, the American volunteers gamely swept their feet through the steps. The air smelled of dust and eucalyptus and the soldiers' cigarettes. Someone put "Erev Ba" on the record player and there was a murmur of approval. More soldiers stood up from the shadowed benches and joined the dancers, the curved line of them moving together and apart with small caressing steps. The Americans moved aside to watch. Helen saw that Dror had squeezed his eyes shut. He stayed that way for a long moment. Then he rose from the bench where he had been smoking by himself, extinguished the cigarette under his boot, and, looking at no one, took a spot at the end of the line. The dancers in their khaki uniforms stepped and swayed in the dusk and Dror moved with them, soft on his feet— pivoting silently in the dark, his forearm in the white cast held gently before him, his palm raised toward his chest in a gesture of unexpected innocence.

After, when it was dark, he sat at the end of Helen's bench and peeled an orange with the point of a knife, working it in a circle with his good hand. A few dancers still moved in the dim light shed by the canteen. Dror passed sections to the two soldiers who sat between him and Helen; they passed a portion to her. A deep, stunning sweetness.

When she turned, Dror was walking away.

In the morning the volunteers were driven in a battered blue bus to five points of interest in the desert—this was the educational compo- nent the volunteer coordinator had made much of, sitting across a desk from Helen in London two months and a thousand years earlier. The volunteers would visit Masada, the Dead Sea, Ein Gedi, and the pro- posed site for a nature reserve at Hai Bar, ending with a tour of Ein Ra- dian. Days' worth of sightseeing, crammed into twelve hours; it turned out the kibbutz needed the bus for the rest of the week.

They'd planned an early start. But the bus driver spent an hour on some unspecified repair, his legs sticking out from beneath the belly of the bus while Dror and the man from the kibbutz and an Israel Tourist Bureau guide sat cross-legged, alternately smoking and spitting sunflower-seed shells and occasionally passing the driver a tool. Helen sat in the dust among the others, waiting. One of the American women tried to make conversation with Dror about her impressions of Israel, before lapsing into that wounded silence the Americans fell into when they suspected an Israeli thought them trivial.

The sun was high by the time they approached Masada through the rocky, lifeless desert—and the sight of the mountain through the bus windows extinguished all conversation. They filed out of the parked bus quietly, into a crushing heat.

Helen had seen higher mountains, yet none so forbidding as this plateau of pale rock. Its rough cliffs, bare against the horizon, issued an overpowering silence.

They climbed wearing shorts and hats, their sandals pale with dust. The Snake Path was narrow, and the morning grew still hotter as they hiked up the steep side of the flat-topped mountain. None of the volunteers had brought enough water for this hour of the day, and they made their way slowly, sweat drying to a salt scrim on their skin.

At the top of the mesa, the sun pressing without mercy, the guide gathered them. Far below the plateau, the brown-gray desert seemed to vibrate in the heat. The Dead Sea was a faint purple line in the distance. Dabbing his forehead with his folded cloth hat, the guide began his recitation. In the first century, he said, after the Romans had destroyed Jerusalem and killed or enslaved its Jews, a group of Jewish zealots had fled to this spot to make their last stand in one of Herod's famously impenetrable and well-provided fortresses. Here on the mountaintop were storerooms, cisterns, living chambers, bathhouses; a few had been excavated and more archaeological work was planned, the guide said —for now they would need to imagine much of what he was describing.

She felt Dror watching her. She met his eyes; his gaze flattened and moved elsewhere.

The mighty Roman army—the guide intoned—which had vanquished all of Jerusalem in a matter of days, staged a siege for more than a year in this searing desert before it succeeded in bringing about the fall of this small community of Jews atop Masada. While the Romans suffered in the heat below, the Jews above drank the plentiful water from the cisterns and lived off food stores laid away by the notoriously paranoid Herod. The Roman camp called for reinforcements, brought in engineers, rationed water—all to defeat the last tiny gathering of Jews still daring to practice their own religion. And when the massive Roman division had at last completed an earthwork to breach the walls, and as the Roman soldiers prepared battering rams and lit fires around the mountaintop, the Jews finally knew their situation was hopeless. Their leader, Eliezer, gathered the men. It was time, Eliezer said, to deny the Romans the chance to murder or enslave them. "Let us at once choose death with honor," the guide recited, "and do the kindest thing we can for ourselves, our wives, and our children, while it is still possible to show ourselves any kindness." Each man, Eliezer urged, must kill his family. Then, in an order to be determined by lot, the men would slaughter one another. The final man standing would kill himself—but only after setting fire to the food stores so that the Romans would be denied that prize. Only one food storeroom and water cistern would be left intact, to mock the Romans with its bounty. Let the Romans find the food and the brimming cistern, and the bodies tenderly laid in a row. Let them know that the Jews had chosen death, rather than slavery to the Romans and their gods.

Not long after, when the Romans broke through the walls expecting a pitched battle, they found themselves facing smoke and silence.

The guide pushed himself off the stone wall he'd been leaning against. Today, he told them, Israeli soldiers are sworn in at dawn on this mountaintop to the motto "Masada shall not fall again."

On all sides, the plains below them wavered in the heat to the far horizon.

"Still," Avi, the short, stringy American, muttered to two of his fellow volunteers, "how can anyone kill someone they love?"

The guide glanced up sharply.

Avi, reddening—he hadn't meant to be overheard—nonetheless continued. "I mean—what sort of man can do that?"

Dror let out a small sound. He dropped his cigarette and ground his heel hard into the dirt. Pocketing the butt, he turned away from the American.

That guide said nothing for a moment. Then he spoke in a low, quick voice. "Have you ever had to contemplate letting loved ones die at the hand of someone who hates them?"

The American, silenced, turned to the view.

Checking his watch, the guide motioned with his head toward the Snake Path. The volunteers began the descent without another word. In single file, they picked their way toward the desert floor.

Ahead of Helen, Dror jogged down the twisting footpath. Next in line behind him, she followed heedlessly, matching his punishing pace regardless of the sliding of her feet on the steep pitch, the sun pounding her head. Twice someone called her name from the slow-moving line behind her, but she didn't turn. With each jarring step she slipped free of the first century and martyrdom, the grisly story sliding off her hot skin as she let gravity carry her down the mountain. Dror met each turn of the path as though he'd been born to this—his birthright to run down a mountain without breaking his neck. She knew she was unsafe at this pace, but she didn't slow. She didn't care if she broke a bone. She wanted to break a bone. She wanted to wing down this mountain and stumble through all this stark parched bright impossibly romantic desert air to break herself on those stones. So he'd have to stop at last and speak to her.

The mountain was running out on her, her legs pounding, the flat plain approaching with fearsome speed. She didn't know what she would do if she caught up to Dror, only that it was urgent that she do so.

He disappeared into the bus.

She stopped in the lot, her breath loud in the silence. Slowly the heat claimed her, as if some essential boundary between her body and the desert had been erased. She stood, heart beating steadily, as the footsteps of the rest of the group became audible on the rocky path.

HALFWAY TO EIN GEDI, she rose from her seat and made her way to the front, where the guide was tracing a route on the map with his nicotine-stained thumbnail and conferring with the driver. When the guide looked up at her, she wasted no time on pleasantries. "If all the Jews died," she demanded, "how do you know what happened up there?"

The man tapped his worn map and sighed. Atop Masada, he'd been solemn. Now his grave demeanor had spent itself. Brusquely he said, "The historian recorded it. Josephus Flavius. And Josephus knew because two Jewish women, one old and one young, hid in a cave with some children during the killing. In their cowardice they were caught and made slaves by the Romans, and the women told their story to Josephus." As the bus rounded a shuddering curve the guide squinted at the roadside, drew on his cigarette, and exhaled meditatively past Helen's face. "They were traitors. But they did at least the good of keeping the story alive."

Someone in the back of the bus was complaining about a stuck window. Someone else began to sing and was silenced by a volunteer who said she had a headache.

"Why?" Helen said.

"Why what?" The guide, who had turned to speak with the driver, glanced back at Helen.

"Why were those women traitors?"

From the corner of her eye she saw Dror look up sharply from his seat across the way, but she didn't turn to him. "*Why* was it cowardly to want to live?" she charged.

The guide gave her a weary look. With a slow shake of his head, he returned to his conversation with the driver.

On the lurching walk back to her seat she passed Dror, who paid her no mind.

That night on the base she felt a wild disappointment. For the first time she considered leaving. The desert that she'd imagined speaking to her in fact spoke a language she didn't understand at all, a foreign tongue of whispers and implications.

She left her bunk. The night breathed traces of desert plants whose names she'd never know. The single bright bulb outside the dining hall lit the eyes of a jackal on the far side of the fence and she turned from it. The silence of the base had deepened to its midnight pitch. A man appeared from the far side of the dining hall, a uniformed figure. He approached her with a hesitant step, the cast on his arm catching the dim light. An impulse took her—to run from the sight of him.

But she hesitated, and he was in front of her. He stood perfectly motionless, as though to compensate for having fled down a mountain to escape her.

She lifted her chin like a soldier standing at attention—she meant to mock him. The air between them was alive. She could feel him through it.

A question passed over his face. Then he stepped forward and kissed her.

The night sky shone beyond the horizon of his tight, dark curls. Her hand, rising, found only the plaster encasing his arm, cool and smooth as though he were made of stone or weathered bone.

A breeze. A lone cypress bent, occluding the stars.

Then, with a hushing sound, the cypress swept back over the sky's thick stars and she found the living skin of his inner arm, then his warm body reaching, and something gave way.

SHE KEPT IT SECRET. She knew he would want her to. The way his voice still lightened with surprise when she greeted him, as though in the interval since their last meeting she might have forgotten his name or vanished; the way he scooped her toward him from the small of her back; the quiet, delighted pitch of his laugh when she teased him for his stern behavior with the volunteers; the way he seemed to be laughing not only at her words, but at laughter itself . . . all of this was to be kept between them. He didn't have to tell her this. Even had she wished to speak of it, with what words could she have explained that she'd changed—that her body had changed—that every molecule in her was alive, aligned, iron filings to a magnet? She chopped vegetables every day and doled leben into buckets and picked spent bullet casings in the pressing heat, but everything around her had been redrawn. The world was a geography of hidden places, the spaces where they could meet unseen punctuating the endless barren stretches where she pretended not to notice his low conversation with the other officers as he entered the dining hall, or the way he raised his head silently at a jeep moving on the horizon.

She spent her days weighing the distance to the next time and place they'd be alone, and it seemed to her when she set down her knife and looked at the desert beyond the kitchen window that everything was waiting to give way—to buckle and rise transformed into something else, something yet unseen, some new way of being in the world— some new incarnation of rock and sky and cypress tree and fuel tank that would reconcile everything. There was the light shearing off the kitchen's long window, and the fine shimmer of heat across the jeep's windshield, and the thin cold juice of pear nectar at the canteen at dusk, and softness at the core of everything.

IN JAFFA THEY STEPPED OFF the bus into sleepy afternoon heat. It was the first time their days off had coincided. All the way from Be'er Sheva they sat side by side, their legs brushing. He'd teased about her inability to pronounce the *r*'s of his name properly; she'd rebutted by imitating his pronunciation of hers—*Helen Vatt*—as he unwrapped the pitas and salted cucumbers he'd packed for their bus ride. Once far enough from Be'er Sheva that they no longer chanced running into someone from the base, he took her hand and held it. As they watched the landscape change from desert to rocky farmland to coastline, he sang to her under his breath—something in Hebrew, then something in Polish that made him tap a rhythm gently on his knee and then stop singing.

At the sight of him in civilian clothing—a short-sleeved cotton shirt, his arm pale where the cast had been removed, a rolled beach towel tucked beside him on the cracked vinyl seat—she felt a tenderness she masked by calling him Frankie Laine and refusing to explain herself. As she laughed at his puzzlement, words she'd been forced to memorize as a schoolgirl came to her. *How beauteous mankind is.*

He knew his way to the shore and led them toward it, stopping at a dim storefront restaurant near the clock tower to buy lunch, which they ate on a low rock wall overlooking an orange grove and, beyond it, the sea. On a whim she added a dark green harif sauce to her falafel—Dror, staying her hand, said, "Are you sure?"—but she'd spooned it on all the same, determined to dispel any notion he might still hold of her as an English flower. At her first bite, the harif burned so badly, her eyes watered. "Holy God," she coughed, and Dror, laughing at first but then attentive, had plied her with water from his bottle until the burning subsided. With his thumb, carefully, he wiped the sauce from her upper lip, and when her mouth still stung from the spice he went back to the owners of the restaurant for a cup of ice.

Just off the coast, solitary Arab fishermen stood with rod and line on the Andromeda rocks, each man deposited on his own perch amid the surf to collect the day's catch, until his friends or family retrieved him in a rowboat. Under their gaze, Dror led her down to the sliding waves.

She'd swum in an ocean before but was unprepared for the swiftness with which the warm waves lifted them, now holding them in the palm of the sea, now slipping them down, farther than she expected. She grabbed Dror's hand, and he pulled her to a sandbar and cradled her there as the waves lifted and sank—and something wild settled in her.

After a long while he said in her ear, "I can rest with you."

Later he lay beside her on the narrow towel, drying in the sun: a man who could have preened, had he chosen to. Spare and muscular from his training, nothing wasted, his features like something carved. She rested her head on his chest. With the pads of her fingers, she tapped his heartbeat back to him. He clasped her hand to his chest, stopping her.

The wind shifted, bending the branches of the orange trees, gusting out toward the water. Without warning a honeybee lit on the heel of Dror's hand and crawled into the tender gap between their two palms. Instinctively she bucked back, pulling their hands apart.

The bee—a compact creature, its wings pressed back, helpless against the wind—clung to Dror's palm, the last solid thing between it and the vast ocean.

He stood carefully, cupping it. He walked against the wind toward the orange trees, sand clinging to his legs, carrying it to safety.

He returned, studying his hand.

"It stung you?"

He nodded.

"But it'll die!" As soon as she spoke the words she heard their absurdity. As though the world owed its creatures fairness.

He turned and jogged down to the water, entered, and stroked his way through the waves for several minutes before leaning back and letting the water carry him.

A small distance from shore, a boy in a rowboat had pulled up to one of the Andromeda rocks and was handing a basket to the fisherman, who laid down his rod to receive his lunch, clasping the back of the boy's neck in thanks. At the water's edge, two girls with long braids walked hand in hand. Higher up on the shore, a middle-aged man with leathery skin trudged slowly beneath the orange trees, carrying a closed vendor's tray—presumably on his way to an afternoon's work in some neighborhood more likely to yield customers. Catching Helen's eye, he brightened, then beckoned, sweeping open his tray against his ample belly, and began to address her in Arabic. Stepping closer, she saw that his tray contained an assortment of modest artifacts of tarnished metal, a few of them with embedded stones of a beautiful blue, a few with empty sockets where stones had once been.

"Quite lovely," she offered—but shaking his head at her attempts to address him in English or Hebrew, he smiled with stained teeth, and gestured enthusiastically toward the street where the restaurant was —then beyond, toward a narrow alley behind it. His cart: in his cart he had more, in his cart he surely had what she wanted.

"*Gveret, bvakasha,*" he said, and repeated the words: *Miss, please.* It seemed to be the only Hebrew he knew.

She let him lead her, repeating his two words, farther from the shore and then onto a side street—she wasn't sure the man would have anything worth purchasing, but she thought all the same that she'd like to surprise Dror with a gift. In the man's small wooden cart, as battered and stained as the objects he vended, there was a basket. After some fumbling, he opened its lid to reveal a jumble of larger objects: pitchers, metal cups, ornamented lockets. She spent a long while sorting his wares, the man breathing nervously behind her, before selecting a small silver-colored picture frame patterned with grapevines.

She paid without bargaining—surely more than the thing was worth, but the sum was still low—and, with a wave to the satisfied vendor, returned to the beach.

"Helen!" Dror, still wet from his swim, a towel over his shoulder, broke away from what seemed to be an urgent conversation with another man—the owner of the restaurant where they'd bought lunch. He ran to her. The expression on his face—incredulity and fury—tightened her body.

"What?" Inadvertently she laughed.

"What were you thinking?"

She turned. Behind her the old Arab man had disappeared.

"He had his wares in his cart."

"So you just followed a man you didn't know down an alley?"

"I didn't just"—she looked at him. "Well. Everything's fine, isn't it?"

"Do you have *any* understanding?"

She opened her mouth, then closed it. She could make no sense of Dror's fury. He'd gone from tenderness to tight-lipped rage in what seemed an instant.

"A blond-haired English girl," he pressed, "out for the day with an Israeli Jew. You'd be a perfect candidate for an attack."

"Dror—he was a wheezing old man."

"You can only say that for sure now, on the other side of it. If you want to ignore the dangers then you might as well—"

"How is it any different from the man who sold us lunch?"

"I've bought lunch from Ahmed a dozen times. Everyone knows

him. He was about to help me search for you right before you showed up."

She didn't know how to answer.

"You need to think about what could have happened to you."

He spoke like an adult scolding a child. Yet he was twenty-four — only five years older than Helen.

"I don't see," she said to him quietly, "why the thought of me being in danger should make you look at me as though you hate me."

They rode the bus into the desert. The heat of the afternoon pressed on the metal roof; she angled her head closer to the window, which she'd slid open as far as it would go. When they'd traveled most of the distance to Be'er Sheva, Dror lifted a hand and laid it atop hers — but it was a heavy, dutiful gesture. After a moment, she slipped her hand away.

Arriving at last at the base, she thought they'd part ways — but he led her instead to the empty barracks on the deserted northern side of the base where they'd spent stolen hours these past weeks.

Just inside the door she balked.

"Don't touch me," she said, "if it's torture for you." She meant to sound wry, like a woman in a movie, but her voice wavered.

He broke away from her and pushed through the thin metal door. A blare of sunlight — then it banged shut behind him, leaving her in the dark.

She found him smoking outside, glaring at the empty stage of the desert. He didn't turn at her step. "I need you to understand," he said. Of course, she thought. Staring at him, she tried to imagine what his mother and sister would have looked like — those same dark eyes and curls on softer features.

"I'm sorry, Dror, I —"

"Don't be sorry." He dropped his cigarette to the dirt, ground it under his sandal. "When I kiss you," he said, "I'm just one man. I'm not carrying all of them with me." He paused, waiting for her to understand. "This week I hardly thought about my family."

She'd no answer for the simple grief in his statement.

A long moment passed. She heard her voice. "Are you lonely with me?" she said. "Because I'm not a Jew?"

He didn't answer, and to her own surprise when she spoke again her voice wasn't gentle, but accusatory. "Can't you trust me?"

"It's not a question of trust. It's"—he breathed. "I don't know, Helen, whether you understand all that you're touching when you touch me."

"You're right. I don't. The Nazis made your world a horror, and now after everything you went through, you've decided that world is where you'll stay? Do you *want* to live in a world where no one can cross any lines or—or touch each other, Dror?"

He spun to face her, then stopped, his face lit with fury.

She said, "You think I'm heartless."

He inhaled slowly through his nostrils. "Yes."

She was shaking, but her words came steady, as though they cost her nothing. "I'm not. And I didn't think you'd be one of those who confuse truthfulness with heartlessness."

A cluster of goats picked its way across the plain beyond the barbed-wire fence. A slight boy in a white headdress followed them, a stick dangling unused at his side. Nothing else moved on the horizon.

"You're right," Dror said. He watched her. After a moment he said, "When you see what makes no sense to you, you say something." He paused. "Don't stop doing that."

His handsome face had softened. She felt his grief rest gingerly in her hands.

She wanted to apologize—tell him how wrong she'd been, ask him please to tell her more, tell her all of it until she could feel what he felt.

He held himself apart another moment. Then reached, blindly, for her face.

That night she lay down with him on the rough blanket, with the feeling of sliding from a great height. He met her there with a solemn welcome, his hands on her body indelible.

THEN ONE EVENING LATER THAT WEEK, their secret was no longer a secret. At the canteen there was whispering on the bench: Nurit from the kitchen sitting with flirtatious Dov from the bomb unit; both shaking heads at something Avi the American volunteer was saying. Seated beside the trio, Muriel listened long, with arms wrapped round her torso, before issuing a vehement verdict.

From where Helen sat, alone on the end of her own bench as though adrift at sea, only one word of Muriel's speech was audible: *Dror.* The name a rasp of betrayal.

For a hypnotic instant Muriel's eyes fastened on Helen's.

Dror sat alert amid the gathering at a distance from Helen, his untouched soda in his hand. She saw that he'd felt the change as well. She watched a wary hope on his face dissolve to something dull, before re-emerging, a moment later, as anger.

Then Avi turned to Muriel and, loud enough to still the activity at the cashier's table behind them, said, "Well, it's not as though non-Jewish volunteers are part of our effort."

Dror tapped his soda bottle with his fingertips. He tapped again. Then he stood, and the words he spoke were addressed to Avi and to all of them, the two dozen soldiers in uniform, their young faces turned to Dror in trust and dread, as to an admired elder brother.

"The non-Jews are here by choice," Dror said. "We talk all the time about heroism. How many of you would have *chosen* to give up safety?"

There was no answer, but the faces around the canteen rebuked him.

Dror turned and left the canteen.

Helen didn't move from her bench until every one of them had left, none offering more than a quick glance in her direction. Even to her ears, Dror's argument felt thin. The Jewish volunteers had chosen to give up safety too. Walter from Canada and Maria from Italy, and Avi who had been Abe and his fellow Americans, and of course David from London: all had left places where they could have had comfortable lives, and all planned to stay in Israel. For them, this volunteer stint was a way to launch their new lives as Israelis, tossing them headlong into a society where everyone had to be willing to pitch in because the coming of war was inevitable. They'd come here because, as she'd heard Avi say grimly to one of the other American volunteers, safety no longer had meaning for him once he knew how easily Jews could be murdered. They weren't here, as Helen was, for a few months, a year, a rebellion en route to adulthood.

A week passed before it began. A week when Dror's voice whispered her out of sleep in the hot, quiet barracks and he buttoned the blouse of her uniform with absurd care. A week of averted eyes even from the girls who had once been friendly to Helen; of silence when she carelessly splashed mop water onto the kitchen floor—the cook's reprimands muted out of some uneasy respect for Dror. A week of tensions blanched invisible by the bright light of Dror—his smile upon seeing her, his touch like the courtship of something precious. She lay in the barracks beside him, the pulse visible in the skin of his neck, and her fear evaporated. Here she was at the center of things. Here she was, at last, where it was possible to lie naked and at rest, to look into the dark eyes of the man beside her and know they'd pledged each other the gift of truth. For the first time since childhood, she realized, she didn't dread living in the world. She said it aloud in the still air of the barracks and listened to the two Hebrew words drop peacefully from her, like twin stones into the quiet desert: "I'm alive."

She woke to Dror watching her. Instinctively she sat, pulling the rough blanket over her breasts.

"Do you know how many of us died?"

At first she thought she'd misheard.

"One out of three." He spoke quietly but with an intensity she instantly feared. "One out of every three Jews in the world. In my country, in Poland, nine out of every ten of us died."

She waited. He was watching her with an emotion she couldn't identify. "Including your mother," she said quietly. "And Nessa."

He blinked. "Do you know how many of us died here just after that, in the war of independence? When we were attacked from five fronts?"

"Dror," she said. "You sound like you're making a speech."

Dror stood, and she saw that he'd dressed while she slept. Slowly he paced before her, as though interrogating a suspect. Then he stopped. "I want you to know what you're stepping into."

She watched him. *Don't forget I've lived through war too,* she wanted to say, then was ashamed. She remembered little of the Blitz: her mother's arm pulling a heavy curtain to shut out the blaring, wailing world; a confusion of green sliding past the train window; the smooth handle of her tagged suitcase and a kitten that lived in a garden shed and a large silent woman who'd already taken in three other children. The embarrassment of forgetting how to tie her shoe; the older girl who showed her how.

"What I'm talking about," he began as though reading her thoughts, "isn't just a war that begins and ends, Helen—and it's something England can't have prepared you for. You name a country, and I'll tell you about a time it became obsessed with killing Jews. Do you know, in Russia the Nazis recruited local farmers to help drown Jews, before they settled on more efficient means. Thirty thousand in two days at Babi Yar." He paused. "Drowning," he said.

"Dror," she said. "Stop."

"I want you to try to imagine it."

She stared at him.

"*I* imagine it," he went on. "Drowning has to be done individually. Can you imagine what it takes to hold a child down by the hair, a woman, a man? And not for just a second, not the sort of thing you can do with a moment's adrenaline before you have time to think about it. With drowning you have to hold"—his voice cracked. "You have to do it until the struggle for life has stopped."

She did not want to imagine and couldn't help it. She felt the tendons of her neck constrict. Near panic, she raised her palms to repel the horror—to repel him?

He sat down opposite her, so quietly he barely made a sound. "I need you to understand," he said.

"Why are you doing this?" she said.

He closed his eyes.

She sat opposite him, the blanket to her throat. For the first time, it occurred to her to wonder whether she might be luring him into something wrong. Suddenly the softness of her own breasts, the warmth of her skin, seemed untrustworthy, as though they might lead him astray in a world that required hardness.

Pushing the thought away, she reached for him, and let the confusion bleed out of her. She thought, *With this touch, and this and this. I lead you to me.*

The following night, they crossed the endless open distance from the canteen to his quarters with his hand firmly holding hers. It was the first night they spent together in his room and they let themselves be seen entering the officers' building together. Their lovemaking that night was slow and deliberate, a declaration. When they'd finished, she didn't sleep. Outside, the black sky towered above the desert, the stars

compounding to infinity. She watched Dror blink at the ceiling, his dark
eyes bright.

ON THE FIRING RANGE THAT week she dropped bullet casings into
a sack, each making its muffled clink under the beating sun — her sweat
trickling down her back and breastbone, the desert horizon with her
always. There was no escaping the horizon. No softening it, or clouding
what was real. This was why she was here — she'd struck the flint of it.
This was why she'd had to leave England. She'd come here in order to be
in a place where polite lies weren't possible. And here was the reward —
here was what she'd craved — a love synonymous with honesty. Hadn't
Dror brought the harshest truths and laid them before her? As spent
casings slipped her fingers, she conjured his image on the empty plain: a
man unbending, his heart somehow still willing. The promise she made
to him was sewn like a sinew into her body: I will never lie to you.

WHEN HE HANDED HER THE dusty volume at the end of that week,
she turned it away. "There's no need for that, Dror," she said.

They were in his room on the base. Another day off for both of them;
she'd thought the timing a coincidence until Muriel shot a comment
through the dark over Helen's bunk about Dror the high and mighty
who was rigging the volunteers' schedule for his own *pleasures*. None of
the other girls had answered. Other than Muriel, the soldiers avoided
any mention of the situation, choosing to navigate around Helen during
the daytime as though she were invisible. If they met her gaze at all it
was with absolute neutrality. Everyone seemed to be waiting for some
unspecified signal that would tell them the crisis had passed.

Now, in his room, dressed in his civilian clothing, Dror pressed the
book into her hands. "I found it in Be'er Sheva," he said. "I've been trying to explain in my own way, Helen, but—" He drew a long breath.
"You've told me you love books. Maybe this is how you'll understand."

She stared at the title. *The History of the Jewish People.* She laughed
aloud, deliberately, to show him she didn't take his sober mood to heart.
But when she glanced up his face was stern. He looked, for an instant,

like the officer who'd given the grim welcome upon the volunteers' arrival at the base.

She lifted a hand and saluted him.

He didn't laugh. "This is important. I need you to know what you're
walking into."

The book was used: its cover worn, the lettering of the title faded.
"Do you understand how absurd this is, Dror?"

He didn't answer.

"You want me to read Jewish history so I can decide whether to love
you. But I already know," she said, "I already know everything I need to
know about that."

He was silent. She'd known she would need to speak the words first.

For a moment she thought he would lower himself to the edge of
the bed where she sat and speak them back to her. But he stood, his
face etched with a tension she didn't understand. "You don't know what
you're doing."

Her voice snapped. "You're wrong and you know it, Dror. You sound
like a person at a podium. That"—she gestured toward the book, she
spoke wildly—"*that* has nothing to do with love. That's fear. You're just
afraid of"—her hand swept through the air at Dror, at herself—"of
this." Yet even as she spoke she wondered: Was she accusing him, or herself? Hadn't she been relieved, just a bit, when a feeling she didn't know
how to contain had been pruned back by his anger, that day in Jaffa?

But a look of nausea crossed his face and she saw her words had hit
home.

"Helen. What do you think life could bring that would frighten me
now?"

Not a footstep disturbed the quiet of the barracks.

"Please," he said.

HE'D BROUGHT HER DINNER IN his room, setting it on a tray beside her as she sat reading on his cot in her thin sundress. Carefully
he arranged napkin and fork, then turned the room over to her with a
tenderness that might have been comical under other circumstances.

She paged through the book resentfully, like a child forced to fulfill the terms of an unjust penance. Outside the single window of his room Dror was visible, leaning against a tree in his blue short-sleeved shirt, smoking one cigarette after another. He wanted her to embrace his history, she knew, or to flee him then and there—before they were so tightly knit together that no surgery could separate them without devastating both.

She scanned the opening, the words falling away from her senselessly. Dror wanted her to weigh every sentence? Fine. She forced herself to a second page, a third. Dror wanted a fair-minded inquiry. But for once in her life, Helen did not. She knew the ending she wanted for this story, and she was going to head for it regardless. She would read Dror's history book, and she would tell him—no matter the horrid truths on these pages—that despite all evidence and logic they could still be together.

She tested a pen on the notepad he'd brought her, wrote her name in sharp, angry letters. After several minutes, she wrote a sloppy row of headings to keep track of the time periods she was reading about. *Israelite Kingdom. Diaspora Beginnings. Greeks and Hellenization.*

The story of Mattathias and the Judean martyrs caught her, and she read despite herself. *In the isolation of their desert exile, the truth was evident: speaking their beliefs directly meant annihilation.* She absorbed the words, and read on. Her anger faded. Whatever message she'd wanted to impose on the history dropped away—she'd recall it later. For now the stories themselves, set in a stark, familiar landscape, had all her attention. As she read, she wrote down names and dates, as though echoing harrowing facts with her pen would seal them into her memory and there make sense of them.

Outside Dror stamped cigarette butts into the dirt, and paced.

How soft she had been, then. Every breath she took—shifting on Dror's thin mattress, reaching to turn a page—was still an exchange, a question, a hopeful sampling of the world.

When he came with two glasses of mint tea, she shut the book and folded her notes out of view. "This is pointless, Dror."

He shook his head mutely and stirred her tea, raising a whorl of dark leaves from the bottom of the glass.

"Tell me about your sister," she said, watching them settle. "That's the Jewish history I want to know, Dror. Your history."

With the deliberate motions of a man coaching himself not to smash the objects in his hands, he set the tea and spoon quietly on the tabletop. "We can talk about everything," Dror said softly, "after you read."

She read on in a fever of concentration, through afternoon and evening. She read into the night by his bedside light. He slept beside her, his body cupping hers, moving only to pull a pillow over his eyes when the light disturbed him. The fingertips of his hand rested, trusting, against the skin of her thigh: the first touch he had allowed since handing her the book.

She read until the starred black sky gave way to a deep predawn blue.

She finished and shut the book, and only then did the tears of frustration rise.

The single page on which she'd taken notes was filled on both sides. She had turned it, written on the back; filled in the margins; inverted the page and filled it again upside down, writing between the lines she'd already penned.

Dror, waking, rose and brought her breakfast: leben, pita, a sliced and salted cucumber, all laid out neatly on blue plastic dishes from the mess hall. He set her coffee before her with care.

"What did you learn?" he said softly.

She'd never before seen him afraid.

"Did you read about Dreyfus?" he said. "About the White Paper?"

She nodded.

"Did you see"—he was watching her carefully—"how things changed without change? How it only gets worse—how the trap closes harder each time? Helen, *why* do you want this in your life?"

She didn't speak.

"Do you see?" he repeated.

"See what? That you want me to think loving you is a curse?"

"I need you to see the truth."

"Which is that you're trying to scare me away." The words hurt her throat. "You don't want to let go of"—she gestured, her fingers splayed —"a milligram of the horror."

Her fingertips caught the edge of her coffee cup and it spilled—over her legs, over the handwritten page beside them, blurring the bright blue ink so long lines of her words bled to the margins and were wasted.

Then she was crying, and with a choked sound he pushed book and page and coffee cup from his cot, and when they made love his voice was like the hush of a rainstorm in her ears: *I'm sorry I'm sorry I'm sorry.*

ONE AFTERNOON MURIEL CORNERED HER without warning beside the outhouse. She grabbed Helen's arm, hard, and there was no pretense of goodwill. "Don't you know he's going to work in intelligence? Don't you know they want him—after they saw what he could do as a commando? Did he tell you he starts in June, he's going to spend half his life undercover in other countries if they ask him to? Or that his wife will never know what he really does? Have you even heard of the Mossad—or is England too pure to need that sort of thing? Then I'll explain: these are the men who leave widows, and you'll never see a memorial for them because their work doesn't exist."

Muriel's grip had stopped the pulse in her arm. Helen tried to wrench away. But Muriel only gripped tighter as though in a trance of vindication—and Helen was aware, even then, that Muriel would regret her words after her wildness had subsided. "I supposed he wouldn't have bothered to tell you that. But he told Uri before you ever arrived here on your precious noble vacation, he told Uri that he wants to devote his life to national security. To doing what *our* people need so this country doesn't become another trap that closes on the Jews."

At the echo of Dror's words, Helen no longer noticed the pain in her arm.

"He's ready to throw himself off a cliff for this country," Muriel went on, "and he'll do it the minute they ask him to. Probably they'll start him doing intelligence in eastern Europe, maybe just for a few months, maybe a few years. Is *that* who you thought you were having your little fairy tale with? Or did he forget to tell you you'll always come second? He'll never love you the way he loves *us*."

She left Muriel and ran, not caring who stared, to Dror's room, where she found him on his cot, reading a newspaper. "You're going to leave me. You're going to run off and get killed for the country."

Slowly he folded the newspaper and set it aside.

"Muriel told me. You're planning for me to be a war widow, that's what you're preparing me for?"

The sorrow in his eyes confused her. She shook her head—wasn't he going to deny it? She'd run here counting on the fact that he'd tell her it was a misunderstanding—that she could fall into his arms with the relief that they'd leapt another hurdle together.

"Helen," he said quietly, "I didn't lie. I want to work for the country if they'll have me. But—"

The conversation was happening too fast—she couldn't take it in. Something in him was alien to her—she was a foreigner here after all. But then, hadn't she always been? Loneliness gripped her—a physical need for the sound of rain. England. The rockscape outside Dror's window made her heart race as though it would give out if she couldn't see a bit of green. What if she *was* afraid of it all? The thought came to her: I can't do it if I can't be sure of him.

She raised her voice, louder than she needed to. "What you're saying, Dror, is that I'll always come second. And I'll never understand you because I'm not Jewish. I'll never be as—"

"You're"—he rose, stepped toward her, gestured uselessly. "Helen, everything I *do* is to be honest with you. I want you to know the worst, so you can run away now if you need to. But that's not—if you decide to be with me, Helen, I see now that we can make this—"

Her only thought now was to wound him, so he would hold her once more—so he would whisper his apology for the unbearable images Muriel's words had conjured: Dror lost. Dror missing. Helen alone in an empty kitchen years from now, listening to the radio in a country she'd never understand. In a ragged voice, she spoke the ugliest words she could find. "There's a hole in you where your heart once was. And in its place, you've put history."

A blast of silence. His eyes were closed. He said, simply, "No."

He opened his eyes and looked at her. "*You're* in my heart," he said. "But you're right too, Helen. I'm not who I was. I—"

It took her a moment to register that his voice was breaking.

"I *hated* it," he said. And then, louder, "I hated it. Do you think I didn't know when it was happening to me? Do you think the world can operate on your heart without you knowing it?"

His voice was breaking for himself, she realized—and she despised herself for forcing him to see what she saw. And she loved him as she

hadn't loved a human being in her life—felt his blamelessness so powerfully that she would willingly have lain down on the painted concrete
floor and rested her head on his worn, motionless boots.

He'd finished. He stood for a moment. Then he opened the door and
motioned her out.

AND THERE WAS A SOLDIER sketching the silhouette of Masada
from the hood of his jeep. She left her suitcase and her ticket for London in the car she'd rented to drive herself out of the desert for the last
time. She could feel the iron in her smile, but she saw the soldier's eyes
soften with foolish hope as she approached, in the skirt and blouse that
were foreign on her body after her months in uniform. And she took the
sketch from his hand with a grim, hard grip.

HOW DID YOU COME TO HISTORY?, Aaron had asked her, that first
long day of work at the Eastons' house.

She gathered her coat. Her satchel. Her cane, the finish worn away
on one side of its knobbed handle. She turned off the overhead light,
and locked her office door.

Outside, in the dimming afternoon, she leaned her cane against a
railing, and with both hands labored to button her coat against the chill.
She reached the top button. Put her hands into her pockets, and rested.
Then worked one glove onto each hand, retrieved her cane, and began
the slow walk to her car.

12

December 6, 1663
7 Kislev, 5424
London

S HE SLID OPEN THE BED CURTAIN, the wooden rings clicking.

The stone floor was ice. She firmed her bare feet on it and
stood, her breath weightless in the dark room. From the truckle bed, the
heavy sounds of Rivka's sleep. She reached and found the windowsill.
Stood a moment before the panes that admitted not light, but rather a
thinning of the dark.

A pale smudge of moon was visible above the city wall, and a small
commotion passed briefly on the street below her window—the brief,
raucous laughter of men on their way back from a tavern. She wrapped
her shawl tight about her shoulders, then followed the wall until it
opened to the cold stair.

Without its warming fire, the rabbi's study was hollow. She lingered
a moment at the threshold. Even now, it was this instant she most treasured: the moment when she entered the dark room. The bound volumes, arrayed silent on the cloaked bookshelves, waited. She stepped
across the threshold, drew one long breath. Then, swiftly, found candle
and striker in a drawer near the hearth. Revealed, the room shone with
a brave brightness. The volumes she'd retrieved most recently from the
bindery lay on a table where she would read from them to the rabbi on
the morrow. Setting the candle in a dish, she drew the curtain covering
the closest shelves and slipped her hand across the spines, her fingertips
slowly crossing the fine rivulets of each leather binding. The first book
she touched was in Portuguese: *Consolação às Tribulações de Israel.* The
next, *Ketseh Ha-Arets,* in Hebrew. The next in French, *Les Principes de la*

Philosophie; then *Sidereus Nuncius*—written in a dense Latin that had, for most of the past month, confounded her, only slowly yielding to her attention.

Something had sprung alive in her these years—slowly at first, then more powerfully with every passing day. Surely the rabbi must know it? Something had seized her. The city, its books.

At least once each month now the rabbi required her to venture into London to arrange for the binding of the books the Amsterdam community continued to send, or else to purchase new texts with the income the rabbi's nephew provided. Ester had long feared a day when the rabbi might realize his folly—for the number of books in his library grew at greater pace and far greater expense than the needs of the household might justify. The rabbi himself could study only some few hours before fatigue overtook him, and the students knocking on his door had lately diminished to a mere rill, the HaLevy brothers being two of only five pupils who arrived at the threshold at intervals through the day, if at all. Yet outside this matter of amassing books, the rabbi's mind seemed intact—and, Ester reasoned, one who had spent his life so meagerly surely merited the chance to indulge himself in such extravagant purchases of texts now, when at last he was provided with the income to do so.

With each of Ester's forays into London, the city seemed to grow and brighten, its streets threading into a dense map that she'd walked first with caution, and now confidence. She lingered at booksellers' tables to inhale; how strange that she could ever have forgotten the smell of books—as though her years of mourning had blotted her senses. Now, the squared Latin and English letters delighted her; she relished the feel of each word as her mouth silently shaped it. All about her, strangers slid their fingers along lines of print, their touch curious, reverent, even tender. How intimate the love of books had always seemed to Ester; yet among Jews the holiest books could not be touched by human hands. No woman could approach the Torah, and even a man could touch its scrolls only with a wood or silver pointer. Here, though, among the Gentiles, even the holiest words could be caressed. When the rabbi's errands first brought her to the booksellers' stalls at St. Paul's, she hadn't dared approach the Christian texts. It had taken her weeks to embolden herself to lay hands on one—and then a second, and a third, opening each book's quires and standing long minutes before the pages. At first, as though the words might burn, she'd read without allowing her fingertips to graze the printed letters. Then, she'd touched. *We have thought fit, by this book, to give an account of our faith . . .* What strange voices these were, questing inward, as though truth were to be found not in the instruction of the community but in a single spirit and mind. With effort she deciphered the careful sentences of an English Christian named John Jewel. She turned page after page of a text called *Summa Logicae*—and though the meager instruction in Latin she'd once gleaned from her brother's lessons was inadequate to the more difficult passages, still she sifted the fragments of each argument until she felt she could glimpse the shape of the whole. And here was a book written by a pious Christian woman known as Julian of Norwich, whom the Christians—could such a thing be true?—had walled into their church to live out her life there, bringing her food and necessities so that parishioners could come lean into the small window in her stone prison to confess and receive her wisdom. On page after page, the woman gave account of her own visions.

At the bindery, an establishment warmed as much by the bodies shuffling its narrow aisles as by the low fire in its hearth, she stood alongside strangers at tables piled with parchments, loose quires, and pieces of leather binding. Expensively bound volumes were stacked high here and there, waiting to be claimed by those whose gilt initials adorned the spines alongside the names of the authors. There was a peculiar political work by Van den Enden—a description of the ideal society, passages of which she committed to memory. A copy of Robert Burton's *Anatomy of Melancholy*, with a heavy swirl of ink on its frontispiece, lay awaiting collection for weeks; when she visited it, she took to parting the book's thick girth with the wedge of her fingernail, and whatsoever page it might fall to, she studied that passage to glean what she might. So too did she linger with a set bound in dark green leather, the edges of the pages marbled in reds and purples. Descartes. Galileo, William Alabaster. William Shakespeare.

And when the rabbi sent Ester about London for ink and paper or quills, she rushed to each errand, then bundled the rabbi's purchases under her arms and wandered where she pleased. How different these excursions were from the rounds she made with Mary to dressmakers and cordwainers—hours so thick with Mary's gossip that Ester barely glimpsed London's riches passing outside the window of the da Costa Mendeses' coach. But set loose on her own in London, she watched a brightly painted barge and a worn herring-bus being unloaded by a crew of men; passed a tall Moor with dark lips that opened to a bright and still brighter smile as she neared him, until they both laughed aloud before parting without a word. She stopped at the cart of a fat, whiskered woman and bought from her a plum, not for its small bitter heft but for the opportunity to memorize the Englishwoman's gestures and the satisfied way her mouth gathered itself when she'd finished speaking. She watched two apprentices squatted together beside the river, saw them shimmy their closed fists and fling forbidden dice at the bare earth between their kissing knees. Nearby, three men watched, and banged together their metal mugs of posset, hob and nob, as they toasted a long list of sins soon to be restored to England with the return of the king: dicing, bowling, bear-baiting—each sin saluted by the men with a three-voice chorus of "a very rude and nasty pleasure."

Back on Creechurch Lane, she labored hour after hour at the writing table as Rivka came and went from the room. Her quill, working under the rabbi's unseeing gaze, answered his quiet words with a dry creaking of its own: the small noise of some lowly creature doing its delicate work, scratching to gain entry. *To the Esteemed Yochanan Yisrael,* she wrote. *To the Honored Rabbi Abraham ben Porat.* At the rabbi's direction she sent a query to a kabbalist in Hameln concerning the numerology of a verse of B'reishit; pages of dictation addressed to obscure young scholars who had directly or indirectly requested the rabbi's advice; a question to the Council of Four Lands in Jaroslaw regarding their ruling in a case in which Ashkenazic Passover dietary law had been violated—and through this she understood that the rabbi consulted even the Tudesco rabbis, and held no bias against them, unlike those Sephardic rabbis of Amsterdam who forbade any congress with the hordes of impoverished Ashkenazim.

The learning that spooled from Ester's hand made her feverish— yet there was no fever in the rabbi, only a patient concentration that seemed not to dislike Ester's presence but to welcome it. Inking his words, she felt the rabbi's mind: clear, absorptive, and without pride —his reasoning featuring neither the brilliant rhetoric nor the sudden accusatory turnings that distinguished the speeches Ester recalled from Amsterdam's celebrated rabbis, Aboab and Abendana. Instead, Rabbi HaCoen Mendes issued opinions in gentle terms that offered a humility so simple it seemed to Ester—the fresh ink trailing the progress of her hand across the paper—something like glory.

Though, of course—so the rabbi concluded his missives—those he advised could surely think of better arguments themselves, and must remember to reply to their aged friend in London and share their own wisdom with him.

When the rabbi's letters were finished for the day, he requested that she read him commentary. She pronounced for him sentences of winding logic in Aramaic, puzzling out their meaning while the rabbi considered. "Do you hear the argument the other side makes?" he might ask, after a long silence. "Do you see why they debate such a preposterous conjecture, though the situation will never arise in this world?" She heard, and saw. And remembered: so young, her shoes hardly brushing the wooden floor of their house in Amsterdam, her breasts not yet budded, the spring air damp and riveting on her skin. "What is the purpose of study?" the rabbi had asked. She'd said, "That the spirit be clothed in reason, which is more warming than ignorance." The rabbi had corrected, gently, "Yet the text we studied said knowledge, Ester, not reason." And she'd countered, "But reason is more warming, for it seeds knowledge. But knowledge can grow nothing outside itself."

The rabbi had smiled then, though with a furrowed brow. "You have a good mind," he'd said after a moment.

Words that wisped about her and warmed her still, all these years later, as she and the rabbi labored together.

Only yesterday, he had instructed her to pull from the shelf a heavy volume, Augustine's *Confessiones*. "Read," said the rabbi. Slowly she'd spoken the Latin words aloud. The afternoon filled and brimmed with them; the afternoon was suspended like a great heaven-kissing bird that did not need to flap its wings. *Noverim te, noverim me.* The rabbi interrupting only to correct her pronunciation. When she'd closed the book, he said, "I dread their priests, yes, Ester. Yet I read such works in Lisbon in my youth, and though many think me in error in this, I fear neither such books nor the language in which they're written. If Latin is the language in which the world arrays its beliefs, Jews may also speak it. Nor do I grant the irons that closed my eyes permission to close my mind. When any man of any nation cries out in his wish to know God, then his questions merit considering."

She fingered the spine of the book before her. Whispers overheard on Amsterdam's barges tickled her memory. She said, "Even the questions of one such as de Spinoza?"

The rabbi's face tightened. But Ester continued, searching her mind for the wisps of scandalized conversation she'd overheard as she sewed mutely in a neighbor's parlor after the fire. "People said he believed even a tree or a fight might be God."

She'd but one recollection of Baruch de Spinoza from childhood —doubtless she'd seen him at later times, surely they'd passed on the street, surely he'd been in the synagogue gallery while she'd stood in the balcony. Yet her sole memory was from years before his exile. He'd been older than Ester, perhaps of age thirteen or fourteen, and that afternoon he had been tasked with escorting the rabbi from the synagogue to her family's door. She remembered only dark, heavy-lidded eyes, quietly taking in all. And a figure that seemed, in retrospect, too slight, too timid, too gentle, to support such devilishness as she would later hear was burning in his spirit.

"De Spinoza," said the rabbi, "flaunted his doubts." He chose each word with care, as though reluctant to speak at all. "I failed to sway the other rabbis to a gentler course. And I failed to persuade him to hear reason." The rabbi turned his face intently toward Ester. "De Spinoza chose exile and therefore death."

Yet—Ester thought with a vexation that surprised her—had it not been whispered that the heretic, who'd spurned his Jewish name, now carried on his curious debates in alehouses and binderies as Bento—or even Benedictus—de Spinoza? Was it not whispered that he studied gladly with the former Jesuit Van den Enden, whose own thoughts were said to border on atheism? How then must de Spinoza be counted among the dead?

From the kitchen, Rivka's call: the evening meal was prepared. Slowly the rabbi freed himself of what had troubled him. At length he turned to Ester with a peaceful countenance. "I believe it no danger to your faith to read the words of a Christian. Yet it would be wise not to

reveal that I've introduced you to such books. Word that I have permitted a girl this knowledge might stir our good cousins in Amsterdam to
force an end to your labors on my behalf, which they seem for the time
to have forgotten."

It was the first he'd spoken of her sex in all these years, and she received his speech in silence, afraid any word of hers might jar him from
his indulgence, and at last make plain to him the impropriety of this
new life he'd permitted her.

Now, in the glow of candlelight, the books lay before her: Augustine,
Descartes. Atop these volumes rested her own hands, no longer chafed
from constant housework: strange and delicate things with a fixed desire of their own. A desire to touch each page, each line of ink.

More than half the candle remained. She could read an hour before
it guttered, longer if she took another candle from the drawer. How
many had she burned already this month? Her hours of night reading
seemed to grow ever more necessary, for each day's study compelled
her to explore these volumes further, and with a fierce attention impossible when others were about. On nights when she could rouse herself
after her first sleep, she forced herself from bed and down the stairs to
the rabbi's room. Once there, she studied until she could read only by
brushing tears of strain from her eyes. In vain were her most solemn
determinations to burn only one candle; for when that candle guttered,
she lit another—and after all, was the household's allowance not abundant enough to pay for but one more? She'd use the rabbi's coins to purchase replacements the next time she was sent abroad in the city. Praying Rivka wouldn't discover the depleted drawer until Ester had filled
it once more, she sighed a long, peaceful sigh, and opened *Confessiones*.

The remaining half-candle spent itself as she puzzled over Augustine's fervor. She sought something here that she couldn't name, and
felt it elude her narrowly. She turned to Descartes—a second and third
candle, thin smoke wreathing and rising. And back to Augustine, until
she knew long passages by rote—for if Latin was the language in which
thinkers clasped hands, she'd study it until it opened its secrets to her.
So she read on, a great and solemn feeling moving through her body:
a scaling fatigue, a scaling curiosity. Only when the fourth candle went
out—the room's hollowness suddenly magnified a thousandfold by the
dark—did she rise and shut the books, returning each to its place by

feel. Through the towering silence she slipped quietly toward her bed, her head light from exhaustion, the dimensions of the household seeming to grow and shrink about her.

AT DAWN SHE WAS A STONE, unmoved by sunlight or the twitter of starlings on the roof, responding only to the slap of Rivka's open hand on the wall beside her bed. In the kitchen she mixed Rivka's pale batter, the upper limits of her vision darkening if she raised her head too quickly, as though curtains threatened to close on a stage. A question floated in her mind, knocking against the side of the wooden bowl with each turn of her spoon. Why, when the rabbis wished to understand God's will or Augustine the construction of man's soul, did they not reason as Descartes did, taking nothing as given? Must true inquiry proceed from texts and traditions already established, or could the mind on its own perceive all it needed to fathom the world? And which path of inquiry led more straightly to truth? The spoon knocked, the questions knocked, her lips shaped single words of Latin.

Rivka was before her. "What animal of the night," she said in Portuguese, "has crept into the house and used every candle in the rabbi's study?"

Ester stared, dumb, Rivka's square face a senseless blur.

"Or has the rabbi found himself fond of lighting the night, though he lives in darkness even so?" Rivka's voice brimmed with strange anger. Ester could focus only on the vein-webbed nose, the large dark pores — she could absorb only details, not the whole of Rivka's tired face. "Is it *he* who's left wax drippings on the table for others to clean?"

Ester clutched the bowl to her chest. And then at once, as Rivka continued, Ester saw the face before her in its entirety, and everything writ on it: a fury and anguish she'd never before seen in Rivka. "We live in this terrible city," Rivka said, "in this terrible cold house that worsens his health, so that he can teach. Yet you spend the house's money on candles for your passing whim for study."

She'd no answer.

"If he wishes to have you scribe in place of a man"—Rivka drew breath—"then I will honor his choice. I won't deny him your labor. But I won't have you steal from the only one"—Rivka's voice turned dangerous — "the *only* one among your precious Sephardic lords and ladies kind enough to take in orphans."

"Rivka, I'm not like those —"

"You will be!" The harshness of the words seemed to surprise even Rivka. When she spoke again her voice was steadier. "You will be," she said again. "It's your due, Ester. You're Portuguese. When life opens a door you'll marry. Any would. And you'll forget the rabbi, as the rest of them do already."

At a soft shuffling on the stone floor, they both turned.

The rabbi had emerged from his room. He stood in his thin robe, the bones at his throat painfully sharp, a tuft of white emerging from the collar of his undergarment. Softly he addressed Rivka. "It's for the furthering of my wishes that she reads at night."

Rivka looked stricken.

"Ester studies at night," the rabbi continued, "that in the day she might better fulfill my needs for a learned scribe. So great is her devotion to my unworthy house of learning." He turned his face toward Ester now, and it seemed to her that it was as innocent as a child's. "But, Ester, I owe my apology. I was careless, and failed to make plain that you must not do this. Read only during the day, please, for not only does candlelight burn the household's income, but too-prolonged study withers the bloom of health."

Rivka's voice had thickened. "You've known of her night reading?" she said slowly.

The rabbi's smile was weightless. "A man of my age sleeps little, even when cared for as though he were a king." At Rivka's silence, he continued. "I have not merited such care as you offer me, Rivka. I'm grateful."

Rivka closed her eyes for a long moment as she stood opposite the rabbi. Then she opened them and, without a word to Ester, retreated softly to the kitchen.

That morning the rabbi tutored pupils, and when alone he sat in his chair, seeming to sleep. Often Ester was on the verge of thanking him for what he'd done. But what words could express her gratitude? Instead she sat by his feet, stoking the fire that warmed him as he slept, rearranging the blanket when it slipped from his shoulders, replenishing the water in his cup, though he barely sipped it. So absorbed was she in these tasks that she nearly forgot Mary's summons, and was still tugging the laces of her dress with one hand when she opened the door to Mary's knock.

Mary, black curls carefully arrayed over powdered white shoulders, frowned at Ester's drab dress. "That one again?" she said. "Well, all the better that we go to the dressmaker!" Turning back to squint at the street, she added, lightly, "Mother accompanied me to two gatherings this week, but says to tell you that you'll now need a dress suitable for more than errands."

Ester hesitated. Was this Mary's way of telling her Catherine's health was declining? She opened her mouth to ask—but Mary left no space for inquiry. Already she was leading Ester into the absurd coach—for who, in truth, required a coach to traverse the narrow cobbled streets of the city, when a person on foot could weave through a crowd in half the time? Yet Mary adored the conveyance.

As Ester settled on her usual bench, Mary launched into gossip. "Did you hear that Isabella Rodriguez said Pierre Alvarez is courting Rebecca Nones?" Having chosen the forward-facing bench as always, Mary spoke with eyes fixed on the traffic outside the coach's window. "And did you hear, Pierre Alvarez wore perfumed gloves that made Rebecca sneeze, and because Rebecca hadn't a kerchief on which to wipe her nose, when no one was minding her she dried her nose on a red-pollened flower he'd given? And after, Rebecca walked about with a red stain upon her nose—and none liked her well enough to brave her temper and tell her of it, not even her gallant Pierre—did you hear of it?"

So Mary spoke always, posing each declaration as a question, soliloquy in guise of conversation. Ester found it simplest to make no answer.

Now with a sudden glad cry, Mary rapped for the driver to stop. On the street were two girls from the synagogue—both well-dressed, though neither so expensively as Mary. Leaning from the window, Mary beckoned them into the coach. As they climbed up, they glanced with surprise at Ester seated opposite—then settled on either side of Mary in poses of eager attention. As the coach resumed its rolling, one of them—a round-faced girl called Emilia, with pretty, lush brown curls—complimented Mary's gown and hair so thoroughly that even Mary began to look restless. Then, turning to Mary at such close quarters that Mary blinked, the girl said, "How is it, Mary, that you refused Joseph

Levita? Isn't it true his family brought him to visit in the hope of a match with you?"

Mary, recovered, smiled airily. "He was a pimple."

On either side of Mary, the two girls' eyebrows rose in disbelief. Levita and his family had made an appearance in synagogue a few weeks earlier. Ester herself had seen the young man in question, and he wasn't ill-favored.

"Is it that he's Venetian?" The other girl, sallow and thinner than Emilia, cut in. "My father would let me marry a Venetian Jew if he liked the man. Why didn't yours?"

"Perhaps my father thought he wasn't good enough," Mary lilted. She was enjoying the game, but what lay beneath her coy words was murkier. If Rivka's account of synagogue gossip last week was correct, the Levitas, under closer inspection, hadn't proved as wealthy as the da Costa Mendeses had first believed. Mary's father had dismissed the suit immediately, against Catherine's wishes.

Emilia was staring at Mary. "Then *who* catches your fancy, if not Levita?" The coach rolled a moment in silence. "Not Maria Olivera's cousin? Rebecca Cancio saw you speaking to him and his sister last time they came to London."

Mary busily looked out the window, but the small, involuntary smile on her lips said she considered this one something other than a pimple.

"But he's already promised to someone in Amsterdam!" Emilia exclaimed—not, Ester noted, without satisfaction. "Didn't you know?"

Mary laughed lightly. But after they'd deposited the two girls at their destination some few streets beyond the synagogue, she sat back at her window with a loose sigh.

Later, while the dressmaker draped fabrics around Mary in her well-lit workroom, Mary gazed languorously at the nearest window, making only distracted answers to questions about pleating and the positioning of lace. Leaning to reach for her purse, she dragged it across the table by its strings—then put the purse to her lips and slowly bit the smooth wooden clasp open with her small even teeth in a gesture of such drowsy amorousness that even the dressmaker, her sealed lips bristling with pins, averted her eyes.

When it was Ester's turn to mount the pedestal in her shift and be fitted for a busk and a dress, Mary sat on a cushioned stool and stared at Ester's body with a childlike curiosity, a wishfulness set loose on her face as though she were a girl too timid to ask a question of an elder sister.

Finally, reaching to finger the linen at Ester's knees, she said, "Do you think love real?"

It was the first true question Mary had asked her, and so surprising that Ester couldn't help laugh.

"I mean," Mary continued slowly, ignoring Ester's laughter, "do you think love can be made to happen with whichever man our minds choose—so it's a thing a lady may direct as she pleases? Or is it a thing outside control?"

The dressmaker, a neat and weathered woman with a silver-shot coiffure, had paused. But Mary disregarded her, all her attention now on Ester.

Quietly, the dressmaker resumed lacing a fencework of stays about Ester's waist.

"Outside control," Ester said slowly. "And so folly to seek."

"Well, of course I don't mean a person ought to *marry* without thought," retorted Mary, her voice quickening as though to tamp down Ester's words. "Of course I mean we must choose sensibly in marriage. But I said love. And just because a thing is outside control doesn't mean it's folly. Maybe love is"—Mary waved vaguely—"*good*."

The word sat amiss with Ester. Without considering whether she ought, she spoke what prickled in her heart. "It's a danger to a woman even to feel love."

In the silence, the sound of the dressmaker winding a length of thread.

"You're wrong," Mary said.

Was she? She knew she feared her own words to be true.

Abruptly, with a brisk tug from the dressmaker's hand, the world stiffened. As Ester attempted, gingerly, to breathe, Mary came and stood beside her.

"You're wrong," Mary repeated softly. "And you know it—you're lying to me, wicked girl." She reached up and pinched Ester's cheekbone, hard enough to leave a mark. Ester saw it in the dressmaker's glass.

"Don't ever do that again," Ester said in a low voice. "Or I'll leave you and not return. I'm not your servant."

Mary's face flushed with confusion.

At the faint sound of knocking from the front of the shop, the dress-maker disappeared.

"Well," Mary blurted after she'd gone, "do you think my mother a fool?"

Ester drew a cautious breath. Was Mary in truth asking her to speak aloud what was whispered at the synagogue: that Catherine was chok-ing on the air of a city her husband refused to leave?

"Your mother," Ester said slowly, "struggles to breathe in London. Yet for her husband—"

But the words had hit too tender a spot. Pain bloomed in Mary's eyes and Ester saw, too late, that Mary had wanted only the answer *no*.

Mary turned on Ester now. "And what did *your* wise mother counsel you about love?"

The dressmaker had returned. She dropped a cloud of fabric over Ester's head and resumed her pinning. Ester endured it, her lips pressed tight.

After a moment a soft *tsk* escaped Mary. Then Ester felt the pedes-tal take Mary's weight. Positioning herself quietly behind Ester, Mary unpinned Ester's cap.

"A comb," she said. The dressmaker produced one, then at a sum-mons from the shop's front room disappeared once more.

Frowning with concentration, as though Ester's hair had all along been the true subject of their conversation, Mary parted Ester's locks above each ear. With inexpert gestures, she began to divide and gather, now and again nipping Ester's ears with the wooden comb. "Sorry," she muttered as she worked.

Hands in her hair, stilling Ester. How many years since the house-maid Grietgen had plaited Ester's hair, her hand lingering with affec-tion on Ester's finished braids? How long since Ester had had a friend? A strange submissiveness took her. The fine teeth of the comb Mary was using were never intended for hair so thick or wavy—yet despite Mary's savage tugs, Ester closed her eyes. For a rushing instant, then, her spirit lifted, and she wished to explain all, so that Mary herself—with her airs and languid sighs—would hear Constantina's drink-mudded voice, speaking on into the quiet night. Would understand exactly what love could wreak.

"She counseled me," Ester said, "not to be a fool."

Mary's hands slowed. "My mother thinks *I'm* a fool," she said. For a moment the comb stopped moving in Ester's hair. "I'm not."

The comb resumed, its motions more tentative.

"Do you wonder, ever," said Ester quietly, "whether our own will alters anything? Or whether we're determined to be as we are by the very working of the world?"

Mary snorted. "I wonder only whether you expect anyone to understand when you speak that way."

"I mean," Ester said, "do you think we can't help what we are?"

With a vigorous tug at Ester's hair, Mary said, "I choose what I am."

She knew she oughtn't answer. But pity for her own state was climbing dangerously in Ester's chest. She'd no doubt love was real. Nor that it was a storm that flung a few to safety, but most to wrack. She wished that she, like Mary, could throw herself full-bodied at dreams. She wished to *be* Mary — to be any woman other than herself.

Most of all, she wished not to recall her mother's drunken voice.

London. Constantina, swallowing the burgundy liquid in deliberate gulps that seemed to hurt. Constantina, throwing herself back on her bed, casting her long dark hair, loosened, across her pillow. *London is where* he *lived.*

"My mother," Ester said before she could stopper the words, "was born from an unwise love."

Mary's mouth fell into an uncertain, half-mocking smile: Was this true? Was Ester confessing what none ought to admit, even if it were so?

Sternly, Ester continued. "She told me it. Though wine blurred her telling."

At this further scandal Mary uttered a half-choked laugh, then stifled it. Something solemn flickered on her face: gratitude. She moved her hands gingerly about Ester's head, as though not to disturb this unfamiliar, astonishing honesty.

Ester watched in the glass as Mary worked. Yes — she'd speak the truth. The parts, at least, that she felt certain she recalled. Constantina, whispering in the quiet house — Samuel and Isaac away, the maids dismissed for the night. Constantina, uncorking a bottle with a grunt of effort. Long, tapered fingers on ornate cups — one for her, one for Ester. A few small, warming sips, and her mother's silvery, conspiratorial laughter. *Do you know, Ester, why I keep a book of English verse I no longer care to read? That book was my own mother's, Ester. A gift from the man she loved. But she could no longer bear to open its pages. I claimed it, Ester, because I was certain England would be my home when he called for me.* Constantina's dark eyes, trained on the dim ceiling above the curtained bed. *When he called for me. My* true *father.*

"My grandmother," Ester enunciated, "hailed from Lisbon. Yet the man she married—a merchant twice her age—brought her to live for some years here in London. And while here, she loved an Englishman, not her husband."

Mary pulled the comb through Ester's hair, making barely a sound.

"My mother was born of that love," Ester continued. "She was raised back in Lisbon, calling another man Father, yet her own mother whispered her the truth all her life." In the glass, Ester found Mary's eyes. "My mother was born of a great love, Mary. But that love failed to offer sustenance."

Constantina: her almond eyes, the extravagant dark tumble of hair on her shoulders. Pulling drunkenly at the cord to release the drapes about the bed. Bidding Ester to unlace her gown, which Ester did gingerly, afraid to touch her mother's velvety olive skin lest this sudden intimacy vanish.

Only once, Ester! I met my true father only once. My mother sailed with me to London to find him. And his eyes, Ester, my father's eyes, weren't mere brown. They were lit like jewels of moss and wood.

Mary's hands had forgotten their work. "Why?" she charged.

Ester hesitated, then pressed on. "My mother said it was a love that made both rue that they were bound in wedlock to others. He was a man not high-born, but vaunted for his wit and perception in all he created. Yet he was restless in all that might cage him. As was my grandmother. But in the end they brought each other only torment. My grandmother, Lizabeta, returned to Lisbon with child."

"But then they saw each other again," Mary demanded. "Didn't they?"

Ester nodded. "Though not for years. Only after the Inquisition in Lisbon took Lizabeta's own father. She woke my mother in the middle of the night and they stole away without permission. They fled by ship to London, where they searched long for the Englishman. But his friends turned from Lizabeta and would not promise to bring him."

"But they found him, in the end?" Mary said. "They did find him."

"My mother was only a girl, Mary. Surely she invented or misunderstood much."

"No, she didn't." In the mirror, Mary's reflection was rapt. "Tell me."

For a moment Constantina's whisper filled Ester's ears, an ocean in a seashell. *My own mother sang it to me as she rocked me through the stormy passage to England, Ester. My mother sang to me. "I know your father's soul. He is a great man. You were born, Constantina, from a great love."*

"She said she felt her true father's goodness, though he was careworn. She said that standing between my mother and this man was like standing in the current of a river. She said it was a soft, endless . . . push, which slips you off your feet if you're not anchored to something."

Mary was nodding; this was a tale of love such as she'd hoped to hear. It seemed to take a moment for her to perceive that Ester had fallen silent.

"And then?" Mary said. "He took them in, didn't he?"

Ester turned from the mirror. Constantina's long-ago words thrummed in her head. *And I hated him for not breaking the world apart so he could be with us.*

"No," Ester said.

When she looked back at the mirror, she saw that Mary's expression had curdled. "Didn't he know the danger for them? In Lisbon?"

"My grandmother chose not to tell him."

"But that's—" Mary stopped, unable to stitch words to this absurdity. After a moment she said, simply, "Why?"

"My mother herself could never understand it."

"Because it can't be understood, Ester!"

"I know Lizabeta charged her Englishman with all his old promises of eternal love. Yet though the man answered her in the same terms, he shrank from her and spoke of the constraints of his life, and begged time to consider. He even offered money for their support—but this Lizabeta in her pride refused. She said nothing of the seizing of Jews, the priests flaying my grandfather until ribbons of skin danced."

Ester could still recall Constantina's voice, sailing high in wonder and bitterness. *Why wouldn't my mother tell him of the danger? Why, Ester? Was she determined to test love to the fullest? But Ester, the world had no stubbornness like hers!*

She stood behind me, arms about my shoulders, her heart beating against my back. And her Englishman wept on that street as I'd seen a man weep only at a death, and his eyes filled with the sight of me in my mother's arms until the seeing harrowed his face, so that he seemed to wane and age.

"My grandmother," Ester said, "wished not to trap her love into taking her. She said a heart is a free thing, and once enslaved will mutiny. She said she wished the Englishman's eyes to see her ever in beauty and joy, and never as something pitiable, for his memory of her was her greatest treasure."

Mary absorbed this. Then, defiant, she shrugged. "*I* would tell. And then, my love would save me." With a vexed expression she returned to work on Ester's hair, asking only after several moments' silence, and then sullenly, "What then?"

"Lizabeta and my mother sailed for Lisbon, and the Inquisition."

"And then?"

"I believe," said Ester, "my grandmother later had other loves, though not like her Englishman."

Mary tittered unkindly. "*Other* loves? Does your rabbi know what manner of lineage he's taken under his roof?"

Ester raised her head. "I believe so, Mary."

Mary returned to working the comb.

But with a boldness that startled her, Ester spoke on. "My mother," she said, "thought herself wiser than her own mother. She left Lisbon, and married my father without affection, because she thought him dull and therefore unlikely to spurn her. Nor did she remain faithful when faithfulness did not suit her. This she confessed to me freely."

Constantina, in the flickering candlelight. *So you see, Ester, I learned from what befell my mother. I remade my heart. I learned to conduct myself in love so it could not betray me.*

Had Constantina believed, on that drunken night in Amsterdam, that she spoke to Ester of love? But there had been no love in her words, only rage. As dawn drew near, bringing to an end those strange candle-lit hours when the gates of her mother's trust had inexplicably swung open, a stark sobriety had gripped Ester. Solemnly she'd listened to Constantina's final recital of betrayal, and sealed it into memory.

On my last visit before my mother's death, Ester, do you know what she dared say to me? She chided me. Can you imagine, Lizabeta chided me for my anger? I, who was nursed on her sorrow. Yet she said she'd not succeeded with me—for she'd hoped to teach me to despise a prison, be it made at the hand of the Inquisition or by my own heart.

I told her it was precisely to avoid a prison of the heart that I acted as I did. I told her: I act such that love will not fail again as it failed us before.

But she shook her silver head as if I were the fool, and not she. She said, "Love didn't fail, Constantina. Only one love did. It failed because we asked too much of it, he and I. We each, in our own time, asked it to remake the world."

She spoke as though she wished to burn this new truth into my heart, and in so doing erase the one already burnt there. She said, "I wrote to your true father just before he died, when you were but ten years of age, and we were at last safely escaped from Portugal, and I told him all. He'd not known what was happening to us in Lisbon, Constantina. The full truth of our situation hadn't been told of in England. His reply wept in words. He said he would have done all to help us if I'd but told him. But Constantina, I could not. For love does not set shackles, nor entrap. Nor could I live in his London as his shadow, a woman kept in secret, without him by my side. Don't you see? It was the very shape of the world that defeated our love. There is no bitterness in my heart. Only sorrow."

In the dawn-silted room in Amsterdam, Constantina had drained her cup, vexed, and set it carefully on the table. She stared at it as though confused. Then, fiercely, she gripped Ester's shoulder one final time. *I shaped my heart, Ester, so as to be no fool.*

Drowsiness and wine must have unmasked Ester for an instant in that reeling room, allowing her emotions to show unbidden. She would always rue this. For Constantina had flinched, as though in the pity on her daughter's face she'd finally glimpsed the bitter knot of her own spirit.

It was the only time Ester would see regret drain her mother's cheeks.

Barely six weeks later, the fire.

Samuel Velasquez, turning now on the stair, his dark eyes seeking the door where his wife slept. Racing the racing flames.

Without meaning to, Ester lifted her hand as though to call them both back.

At the sound of Mary speaking her name, she opened her eyes.

"What of your mother?" Mary prompted.

She could not now recall how much she'd spoken aloud. To satisfy Mary she said, simply, "She forgave nothing. Touching the mere hope of a great love misshaped her."

Her hand trailed in empty air. She lowered it.

In the dressmaker's glass now, she saw that Mary had finished. Ester's hair was drawn back elegantly at the front, cascading at the sides. Soft spaniel ears brushed either cheek. A heavy bun weighted the back of Ester's head.

Behind her stood Mary, hands stilled at her sides.

"There," Mary said. Her expression was uncertain, as though she'd just been privy to something for which she had no name.

The dressmaker's shop was silent. They stood on the pedestal.

Mary's voice was barely a whisper. "Have *you* loved?"

"No."

Mary shook her head slowly: nor had she.

Slowly Mary straightened. She looked not at Ester, but at their reflection in the glass. She said, firmly, "*We* choose what we are, Ester. I choose." After a moment she added, "And so do you."

Ester opened her mouth—she wished to argue with Mary: *my mother believed herself in control of love, and the error consumed her.* Yet her voice was stopped by a craving: To trust desire as Mary did. To reach for love and call it good.

There was a long silence. Mary's hands rose to tuck an invisible strand of Ester's hair, and lingered a moment as though in search of another. Yet as the moments passed the motion of her hands grew chary, then stopped altogether—as though she feared to touch for too long something so fascinating and so tainted.

"There," Mary repeated more lightly, and stepped off the dressmaker's pedestal.

SHE RETURNED FROM THE DRESSMAKER as though fleeing a storm. The door of the rabbi's house closed heavily behind her; she pressed it shut as though buttressing it against a wind. All her senses were rushing.

A low fire burned in the hearth. The rabbi was asleep in his chair. At length, the pounding of her heart relented.

On the table beside the door was a sealed letter, delivered in her absence and left there no doubt by Rivka for her to read to the rabbi.

She took the small knife from the drawer and cut it open, and read the message penned in a cramped hand.

To the Rabbi HaCoen Mendes of London,

With the blessings of G-d I greet you. I, being a cousin of the late mother of Catherine da Costa, and so not unfamiliar with the better families of London's Jews, though my own meager widow's means permit me only a modest living here in the country, write to you with esteem and with a proposal that will delight you. In conversing with a member of your congregation at a gathering in which I was most graciously included, I overheard a tendency toward warmth in discussing a member of your household. To speak plainly: I suspect there may be fertile ground for a possible match between your charge, the orphan girl Ester Velasquez, and a young man of this London congregation. You will understand, of course, the boon to the Velasquez girl, whom I am told lacks even a dowry. Through this marriage she might enter into a life as a mother in Israel. Although the match be unlikely due to her poor means, I urge you to consider engaging my services, and as swiftly as you may, so that the young man not lose his interest, and in turn I will bend all my notable efforts to its success. The young man of whom I speak naturally wishes discretion—it seemed to me he was surprised by my offer of intervention in the matter, though perhaps it pleased him as well. May I then pursue this matter, and come to call when I am next able to journey to London? My fee for the match would be within bounds of what is properly accepted, though surely such a gift as a marriage for such a girl lacking prospects is without price.

Awaiting your reply with esteem,

Isabella Mendoza

She held the letter. A feeling like ice spread in her chest. Could a stranger so easily unmake Ester's life—marrying her for a fee to a faceless youth, and in one stroke parting her forever from the rabbi and his quiet fireside, from her books?

The thought grew until it filled her: *not yet.*

The rabbi was stirring. As though able to sense his least motion from afar, Rivka entered from the kitchen and knelt at the fire, adding wood and stoking it high. Ester set down the letter.

At the rabbi's quiet call, she answered, "Here I am."

He beckoned her to a seat by the fire. For a long while, then, the rabbi sipped the tea Rivka brought. She waited for him to ask about the letter; then, as the moments passed, she realized he did not know any had been delivered.

The fire crackled. Rivka had piled the wood high, as though to supply all the warmth the rabbi's meager body could not. For a long, silent time Ester sat opposite the rabbi near the blaze, until the heat made her eyes ache. Did his eyes, she wondered, suffer from the heat of the flames as did hers—or had the iron that extinguished them robbed them not only of sight, but of all sense of pain? And if he'd become insensible to pain, was he also deadened to desire for all that he could no longer have?

A snap from the fire assaulted her.

The rabbi spoke softly, without moving. "I believe," he said, "that these stone walls are safe from fire."

Even blind, he'd felt her startle.

"Let us read," she said, more briskly than she intended.

Hadn't she struggled only hours ago to find words for her gratitude to the rabbi? Now vexation propelled her into motion. She stood, crossed to the table, and took up a thin volume, a commentary on Jonah that she and the rabbi had begun discussing some days earlier.

"Something troubles you," he said.

She could barely persuade her voice to sound. "No," she said quietly.

The rabbi fell silent. Then he said, "I believe my mind is too dull this afternoon to read commentary."

She laid the book down.

"Perhaps," he said, "we ought to sit and recite psalms."

A physick he was prescribing for her, not for himself. Her throat constricted with feelings she'd no name for.

"The words of prayer are like birds, Ester," he said gently. "They soar."

She did not believe prayers were like birds. Birds could fly out of a burning house. If prayer had flown, then her father would still live

—perhaps, through her father's devotions, even her mother would have survived—even rageful, bewildered, bereft Constantina. If prayer had flown, Isaac would not be dead.

Before she knew what she was saying, she turned to the rabbi. "What do you see," she said, "behind the lids of your eyes?"

For the first time there was unease beneath his silence. She felt a hard, thin satisfaction she was ashamed of.

"I shall not, at this moment, answer this question," he said. "But I will tell you what I learned after I lost my sight, in the first days as I came to understand how much of the world was now banned from me —for my hands would never again turn the pages of a book, nor be stained with the sweet, grave weight of ink, a thing I had loved since first memory. I walked through rooms that had once been familiar, my arms outstretched, and was fouled and thwarted by every obstacle in my path. What I learned then, Ester, is a thing that I have been learning ever since."

She stood rooted by shame, dreading his words.

"The distances between things are vast," he said. "They are vast."

His blind eyes were turned toward the fire.

"Ester," he said. "Do not rue your lack of freedom."

Had he read her thoughts? That morning after Rivka had confronted her, she'd searched the drawer in the rabbi's study, hoping to find even a single candle rolling inside. But Rivka had left not even a rushlight.

"You learn as no other women do," the rabbi said, "yet you wish for more. Your mind is eager, Ester—and though all Amsterdam should disagree, I will say this eagerness is given to you by the divine. But it must have limits. Sometimes a soul must content itself, purify itself and burn inside itself, without receiving all it desires." He turned to her, and she felt his attention, penetrating and sober. "The Jews of London, Ester, do not want me. They believe I come to scold them about the traditions they've disdained. Soon they'll acquire what they wish: a respected rabbi for their synagogue, one who offers grandeur and a reminder of our tradition's glory. Under such a rabbi they'll return in their hearts, slowly but after a time fully, to the tradition. But they do not wish to be guided by one such as I." The rabbi was still turned toward Ester, his face white in the firelight. "I will do what's mine to do," he said. "I will be their servant for as long as they tolerate my presence. It is not my place to argue for a grander welcome for my learning."

"But you deserve their respect," said Ester fiercely. "They ought be assembled before your door, awaiting the chance to study with you, entreating you to deliver sermons. You're a scholar who endured torture for the sake of your faith—and they persist in wearing crosses in the streets of a city where they need fear no Inquisition." All her love of the rabbi rose in her, hardening instantly to a wish to fight on his behalf. "What right have they to disdain a martyr?"

He flinched at the word. After a long moment he said, "I was no martyr."

"What I mean is—"

"I begged," he said.

There was a long silence.

"I used what words came," he said, "in Lisbon. I do not believe I recanted my faith under the priests' instruments, but neither did I proclaim it. My words tumbled without sense." For a long moment he was quiet. "For a reason I've never understood, they released me. Perhaps they felt a moment's pity, for I was yet young. Or perhaps in my moanings I uttered those very words they so cruelly wished me to speak." The rabbi sat motionless. She watched some struggle pass across his face, and fade. "I do not recall ever speaking the name of their lord," he said. "But it may be that I did. For I can think of no other reason I was allowed to live.

"Yet speaking their words would hardly have been more cowardly than what I am certain I did." He winced, his eyelids wrinkling as though they could yet shut out vision. "I begged for life. After my father and mother had asserted their faith."

Without thinking, Ester stepped forward. She set her hand on his arm and rested it there. The rabbi, motionless, allowed her touch.

"They let me go, saying my sight would be a small price to pay for my life. Before he took my eyes, the youngest priest said, 'Look now, so that your last vision ever stay with you and remind you of the truth you learn today at God's hands.'"

He sat undefended like a child. His shoulders were thin, his frail neck exposed.

"It was as he said. It has stayed with me always. I see that last sight even now, Ester, at this moment."

She did not ask what he saw. She vowed never to ask.

The fire burned softly, the air over the hearth a fine shimmer.

"The psalms," the rabbi said.

She went to the shelf and retrieved the small worn book, which awaited her there as though no violence had shaken the room.

"Number thirty-three," he said.

She chanted with the rabbi.

Later, after Rivka had persuaded him to take the air outside and led him slowly to the street on her arm, Ester stood alone in the study. A long while she stood.

Then she unfolded the widow's letter.

Did she wonder which young man might have spoken of her in the presence of Isabella Mendoza? Yes. Yes, perhaps she did. She could not deny it. She wouldn't pretend Mary's foolish yearnings had no kin in her own.

But she could ill afford to be like other girls. And she'd not yet learned of a woman's passion that did not exact a fearsome price. Had the widow who wrote this letter herself once allowed her senses to rule her? Whatever choices this Isabella Mendoza had made, whatever hopes she'd dared, they hadn't sustained her. It was now her business to insert herself, for sustenance, into the forming of further matches, whether or not they might serve as traps for the souls thus bound.

It is a danger to a woman, she told herself, *even to feel it.*

Did she believe it?

She reread the letter, and dropped it into the fire.

Just so — in the space of a heartbeat — she'd betrayed the rabbi.

Breathing deeply, she watched it burn. It curled in the flames, half rose in the heat, and subsided: the single page that could have expelled her from this narrow perch of home.

The fact of what she'd done pierced her even as she watched. Yet if she could have hastened the dissolving of the paper to ash, she'd have done so. She watched the last of the widow's letter to the rabbi form a fine dark webbing of ash, then collapse onto the orange coals beneath it.

The choice sat ill in her body, like a physick she had chosen on impulse to swallow. It was too soon to say if the body would rebel.

13

December 16, 2000
London

Well, Marisa, you've got me curious. First your report of planned excursions to the north, then the news that suddenly you're leaving your kibbutz program . . . and then you tell me you've planned a visit to the desert. Then silence. I'm thinking you've converted to Orthodoxy and are currently wearing a headkerchief and on your way to mothering eight children. Or else you've formed a punk band and are living the high life in Tel Aviv.

Am laboring away on the documents here for the ever-charming Professor Helen Watt. Some of the documents are pretty mundane, others interesting, but we're only starting to put together a picture of what they are, let alone why they were under a staircase in Richmond, which in those times must have been at least a half day's travel from London. There are some as-yet-unexplained references in one of the documents, which Watt seems to feel will be of earth-shattering importance. I'm not yet convinced, though it does seem we may have run across evidence of a woman scribe. That's going to make waves when we publish. There's no doubt this will advance the scholarship in the field, and it's pretty much guaranteed that whatever papers we write on this material will be published . . . which somewhat eases the pain of dealing with Watt. A few times I've thought she was about to ease up and behave like a human, but I've been sadly disappointed. She's the sort of person you can't imagine having an actual home. It's as though she turns a corner leaving her office and is shelved overnight in some storage unit for the terminally pedantic, and only materializes again on her return to work the next morning.

God save us (note, please, how British I'm starting to sound) from the doyennes of academia. She refers to the seventeenth-century hidden Jews as "crypto-Jews," which she pronounces like she's talking about some specimen under a microscope. She calls the Ketuvim "the Hagiographa," maybe to make sure I know she's not one of those sentimental religious types. She studies Jews like we're her favorite insect pinned to a wall. Well, I'm just going to have to develop that British stiff upper lip. I'm glad to be working on this project. And she needs my skills.

That last part was a lie. Or maybe it wasn't. Maybe Helen Watt would abruptly turn to him this very morning and give him credit for being something other than a page-turner?

Unlikely. He'd caught her rechecking one of his translations just yesterday. What was the point of hiring a grad student with eighteen combined years of Hebrew and Spanish and Portuguese study if you didn't let him do so much as render a translation?

But then, what was the point of disdaining work, even as a page-turner, if you'd made no serious headway on your dissertation in a year?

Around his thoughts went, like a bus on a roundabout. It took so little to start his mind on this course, the sickening sweep of his months in London raising bile in his throat. The weeks he'd wasted in the library trying to make something new out of Shakespeare's use of the name Bassanio in *Merchant of Venice,* and tracking down every possible connection between Shakespeare and the Jewish Bassano family then in the London court—only to discover that another scholar had already mapped the entire terrain of that blind alley . . . and by the way, the Bassano family wasn't actually Jewish. The months he'd devoted to *The Tempest,* following some glimmering notion about Prospero's references to magical books and a magic garment, which Aaron theorized might be derived from possible Jewish sources—only to realize that there was no evidence of any Jewish derivation . . . and, worse, to discover along the way that in fact he didn't understand *The Tempest* at all, because he couldn't honestly believe Prospero's relinquishment of his magical powers. And if Aaron couldn't take seriously the culmination of the play's drama—if he couldn't agree that a man like Prospero would ever willingly break his wand, and in doing so renounce his power to dazzle and wreak revenge and draw those he loved irresistibly to him — if Aaron failed to understand the very surface of this text, despite the fact that a significant portion of humanity seemed to think it was Shakespeare's towering achievement . . . then how could he hope to glean any of what lay beneath?

He'd abandoned *The Tempest*.

Darcy had consoled him. That is, Darcy had come as close to consolation as one could expect from a British academic. Darcy had combed his thin gray hair back over his bald spot with the fingers of one hand, and counseled him with a mildness that Aaron suspected was as close as the man came to warmth: Dark nights of the scholarly soul were sadly unavoidable for those who chose the rigorous path. Aaron would carry through in the end.

With a clap on the shoulder and a gesture at his clock, Darcy had ushered Aaron out of his office and his afternoon.

It would have been far simpler, yes, for Aaron to engage in small ideas, rather than try to say something fresh about the Bard, to whom academic crackpots flocked like iron filings to a magnet. Once, over beer and chips at a party, a fellow who'd been sizing up Aaron's Bard-olatry credentials had boasted that he himself had disproven all three leading theories about the identities of Shakespeare's Dark Lady and Fair Youth, and would soon be the one to unearth the true identities of Shakespeare's female and male paramours. When Aaron had questioned the guy, though, he'd gotten cagey, guarding his ideas as though Aaron were angling to steal them. He needn't have bothered; in Aaron's opinion, obsessing about the identity of long-dead individuals — even presuming you first made the leap and assumed Shakespeare wasn't just writing imaginatively in those sonnets but was talking about actual people he'd admired or loved — was a complete waste of time. Discovering which particular individuals caught the Bard's fancy and what sort of relationships might or might not have ensued would cast no real light on Shakespeare's significance. Let the Dark Lady and Fair Youth sonnets speak for themselves over the ages, universal messages that needed no external context.

Yet hadn't he just argued the irrelevance of his own dissertation? How was finding links between Shakespeare's writings and a long-lost Jewish community any different? Perhaps he ought to thank Helen

Watt for allowing him temporary shelter in a time period a full fifty years after the Bard had had the good grace to expire.

In an e-mail written more than three weeks ago, Marisa had mentioned a possible visit to London this coming summer, to attend a friend's wedding.

He pictured her.

He pictured her in his London flat, setting her travel bag on the floor.

Looking at him. And abruptly laughing.

He pictured her naked.

He pictured her reclining.

He pictured her reclining on black velvet drapes in a portrait painted by Rodney Keller.

He wondered whether Rodney Keller was gay.

A bus on a roundabout.

He set his fingers on the keyboard once more.

Unfortunately, there's a wrinkle in the process. We're not the only ones working on these documents anymore. The head of the History Department is about to give another team access. And don't even ask: nobody is about to offer to collaborate. Helen Watt was ready to explode when she got the news (I could tell, clever fellow that I am, because her lips got three microns thinner when the competing scholar's name was mentioned) but I'm guessing she's scared. Maybe she's human after all. Me, I'll keep slaving away on the papers all day in this reading room that's quiet as a cathedral. Got to be both painstaking and fast. Do not hurry; do not rest. So said Goethe. I don't rest, but it's a lot of rough hours conversing with nothing but three-hundred-year-old paper and my computer.

His fingers rested on the keys. He tried to think of some way to describe what he felt, day after day, in the rare manuscripts room. The massive silence; tables of very thin students with very bad posture; a page nested before Aaron, on a furrowed pillow on which he'd have loved to rest his own head. He tried to think how to tell Marisa what it was like to sit reading documents he was forbidden to lift or move, making notes with a pencil stub grooved with some unknown scholar's tooth marks, until he was a coiled spring—until he felt that some mad idea was about to break in him like a wave and he would jump from his seat and follow it, whatever the consequences. A state at once intolerable and intoxicating. He searched for words that would be true and also acceptable to Marisa. There was nothing. Then abruptly his fingers sprang into urgent action on the keys, and he watched the words appear on the screen.

Never underestimate the passion of a lonely mind.

He planned to delete the sentence. He'd typed Helen's words only to feel them out, like trying someone else's gloves on his hands.
Then he knew that he would keep them, send them as his own.

If I read your last e-mail right, you're nostalgic for London. Well, there's a welcome waiting for you if you want it.
　—A

He hit Send, watched the computer release his message into the void of the irretrievable.

INSIDE THE RARE MANUSCRIPTS ROOM, settling alone at the long table, he wearily regarded the pencils Librarian Patricia rolled onto the table. "No offense," he said to her, giving her a smile, "but these are killing my knuckles." He raised a hand and ruefully indicated the red-gray calluses left behind by yesterday's work.

Librarian Patricia turned her dispassionate gaze to his shirt pocket, where a round pencil of his own was peeking out: contraband. With the slightest flicker of satisfaction on her impassive face, she plucked it from his chest and turned her back—leaving him to a faintly inked letter dated 1659 and three sharpened brown pencils, notched into painful hexagons, each no longer than his index finger.

"Hey!" he said, his indignation real this time.

She didn't turn back.

"You flirt!" he muttered when her stodgy figure was out of earshot, and his own humor righted him.

He worked. The first letter was in Portuguese and he dispatched the translation within a half-hour, dry-gulping two ibuprofen as his temples began their daily throbbing.

> March 18, 1665
> 2 Nisan, 5425
> Amsterdam

To Rabbi HaCoen Mendes,
Surely you will not remember your undeserving pupil from so many years ago, yet I've not forgotten your tutelage in my youth. Your learning was ever a light to those privileged to study at your side, and your pupils spread that learning as mirrors multiply one candle and make it a thousand.
I am but an unimportant scholar in the kahal of Amsterdam, yet it is an abundant blessing to labor here in support of the great rabbis and to be asked to respond to a letter such as yours. You will be honored to know that the Rabbi Solomon de Oliveyra concurs with your methods for teaching Hebrew, and he refers you to his work on the subject, Sarsot Gablut, which perhaps you have not yet encountered. With regard to the other questions you posed, debate continues here regarding whether the messianic age comes in this year of 5425 or the coming year, yet whichever be true, the fervor of many here, including myself, rises. Even the Rabbis Aboab and Oliveyra have written prayers that are included in new books dedicated to the imminent coming. From the words of your letter, I understand that you and many in London have not yet woken to the coming of the Redeemer, yet I am told your city is hushed in contemplation of the portent seen in your night skies, as it is in our skies here in Amsterdam. Though I am unfit to persuade a learned man such as you, still must I try to impress upon you the import of a sign your eyes cannot behold. The significance of G-d's bright beacon to our heavens cannot be mistaken. With eyes lifted to the hills,
Yacob Rodriguez

Aaron finished the translation and made notes on a separate pad. The involvement of Aboab and Oliveyra in the false-messiah hysteria was already well documented, but this was a nice piece of evidence regardless. Might be part of a paper one day.

He requested the next letter, this one with a somewhat earlier date, and after a break to stretch his legs and get a soda he sat back down to the new document.

> March 13, 1665
> 26 Adar, 5425
> Amsterdam
>
> To Rabbi HaCoen Mendes,
> Rabbi Isaac Aboab da Fonseca has received your report regarding the progress of the congregation's return to tradition in London, which shall with G-d's will prove favorable. Rabbi Aboab has instructed me to dispatch this reply to you, as his labors on behalf of our blessed community here in Amsterdam leave him little time for such correspondence.
> You and I are not acquainted, yet I have been assured of your merits and your sufferings under the cursed Inquisition, and the long devotion you have shown in your work in London, such as will be rewarded in the world to come. I am, however, obliged to tell you that the new-formed Mahamad of London has already reported to us all that you describe in your recent letter, and now that the honored Rabbi Sasportas will soon be installed in the community we will of course be honored to receive such communications from him. You must not strain your health to produce such an account as you have given. Your age merits that you rest, and you may do so glad in the knowledge that your congregation's esteemed leaders do all that is required. Benjamin HaLevy, whose name as you know is held in high respect, tells us of the Ets Haim house of Jewish learning lately founded in London with generous gifts by men such as himself, and he reports that he long ago removed his two sons from your tutelage and has set them to study there, to be examples to the community of the strength of the Council's institution of Jewish learning.
> Happy is the teacher whose students grow beyond his reach, so you are to be praised, for surely these two young men of Israel have learned all that you had to teach them.

On the matter of your inquiry as to whether we might publish a book of your teachings here in Amsterdam, I will say that of course we will be honored to do so if it is deemed suitable. You are aware, no doubt, that the London Mahamad, in its growing labors to safeguard the strength and virtue of the Jewish community of your city, has banned the publication of any work without its prior approval, but I am certain that when you show the Mahamad the work of your hand it will quickly approve its publication. I respectfully await word of your Mahamad's authorization.

Lastly, in response to your question, I am asked to relate to you that all congress with the heretic de Spinoza is forever banned, and this ban is not subject to any limitation. The passage of time does not lessen the dangers of exchange with him, nor does it make him more likely to be persuaded of wisdom. He has left our city and our souls are eased for it. Rabbi Aboab has instructed me to make this matter clear.

In trust of the coming of the Redeemer, whose rumor reaches Amsterdam even now, and I a young man who trembles at the approach of Eternity,

Avner Ben-Samuel

Aaron finished the translation. The retort about Spinoza was an eye-catcher, of course. He wondered what Helen would make of that. Had someone—Aleph—wished to contact Spinoza, despite his excommunication for heresy? It seemed unlikely. Probably the rabbi, who might plausibly have taught Spinoza as a youth in Amsterdam before his apostasy, had wondered about the permissibility of dropping a line to his old student. In any event, this would make for another paper—*any* authentic document that mentioned Spinoza, even the thinnest reference, could be spun into a publication. It should have put Aaron in a good mood—yet he couldn't deny that this letter irked him. Couldn't Aboab or Oliveyra have at least done HaCoen Mendes the dignity of answering him personally? Or didn't seventeenth-century rabbis believe in professional courtesy? It was no shock, of course, that HaCoen Mendes was being supplanted—the London community had, inevitably, organized itself, and had invited the acclaimed Rabbi Sasportas to be their synagogue's first Haham. Their loss, thought Aaron. Within the year the great Sasportas would have fled the plague and London, never to return. London's Jews would have done better to skip the celebrity rabbi and stick with someone like HaCoen Mendes.

He called up the next document by its code: RQ206. A few moments later, Patricia set it — a stack of six or seven handwritten pages — on the cushion in front of Aaron.

> March 23, 1665
> 7 Nisan, 5425

> To Daniel Lusitano,
> My distress grows with every hour I meditate upon your letter. And so I hope you will forgive the crowding of one missive atop another, as my thoughts crowd like sheep at the pasture gate when a wolf prowls. In my own darkness I see perhaps too vivid a picture of the error that lies before your community in Florence. It is an error not only of soul but also of body, for they that muster for the next world before it has come can only betray their lives in this one. Long have I heard rumor of Sabbatai Zevi and yet I remained foolishly silent, and I can only rebuke myself that it has taken a new report of the threat from my beloved student to awaken me. What small help my thoughts may offer is ever at your disposal, and so I set forward the following additional arguments.

Aaron read on. HaCoen Mendes laid out his case patiently, if laboriously. Sabbatai Zevi was a pretender; the true Messiah, sent by the Almighty, would be recognizable by certain traits, among them a lack of ambition for earthly power. As Sabbatai Zevi declared himself Messiah among Jews from Smyrna to Salonika to Aleppo — and as his fame drew adherents in congregations throughout Europe — he was an increasingly dangerous manipulator of the people's desperate hopes.

Aaron had read this sort of argument before, and found himself skimming. But when he reached the fourth page, he set down his pencil.

He'd seen cross-written documents before. It had been a common enough practice, where paper was scarce or expensive, for the writer of a seventeenth-century letter to complete one page, turn it upside down, and ink another full page between the lines already written. But he'd never seen a cross-written document like this. In its orientation on the cushion before him, the page of Portuguese offered itself first to his eye. Yet midway through the page another text rose up, sprouting between the lines like a counterargument arising from unknown depths. The page grew abruptly crowded, the rabbi's Portuguese interspersed with another message, upside down. Aaron leaned closer. The upside-down writing was in Hebrew, with the exception of one line in English. It was Aleph's familiar handwriting, yet different—the words slanting from haste or urgency. He turned the other pages as swiftly as he dared, scanning both texts, trying to understand what was before him. Two messages, Portuguese and Hebrew, proceeding in opposite directions, their logic converging and then separating, their conclusions farther and farther apart.

"Patricia," he said.

She didn't hear, or if she heard perhaps she wished him to announce his dependence more clearly.

"Patricia," he called softly, the humility in his voice unfamiliar.

She came.

"Please." He motioned impotently with his hands: invert the document.

She stared. After a moment she seemed to understand. She pulled cotton gloves from a pocket, lifted the pages, and resettled them efficiently on the angled cushion. As Aaron gripped the nub of a pencil and began transcribing the Hebrew, Patricia lingered a long moment at his shoulder—as if mesmerized herself by the urgent counterpoint of the two languages on the page.

Ignoring his burning knuckles, he copied out the Hebrew on the fourth page, searching it for meaning—it seemed to be the end of a declaration or confession, but of what nature and of what kinship to the Portuguese text he couldn't say, nor could he guess the significance of the English quotation at its end. Some time later he had Patricia invert the letter so he could read, beginning to end, in Portuguese; then had her invert it again so he could read end to beginning in Hebrew. He rechecked his transcription, crossing out and adding notes.

Over and over he returned to the sixth and final page of the Portuguese letter. Below the rabbi's sprawling signature and the initial of the scribe Aleph, was the word, decorated with a small, elegant scroll, *Finis*.

But turn the page upside down and, in the same elegant hand, the Hebrew read, *Here I begin.*

Here I begin.

I am one soul in a great city.

I am the hand that moves over the page.

The rabbi speaks. I write. This has been my task and my refuge. I scribe for a man not honored by those who ought honor him.

I would do him honor.

But I do not. Instead I pose questions forbidden to men, though I myself am blameless of violating the law.

The words that leave my hand are my life.

I've brought forth no other life in my days, and believe I shall not.

This day, Manuel HaLevy, a man of a temperament to use a folio of verse to wipe his boots, came to the rabbi's study to scoff at his own brother's cruel impressment onto an English ship. I have observed this HaLevy these years, and know the force of his contempt for all of more delicate temperament.

When I refused his offer of marriage, he asked me what I am.

I gave this answer: I am an empty vessel.

It is not so. For if desire be the essence of man, it must also be of woman. I am a vessel that brims with desire.

I write. Were the truth known of what I have wrought in the rabbi's place, I would be counted among the most wicked of souls. Yet forgiveness I do not ask. If it be the nature of God's universe that our lives must be made false to remain true, then be my conscience clear and scoured as my heart.

Where words are scarce they are seldom spent in vain, for they breathe truth that breathe their words in pain.

As soon as Aaron had checked over his full translation, he stepped out of the rare manuscripts room and left a message on Helen's telephone. Several minutes later he left another—then a third, feeling vexed to the point of madness, in which he read to her answering machine the first lines of the cross-writing. He was considering leaving a fourth when his phone rang.

"Mr. Levy?"

How long was it going to take for her to use his first name?

In his phone messages he'd said things that would have piqued any historian's curiosity. Yet now Helen didn't ask him a single question. She simply said, "I'll meet you at my office."

Walking across a series of narrow courtyards toward her office, weaving between drifting clumps of students, he took a moment to imagine Helen Watt as a child. *No thank you, Mother, I prefer to wait and open my Christmas presents next month.*

She wasn't in her office when he arrived. He leaned on the wall beside her door, then after a time slid down to sit cross-legged on the floor of the empty hallway. He tugged his laptop out of his bag and opened it.

Aaron,

I don't want to be in touch with you right now. Sorry to be abrupt, but I'm telling you directly to spare you the experience of sending e-mails into a void.

Marisa

The words made no sense. He read them again. He closed his eyes, opened them, and found the words still on the screen.

At the sound of Helen Watt's cane he shut his laptop, stood, and mutely followed her into her office.

As she settled at her desk, and he into the wooden chair opposite, he thought for an instant that Helen looked unwell. Then, under her unblinking stare, he decided he'd imagined it.

"Tell me what you found," she said.

He began his description of the cross-written document—and the act of speaking righted him. Marisa's bewildering, eviscerating e-mail receded . . . surely it would make sense later. As he addressed Helen, the full force of his excitement returned to him. Two texts singing together in harmony—it was a work of art. It read almost like a poem, he told Helen Watt: a personal diary meted out in crisp lines that stood apart from one another like islands. Perhaps it was simply something scribbled by a seventeenth-century woman in a meditative moment— but it had the feeling of a coded message. Certainly it hinted at some intense human story behind this collection of documents ... yet that closing quote, for which Aleph had switched to English, was from Shakespeare's *Richard II*—Aaron had already checked it online. And that phrase about desire—he'd have wondered if it might be a reference to Spinoza's *Ethics*, only *Ethics* wouldn't be published for more than a decade after this was written. Still, what were they to make of this sort of philosophical language? Wasn't such discourse banned to Jewish men, let alone women?

When he'd finished, Helen Watt said nothing. She was staring out the window, her face stony with some fierce inner focus.

He decided to wait out her silence. If she could act as though the earth hadn't just shifted under their feet, so could he.

Then, the clock on her desk ticking with obstinate stupid slowness, he couldn't. Something had pricked a hole in his confidence. Marisa's words flew back into his mind and lodged. How could he have so offended or disappointed her that she couldn't even tolerate his e-mails? The very thought of Marisa was, abruptly, a body blow. He shook his head involuntarily, ignoring the sharp glance this drew from Helen Watt.

Who had still said nothing.

However disoriented he felt, Aaron was not confused—not in the least bit—about the document he'd seen today. Didn't Helen understand what he'd discovered? *All* forms of diary were extraordinarily rare in early-modern Jewish communities. There was no Jewish Augustine, no Jewish Julian of Norwich. There was Leon of Modena, true; but the only known diary by a Jewish *woman* of the early modern period was that of tedious Glückel of Hameln, filled with moralistic pronouncements and details of dowries. Didn't Helen see what they had in their hands? If there were more notes like this in the trove—more personal margin-scribblings or cross-writing, or maybe even a more coherent passage by Aleph in which she'd explain what the hell she'd meant by that cryptic *counted among the most wicked of souls*—maybe this could be the new Glückel, except without Glückel's plangent materialism. A young, philosophy-dabbling, melodramatic Glückel; *that's* what he'd write up for his dissertation.

"This could be the new Glückel," he said.

She didn't answer.

"And combined with the information in HaCoen Mendes's letter about a Sabbatean crisis in Florence . . ."

Still Helen refused to respond.

He continued sharply. "Florence being a community that's been thought of until now as a fairly safe haven from Sabbateanism. Making this find doubly important."

Helen inclined her head. "Correct on all counts."

He stared at her. She still wasn't looking at him. He made no effort to mask his anger. "This could be the new Glückel *and* we've got fresh information on the influence of Sabbatai Zevi in Florence. One of those things alone is a huge find. Together?"

Still looking at the window, she said, "I'll check the translation of the Portuguese first thing in the morning."

He sat straight-backed in his chair. Again, some vague agony—something to do with Marisa that he hadn't yet wrapped his mind around—thudded dully inside him. With effort, he held himself perfectly still. "That's all you have to say?"

Helen stared at the window as though she hadn't taken in a word. As if waiting for him to leave. As if she too had decided she preferred not to be in touch with him right now.

"So you won't believe it until you double-check to see if my Hebrew vocabulary is up to scratch?" His hands, loose at his sides, felt hot. "Is that it?"

She raised her eyebrows in the manner of one annoyed by a far-off sound.

"Well," he said, "if you're not going to trust me as a scholar, you ought simply tell me that right now."

She glanced at him, surprised, as though the question of trust hadn't occurred to her. She spoke with unexpected mildness. "I'm simply stating that I intend to check these translations before we proceed further. It's a matter of prudent scholarship."

Fuck prudent, he enunciated in his thoughts. *Fuck you.*

She resumed her inward focus, as though too preoccupied to notice that the other person in the office with her was staring at her with as much hatred as he'd ever felt for another human being. His fury had lifted him almost out of his seat, his hands clenched by his knees as though he were being threatened with fists rather than her bludgeoning indifference. Helen Watt, imperious expert in Jewish history—a woman with Masada framed on her wall, as though to prove she loved the Jews and their suffering. How sick he was of English people who loved martyred Jews. How sick he was of her. He would not leave this office without being acknowledged. "Do you see what this could mean?" he repeated, and this time he didn't disguise the demand in his voice.

She turned to face him so suddenly, his body braced as if in self-defense. Her voice was extremely quiet. "Yes, young man. I have seen it all along."

There had been, perhaps, a point when he could have stopped, when he could have prevented a conflict that would change everything. But as he opened his mouth to answer her, he knew that point, if it had ever existed, had passed.

"You could've hired a child to turn pages for you," he said. "You should have. They work cheaper than postgraduates, and they don't mind being ordered around by someone who hasn't a vestige of consideration. Even better"—he continued, not caring anymore, wanting only to fire back at the blanched, haughty woman to whom he'd been enslaved because of his own desperation—"children don't challenge Brits who get their kicks out of dissecting other people's histories without the least—"

She cut him off. "I have as much right to research Jewish history as you. Perhaps more, if you count years of—"

He didn't care. He wouldn't care. "Spoken like an old-fashioned colonialist."

He had, at intervals throughout his life, burned himself badly through an inability to control his temper once he got started. He could go years without an incident—he could go so long that he came to believe his Teflon Man moniker. And then, without any warning he himself could see, he would erupt as though there were no such thing as a consequence. Thus far he'd damaged himself very little, allowing his temper to fly in the faces of those who held only paltry power over him —so he'd been able to proceed with full confidence to the next mentor, the next study group, leaving in his wake only a thin trail of muttering TAs or resident advisors, whom he would never use as job references and whose ill opinion of him would never reverberate into his future. Now he felt it happening with Helen Watt and had no wish to stop it.

He wanted only to blow the flames higher, to see how high they could rise—how quickly this whole enterprise, the entire fantastical trove under the staircase, this golden chance to save his stalled academic career that gave this bitter woman such intolerable power over him, could blow to ash.

Faint pink patches had arisen on Helen's cheeks. "Mr. Levy, you are on very shaky ground."

"Bullshit." He got up out of his chair. "Bullshit," he said again, as though it were necessary to repeat this from his new vantage point. The word strengthened him. The way her nostrils flared—as though everything about him were odious—strengthened him. "This story, for example, belongs to the global Jewish community. *Florence. Sabbatean crisis.*" He spat the words. "*Rabbis sending advice across Europe.* Yet you go along with Jonathan Martin's plan to skirt the Freedom of Information Act, because you don't want to share this with Jewish scholars. You don't want to share it with *anyone.*" He was arguing against his own interests now and he didn't care. All he cared about was humbling her. And something else, something seductive suddenly flurrying inside him —the prospect of succumbing to reality. There, he'd thought it: so he *wouldn't* get a Ph.D. He didn't need Shakespeare, he didn't need Helen Watt, he didn't need drizzly England and its sodden queues and waterlogged personalities. He didn't even need history; he could make his life without it.

The only pinch of regret he felt, as he spoke on, was at a momentary image of the documents, packed so carefully on their shelves in that stairwell in Richmond. The tide of lines on paper, written by a steady unknown hand, speaking to him across the fraught silence of centuries.

He blinked it aside.

"The university," he said to Helen, "has gotten queries from the Jewish Theological Seminary in New York. From Harvard's Judaic Studies Department. The Patricias whisper about it, you ought to know. If you love the pursuit of Jewish history so much, the least you could do is urge Martin to expedite the release of the papers so a larger pool of scholars can tackle them. Yet you haven't raised a finger."

Helen's posture was taut. "This is not a *Jewish* story. This story, whatever it proves to be, belongs to all of us."

"Awfully convenient of you to say that," he spat, "as you cooperate in elbowing everyone else away from the table. What, did you spend a summer in Israel? Just because you once read a Jewish newspaper or ate a kosher hot dog or maybe"—some instinct propelled his words forward, the line of his argument a heat-seeking missile—"once for a month you had a Jewish boyfriend, it doesn't mean that you own this history." He swallowed. "Exclusively."

On her cheeks, the flush had deepened. "You believe I'm just profiteering from someone else's heritage?" Her voice was neutral, as though his answer didn't matter to her.

He didn't have to say more. He knew, in some confused way, that he'd hit a target, and the satisfaction that spread in him pushed aside all else, keeping at bay for the moment the wave of regret he knew was coming.

"Well," she said, and was silent.

"I'll go, then." He picked up his bookbag. "Perhaps we can have a more sensible discussion about this tomorrow." He knew they would not. He would walk out with his head high, organize his papers, and give notice to Darcy that he was no longer in Professor Watt's employ.

And then, after he'd done that, perhaps he'd just go ahead and tell Darcy he'd be taking a leave from Shakespeare. Why not? Did he dare? And who would stop him?

As he slung his bag over his shoulder, he imagined a phone call with Marisa—in his mind he'd already reached out across the miles, persuaded her to talk to him—in which she'd celebrate his explosive liberation from academia. Perhaps, now that he'd shaken loose some old and outdated version of himself, she'd even encourage him to join her on some adventure in Israel or travel with her around the world. What was there to stop him from choosing some completely different life, after all?

Nothing but the fact that he'd never wanted a different life.

He felt his exuberance crest. The total, pool-still silence of something at equipoise. And the beginning of what he knew would be freefall.

Had Marisa guessed this about him, then? Had she, out of all the women he'd slept with, seen through his cool and his vanity and understood what he'd long secretly feared: That underneath it all, Aaron Levy lacked the courage for an authentic life? That he had not the slightest idea who he was without praise, without steady advancement toward a degree and title, without organized competition for some elite goal?

A secret no one had yet guessed. Except Marisa—who had summarily decided she wanted nothing to do with him.

And, perhaps, Helen. Yes, Aaron thought: Helen had guessed.

And even now, as his adrenaline drained, as he stood before Helen Watt with his hands loose at his sides and his heart still pumping hard, Aaron was beginning to fear what he'd done. A stunning sobriety broke over him, washed him cold from head to foot. The arrogance that had always granted him a safe landing from every exercise of boyish temper had finally blown a hole in his career that could not be patched. Darcy would hear of his behavior. The question of whether to continue his studies might not even be in his hands. What in him had desired this, had inexorably pushed toward and past this brink?

Helen was talking. "Do you imagine, young Mr. Levy, that if I *had* been involved with a Jewish man I'd necessarily have some sort of blind possessiveness—that condescending *colonialist* viewpoint you and your cohort make your careers describing?" Her blue eyes were ice. Instinctively, he folded his arms across his chest to warm himself.

"I was," she said. "I did love a Jewish man, Mr. Levy. Does that make me less capable of honest scholarship?"

Aaron concentrated on her words only with effort. They made no sense to him, just as it would have made no sense if she had told him she'd had a former life as an acrobat or circus clown. He wanted this conversation over. He had no idea how he'd gotten into it, he had no desire to hear whom or what Helen Watt had loved, if she was even capable of such a thing. He wanted only some quiet in which to marvel at what he'd done, and what it might mean.

"Well," he said to Helen, "life is complex."

She stared.

"Perhaps," he muttered, "perhaps if he hadn't broken it off with you, maybe—"

With a white hand, she gripped her cane. She stood with difficulty to her full height, somehow taller than Aaron remembered, and held herself there. "What makes you think, Mr. Levy, that he broke off with me?"

With a sensation like startling from a dream, Aaron woke to the knowledge that he had gone dreadfully wrong. He wanted to vomit.

"He didn't leave me," she said, with a peculiar intensity. "I left him."

Aaron leaned hard against the wall as though it might open and offer an exit. He didn't want to ask her why she'd left, or when, or what it mattered. He didn't want to know. But he couldn't draw his eyes away from her flushed, living face.

AND SO, WITH A FEW words she seemed to have chosen not to take it to the grave, after all, but to place its bare outlines in the hands of Aaron Levy—a youth without the maturity to see or care. A pointless, empty choice.

Over the years, in a process so gradual she'd barely felt its motion, she'd come to understand that beneath it all, Dror had been trying to tell her something. That he'd loved her enough to want to offer her a way out. It was she who'd wavered, who'd stolen, who'd run. It was she who'd chosen to believe in Muriel's jealous words; in the soughing cypress tree that told her she was alien; in the jarring, distorted reflection of her own pale face in the barracks' dented mirror.

Dror had followed her from his quarters. He'd called Helen's name despite stares from all directions, he'd caught her arm despite the uniformed soldiers straining to hear—and he'd said to her in a low voice that was only for her, "This is who I am. This is my world. If you'll have me despite everything, I'll marry you in an instant." He'd held her eyes as though the two of them weren't on a stage before the entire base—before the entire empty, ringing desert. "I love you," he said. "I haven't said those words until now, because I've wanted to say them to only one woman in my life. I've wanted to be sure." His face was fierce with concentration, his dark eyes fastened on her with unspeakable tenderness. His hands encircled her as she faced him. "Can you understand that?"

His hands on the small of her back. His face, broken open, shocking.

He stepped forward to seal her fast in his arms. Yet as his embrace closed on her, his trust seemed to take on physical weight, bearing down on her—and her heart raced hard and then harder, until it was loud in her ears and she feared it—a foreign-tongued stranger speaking too fast, too urgently, whether of love or terror she didn't know. She'd broken away and left him there.

"WHY?" AARON LEVY SAID, his mouth so dry the word barely sounded.

Helen looked at him for a long time, her face suffused by some combination of emotions he felt unqualified to understand. She turned, then, and gestured simply at the framed sketch above the mantle.

The faded silhouette of Masada offered itself, its mute lines clear testimony for those who knew to read what was written there. A stark choice. Self-immolation or slavery. Freedom or life, but not both.

"Because," Helen said, "if we had been there, he would have cut my throat."

Part 3

14

February 6, 1665
21 Shvat, 5425
London

WITH THE TOE OF HER SHOE, Ester tipped away the loose half-cobblestone someone had used to anchor the pamphlet against the day's unseasonably warm gusts. She picked it up from the rabbi's doorstep and read it. *A Proclamation from the London Mahamad.*

Softly, she laughed. She needed no proof to know it was Mary who'd laid it at the door during the hour Ester had been out arranging to send a letter. As blithely as Mary changed dresses to suit her needs, so now had Mary fashioned herself as the Mahamad's unofficial courier, delivering its decrees to the Jewish homes clustered on Bevis Marks and Bury Streets and Creechurch Lane—a task that, by no coincidence, obliged Mary to visit the door of every Jewish house, pausing where she wished to collect gossip or to make show of her charms to any who might have an unmarried cousin or nephew. Ester could imagine the distracted haste with which Mary would have deposited the pamphlet at the rabbi's household, without troubling to knock. None of what she sought was to be found here.

Ester read the first page of the pamphlet, the Portuguese ornamented with the occasional Hebrew phrase. *Be it known that the Jews of London shall not cavort at brothels in the manner of London society. Nor shall their women appear outside their domiciles with their flesh exposed, nor shall they allow strangers to see their hair but instead shall keep it covered on the byways of the city.*

Ester would have wagered any sum that Mary had delivered this announcement with a shawl drawn piously across her bosom . . . and that beneath the shawl, the rise of her powdered breasts had been adorned with crescent-moon patches. A few hours laboring for the Mahamad was all Mary would tolerate before she moved on to sample one of the city's gaieties. Indeed, a few hours' sobriety seemed more than most of London would willingly endure. So thoroughly had London remade itself since the restoration of the royal court that Ester found it a strain to recall the city that had come before. Now the king and his famed lovers had made an art of raucousness, and it seemed all London followed. Not a food or song or deed or costume was left plain that might be somehow adorned. Torrents of lace and ribboned love locks festooned gentlemen everywhere but among the Puritans and Quakers; women young and old promenaded the city under the weight of expensive and brightly colored fabrics such as had been banned under the Puritans; and an overfullness seemed to strain the city's very walls, as though each satiety had to be challenged to see if the body that was London could be made to sustain yet further pleasure.

Against this abundance the synagogue's new Mahamad had swiftly set itself, a bulwark against all it deemed grotesque. With the elegant and austere Rabbi Sasportas—newly imported from abroad—now walking openly in his dark robes and skullcap on London's streets, and with the wealthier members of the congregation talking of constructing a new and grand synagogue building suitable for such an esteemed rabbi, London's Jewry daily seemed to Ester more and more like Amsterdam's. The small ring of men who'd lately formed the Mahamad spoke up stridently from the men's side of the synagogue, issuing warnings against praying with Tudescos and against the self-declared Messiah Sabbatai Zevi, and proclaiming new community standards for dress, dance, music, and of course attendance of the theater. Indeed, Constantina's long-ago pronouncements about Amsterdam's Jews now kept Ester jarring company. *See how these men of the synagogue set themselves up as judges.* It remained true that all had not yet submitted to the community's new rules; a mighty argument was even now in progress, Rivka had reported, because Sasportas had threatened to expel two men of the community who refused circumcision. Indeed, many of the synagogue's men and women nodded respectfully to his sermons and then ran their households as they pleased, and the young winked at the Mahamad's proclamations and flung themselves at London.

Still, it was the Mahamad's impositions that had helped set Ester on the very errand she now returned from. Only yesterday she had entered the rabbi's room to find him seated idle beside his fire, as he was so often of late. So few pupils came now to the rabbi's doors, choosing instead to learn under Sasportas or to join with the sons of the wealthy at the Ets Haim. As Ester had looked on at the rabbi pressing his empty hands together lightly and parting them, pressing them and parting them, a thought had seized her.

"Isn't it time we compose your teachings into a book?" she'd said.

The rabbi had turned to her slowly—and as he did she noted yet again how the winter seemed to have sapped his strength, though he never complained. But his body was more bent, his face even paler.

"Your commentaries about the Torah," she said. "Or the Mishnah. We'll print them. Your words will be preserved. They'll go out to other students, even far from here."

A great stillness came over him. When he spoke, something had kindled in his voice. "Perhaps," he said, "my words might indeed help students see the wisdom in the teachings of those greater than I." He listened long to the fire. Yet a moment later the spirit animating him seemed to subside. "No, Ester," he said softly.

"But why?"

"The learned Rabbi Sasportas's authority is new, and tender. It would not be right for me to raise my own voice now." The rabbi shaped his next words carefully. "Surely too the Mahamad must approve all publications issued by Jews of this synagogue, and would not allow the printing of mine without Sasportas's approval. I should not wish him to think I were endeavoring to supplant him."

Nor, Ester knew, would the rabbi wish to give the famed Sasportas an opportunity to step into the path of sin by blocking a rival's publication. Never did an ill word regarding Sasportas escape the rabbi's lips, though Sasportas, in all his months in London, had not called on the rabbi. Neither did the rabbi make judgment of Sasportas's teachings —though on more than one Sabbath, peering through a gap in the curtain, Ester had watched the rabbi's face tighten as Sasportas, with his thin nose and high forehead and mellifluous voice, recited a magnificent sermon that praised, condemned, and promised, yet gave no warmth.

The silence muffling the room was impenetrable, London's din a distant memory. Palm to palm the rabbi raised his hands, and lightly pressed them together.

"Perhaps," Ester ventured, "the press in Amsterdam might print it? I'll write to Rabbi Aboab."

A ripple of longing disturbed the rabbi's expression. She could feel his wish moving in the still room: To teach. To be heard.

"Thank you," he said.

He'd permit it. She blushed at his simple gratitude. "All your pupils will be pleased," she said. "They wish your words to spread."

A pained smile lit the rabbi's face. "Not all, Ester. But I thank you nonetheless."

She waited. The rabbi didn't speak. "You refer to de Spinoza?" she said.

The rabbi nodded.

Would he rebuff her curiosity? "What sort," she said slowly, "was he?"

Rivka entered with the rabbi's coffee. He waited until she had departed to answer—then spoke slowly. "I knew always, even when de Spinoza was a boy, that he exceeded me in intelligence. Yet could I only have imparted to him more of the beauty of our learning, I might have saved him from the path he chose. I failed to do so." The rabbi paused, then continued with conviction. "But what a sage he could have become, Ester . . . and still might become, if only he wished it. Had they not banished him, he might yet be one of our great lights." The rabbi turned his face intently toward Ester. "He visited me once, just before the ban. I'd sent word I wished to speak with him. I felt he might yet remain among us, if he only mastered his desire to so sharply rebuke those he thought in error. Yet though he addressed his former teacher with extraordinary politeness, he heeded naught I said. To my face he even carried his heresies further than I'd feared, further than I believe the other rabbis knew. *Deus sive Natura:* God or Nature. This was the spike with which he would pierce our tradition. God and Nature, he claimed, were indistinguishable—and he went even beyond this, he took pains to explain to me that we therefore are creatures determined by nature, lacking will of our own. In one breath he denied miracles, the holiness of the Torah, the soul's endurance, heavenly reward or punishment. I believe, Ester, that in speaking to me thus he felt himself to be offering me a gift of truth." A stain of regret on the rabbi's face. "I could not persuade him."

The sounds from the kitchen had died, creating a fragile lull.

"It is a shame upon the Amsterdam community," the rabbi said, "that they could not hold one of their own sons. They would not bear his views of God. I endeavored to dissuade them. I went to the synagogue and said to all those assembled, the rabbis and the men of the Mahamad, 'God himself has not struck de Spinoza down. Indeed, God countenances his rebellion, allowing de Spinoza to continue to walk this earth—for God knows truth always defeats misunderstanding. So must we welcome even a heretic in the byways of our own congregation until he sees truth.' Yet even without knowledge of the new heresies de Spinoza had confessed to me, they closed him out from life. They said, 'God's jealousy will smoke against him.'"

Ester's heart beat strangely. She spoke, her voice too avid. "Which of de Spinoza's heresies so enraged the rabbis?"

The rabbi raised a hand as though to deflect the question. Then his hand fell to his lap. Quietly he pronounced the blasphemy. "That God does not intervene on our behalf."

Yet in the same instant, something within Ester said, *That God is afraid*. She barely understood her own thought—yet it pinioned her.

In a rush she said, "I wish it could come to pass that you might speak with de Spinoza further. To impart more of your thinking."

A faint smile crossed the rabbi's pale lips. "I do not believe, Ester, that my arguments could win him. But I would dearly like to hear my old pupil's voice. I would like to tell him, at the least, that I endeavored to persuade the others to let him stay."

She understood that he'd say no more.

Yet as she settled a blanket across his knees, and placed his neglected cup of coffee into his thin hands, a question rose in her: what if she herself could converse with de Spinoza—a man who dared challenge the rabbis?

She knew in an instant what she'd ask. She'd demand explanation for what none, not even the rabbi, had yet been able to explain to her: how a just God might willingly make a youth—a child—an instrument of death. Isaac, her Isaac, was all the proof she needed that God was either indifferent to human life, or else must have no power to alter its course. Had de Spinoza come to believe God—*God-or-Nature*—indifferent?

The God the tradition spoke of must necessarily wish for the well-being of His creations. Either there was no such God, then . . . or perhaps there existed only a God who could do nothing to alter the world's evils.

Then did God quake in helpless fear at the roar of fire, the cry of a mob? Did God too tremble at times with rage and confusion?

It was for the rabbi, she told herself, that she added to her letter to Amsterdam an inquiry about contacting de Spinoza. Should the response be positive, she'd surprise Rabbi HaCoen Mendes with permission to write to his former pupil. So she persuaded herself, as she addressed the letter to one of the very Amsterdam rabbis who had banished de Spinoza. And perhaps, she reasoned as she watched the ink dry and lose its shine, the Amsterdam community's ferocity toward de Spinoza had been in part a show, meant to serve as a warning to others. For could those rabbis truly be possessed of such fury for a fellow Jew —for his mere *ideas*? Wasn't such lack of tolerance the manner of the Christians, rather than the Jews?

She sealed the letter with a pang. None yet had been able to answer the questions that blew in her sometimes like hail. She'd seized now on the hope that the heretic de Spinoza might.

She'd carried the letter to the courier this morning, her brother's words rumbling within her even as she walked, forgiving her. *You're like a coin made out of stone . . . a house made out of honeycombs or feathers or maybe glass.* If only Isaac's impish spirit could steal its way into her, replacing the clenched, balking soul she herself possessed. The wrong one of them had lived, for Isaac had been finer than she.

She'd sent the letter to Amsterdam; there was no calling it back.

She stood at the threshold, the Mahamad's pamphlet in her hand . . . *nor shall they allow strangers to see their hair but instead shall keep it covered on the byways of the city. Nor shall the members of the community take their entertainment in the theaters.*

Stepping indoors, she closed the heavy door behind her and shed her cloak; then dropped the pamphlet into the rabbi's fire and watched as its edges curled. Yellow flames with dark cores danced through the words, two at a time, ten at a time. Then the page heaved, blackened and whitened at once, and dissolved.

"It's a puzzle."

A soft sound escaped her. She'd thought the rabbi asleep.

He sat in the shadowed corner. His face was raised toward the empty light of the window across from his chair. He reminded her of a bird awaiting a current that would lift him into the white sky. He spoke softly. "Why does God create in fire a hunger for paper . . ."

She tensed.

". . . and yet that hunger is never sated while the fire lives?"

He waited for her response, then sighed. "I will pray to understand God's mysteries."

"I was burning a proclamation of the Mahamad," she said softly. "It regarded only women's clothing and theater and such matters."

"I am certain," said the rabbi, "that you burn only what must be burned."

She didn't answer. She let the noise from beyond the window reign. A laden dray passing down the narrow street, a cart edging past in the opposite direction. A clamor of iron-clad wheels on stone. "A woman visited here while you were out," the rabbi continued. "The widow Isabella Mendoza. She's in London to see a cousin, but wished to speak to me. She claimed she'd sent more than one letter this past year proposing that she find a match for you. She was sorely insulted to receive no reply."

"Perhaps," the rabbi said, "her letters were lost in the delivery?"

Outside, a vendor calling for kitchen scraps: *Any kitchen stuff have you, maids, any kitchen stuff, any—*

"I'm sorry," she said.

He considered, then nodded. "I believe you, Ester. And forgive."

She waited.

"I told her I would think about her offer and give my reply."

She stiffened, her spine a stave. She pushed her palms away from her body as though to shove away the words. "I don't want it," she said. "Not now."

The rabbi's face was turned toward her. She felt the growing weight of his thoughts.

Could she walk out right now without his knowledge? Leave him to address the empty room?

"Then what is your wish for the future?" he said.

She spoke more quickly than she'd intended. "I have no wishes."

A flicker of a smile crossed his face at her defiance, but gave way to solemnity. "But what of marriage?" he said.

The sounds from the street had drained away.

"I will die," said the rabbi in the silence.

She took a step toward the door but could not bring herself to leave him alone.

"This household will dissolve," he said. "My nephew will not maintain it after my death." He raised a hand to his temple, and his splayed fingers prisoned his face. "I've been selfish. I've ignored your well-being for the sake of my own."

"But—"

He lowered his hand. "The skills you've practiced here are useless to a wife. They will repel suitors, as I've known. And yet I've let you continue, and so dimmed your prospects. Ester, you are"—he gestured—"a remarkable pupil. Perhaps you don't know it, but I, who have taught many, do." His mouth worked. "To study with an able mind is to escape prison, for a time."

With a resolve that filled her with dread, he continued. "I so prized your love for learning and my own, I let myself forget the cost to you. Marry, Ester. You have my permission, my urging. And my apology."

"For what?"

"For allowing you to blight your life."

"It was my wish," she said. "It *is* my wish."

He shook his head. "It's fear that speaks in you now. You've lost much, so you fear losing this home as well. I understand. But Ester, there is no other future for you. After my death, Rivka can go on to wash or bake or labor in the household of a wealthy family. And you? Is your constitution strong enough to labor all your days for bread? Rivka thinks it isn't, and I believe she speaks honestly. She reports you grow dizzy with the exertions such labor requires." Slowly, slowly, he shook his head. "I cannot be selfish any longer. I cannot condemn you to such a life or such a death."

His words closed on her, a heavy lid.

"In years to come," he said softly, "you'll be glad of the choice. You'll have someone to see after you in your old age, Ester, as I've had you." He turned in his seat, and raised a hand toward her. "I won't deny you the blessing that you and Rivka have given me. I say it even though I know the loss of our study together will grieve you." He pressed his lips together. "It grieves me."

"Perhaps," he began, and halted. "Perhaps long after I'm dead, after you have raised children, if it is the will of God, you may find some small leisure for study once more."

She spoke, the words hollow. "You'll be left in darkness."

He nodded. Then added, "I'll do what is in my power to secure you a good match."

She laughed aloud.

Startled, he seemed to choose his words with care. "Your mother was spoken of as a beauty. Surely you cannot be so ill favored that a husband wouldn't wish your care."

How strange that the rabbi could know her these years, yet have no notion of the color of her eyes or complexion. "My form is neither pleasing nor displeasing," she said. "But I've let the world see how little I care for its verdict."

"The widow Mendoza," he said slowly, "tells me there is some young man of the community who, she promises, won't shun you for the work we've done together, provided you now turn your attention away from it to tend his home. She was careful not to give me his name, as neither I nor the young man in question has yet employed her or agreed upon a fee. So at the moment, Ester, I have only her word on the matter. But I think, whether or not her meddling was wished for, she's sincere in believing a match might be possible."

The rabbi's face was inscrutable. The fire beside him had settled to coals. Ester made no move to revive it.

"I understand well your wish to study, Ester, but you must consider your choices. I cannot pretend God created you a man, who might earn his keep as a scholar." He paused. "God has planted in us endless hungers. Yet we master them in order to live. So I was forced to master my own wishes, after the loss of my sight made it impossible that I would become the scholar I wished to be, or the father of a family." His voice had dropped to nearly a whisper. "I'm sorry. I led you to believe you could be a scholar. You were a fine one."

A helpless fury took her. "As were you," she said. "But now there will be none to write the words from your lips."

He bowed his head. "I won't force you to marry, Ester. But neither will you scribe for me any longer." In the thin light from the window his skin was almost translucent. "In my selfishness I've sinned against you. I ask your forgiveness."

In a blinding swath of tears she rose, not knowing where she went. She took her cloak and left, the door standing open behind her.

OUTSIDE, A CITY TORN BY warm gusts. The heavy sea-coal smoke had lifted visibly, like a draped fabric suddenly lofted high over the city. Above the street, sheets of it shredded slowly, floating like the tissue of some living thing. The noxious odors of the kilns and tanneries were being blown far off to the countryside today, it seemed, and a fresh wind was blowing in, leaving the air bright and confusing. All of London was in the streets, nags pulling clattering carts to the distracted calls of their drivers, flocks of pigeons rousing and settling in great restless waves.

She cast her way along the alleys, her vision still blurred. Where now? She'd no destination in mind. She knew only that she had to escape this congestion of noise and traffic. To the park, then — she'd been there twice with Mary, who loved to show herself beneath its leafy canopies. She knew the way, though she was accustomed to seeing it pass from the window of Mary's coach. She walked swiftly to stop her eyes from filling: Cheapside, Newgate, Holborn, but as the streets narrowed, the people seemed only to grow in number. In her blindness it seemed that the rills of strangers emerging from side streets had come only to gape at the unnatural girl from Amsterdam who would not wed. She shook off the thought — she was invisible amid this tide of city dwellers.

Reaching the park, she saw its paths were already full, as though this first taste of spring warmth were a universally acknowledged holiday. Workers in stained aprons or smudged eyeglasses were out taking the air, and the menagerie included animals as well as people: spaniels trotted on the leash, solemn greyhounds paced before gossiping owners, and a shirted monkey in a harness trailed the old man who pulled it, making its way along the path with jerky, wheeling steps. Coaches and horses lined the edge of the park, and amid them, she saw the da Costa Mendeses' — Mary, she thought with a burst of self-pity, must have found some other escort, one better suited to her temperament.

She cast her way along the path. Strangers walked before and behind her, shouts of jollity rose up from knots of people, the smell of churned dirt was in her nose. Across the open greenery strolled cross-tides of Londoners, some in finery: painted faces, elaborately curled wigs. Gatherings of the well-dressed and the plain drifted, separating and reattaching like the flocking birds, like the smoke high above.

How long did she walk? Fear crowded out thought, and without thought there was no time or sequence, only faces, and the rhythm of her feet on soft dirt, and more faces, and the babble of strangers.

Then, among the faces, Mary's—and then, dizzying her, others she knew. She stopped as they hailed her: four couples carrying parcels—food for a midday meal in the open air. Mary, on the arm of Manuel HaLevy, glanced at Ester and then away. There was a tight expression on her face that Ester hadn't the heart to wonder about, though perhaps it had something to do with her companion. Manuel HaLevy, in turn, stared at Ester in the keen hard-eyed manner Ester had all but forgotten, for it had been more than a year now since the HaLevy brothers had last visited the rabbi's home. Nearly tripping on his elder brother's heels was Alvaro HaLevy, grown from a puppyish boy to a puppyish young man. On his arm, a tall, impatient-looking girl whom Ester had seen in the synagogue, the daughter of the Cancio family. Alvaro stared at Ester as though she'd stepped out of a dream. A look of misery and longing swept his face and he faltered, forcing his companion to stumble to a halt.

"Good afternoon," he said to her in English.

She answered with a nod.

Instantly he was alert. "You're not well?"

With his fawn-colored coat and matching boots, his soft curling wig and pale cheeks and slight body, he looked like a boy playing at adulthood. She told herself to move along; she'd no wish to speak to him. He couldn't help her.

"You're unwell," he affirmed, eyes widening.

"I'm well in body," she said.

He turned to his companion and with a few words detached himself. With a glum expression, the girl followed the others to the bench they were making for, looking back once with visible curiosity.

"Even if you don't wish for my company," said Alvaro, falling in beside Ester, "I thank you for the excuse to step away." Ester was surprised at the soft mischief that lit Alvaro's face, though in an instant he'd sobered, as though afraid of his own honesty.

"Why not go to her," she spat, "and enjoy your wooing."

He opened his mouth to speak, then closed it.

She shook her head, shamed by her own spite. There was no need to vent her fury on one who would never be bold enough to defend himself. Yet she hated him for the simple reason that, regardless of his lack of boldness, the broad road of life lay open to him. She stopped on the path and turned to face him. "Why do you walk with me?" she asked in a low voice. "Go to that one"—she pointed to the beribboned girl on the bench—"or another girl. Go to ten girls, go to a hundred. Find a bride."

His shock showed on his pale face. But instead of hurt or anger or bewilderment, he had turned alert. He was reading her expression, hesitant, as if seeking permission to speak as he wished. "I would marry," he said, "if I were wise enough—"

"*I* would not," she snapped.

He held her gaze uncertainly, as though his eyes might utter the words his lips dared not speak.

The others had decided to set out for a farther spot and were calling for him to join; Ester heard Manuel shouting some mockery to his brother, though his words were lost to the breeze. Alvaro's companion had stood from the bench, her irritation legible in her stance even from a distance.

"I'm cursed," he whispered to Ester. "I shall never have what I wish."

"Why?" she said, loud. And as she saw his eyes widen with struggle, the thought struck her that he was her unnamed suitor.

A pitiable trust washed his face, and she had no answer for it.

Around them, strangers' voices like surf.

"I'm cursed," Alvaro repeated at last. His shining eyes dropped from hers.

She watched him return to the young woman at the bench, who took his arm and hurried them down the path toward the others.

A sick feeling in her stomach.

She could marry a soul like Alvaro. He would be kind to her. He had wealth. Her life would be graced.

Yes—but had the widow Mendoza not said that this suitor required that Ester renounce her studies?

Once, before the fire had burned away all pretense, she might have become the sort of wife who would shutter her desire to learn, keep a civil tongue, profess happiness with what was available to her. She was no longer that person. The human heart—her mother's, her grandmother's, her own—was a chaos of desire. And she could counter it only with the life in her mind. By living in words and books and cool reason. Recording the map traced by her thoughts, though it be an infinitesimal gesture, small and unseen. A fingernail's scrape on a prison wall.

The prospect of sheeplike Alvaro HaLevy and a house full of his children, their eyes trained on her while she pretended to be what she was not, made her walk faster. She couldn't marry Alvaro. She would come to punish him out of her own discontent.

She was unnatural; so it must be.

She walked on. After a time she recognized the crawling in her belly as hunger. She'd no money to pay the vendors who sold rolls and oranges from laden trays. She'd left the rabbi's without anything but her thin cloak. Now the air was cooling, and although the park was still alive with those loath to let go the day, the crowds had begun to depart.

A weightless dusk stole over the green. What had she imagined—how did she think to sustain herself? Away from the food and shelter of the rabbi's household mere hours, and already she faltered. The truth choked her: the rabbi had been correct. What choice did she have in this world, but marry or else give her life over to the crushing labors of a housemaid?

For some moments, without realizing it, she'd been watching a portly woman walking slowly in a cloak and dressing gown. A sable tippet was draped about her shoulders, her hands were buried in a fur muff, and a black felt mask covered the upper part of her face. Some lady of wealth, no doubt, unable to resist the freedom of the balmy air but loath to be recognized in her dressing gown—another soul leaning for just a moment into the freedom of the damp, greening park.

As their paths converged on a shallow rise, Ester noted something familiar in the ponderous gait, the soft jowls, the head held obstinately high. Ester reached the woman, who stopped her laborious progress.

From behind the mask, watery dark eyes found Ester. "Today," the woman said after a moment, "London's air may be breathed."

Catherine da Costa Mendes, Mary's mother. From behind the black mask, she gazed into Ester's eyes with the peaceable blankness of one struggling too much to judge or be judged. The sloping path, Ester saw, was her master.

"I'm glad to see you well enough to venture abroad," Ester said. Such direct reference to Catherine's health, she knew, might be improper. But she'd no strength in her for delicacy.

Catherine snorted in grim appreciation. "I'm not," she said, "well enough. Yet I chose to accompany Mary on this excursion. And Mary awaits me now, I'm sure, with little patience." With her chin, she indicated the edge of the park, where her daughter was presumably already seated in the waiting coach. A moment later she looked back at Ester— and a silent acknowledgment of all that Mary was and was not passed between them.

Catherine leaned heavily on her walking stick, each of her soft breaths audible. The light was fading, and the park was fast emptying of the women who considered their honor too precious to be left out after dusk. A trio hurried past, lifting their trailing gowns, their speed curtailed by their elegant shoes; they glanced at Ester and Catherine with curiosity. Ester watched them cross the last margin of grass and reach the street, one turning to the others, her speech indistinguishable from this distance save a high laugh of relief. Most of those wandering the paths about them now were men, and the better dressed stepped briskly.

"You've been walking without purpose," Catherine said. "I've seen. But surely you have one."

"I've come to see the greenery," Ester said.

She could sense that Catherine was taking her measure, though the older woman's eyes were hidden behind her mask.

"Let us not be polite," Catherine said. "I no longer have breath for lies." When she was able to continue, her words were flinty. "Lies served me, in my time. Now they peel away. Nor do I have tolerance anymore for idle gossip . . . a change that vexes my daughter greatly." She breathed. "The least of the thousand things that vex her, to be sure." She searched Ester's face and nodded at what she found there. "You and I risk nothing by speaking the truth. It will not take long, you see, for any words you speak to go with me to the grave. And I"—a fierce expression tightened her face for a moment, before loosening its hold—"I should like to hear truth."

The park was quiet. Even like this, masked and struggling for air, Catherine still had the erect, stern bearing of a woman whose judgments others feared.

A broad laugh broke the surface of the quiet. Two women, dressed in low bodices and scarlet skirts that advertised their trade, were leading patrons into a stand of trees.

Ester spoke first. "Why do you press Mary to choose me as a companion? When she summons me now, she tells me it's upon your insistence."

Catherine bowed her head, then spoke with slow force. "You may think of me what you wish for what I'll now say. But know that I am no fool easily swayed by shadows and portents." She waited for Ester's nod of acquiescence, then spoke without pity. "I dreamt I was in my grave. And yet I saw through the eyes of a bird on the rooftops, and I saw that Mary was in need of aid. I dreamt I flew from roof to roof looking for one who could help my daughter." She breathed. "There was no one. So the dream ended, Ester. With no one."

The twilight had inked Catherine's mask to a yet deeper black. For a moment Ester indulged the notion that someone else looked out from behind it—someone dear to Ester, someone she belonged to. Could Catherine know how near her vision had trod to Ester's own dreams, which too often raked her sleep? Her mother in her green dress, with her wounded glance; her father with his velvet eyes, calling her name. Her brother upon the docks, his voice echoing with some urgent request.

To push back shadows with the hard edge of reason, she spoke. "I don't believe dreams instruct us," she said. "They confuse and weaken, and are false signs."

Catherine weighed Ester's boldness for a moment. "You're wise, perhaps, not to heed them," she said. "Nonetheless, I have not forgotten this one dream, which differed from any other that has visited me in all my years. Mary will need a friend. I want you to be one to her."

Ester drew a sharp breath. How foolish she'd been to think for even a moment that Catherine might care for her well-being. To a woman like Catherine da Costa Mendes, Ester could never be other than a servant —a salve for Mary's troubles.

"Mary has all she needs," Ester said, obstinacy rising in her voice. "Even if she doesn't marry, she'll have an inheritance and everything she requires. It's not she who deserves pity."

She'd rarely dared utter the word, not after the deaths of her parents, nor even of her brother. But now a toothed hunger seized her. *Pity*. A charity none save the rabbi had troubled to offer.

Catherine took a step back as if to shield herself from Ester. "I birthed five children," she said. Below the outline of her mask, the set of her mouth had tightened. "Did you know that? Only Mary, my youngest, lived past six years."

Ester's face would not submit to her will.

"Hear me, Ester. I cannot be mother or shepherd to another soul. The world has crowded all but the last breath from me. I've no pity to spare for you, though you might merit it." Catherine breathed. "I've no pity left," she murmured, "for any on this earth." A moment later she added simply, as though to explain something to herself once more, "It's spent."

"What of your husband?" Ester said. "He can help Mary."

"My husband," said Catherine, "will hardly think of Mary after I die. He remembers her but little now, while I am still living to remind him. So I require another to look after her—and I cannot entrust the task to a girl with her own prospects."

A high laugh escaped Ester. "I have prospects, though it must surprise you. I have a suitor. And yet I've told the rabbi I refuse to marry."

Catherine pursed her lips. "Then you're a fool. How will you live?"

Ester said quietly, "I wish to study."

There was a small sound of surprise from Catherine. After a moment, she lifted her walking stick and continued up the rise.

Slowly they climbed. To one side, behind bushes, the rustle of some struggle on the grass—a dim cry of ecstasy or dismay. The park was transformed; lanterns had been lit by figures gathered on the edge of the green, but the safety they promised was still distant, and the calls of those who held them were remote and the names they called as unrecognizable as if in another tongue. Ester moved through the dark,

matching Catherine's slow pace; whatever fate might bring, they would
be at its mercy.

Abruptly, Catherine stopped. "I *have* seen it," she said, "though perhaps never so brazenly as you might wish to imagine. A woman may in
some circumstances acquire what she desires without the protection of a
man." She regarded Ester. "If you find a way to live as you wish, unnatural though it might be, you'll carry on your shoulders the weight of a
thousand wives' wishes. Though aloud all may curse you as a very devil."

The boughs overhead had nearly dissolved against the sky. In the
dark, Catherine's face and her mask seemed indistinguishable.

"Then look for any window that opens, Ester." A soft, rasping cry for
breath. "Any crack through which you may lever yourself." In the silence,
then, a rustle of cloth: Catherine, leaning hard on her walking stick
with one arm, was raising the other. Cool, trembling fingertips brushed
Ester's cheek, once, before falling away.

They reached the verge of the park, and left it behind.

From the da Costa Mendeses' coach window, her shoulder jostling
gently against Catherine's, Ester watched the city settle into night. On
the bench across from them, as they bumped through the streets, Mary
peered curious and sullen, first at her mother, then Ester. Outside, the
winds that had whipped London into unrecognizable form had subsided at last, and all was still.

WHEN SHE ENTERED, THE RABBI was by his fire as though he'd not
moved in all the hours since her departure. Rivka had piled his hearth
high and the room danced with an orange light not customary for this
hour.

"God has preserved you," the rabbi said hoarsely. "I could not rest."

She closed the heavy door softly behind her. Slowly she hung her
cloak on a peg.

With effort the rabbi stood from his chair. His form was skeletal,
and it unfolded painfully. "What angel saw you safe past the thieves and
cutthroats?"

"I won't marry," she said.

There was sorrow on his face. "It's as I thought," he said. "Ester. I've
wronged you."

She said nothing.

For a long time there was no sound other than the hollow rushing of the fire. Then the rabbi groped for the walking stick that leaned against the wall. "As you are silent, so will I be."

Slowly he began his progress across the room to the hall, to his dim bedroom.

She wanted to follow at his heels, light a lamp he didn't need, set the pillow beneath his head. Instead she lit a rushlight in the hearth and, holding it before her with wintry hands, climbed the stair.

15

December 17, 2000
London

S HE LIFTED THE PAGE CLOSER to read the too-faint printout.
Here I begin.
She had, right here on her desk, a piece of autobiographical
writing by a seventeenth-century Sephardic Jewish woman. Aaron had
been correct, of course: this was a remarkable find, she'd known it the
moment she'd heard his final telephone message yesterday morning.

Only that message could have compelled her out of the torpor she'd
fallen into upon her return from Dr. Hammond's office. As always, she'd
taken the first appointment of the morning so as to be past his chastise-
ments early; she'd planned to drive straight from his office to the rare
manuscripts room. Instead, leaving Dr. Hammond's office, she'd been
seized by an insurmountable fatigue that left her scarcely able to focus
on the road. She drove clutching the wheel, only half aware of the other
cars drifting around hers — a sudden fragility caging her as though she
must not, at all costs, be jostled into reconstructing Hammond's words
— or worse, the expression with which he'd said them. Without meaning to, she drove not to the university but to her home. She climbed the
impossibly steep steps and unlocked the narrow door to her flat, every
movement leaden. In truth, she hadn't slept properly for weeks. Was her
fatigue the crack Dr. Hammond had perceived in her armor, his cue that
today was the day to press his point at last, insisting that she comprehend? She entered her flat. Gained the kitchen and then the long, cool
hallway. Reached, finally, the bedroom, where she lowered herself onto
the bed she'd slept in for forty years. What if — her thoughts turned
slowly, shadows moving in the depths — she didn't go to her office to-

day? What if she simply chose not to face the mountain of exhilarating, terrorizing documents she now knew she wouldn't have the strength to climb? Shutting her eyes, she let the clock's tick slowly fill her hearing to the brim; and under its weight she finally capitulated, and slipped into the sleep so many nights had denied her.

It had taken that third message—the one in which Aaron impatiently recited several lines from a document he urgently wanted her to see—to rouse her. She'd steeled herself into her shoes, into her car, through traffic. Greeting him at her office, she'd barely been able to speak, let alone find the proper words to acknowledge what was plain: Yes. He was right. Yes. This cross-written document he'd just discovered did violate everything that was known about the lives, literacy, and worldview of seventeenth-century Sephardic women.

She owed Aaron Levy, at the least, a strong show of appreciation. Instead, right here in her office, seated opposite him, in full awareness of the potential of the discovery they were making together, she'd lost him.

He'd brought it on himself. But if she'd ever imagined there might be pleasure in seeing Aaron Levy's arrogance humbled, she'd been wrong. For once he'd made no eye contact, his lean frame bent in defeat. He'd handed her his translation, mumbled "You need a new printer cartridge," and left her office without another word.

After Aaron had left, she sat in her office, listening to the steady thrum of the heater, her hands loose on the fabric of her skirt, her eyes unable to settle on any one thing. It had taken her a full ten minutes to calm herself enough to turn to the pages on her desk. When she did, she was stricken to see what Aaron had been referring to: the printout of the transcription was so faint as to be barely readable. The imprint of a seventeenth-century mind and spirit, lost for almost three and a half centuries and finally salvaged ... only to be thwarted by her drained printer cartridge. It was almost funny. But nothing was funny to her, nothing had funny for years. Was that the problem? Was it her humorlessness—her stiffness—that had prevented her from giving Aaron his due when he'd presented his findings? Was that why he'd left with that humbled air she never expected from Aaron Levy, his moment of triumph turned to defeat? When had she become such a mirthless, ungiving person?

She knew when it had become irreversible. She remembered precisely when it had happened. It was the spring, four years ago, shortly after she'd learned of Dror's death. She'd read of it in an article so brief it was barely an article, just two paragraphs in a newspaper she'd found on the Internet while searching for Dror's name — something she'd still been in the habit of doing from time to time, at her computer on the small wooden desk in her bedroom.

The news report, which had been published three months earlier, referred to Dror as a "businessman" and this almost made her laugh aloud, before she read further.

Dror, the report said, had died when his car accidentally went off the road somewhere outside Moscow.

At first she'd not believed that Dror could die without her knowledge. She, who had no patience for theories of the paranormal, could not comprehend that the world could be emptied of Dror's face, his body and hands and eyes, without her sensing it. Yet there were the words.

It hadn't been an accident — of that she felt certain. If Dror's car had veered to its destruction, it was because he'd been run off the road while doing something covert, something he or his superiors hoped would save lives.

His body, the report said, had been released by the Russians in exchange for something. Later, she wouldn't be able to recall what. In the weeks to come, drifting off to sleep or waking in the middle of the night, she became confused, even, about which one of them had died. She'd be stricken in half-sleep by the image of Dror pausing somewhere amid his work or even at a meal with his vibrant family to recall Helen with a pang of sorrow — and the desire to spare him that grief rose in her like dark well water until she woke, drowning — and sat awake in her nightdress, disoriented, turning the pages of her volume of Shakespeare's sonnets.

> *Nay, if you read this line, remember not*
> *The hand that writ it, for I love you so*
> *That I in your sweet thoughts would be forgot*
> *If thinking on me then should make you woe.*

She'd readily have sacrificed her place in Dror's heart—erased all memory of herself—if it would have eased him. But Dror had never forgotten her. Of that she was certain.

That spring was when she'd first felt the drag on her foot. It had started with the lightness of a touch, slight but insistent—as though someone who loved her with a great and abiding gentleness had rested two fingers on the top curve of her right foot as if to say, *Are you certain?*

She'd had to lift the foot consciously, the light press of the fingers giving way without protest: a loving presence that did not overrule her.

Then the whole foot grew reluctant. She'd stand up out of bed to find its weight grown heavier each morning. But though it dragged, she insisted on walking forward, and always it submitted to her will.

The doctors used words like *radiculopathy* and *idiopathic*—terms that sounded like jeers until she registered their meaning: not that her symptoms were *ridiculous* or *idiotic*, but rather that the doctors couldn't pinpoint their origin. Still, she knew that because her doctors couldn't explain her symptoms they disbelieved her, not directly but faintly, with a patronizing politeness she felt was worse than mockery. Only a year later, after she'd grown pale and stiff and had mastered the art of masking both pain and tremors before her colleagues, had the diagnosis been pronounced. She'd received it wordlessly, to the discomfort of Dr. Hammond, who seemed unnerved by her failure to ask questions. But she'd asked nothing then. Just as she'd asked nothing of Dr. Hammond yesterday, rebutting his lecture with silence.

It was Friday now, and almost noon. She sat at her desk, Aaron's transcription in her hands. The echo of yesterday's argument still rang in her mind. She couldn't reconstruct the channels through which Aaron —or perhaps she?—had arrived at the subject of Dror. All she could retrieve was the feeling of it: like something rising up inside her and spilling—unstoppable because she didn't want to stop it.

She told herself to focus. She'd nearly finished fighting her way through a dozen student papers from her Early Modern History course; she needed to clear her desk and her mind for the documents, which she expected would consume all her remaining force. In truth, attempting to work her way through the documents quickly enough to fend off Wilton and his team was hopeless. Aaron Levy would presumably announce his resignation in an e-mail today—that was the style of his generation, to communicate via the safety of pixels on a screen. Or perhaps he'd simply fail to show up to the rare manuscripts room, leaving the obvious unspoken. She couldn't say at the moment whether she was sorry to see him go. But it was clear his departure would be a significant blow to her work, possibly a fatal one.

Fretfully she raised the transcription to the light, the better to read the faint print.

> *The words that leave my hand are my life.*
> *I've brought forth no other life in my days, and believe I shall not.*

In the dim light of her office, she was seized by an irrational premonition. She half rose from her desk to shake it. The transcription in her hands frightened her. She eyed it charily, as though the faint words on the page might have the power to overturn not only the received wisdom of seventeenth-century scholars, but what she thought she knew about her own life.

A loud knock.

She took up her cane, attempted to steady herself. Then, obedient as a girl, opened the door.

"Good morning," Jonathan Martin said.

"Good morning." Her voice sounded thin.

Despite not being particularly tall, Jonathan Martin occupied Helen's doorframe with a tall man's authority. Beneath his thick, graying hair, his face was lined but notably healthy-looking—how was it that Martin always looked sun-tinged, as though he'd just returned from vacationing in some warmer clime? He stood before her: fashionable rimless glasses, thick gold wedding band, the line of his shirt straight where it was tucked in beneath his open jacket—no trace of the paunch one would expect in a man his age.

His smile made her flinch.

"I thought I'd let you know that Brian Wilton and his group begin in the rare manuscripts room today. I trust their access to the documents won't interfere with yours."

"Do you?" she said.

"Of course I do," he replied. "Adding Wilton's energies to the mix is all for the good of the work."

She stood as tall as she could. "Don't you *for-the-good-of-the-work* me."

"I'm a bit surprised at your possessiveness," Martin replied mildly. "The more people studying these documents, the better, don't you think?"

Of course she didn't think, and neither would Martin or any other ambitious academic in her shoes. But she held her tongue. Jonathan Martin was a master at his game. He knew that whatever her reputation—and her staunch defense of departmental requirements, her insistence on diversifying the list of acceptable qualifying languages, and a half dozen other hard-fought battles over the years had indeed earned her a fierce reputation—Helen Watt did not make scenes. She might frost an opponent with disdain, yes, but she could be relied on not to shout into the wind. Martin had her boxed, and evidently he'd come personally to deliver his message in order to enjoy it. Helen, it seemed, had rankled him over the years more than she'd known. Under other circumstances she'd have considered this a compliment.

Martin was watching her from behind those rimless lenses. "You'll be retiring this year, won't you?" he said. "And we all know these documents will take more than a few months to study."

"I can still work after I retire," she said evenly. "I can translate and publish without being on the university's dole. All I require is ongoing library access."

Martin smiled again, at a dimmer wattage—his setting for compassion. "It's not practical, Helen. You're a practical woman."

It stung, as of course he'd intended it to sting: the use of her name, the implied intimacy with her qualities, and—after two and a half decades in which she couldn't recall Martin referring to her as anything but a "scholar" or "colleague"—the reference to her as a *woman*. All intended to erode the pilings on which she stood.

She watched Martin walk down the hall and, with a dapper knock, disappear into Penelope's office.

THE RARE MANUSCRIPTS ROOM WAS already inhabited, as she'd expected, by Wilton and his three postgraduates. They were bent over the center table together, two on each side. There was one woman, mousy with pale pink lipstick on her thin lips, and two young men—and of course Wilton himself, barely older than his students. How long had it been since her path had crossed Wilton's? Perhaps two years—had it been that long since Helen had stopped attending faculty meetings? She noted immediately that all three of the men, including Wilton, had gorgeous hair. Wilton's was a dark glossy brown and proceeded in ripples from the crown of his head, whorling down to brush his ears. Where did a historian get such hair? Luxuriant without being effeminate. His two male acolytes sported more modest coifs, but it was clear neither was indifferent to style. Only the girl looked wilted enough to be a true work of nature.

Until this moment she'd had nothing against Wilton, except perhaps that he was a type. As a postgraduate he'd laughed heartily and with apparent sincerity at his mentors' jokes, concurred wittily with the majority at such meetings as postgraduates attended, and volunteered his labors more regularly than any of his cohort. Despite this, he'd been well-liked among his fellow students. Once she'd been sitting on a bench near the entrance to the department, catching her breath unseen before venturing the walk to her car, when Wilton had clasped the shoulders of two other male students not twenty yards from where she sat (so invisible was she) and, jerking his head in the direction of the portly middle-aged secretary who had just passed en route to the car park, muttered something about being able to tell a battle-axe by the number of hooks on her brassiere. "There's not a female in the History Department," he'd intoned, "with fewer than three hooks. Our tragedy is not to be in Romance languages. Did you see Castleman's latest protégé at the holiday party? A silk blouse and straps made of dental floss."

The others had chortled and Wilton had been in the midst of clapping one on the back when he'd seen Helen on her bench, looking directly at him.

He'd had the decency, she recalled, to color. But she was certain the incident didn't stay with him long. Such men didn't concern themselves greatly with remorse. Aaron, she thought, would fit right in. In fact, if he had any sense he'd join their group.

Steeling herself, she stepped past Wilton's lavishly tressed crew, resolving not to crane her neck in a transparent attempt to learn which documents they were reading. Yet even with her eyes fixed forward, it was a simple thing to tally the magnitude of her defeat. Pencils scratched audibly from Wilton's table—formerly *her* table. Four pencils jotting notes; four brown cushions. Wilton's team was translating *four* documents at once. She could not possibly succeed on her own in ferreting out Aleph's story before Wilton's team did.

She didn't bother telling herself it shouldn't matter who was first. It mattered deeply. She wanted to ball her stiff hands and turn all their hair-gelled heads with a harsh cry: This is *mine*.

She'd stopped walking. Without intending to, she'd turned back, a few paces beyond the end of their table, to face them.

All three postgraduate students were looking at her blankly. Wilton glanced up, offered a vague nod, and had almost returned to his work when he recognized her and froze. After a delay of a millisecond, he offered a pained smile.

He lifted a hand, then—what *was* he doing?—and offered a casual salute, no doubt meant to appear jovially competitive. *Hail, fellow, well met, and may the best scholar win.* It was a sporting gesture: nothing personal, of course, but naturally he wouldn't wish to hear her theories about the documents until he'd established his own . . . after which, it need not be said, he'd be able to claim full credit for them, for there would have been no collaboration.

She let his gesture bounce off the stiff planes of her own face, and fall.

He smiled again, more briefly this time, and with an uncertain tug at one cuff of his blazer returned his eyes to his work.

Helen crossed to the librarian's desk, where she took a pencil stub and paper slip, wrote the number of the document she wished to view, and passed the slip over the desk to Patricia Starling-Haight.

Patricia glanced at the number. "That's in use," she said.

Helen felt her lips part drily with surprise. A few hours in the library, and already Wilton had arrived at the document it had taken two weeks

for her and Aaron to reach. She would not have thought her obsoles-
cence would be so swift.

She waited to speak until she was sure she'd mastered her voice. "I'll
take the next document in the catalogue, then."

Patricia didn't move. "Why don't you ask him if you can see the one
you want?"

Helen raised her chin. What was the point of all her strict upbringing if she couldn't at least muster imperious dignity where the situation
called for it? "*He*," she said, "is not my ally in this matter."

Patricia's lips tightened into a small ring of mirth. She lowered her
spectacles and stared at Helen. Helen could not recall the last time
someone had laughed in her face.

"I was under the impression that he was your *sole* ally. Frankly it was
good to see you had one."

From across the desk, Helen looked into Patricia's face. She had been
looking into Patricia's round, staunch face from across this desk, she
realized, for two decades. Only now did it occur to her, with an absurd
shock, that for all that time Patricia had been looking back.

"Professor Martin," said Helen in lower tones, "has made his deci-
sions regarding access to the documents. I am laboring alone."

"A pity," Patricia said. But there was no pity on Patricia's face—and
Helen recognized, as though looking in a mirror, another woman who
didn't waste useless sentiment on herself or others. In place of pity,
though, something else animated Patricia's expression: honest interest.
Even the possibility, however faint, of a tough camaraderie. It occurred
to Helen for the first time that Patricia was close to her own age, and
that Patricia's orderly desk held no photographs of children or grandchildren.

"I've always thought you were one of the only non-egoists in this
place," Patricia said, her blue eyes steady. "Perhaps the sole faculty member who cares more for the past than for his own selfish present."

Helen found her voice. "Well, that's—"

But Patricia wasn't finished. "I tolerated his ill breeding in part because I believed him accountable to you." On her pursed lips, the merest
hint of a wicked smile. "Shall I confiscate his smuggled pencils now?"
she said. "Or shall we start with the mobile phone in his bag? Or the

utility knife our American Boy Scout insists on carrying on his person, or perhaps the pens he's hiding in his pockets?"

Helen turned. At a small table tucked between two projecting book-cases near the wall sat Aaron, his familiar lean form bent over a thickly inked document on a brown velvet cushion. His wooly dark head was bowed, and he was biting at the end of a pencil. Even from behind, his anxiousness was clear.

She was stunned by the relief she felt at his presence.

He raised his head, and for the first time, his face was free of ego, of hostility, of anything other than quiet, humbled uncertainty. They looked at each other. After a moment he tilted his head. It was his apology.

A laugh escaped her, a bark of reprieve.

His old cocky grin lit his face. He turned back to the document without a word.

Helen turned back to Patricia, conscious of the warmth on her own cheeks. "It seems," she said, "that I misunderstood to whom you were referring."

"It seems," Patricia said, with an admirably impassive expression, "that you did."

Leaving Patricia at her desk, Helen went to the table where Aaron sat. She read over his shoulder. The Portuguese letter was right side up on the cushion, the Hebrew inverted.

"What do you have?" she said, lowering herself into the chair beside him.

"I'm rechecking my translation now," he said in low tones. "Making some minor changes. But you need to see something else." Beside him was a second cushion with another document; he slid it toward her. "I got Librarian Patricia's unprecedented permission to have two documents out at once, don't ask me how." He raised a finger to his lips as though to swear Helen to silence. "I think she has a crush on me."

"I very much doubt that," said Helen.

How had they gone from ashen-faced anger to this strange new comfort? She wasn't sure what had happened, or even whether it was a good thing. But she knew she did not, at this moment, want to be sitting alone at this table.

"I asked to hold on to the cross-written letter," Aaron said, "because I didn't want to risk returning it and having *them* get to it before you could see it."

"You mean Wilton's group?" Helen said, intending to sound unconcerned.

Abruptly, Aaron turned to look at Wilton and his students. He turned with his whole torso, so no one in the room could miss the fact that he was looking them over.

Two of the male postgraduates looked back at Aaron uncertainly. Aaron answered with a Cheshire cat grin.

Dropping audibly back in his seat, he turned to Helen. "Bunch of weenies," he said, loud.

The rare manuscripts room was silent.

Casually, as though the entire room weren't listening, he added, "Speaking objectively, of course."

She regarded him. "I assume that's American for *May the best team win?*"

"No," he said. "It's not."

She felt their eyes on her back: Wilton's group, trying to sort out whether they'd just been mocked or invited into a joke. A faint smile formed on her lips.

It lived only a moment. Despite Aaron's bravado, she knew more than he did. Jonathan Martin could cut off their access to the documents at any point. Aaron would have to make his way in this department. He shouldn't burn bridges for her sake—a fact that surely would occur to him soon.

But here he was beside her, at least for the moment. "What's the other document?" she asked him.

"You're going to like this," Aaron said. He pulled the second cushion closer. She saw there were dark half-moons under his eyes. He looked tired, and boyish, and honest. She couldn't reconcile it with the Aaron Levy who had departed her office the day before—even then, even chagrined and defeated, he'd still had a self-righteous air. But now, for the first time since she'd met him, he looked cracked open—like a man who was out of ideas, and could only wait attentively for what might come next. When he spoke, his voice was quiet at its core, as though tempered by some setback larger than she herself could have inflicted.

"You know the Manuel HaLevy referred to in the cross-writing?" Aaron said to her quietly. "It sounds like there was a scandal involving his younger brother. Which is why the older brother came looking for him. And there are some interesting hints as to the nature of the scandal."

She lingered one moment before turning her attention to the document. She realized she understood nothing about Aaron, except that for some reason he'd bent his neck and knelt beside her on the chopping block. Had he nowhere else to go?

Good God, they had something in common.

16

March 20, 1665
4 Nisan, 5425
London

To congregate long here might be folly. Yet the sun warmed the cobbles outside the synagogue with a boldness that seemed to captivate all of them—even Rivka, who lingered heavy-lidded at the rabbi's elbow. Ester, too, lagged among the small crowd, drifting at the edge of a circle of older women.

Observed singly, the men and women milling on the street might have appeared English, albeit with some foreign ancestry. If their complexions were slightly shadowed or their faces cast in a strange mold, such differences were still readily overlooked in light of a man's coiled English wig or a woman's English dress. Yet though London's Jews might go unremarked one by one, together they were recognizable in an instant: dark-lashed almond eyes, bent noses, mouths tipped downward at the corners with some old, bittersweet knowledge.

Were they safe?

They gathered, scattered, regathered. Birds on a rooftop.

A few women near Ester were trading news of far-flung family. Ester stood half-listening, blinking at the unaccustomed brightness. Only the esteemed Rabbi Sasportas seemed immune to the seduction of this day's sun. It had become his habit to depart promptly after prayers and take his meal behind closed shutters—even now, he and his small retinue disappeared around the corner without a backward glance. Sasportas, with his heavy arched brows and ebony skullcap, the weighty pouches beneath his dark eyes, seemed to have expected a congregation that would reverently accept his authority—not politely praise his sermons, make rich gifts to the synagogue's coffers, then climb into waiting carriages and go off to their business, throwing off the Sabbath despite whatever thunder Sasportas might fling at them in the following week's sermon.

Ester listened dumbly to the women, whose talk had turned to the need for a new synagogue building—one with a proper women's balcony. Today, as it did each week, the Sabbath respite found Ester unsteady on her feet, as though she'd just stepped off a ship with surf still ringing in her ears. All week a tide of housework rose about her, sliding her this way and that as she fought with breath and limb to stay afloat. Bread and meal, ale and fuel, mending thread and needle. A full partner now in domestic labor, Ester understood at last how much Rivka had spared her while she still scribed for the rabbi.

On wash mornings she was wakened by Rivka in darkness to set a buck-basket of linens soaking in lye, then work in the kitchen while dawn came and went. On market days she walked until her feet were numb. She could negotiate prices of coal in English now and even had come to understand the repartee of the vendors in the city's marketplaces. But any more delicate thoughts scattered at the least interruption, and the books on the rabbi's shelves might as well have been behind a locked door. She was a body, laboring. Even at night in her bed, when the tide of work had ebbed and her thoughts ought have convened, they failed her. Verses that had once played in her mind now vanished—a whorl of words, dipping and spinning, gone. Sleep, of all things, had overmatched her, closing on her like shutters of oak. Passing the rabbi in his study, she'd pause only to add wood to his fire or bring him his meal. In his accustomed chair he sat, the light of his face dimmed, attending to her tread as she neared and departed, as though listening for a signal that the wrong he had wrought had been undone. She did not linger. She returned to the kitchen and washed the salt out of a block of butter. She broke up and pounded cakes of sugar, set new-milled flour to dry. She heard from Rivka one morning of the death of Catherine da Costa Mendes, and then—in tandem with Rivka, their bodies folding and turning as one—wrung a torrent of water from a sheet, and set it over the basket to dry.

In the enticing sunlight now, Mary's father, the olive-skinned and black-wigged Diego da Costa Mendes, stood conversing heartily among the men. He gave barely a glance to Mary, who stood among a cluster of beribboned girls. Mary herself gossiped gamely with her companions, yet something in her seemed newly tentative—in the snatches of conversation Ester overheard, Mary entered others' witty exchanges like a house-breaker, her words landing with graceless haste. In truth, Ester had had little chance to speak with Mary directly since Catherine's death. When Ester had carried Rivka's offerings of food to the house of mourning, the da Costa Mendeses' servants had accepted the gifts, but Mary herself had not emerged to converse—nor had she made any reply to Ester's soft greetings in the ensuing weeks, beyond a brittle nod. And Ester knew better than to join Mary's cluster of friends here outside the synagogue—the other girls had long made plain without words that Ester wasn't welcome in their gatherings. Their eyes fled her silver hair, as though her apparent ineptitude in the area of marriage might be contagious.

All Ester knew now of Mary's state was what was evident to everyone: whereas other widowers might worry over the welfare of a sole surviving child, Diego da Costa Mendes seemed to take no note of his daughter. There was little doubt he'd soon choose a young wife to bear him a new family. Only last week Ester had heard one of the synagogue's matrons say there was a lady whom Diego da Costa Mendes courted in the countryside—indeed he'd traveled there twice in the scant weeks since Catherine's death. "In the *countryside,* did you hear?" The matron's voice had dropped to a disapproving whisper. "And Catherine of blessed memory suffering all those years in the London air, and he unwilling to leave." The circle of women had shaken heads, yet said no more—for though there was little affection for the da Costa Mendes family, none wished their enmity.

Half dozing now at the verge of this cautious, all-judging circle, Ester caught fragments of the chatter of the nearby cluster of Mary's friends, their restless noise amplified by the stone wall beneath which they gossiped.

"It's sheer obscenity," said Emilia Valentia, her words gilded with delight as she played with one of her long brown curls. "So all say, and I'm certain it's true."

"And she *attended*?" said the tall, angular Cancio girl, and she led the others in a gust of laughter. The girls prolonged their merriment as though for an audience, their gazes flicking now and again across the narrow street, where several young men of the community stood in studiously casual poses of their own.

"Are you certain?" the Cancio girl continued more quietly, her surprise evidently genuine. "How could her father permit it?"

"But he accompanied her!" exclaimed Emilia. "Along with her mother! The entire family, together!"

Sarah Cancio, the heavyset matron beside Ester, had been attending to the girls' conversation as well, and now she leaned out of the group of older women to nod approvingly to her daughter. "Theater is obscenity," she called out briskly. Beneath her powder, streaked by sweat, she had an honest, impatient face. "A wretched influence for a girl, worse for her reputation. It was vile enough before they permitted women on the stage. Now who can say what audience of drunkards gathers there?"

The Cancio girl frowned and stepped deeper into the cluster of her friends, seeming to reconsider her own disapproval now that her mother had affirmed it. "Yet half London's gentlemen go, Mother," she protested. "And you say you wish me to marry well?"

Her mother gave a grim laugh. "You won't find any among us to escort you to that cesspit. Let the Christians throw their souls to the dung heap with such entertainment."

Firm nods among the other women concluded the matter: theater was not for the daughters of the synagogue.

As though at a signal, the gathering on the street at last began to disperse—the older women trading quick embraces; the girls offering hasty kisses on the lips and tidying one another's curls one final time in parting. As her friends found their families and departed, Mary trailed behind, eyes trained on her father. Diego da Costa Mendes spoke on with his companions. His daughter, Ester saw, had become as invisible to him as his ailing wife once had been. Perhaps she'd always been so.

Pain flared, sudden and unbearable, on Mary's face. Then, abruptly, her expression shut. Without warning, she turned.

"Why are you staring at me?" she charged Ester.

So accustomed had Ester grown to passing unremarked, she'd almost forgotten she herself was visible. She hesitated. Then said, "Because your father won't pay you mind."

For a moment Mary's hands worked at the fabric of her bodice, as though searching for some other place to alight. It occurred to Ester that Mary might slap her.

Instead Mary's hands alit, painfully tight—one, then the other—on Ester's wrist. "*We'll* go."

"Go where?" Ester said. But as soon as she uttered the question, she read its answer in Mary's defiant expression.

TWO DAYS LATER, ESTER CLIMBED into the coach to find Mary scanning the street through the coach's window. Mary was dressed in a blue satin that showed her rosy skin and black brows to advantage, and she sat with stiff posture—her stays, Ester saw, had been tied tight as was now in fashion, and pinched her waist cruelly. On her bosom rested a small silver cross Ester had never before seen. Many of the congregation wore such adornments when they ventured about London, but Ester was certain Mary hadn't worn such a thing while her mother lived. With a reflexive, agitated motion, Mary stroked the cross with a single finger, as though she were with each touch mustering courage to issue the world a dare that frightened her.

As Ester settled on the bench, Mary glanced past her. "What concern's it to *her* if we go?" she muttered.

Following Mary's gaze to a high window of the rabbi's house, Ester saw Rivka's shadowed form there, watching.

"She allowed me the day free of work," Ester said. "So I might accompany you."

Still staring at the form in the window, Mary cupped the cross in her palm. "You speak as though she's done me a charity."

"The demands of the house are a greater burden on Rivka without help," Ester said.

Mary snorted. "I'm raising up a member of *her* household. I'm not the one in need of her charity." She glanced at Ester. "Or anyone's!"

The carriage began to move. Ester said nothing.

"And if you think this such frivolity, why are you here?"

The street slid slowly past the carriage's window. Not knowing whether she meant to be kind or cruel, Ester heard herself say, "Because of your mother."

"What about my mother?" Mary shot back.

Ester hesitated, then spoke the words as gently as she could. "Your mother had a dream. She told me of it. She asked me to watch over you."

Mary's expression froze. "I don't believe you," she said.

Blinking, she turned to the driver—a sallow-faced, taciturn man. "Faster!" He chirruped to the horse and they lurched forward, down the narrow street and on toward Westminster.

Mary's words came quickly. "If my mother had known *your* mother was born out of wedlock, she'd not have allowed you with me."

It was the sole mention Mary had ever made of their long-ago conversation at the dressmaker's, and Ester knew the words were meant to wound—yet she registered, too, the other message they carried: that Mary had kept Ester's secret, even from her mother.

"Your mother welcomed me," Ester said, "even though she knew I'd no prospects."

"That's right," snapped Mary, "you've no prospects."

Ester said nothing.

A moment later, Mary let a hand flutter in mute apology. She said, not unkindly, "You *could* marry, I suppose." The notion seemed to give her energy. She turned to face Ester. "It's not impossible, you know, even with no dowry. You could care for an older husband. Or even perhaps have children, and if the husband is wealthy enough you might have servants while you directed the household. You could forget everything that came before your wedding day—that would be a life. Imagine it!"

The carriage crawled on along the street. Ester imagined it.

When Mary spoke again, her voice was soft. "How did she think you could help me?"

"I don't know," Ester said.

They watched the city pass. Mary gave a sudden snort. "By escorting me to obscene comedies?" She laughed then, a crazy, dark laugh. With a pang Ester recognized it: the laugh of a grieving girl, who would pull a house down on her own head to see it fall.

Even before they entered the broad carved doors of the theater, the sour smell of the assembled audience reached them. With a white hand-kerchief wrapped around her hand, Mary fingered the necessary coins with difficulty and passed them into the dirty palm of the fat-faced fare collector, who winked at Mary before taking the money. "Don't see many like you pay to watch from there," he leered as she passed. Mary retorted with a bright smile, behind which Ester saw a flicker of worry.

They were late—the entertainments were underway, the crowd pressed forward, and as Ester followed Mary into the throng, she saw that in her bravado Mary had purchased entry to the pit, among the roughest crowd. But there was no time to question Mary's choice, or how far she'd carry it. At the front of the theater the rope-dancers had begun their midair ballet: two sturdy men, faces blank with concentration, working their way in and out of the shadows over the stage. Ester had seen rope-dancers in Amsterdam, yet those had clowned and gibed as they worked. These men were solemn, even menacing, tumbling in slow, smooth spirals high above the crowd like priests of some silent and powerful religion. Over the thin accompaniment of a flute and a toneless drumbeat, the creaking of their ropes was audible. Their bodies furled and unfurled, a somber rite sculpted in air.

She pressed forward, trying to catch Mary—but Mary was piloting herself to the front of the throng, threading between the backless green benches, undaunted by the smell of open piss-pots. Bodies pushed back or gave way as Ester forged ahead to keep pace. She didn't dare look about her, but kept her chin tipped up and followed the flight above the stage. Underfoot, the crunch of oyster shells, the slick of unseen puddles. Few seemed inclined to sit—some stood on benches, many in aisles. Men jostled about them—one blindly cuffed Ester as she passed and then was hugged about his neck by a companion who shouted in his ear, "Can't tell the difference between man and wench? You need to feel for the soft bits, sirrah!" and then men on all sides let out shouts of laughter as Ester shoved blindly forward. She hurried after Mary, calling her name fruitlessly in a sharp whisper, and reached the edge of the stage an instant after her.

They stood catching their breath at the front of the pit. In the throng pressed about them, there was only a scattering of women, and it was no difficult thing to glean their livelihood from their attire. Above, in the dim and distant galleries, well-dressed ladies sat beside well-dressed gentlemen; a few had been so bold as to lift their masks to peer more closely at the rope-dancers. Ester lowered her gaze from the galleries just in time to see an orange go sailing through the air, launched by some unseen hand in the pit. It barely grazed the rope of the dancer it had been aimed for, but his body flinched from it like a mussel contracting into its shell, and for a moment he swung wide, fighting for control, his shadow looming and shrinking against the theater's wall like a man swaying on a gallows. Looming, shrinking, looming, before regaining at last his slow deliberate dance.

Beside Ester, Mary watched as in a trance.

With a dull beat from the unseen drum and an abrupt spin downward, both dancers hit the stage feet first, bowed with abrupt violence, and disappeared behind the proscenium. At this signal, costumed players swarmed the stage and shouted in unison—"And now let us all praise honest men!"

"An honest man indeed am I," intoned an actor from the center of the throng.

The play had begun, the players' speech nearly drowned by the bawdy laughter that rolled from the audience behind and above. An actor playing a character named Roderick Rogue made his way about the stage codpiece first, his face made up like a clown's. To Ester's surprise, she understood most of the rapid English banter. "If she a fool would marry, I swear I'll fool her grandly." The throng in the pit rumbled appreciation; scattered applause sounded from the balconies. The players, warming to their task, seemed to hit each new rude line at ever-higher volume, drawing encouragement from the crowd, hauling their tale from lowest humor to a plateau of dull moral pronouncements, only to plunge gleefully back again, like a ship that regained speed in the trough of each wave.

"Be a man's fortune not in his own hands?"

"And I pray, look what lies between mine!"

On stage amid the costumed men now appeared two women players in low-necked gowns, one with blond ringlets and one with brown. Cast as innocents, they parried each assault on their honor with unctuously feigned ignorance. Ester saw nothing especially provocative about them —surely their dress was hardly more immodest than that of the women in the theater's balconies—yet by simple virtue of their elevation on the wooden platform they seemed to goad and tempt the men in the pit beyond endurance. A sea of work-rough hands extended each time one of the women neared the stage's edge, as if to grab her by the ankles should she step too close.

"Vile," murmured Mary, moving so close, Ester could feel every breath she drew.

The stage cleared of other players, and now a lively man of indeterminate age with a long curled wig stood at the center, his thin face sweaty and cheeks pink as from liquor. He made a grand speech, part of it seeming improvised, as though he'd been tasked with engaging the audience while some transformation was achieved behind the proscenium's curtain. His speech, beginning with a rumination on love, "a man's worst and most delicious folly," and proceeding to detail the ideal lover's qualities, soon turned overlong. Amid a winking repetition of the requirement that a lover be generously endowed in body, a piece of refuse sailed at his head. He batted it away and continued unperturbed, which provoked further assaults from the pit, yet he went on until he'd done with his speech and exited, sweeping the refuse from the stage with the insides of his feet, making a gay dance of it. Three players emerged in his wake, then, and sang a rollicking song. "If she be not as kind as fair, but peevish and unhandy . . . Leave her, she's only worth the care of some spruce Jack-a-Dandy."

From behind, a callused hand crept about Ester's waist and immediately began to search higher. Panicking, she dug into it, hard, with the tips of all her fingernails; it withdrew in haste.

"We should leave," Mary whispered faintly. Yet she stood transfixed.

And then the singers exited and a strange vision greeted Ester's eyes.

A woman—the blond-ringleted player who'd sashayed about the stage in a bright yellow gown moments earlier—had now emerged onto the proscenium stage in a man's attire. Her hair had been gathered back and knotted behind, her breasts were concealed beneath a heavy doublet, the slenderness of her arms was masked under gilt sleeves. She might have been a particularly tender-faced courtier.

The calls of the crowd grew so loud, her words could barely be heard; she obliged by ceasing all speech and adopting a wide stance, allowing them to take in the oddity of her split legs.

"The fish has a forked tail!" a man shouted, and the player swiveled prettily in response.

The theater shook with the men's answering roar—a sound that went on and on, beating in Ester's ears.

The crowd at length quieting, the player resumed her speech. Screwing her flushed face into a facsimile of determination, she intoned her character's purpose. Some turn in the plot, the audience was made to understand, required that she perform this subterfuge: she would masquerade as a man and, by deceit, gain her suitor's confidence and learn his true feelings for her.

A woman in breeches. What power the maiden in this play had seized in one stroke, with a simple change of costume. Yet for her, the deception was all for the sake of a passing vanity: to learn the mind of an insufficiently complimentary suitor.

Had Ester such a power, she thought, she would use it otherwise.

The woman ceased her speech. And then, with a simplicity that stunned Ester, she walked out from under the proscenium, and onto the thrust stage, like a figure stepping out of a framed portrait and into the living, breathing world. And as she posed just out of reach of grasping hands, and as the other players emerged from the wings to be fooled by her costumery and the absurd story of the play wound on and on, Ester laid her hand on the stage to feel that it was real.

An idea came to her then, as simple as it was impossible. She gripped the wood until her fingers ached.

The play was ended. The audience broke up about them and poured out of the theater; the flushed, restive throng turned into men and women blinking at the bright haze at the theater's opened doors. They stepped out into the city, singly or in clusters.

Ester's hand remained on the edge of the empty stage. She could feel the theater growing quiet behind her. She let her gaze rise to the soaring dome of the roof, the emptying galleries with their elaborately carved posts. Here and there she could make out a lady's mask—delicate arched eye-holes and blank velvet face—lying discarded or forgotten.

A soft cry beside her. Ester turned, in time to glimpse Mary's face gone pale, barren and unknowable as the moon. Then Mary slumped against her.

Ester caught Mary in her arms, but could hardly hold her. Staggering back, Ester looked for a clean place to lay her. But the floor was a mess of oyster shells, and a piss-pot in the corner had overflowed, fouling the floor. With effort she pulled Mary, legs trailing, to a dry patch, then took off her own shawl and bunched it under Mary's head.

Mary's breath was shallow. Crouched awkwardly above her, Ester watched her eyelids flicker. At the far edges of the proscenium, figures moved here and there: the players setting costumes in order for tomorrow's performances. Ester cast about for help, to no avail—the remnant of audience still trailing from pit or gallery paid her no mind. Without help she'd never succeed in carrying Mary's limp weight to the coach waiting outside, nor dared she leave Mary here alone while she summoned the coachman for assistance.

Something small and hard hit her in the center of the back. She turned in time to see one of the players retreat, his slim form disappearing behind the curtain. By her feet was the cloth-wrapped object he'd thrown. She opened it and saw a dirty cube of some whitish substance. She gave it an uncertain sniff, and immediately recoiled: hartshorn. She held it beneath Mary's nose and watched her jolt awake, her lids fluttering and her lips shaping a curse.

Mary gazed at the balconies, the fouled floor, the stage, before at length seeming to recognize her surroundings. Registering the amusement on Ester's face, Mary swore again, louder. She raised herself on her elbows.

"A disgrace," Mary muttered—though it was unclear whether she was referring to the play or to her own position amid the shell fragments. Attempting to rise too swiftly, she lurched against a bench. With a scowl, keeping her eyes fixed ahead so as not to admit the indignity, she awaited assistance. Ester helped her stand, and kept a hand on her elbow to stabilize her until Mary, surveying the theater with head held high, shook herself free.

"Let me loosen your stays," Ester said.

"Don't be absurd," Mary said. "I simply overtaxed myself." When Ester shook her head sharply Mary added, glancing away as though in embarrassment, "In the garden this morning. Working."

Ester couldn't restrain a laugh. "Since when does Mary da Costa Mendes work a garden?"

"I'll claim that, my does." A man—the slim player who had thrown the hartshorn—was striding toward them on the thrust stage. Still cleaning the paint off his face with a soiled cloth, he hopped to the floor of the pit and extended a palm. Ester gave him the hartshorn.

He lowered the cloth. This was, Ester saw, the same man who'd borne the storm of refuse on stage and kept on with his rambling monologue about love. Yet shed of the puckish spirit that had animated him on stage, he was barely recognizable. The gaudy paint he'd worn still marked the channels of his face, so that he appeared petty and carved by age, a man divided into pieces. In place of his flowing wig, his own graying brown hair showed, slicked back from his face, and the years that had been disguised by his youthful grace on stage were now evident. Instead of an elaborate doublet and hose, he now wore the threadbare clothing of a man fallen from wealth. His silk shirt was darned, his velvet breeches worn.

He took in Mary, from the crown of her glossy head to her pretty mouth to the patches on her breasts, the fine shoes nested in pattens. A rakish smile lit his face. Swiftly he wiped the remaining paint from his cheeks and neck. "You're the third to go down since Lord's Day," he said to Mary. "But most of the fainting sort pay to do it in the galleries rather than the pit."

Mary's wan face had gained color; Ester watched her cast about for a witty answer. "I prefer to faint closer to the ground," she said after a moment.

"Aha! Beauty *and* wisdom." The man extended his arm. Flushing, Mary took it, and he strolled a few paces off with her as though they were on a promenade, rather than in a pit. "And you fainted, I take it, due to the power of our disquisition." He enunciated as though still on stage.

"She fainted," Ester offered, "from the shock of the crowd."

"Or it *might* have been due to the dazzling wit of the actors," he said archly to Mary. "Only you, being the proprietor of the faint, are in a position to know."

Already a flirtatious pout was forming on Mary's lips.

"Shall we go now?" Ester said. It felt urgent to dispel this stranger's charm before it took further hold.

Mary shot Ester a sour look. At this, the man turned on Ester a bright, magnanimous smile — as though she were speaking out of envy. "You can join us as well if you like. Unless my acting so offended you?"

Ester countered with an overseriousness even she could hear. "It's not any insult to your acting to say you recite the lines of a middling play by a middling playwright."

His laugh filled the hall. "Yet it's not any compliment either. I shan't ask your opinion of my acting, dear lady, for I fear it. Perhaps your other admirers enjoy barbs. But I like a lady sweet." He looked only at Ester as he spoke, but she watched his words have their intended effect on Mary, who smiled a soft, blushing smile.

Behind Mary and her companion, other players began to drift across the stage. A woman with pale frothed hair and tired eyes approached from the proscenium—hardly recognizable as the brazen actress who had just walked the stage in breeches and, with a foolish pretty speech, cracked the sky over Ester's head.

The woman, jumping down neatly from the stage, murmured, "See you tomorrow, Thomas my love," and—paying no notice to Mary on his arm—kissed him carelessly on the lips and hurried off. Mary stood agape, her expression of resentment giving way gradually to a sparking, curling curiosity.

On the stage, two men who'd emerged behind the woman lingered, clearly awaiting Thomas. One, a tall, bearded, Spanish-looking man, scowled impatiently at Thomas. The other, a slim, short-haired English-man in modest but tidy attire, had a light cap of hair and no beard. His expression was alert, his gray eyes quiet, and he observed Thomas with a thoughtful detachment that made Ester wonder if he were a student of the ministry.

"Thomas, man, what might you possibly want with two Jewesses?" the darker man said. His voice was low and amused, but as he spoke his lips curled in a half smile that seemed to Ester more dangerous than mirthful. He'd a narrow face, pale, unblinking eyes, a thick, cropped beard.

Thomas let out a shocked laugh. "Jewesses?" he echoed. Turning, he searched their faces. "But this one wears a cross."

"So do all their people who wish to hide what they are," said the darker man.

"Is it so?" said Thomas, peering into Mary's face with eager fascina-tion. But for once Mary looked away.

Alarm rose in Ester. "It is," she answered bluntly.

Thomas whistled. "A Jewess. And hens make holy water. Who thought I'd find myself a Jewess?"

The slimmer man, who stood slightly behind the others, spoke up quietly. "An honor to make your acquaintance," he said. "I'm John Til-man. You've met Thomas Farrow. And this is Esteban Bescós."

But Thomas, still laughing, was uninterested in niceties. "Heaven strike me." With his free hand he thumped the proscenium stage as though celebrating his good fortune. "A cross-wearing Jewess, and her dour keeper." He gestured vaguely at Ester—then stepped back a pace from Mary, though still holding her arm, to examine her. In confusion, Mary shrank from him—but Thomas waved to show himself harmless. As Mary straightened herself self-consciously, Ester saw Thomas's gaze fall on Mary's jeweled ring and the pearl-set bracelet draping one of her wrists.

"She's recovered now, thank you." Ester took Mary's free arm and made to depart.

Holding Mary by one arm while Ester led her by the other, Thomas kept pace with them on their way to the door. The other two men fol-lowed at a distance. "But you still have no praise for the players and all our philosophy?" he charged Ester, though his words were all for Mary. "'Tis a deep philosophy," he added, with another glance at Mary's ornate jewelry, "that lurks beneath all our wit."

"No praise," said Ester, and she pulled the heavy door open with her free hand.

"None?" he cried, and this time his indignation seemed real. "Your ignorance insults!"

"None." She banged her elbow as she tried to hold the door wide without letting go her grip on Mary. "Though if you must shout such nonsense and call it philosophy, this theater is a fine ringing shell for it." She pulled on Mary's arm.

Stopping beside Mary on the threshold, Thomas replied airily. "It's fortunate for the play it wasn't subjected to your foreigner's English," he said. "Else we'd have witnessed for the first time in history an English play hanged, drawn, and quartered."

Bescós snorted his appreciation.

"In my English," said Ester, her words tight, "your play would have enough weight to make impress in the minds of the listeners, not puff them full of a meal of spun sugar, so they leave with their bellies seem-ing full, only to feel their hunger a few minutes thence." She'd never spoken thus in English, nor had she dared so accost an Englishman. But in her impatience to return home, shyness no longer gated her speech, and the English that had grown in her these years easily breached its confines. "Once your audience realizes the play's failure," she went on, her face hot, "they're no longer in purse to purchase any true meal for the soul or the body, while you retreat with their shillings to purchase drink sufficient to float an armada. A comedy is a fine treat, so long as you serve it with no pretension. Call it entertainment, sir, but not philosophy."

Bescós was laughing loud. "This is something like!" He cuffed Thomas's shoulder. "She understands the principles of your trade."

Thomas made a show of dusting himself off, then replied with a mute punch to Bescós's arm.

Ester tugged Mary one final step into the clouded light of the street outside the theater. There Mary broke away from Ester with a look of fury. "Her rudeness," Mary said to Thomas, "is considered a burden among our community. I alone agree to go about the city with her; the other girls won't." At Thomas's laughter a still deeper flush rose on Mary's cheeks. With defiant formality—as though she spoke not only before Ester but before the whole congregation—she extended her hand and announced, "Mary da Costa Mendes." For an instant she faltered, then —with a furtive glance at Ester—added, "And Ester Velasquez."

"Mary!"

But Thomas was laughing. "My pleasure to learn your name, Mary. I see from your friend's anger it's a forbidden pleasure, which makes me like it the more. In a name lies truth. And," he added, "I'm eager to know the truth of you."

From behind Thomas, Bescós gave a bark of laughter. "You must not begrudge our actor friend his pronouncements about truth and philosophy. He reminds all at least once a fortnight that he was sent by his too-hopeful father to study at Oxford during the battles. But his principal work there, I'm afraid, was to publish pamphlets saying the Parliamentarians enjoyed relations with their horses."

At this John, until now silent at the back of the gathering, spoke up. "These are ladies, Bescós!" he said.

"Yes, Bescós, he's right." Thomas made an obsequious bow to Mary, ignoring Ester. "Please forgive us, the theater makes us forget ourselves."

Ester looked once more at John. He had a sculpted face, faintly pink cheeks. Seeing Ester watching him, he gazed at her seriously for a moment. Then a smile lit his face, replacing its solemnity with a fleeting boyishness.

"Lady Mary," Thomas intoned, "have no fear of our John. If he makes judgments on us, he does not press them, though he seems prim as a very magistrate — a profession we must be certain not to mock overmuch, as his father serves that function. But every knave needs a foil, and John is mine." He turned and spoke over his shoulder as he walked again. "Aren't you, John?"

John answered with a tolerant laugh — but Thomas persisted. "What would your father say, John, of your choice of friends?"

"My father isn't here," said John carefully. "But if he were, he would take care to collect all the evidence before passing judgment."

Thomas laughed. "And have *you* collected the evidence needed to judge us?" In turning to address John, Thomas steered Mary carelessly close to a wall lining the alley. Her wide sleeve brushed a clay pot containing some loose dirt. It teetered, then toppled from the nook where it had been nested; John caught it with quick grace before it hit the pavement, and set it back in place without a word. This time, though his reply was mild, the smile he turned on Thomas had something stiff in it.

"My father is the magistrate," John said. "I'm only his son."

Bescós was facing both his companions, and this time there was more flint in his words. "Yet any magistrate or man of reason might question the folly you both display," Bescós said to them both, "in calling a Jewess a lady." He turned then, and looked full on at Ester. His gaze was cold, and as it continued unrelenting, Ester felt her own stare waver. Only then did Bescós give a slight smile.

She felt a thread of fear. Pulling Mary's free elbow, she turned for the coach. This time Mary came. Behind them Ester heard the men follow, like a pack trailing a scent, but she didn't turn. On the next street, their coach was waiting, the driver waking from his sleep as Ester rapped on the lacquered wood. Mary climbed in and Ester followed, closing the door firmly — yet by the time she'd latched it Thomas was at Mary's window, speaking in a rapid banter that elicited a giggle. Ester turned away in vexation, only to find someone at her own window. John's face was serious but his brows arched — poised, she thought, between humor and concern. He gestured with his head toward Thomas. "His tongue runs on pattens," he said.

In her confusion she tested the door and found it shut. Uneasily, she looked across the coach, where Mary leaned out her window, both elbows propped on the frame, the bustle of her dress shoved in Ester's direction. Thomas was getting his display of Mary's graces now if he hadn't had his fill earlier.

Ester glanced back at John, still at her window. His eyes were a flecked, filtered brown. Light in a sieve of tree branches.

"Do you always speak thus?" he said. "Direct as an arrow, with no fear of judgment?"

"Mary." She tugged on Mary's bustle. But Mary swatted her hand away without turning.

"'Tis a rare thing," John said.

"Go," Ester called to the driver.

"A minute!" cried Mary, and Thomas joined her laughter.

On her hand clutching the sill of the coach's window, Ester felt a touch. John had set his hand on hers. Gently he began working one of her fingers loose of its grip on the wood.

She stared as he released one white knuckle, then began patiently on the next. The purity of his focus so riveted her that for a moment she forgot to pull away—the light weight of his hand on hers was astonishing. Absurd.

He released the third finger, and the fourth.

A bitter laugh burst from her. "Should you wish some coins for your service in seeing us to our safe departure," she said, "you may go to the other side of the coach, where the favors flow freely—or so your companion seems to think."

Her words didn't dissuade him from his labor.

"I've nothing for you," she said weakly.

He'd worked loose her last finger. Now he lifted her palm lightly, and set it down again on the polished wood of the coach's window. For a moment he smoothed it, studying the long, thin fingers with their wash-roughened knuckles and bitten nails—as though her hand were a creature deserving of tender pity.

"There," he said. When he looked up at her, it was with an expression of quiet delight, as though his own daring had taken him by surprise.

Raising his hand before her, he clenched it into a fist—then slowly spread his fingers wide, as though in demonstration: *like so*. A gesture of such untroubled simplicity, she could not comprehend it.

Mary spoke some word to the driver, and the coach started along the street.

Ester looked straight ahead. When at length she turned, Mary's lips wore a ticklish smile.

She knew she ought to say something to Mary. But her mind had been rinsed clean.

"I believe," said Mary, "that I'll require your presence at my home. Tomorrow, noon."

"Why?" whispered Ester.

Mary shrugged prettily.

"Why?" repeated Ester, finding her voice.

"I need a companion, as I'll be receiving a visitor." Mary had turned to face her. Her eyes, a rich brown, were wide with elation.

"You told him where you live? *Thomas Farrow?*"

Mary grinned with sudden abandon. "Yes!" she sang.

Ester couldn't hold back a laugh. Whether Diego da Costa Mendes would accept a Christian suitor for his daughter Ester couldn't guess, but she'd little doubt as to how the man would respond to the prospect of his daughter being courted by an actor. "Your father will send him away without a word," she said.

"My father is gone these three days."

Ester drew in her breath. The foolishness. Had she the freedom Mary enjoyed, she felt certain she wouldn't squander it on flirtation with such a man.

Without thinking, she'd spread one hand on her skirt, and with the other now felt the skin of her knuckles. It was rough, cracked from laundering. She balled her fist tight. "Don't act a fool," she muttered.

"I need you as my companion," said Mary.

"You want me to act the duenna to appease gossip—so you can flirt with a paltry man to spite your father."

Mary's face darkened. She stared out the window. In a low, dispirited voice she said, "Didn't my mother ask you to be my companion?"

"Her aim was to save you from folly, not invite it."

Mary didn't answer.

Ester pressed on, her voice rising to a pitch she couldn't justify. "To make my meaning clear," she said, "I care nothing if you trollop yourself about with such as Thomas Farrow. But don't imagine my presence will save you from gossip. As you yourself noted, I carry my mother's dishonor. Not that I care for such a thing as reputation." She said the last as bravely as any dolly on London's streets—as though respectability were nothing to her. Yet she knew all too well how its public loss could be used against her. Mary knew too. An unblemished reputation was the key to what all sensible women aspired to: marriage, safety. A life like those masks lying forgotten in the theater, serene and unreadable.

Was such female happiness real or feigned? No matter; Ester was barred from it by circumstance. By temperament.

But perhaps a different sort of happiness might yet be hers, in the confines of the rabbi's study.

The coach had stopped abruptly. There was shouting outside, the noise of a small crowd. But Mary's attention was fixed only on Ester. "I ask no charity," she was saying. "I'll *pay* you to serve as my protection against the gossips."

The tumult from outside rose, jeers and raucous cries; the driver was conferring with someone and laughing loud. But Mary kept her eyes on Ester. "Ten shillings for tomorrow," she said.

Ester almost laughed. Was it worth so much to Mary, this meeting with Thomas? A dalliance with a man whom any could see would make a ruinous mate? Did a woman's desires so war with sense?

All the more reason, then, to banish them from her heart.

"I'll meet Thomas even if you don't come, you know," Mary said. Then added more softly, "But it's best for me, Ester, if you come. You know it is. I'll pay you, and that makes it a simple employment, doesn't it —one whose only requirement is your presence." Her lips curved. "And this way, you see, my choices won't be your responsibility. *Or*"—she added—"your business."

Ester's heart beat once, twice—and on the third she knew she'd accept. Was it craven? But there was no stopping Mary. And surely the money could appear at no better time: coins for candles, and ink. For the plan forming in Ester's mind.

Mary nodded briskly: the agreement was sealed. She rapped on the divider. "Why are we stopped so near home?"

The driver called back, his voice rich with amusement. "'Tis a second theater now."

"What sort of theater?" called Mary.

But it was a white-haired, round-bodied woman standing outside her window who answered. "Two lads, miss, caught together in a dalliance at the Rose Inn. And one soon to find himself in great trouble, for his father comes and will have none of this new morality between men." A fresh wave of noise arose from ahead of the coach. "See here how they pull the one out?" The woman's merry laughter obscured whatever she said next.

Ester spoke to the driver through the flap. "And you've stopped our coach to watch?"

"Not I," he said mildly. "Look yourself."

Ester hesitated, then crowded beside Mary at her window and understood the driver's meaning. The narrow street was blocked with people craning as though at an entertainment. A jumble of dray-carts all pointed like a bristle of spears toward the doorway of an inn, where a slim, muscular young man had staggered out in a convulsion of laughter. He was naked save the sheet he held to his groin, but at the sight of the gathered crowd he made a ball of the sheet and threw it at them, his member bobbing half-mast like a flag in a brown thatch, and as Mary leaned against Ester to see better, he flung his arms wide and bowed so low, the men behind him roared with laughing disgust, and someone ran to restore him his sheet, but he refused it.

Even through the rigid stays of Mary's dress, Ester felt Mary's shudder of laughter.

"Here?" A man's voice was shouting in the din. "Show me my son!"

The crowd settled into a sharp hush as a man pushed his way to the front. Ester saw with a start that it was Benjamin HaLevy.

A fringe of white hair showed beneath HaLevy's dark wig, which rode askew above his dark, handsome face, so similar to his son Manuel's. His nostrils were flared, his mouth dreadful in its severity. Two burly draymen in his path stepped back before his fury.

Without thinking, Ester rocked back from the window and stumbled her way out of the coach and into the thicket of the crowd. Beside her a low voice sounded, a man chuckling to his companion. "See now the Jew. He'll whip his son for sporting with another man, though the king's court itself is reported to be full of such games."

"I'd whip the buggerers myself," laughed the other.

"I too! But even so the Jew is different—he hates all royal notions, for he hates the king."

Hastily Ester pushed forward, ignoring sounds of protest, aiming to where the crowd was thickest. As she broke through to the front, she saw Benjamin HaLevy pull Alvaro from the tavern. Alvaro's doublet was askew and half-buttoned. His father's fist was bunching the fabric of the son's blouse so it tore. But it was Alvaro's thin body, not the cloth, that seemed to rend—and when Benjamin HaLevy released his grip and strode away, Alvaro stumbled behind as though the cobbles beneath his feet were less than solid. Pausing an instant for balance, he gazed about in slow comprehension at the hooting, bucking crowd, and Ester wanted to take him in her own thin arms and race him to some imagined place of safety.

Then his eyes found Ester's and fastened on them in relief and desperation, confessing mutely to her, in a language she at last understood, that he was cursed.

THE RABBI SAT BY THE FIRE.

She thought: he hasn't moved since I departed hours ago. She thought: he's barely moved since he banished me from scribing; without any to help him study he might as well be in irons. She thought: even now, his imprisonment under the Inquisition continues. This time by his choice.

Did she blame him? Would that make it easier to do what she was about to do?

She entered the house and shut the heavy door behind her. The rabbi turned patiently toward the sound. She thought: his beloved face.

His eyelids were pale parchment; his form thin, frailer even than she'd noted before. There was no restlessness in his expression, nor hope. Nor rage at the heavens for the life stolen from him.

He was her friend—the only one in the Amsterdam congregation who'd understood her plight, and Isaac's, and tried to save them. And he was her teacher—his mind like a sounding line probing the depths of each verse and text. But she could no longer lie to herself, so with a pang she let herself know what she'd felt in those last months of her studies with him: that she understood the texts they'd read more deeply than he.

The thought that her abilities exceeded the rabbi's made her wish to protect him all the more. To fortify herself, she summoned the image of Alvaro's pleading face: a boy who would sink because he was not hard enough to deafen himself to jeers, turn, and strike his father's hand from his collar.

She addressed the rabbi. "A letter comes this day from Florence." She spoke as though indifferent. "How shall I dispose of it?"

The rabbi was silent. How many weeks, she wondered, since he'd received any letter? Without recourse to a scribe, his correspondence had withered.

"Perhaps you prefer I don't read it to you."

She felt his mind in its loneliness. She felt it turning her words, sounding the depth of her anger. "Read this letter to me," he said softly. "Please."

She moved toward him, but stopped midway across the room. She withdrew from the pocket of her skirt a paper—the playbill from the theater. A pang of doubt took her. She unfolded it quietly. *The Lovers' Masque*, the paper said. *A Spectacle of the Foolish Hearte.*

"From whom is the letter?" said the rabbi.

"From one Daniel Lusitano," she said. A name she'd culled from memory during the last of the coach ride. The Lusitano sons, former pupils of the rabbi, had been some years older than Ester, but had left Amsterdam long ago when their father's trade called him to Florence.

"He says"—she was speaking more loudly than necessary, she realized. She lowered her voice—"he studied with you in Amsterdam."

Slowly the rabbi nodded. "I remember," he said.

Her throat was dry. She continued. "To the esteemed Rabbi HaCoen Mendes," she said. "I write with my soul torn by the folly of the people I dwell among: this congregation of our people in Florence, which has served as a beacon of learning to those in darkness, yet now welcomes its own destruction. I turn to you now in respect and admiration." She looked at the rabbi as she spoke—she looked directly at his closed eyes and willed him to see her. "For your learning is great," she added. "Greater than many rabbis whose fame exceeds your own."

The rabbi listened, his brow furrowed.

She continued. "Florence's Jewry approaches a schism, I fear. Here the multitudes of our people turn their hearts to the imposter Sabbatai Zevi. They follow his claim to be the Messiah, whom we have awaited with such patience and through every trial and persecution. Even the rabbis of our community begin to turn their hearts to him. I have spoken with those I hoped I might persuade, but my reasoning makes little mark on them, for they still stand ready to join the multitudes in following Sabbatai Zevi.

"Though I was never the wisest pupil, still I recall fondly the steady light of your teachings in Amsterdam, and I feel certain you would deem this man Sabbatai Zevi an imposter. I beg you, please, to send some words that might help me persuade the people against this folly. There are those who sell their belongings to prepare for their removal to the Holy Land on the day he will declare himself the Messiah. There are those who speak of unearthing the graves of beloved ones so their bodies may be revived to life at the approaching end of days. I fear for the Jews of this city and"—she faltered—"this city and all the lands this false leader touches. I fear the people will not be able to return whole, once they lean their weight on false faith.

"Your respectful servant, Daniel Lusitano."

She waited. Had it not been enough?

"I've heard much rumor of Sabbatai Zevi's claims," the rabbi said slowly, "and the madness of some of his followers. I did not know it had reached Florence, nor that the wiser minds of that community were susceptible to it. But why does he not turn for aid to one of the great rabbis of Amsterdam? Or to Sasportas, whose authority exceeds mine?"

She kept her voice even. "Perhaps your student trusts only in his teacher."

The rabbi stirred in his chair. "Let it be known," he said, "that I oppose the following of Sabbatai Zevi as dangerous."

He was asking her to begin a letter. Yet she couldn't bring herself to move.

He waved at her, his face taut, distracted. "I wish you to write a reply for me."

She stepped to the writing table. She let herself down onto the chair as though sinking from a great, vertiginous distance.

The rabbi had lowered his face into his hands and remained in that posture for a long moment. Then he raised his head and spoke. Quill in hand, she took down his words in a hasty scrawl. *My dear Daniel, You may be assured I will attempt to do as you have asked. With full heart, I offer the arguments that seem to me most true. You have my blessing to improve upon or alter my words as you see fit, trusting your own wisdom as to how best to use them, for it is G-d's work that you do and you will know better than I what will sway the Jews of Florence.* She struggled to keep pace with his words, ink staining her fingers. *The argument against the claims of Sabbatai Zevi may be divided into three portions, which I will attempt to set out for you now.*

When the rabbi had finished, he had her read his words back and take his corrections. When he was satisfied he rose, his hand reaching to the wall for support.

Once she would have stood to help him. But the set of his face told her the rabbi did not welcome her help.

"I'm troubled by this news," he said. "I'll sleep now. Copy the letter, and send it."

"I will," she said.

He felt his way toward the doorway, a long, labored process. Near the door he turned to her, his face heavy and unreadable. "Tomorrow you will take down a further letter to the rabbis of Amsterdam, alerting them to the danger of Sabbatai Zevi's rise. You will scribe for me until this matter is resolved, and only until that day." He paused. "I will not ask you to write to Amsterdam and send for a scribe to do this work in your place. I will not ask you to do this thing, because I know you will not do it. And as the only remaining guardian of your soul, I do not wish to be responsible for your lie." His face was tight with vexation, though whether at her or at himself or at the congregation of Florence she didn't know. He left.

She spread her palms on the writing table's cool, smooth surface. Did these hands belong to her? The very words she'd once hurled at her brother accused her: *You ask me to spit on the one man who's helped us.*

Yet how easily she betrayed the rabbi now.

Tears welled. She banished them.

After a moment she set the rabbi's letter to one side, drew a fresh piece of paper from the drawer, and picked up the quill. She wrote the words in a rush.

To Franciscus van den Enden,

I have read with much interest of your work with Plockhoy and of your notions of the ideal society. Yet while your political philosophy is a rich terrain, there are other matters I wish to discuss with you and the philosophes of your circle.

I will speak plainly and ask that you judge such directness a mark of respect. Some say you go so far as atheistery, and that your association with Benedictus de Spinoza emboldened him to leave his people the Jews. If this is so, I will not judge it for ill, for the notion of the divine is to me a puzzle not yet answered and many are those who strive honestly to solve it. It is evident, by proofs I will gladly formulate should you choose to engage this discourse, that the twinned concepts of divine will and infallibility do not withstand study except where shrouded in obfuscating mystery by men whose imaginations insist on this comfort.

These words alone are a heresy, yet my questions range beyond what I write here. Among my strong desires is the wish to understand the notion of determinism rumored to be held by de Spinoza. Are you in agreement with it? And in your thinking how far do its consequences reach—does man hold no remnant of free will? And might determinism limit even God, if one may still speak with you of God? Does God possess will, and the power to execute that will, or is God something other than what every manner of faith has conceived? I beg to enter into an exchange with you on these and other matters. I assure you that your reply will not stray from my hands, but will be seen only by myself. Well do I understand the perils of metaphysics, and the dangers to philosophers whose work too sharply interrogates faith. Yet I ask of you whether a thinker might join in your circles from a distance. For even though I respire the air of another clime, I gladly conspire with you, as all we men of philosophy breathe the same air of questions wheresoever we reside.

Awaiting your reply,

Thomas Farrow

It was with a grim smile that she signed Thomas's name as she imagined he might: with a swaggering flourish. At least, she told herself, she did that one goodness. She told no lie under the rabbi's name.

WHEN ESTER OPENED HER EYES it was to a ripened day. Rivka, who must have been informed by the rabbi that Ester was again in his service, had left her abed, wordlessly hefting the load of housework upon her thick shoulders once more.

The world was changed. She lingered to feel it. She sat at the edge of her pallet, legs crossed inside her shift, feeling the breathing warmth of her own body. Her palms and fingers flexed, and were miraculous. Her hands belonged, she thought, to her. The warm, smooth soles of her feet met absurdly, like clapping hands. She clapped them. Then rose, washed her face in the basin, and let the diamond-drops slide from her face down her neck. She dressed and descended the stair and stepped out of the house into the noon light like a creature emerged from a chrysalis long outgrown.

A breeze pressed at her skirts, riffled the hair she'd carelessly pinned at her neck—she laughed in London's sooty, braying face. And walked to Mary's house in a cool blaze of words: a rebuttal she might compose to Solomon Sivani's pompous assertions about the nature of time in the Torah, which she and the rabbi had discussed more than a year ago. And then perhaps a letter to Lodewijk Meijer—for months ago, standing at a bookseller's stall outside St. Paul's, she'd read a preface authored by Meijer, and still recalled some of its phrases. She'd return to that same stall tomorrow; perhaps that volume or another was still there; perhaps through serving as Mary's companion she might dream of mustering the coins to purchase it: de Spinoza's *Principia Philosophiae Cartesianae*. The passages she'd read had seemed to her cautious in the extreme, with no trace of the heretic's rumored audacities—but perhaps upon closer inspection she'd find some hidden fire in those pages. The thought carried her through the grand carved doors of the da Costa Mendes home, where a maid held out a hand for Ester's cloak. As Ester gave it over, her own work-roughened hand brushed the maid's, and Ester looked up into the blunt fatigue on the maid's doughy face. Swiftly, before pity could overtake her, Ester turned away. To feel guilt over her own escape would drown her. She'd found a spar of wood to cling to, a thin chance at life; she couldn't falter at the sight of yet another drowning stranger.

In the da Costa Mendeses' sitting room, fragrant steam wisped from a china pot on a low mahogany table.

"You're here at last." Mary's voice was bright with tension. The nervousness animating her powdered face made odd contrast with the dainty dress she wore: a rich blue threaded with pink silk ribbons at the bosom, cascading with lace below.

Thomas, lounging on the broad velvet seat beside which Mary stood, turned and offered Ester a wide grin. Then his gaze slid across the room, where Ester saw the cause of Mary's distress. Standing in the tall window's sharp light were Thomas's two companions from the day before. Bescós stood with a teacup in his palm, surveying the tableau of indolent Thomas and straight-backed Mary. Beside Bescós stood John, looking at Ester now with a query in his mild eyes, his cup cooling untouched on a side table.

Thomas raised his cup. "To the beauty of our hostess," he said. Ester sensed it wasn't the first time he'd made this toast.

Mary attempted a smile, and failed.

Atop the virginal, beside a matched pair of celestial and terrestrial globes, lay a square of tent stitch—the needlework resting on the polished wood as though forgotten there by a casual hand. It was work of maddening delicacy, floss silk pulled through the thick white satin, with tiny silver spangles and seed pearls accenting the nearly finished design: a pattern of flowers, butterflies, caterpillars. Ester hadn't known Mary's restlessness could birth such elaborate handiwork.

Thomas, oblivious to this display of fine feminine needlework laid out for his benefit, was engaged in dragging an embroidered stool near with the toe of his fashionable boot, an exertion that would have proved unnecessary, had he merely leaned forward to take hold of it with his hand. Succeeding at last in maneuvering it to his satisfaction, Thomas propped a heel on the stitched cushion. Ester could see the sole had been patched.

Mary stepped forward, her eyes narrowing at Ester, her message clear. Turning to the pair at the window, her voice pretty yet each word a dagger, she said, "Ester and I didn't expect your company as well as Thomas's."

Bescós laughed full and long. "Neither did Thomas," he said. Then, without budging from the window, he fell back to surveying the room's rich tapestries and elegant decorations. Indeed, Ester herself was struck by the wealth of the household. Only once, meeting Mary for an excursion, had she entered the da Costa Mendes house, and even then she'd ventured no farther than the house's threshold. At all other times, Mary had collected her at the rabbi's doorstep. Now she couldn't help but stare as well: silver and tapestry, mahogany, richly framed art.

"We followed Thomas here," said John, "so that we might fetch him back to the theater in time." His speech sounded so softly in the room, it put Ester in mind of a Quaker preacher she'd once heard on a London street—a man who seemed to meditate before choosing each phrase, perched though he was on a crate amid the city's traffic—as though he believed each utterance could do harm or good.

As John spoke he shook his head apologetically at Mary. "He departed our company at the inn with his mind already bright with wine. And he's needed on stage in little more than an hour. The players have had to proceed already once without his part. Should he be absent once more, his position at the theater will be forfeit. So, we followed."

Thomas, listening with a sleepy half smile, bit his thumb at John. His cheeks pink with whatever he'd drunk at the tavern, he caressed his short beard and returned to a survey of the room's tapestries. Now and again he glanced over at Mary, who stood beside the virginal—but whatever designs he had on her seemed, for the moment, second to his study of her father's furnishings. Thomas watched wealth, it struck Ester, the way some men watched a sunset.

There was a step in the hall: a matronly servant entering with a deliberate bustle. She crossed before the company to the teapot, lifted its lid, and said to Mary stiffly, "You'll want more water, then?" Without awaiting an answer or bothering to shield her hand with a cloth, she took the hot pot to her bosom. "I suppose your father will be wondering, Mary, what guests stayed to enjoy his household's hospitality, him being absent?"

Mary lay a finger along the etched metal surface of the terrestrial globe, rolled it slightly forward and back, then spun it, hard. The force of the motion set the stand's metal legs rocking, raising an outsized din from the virginal, whose brass strings thrummed in a dire voice as though at some dreadful injury. The low notes died last.

"My father courts his new love," said Mary, "as you well know, Hannah. He won't return this fortnight."

At these words the servant let out a small, pained sound. Whatever disapproval she might feel concerning the daughter's behavior, it was clear her distress at the father's exceeded it. She departed without another word.

Mary stepped quickly to Ester. Grabbing her arm, Mary hissed, "Take them to the garden."

Ester glanced at Thomas. "Are you certain?"

Mary's face gave the answer. She pointed to a passageway to the left.

Without fanfare Ester addressed the pair by the window. "To the garden," she said.

Bescós pushed off from the wall with a short, sharp laugh.

She led the two men down a brief hallway and out a door that opened onto a tiered, well-kept patch of flowering shrubs, its merry pinks and winding ivies hemmed by thick walls. Exotic plants with delicate blossoms unfamiliar to Ester curved in modest rows; hedges of briar rose shaded the path. This must have been Catherine's garden, abandoned by its maker during its winter sleep. Some invisible hand had kept up its faithful tending this spring. With a start, Ester realized whose. The pruning was inexpert: one hedge sheared too closely, another trimmed halfway up and then forsaken. Ragged, fitful weeding, the mute language of a daughter's devotion.

Beneath the damage done by Mary's unsteady hand, Catherine's stately design was still everywhere in evidence: a brief allée of trees, pleached into two walls and entwined to form an arch; urns of fragrant plants, an elegant illusion to distract the mind and senses from the fact that there was but a circular gravel path to tread, round a bit of greenery roofed by the drifting smell of the tanneries and the needling sounds of cart traffic from just beyond the wall.

Ahead, along the perimeter of the garden, strode Bescós. John, Ester saw, had determined to walk with her. They stepped slowly along the path. After a moment she turned to him, found him watching her, and looked down again—but a moment later his soft, sudden laugh lifted her gaze.

With a gesture he directed her attention toward a bush of silvery cotton lavender that had been trimmed into a neat globe. There, tucked in the shadow beneath the plant's stout curve, lay a small embroidered pillow with a design Ester had seen not three minutes earlier. The pillow had been cut open and one panel carefully removed, the wool stuffing left exposed. Beside the pillow, in the dirt under the bush, lay a small silver scissor.

How deliberately, how delicately Mary must have worked to unstitch just enough of that panel to make it appear to be her own handiwork —mounting the cut panel onto a tent frame, setting a needle upon the thread, and laying it atop the virginal as though she had only just paused in her work upon Thomas's arrival. A labor of deceit to rival the labor of the embroidery itself.

John was laughing with his mouth open and his shoulders gathered: a gentle mirth, his cheeks pinked, his eyes bright. Only when he fell silent, concern flooding his face, did she realize that she herself hadn't been laughing, but rather staring at him.

But now his consternation over her solemnity was absurd—she couldn't control her face. As if striking a silent agreement, they laughed together: a soft conspiracy among the strict hedges and tamed herbs of the garden. Her voice sounded out above his, high and girlish.

What was it that made him seem so unburdened? His eyes were clear of suffering, of grievance. She'd never seen such clear eyes, a rain-washed brown, with room to take in all that they saw.

She bit down on her lip until she tasted iron. "You mustn't try to know me," she said.

His brows arched high. "Why?" he said.

How to explain that for just an instant he'd reminded her of carved wooden angels she'd seen here and there in London, set high in lofty arches or on the posts of grand entrances—creatures whose faces shone with a mesmerizing trust? And each time she glimpsed such angels she felt certain that, should she but touch them, their innocence would dissolve.

She stood opposite John, wanting to turn away and wanting the feel of his hand on hers once more. "If you knew me," she said, "you'd run from me."

"Perhaps," he said, "you think so only because you don't know me."

He stood before her, arms loose at his sides. It seemed to her that he'd just issued a challenge, though whether to her or to himself she didn't know. She felt there was something she ought say in response. Then she saw that what was required was that she say nothing.

A moment passed. Another. Something between them turned.

Bescós was coming. She broke her gaze from John and walked.

"Tell me," she said, as though they'd been discussing the matter all along. "Did your friend Thomas truly learn nothing at Oxford?"

John fell into step beside her. "During the siege of Oxford, he was among the students who studied with Harvey."

"The anatomist? The author of *De Motu Cordis*?"

"Yes," said John, surprised. "Harvey had a great following among the students moored there during the war."

"Yet your friend shows few traces of cherishing his education."

"I fear that's true," said John, as Bescós reached them. "I believe the only lesson Thomas took from Oxford was that he detested schooling. And the only lesson he drew from Harvey was after Harvey's most brilliant work had been damned for contradicting Galen. Harvey declared, then, that humankind was but a collection of mischievous baboons." He grimaced. "I believe Thomas has lived since then to prove Harvey correct."

Bescós was smiling a small, satisfied smile. "Thomas and I are united in one thing, at least," he said. "We believe Harvey was correct about humankind." He looked past Ester, and fixed his gaze on John. "You, on the other hand, take a daintier view of the human spirit."

"A kinder one," John said.

"No," said Bescós, a sudden edge in his voice. "'Tis kind to tell the truth rather than pretty falsehood. 'Tis kind to wring a runt's neck, put the weak and deformed out of their misery, recognize that some of humanity is lesser and dispatch with it. You think you have a tender heart, John, but you lie to yourself. Those who hold your precious view of humanity only lengthen the suffering of those ill-fitted for this world. Harvey was too generous in his estimation—the baboon at least demonstrates some sense regarding its fellow creatures. It cannot be said of mankind." He turned, and disappeared into the house.

Only when he was gone did Ester realize she'd risen to the balls of her feet while he spoke, as though to flee.

An unhappy expression passed across John's face. "He and I spoke earlier of my opinion that soldiers who turn deserter amid hopeless-seeming battles should be spared execution. I argued that many are pressed into service yet not of a temperament to be heroes. You may guess Bescós's response. I try to forgive him his ferocities."

She shook her head slowly.

"I'm sorry," John said. "He's a creature of blunt thoughts and no courtesy."

"Then why do you name him a friend?"

He looked surprised. "Bescós is Thomas's friend, not mine."

"Yet you keep his company."

"When I must. And in truth Bescós does no harm despite his bluster, and at the inn where we board I've seen him buy supper for poor students while men of more seeming-refined manners and greater means turned their backs. His generosity is of a rough sort, as are the opinions he holds. But I know him to be guilty of nothing more than restlessness —and in that, I fear, he's no different than most who come to this city in pursuit of their future." He thought a moment. "Do you keep Mary's company out of true friendship? You seem little alike."

From the house, the faint sound of Mary's giddy laughter.

Surprising herself, she looked directly at John. "Mary pays me for my presence here today."

John laughed his surprise. Then he said, "Allow me to try to make your hours of employment pass lightly."

But she wasn't ready to join his laughter. "Mary, unlike your companion"—she indicated the door where Bescós had disappeared—"doesn't disdain any for the faith he was born to."

John absorbed this. Quietly he nodded.

She led him back into the house, in time to see Thomas and Mary tumbling like children from some back passage—Thomas's lips cherry-red, Mary giggling in a merry register. Thomas, his face flushed from more than wine, bowed his way cheerily out the door before turning to the street with a sated expression. There Bescós awaited him. As soon as Thomas appeared, Bescós turned his back and began to walk away.

"A moment for farewell," John called.

Bescós stopped midstep. Slowly he turned back. "John, my friend," he said. But his expression had nothing in it of friendship. He stared for a moment at Mary, then at Ester. "Surely you know I give courtesy where it's necessary. None is necessary here."

Mary looked confused, as though she'd heard the words yet didn't know what they signified.

John shook his head. He bent to kiss Mary's hand. She received the gesture numbly. He did the same, swiftly, with Ester, his eyes lighting on hers for only a troubled instant. Then he left, striding swiftly to catch his companions. When the three turned the corner, Ester saw John was addressing Bescós earnestly.

Ester watched them go. At length she turned back to Mary. If naught else, she'd say what she saw. "Mary. Your father wronged your mother, and he wrongs you now. Yet you mend little by—"

"You know nothing," Mary countered dangerously.

"Perhaps. But Mary—" How much to say? Did warning ever stay any hand from reaching for what it desired? What, indeed, had Catherine imagined Ester might do to correct Mary's course?

"You asked once," Ester said, "what my mother counseled me about love. But it was her life rather than her words that gave the plainest counsel. My mother was so angered by love's failures, Mary, that she navigated with spite as her compass. But if you'd seen her, though she was beautiful, you'd have understood how easily the blade of spite turns in one's hands, and cuts one's own palms. So that one can grasp nothing, Mary. So that life is . . . no longer life."

For a moment Mary seemed to be listening. Then she shrugged.

The ways women comforted one another were foreign to Ester. She'd had no sister, nor any friend bold enough to lay a finger on a troubled spirit for the purpose of salving it. Searching for words, she found only her own mother's wine-rich voice—and was surprised to hear there, amid Constantina's midnight litany of betrayal, a portion of mercy. *Some women, Ester, like to believe their hearts are made of glass, which must shatter if they so much as think of a sin. Oh Ester, shatter!* Even now, Ester could hear the wretched fury cracking her mother's words. *Such women believe their delicate hearts are a sign of virtue. But—Ester, know it!—they're a sign of nothing more than luck. Ester, hear me. Only the strong-hearted live on, after luck dies.*

What she wished to tell Mary now: a woman must have a heart made of something tougher, or she dies when a first blow comes.

What she wished to tell Mary: forge your heart.

But Mary stood apart from her, eyes still trained on the receding horizon of respectability. "Do you think my mother would be very angry with me?" she whispered.

For an instant Ester returned to the windy evening beneath the trees, the sound of Catherine da Costa Mendes's labored breathing as she struggled up the park path. The tired gaze through the black velvet mask. Ester said, "Your mother didn't linger on what she regretted. Nor should you."

Mary stared down at the paving stones between her shoes. "I don't regret it. Only—" She stopped herself, then glanced up at Ester once, searchingly, as though some suffocating weight, a cloak of heaviest lead, were only now settling on her.

She bit her full red lip and turned for the house.

THE RABBI WAS WAITING FOR her upon her return. He sat in silence until she'd hung her cloak.

"To Daniel Lusitano," he said.

The rabbi had had Rivka set out fresh paper.

"My distress grows," said the rabbi, "with every hour I meditate upon your letter."

She lowered herself to the writing table.

"And so I hope you will forgive the crowding of one missive atop another, as my thoughts crowd like sheep at the pasture gate when a wolf prowls."

She wrote.

"In my own darkness"—the rabbi continued, and she saw he'd rehearsed this letter in his mind—"I see perhaps too vivid a picture of the error that lies before your community in Florence. It is an error not only of soul but also of body, for they that muster for the next world before it has come can only betray their lives in this one. Long have I heard rumor of Sabbatai Zevi and yet I remained foolishly silent, and I can only rebuke myself that it required report of the threat from my beloved student to awaken me. What small help my thoughts may offer is ever at your disposal, and so I set forth the following additional arguments."

Her hand slowed on the page. "You should rest," she said. Could he hear the regret that snagged her voice? "I'm certain he'll write to you again soon. You can add to your arguments later, without taxing yourself to compose them now."

His thin nostrils quivered. "You'd now stand in my way?" he said.

She'd never seen him angered. He'd registered her betrayal, she saw, even if he didn't know its nature.

"I'm ready to write," she said.

Her quill moved across the page at the rabbi's direction. The letter was long, full of careful argument, clarification, gentle insistence, and one flare of passion. *To follow this man is to follow the very false god warned against in the commandments.*

His distress was her doing. She wouldn't pretend otherwise. He was the only one who had tolerated her desire to study, even loved it. And here she was, dissolving the ground he stood on. An impossible price for her freedom. As she wrote his words, she pledged: *I'll repay you.*

And did her body still hum from the morning? Did John's clear eyes, his living form, float through all the extremities of her body, did the sound of his laughter in the garden linger? She'd banish it. She hadn't done this great wrong to the rabbi so that she could waste her freedom on distraction.

When he'd finished, his face was solemn. The effort of the letter had emptied him. What's more, she understood now what he'd ventured: however carefully phrased, his words could only be understood as a charge to be levied against the esteemed leaders of the Florentine community. Yet for the sake of his student, and for the sake of stemming the tide of Sabbatai Zevi's followers, he dared.

"Copy it now," said the rabbi.

Her hand moved thickly on the page, composing a letter that would never be sent.

A knock upon the front door. Before Ester could rise, Rivka had emerged from the kitchen to open it. A muffled exchange, then a familiar figure swept into the rabbi's study, his cloak still upon him.

"Manuel HaLevy," Rivka announced flatly.

Ester hadn't seen him since the day in the park, and then from a distance.

"Welcome," said the rabbi, lifting his face. "It's been a great while since we've learned together. I trust your business goes well?"

"Well enough," said Manuel. "I trust you're also well enough," he added, a strange humor in his voice. His eyes took in the rabbi, the remnants of his tea, the fire. They shifted, appraisingly, to Ester.

She laid her hand atop the letter she was writing, though the ink stained her palm.

"My brother, you've perhaps heard, has been pressed this day," said Manuel. "He leaves this hour for a warship of the king's navy."

The rabbi let out a sound of surprise. "But could your father not prevent this? Isn't he a man of some standing, even among the Christians?"

"It was my father," said Manuel, "who summoned the agents to seize him. They're crewing a warship this day, one that goes to the Americas to oppose the Dutch, who menace our interests there."

"It's an enslavement," said the rabbi, rising slowly from his chair. "No less."

Ester looked from the rabbi, who still held to his chair with one hand for support, to Manuel. "What does this mean?" she asked.

The rabbi spoke heavily. "You may think I know nothing of the world, Manuel HaLevy. Yet when I lived in Amsterdam I yet heard tidings from those that traveled. The life of the impressed man is a life of labor so cruel that the men are shackled when the ship docks, so that they will not escape. A wretched life. And for one like your brother, without seafaring experience, it must be a short one, may God prevent his death. Can this be what a Jew wants for his son or his brother?" Letting go the chair, he took one step toward Manuel HaLevy, then stopped; his face, contorted, trained on a spot that was not precisely where Manuel stood.

Manuel shrugged, as though the rabbi's fury had no power if not aimed true.

"It's because of your brother's nature," said the rabbi. "Is it not?"

Manuel laughed softly. "Yes," he said. "It is."

From behind Manuel came a burst of Rivka's thick Portuguese. "So you have no heart? The creatures of the deep will eat his body."

Though he'd startled at her vehemence, Manuel didn't so much as glance at Rivka. "Only God knows my brother's fate," he said to the rabbi. "And with a bit of labor my father believes Alvaro might remake himself as a new man. Or else fail to. But in either case he will do so far from my father's house."

Rivka, crossing swiftly to the rabbi, helped him to his chair.

"Why are you here?" Ester said.

"Upon my father's request," Manuel said, "the sailors agreed to allow my brother some hours to order his things and make farewells. Alvaro asked a servant of our house to bear the news here. But I found it more practical to bear the news here myself. Perhaps I was in need of some air." He looked at Ester steadily now, his gaze carrying a message she could not read. Then he laughed, breaking the spell. For a moment his mouth formed a tight bud. "I believe my brother hopes for a farewell from you before he departs."

There was something about Manuel that arrested Ester. His thick pale lips, those brass-colored eyes under the fringe of dark, glossy hair. The straight nose and high cheekbones, the heavy frame of his face looming above her where she sat. He was a man, yes—but also a boy. She could almost imagine him at an age of bewilderment, watching the world silently through those strange eyes of his . . . slowly arriving at his first resounding conclusions.

Rising, she tucked the page she'd been writing under a stack of blank pages and took her cloak from its peg.

"Ester," said the rabbi. "Carry a note from me to the boy's father. Say, *Alvaro's nature may sin, yet the sin is not against you. Let the sins of VaYikra be dealt with by God and not by man.* Tell him"—briefly the rabbi's voice rose, then grew hoarse. "Tell him, *It is not for us to stone the sinner, for we are not the holy ones who dwelt in the desert, but to trust in God to punish or forgive.* Write these words, Ester." The rabbi's voice shook. "Write, *The exile you force on him will be his death.*"

THE HALEVY HOME WAS KNOWN to her, though she'd never entered it. Its brick front surveyed the street: severe windows, a peaked roof made of slate, not thatch. A showpiece of wealth.

Her hand had not yet touched the ornate knocker when Alvaro himself opened the door. He was dressed in white like a penitent, his loose shirt only half-tied at the neck and hanging over his hose and breeches.

He greeted her without words, gesturing her into the house's entry, so she understood that there was no time for pleasantries. Standing against the wall as though he required its support, his blouse draping his still-boyish body, he might have been a painter's portrait of a lovesick youth—yet his eyes were desperate. She saw that his spirit was already shackled to the deck of an outbound ship, the solid rock of his life slipping past reach.

From deep in the house she heard the irregular thump of activity. Then a pall punctuated by a clatter of words from a back room—the sounds of a household furiously rending itself. A thin, white-haired servant emerged from an inner doorway; startled by Ester's presence, she stared for an unguarded instant. Her face plainly expressed her anguish —though whether the son's deeds or the father's troubled her more, Ester could not guess.

Ester beckoned to the woman and handed her the rabbi's note. "For Benjamin HaLevy."

The woman pursed her lips and disappeared, note in hand.

"You wished to see me," Ester said to Alvaro.

"Yes." He nodded. "It's just, I need"—he spread his hands. What he needed none but his father could offer. He lowered his head. "You've always been kind to me. Perhaps you know a psalm."

She wouldn't deceive him. Nowhere in her twenty-seven years had tidings reached her of God stepping from the pages of the holy books to guard the paths of the righteous. What hope were words of divine protection for Alvaro then, who'd sinned according to those same books?

He drew a full breath, held it, then continued. "You know now what I am." He raised his head and let the full weight of his trust rest on her eyes. "I wished always to tell you. Now you know it. My father's house is cursed with a buggerer." At the word his face fell, but he continued. "I'll ask no blessing, then, for what blessing does one such as I deserve?" For a moment his voice strengthened so she could almost believe the brave words; then she saw Alvaro's pooling eyes.

A soft tread in a nearby passageway. The servant to whom Ester had given the rabbi's note entered. "Here," she said. Gently she placed the rabbi's letter back into Ester's hand.

"Isn't there any reply?"

The woman, her gray hair tied in a dry knob at the back of her neck, shook her head. "None." Her face worked for a moment, as though she wished to say something else entirely. "None at all," she said, and then departed, the look of tenderness she cast back over her shoulder unseen by Alvaro.

Alvaro stood perfectly still, listening, as the servant's footsteps faded. The sight of him, motionless in the shadowed entryway, made Ester shudder—and for an instant she was taken by the tall gray waves of the long sea passage that awaited him, the bitter wind, the unforgiving order of a ship at sea. She saw in her mind Alvaro's still-youthful face, the pale down on the lobes of his ears, the nails of his fingers bitten to the quick—Alvaro, stilled by a fear so deep, it was indistinguishable from prayer. She saw his body heaved over a rail by strangers. Soft limbs spiraling through lightless depths, away from the distant, shimmering surface.

She forced words from her lips. "This blessing," she said to him. "To dream such glad dreams that you wake laughing."

She watched him surface to her words.

From deep in the house, a servant's summons.

TO HER SURPRISE, MANUEL AWAITED her on the street. As she walked past him with a tight nod, he fell into step beside her.

Down St. Helen's Street they walked. His manner was serious, as though he'd some important business to conduct. After one brief glance at him, Ester didn't look again; she'd no notion what his presence signified and didn't wish him the pleasure of seeing her confusion.

They passed Fletcher's Hall, and turned onto Bury Street. By now she could not deny she was walking home with him as her escort. He strode beside her in his fine cloak, slowing his steps when necessary to match hers. He clasped his hands heavily behind his back, as though he were an older man, ponderous with his own success.

At the corner of Creechurch Lane she stopped. She was on the verge of opening her mouth to curse Manuel for a killer.

"A day," he said, "of much turbulence."

She checked his face for remorse. There was none. Only the fatigued practicality of a young man who'd already accepted the necessities of this world.

"A cruel punishment," she said, "for a harmless soul. Why must your father dispatch him in such a manner?"

Manuel smiled—indulgently, she thought, as though addressing a foolish child. "You champion him now. Yet I saw you spurn his puppy-ish admiration."

Ester shook her head violently—she would not be implicated, if that was Manuel's purpose. "I never wished him harm. And I didn't know he wanted to marry me only in order to mask what he was."

Manuel laughed. It seemed to her that he took a very long while with his laugh, his eyes raised to the upper galleries of the houses and on past them to the city wall and the distant silhouette of the tower. Then he lowered his gaze to evaluate her again in that manner that had struck her before as detached, but now seemed more like the gaze of a merchant carefully watching the horizon, whence approached a ship in which he had made a certain investment. "He was never your suitor," he said. "I am."

She laughed.

He said nothing.

"You lie," she said.

He shook his head, enjoying her anger.

"But you dislike me," she said.

Only now did his smile soften, and turn rueful. "Perhaps I did dislike you, before. But such feelings are changeable, and the thing I first disdained in you is the very thing in which I now take greatest interest."

After a moment Ester mustered her voice. "Is this a proposal of marriage? If so, it is a dry one."

He tipped his head toward her, eyes still fastened on hers. "Would you like it to be?"

Her throat was tight. "Don't young men woo with talk of love? Or am I so outside the world of love that I've failed to note that men in this land propose like actuaries?"

"Perhaps others do," he chuckled. "I can tell you only what I propose. I would, in marrying you, promise you neither fidelity nor obedience, nor any part of my heart but that which you earned through a change in your own demeanor—and your demeanor, I need not tell you, alarms all men who are not of intrepid constitution."

She spoke past her confusion. "My *demeanor*, as you call it, will not change. Nor will I marry you."

He nodded briskly. "Yes, I understand that's your belief. But time will press you to marriage, and that time will come soon. HaCoen Mendes hasn't much more life to live." At her sound of protest, he raised his voice, insisting. "You know it. After he dies, you'll be left without money or protection. You're a quick student, I'm certain. You'll marry, and the man you choose will be me."

His smile maddened her—how lightly he sported with her fears, with the precariousness of her position. "Do you expect me to be a gull for this prank of yours? Why would any believe that Manuel HaLevy, son of one of the wealthiest Jews of London, has no greater dream for himself than to marry a woman whom he does not love, and who is, besides which, without wealth or any desire to please a husband? Or can it be that you, alone among mankind, enjoy plunging your face into thorns, rather than roses?"

"Roses," he said, "die."

And thorns endure the winter. It struck her for the first time that he might be serious.

"My mother was a weak woman," he said, "though in my childhood I thought her kind. Nonetheless she slipped from this world with hardly a struggle." His eyes were hard; there was no room in them for contradiction. "Women die easily," he said. "I'm sure it can hardly have escaped your notice. They die of the everyday rough use of the world, they die in childbed, they die because they have not the endurance or the taste for this world that men do. They die, and they do not resist dying, like sheep. No. Less than sheep." His voice quickened, like a student philosopher rehearsing a disputation. "It vexes the mind that God would create a creature and give it so little will. Even a flea argues more strongly for its life than a woman. Perhaps when a rabbi can explain God's purpose in making women thus, he will earn my admiration. If even a *priest* could explain it, I would give him my allegiance in an instant. And don't pretend surprise at my blasphemy, Ester, because I've seen your face as the rabbi recites his prayers and I know you share it. The rabbi's words don't explain the way women die." He stared, for a moment, at the low clouds. "It vexes the mind," he repeated.

But she saw it was not his mind that was vexed, but his heart. A thing that might, like an animal, prove docile or dangerous.

A scrap-metal vendor pushed his rattling cart past; two housemaids walked by, giving curious glances. He paid them no mind.

"Such weak womanly souls," he continued, "are deemed desirable. But in truth they're cowardly, betraying all promises of life and sustenance. The promise of a weak woman," he said, "is worthless. I seek a woman who will not murmur *the Lord in his wisdom* and gently expire, but fight with clenched fist and jaw to remain in the world and in my household and raise my children. I want no faint woman for my wife, though such I may seek for pleasure." He was silent a moment, then stepped nearer. "I've seen your face set against all of London like a rock set against the sea." She was shocked to see true pleasure on his face. "You make no effort to mask how little you care for the opinion of others." He raised his hand; she couldn't fathom its motion toward her. At the touch of his fingertips on her cheek she flinched, but he only gave a low laugh. "When you come to marriage, you'll come with gratitude, and you'll apply to it the strength you now apply to scorning it. Affection will follow on the heels of marriage." He spoke sternly but his eyes were watchful. "When you cease your scribing and bookish pursuits, and turn from the unnatural to the natural, you'll bear children. And even your essence will bend, your temper will ease to that of a mother. Nor will I tolerate"—one eyebrow rose as his voice lowered—"a difficult woman."

"Then," she said, "let us spare you that fate without further discussion." She turned to leave, her thoughts in disarray.

"No," he said. "I've set my mind. You wield your puny might like" —he laughed—"like a child's fist cocked at a man's world. It pleases me. I said so, unthinking, in the company of the widow Mendoza, but I wasn't displeased that she took it as profitable business to make inquiries. Though"—he twisted his lips—"you drew a conclusion that was comic, don't you agree?"

Tears rose in her eyes, though she couldn't have named what drove them there. "You can't want me," she murmured.

He spoke to her gently—for the first time she saw that he had in him a great store of gentleness. "You've spent too many days with

Mary's petty criticisms as your only mirror. Look again. You'll see there's no blemish in you." His words trailed as he considered her. "Once you've done what women do to their hair" . . . he gestured at her head . . . "and erased this false augur of age that you wear" . . . reaching up, he tugged at a lock of her hair, then released it softly. "There is life hidden there."

She wished to flee but could not.

"You have a beauty of a sort," he said. "But more important than that, you have enough manly strength in you to match me."

She found her voice. "Do you love men, then, like your brother?"

He laughed at the taunt. His large frame loomed before her, commanding. "My brother and I could not be more opposed in temperament or desire."

She did not doubt him.

All amusement was gone from his face. His jaw was set. Fear mixed in her with an unfamiliar longing for protection. What would it mean to stop fighting for what none other than she believed in, and accept the shelter that was offered?

"I'm not a selfish man, Ester. You see me standing here before you." For a moment his face bore a wistfulness strange for one so accustomed to the fulfillment of his wishes. Then he raised both hands, palms up, in a gesture so emphatic it could not be submissive. "I want your ferocity for myself. That's true. But I want it also for my sons. I want," he said, "a woman of will."

On the corner of Bury Street and Creechurch Lane, carts trundling past now and again on the uneven stones, he waited for her answer.

She said softly, "You won't have me."

"What are you, then, if you refuse to be a woman?"

She faced down the narrow street, a darkened strip beneath overcrowding balconies. "An empty vessel," she said, though she knew not whether the words were meant to spite him or herself.

"Yet," he laughed, bowing his farewell, "you are not."

She walked home alone, gripping her cloak tight about her, thoughts piling and slipping. Manuel HaLevy understood her more truly than any—he saw she was no docile creature, nor did he wish her to be. And his warning echoed the rabbi's: she'd have no livelihood, no protection from hunger and need after the rabbi's death. Why, then, not marry him, under such terms as he offered? But her nature, it seemed, was unnatural. What she wished—she could not help it, the wish persisted darkly inside her—was to be a part of the swelling wave she felt in the words of the books and pamphlets lining the tables outside St. Paul's, the piles of fresh-bound quires at the bindery. What she wished was to struggle with all her force to urge that wave along, so that she might herself sweep and be swept in its furious progress— driving against the shore to smash some edifice of thought that stood guard over the land, throw herself against it and watch it crumble. For some new truth lay beyond it, she was sure of it. A continent awaiting discovery.

How to explain to all the world that her own vanity—her preten- sion at philosophical thought, which a man like Manuel HaLevy would trample—was more valuable to her than the safety he offered?

She'd reached home. The door shut hard behind her, and in its wake quiet reigned. The rabbi had retired to his room, the fire in the study had gone to embers.

A woman's body, said the world, was a prison in which her mind must wither.

She forced herself to stand still in the center of the room, palms resting lightly on the fabric of her skirts. She would not permit herself another step until she calmed herself with reason.

Nature gave a woman not only body but also intelligence, and a wish to employ it. Was it then predetermined that one side of Ester's nature must suffocate the other? If two of God's creations were opposed, must it be that God decided in advance that one was more perfect and there- fore must be victorious? Did God determine before each storm that ei- ther the wind or the oak tree must prevail, one being more dear to Him?

Or perhaps, rather, the storm itself was God's most prized creation —and only through it could the contest between wind and oak tree be resolved, and one proven hardier. Perhaps—she trembled at her own heresy—the storm itself was God. And God was only the endless tu- mult of life proving new truths and eradicating old.

Then it was only right that she do as her spirit told her, and let the struggle itself answer the question of which was the stronger: her will or her womanly nature.

Still dressed in her cloak, she crossed the room, sat at the writing table, dipped a quill, and wrote quickly, as though the words she set on the paper might be spied and seized from her.

To the esteemed Thomas Hobbes,

I write to inquire whether I might engage your illustrious mind in discussion. Although I am unknown to you, I believe myself to be one such as you may trust: a companion in inquiry, and no part of the powers that would condemn a thinker for incredulity or atheistery.

My interests in metaphysical inquiry are many, but of late concern the question of extension. If I may embolden myself to do so, I would like to inquire as to what relationship you find between the divine and natural worlds, and what beliefs you hold in the matter of providential intervention. I myself, as you surely intuit, hold thoughts in these matters that are other than those commonly held. I am in disagreement not only with the notion of divine dominion over nature, but also with the belief in its expression through miracles, the which notion seems to me the facile recourse of a poor mathematician whose numerical proofs, having failed to arrive at a wished-for sum, may yet be solved by the sudden mysterious introduction of a new number to right the balance.

It is my keen wish to discuss and learn from my fellow thinkers, so that where I err I might be corrected, and where I possess a spark of understanding it might be fanned. Yet an infirmity of body bars me from traveling to your door to converse with you face to face as two gentlemen ought. It is my hope that you will take my word, insubstantial though it must seem, for surety. It is my hope that you will answer my letter.

So she wrote, and signed the letter *Thomas Farrow*, and when she had finished this letter she set it to dry.

There on the desk beside it, written in her hand, lay the rabbi's letter to Florence. Slowly but deliberately, she turned it on the wooden table. She dipped the quill heavily, and drew the nib across the paper between the inverted lines of the letter, shaping a ribbon of blue-black ink to ease her own thoughts.

She wrote, in Hebrew, *Here I begin.*

17

December 22, 2000
London

HE'D ARRIVED THIS MORNING TO find the rare manuscripts room strafed by shafts of sunlight, and empty with the exception of the necessary Patricia. He'd requested a document, and Patricia had brought this bill for provisions, written by an anonymous merchant in December 1664—so much money for so many sacks of flour and a barrel of something illegible. The paper was moderately damaged, and Aaron let his eyes slide over the letters with their brown halos. Nothing of interest.

An English sort of quiet reigned in the hall—reverent and fraught. *She doesn't know what she's missing,* he told it.

Only last night, making room on his kitchenette table for a sheaf of transcriptions of Rabbi HaCoen Mendes's letters, he'd moved aside a stack of dissertation research notes (and how foreign his dissertation now revealed itself to be: a work written in Sanskrit by an earnest scholar who vaguely repelled Aaron) and, in doing so, dropped his Signet Shakespeare to the floor. Picking it up, he'd browsed the sonnets until one stopped him:

> *Nay, if you read this line, remember not*
> *The hand that writ it, for I love you so*
> *That I in your sweet thoughts would be forgot*
> *If thinking on me then should make you woe.*

Staring at the lines, he'd felt a sudden gust of anger. Yet again, he didn't fucking get it. Or maybe Shakespeare was bullshitting. Wasn't love, by definition, the wish to be remembered? Nowhere in Aaron's notion of love was there anything remotely resembling the willingness to erase himself for the sake of the other's ease.

No matter; Marisa had erased Aaron without his help, for her own ease.

He blew out a long breath, and admitted it: she didn't love him.

Beyond that thought was a vast, featureless terrain.

After a while he saw that he could traverse it all day without arriving anywhere.

There was a pencil in his palm. He took it between his fingers, bore down with his bruised knuckle on its ridges, and like a miner picking his way toward an unknown destination began to write—slowly, steadily, filling the void with work.

Was that what sadness did to a man?

He transcribed meticulously, responsibly, avoiding shorthand that could create confusion later. The lone scratching of his pencil on the page livened the silence, humanized it, comforted him.

Good Lord. He was growing up.

Women loved that.

By noon, he'd transcribed two documents, neither of any importance. Household detritus: A bill for bookbinding. A note about the timing of a pupil's next lesson.

He stood from his table, his body stiff with the morning's labor. He wanted another look at that cross-written letter. Something about it bothered him, though he couldn't say exactly what—something he couldn't get at by staring at the transcription on his laptop. The Hebrew words were taut and carefully chosen, as though each sentence had to arc around some invisible obstacle before setting down lightly on some delicate, all-important point.

At the desk he gave Patricia a perfunctory smile. "Document RQ206, please," he said.

She shook her head. Her gray hair, pulled back in its usual tight bun, looked like something she'd applied to her head with a paint scraper. She appeared, if possible, more irritated than usual. "That won't be available until one o'clock."

He turned to scan the long room with its rows of tables, populated at this hour only by a pair of classics postgraduates. "But I'm the only person here working on the Richmond papers. Who's got the document?"

"It's unavailable," she said. "Until one o'clock." The repetition seemed to satisfy her.

He blew out air. "I'll take the next available document, then."

He worked for another hour before Helen came in.

"Where were you?" he said, rising. "I thought you were going to be here more than an hour ago." He knew he sounded accusatory, but in truth he felt himself relax at the sight of her.

Helen set down her briefcase. At first she didn't answer. A tight anguish curved her lips. When she spoke it was quietly, though they were alone in the reading room save Patricia, bent over her glowing computer screen.

"I just saw Wilton and one of his students in the lift, with a camera. Coming *down*."

Down from the conservation lab.

Aaron swore.

At the circulation desk he stood over Librarian Patricia, backing up a step only when she looked up from her computer. A tall man occupying space: now there was a dissertation topic he could have done justice to, if he hadn't stupidly chosen a death match with Shakespeare. He knew just how to move in space with women, at least those within shouting distance of his own age: when to prop an arm and lean slightly over them as he made a point. When to sit back and let them come to him.

He wasn't quite as sure of himself, though, with these older women.

He set the fingers of one hand lightly on Patricia's desk and spoke in what he hoped was a casual tone. "What's up with the paparazzi in the conservation lab?"

She looked at his hand. He didn't withdraw it.

"One photographer is hardly paparazzi," she said. She turned back to her screen. But her distraction showed in the fitful way she moved the computer mouse, and he could see that he wasn't the source of it.

He didn't move.

"The document in question is being photographed," she said after a moment. "Along with a few others."

His hand faltered on the desk. "They can *do* that?" he said.

"They can," Patricia sang under her breath, "if Jonathan Martin wants them to."

"And Conservation Patricia let them?"

Librarian Patricia stiffened at the nickname, but he was too aghast to care. He thought quickly. He'd double down. A little camaraderie to sweeten the pot? He said, "I'd think she'd zap them with her laser-beam eyes."

Librarian Patricia stared at him. Her eyes were a pale, steady blue. She'd taken off her glasses. Slowly she folded them, with a soft dual click. A sound understood the world over to mean you were in trouble with the librarian.

"Of course," he began — and before continuing he offered a sheepish smile to ensure that she'd get the joke, and understand both that this was a compliment, and that the flirtation was recreational only. "*Your* eyes are lethal, too."

She blinked at him.

He leaned forward conspiratorially, bracing his weight on his hand. "You don't find me charming," he said in a low voice.

She leaned forward as well, her gray head nearly brushing his. "Shocking," she said, "isn't it?"

Her breath smelled of stale coffee.

She turned back to her computer.

After a moment he withdrew his hand and left.

"Well?" said Helen, back at the table.

He jutted his jaw. "She might not actually have a crush on me."

Her face was clotted with a desperation he only half understood. She brushed past him and went to Patricia's desk. After a moment Aaron followed.

Helen was addressing Patricia in a hushed, urgent tone. "They photographed RQ206?"

Patricia referred to her catalogue. She sighed. "Yes. And the next few in the series."

He watched Helen and Patricia exchange a look. It was like watching two weather-beaten lighthouses flash at each other across a wintry bay. A silent, fleeting exchange to which he had no access.

Helen turned to Aaron and nodded, her jaw clenched. Patricia had turned away in what might have been a gesture of tact or even sympathy

—he might have known how to interpret it if only he understood Brits. Or older women.

Maybe people. Maybe what was missing was that he didn't understand people.

Wilton was going to scoop them on the Sabbatean crisis in Florence. Aaron had trusted they'd be the first. But what hope did he and Helen have of that, when the other team had four able-bodied researchers to work on the project—not to mention a shortcut to publication in the form of Jonathan Martin, who had only to lift the phone to get the attention of the editor of *Early Modern Quarterly*? Wilton's choice to photograph this week, when most academics were drifting off to start their boozy holiday rounds, might even mean the editor had agreed to look at it over the Christmas holiday. Wilton was going to rush out an article on the cross-written letter and whatever else he'd read, before he'd even finished going through the documents. It might not be the most thorough scholarship, but it was a brilliant move. Anyone who wrote a second article on the Richmond document cache would merely be deepening Wilton's work—a follower on the trail Wilton had blazed.

Their only hope, Aaron thought, was that Wilton's group hadn't yet figured out the gender bombshell. He consulted his notebook. "I wonder," he said, "have they photographed RQ182?" The letter from Yacob de Souza carrying the request that the girl be replaced as the rabbi's scribe at earliest convenience.

"That and the cross-written letter were the first two documents they requested when they came in this morning." Patricia lowered her reading glasses.

"Well," Helen said.

Something on Patricia's desk seemed to require her attention. She busied herself with it; yet though her face was averted, her posture was intent, as though she were silently counseling some course of action.

Helen said, softly, "The next document, please."

Nodding her approval, Patricia left to retrieve it.

They worked for a half-hour in silence. Making his way through the document before him, Aaron transcribed a trickle of useless material—a statement of household accounts in Aleph's secretary hand, the flourishes atop the capital letters torqued back so far, they looked like coiled creatures about to fling themselves across the page. *For two vessels of whiting a summe of 4d. For 1 lb coffee 2s 6d.* He noted again that there were no entries for income from students—an indication, perhaps, that the rabbi's stream of pupils had dried up? Now and again, he paused in his work and watched Helen furtively. He'd never before taken the opportunity to watch her write. Her white knuckles pushed the stubby pencil across the pages of her notebook in a glacial scrawl so determined, he could imagine its lead point carving valleys and leaving behind boulders. If he'd noticed her writing style earlier, he thought, he'd have been more fearful of her.

At twelve-thirty, Librarian Patricia, unsolicited, approached their table. She set a cushion before Helen: the next document in the series. Never mind that Helen and Aaron were each already at work on a document. She departed, then returned three times more, bearing more documents. Six at once: a flagrant breach of library rules. Patricia arranged the new pages in a straight line before Helen without a word. Then, without looking at either of them, she laid a bare weathered hand on the tabletop, patted it once, and retreated to her desk.

"Jesus," said Aaron. He turned to Helen. "She has a crush on *you.*"

Helen had risen and was busy scanning the documents.

"You two are friends?" he persisted. "I never see you talk."

Helen slid a cushion closer and squinted at it. "I hardly know the first thing about her," she said distractedly. "Nor she me. Sorry to disappoint you."

He pointed at the six documents on their identical brown cushions. "Well, if you don't call *that* friendship . . ."

She faced him. "*That,*" she said, lowering her glasses to the tip of her nose, "is British for *May the best team win.*"

He looked at her, but chose not to laugh at the irony. What could possibly be the point in racing through the next documents? Speed didn't matter anymore. Wilton's team was going to press with the story of a female scribe *and* the previously unknown correspondence about the Florentine Sabbatean crisis: two huge findings, which he and Helen had had the naiveté to hold back until they'd done a proper job of working through the cache of documents and forming a coherent picture of who left it and why. Just like that, with no fanfare, their work had become irrelevant.

Failure. This time he didn't recoil from it, but poked at it like a miss-

Check Out Receipt

Lake Forest Library
847-234-0636
www.lakeforestlibrary.org

Thursday, June 10, 2021 3:39:33 PM
Considine, Maria

Item: 31243006047145
Title: The weight of ink
Call no.: FICTION KADISH
Material: Book
Due: 07/01/2021

Total items: 1

You just saved $17.00 by using your library. You have saved $119.11 this past year and $1,927.62 since you began using the library!

Thank You!

ing tooth, carefully prodding the sickening metallic taste, the blank, textureless surface.

Then he turned back to his work. He'd never done that: sit down to a task even though he knew he wasn't going to win. He wasn't sure he understood himself. But what else did he have to do? The horizon was bare.

Ignoring the new documents for the moment, he surreptitiously pulled out his laptop and positioned it on his thighs beneath the table. Despite Patricia's transgression of reading-room rules, he had little doubt she'd throw him out for such a flagrant violation. Helen Watt, on the other hand, seemed too focused to care. On his computer screen he pulled up a translation of the original cross-written letter.

Start at the beginning, he counseled himself. Like a good Cartesian thinker, he needed to approach the evidence with systematic doubt. A return to first principles: what, in all the universe, did he know for certain?

He read Aleph's words.

> I pose questions forbidden to men, yet I am myself blameless of
> violating the law.

Very clever, Aleph. You're a woman, so you can't be accused of doing things "forbidden to men." Clever, but by no means revelatory. Somehow he'd had more respect for Aleph than this. Somehow he'd expected her to do more than doodle upside down on her boss's letter in breathless hyperbole about how very terribly mysterious her scribe work was. "Come on," he muttered. "Give me something better."

He felt Helen's eyes on him but didn't lift his gaze from the screen.

> I gave this answer: I am an empty vessel.
>   It is not so. For if desire be the essence of man, it must be also of
> woman. I am a vessel that brims with desire.

He read the Hebrew text in full, then the final line in English.

> Where words are scarce they are seldom spent in vain, for they
> breathe truth that breathe their words in pain.

He'd been through all of this with Helen multiple times, but it felt as obscure now as the first time he'd read it. *Richard II* had been in circulation since before 1600, so certainly Aleph could have seen it performed or read it in quarto. Still, the quote felt as disjointed as the rest of the cross-written text. Maybe, Aaron conjectured, the business about forbidden questions was a sly reference to Sabbatai Zevi — maybe Aleph had been drawn to Sabbatai Zevi's movement against her boss's better judgment. Or maybe all the grandiose confessional language was simply Aleph metabolizing the fact that the rabbi wasn't supposed to have a girl scribe? Still, the soap-opera references to the day's events, the business about *the most wicked of souls* — it all felt paranoid, overblown. Possibly even a bit psychotic.

Still, even as he thought that, he imagined the shadowy girlish figure of Aleph herself lining up behind Helen and Patricia, all shaking their heads in disapproval at the obtuse American: why did he assume everything was as it appeared on the surface?

I pose questions forbidden to men.

Why? *Why* was it forbidden for men to ask about a Sabbatean crisis in Florence — assuming that's what Aleph was referring to?

"Helen," he said.

Only when she stared at him did he realize he'd called her by her first name.

With the tip of his pencil he tapped the line on his screen, angling the contraband computer so she could see it. "What do you make of that?" he said.

There was a silence, during which Aaron had a chance to appreciate something he'd overlooked about Helen: she was the sort who'd never berate a student for asking her to look at material she'd already looked at ten times before.

"She's saying," murmured Helen, "that it's the rabbi who's guilty of violating the law, not the scribe who sets down his words. But of course underneath that she's being mischievous and saying that *she's* not sinning because she's not a man. She's speaking through riddles."

"Yeah," said Aaron. "Okay." Clearly Helen didn't think there was anything amiss.

Helen was watching him.

"Okay, *what?*" she said.

The words burst out of him. "*Why* is it forbidden to men?"

Her gaze drifted to the high ceiling. Then back to him.

"Good question," she said.

They sat together at the table.

"Do you think she could be talking about something else?" he said to Helen. "Some other kind of questioning, something that *was* illegal?"

"It's possible," she said.

"What questions couldn't a person ask in the seventeenth century?"

Helen responded with a dry laugh. "Where do we begin? In the 1660s you could be imprisoned for promoting Catholicism when the king swung Protestant, and Protestantism when he swung Catholic, and the minefield was worse for Jews. French authorities searched bags at the borders to check for banned books—woe betide you if you were caught smuggling ideas across borders. Atheist remarks could get you butchered. And think about what happened to Johan de Witt, a voice of tolerance and political moderation! He and his brother were torn literally to pieces by a mob. Only the landlord's decision to lock Spinoza inside the house that day prevented Spinoza—who was out of his head with horror and grief—from confronting the mob holding a sign saying *You are the greatest of barbarians,* and meeting the same fate himself."

Aaron gave her a moment to return from the terrain her speech had carried her to.

"I just think," he said quietly, "that Aleph is up to something."

"Why?" countered Helen, but the sharpness of her tone was nothing personal. She was going to interrogate his idea; it was what they were there to do.

Even to his own ears, his arguments sounded thin. "Why the cross-written document? Why the sudden urge to save paper?"

"You've seen the meticulous household accounts. Perhaps she was just being mindful of expenses."

"Still," insisted Aaron, "we've read through dozens of HaCoen Mendes's letters that she wrote for him, and there's no precedent for her using one as scrap paper for her own musings."

"All right. What do *you* think she was up to?"

He slowed; here he was on unsure footing. "Maybe it's a commentary of some kind."

"How so?"

He tapped the computer screen once more. The straight lines of text failed to re-create the feeling he recalled from the original letter: an overgrowth of words sprouting from the cross-written page. "You know how a page of the Torah is laid out for study, right?" he said. "There's the main Hebrew text of the Torah—just a verse or two—and then framing it, in tiny script all around it, there are blocks of interpretation and counterargument. Well, this just reminds me of it. As though the inverted lines are a commentary on—or maybe more like a response to —that Florence letter."

Helen's silence felt like a lucid, steady current. She didn't say aloud *I take you seriously*—yet as the seconds passed without reprimand, Aaron felt loose-limbed with relief.

"I want you to see this," she said.

She moved her cushion closer to him. He read.

The hand was unfamiliar; the letter, written in Latin, dated April 17, 1665.

> To Thomas Farrow,
>
> Being the recipient of two of your letters, I am compelled to offer a reply. Your intelligence is sound I am sure, but you err in thinking I will rush into discourse concerning such propositions and proofs as you contemplate.
>
> I am not of a mind to engage in disputation with persons unknown to me. Nonetheless I feel compelled to warn you that your arguments are dangerous in nature. I do not entertain such notions as you suggest, nor do I welcome further correspondence.
>
> Faithfully,
>
> F. van den Enden

"Who's Thomas Farrow?" said Aaron. "And why does Van den Enden sound familiar?"

"No idea about Farrow," said Helen. "But Van den Enden is a name you surely once memorized for an exam. He was a former Jesuit and a convener of radical circles in Amsterdam—he tutored Spinoza and was one of Spinoza's influences. Van den Enden was known mostly for his political theories, and in the end got himself executed for conspiring against Louis XIV. I've no idea, though, what he might be responding to here. Nor do I have any idea what this letter is doing with Aleph's papers. Perhaps Farrow or Van den Enden had some connection to the rabbi, or to whoever put the papers in the stairwell in Richmond. Or who knows—perhaps someone entirely unrelated threw this letter into the Richmond cache at a later time." She wrote the two names deliberately on her notepad. It took her a long time to shape the letters: *Thomas Farrow. Franciscus van den Enden.* "I can go over to the archives tomorrow," she said, "and start a records search on Farrow."

For a moment Aaron worked his neck in a circle, thinking. "I still can't get used to the notion," he murmured, "that you Londoners can just do a search for records of some nobody who lived in the seventeenth century. A paper trail for everyone going back into the mists of time." He slid the cushion and its document away. "Sometimes I wonder how you people breathe in this country."

She pulled the cushion back toward her protectively. "What's wrong with having good records? Historians thrive on records."

"No offense, it's just that the English are pinned under the microscope from the moment they're born. Everyone knows about their heredity. Their *lineage.*"

Helen responded with a small sniff and turned back to the document.

Had he sworn to stay out of dangerous territory with Helen Watt? Fuck it. "We," he dimpled at her, "don't give a rat's ass about lineage."

"Yes," she said thoughtfully, pencil in hand. "It's one of a very finite number of things I've always respected about America."

He straightened. "See that?" he said.

"See *what?*"

"You English can't give a compliment. Not a real one. You don't know how to do it."

She turned fully in her seat to face him. "And how, Mr. Levy, do you suggest I compliment you? Please. I'd like precise instructions."

He leaned back in his chair. "*I like you,*" he enunciated.

She looked at him over the rims of her glasses, her eyebrows arched. He almost laughed at the perfect pose of English discomfiture, but held back.

"Go ahead," he said. "I dare you." He exaggerated each word now, as though teaching elocution to a foreigner. "*I like you, Aaron Levy—you're a decent human being after all.*"

Her mouth had shut. She opened it, after a time, to say only, "You're a bigger fool than I'd thought."

"That was close," he said. "We'll try again some time, okay? Don't feel bad, you almost got it."

When she was busy with her work again, he turned to his laptop once more. Let Helen go to the archives, he thought. He opened his browser and typed in the name.

A hundred Thomas Farrows lit his screen. A Canadian politician. An obituary in a Florida newspaper. He narrowed the search to the seventeenth century. The yield this time, once he'd weeded out the junk, was one solitary link. A graduate student in Michigan named Derek Godwin was writing a dissertation on a Thomas Farrow, circa 1622–1667. Godwin had delivered a paper at a conference three years prior; presumably he, like Aaron, was still laboring away to produce his masterwork. Godwin, according to the précis listed on the conference's outdated website, was arguing that Farrow was an overlooked voice in seventeenth-century thought, a man of slim but prescient output.

Potentially interesting, assuming this was the same Thomas Farrow. Certainly the fellow wasn't getting a friendly reception from Van den Enden. Aaron made a note to find Godwin's address and e-mail him later; he'd do it outside the rare manuscripts room, where clicking away at a keyboard wasn't risky.

Across the room, Wilton's team entered. They settled together at the table farthest from Helen and Aaron, silently positioning themselves so that eye contact with Helen and Aaron was impossible—all but the woman postgraduate, who was the last to the table and took the seat at the end. Aaron caught her eye as she lowered herself into the chair, and she turned away guiltily.

Immediately, Patricia was at their table. As Aaron discreetly tucked away his laptop, he saw why she'd come. Without seeming to look up,

Helen indicated the two cushions she wanted to keep on the desk. Within seconds, the evidence of Patricia's favoritism was gone, and Patricia was back at her desk.

The document that remained in front of Aaron was the letter addressed to Thomas Farrow. On the cushion before Helen was a page Aaron hadn't seen.

It was a simple page, written in the familiar flowing hand. A roster of expenses and debts—again, there seemed to be no income from students. Near the bottom, though, was something that had not appeared on any of the other household accounts. There was the usual letter aleph signed by the scribe ... but trailing down from it vertically was a signature, done not in a flowing hand but in separated Hebrew letters, as though the writer were daring the world to miss this slim path of markings leading toward the bottom of the page. *Aleph samech taph reish.*

And then, beneath that, written horizontally in small Roman letters: Ester Velasquez.

"That's her," Helen whispered. "That's her." And a look settled on her face, one Aaron did not understand: a look laden with regret and sympathy, as one might wear to a reunion with a friend one has wronged terribly, and from whom one does not expect forgiveness.

"Ester." Aaron tried out the name.

Beneath Ester's name, signed with a small flourish by the same hand, was another.

Thos. Farrow.
Let there be one place where I exist unsundered. This page.

Beneath that line, a list of three names, the first two with tick-marks next to them.

Van den Enden
Hobbes
de Spinoza

Helen turned from the page to Aaron.

"Thomas Farrow," he said, "might or might not be a minor philosopher who corresponded with some of the greats. There's a grad student in the U.S. who thinks Farrow's been shorted by history." His heart was beating foolishly. "Do you think it's possible—"

He didn't want to finish the sentence.

Helen was silent a minute. Then she nodded.

TOGETHER, AS THOUGH THEY'D CHOREOGRAPHED IT, they looked over at Wilton's table. For the moment, at least, this document was theirs.

Aaron took out a pad and paper, and began writing swiftly. Helen saw that he was transcribing the page before them, laying out each letter identically on his notepad.

When he'd finished, he set down the pencil and closed his eyes. Then he reached, blind, toward the cushion, and felt for the document with both hands.

She started forward in her seat. "What—"

He opened his eyes, took aim, pinched the lower edge of the page, and before her outreached hand could stop him he'd stood and in the same instant he'd torn the paper—a two-inch gash up the bottom left side of the page, far from the inked words.

She couldn't put it together in her mind, as though she'd witnessed an act of violence done on a living body. "Aaron?"

Aaron had thrown up his hands. When he called for Patricia, it was in a voice so contrite that Helen could have believed it genuine.

"I'm never going to forgive myself," he said as Patricia approached. "I'm so sorry. I'm"—he raised his palms: words failed.

Patricia's eyes found the torn document.

Aaron held out the zipper on his sweater, he zipped it up and down as he spoke as though to demonstrate its unruliness. "It caught on the paper as I was standing up," he said. "I must have leaned forward and the page caught, and then the string weights were holding it down so it ripped as I stood. I'll never wear anything like this again, I had no idea that could happen. I am so, so sorry."

On the other side of the room, Wilton's team looked up. As Aaron went on with his abject litany, one of Wilton's postgraduates turned to his mates with a condescending grimace that said *Bumbling git*. But

Wilton himself, with the charitable air of someone focused on a greater prize than humiliating an already-bested competitor, merely lofted his eyebrows and returned to his work.

The longer Patricia was silent, the harder Aaron seemed to try to fill the silence with apologies. But Helen could see Patricia's face—and she observed, to her surprise, that Patricia wasn't unmoved. Having seen that the damage was minor and didn't affect the inked portion of the page, Patricia seemed satisfied by Aaron's contrition. What's more, she looked impressed that he'd finally seen the worth of the physical manuscripts.

"Perhaps," said Patricia at last, "we need to add another rule to our protocols here." She sniffed. "Though the rules have never seemed to constrain you."

"I'll write the sign for you myself," Aaron said. "*No Zippers in the Rare Manuscripts Room.* I'll police everyone. I'm serious. I'll make this a buttons-and-Velcro-only zone." Helen could almost believe his anguish as he reached a futile hand toward the torn document and said, "Can it be repaired?"

Patricia shook her head. "That's for Patricia to decide upstairs." She regarded Aaron. "*Conservation* Patricia. With her laser-beam eyes."

He accepted the rebuke in silence. "I hope it won't be too much labor for her," he said. "I know she's already busy with other documents, and doesn't have time to jump every time a student does something unbelievably clumsy. Please do send her my sincere apologies."

And Helen saw. "I think we're through for the day," she said to Patricia. And then, surprising herself, she stood and gave Aaron's shoulder a single, awkward pat. "I suspect we'll need to settle our nerves before continuing."

Patricia took the document and left for the conservation lab. Helen heard the door of the lift slide open, then shut.

Aaron was packing his bag. When he turned back to Helen, he wasn't wearing the cocky expression she'd expected. He looked unnerved. "It hurt to do that," he said quietly. "More than I expected."

Helen's hair had escaped its barrette and the gray strands striped her vision. "You're bloody brilliant," she said.

A smile broke slowly over his face. And the haggard mien she'd noticed in him recently—the look that made her think perhaps Aaron

Levy might understand something of life after all—vanished under the onslaught of his grin, as it can only in the still-young.

"That!" he cried, so loudly she startled. "That was it!" Slowly he clapped his hands—big, emphatic, hollow claps that would have brought Patricia running, had she not been occupied bearing her wounded up to the conservation lab.

Helen couldn't mask her embarrassment. Even Wilton had lifted his leonine head and was watching now. "*What?*" she snapped.

"A compliment." Aaron stood opposite her, addressing her with a beatific expression. "I knew you'd get the hang of it."

18

April 10, 1665

To Benedictus de Spinoza,

My name will surely be unknown to you. Yet it is my wish to enter into an exchange with you, out of respect for your philosophy. I am in hope that you will entertain a correspondence with one writing from afar, for as you must know there are those who hunger to understand truth even though they be scattered to all points of the compass.

I have read your text *Principia Philosophiae Cartesianae* and admire it. You establish a firmament of clarity in its pages.

Yet I feel in those pages the weight of much you do not say. Your sentences hold back thoughts as a stone wall might hold back a hillside—only for a time, as the earth grows ever heavier under the saturating rains, and soil and rock must, come what may, unprison themselves.

It has reached me that you assert in private speech that God is nature. If this be so, then as man in all his varieties is encompassed within nature, it must also be that God does not choose any one thing or person to hate or love, as so many claim, but rather is equally present in each member of creation. Therefore God does not enter into any contest between peoples.

This must be correct, by my thinking. Yet it would relieve my spirit to know that another spirit argues this in cool reason.

I wish to understand more plainly, as well, what you mean when you speak of God—for here again, the words of yours that have reached me promise much, yet hold back much as well.

It has long been my wish to converse with you. Yet my own lack

of practice in the foment of philosophical conversation bade me approach your friend Van den Enden before writing to you, in the hope
that through exchange with him I might learn the manner of speech
and argument you employ with one another, and address you as one
less untutored. Yet Van den Enden does not engage my correspondence. It is my hope you will choose otherwise.

I await your response and will then say more.

Thomas Farrow

April 11, 1665
20 Nisan, 5425

To my beloved pupil Daniel,

Your silence troubles me, and so I write again, though perhaps
you may not welcome this intrusion. Yet I remain in great alarm
over your words. I fear what the Jews of Florence will do in service
of Sabbatai Zevi, yet I fear still more what they will do after he is
revealed as an imposter. I have seen what the raising and dashing of
hope wreaks upon the spirit of a community, the shame and divisions
it sows. Sabbatai Zevi will not leave your Florence as it was, just as a
fire does not pass through a stand of trees and leave them living.

Please inform me whether my letters have found you, even should
they have proven of no use to you. I fear for your safety in this mysterious upheaving world. In my infirmity I am able to carry but few of
the duties I would assume were I whole, yet this one duty I carry with
all my heart: my love for my pupils, who are sparks of light in this dark
world. So I beg your forgiveness for this demand of mine to know
your welfare, yet I will not rest until I hear word that you are well.

Rabbi HaCoen Mendes

א

April 29, 1665

To Benedictus de Spinoza, whose thoughts I hold in esteem,

You remain silent, as though my request for conversation hid thorns. Yet you know well, with a knowledge that lives in your very name, that even a thorn can bring welcome truths. If my thoughts are phrased other than is the custom among men of your circles, then I ask you to turn deaf to the defects of my speech, for an infirmity of the body has long barred me from easy exchange with other philosophes where I might learn gentler habits. I seek nothing more than an answer to what troubles me, as do all sick men and all thinkers. Perhaps it will aid your trust in me to know I have made the acquaintance in London of your former teacher, the Jew Moseh HaCoen Mendes. I think him an admirable and wise man, despite his adherence to beliefs I cannot share. He speaks gently of you, and praises your intelligence.

I wish to discuss with you my prior questions, and add to them these: What is the nature of man's obligation to the conventions of his society? If those conventions be in error—as must occur, for the conventions of one society contradict the conventions of another and all cannot be correct—then is a man permitted or even required to act upon his own renegade definition of virtue? Finally, what obligation does one human soul bear to another, in such a broken world as this?

Bacon would have us design a House of Solomon in which philosophers might continuously share their notions . . . for every notion must be tested against the evidence of nature and the reasonings of other thinkers—and if it be barren then let it be set at naught. My thought requires discourse with yours. Is it too bold to hope that you might venture to refine your philosophy through discourse with one like-minded, even if the end of such exchange is the disproof of all I essay? A question unanswerable unless engaged.

Thomas Farrow

April 30, 1665
15 Iyyar, 5425

To Daniel, or if I may call you Son,
It is a comfort to hear the words of your letter and to know that

you live. I feared, I will now confess, that you had succumbed to some sickness like that which lately shadows this London, which the people here dread so greatly that they begin to shun certain parishes of the city, even to the point of diminishing their useful labors and thus their livelihoods.

I am gladdened greatly to learn that my words have proven helpful to you in your disputations in Florence. Nor am I surprised by your request that I further explain how to use the words of Jeremiah and Isaiah to demonstrate the true portents of the Messiah. You were ever an attentive student and I see you remember well how I counseled against the misinterpretation of these passages. This labor will take some weeks, but as you believe it helpful in the loosening of Sabbatai Zevi's grip on your congregation, I shall undertake it. In truth, the work will be a salve to the loneliness of my position. You might find it strange that even now my spirit still rebels. Yet when I hear the labors of this household I still at times do yearn to join my body to some useful labor, to see with my eyes and work with my limbs, for such lifts man's spirits and in my youth did lift mine. Even an old man must guard against the evil impulses of rue and despair. So the acceptance of my infirmities must be a tribute to God, who in his mercy spared me while others more worthy perished, and left me the ability to labor with spirit and mind.

I ask that you write to me often with such questions as trouble your community. In return, I offer you my honesty.

Moseh HaCoen Mendes

א

May 19, 1665
24 of Iyyar, 5425
London

LIGHTNING, AND THEN. TIME ONLY for a single thud of her heart. A great roar cracking over the city, sheets of water down the da Costa Mendeses' window glass. Fury breaching the sky, striking her with childish terror. In each slow fracture, echoes—her brother's hoarse cries, and her own, and her father's silhouette as he disappeared up the fiery stair, calling.

Her mother's name amid a splintering of timbers.

Beside her, the da Costa Mendeses' silver candelabra, heat silently braiding upward from its three steady flames. Only lightning, she schooled herself. Only thunder, and only lightning. It would not strike here. It would set something else ablaze—a tree in a pasture somewhere, far outside the city walls. How cowardly, she told herself, to fear this when she feared nothing else—not sickness nor death. She stood stiffly, her body a raised fist against the heavens. "Strike me down," she whispered, her lips to the cool rushing glass.

The rain sluiced against the thick glass, obliterated the street. The world a gray wash.

From the hall behind her came a murmur of laughter. Thomas and Mary had retreated to another room. Easing back from the window, she slipped her hand yet again into her pocket to feel its contents. Ten shillings in copper and lead tokens, and another five in royal coinage. A fair sum for standing here like a statue week after week during Diego da Costa Mendes's multiplying absences from London, while Thomas and Mary made sport somewhere in the house. Yet the coins in her pocket were still a paltry amount when set against the growing need of the rabbi's household.

For little question remained that the rabbi had been forgotten: the disbursements sent by Mary's father, which had become irregular after the arrival of Rabbi Sasportas, had by now ceased altogether. Perhaps Diego da Costa Mendes felt that Sasportas might be insulted by any show of support for another rabbi, even one of such humble repute as HaCoen Mendes. Or perhaps Diego had simply grown forgetful of the rabbi's need for sustenance. Were Catherine alive, she'd have ensured regular payments were kept up—but Catherine was dead, and in her widower's mind, other concerns were now foremost.

There was grim humor, to be sure, in carrying Mary's coins back to a household her father no longer sponsored. But Ester knew better than to tell Rivka the source of the money she handed over each week. It was a sign of Rivka's growing worry over the household's need that she never demanded Ester tell her more.

But neither this mad dalliance of Mary's, nor Ester's absurd employment as paid companion, could last. A few more weeks, perhaps, and Thomas would tire of trying for Mary's money. Her father would never permit the marriage.

Restless, Ester surveyed the room. Laid carelessly face-down on the seat of a cushioned chair where she hadn't noticed it earlier was a thick bound volume. She picked it up. *Philosophical Transactions: Giving Some Accompt of the Present Undertakings, Studies, and Labours, of the Ingenious in Many Considerable Parts of the World.*

Never had she seen a publication of the Royal Society's transactions, though of course she'd heard talk of them. Men at the synagogue made reference now and again to some discovery regarding the workings of nature, or some new-published study of the tides that would affect their ships. Eagerly now she lifted the frontispiece, a portrait of the king and a man the caption said was Francis Bacon, and turned the pages. "Physico Mathematic Experimental Reasoning." "A Narrative Concerning the Success of Pendulum Watches at Sea for the Longitudes." "An Experimental History of Cold." "A Spot on One of the Belts of Jupiter." "A recipe for mulberry cider contributed by the honorable Sir Thomas Williamson"—this last item being the sort any could see was included merely to gain the Society the goodwill and patronage of the titled fool who contributed it. If only she might air her own thoughts as easily as this cider-maker.

This week had brought two more replies to Thomas Farrow's missives. Each time the letter carrier's knock sounded, Ester had been close by to answer, slipping the letters into her pocket until she'd leisure to read. Although she'd not yet received the reply she most hoped for, an exchange seemed to be beginning at last with Van den Enden, and with Lodewijk Meijer. Both their replies, to be sure, were still cautious, demanding further information: "With whom have you studied this matter?" "Are you in agreement with Hobbes in questions of providence?" The brusque tone of her own letters, Ester was certain, had given rise to such chary answers. Yet it was impossible to discipline herself to speak otherwise. Even in Latin she'd no patience for sentences that simpered like a bent neck, and that required study to determine where lay the cloying ambition, where the hinted insult. *Mine is by nature but a shadow of your more perceptive mind, and so I pray you forgive this query and understand it to be that of a mind that has not glimpsed the light yours has apprehended . . .* she could not bring herself to indulge in such serpentine speech.

Slowly she turned the pages of *Philosophical Transactions.* Like air, like water, such conversation belonged to these men of the Royal Society for the taking—while for the sake of her own halting correspondence she must deceive and betray, and labor for each flare of light to read by. And yet here were men parading their hypotheses and conclusions as though thoughts did not need to be clothed, but could walk about in the world naked and fearless. Her envy warred with her wonder over such folly—for should the king die, or should his fondness turn from one style of Christianity to another, these words lettered on the page might loft their authors' heads on pikes.

At a soft sound, she slapped the volume shut in her lap.

Bescós stood, his eyes upon her—in her absorption in her reading she'd failed to note his entry. Slowly he finished drying himself, using a towel the servant Hannah had surely provided at the door. He rubbed the back of his neck. Then his dark hair, rain-slicked where the hat hadn't covered it. The beard that trailed down his neck to the base of this throat.

The smile on his lips was no smile. "Such a melancholy Jewess."

He lowered himself onto the cushion beside her. The frame of the divan creaked as it took his weight. She could smell his wet hair, feel the heat off him, see the pores of his skin.

She weighed the bound pages in her hands as though they were naught to her. "Yours?" she said.

He glanced, and she saw the surprise register. "The proceeds of the Royal Society?" He gave a short laugh. "Thomas's."

The possibility that Thomas might read such material hadn't occurred to her. Had she been a fool to sign her letters to his name, certain he'd be unknown to the thinkers she addressed?

But Bescós continued. "Thomas would as soon adorn the privy with those pages as read them. Yet his father, as much a fool in his own way, sends such publications with the fervent hope some further education will persuade Thomas to leave the theater and revive the family name. I've little doubt Thomas carried it here in order to hand it over to me and be rid of it." A faint amusement crossed his face; then vanished, replaced by impatience.

There was something about Bescós today. He was distracted, as though waiting for the pans of a set of scales to stop moving so he could read the outcome.

Abruptly, then, distaste weighted the corners of his broad mouth. "A man tires of such silence as yours. Have you no polite chatter to offer a guest? Is there no lady of the court or stage you wish to insult while claiming to praise her? No tale of culinary adventure with which you wish to regale me?"

She kept her voice level. "I speak but poorly the looping language of coquettes, if that's your meaning."

"Yet you fancy you speak *this* language?" he gestured, mockingly, at the volume on the cushion beside her. "Why," he said, "does a woman read what she cannot comprehend?"

Outside, two flickers in quick succession. She braced herself for the sound.

"I know a maiden of fine quality," he said. "She understands her place in this world, and she'd sooner clothe a monkey in lace than trouble herself with such a tome."

Some dissatisfaction was working on Bescós, though it seemed to Ester that the source of his discontent was not the maiden herself. Was it better to ignore his dangerous mood or attempt to disarm it?

She said to him, "Does her father permit the marriage?"

Too late she saw that she should have kept silent—that in presuming to understand him she'd crossed some forbidden divide. She felt the sudden weight of his attention, trained on her now as it had not been before.

"Her father," Bescós said flatly, "wishes her to reach an age of greater maturity. While she possesses more maturity in a strand of her hair than he in his whole head. But I see you think yourself entitled to inquire into the affairs of your betters." With a swift motion, he took the volume from Ester's lap, his great hand pushing hers roughly aside. He flipped the pages. *"I have easily found the principle,"* he read aloud, *"and 'tis this, that this Comet moves about the Great Dog, in so great a circle, that that portion, which is described, is exceeding small in respect of the whole circumference thereof, and hardly distinguishable by us from a straight line."*

He turned to her. "You fancy yourself able to understand such words?"

She feared to answer.

"You do," he said. "I see it. They say the Jews steal ideas as well as silver and blood, and now you show me it's the truth. Yet do you believe this notion printed here? That your eyes might deceive you, and the straight line they show you might in truth be part of a circle beyond your comprehension?"

She said nothing, unsure whether further answer might provoke him.

"*I* believe in my eyes," he said, watching her. "And all the senses God gave me, each one of which proves His word."

She saw that he spoke of God not with passion, but ownership. God, for now, would be the servant of Bescós's restlessness.

"I like not these men of science," he said. "They deny God by worshiping the mind in his stead."

She knew she oughtn't. "Yet," she said, "is man not endowed with a mind so that he might better understand God's work, and even help prevent unnecessary suffering among God's creatures?"

"Ho!" He clapped his hands together twice, loudly. She cringed at the sound. "When I was a boy," he said, "my father sent me to the priests to learn. Do you know what they taught?"

Her gaze found refuge in the rain, still beating against the window.

"They taught that there is no such thing as *unnecessary* suffering. God's punishments are medicinal." He leaned closer, as though inviting her confidence. "The priests schooled us too about Jews. They said you think suffering unnecessary because you don't believe it purges the soul, and you believe in no afterlife."

She spoke softly. "I don't know the theology you speak of."

He brushed away her denial with a lazy wave. "No matter," he said. "The priests will argue it most persuasively with you in their time."

She saw he picked up and set down a threat like a plaything. Was he dangerous, or simply a man who wished to appear so? "There's no Inquisition in this country," she said sharply.

His smile completed her sentence: *for now.* "Your friend John," Bescós said, "is of a sudden strangely fond of the Jews. But then, he's fond of all hunted things, and is fond most of all of scolding the hunters for their cruelty. Yet I'll tell you what I tell him: the king of England is a Protestant as a butterfly is a caterpillar—that is, only for a time."

She rose, her face hot, and stepped away from Bescós. "You should leave this house."

"I think I won't," he said. "I find I enjoy your manner of conversation after all."

A knock at the door, and Hannah hurried to answer, passing Ester and Bescós with a wary glance as though they were yet another scandalous pair in need of supervision.

John entered. "Ester," he called, even as he handed his wet things to the servant. His voice was light, his happiness at seeing her evident. Yet she was too discomposed to answer, or to do more than glance at his confused face. And before he could inquire about her mood, a flurry of laughter approached from the back of the house, and on its tide Mary and Thomas—Thomas with a bottle in one fist and the other about Mary's waist. Greeting his companions as though it were his own home he welcomed them to, Thomas gestured all to sit. "What's news?" he called.

"John's only now arrived," said Bescós, "so he's been deprived of a most learned conversation. Mary's companion and I have been discussing the recent comet. And the gentle correction of the Jews' errors at the hands of the Inquisition."

Bottle aloft, one hand still on the fabric of Mary's dress, Thomas paused. Then he lifted the bottle to his lips—first cautiously, then draining it. He settled onto the couch. "The comet. Let's hear of that, shall we?"

Something fluttered on Mary's face. She blinked at Thomas. Then she sat.

"Provide for your friends, will you, Thomas?" Bescós said.

Thomas held the bottle upside down, letting a few red drops darken the velvet of Mary's father's couch. Immediately, Mary called Hannah for another bottle; while they waited for it, Ester saw Mary rub her fingertips over the stain with an expression both triumphant and bitter.

John was frowning.

"To learn of the comet, my dear Thomas," said Bescós, "you ought read these publications your noble father wastes on you." He lifted the *Proceedings* and smacked Thomas with it. Thomas grabbed at the volume with a rueful cry, but Bescós tossed it to the floor, both men laughing.

John picked it up. After studying it a moment, he turned to Ester and spoke in an undertone. "*You've* been reading this?"

"Yes," Ester said.

"I'd like to know your thoughts," he said. "My teachers speak most highly of the Royal Society."

"You're a student?"

John flushed as though the question were both compliment and accusation. "I was. Or am." He shook his head. "That is, I will be again, if I'm to have my say in the matter."

The new bottle was brought, this time a pale canary wine. Thomas held it to the light and scrutinized it, running his fingers along the elegant raised pattern stamped in wax at its base—the coat of arms of the da Costa Mendes house—as though sizing it up for purchase in the marketplace. He drank, and passed the bottle to Bescós and John. When it reached Mary she took a deep drink herself.

"Come, give it here," said Thomas, gesturing for the bottle again. "Medicine against the plague."

"It's the cats that spread that," said Mary. She took the wine from Thomas and drank again, cringing as she swallowed as though forcing herself. Ester saw that she avoided Bescós's gaze, conducting herself as though he weren't in the room.

"The dogs," said Thomas.

"Cats and dogs," Mary agreed. "And the miasma. Still"—she wiped her mouth daintily with the lace of her sleeve—"my father says we'll see the sickness die out before it strengthens." She flushed, as though she hadn't planned to mention her father. "The astrologers say so as well."

Mary passed the canary. Ester raised it, set her lips on the cool green glass, and drank. The wine was sweet in her mouth and warmed her immediately.

She saw the surprise on John's face: the ladies of his acquaintance, perhaps, did not drink from a bottle. Deliberately, under his gaze, she took a second drink, though it made her cough.

"How goes your wooing, my friend?" Thomas said as the bottle went round.

Bescós let out a warning laugh.

But Thomas persisted. "Have you softened your ways, so as to persuade her father?"

"You, my friend, wouldn't understand such things," said Bescós quietly, and Ester saw that while Bescós might prick Thomas freely in play, the same would not be tolerated in reverse.

"Ach man, give us a morsel," cried Thomas. "How far does this holy *she* permit your advances?"

"Thomas!" John warned. "Show respect."

With a sharp creak of his chair, Bescós sat forward. "What do *you* know of a natural love?"

Thomas's laughter quieted.

"Had I your family coat of arms, Thomas," said Bescós, "had I your *splendid* education, I'd be wed already. Yet see what use you make of them." Bescós's gesture encompassed Thomas, head to foot.

From his seat, Thomas replied with a mocking half-bow.

But Bescós widened his gesture to include Ester, and Mary. "What is it in this household, I wonder," he said, "that so captivates you, and John as well? Each of you entranced by your Jewess."

Ester's eyes fled to Mary, who appeared uncertain whether this was a jest.

"Let me instruct you," said Bescós, still addressing only the men, "in the manner of natural love. It's as follows: like must couple with like. All else is repellent."

Ester could not help but turn to John. He was watching Thomas and Bescós warily and now, blushing, cut in. "You speak as though the company of Jewesses were lesser."

At John's words, Bescós's eyes lit. "Yet how do you fail, John, to call the Jew unnatural? Do you know, man, about the Jews of York?"

None answered.

"It's a fascinating example of obstinacy," Bescós continued, his voice turning light as though he were about to recount an amusement. "They slaughtered *themselves*. Right here in our own dear England, they fled into a castle in fear for their lives, and locked the doors against the mob, and then when the mob made plain it would not leave without Jewish blood, the Jews killed themselves in honor of their own beliefs." He looked at Ester now, a curious smile on his lips. "Imagine that. They saved the Christians the knifework."

The rain drummed distantly on the roof.

"Truly," Bescós continued, "the choices of the Jews have always seemed unnatural to me. If I may say it, they seem born martyrs, preparing their whole lives for the moment when they'll be hunted, while con-

ducting themselves so as to provoke the hunters." He turned to Mary.
"Tell me, would you do as they did? Or would you rather someone else
set the knife to your throat? Or perhaps you'd plead and renounce your
faith."

John half stood, his hands gripping the wooden rests of his chair.
"You insult this company and threaten the ladies."

"Ah yes," laughed Bescós. "The *ladies*. But tell it true, John. Aren't the
ways of the Jews commonly considered fodder for curiosity? Haven't
you heard your own father muse thus about Jews?"

John's cheeks flushed. He gave a brief, reluctant nod. "Yet you take
matters too far, Bescós."

Bescós, sitting back now in his chair, waved a hand. "Well, John. I
retract and repeal any words of mine that might have offended."

John's gaze turned to Ester. She met it plainly, and her trust seemed
to firm his resolve. There was in him, she saw, something that hungered
to be tested.

But Bescós had done with testing. He smiled faintly. "This business
of the Jews is no real concern to me. I've other matters of my own to
attend to. Let's drink, and then we'll haul Thomas to the theater, won't
we, and propel him onto the stage still full of wine."

"See?" Thomas cried. "All ends well."

Slowly John leaned back in his chair, but Ester could see he was not
at peace with Bescós, or with himself.

Mary's nostrils were wide. Her eyes traveled from Bescós to Thomas.
But Thomas was occupied with the sweetmeats Hannah had brought
— these displayed with obvious carelessness on a silver salver, as though
to make plain the servants' opinion of the quality of the persons Mary
had brought to her father's residence.

Thomas selected a large candied nut. "Excuse Bescós for behaving
badly," he said. Then, hesitating before placing the sweetmeat on his
tongue, he added, "Or, don't excuse him." His eyes were bright as though
something at last had pricked him. Seeming not to note Mary at his
side, he chewed, then picked up another nut and, waving it widely as
he spoke, addressed Bescós. "You jest about my study at Oxford, my
friend. But what I learned from Harvey is no jest, though perhaps it
wasn't the lesson Harvey aimed to teach. My head was never fit, true, for

his teachings about the humors or the circulation of the blood. But my head is good enough to remember this: I held the man in respect, and I saw the world abuse him." He gestured with the sweetmeat. "Harvey was correct, all now say, about the workings of the body. And yet what of it? His life was misery. He was called crack-brained, his papers were looted in war. Forty years of work lost. It wrecked his faith in man. So" —Thomas waved the sweetmeat once more—then abruptly dropped it back onto the tray, and showed Bescós his empty palms. "This is the lesson I choose, of all Harvey's teachings: if the world cannot respect such a man, then the effort to be respectable is worthless." Locating the bottle of canary at his knee, Thomas reached for it and began to raise it to his lips, then paused midway. "It's not only sloth that makes me as I am, Bescós, though you know well my love of sloth. Look closer and you'll see I am as principled as any Jesuit—I simply obey a different religion." For an instant he met Bescós's eyes. Then, with a snort, he squeezed Mary's knee and, as she shrieked, lifted the bottle to his mouth.

"Go," Mary said airily to Bescós. "Go now."

Bescós stood. Amusement flickered on his face as he addressed Mary. "You're rid of me. But tell me—next time Thomas visits, shall your father also be present? For surely it's mere happenstance that Thomas hasn't yet been granted the honor of a meeting—and nothing to do with the fact that his beautifully rich Jewess is deceiving her father?"

"Leave her be," Ester said.

Bescós turned to her. "Ah. More speech from the princess of womanly decorum."

"If I was ever schooled in it," Ester said, "it did not adhere to my spirit."

"Perhaps," he said with a cool stare, "you have a spirit like a hot coal, so all it touches shrivels from it."

Mary let out a muffled sound.

Thomas stood. This time he had a hand on Mary's shoulder. "Come, Bescós, what harm are we to you?"

Ester saw Mary's face alter. Out of all the rest, the word "we" seemed to have entered her spirit.

"You're merely out of temper, my friend," Thomas said. And he gave a loud laugh to show they were all in fellowship and no insult would be taken. "And you'll come to see *this* is natural love." He squeezed Mary to his side, but without looking at her. "But when you return to your merrier temper you must bring your bride here to drink with us."

At the mention of his beloved, Bescós slowed. "She's too good for you," he said. But then, a gentler humor returning to his face for the first time, he added, "I'll bring her to you, Thomas. So she can see the poor company I was forced to keep before discovering hers." He turned to the others. With an inscrutable look he said, bowing, "My apologies."

"Now here's my friend, returned to himself," laughed Thomas. "Come aloft, then." And together the two men walked toward the door —Thomas with an expression of relief that made Ester stiffen.

There were men who possessed a force of vitality and certainty that emboldened all who kept company with them, whether for good or for ill. Her brother had once been such, and Manuel HaLevy. Bescós was another.

For all that he might deny it, Ester saw that Thomas had chosen Bescós as his planet to follow. And what might appear to the eye to be moving in a straight line and of its own accord was, in fact, traveling a long orbit around a more powerful body, at every moment gauging its distance to the object of its admiration.

Mary would not be able to see this. She would believe only the most direct evidence of her senses: Thomas kissed her. Thomas groped about the tabs of her bodice, relentless until he gained entry. Therefore he loved her above all others and would do all in his power to protect her.

John was studying Mary. Concern like Ester's own lit his face, as though he too could see what wasn't visible to the naked eye.

"On the next fair Lord's Day, then?" Thomas was saying over his shoulder to Mary, who sat moored on the couch. "And no fear, our combustible Bescós shan't come, he'll repair to wooing of his own." With this he cuffed Bescós's shoulder—but carefully, Ester noted. "And when you'll see him next he'll be in merry fettle."

Mary hesitated, then nodded.

To John, Thomas said, "You'll play companion to our companion?"

Her eyes found John's. What excursion was being planned? She hadn't been listening to Mary's chatter earlier.

John smiled at her bewilderment. "If she'll have me," he said. To Ester he whispered, "The river."

Ester felt herself pink.

Rising from the couch, Mary laughed loud. "Oh, she'll have you, I believe!"

Ester straightened the tray of sweetmeats on the table.

"See how they shy to look at each other," Thomas sang out.

Ester closed her eyes to the rain of laughter. She heard Mary kiss Thomas noisily on the lips, and his hum of satiety, and the light admonitions with which Mary accompanied Thomas to the door in Bescós's wake.

The rain outside was easing; she could hear its faint spatter from the drainpipe outside, and the shuffle of boots on wet stone. Mary, lingering at the door, called her farewells to Thomas.

John had stayed. She could feel him standing a few paces from her. The house was quiet.

"I'm sorry for his words," John said softly. "Bescós. I'll speak reason to him."

He was looking at her, his cheeks as pink as she felt her own to be. "I believe his grievance is with others, not with Jews, though today he seized on the subject."

"Yet what does harm," she said, "is not what truly merits a man's anger, but what he seizes on instead."

John hesitated. Then he nodded, once, as though pledging himself to something.

"The next fair Lord's Day, then," he said. He bowed and kissed his own hand and, stepping toward her, kissed her lips, lightly, as she'd seen Englishmen do with a woman who was their equal.

Mary shut the door behind him. Ester busied herself tidying the cushions.

"Perhaps *now*," Mary lilted, "you won't be so lonely."

Gently, she set a cushion down. She ought to speak reason to Mary once more, she knew. Thomas could bring only danger. Mary's virtue would become a shuttlecock batted about to the delight of all, if it were not so already—for if Mary thought the servants were fooled by the presence of a companion such as Ester, then Mary estimated her servants amiss.

Yet how to speak reason, when it seemed now to elude Ester herself? She addressed Mary in Portuguese. "Loneliness . . ." she began. But how to say it—how to stem this thing in her with words—this warmth filling her so steadily it threatened to expand beyond the confines of her body? This wish to be saved from the path she'd chosen. "Loneliness"—she spoke each word of the lie like a hammer stroke—"doesn't trouble me."

With an agitated motion, Mary tugged a wall hanging into place. "I envy you then," she said, "and pity you. I envy you that you won't ever feel the pains that a woman with a heart feels. And I pity you that with such disdain for life you won't marry."

She hadn't expected such words could sting. "I don't disdain life," she said quietly. "It's only . . ."

Mary turned. "What?" she said softly.

"I don't believe marriage will offer me what I desire."

"Why?" countered Mary.

For an instant, impelled by no logic she could fathom, Ester wished Mary to understand all she would lose were she to become a man's possession. "For one such as me, perhaps to marry is to disdain life."

"There's no sense in your words," Mary said with a wave; yet she was still listening, as though keen for Ester to cast light on something Mary needed to see more clearly.

"There was a woman," Ester began. "Her name was Julian of Norwich."

But she trailed off; Mary would never understand. Instead, seeing in her mind John's serious eyes as he stepped forward to kiss her farewell, Ester began afresh. "*You* wish to marry, I know," she said. "And for you that's well. But Mary, don't entertain a man so besotted by your father's fortune that he barely glimpses you amid the silver plate and hangings"—she gestured at the furnishings. "Should your fortune be considered by one of your suitors, it should not be the main, much less the only consideration—"

Mary broke in. "My father's fortune isn't why Thomas wants me! Are you so jealous that you can't see love?"

Ester went on, the words beating back the unfamiliar thing whispering in her. "He's fond of you, Mary, yes. But while your eyes linger hungrily on him, his look happily to the damask hangings."

"Do you claim to act as my mother then?" Mary cried.

"No—"

"No, because she's *dead*." There were tears on Mary's face. Unwise, enviable tears. Ester wanted to touch them.

Instead she spoke softly. "As is mine," she said. "There's naught but us to advise each other."

"Get out," Mary managed through her weeping. "You may leave, just like that monster Bescós. But—here's the truth, here it is, Ester! Both of you envy love such as we have."

Ester felt her own eyes well. "Perhaps," she said.

THROUGH THE RAIN-SLICKED STREETS SHE walked home, and her lips moved with words that sounded to her own ears like prayer. But if a prayer, then a prayer to a strange god: one who knew, as she did, the bitterness of the world, and lacked the power to alter it. *Kill it. Kill the part in me that desires to be touched.*

She couldn't protect Mary. Not without bearing her bodily from Thomas as one would a child. Mary had chosen her own course. And if accepting Mary's coins made Ester a proprietress at a brothel, what of it? She must steel herself. She must.

Yet even as she thought this, she remembered Mary's hopeful eyes at the instant Thomas had entered the door this afternoon.

What obligation did one soul bear to another indeed, in such a world as this?

So often now she lay in her bed half a night, constructing thoughts she wished to test against the books on the rabbi's shelves. And so often these thoughts—built with such care, the bricks with which she hoped to shape her understanding of the world—had dissolved by dawn. She could deceive the rabbi, but at night she could master the darkness no better than he. So she made what use she could of every moment of daylight she was permitted in his study. Just yesterday, in her desire to confirm the phrasing of Descartes's notion of extension, a question she'd fretted over in the darkness until tears of vexation sprang to her eyes, she'd forgotten that the letter she was supposed to be copying—a fresh bit of advice the rabbi had composed aloud for his former student in Florence—was a brief one. After a long silence—five minutes? more?—

the rabbi had lifted his head, his face turned in her direction as though to catch the rays of a weak sun. "How many pages you turn for my simple missive."

Had she imagined a catch in his voice? But he continued in his usual mild tone. "Perhaps I overtax you?"

Closing *Meditationes,* she'd agreed it might be time to finish their work together for the day.

Sentiment would undo her—each of its ties was a tether that would hold her from her purpose. Men, perhaps, might nourish both heart and mind; but for a woman there could be no such luxury. Had not Catherine drowned in the London air while practicing the virtues of love and obedience? How readily the rules of female behavior—gentleness, acquiescence, ever-mindfulness—turned to shackles.

So, she thought, there must be declared a new kind of virtue: one that made the throwing off of such rules, and even such deceit as this required, praiseworthy.

Or at least forgivable.

Of late, at moments when she looked up from her writing and saw the fatigue and hunger written on the rabbi's face—a face she'd known since girlhood—one small weakness flared keenly in her: the wish to be forgiven.

What obligation, in such a world?

The sips of wine she'd drunk at Mary's had dizzied her. Since morning she'd eaten only a piece of bread and a sweetmeat. When she reached home, she'd give Rivka all she'd earned, though it hurt to set the coins down on the kitchen table. But how could Ester use Mary's coins for candles and books, much though she craved them? Each week Rivka seemed to work harder, washing the laundry of strangers for extra coins—for Rivka wouldn't beg support of Diego da Costa Mendes unless the rabbi's next breath depended upon it. Instead she cooked patiently over the paltriest flame, using and reusing the last ashen bits of coal. She reserved the wheat loaves for the rabbi, and for herself and Ester prepared loaves of barley and rye of a poor grade, though even careful sifting left small stones lodged in the bread. Ester pressed each mouthful carefully with her tongue; already Rivka had cracked a front tooth.

If the growing need of their household was invisible to their former patron, it had been noted by at least one other. Tuesday, when Rivka was out, Manuel HaLevy had come to the house to offer what he termed *a small gift of sustenance*. Handing a bag of coins to Ester with a smile, he'd swiftly turned the conversation to the qualities of the breeze—which, he said, was damp that day but augured well for the trade vessels. So Ester understood that this new Manuel HaLevy wished to spare her shame. Ester had passed the bag back to his hands, inviting him stiffly to return another day and make this generous offer to Rivka, who managed the household. With an undaunted smile, he'd promised to do so.

She feared the debt that would come with Manuel HaLevy's charity, should need someday constrain Rivka to accept it.

Early this morning, watching Rivka labor in silence, upper lip curling reflexively about the broken tooth, Ester had paused for a moment over her own kitchen work to imagine Rivka's existence. No access to reading or writing. No escape to other worlds, nor refuge from the endless river of days. No dream of throwing her thoughts high into the thick-smoked sky in the hope that they might land somewhere brighter.

But how to help Rivka, when the threat of being herself plunged into such darkness struck Ester with dread bordering panic?

She'd reached home. She entered, hung her damp cloak, and stopped midway across the empty room.

There, on the writing table, was a letter, its seal of red wax intact.

Cautiously she stepped toward it. The hand was unfamiliar, but the wax seal told her all: a small thorned rose and the Latin word *Caute*. A rose, she guessed, to signify both the meaning of the de Spinoza family name—"thorned"—and then the need to be cautious—*sub rosa*. Her hands fumbled as she lifted the letter. It was addressed to this household, but the name on the letter was Thomas Farrow.

She broke the seal.

She'd been rebuked before. She had tried writing to Mersenne about Descartes's notion of extension, not knowing the man was years dead; the reply from his housekeeper had been a piece of incredulous fury. But the Latin words inked on this page stung beyond any rebuke she'd yet received.

May 7, 1665

To Mr. Thos. Farrow,

I have received both of your missives, and this reply shall need to serve for both. Your persistence is admirable, but you will permit me to question its purpose.

You express no admiration of my philosophy, yet you pretend to perceive its implications more deeply than I have confessed to, basing such claim on rumor of unnamed source. I am by now familiar with those who wish for their own purposes to distort my arguments, extending them into domains of atheism I do not claim. Should this be your intent, I must warn you to cease. My peace is lately harassed by the persistence of one called Van Blijenburgh, who first claimed as you do to seek truth—yet the man has consumed my hours and days in an exchange whose ultimate purpose, it seems, be to hunt amid my thoughts for what he might vilify.

If your purpose like his be to entrap me in my statements, then know that I do not fear my own thoughts, though the world may. Should you wish to understand my philosophy, you may one day read the works I compose even now and will some day bring to light, wherein I write in clearest logic what I profess. All the satisfaction I shall grant you now shall be but to say this: I do not refute the divine, but only its false depiction, and my thinking is maligned by any who say otherwise.

And this: your argument leaps without method.

I wonder that you know of my connection to Rabbi HaCoen Mendes. I've not written of him, and he remains, I believe, unknown to any outside the Portuguese community of Amsterdam. Nor would he have the ability, given his infirmity, to make his learning known to Christians in England. I wonder then whence you came by your admiration for him.

If it be so that you admire him—if your letter speaks the truth —then we share at least this one sentiment. Rabbi HaCoen Mendes was a man of great heart, though his thinking could not vault the walls within which it was prisoned. If he still lives, I would wish him know I think of him with respect, though the ban against me must mean he will not acknowledge me. It is for his sake alone that I write you this letter, for I wish no other conversation.

If my tone here has offended, I beg you understand that I must respond in this manner, for you wield my logic in such a way as seems intended to accuse me of being what I am not. As what I am brings me already to great difficulty, I wish no further calumny. If atheism be in your own thoughts, then write it under your name, but leave mine unscorched.

Benedictus de Spinoza

She read, and reread. Then she took a quill and, still in her outdoor cloak, wrote swiftly on a fresh page.

Your caution is sensible, and if I erred in leaping too swiftly into debate, I offer apology. That my intent is good you have my word —this I swear not on my own good name (for in this world a name may be easily taken and shed), but on my regard for the rabbi, whose honor I hold inviolable. If you but understood my own need for caution, which I may be bold to say might match even your own, your apprehensions would dissolve. I write my words in secrecy, my thoughts being unacceptable to man. Thus when I write I can bear to write naught but what I perceive as truth. I wish not to lure you to untoward opinions, but to discover together what truths we may.

You fear, still, that I wish to expose your thoughts while risking nothing? So I shall give you my credo on this very paper: such a God as the theologians would have us pray to—a God who in a world of suffering aids some but not others—cannot contain the mercy ascribed to him. Therefore, I say: such God as we pray to does not exist. And to this I add: there is no divine intervention. There is no divine judge. So we must supply for ourselves notions of good and ill. This is the purview and millstone of the philosophe.

So be my fate, now, in your hands. Should you wish to cry my name to the heavens as atheist you may. You may publish this address where I live, and if it is your will you may make my life a hellishness or perhaps end it altogether. Such questions as I explore, spoken in whispers, are not deadly in London today, so I believe—yet should I be known in plain daylight to propound the views I have just stated, they might swiftly prove so.

Now that I have placed such trust in your hands, may our two minds be honest with one another about the shape of the universe?

The rumors of your thought that have reached me, along with your work in *Principia,* prove a gift, as they assure my spirit it is not alone in questing after truth. Yet I say again: these words must necessarily be but a part of all your philosophy: a fence girding and holding back the mountain of your true thought.

Writing the long lines of Latin, she did not hear the rabbi enter. Only when he'd made his way to the fire did she hear the creak of the wooden chair.

"What do you labor at this hour?" he asked quietly.

Her hand was poised above the paper. "I'm copying," she said. "I spilled ink on the work we did yesterday."

The rabbi said nothing, but frowned.

"I'll finish later," she said.

He nodded slowly. He looked as though his afternoon sleep hadn't rested him. He wasn't well. She had glimpsed it now and again lately, but never so clearly as she saw it now: the too-faint breaths he drew, the translucence of his skin, the seed of death already sown in him.

Yet he spent his strength, now, on a labor he believed the world had asked of him. She did not know if she'd cursed him or given him a reason to live. Perhaps these were one and the same.

He spoke. "Your mind is occupied with some troubling thought today."

She didn't answer.

"You cannot study the holy words, Ester, or even scribe them properly, while your spirit is vexed. If you but untie the knot of vexation, the words of the text will enter your spirit, where they may ease all. This is how I have found it all the years of my life." He raised a hand gently to his temple, as though trying to share with her what was within. "When God created the world, He created first of all light. It was a great blow, Ester, to lose it. For a time I felt a darkness greater even than the loss of light. Perhaps you too have felt something like it. But these words —this learning—is my light. I believe it's yours as well."

She saw that he was distressed for her, was searching her spirit for entry. A gift she didn't deserve. The words flew from her lips—a bitter plea. "Baruch de Spinoza was beloved by you, was he not?"

The rabbi inhaled sharply. After a moment, he spoke. "De Spinoza was my great sorrow." He paused. "The Mahamad issued its decree with the approval of the rabbis of Talmud Torah, despite my efforts to persuade all of them. But I believe the severity of their *herem* banished an honest soul irrevocably from the light."

She bit her lip—then spoke softly. "And set him free. To write and think as he wished."

The rabbi stiffened as though smelling something foul. "Understand this, Ester," he said. "De Spinoza was in grave error."

Her throat was too tight for speech. She shook her head mutely—a gesture he could not see.

For an instant, memory summoned the young de Spinoza: a slim, all-observing youth, framed a fleeting moment in the doorway as he escorted the rabbi into her father's household. Whatever heretical thoughts de Spinoza had held in those long-ago years, he'd held them in silence—only allowing his incendiary notions to be known later, after his father's death. Had he deliberately blunted his words in his youth, loath to betray his living father as she now betrayed the rabbi? What selfishness of spirit, she wondered, reigned in her? What commanded her to set her mind free, though it must wound others?

"Ester." The rabbi half rose from his seat; she stood hurriedly, poised to support him should he fall. "A *herem* sets none free," he said. "It separates a person from the congregation, and so bans him from all that is commanded of a Jew, and from all that consoles us together even as it consoled us at Sinai. Such isolation, Ester. What sort of life is possible—with no ground beneath one's feet except the logic of one's own mind?"

His cheeks were pink with agitation. She'd never seen him so disturbed. "I'm sorry," she said. "I didn't intend to—"

"Baruch de Spinoza erred, may God forgive him." The rabbi's words fell heavily. "He suffers for it even if he fathoms not his own suffering. To live without faith is to live a death. I could not make him see." He held to his chair with one hand for a moment, then relinquished this struggle and sank back on its cushion. "I weep for him still," he said. "And will regret always that I failed him."

"Yet he lives," she said. "He's . . ." She hesitated. "Wheresoever he is, he must still thank you in his heart for serving as his teacher."

But the rabbi shook his head. His breathing was ragged; he waited until it slowed. "To us, he is dead. And even in himself he surely feels this grief. The youth we entrusted with the light of the sages' wisdom is no more."

The fire crackled behind him; his breathing grew quiet. The patches of color that had flared so briefly on his cheeks were gone.

He said, "You were the two best pupils I taught."

She stared.

"Even as a child," he said, "you showed a gift I'd perceived in only one other student. Yours was of a different flavor—your mind a straight path, his a labyrinth. But you were alike in so much. I have thought it often, Ester. It is my lot in life to share the light of learning with all who come to me, yet it has also been my fate to see the greatest gifts spilled into dust: one keen and vibrant intelligence lost on an apostate I could not call back from his errors, the other on a woman who can never make full use of such gifts. God has provided for me that I teach His words, and this must be honor enough. It is not for me to determine which of the seeds I plant will blossom, and which lie fallow, or even bear ill."

His face was clouded. "Ester, do not make the error of mistaking death for life."

She could not guess what he knew.

"Write for me," he said.

19

March 20, 2001

London

S HE SET THE WATER TO BOIL, tidied the kitchen until the kettle sounded, and, while the tea steeped, changed out of her nightdress. Taking the first sips of steaming tea at her kitchen table, she located the new edition of *Early Modern Quarterly* in the small pile of bills and advertisements that had arrived in yesterday's post. Before opening the journal she set down her tea, slowly, both hands required to steady the cup. For a moment she surveyed her kitchen: the spotless counters, the white curtains, the low glow of her shaded lamp. The geranium in its pot on the sill.

How much longer?

Forever, she answered. She'd live here in this flat, managing on her own, until the end. She certainly wouldn't be making any preemptive move into one of those dreadful facilities, despite Dr. Hammond's urging that she soon arrange for what he liked to call "eventualities." And if the prospect of a lingering decline, alone in the grip of Parkinson's, sometimes terrified her? Well, she could choose—couldn't she?—not to dwell on that thought.

At present, work occupied her days. All winter, as though adhering to a pact of silence regarding Wilton's upcoming publication, she and Aaron had convened in the rare manuscripts room each time the Patricias released a new batch of documents. In the interludes between, when other long-deferred projects demanded the services of the conservation lab, they revisited translations and did archival research. They'd found no further evidence of Thomas Farrow, and nothing to corroborate any link between Farrow and Ester Velasquez. If Aaron hadn't transcribed that document before ripping it, Helen would have thought they'd hallucinated it. Still, they'd labored together without either acknowledging the increasing likelihood that all was likely to be snatched from them despite their efforts.

A satisfactory approach to life, Helen thought. Dr. Hammond ought take note.

She set down the tea, opened the journal, and found the table of contents.

It took a moment for her mind to register what she saw there. Publication on such short notice was practically unheard of. She'd expected to see the article in the summer at the earliest. With a pang she realized it: the editor must have held space for something by Wilton, at Jonathan Martin's request, from the moment the Richmond papers were purchased.

There was no justification for the anguish she felt at the sight of the words.

Sabbatean Florence and a Female Scribe: A Startling Find Beneath a London Stair

She tried to read, but could not force her eyes to make an orderly progression down the page. Phrases struck her eyes at random. The type seemed to enlarge in places, the over-bright letters striking her eyes — then shrink into inscrutability in others, as though the words were molten and in motion. Only after she'd turned through the pages of the article twice was she able to read from beginning to end, the text cooling into legible sentences and dreadful, orderly paragraphs.

The existence of a female copyist shows our established understanding of Sephardic customs of the era to be incomplete. While we still lack evidence of any further violations of the dictates of the Amsterdam rabbinic authorities within the early London community, it would seem that prior to the consolidation of the authority of the Mahamad in London, there was a period when authority was sufficiently diffuse for one young woman to be permitted to scribe, for a brief time, for a rabbi. (As previously indicated, technical matters related to the conservation process have thus far precluded the examination of the last few documents; should additions or emendations prove necessary once the remaining papers have been made available, these will be presented as soon as feasible in a future paper.)

This Jewish female scribe's atypical employment is surely an interesting historical anomaly, one worthy of deeper research. Yet the words of the scholar whose thoughts she transcribed comprise the most significant revelation to emerge thus far in the cache of documents. The extent of the Florentine Sabbatean crisis, unearthed for the first time in these papers, is news of scholarly importance, with ramifications for the understanding of that community's role in the larger Jewish history of the region. While the absence of prior information about such a significant Sabbatean upheaval in Florence may at first appear puzzling, that absence can be explained by several factors, which deserve brief mention here.

Helen read the whole, scouring each argument for flaws, finding none. The reasoning was lucid, forceful. Wilton laid out the major points more clearly, she had to acknowledge, than she herself might have. He possessed a certain flair, knew how to take the dry medium of a scholarly article and shape it into story. He'd even included a humane discussion of the letter about the homosexuality and exile of a young Jewish man. Aaron Levy would take that one personally—he'd translated that letter only last week, and had foolishly hoped that Wilton's team wouldn't include it in their article. But no. Wilton had jumped every fence, claiming the entire course his own.

The brief missive from Rabbi HaCoen Mendes to Benjamin Ha-Levy, a prominent merchant, not only implies that HaLevy's son Alvaro was homosexual, but argues against the harsh punitive stance taken by the father. Benjamin HaLevy, undeterred by the rabbi's argument, chose to impress his son into service on a ship (this is the exile referred to in the rabbi's letter—see box below for complete text—and this punishment was indeed carried through, as confirmed by the muster roll of the ship *Triumph*, which sailed from England in 1665 and sank with all hands in a storm off the coast of Brazil in 1667). The father's punishment, paired with the rabbi's plea ("It is not

for us to stone the sinner . . ."), maps for us a range of Jewish responses to the looser sexual mores of Restoration London.

The inverted document is the most obscure element thus far
discovered. Although it's tempting to hope for further enlightenment
concerning its vague references, given the lack of a Jewish Pepys to
map the personalities and social intrigues of this community, it seems
unlikely we shall ever discover the full stories behind the individuals
in question. The scribe was most likely the daughter of one Samuel
Velasquez of Amsterdam, and is known, along with her brother, to
have joined the rabbi's household after the parents' deaths (we have
yet to confirm the siblings' given names). We can assume, however,
that this young woman's own education had not prepared her for the
learned discourse to which she had access in the household of Rabbi
HaCoen Mendes. The pronouncements she makes in the inverted
text are most likely a blend of her own thoughts and fragments overheard in the rabbi's conversation. Given the disjointed nature of the
inverted text, it also seems possible that she was merely copying out
lines from a poem or other source unknown to the modern reader.
Certainly a scribe might undertake such an exercise as a memoriza-
tion aid, or even in order to practice penmanship. Indeed the final
lines of the cross-writing invite this explanation; the scribe's use of a
quotation from Shakespeare's *Richard II* implies that she was versed
in popular literature and in theater, and perhaps eager to show her
knowledge of a beloved verse, even in a doodle to herself between the
lines of another document.

While comparisons to the discovery of the diary of Glückel of
Hameln will surely arise, this loose collection of cross-written statements offers none of the access to the details of daily life that makes
Glückel's diary such a rich source. Nonetheless, a young female
scribe's presence on the written page, while a lesser discovery, remains a compelling one. Indeed, her voice in the cross-written document—though occasionally breathless in tone, as any of us might
find ourselves in a heady environment—may be seen as a touchingly
human grace note to the graver matter at stake: the evidence of a
determined Sabbatean faction in Florence.

Multiple works will surely follow this first one: there is room for

a biography of Rabbi HaCoen Mendes, about whom too little is currently known, and there is perhaps a dissertation to be written about
his scribe, as we might glean from it something about the lives of
Jewish women of this community.

At the risk of injecting the personal into a scholarly article, I
must say that it is an honor to be present at such a find, and a privi-
lege to launch what will surely be a rich and multifaceted study of
these documents.

SHE ATE BEFORE DRIVING TO the university. She set her place
without a butter knife, put the milk back into a cabinet instead of the
refrigerator before realizing what she'd done. When she sat she didn't
bother, for once, tucking a napkin about her neck, and the sandwich
she'd made wavered broadly in her hand, scattering crumbs to the table
and floor while she aimed her mouth at it, and she cursed her hunger
and cursed her body, though she could not blame it for its mutiny. Had
she but loved her life, her body, instead of warring against them—had
she but loved someone, had she but allowed a different future . . . ?

She couldn't think.

Her blouse was stained with tomato juice. Perhaps she wouldn't
change clothing—would simply walk into the world like this: stained,
defeated. *Don't you eat?* Aaron Levy had asked, during that innocent
first week in Richmond, when she'd felt so certain that the documents,
once acquired by the university, would be hers.

She ate, yes. She ate in private. This was why. She'd let none but her
doctor see the extent of her tremor.

Except—the realization hit her, a tiny shock—Aaron. On that first
day in Richmond, she'd deliberately shown Aaron her tremor, hadn't
she? Lifting her hand and letting it quake right in front of his face: an
act of aggression, a dare. Why? Had she so wanted a friend—and so
forgotten how to obtain one—that she'd bullied an underling in a play
for sympathy? But it had had the opposite effect: she'd been so unsettled
by the horror on Aaron Levy's face that she'd barely been able to speak
to him the remainder of the day.

She stood, walked to her closet, changed her blouse.

AARON WAS WAITING FOR HER outside the rare manuscripts room. He looked as though he'd taken a bite of something foul and hadn't yet decided whether to swallow. "I've read it," he said.

She mustered a nod.

To her surprise, he reached out and, before she understood what he was doing, took her heavy bag from her. Hefting it on his own shoulder as though the weight were nothing, he breathed a long sigh. "Shall we?" He opened the door for her.

It took her a moment to identify the sensation that came over her as she passed him. Aaron was being protective. She felt *protected*. It was a useless gesture, yes. But she was grateful all the same.

Which made it all the harder, having checked in with Patricia and settled at the table to await their manuscripts, to speak. Still, she owed him this.

"You should join Wilton's group," she said. She didn't look at him as she said it.

The silence with which he received her words was interrupted by the arrival of Patricia, who placed a document before each of them.

When Patricia had departed, Helen spoke again, her eyes on the far wall. "I think he'd have you. You're good."

He still hadn't spoken. She looked at him.

"See?" she said. "That's a compliment."

She'd meant it as a joke, but her voice sounded stifled.

Aaron appeared to be casting about for a wry retort. At length he said, "Thank you."

"I'll be retiring soon, as you know." The words hurt coming out. "I'll write you a reference."

"I don't want one."

The door of the rare manuscripts room opened, and Wilton entered with his group. They made their way down the broad aisle, deposited their things serenely in lockers. To Helen they appeared too bright to look at, beautiful and terrible angels from a painting. But Aaron was looking directly at them, and he wasn't smiling.

Wilton was passing their table. She forced herself to stand. She forced herself to look at him. "Congratulations," she said. "That was a fine paper."

He hesitated, then nodded. "Thank you. I confess, I'm gratified by the reception it's receiving. But that's a tribute to the significance of this find, of course, more than to anything my group has done."

She offered a tight smile in return. She said, "Have you met Aaron Levy?"

Wilton stepped forward and shook Aaron's hand. Then, instead of stepping away from their table, he lingered with one palm on its surface, and Helen saw that he needed to tip the scales a bit so he could rest comfortably in his triumph. Having vanquished her, he'd now offer her some kindness.

Wilton's focus had fallen, she saw, on the document Patricia had set before Aaron. "That's the last of the Sabbatean letters, I suspect," he said.

"How do you know that?" Helen snapped, then regretted her defensive tone.

"The rabbi died on July 8 of that year, in the thick of the plague," Wilton said. "We have the death record from the parish, which is presumably correct. This letter is dated some three weeks before that." He studied the document, an expression of sympathy on his face. "Rather sad to see him go, of course." He glanced up at Helen. "The documents are really quite moving," he said, "aren't they?"

She saw that Wilton wanted her to like him, and she could not help liking him. "Quite," she said faintly.

Aaron spoke firmly. "Maybe it's the last Sabbatean letter, and maybe it's not."

Wilton gave an affable smile. "You're right, of course. It's important to be cautious. But feel free to check the parish records; you'll see the rabbi's date of death."

"I will," said Aaron, in a tone that might have rung defiantly, had Wilton not responded with a resoundingly friendly smile.

"Good man," Wilton said. "Always double-check."

Wilton made his way to his table.

After a moment Aaron sighed and worked a crick out of his neck. He mimicked quietly, *"Always double-check."*

She spoke sharply. "Don't joust with Wilton out of spite. You've got to have more sense than that."

"Maybe I'm not being spiteful. Maybe I have other motives."

"What?"

"Dunno," he shrugged. "Maybe I like you."

She blinked at the light from the clerestory. "You're a bigger fool than I'd thought," she said.

Aaron pushed back from the table. "Tell you what. Write me that letter recommending me to Wilton, okay? I'm not a fool. Write it and I'll hold on to it, and if we can't make headway in a couple more weeks then sure, I'll jump ship. Even if it does mean working with Wilton."

She looked at Aaron. "Why don't *you* like him? He's"—she gestured vaguely in the direction of Wilton, his students, their hair—"he's your sort."

Aaron hesitated. Then said, "I didn't like how he wrote about her."

"Who?"

"Ester."

She watched him pull out his notebook and set to work.

On the table before her lay a document on its cushion—from the look of it, another household account, like most of the documents she and Aaron had read these past months. There were, according to Patricia Smith in the conservation lab, only fifteen documents remaining, ten of which would shortly be available; four being rather more challenging to prepare, for technical reasons Patricia Smith would be delighted to explain if she thought any historian had even a shred of interest. And of course, finally, the document Aaron had ripped, now relegated to the back of the queue.

For the first time in memory, Helen wasn't sure she had it in her to begin work. There was no longer any point in denying the obvious. Even if Wilton should stumble, other competitors would now surely arrive. "What kind of progress do you think we're going to make in a couple of weeks?" she heard herself say. "We're already miles behind Wilton's group."

"You're right," said Aaron immediately. "There's no hope."

Turning, Helen was startled to see him smiling at her. If she hadn't known better—and she did—she'd think he was flirting. "There's something I need to show you," he sing-songed.

It occurred to her he'd gone insane.

"I received this last night just after reading Wilton's article," he said, "and I've been thinking it over." He pulled his laptop from his bag and balanced it on his knees. "I finally got an answer from that graduate student, Godwin."

"Godwin?"

"The one in Michigan who's researching Thomas Farrow. You may recall I wrote to him a few weeks ago. I got a vague reply, not at all helpful. Now I know why." He opened an e-mail on his screen. She squinted at the tiny print. With a frown, he enlarged the font, and, checking that no Patricia was in sight, set the computer on the table. "Godwin thinks Thomas Farrow is the next big discovery on the philosophy scene." Aaron scratched his chin. "He's a little unhinged about him, actually."

Aaron,

It's been a while since your note, sorry. I've been busy. In fact I've finally had a paper about Thomas Farrow accepted, out next year in *Archiv für Geschichte Philosophie.* So now I feel I can speak a bit more freely. Not to be paranoid, but . . . no one wants to get scooped, if you know what I mean.

So you want to know about Thomas Farrow. I don't think I'm exaggerating to say I believe I'm the world's expert—a feat that hasn't been hard to achieve, given that no one seems to know or care about him. I'm hoping to change that, if I can get anyone to listen.

Thomas Farrow was a son of minor gentry in Worcestershire. He had sisters but no brothers, and while his father had a small fortune he was apparently not particularly generous with it where Thomas was concerned. It seems Thomas's profligate ways had made an impression on the father—yet the father somehow remained blind to his son's deeper intellectual nature and potential. This blindness strikes me as rather pitiable, given what we now know about the man.

Thos. Farrow doesn't appear to have attracted the notice of his teachers during his time at Oxford, and his education was interrupted by the war. His occupation during the Interregnum is unknown, but later he was an actor—a minor one, I believe, and already past his thespian prime (if he ever had one) by the time the

theaters reopened under Charles II. But the striking thing is the way
he bloomed as a philosopher in 1665–67. If you didn't know better
it might seem his brief outpouring of work came out of nowhere—
though a thoughtful study of his output makes obvious how deeply
he was drawing on his prior experiences and studies.

I detail all of this in my forthcoming article (due out in next
winter's issue, from what they tell me) so I won't go on here, but thus
far I've tracked down letters by Farrow in the archives of the Royal
Society, and in the papers of Van den Enden and Adriaan Koerbagh. Some of the letters make bold assertions, others contain more
detailed philosophical arguments. It's clear, among other things, that
Farrow took a position on the divine well past where even Hobbes
was willing to go, which was an astonishingly risky thing to do. Farrow is frankly weighing atheism, at a time when that could mean
death. His main concerns seem to be the nature of God and, depend-
ing how that question is answered, the nature of man's moral and
social obligation.

Farrow didn't get much attention during his brief career because
he never made the sort of allies who would spread the word about his
work. The reason, I think, is that he was rude. He didn't kowtow to
other philosophers—none of those long flowery introductions, none
of the "your mind is so great and mine is so paltry" demurrals. He
went straight for the jugular. I've made a great find, if I say so myself:
I've dug up a letter from Thomas Browne to a minor Royal Society
member named Jonathan Pierce in which Browne complains about
Farrow. He says, "This ill-mannered Farrow will unmake your argument in a single sentence brutal short."

A single sentence brutal short. They respected Farrow at least,
yes?

I owe you thanks, by the way. It's been a slog trying to convince
people this dissertation subject is worthy. Without detailing the
slings/arrows of a graduate student's life, which you're surely familiar
with, I'll just say I was in a hole, not sure I'd even be able to get my
Farrow article accepted for publication. Your e-mail threw me a rope
—reminded me that people out there want to know about Farrow.
To me, he is an undiscovered gem, and the fact that his career as a

philosopher was cut short by his accidental death at the age of only
47 is a tragedy. The injustice of his being unknown is something I
want to correct. Farrow may have been considered unimpressive
during his early years, but underneath that unimpressive exterior
there was a remarkable mind working. Goes to show, you never know
which thinkers will turn out to be the real thing till you see what
they come out with.

At least, that's what I'm hoping my advisor will conclude, years
from now.

Cheers,

Derek

Helen read the letter twice. When she turned to Aaron his face was
bright with expectation.

"Do you think there's a chance?" he said.

For an instant she considered pretending she didn't think so, didn't
know what he meant, objected to the leap in logic that he was making.
But the cautioning words she'd been about to speak dropped cleanly out
of her mind. Why had she ever bothered speaking in that manner—
that mincing academic language in which one pretended not to know
what one knew in one's heart, until it had been tested and objectively
proved to death? What had it ever benefited her, to speak that way? And
what, now, did she have to lose?

"It *was* her handwriting," Helen said. "She wrote *Thomas Farrow* at
the bottom of that page."

If Ester had masqueraded as Thomas Farrow, then a world of possi-
bilities opened. Had she used that fake identity to carry on a clandestine
correspondence? What of the real Thomas Farrow—was it just a coincidence that she used his name, or had she known him?

"Can you ask to see the proofs of Godwin's article?" she said to Aaron.

"Already have."

She nodded approval.

"Wilton seems to think the cross-written lines were some kind of
schoolgirl swoon," Aaron said. "But what if everything she said was for
real? What if Ester wasn't being coy, but was telling the truth, as clearly
as she dared, about her decision to write under someone else's name?"

Yes. Yes. Helen could hear the protestations of every scholar in the field: Jews of the seventeenth century had no tradition of confessional literature; they didn't disburden themselves on paper; any literate women put their literacy to use in running a household. Helen didn't care. For no reason at all, she was certain: Ester had cross-written on discarded drafts not to be clever, and certainly not to practice penmanship—but because there was a secret she had tamped down until it was a murderous weight inside her . . . and she needed there to be, somewhere in the world, at least one place where the truth existed.

Helen seemed to have abandoned logic, and so she could not explain why the final lines of the cross-written letter came to her now: *Where words are scarce they are seldom spent in vain, for they breathe truth that breathe their words in pain.*

She spoke the words aloud.

"What do you think that means?" said Aaron.

She shook her head. "Don't know. But I think she's telling us something. About her life. Or maybe," she added after a moment, "about regret."

She'd turned away from the screen, as had he. His eyes were dark and arresting, they were Dror's and his own, and she wanted to hold the image in her mind forever.

They turned to the documents. Their pencils scratched uninterrupted on notebook paper; Helen kept her eyes averted from Wilton's table. After a half-hour, Librarian Patricia appeared bearing a third and fourth document for Helen and Aaron, no longer seeming to care if Wilton's group saw—clearly she'd seen the *Early Modern Quarterly* article too. As they worked, Patricia came and went unbidden like a magical apprentice, bringing and removing documents.

Helen had just turned to her fourth document, another list of household expenses. It was written in Portuguese in Ester Velasquez's slanted hand. Yet again, no household income was listed. The document was dated May 4, 1665. She scanned it quickly, as she did with each before she set to the work of translation. At the base of the third and final page, beneath the usual tally of expenses and the initial aleph, Helen's eye caught a line of cross-writing in a different ink, as though it had been added after the fact. No, not even a line. It was a single word, inked thinly and carefully between the lines of the inventory, like a spider hanging barely visible in a corner.

אהבתי

An assault, a rebuke across the years. An outstretched hand.

The inverted letters spelled the single Hebrew word that meant "I loved."

20

June 17, 1665
London

To the Esteemed Benedictus de Spinoza,

Your brief response to my last missive would persuade any less determined than I that it were folly to continue this exchange. Indeed modesty ought impel me to conclude that you do not consider my crude thoughts worthy of your time. If this indeed be the reason for your refusal to engage in dialogue with me, then I must apologize and retreat. But in my stubborn folly, Sir, I maintain that despite the flaws that surely mar my argumentation, it is my wish to weigh the merits of atheism that makes you refuse to debate with me. It may be that others, be they the enemies of toleration in your land or even spies of the Inquisition, have endeavored to entrap you into such speech. It is natural you might fear that I claim loyalty to some cause hostile to free thought.

Yet I swear, though it bereave my heart, that I labor to shed all loyalty save that to truth. For every loyalty, whether to self or community, does impose a blindness, and each love does threaten to blur vision, as few can bear to see truth if it harm that which is dear to us. In separating you from your community, mayhap the ban issued upon you in Amsterdam offered a manner of freedom. Vanishing from your people's reach, you shed the unbearable sorrows of the martyrs of your people, which any soul must be stirred by. While you were yet beholding such sorrows, surely some thoughts—those with thorns that prick one's own people—would seem unutterable.

I am gladdened to believe that you employ your freedom now to loose your tongue and pen, and speak as you could not before. Yet caution follows one everywhere, for this world is not a safe one.

If there be any further freedom than the one granted by excommunication, perhaps it is the freedom not to exist.

Existing, you and I and all thinkers are in danger. Is this why you say less than you believe? You insist you do not argue against the existence of God. Yet I would therefore know what manner of divine existence you claim. The folly of those who cling to notions of divine intervention is evident every instant, for the babe born deformed did not merit the life of pain that awaits it, nor do those who dedicate their lives to purity merit the torment and suffering they are so often meted. Therefore it must either be that God cares naught for suffering, or that God lacks the power to provide more tenderly for creation. Unless immortality exist to balance these equations after man's death, they remain unbalanced. And as I endeavor to dismiss all for which I can locate no proof, and as I have yet located no proof of life after death, then these thoughts must lead me toward either a theism in which the divine possesses power without mercy or justice, as though a vast infant ruled over the universe dispensing decrees at whim; or rather toward the thought that the force commanding the universe possesses will but no power, for which notion I might be charged with atheism. It is from this stance that I embrace your conception of God as nature. Yet I remain unsatisfied with my understanding of this notion.

In your second missive you offer me a crumb of your philosophy as though to dismiss me with it: you say that God is substance. Sir, I remain hungry. Of what manner and purpose be this substance?

I have seen the blinded eyes of the rabbi HaCoen Mendes. In questioning faith, we scathe all faithful such as he. How cruel, then, must seem the atheist to the martyr.

Yet without willingness to speak honestly, does the philosopher not take irons to the eyes of truth?

T. F.

She set down her quill and read over the words. Would she dare send such a thing? She'd written the words to see how far she ventured to speak her mind.

The rabbi slept in his chair. Even when Ester could find in herself no belief in the God of the psalms or prayers, she believed in the holiness of Rabbi HaCoen Mendes's spirit. She, in her deceit, must then be his truest enemy.

Yet the change she noted lately in his arguments was undeniable. On his own behalf, she'd long observed, the rabbi dared little, muting his disagreements, ceding to other authorities. Yet on behalf of her imagined Daniel Lusitano, he spoke with his own authority. His face livened; his language was sharper, tearing falsehoods apart. Only in his love for his students, Ester saw—first de Spinoza, and now Daniel Lusitano—could the rabbi thus assert his thoughts. And as she penned his words onto pages that would never be sent, she felt her hand transcribing a wakened, vigorous spirit.

So she justified her own treachery, further proving her baseness.

She slid the page she'd been writing beneath the letter it had rested on, which had arrived two days earlier.

June 5, 1665

Ester,
   You will find here the sum of £7 to maintain the household of
Rabbi HaCoen Mendes, and those who live with him. I know you
will not be so foolish as to refuse such aid, for though you might
deny yourself, you won't deny those in your household.
   Consider this gift, and from whom it comes to you.
   I leave soon for the countryside, which is untouched by the seeds
of the plague that sprout now in some parishes of the city. At present
I plan to go alone. That need not be so.
   Manuel HaLevy

Half the coins that had arrived with Manuel HaLevy's letter had been spent immediately on household provisions. The rest Rivka was carefully husbanding. Ester had not yet replied.

She drew out a blank page now.

To Manuel HaLevy,

I thank you for your letter, and for the support it grants us in our need. Your act is generous beyond expectations. We could not hope for more.

She sat for a long time, searching for further words that would not betray her. Beneath Manuel's letter lay a page inked to de Spinoza and signed under a man's name—a letter that told the truth of her spirit. Yet the truths of her body were undeniable: the hunger in her belly, the ache of her feet from treading the streets in shoes worn past repair. And another hunger she hardly dared acknowledge.

I cannot consider your offer of marriage, she wrote slowly.

At the sound of the clock chiming the hour, she rose and washed the ink from her hands. Upstairs she hesitated a moment over a dress Mary had had her purchase long ago, when Catherine first insisted that Ester accompany her daughter. She'd worn it but few times, yet surely it would still fit as she recalled, the elegant cloth falling away smoothly from her waist? For a moment she ran her fingertips along the pale blue taffeta.

Stilled, one hand on the crisp fabric, she acknowledged it. Yes: she betrayed herself, and hoped. But for what? That an Englishman with kind eyes forgive her for being a Jewess? That he love her . . . and then what? Marry her? And in his kindness make her relinquish, more gently but as surely as Manuel HaLevy would, the thing that animated her spirit?

She turned and pulled her plain daily dress from its hook, nearly tearing the seam when the fabric caught. Cursing, she watched the figure fumbling over the buttons in the narrow glass. A hate welled up in her for her life.

A sound from the street; the da Costa Mendeses' coach arrived. Hurriedly Ester descended the stair, as Rivka opened the door to Thomas Farrow.

"Good morning," Thomas sang.

His worn red doublet was unbuttoned to show a waistcoat of blue silk, his breeches open at the knee above blue hose, red-heeled shoes with their red lining turned down in the shape of a bow. He stared frankly at Rivka—as though he'd heard of thick-bodied, scant-haired Tudesco Jewesses with smallpox-rubbled cheeks and whiskers on their chin, but had not until now believed that such creatures existed. Rivka, in turn, stared back: first at Thomas's bright attire, and then up at his face, its own fainter smallpox scars nearly masked by an application of ceruse—the patent, careful vanity of a man pretending to be younger than he was.

Slowly Thomas doffed his black velvet riding hat to Rivka, who didn't twitch a muscle in response. It occurred to Ester that Rivka wouldn't weep to see Mary's reputation trounced, nor by such a man.

Ester parted the leather curtain and entered the coach, settling beside John, who greeted her, quickly shifting to make room. He too was dressed in doublet and hose, but the difference between Thomas's attire and his was the difference between a peacock and some self-contained brown-and-white river bird.

"A fine day," John said to her as the coach began to move.

"Yes." He sat too close for her to look at him. Instead she looked at Mary, seated beside Thomas on the bench opposite. Mary had dressed in a pale yellow moiré with a petticoat of peach silk. Adhered to her cheek and bosom were several small black velvet patches—one in the shape of a galloping horse, another a boat with sails swelling, and a crescent moon on her breast. Seated together, she and Thomas were a pageant of color and fashion. But the expression on Mary's face differed entirely from that on Thomas's. Her lips were parted distractedly, her eyes shining and unfocused—Ester saw that she'd used belladonna drops to dilate them, sacrificing the day's vision for the chance to seem to Thomas more melting, more womanly.

Yet who was Ester to judge Mary? She herself had yet to say more than a single word to John. She knew how to block the path to flirtation, but not how to open it.

Over the clatter of the coach's wheels, Thomas addressed them. "I was of a mind that we might see the lunatics on show at Bedlam, or the puppets at Charing Cross. But those places are too thronged up, and Mary fears the plague." He accepted a jumbal cake from the small

sack Mary offered, chewed, then took a flask from his pocket and un-
stoppered it. "So I thought the India House, but Mary's so afeared of
serpents, she might faint to see the great one they have there. So this
decided me: today we go up the river and down it." He drank again.

John's whisper brushed Ester's ear. "The plan was ever the river, but
he struts thus for Mary. Thomas's London is made of theaters and alehouses."

Grateful to have grist for speech, Ester whispered back in a rush.
"Yes, though it's Mary who'll pay for the boat, I'm certain, and food and
drink."

John didn't answer. She ventured a glance. He was watching intently
out the window, his cheeks bloomed pink.

She hadn't meant to shame him. It was absurd—what did it matter
to her if he himself didn't pay for their outing, but allowed the da Costa
Mendes fortune to provide all?

She'd no understanding of his air of protected English decency. Pro-
priety, the notion of a fair world with codes that must be upheld—it
seemed absurd to her. The piercing practicality of a man like Manuel
HaLevy, Ester had to acknowledge, felt to her more honest. Yet the
thought that her words might have stung John's pride made her frantic.

She wished to understand him—and it seemed to her that he was
as hidden as she.

She turned, abruptly, to face him. Almost comically he started back
from her.

"Why are you here?" she said.

His expression tipped between laughter and alarm. "On this bench?"

"In London," she said.

"I respect my father's calling," he shot back—as though this defense
had been spooling out in his mind even before she posed the question.
"But he wished for me to align my studies to follow in his profession.
He's a virtuous man and held in much honor, but I told him I wished to
study more widely. If I return to his profession, I wish it to be as a man
with his eyes opened to the world."

"And what do you study?"

"Poetry, history, art, a bit of natural philosophy." He laughed a quick
laugh, as though expecting her to demean these pursuits. "I completed
my university studies months ago, but with the universities wholly con-

cerned now with theology and law, a man who wishes broader learning must find tutors. I linger in London on the last of my allowance to attend lectures as long as I still may. Each week now I receive a letter calling me home to my father's estate, yet I've no wish to return before I must." He searched her face; what he saw there seemed to reassure him. "I hold my father's wisdom in esteem, yet his thinking is like the gardens of his estate," he said. "Each plant or tree is trimmed into stately form, yet each is rooted in only its place in the landscape and has touched no other." He glanced at her once more, then out the window, a flush of a different sort spreading on his cheeks.

At a stair on the river, their driver called the horse to a halt. A brief conference; then Thomas and John stepped down from the coach and left them. Mary sat doll-like in the carriage, blinking.

"Shall we step out?" said Ester.

There was no response, save a small huff of air meaning *no*.

"What troubles you?"

Mary's voice was tight. "Not a thing." Her gaze was fixed out the window and she didn't move — not even a few moments later when the coach swayed with Ester's descent.

Puddles from the recent rain edged the road. Beneath Ester's shoes, brown water seeped between the cobblestones. Nearby, at the edge of the stair, John and Thomas conversed intently with a whiskered man, who stood with arms folded. They weren't alone in bidding for the whiskered man's services; two other men waited behind Thomas and John. Beside Ester, the driver of Mary's coach stood on the street with one hand on the horse's harness. He was picking his teeth and gazing at the river traffic.

Thomas looked displeased as he and John returned to the coach. Seeing Mary still lost in some reverie, Thomas rapped sharply on the side of the coach, startling her. "A hard time of it," he said, "to find a boat to take upriver. The rich are leaving the city again as they love to, for fear of sickness, and in their petty panic claim all the boats. Our good man of the river insists we hire his horse to pull the skiff against the current, or he won't let us have his boat — for he can earn more money by hiring both to us, and he knows well that his three-quarters-dead horse is no good for city use. He's had his way with us too, for there were more looking to hire his boat should we have refused. Imagine, to hire a nag when we've got this one standing idle." Thomas looked regretfully at Mary's father's fine horse. Cuffing Mary's driver jovially on his shoulder, he said to the man, "You should hire this one out while we're upriver. A bit of silver for your own pocket."

The da Costa Mendeses' driver shielded his eyes from the glare and said nothing. But Mary, who had climbed stiffly down to the wet street, signaled him to go. Accepting his dismissal, the driver mounted his seat and *tch*ed the horse slowly into the city streets and out of sight.

Mary watched him go. Then turned to Thomas and said in a pointed tone, "How much for the boat?"

Thomas hesitated. With a quick glance to John, he said, "Six shillings."

Mary pulled an embroidered pocket from the placket of her skirt. She counted the coins deliberately into his hand.

Thomas gave the coins a high toss and caught them, a jaunty gesture. Now that he'd received them thus from the air — as though they were a gift from the fates, rather than from Mary — his mood seemed restored. He clapped John on the shoulder. "It's fortunate the river only goes in two directions," he said. "Our boatman is so drunk he can't find his arse with two hands."

"Thomas, man," John protested.

"They've heard it before, John," he said. "You need to stop being afraid of women." Coming up alongside Mary, he smacked her bottom. She winced and said nothing, which seemed to irk him. Faced with her silence, he shrugged after a moment and turned to the river. "We'll have a leisurely trip, then."

John wore a sober expression. "So many fleeing for the country," he murmured. "Has the sickness reached new parishes?"

"But they go for nothing, John," Thomas laughed. "Flying off in little boats. They do it each time some new fear visits the city. And do you know who rejoices? The thieves. The richer a man gets, the richer he is in fear, so at the least shadow he abandons all his worldly goods except what he can carry. All those frightened gentlemen will have their lovely silver plate robbed out of their houses by the time they return. If I only had a skill for thievery I'd be running off this moment to start the plunder — and if I received a clap on the shoulder, I'd just split my wealth with the magistrate." At a sound of protest from John, Thomas laughed.

"No harm meant to your father, I believe you that he's honest, but if so, then he's the single honest one in all of England."

Only Ester saw the bitter twist that, for a moment, overtook Mary's face: *why steal when all is being given you?*

They walked together to the muddy stair and down into the rocking skiff, Thomas first. In her simple dress Ester was able to climb in with ease, but in her stays and busk Mary struggled and nearly overbalanced, and John and Ester braced her on either side to settle her onto the seat, which she clung to with both hands, though the very wooden planks seemed distasteful to her.

The boatman untied the stout rope from the cleat, attached it to the halter of his nag, and began trudging along the stone path at the water's edge, the nag following, skiff in tow. They started against the current.

The river was wide here, and slow. "Temple Gardens," John said. Leaning forward, he named each sight as it came into Ester's view. "Whitehall . . . Westminster." Towering stone greeted her, a prospect unimagined: dreams of height and grace, invisible from the alleys she daily walked. What a city the birds must see, high above humanity, above all that hammered and smoked. As she watched the vista glide silently by, John laughed.

"London," he said, gesturing as though introducing her.

And could it be that the London that had loomed over her all these years was small enough to be displayed in that single broad sweep of his hand — and to be left behind now in a matter of only moments? But it was: the city wall, an instant of cool shadowed stone, and they were past. Outside the wall, buildings soon thinned. Paltry streets, a few houses, taverns: rivulets of London spilling into the countryside. Then even these gave out. In the growing quiet, a passing boatman sang a verse; the hooves of the nag plodded on the tow path's soft dirt. Gone were the haze and stench of the tanneries, replaced by air pure and wet.

That such air could exist, and so close to the city. It was an astonishment that refused to fit into any plane of Ester's thinking. Her heart grieved, for a moment, for Catherine.

In the green distance, windmills worked, and on grassy hills the whitsters in their pinned-up skirts laid out blinding spangles of laundry. At water's edge, where the tide must flood and recede, abundant weeds bent in the direction of the current. A silent, stunning freshness. Never had Ester felt a place to be so alive. Birds darted at the verge of the river, and the water was starred here and there with insects that seemed to walk on its very surface. All about them was green. Even the metal gates along the shore were overgrown, caked so thickly in moss one might have broken off pieces of it to eat. How absurd, that she could imagine eating it. A hunger such as she'd never felt took her. If she could unmake her entire life and remake it, she thought, she'd do so in an instant— she'd stand and dive from this boat, plunge into this slow-moving river, and find herself as alive as the water and the air. It seemed immaterial that she couldn't swim. For the moment she felt persuaded that the water wouldn't kill her, but would bear her easily beyond the scarred world she'd too long inhabited.

The horse stepped slowly, the breezes blew and settled, the rope creaked, the skiff swayed.

At Barn Elms, John took her arm and helped her to shore. Behind them, Mary said something indignant, calling Thomas back from where he'd stepped ahead of her up the bank.

"One fair hour," the boatman called. Even from several paces away, Ester could smell the ale on his breath. "That's all that's paid, and that's all I'll stand guard over this boat, for I've got business on the river today and won't lose it to your dalliances. This boat leaves in one hour, no matter if it's empty."

Thomas took Mary's arm. "Kiss my parliament," he muttered to the boatman. They hastened into the park.

But John knocked his forefinger once against his lips, then led Ester in a different direction.

The ground was marshy and her feet were soon soaked. She hadn't worn pattens and neither had he, but neither turned back.

They reached an open field. Flitting over it, resting on branches, stilting amid the grasses, was a stunning array of birds: dun and white, speckled, gray-throated, and rust-winged. A breeze faintly combed small dark pools on the ground. Trees lined the field's edges, with trunks mantled in pale green moss. A hushed, witnessing world.

On one side, a few paces from her, the field's border was marked by a low fence of pleached saplings: a living thing, the young trees braided together by some human hand and grown about one another to an entirely new shape. She went to it and laid a hand on the twined wood to feel its springy resistance.

"I didn't know England could be this," she said.

John was grinning. "*All* England is this!" he said.

She laughed in his face.

"No, I meant real England," he said, unhappy. "Not London. London is . . . brilliant and clattering and foul. It has the jewels of the world's learning and also the world's dirt, all in balance. But though I love the city, it's a dream from which a man wakes. From which *I'll* wake." A shadow passed over his face, but then its bright ardor returned. "*This* is England, Ester."

Farther down the field, a young deer appeared: velvet nose, flecked brown coat, watching them through one shining black eye.

"Walk straightly toward it," John whispered, and they did, they stepped slowly toward it, his hand on her elbow, both of them tottering and catching each other as they crossed the mud, until they could see the deer's eyelashes and hear its soft breath. Only then did it turn and move off slowly, as if it wished them to know it wasn't frightened of them.

In that heartbeat she felt she understood Mary's desire to give a man all.

She turned to face John.

He looked startled. Then, as she prepared to speak, he set his lips on hers. A quick kiss.

"You meant to say?" he whispered.

His face was absurd, full of happiness and longing. She raised her hands to her own face, feeling the same expression mirrored there.

But she wasn't the kind of woman he thought she was. He had to know.

"With you, I feel set loose," he said. His countenance was alive—it seemed to sift light like the river water, shining with hidden currents. Blinding her. "I like to be in your company," he said. "I like it very much."

Why? What could he desire in her? She stood on her toes and set her hands on his shoulders, and she kissed him to find out. He answered more softly than she'd expected, a kiss that tugged inside her. To push it away, she said, "You don't know who I am."

"But I do! I know your soul. Ester, am I too bold to think that you and I are people who understand such things?"

Her speech stumbled. "If you knew my soul—if you knew it, John, you'd know it's lived so great a time without light, it no longer believes in what can be seen by it."

But he was laughing, as though her very stumbling delighted him. "Ester, you damn yourself as though you're the very devil. But I'm not Bescós." He spoke slowly to be sure she heard him. "You are no less pure for being a Jewess."

She felt ages older than he—centuries. She felt her own words turn her to dust. Yet she made herself say them anyway, to rip that veil of trust from his face. She said, "I'm not at peace with this world. I—I find what freedom I have here." She tapped her temple.

"Tell me."

Her voice wandered. "I think . . . about the world. About . . . God, and questions."

His brow furrowed; he seemed on the point of asking her something. Then his expression lightened. "I understand," he said softly. "I understand enough, Ester, to know that anything you'll tell me cannot trouble me, because I see your spirit." He laughed, startling her. "Ester, if you believe I've spoken thus to other women, it's not so. I felt something the day I first saw you. I felt liberty, such as I never felt before. A premonition of a new sort of joy."

She didn't know what such words cost him. Or whether he understood their power to save or destroy. All she knew was that against such dizzying gentleness she was a cribbed, fearful creature. She hardly realized she spoke aloud. "Yet will you love a woman, if she prizes truth over softness?"

"If you love a truth, Ester, I'll love you the more for it. And if I know not this truth, I'll learn it. And if I can't learn it, then Ester, I'll tolerate it. That's the love I bear you! But what manner of truth is it that gives you such misery? Speak it and share its weight."

Silently she sifted words. "A truth," she began at length, "for which I've traded my honor."

His face flooded with color. It took him a moment to speak. "You're not a virgin?"

"You misunderstand."

A woeful expression took him. "Then I owe you an apology. Ester, I've insulted you."

"You haven't!" she cried, impatient. "What I say to you, John, is that I've lied about what I am."

He was silent. Then, slowly and with an expression of relief, he nodded. "Yet to be a Jew in this world, I understand, is a danger. If a Jew speak the truth of his faith in the wrong moment, though that faith harms none, he brings down untold wrath. It's an argument I've tried to engage with my father in matters of the law, for it seems to me that the penalties for untruth ought not be enforced on those whose very nature puts them in jeopardy, should they speak true. Ester, hear me. If a Jew tell a lie because the truth of his faith cannot be tolerated by those around him, shouldn't one then prosecute the world rather than the Jew?"

Meadow and tree and ivy—the lushness surrounding him as he spoke was impossible. If he forgave her, thinking she spoke of hiding her Jewishness, would he forgive when he learned that what she hid was her sex?

She would later rue her cowardice at not pressing on until she'd spoken all. But it was too late—she had succumbed to hope, and with it, timidity.

"Will you remember," she said quietly, "that you spoke thus?"

He said, "I won't forget."

Her vision starred with tears.

"I know you, Ester," he said, "though you think I don't." His arms were about her. "You're honest. And I see that unlike most women and even some men, you've the strength to watch over yourself—though that strength must have come at great cost."

There was something in his admiration—something too rapid, even boyish—but she could get no purchase on it. She wished to tell him every road she'd stumbled down before alighting in this green field. She wished to explain to him that she was not a woman accustomed to crying.

And she thought: don't trust love unless you can see what it costs the lover.

And she forgot the thought.

At a shout from the riverbank they turned. Thomas was running toward the shore from a distance, cursing the boatman, who was making a great show of tugging the rope to turn the skiff downriver.

"We come, man!" Thomas shouted. "You've sped the clock."

As they approached, the man untied the famished-looking horse, then threw the boat's rope heavily to Thomas. His voice was slurred. "You'll return't to my man at the stair where you found me," he said, "and you'll go direct, or I'll have twice my pay."

"You've been paid for an hour and we're here not half that," said Thomas.

The boatman muttered something—all Ester heard of his complaint, as she reached the shore, was *and through standing over this boat.* He ambled away, leading his horse.

Ester climbed into the boat, followed by Mary.

"Take your near-dead nag," shouted Thomas. He made a rude gesture behind the man. Then, stepping with one foot onto the boat, he seized an oar and mimed as though to use it as a club—a gesture lost on the boatman, whose back was already turned.

"Thomas," said Mary.

He didn't look at her, but set down the oar, steadying the boat long enough for Mary to settle onto the seat beside Ester. Then he climbed in, drank heavily from his flask, and wiped his mouth on his sleeve, his gestures animated by some pent fury.

Standing on the bank, John pushed them off and leapt the boat's gunwales, then settled on the narrow seat at the front. The river carried them.

Mary was staring at the current. Her eyes had regained a hard focus, the effects of the belladonna drops gone. A front lock of her hair had uncurled, and she chewed slowly on its end.

The boat traffic traveling upriver had grown heavier during their outing, as though some unseen tap had opened and London begun to empty of its people even as Ester and her companions returned to it. Some of the barges and skiffs they passed were heavily laden with hastily packaged household possessions, even fine furnishings.

"See the rolled tapestries stowed aboard!" John said, gesturing at one boat. "The river's full of the uppermost sorts fleeing, and they'll be sending back their servants to load up their households into wagons. I'll guess the roads will be full of carts."

Ester didn't know what made her speak thus, but she didn't seem able to help herself—something pushed her to be sure of John. "Is your family of the *uppermost sorts*?" she asked.

He laughed uncomfortably. "Yes," he said.

But Thomas hooted. "You *are* a little fury."

Mary continued to look toward the deep center of the river.

Thomas hoisted his oars out of the water and rested them on the gunwales, letting the current carry the boat. "Little silver-haired fury with the great gray eyes," he said. "You're either a fairy or a witch, and John and I disagree as to the correct answer." He drained his flask, then spoke again, a bite in his words that Ester had not heard before. "Your John is *indeed* the uppermost sort, Ester. As am I, if you wish to know. Perhaps Mary doesn't know that as well—that I have prospects of my own, elsewhere." He looked only at Ester as he spoke—she could make no sense of it. "Your John there was to be the third in the line of family judges. He might still—only John fancies himself a man of poetry and hasn't yet settled his mind on whether to throw away his fortunes alongside the rest of us in London, or go safely back to his uppermost sort of people. Tell me, John, has your mother written yet to beg you return from dirty, diseased London?"

From the seat where he watched the river, John turned. His cheeks were pink but his voice steady. "I'm my own master," he said.

For several minutes, they floated downriver in silence. As they neared the city, bits of wood and paper and offal appeared once more in the current, and here and there excrement. After a time Thomas resumed rowing.

Without turning her gaze, Mary addressed Ester quietly enough so the men could not hear. "My father writes that he won't return to London until after the sickness lifts."

"Doesn't he ask you to join him?"

"He asks," said Mary. "But I won't go. He has a new lady."

"But"—Ester shook her head, puzzled. "Your father's new lady doesn't wish you to join them?"

Mary spoke haughtily. "I don't go because *I* don't wish it," she said. But behind those words some other unvoiced reason seemed to hide.

The wall of the city loomed, and they were within London once more. Ester twisted to look back at the green hills, but already they were vanishing, occluded by the river's thick traffic. The heavy odor of smoke wafted over the water. She closed her eyes to hold the colors: the green of moss and grass and tree, the deer's soft brown coat.

"Thomas." John's voice roused her. "You're passing the stair." Ester opened her eyes to see John pointing—the set of stone steps where they'd acquired the boat was even now receding in their wake.

Yet Thomas rowed as though he hadn't heard. He kept them at the center of the river, in a current thick with paper rubbish and some soft floating black mounds whose origins Ester didn't wish to know.

"Thomas!" John called.

Mary's eyes were on Thomas now, and her upper teeth bit so firmly into her lip, Ester was surprised it didn't bleed.

They were approaching the bridge. Even from this distance, Ester could hear the water boiling under the starlings.

John turned on his seat, his arms braced on the sides of the boat, and cried to Thomas over the din. "You don't mean to shoot the bridge, man? Not with ladies on board."

Thomas did not answer.

"It's not done!"

Thomas steered them to the center of the river. Ester felt the boat quicken as a swifter current took it.

"Thomas." John half-rose in the boat. His voice, lowered, took on an urgent note. "Take that hazard with your own life, not theirs. Take us to a stair."

The traffic of boats about them had thinned. Those heading downriver were docking to discharge passengers, leaving only the boatmen to brave the rapids that crashed between the bridge's starlings. Some of the boatmen, rough-looking men, glanced curiously their way as they joined the queue of boats in the center of the river. On the Southwark bank, a small knot of people had stopped to watch them. Ester knew why. The bridges' starlings were many and some of the passages between were blocked by mills, and the restriction of the water's course so raised the river's level on the bridge's upriver side, and so lowered it on the downriver, that a waterfall coursed beneath the bridge. Boats attempting to pass beneath London Bridge smashed on the starlings; they smashed inside the bridge's stone arches; those that made it through might capsize in the precipitous drop on the other side. It was a passage dared only by practiced boatmen.

On shore, someone was pointing at Mary and Ester and shouting something unintelligible.

"Thomas!" John yelled again. But Ester could see it was too late.

Thomas was working the oars with a harsh smile. "Let's see how this boat can dance, shall we?" Mary gripped Ester's forearm so tightly that Ester cried out, as with a grunt Thomas gave another vicious pull at the oars. "Shall we put a few scratches in the man's precious vessel?"

"Thomas!" Mary screamed—but he was intent on the starlings ahead. Now the water was a black glassy chute rushing them forward, and Thomas could not have turned them back if he'd wished to. Ester could see the opening he'd chosen: a dark, churning channel of wet rock and spume. Above them the bridge loomed with its tiered shops: a small city perched over the roiling river, yet its sounds were obliterated by the rushing of water. Ester had an instant to view the muted buildings, their glinting windows, their smoke-haze—a last glimpse of daylight. And Thomas's face, a hot fury settled there. John, thrown forward in the boat. John, clinging to the boat's gunwales at a strange angle as the bow dipped steeply, then the stern flung itself high, and they pitched into the dark—Ester's chest slamming the boat's floor and Mary's weight a blow atop her. Water whipped, cuffing Ester's cheek as the boat crashed, then jolted, one way then another, and she thought, *Now is my death.* The pang of regret she felt shocked her.

A grinding, a reckoning with unseen stone, a cold flood. And then, they slipped.

A long slide, into bright, bobbing light.

The skiff half-turned and listed as the current shoved it onward. Then, improbably, it righted, low in the water.

The world returned to her: color and foam and, last of all, sound. As the boat lurched in wave after wave of the bridge's spew, Ester helped Mary raise her head to vomit over the side of the boat.

Thomas and John were bailing with their hands. Two boatmen in nearby skiffs rode close. One was laughing. The other, grave, tossed a bucket for bailing. "'Sblood man, what provokes you to take ladies beneath the bridge?"

Thomas stopped his work for a moment. "These," he said, "aren't ladies."

Ester's eyes met John's. John said to the boatman, "We need to get these ladies to shore, and our friend to a quiet bed to sleep until the drink leaves him."

The boatman moved close until he'd grabbed the side of their craft, then extended a hand to Mary. But she was clinging to the far edge and would not take his hand. Her dress was soaked and clung heavily, the patches on her cheeks were gone or askew. She heaved again over the side, her eyes shut against the rushing water.

When she'd finished she spat quietly and said to Ester, "I'm with child."

The boatman was waiting.

"A moment," Ester called. "Please." The man turned to give them privacy. Quickly, pushing Mary's wet hair from her cheeks, Ester whispered, "Does Thomas know it?"

Mary snorted, but her derision was cut short by a dry convulsion, which racked her body even though her stomach had already disgorged its contents. When this had passed, she sank against the ribs of the boat. "Of course he knows. Why do you think"—she gestured back at the bridge. "I told him at Barn Elms," she whispered. Then she lifted her face and met Ester with a defiant stare. "He'd said it couldn't happen if I didn't"—she stopped, gestured emphatically, and waited for Ester to understand.

After a moment Ester did. *Take pleasure.*

"And I'd heard the same as well. So I took care not to."

A gull wheeled above them, arcing over the bridge before sweeping back downriver. They followed its flight until its gray body faded against the horizon.

A last small spasm gripped Mary. When it had passed, she spoke as though to herself. "I told Thomas my father will disown me." Her gaze had settled once more on the water. "So we'll simply earn our own sustenance. Once Thomas accustoms himself to the idea."

Ester allowed the words to go unchallenged.

With John's assistance, they clambered out of the half-sunk skiff and onto the rocking craft of the solemn boatman—first Ester, then Mary, stiff in her ruined dress. Thomas, still in the skiff, paid as little mind as if they were strangers.

So all Catherine's effort to protect her daughter—and Ester's paltry, stumbling attempts—were for naught. Mary would now need to become a different sort of creature from the petted girl Catherine had raised. A woman whose life Ester could not guess at.

The man rowed them to shore, where they waited silently, Ester wrapped in the rough, smoke-smelling blanket that Mary had refused, despite her shivering. Ester could hear John's voice over the water as he bailed. Thomas, now standing athwart the half-flooded boat while John worked, was singing aloud some bawdy lyric—and he hooted at John's calls for him to join in the labor, until John gripped both gunwales and rocked the skiff, hard. Thomas splashed down in the center and set to work.

At length both men reached shore with the bailed skiff, and at the stair they were able to tip it and drain the remaining water. The boatman who had rescued them agreed to have his son and nephew carry the skiff overland back to the stair above the bridge—this in exchange for more of the coins Mary counted, clutching her sodden skirts and speaking the numbers crisply aloud so that Thomas, standing a few paces away with his face toward the flowing river, could not but hear: three shillings, two pence.

By the time she'd finished paying, it was raining. To warm themselves they entered a nearby inn, a low-ceilinged room heavy with the smells of candle wax and damp wool. Some whispered conversation had sprung up between Mary and Thomas on the brief walk there—Ester could not tell whether it was a fight or a reconciliation, but the two settled at their own end of the long wooden table.

John, sitting beside her, ordered bread and beer and grouse soup.

The candle on the table burned a bright yellow. John laid his hands on the scored wooden surface. "At heart," he said, "Thomas is a good lad."

Ester sat straight on the hard bench. "Thomas is well past youth, yet you call him a lad."

John smiled. "I think he would like that."

"Perhaps. Yet his love of youth is all for himself, and doesn't extend to a brat."

John looked uncomprehending. Then he turned to the far side of
the table, where Thomas and Mary sat unspeaking—Thomas squinting
into a tankard, Mary with an air of taut determination Ester had not
seen before.

John shook his head slowly, understanding. He opened his mouth
—she saw him ready himself to say *Thomas will do what he ought.* But
he hesitated.

"Let us not lie to ourselves," she said.

He conceded.

She shook her head to clear it; she hadn't intended to argue. For
once, she'd no desire to reason or muster evidence. She wanted, instead,
to say something to him. Yet she'd no words.

She tried again. "Let us not lie."

"I'll not lie to you," he said. "Your honesty is a . . ." He drank his ale,
set it down. "Your honesty is a beacon." He regarded Thomas and Mary
for a moment, and shook his head slowly. Then—as though shedding
the events of their return down the river—he smiled softly at her. His
hand patted the table. Once, twice. Three times. "I want to show you all
the still places and the lakes, Ester. I want to show you England." And
there was something fervent in his expression, as though she were an
ideal of such purity it was a fearsome joy to pledge himself to it.

A woman brought the soup. Closing her eyes, Ester warmed her
hands on the bowl. She understood she ought to remind him of the
obstacles to a love such as theirs—between a Jewess and a Gentile. But
she'd no more words to dissuade John from his determination to love
her—nor did she wish any longer to turn him from it. She no longer
wanted to be the aching, watchful person she'd become. For the first
time she thought, *I understand why we sleep. To slip the knot of the world.*
Sitting beside John, with her palms braced on the hot bowl of soup, she
wished for forgetfulness—and for a moment she let herself slide into
a dream. A falling, sickening feeling; a feeling of great and dangerous
liberty. Her body remained on the hard bench—she felt John's knee
against the damp fabric of her dress—yet in her mind they were in a
boat. Sailing, somehow, back upriver—away from all that fastened her
to the city of London, away from duty and hardship, to where the water
was bright and sun-teased. The rocking ribs of the boat. Her own ribs,
cradled by the sparkling current; a cradle of rushing sound, John's voice

rocking her, and a rain of light behind her eyes. And the world, green and green and green.

A wildness took her. She opened her eyes.

"If," she began. Then she stopped. His right hand was on the table. She slid her left hand toward his until they touched. With her right, she lifted the candle in its holder and raised it high. As the first of the hot wax hit his hand, he startled—but he obeyed her stillness and kept his hand beside hers as she traced the wax over his hand and her own, his and her own: a searing drizzle that left no burn, but cooled to a fine tracery that would seal them together until they broke it apart.

21

A T TWO O'CLOCK, LIBRARIAN PATRICIA had assured him that her colleague from the conservation laboratory would be downstairs soon. At two-thirty she'd repeated the assertion. After that, she'd refused Aaron's increasingly pointed queries. Even Helen's polite prompting failed to persuade Librarian Patricia to lift the telephone once more to muster her colleague from her roost in the conservation lab.

At nearly half past three, Conservation Patricia, with her faded red-brown hair and narrow, severe-looking face, approached their table. She had the air of someone who had reached the limits of her patience—had reached it, plainly, before cracking an eyelid that morning. In comparison Librarian Patricia looked downright kindly.

"I'm told you have some need of me?" she said, surveying both of them.

"We're wondering," began Helen, "whether there are any remaining documents—anything that hasn't yet been released for viewing—dated after July 8 of the first plague summer. That would be 1665."

"Do you honestly imagine," said Conservation Patricia, "that I need to be told the dates of the plague?"

Helen tipped her head. "My apologies. I'm accustomed to dealing with people who do."

Mollified, Conservation Patricia opened the folder that was tucked under her arm, and consulted a page. "We're still processing the final documents. However, none is dated later than July 8, 1665, with only one potential exception. There's a document that we haven't yet opened, for the simple reason that no one ever has—the wax seal, which we believe to be the original, is still intact. The humidifying chamber is currently in use, but when it's next available we'll use it to facilitate removing the letter's seal, and then gradually soften the paper to prevent it breaking at the creases when unfolded. It's a slow process. I've no idea what the date of that document will be. Otherwise there's nothing left in the laboratory after that date."

So Ester Velasquez's writing *had* stopped with the rabbi's death.

Aaron watched Conservation Patricia retreat to Librarian Patricia's desk, where the two conferred, presumably comparing methods of beheading researchers who chewed gum.

Had Ester died in the plague? According to Wilton's paper, the parish records had noted the rabbi's death—but there was no mention of any female Velasquez in either the plague year or the subsequent decade. Had Ester died an unrecorded death, in the most chaotic weeks of the plague? Or had she survived the plague to vanish into silence—her scholarly life extinguishing the moment the rabbi's death ended her access to writing? Was the evidence of her own death to be found in the London registers of a later year . . . recorded, perhaps, under a married name?

Aaron returned to the document on the cushion before him. They'd each read it a half dozen times. In truth, there was no justification for holding on to it all afternoon except the feeble wish to delay Wilton and his group from getting their hands on it. He stared again at the single word. *Ahavti. I loved.*

Past tense. Whatever the nature of that love, it had been done with by the time Ester put quill to paper to slip that word between the lines of the household accounts.

I loved, Aaron thought. The words made him feel old. He looked at the document before him. He felt an urge to remove it from its cradling cushion and rest his head in its place.

Well, he thought numbly.

Well.

Perhaps Ester Velasquez had simply died an obscure death in London, either during or after the plague, as Wilton's article had implied.

But then, hadn't Wilton seemed a bit too eager to brush off Ester's story—a bit too preoccupied with the larger prize of Sabbatean Flor-

ence to have given Ester's fate sufficient thought? What if Ester Velasquez's death was absent from the London registers simply because it
had occurred elsewhere?

ONE PHONE CALL AND TWENTY minutes later, he was on a bus to
Richmond upon Thames. He'd made up an excuse for leaving the reading room early—no reason to raise Helen's hopes until he had something concrete to show.

He exited the station with the late-afternoon throng, walked the ten
minutes up the hill to the building that housed the town hall and museum, and, through a warren of narrow bulletin-board-lined hallways,
found the Local Studies office, where he was greeted by Anne—a girl
younger than he'd guessed from her mature, professional manner over
the phone. Yes, she had the records he'd requested. Yes, she could keep
the office open another half-hour for him, as she'd promised on the
telephone. The Local Studies office was supposed to be closing, but as
she had work to do here anyway . . .

As she spoke, she busily cleared a small area of table for him in the
cluttered space. The room was large but crowded with shelves and tables, all laden with files. Visitors, he gathered, were sparse even during
normal hours—his mere interest in the archive's offerings was com-
mendation enough to merit keeping the office open late. Still, Aaron
also noted the furtive glances Anne stole as she arranged a workspace
for him, and the way she fled his gaze when she addressed him. He
was used to this sort of response—but he rarely took a second look at
someone like Anne. Yet he paused now to do so. She wore no makeup,
and her buttoned blouse offered only the slightest guess at the contours
of her breasts. Returning to him once more, she wordlessly set a pad
and pencil in his reach. Was this the way such girls flirted? It occurred
to him that it might be; bewildered by sexuality, they wooed a man with
their reliability.

As he sat, Anne returned and silently deposited three thick volumes
in front of him.

How had he ever overlooked shy girls? It struck him that the fact
that he wasn't attracted to them just might represent a flaw in his character, not theirs.

Seated at the table, three original seventeenth-century record books stacked before him, he considered for a moment his own proud record of acquisitions, and was startled. Could that be right? That he hadn't so much as kissed a girl since Marisa? He scrolled through the past weeks —then on backward through the three months since she'd cut off contact, the five months since he'd seen her—and came up blank.

In his distraction, he opened the topmost record book and turned its soft, thick pages. Parish register, Richmond, Surrey. It was the same sort of textured paper he'd grown accustomed to in the rare manuscripts room, only without the high security guarding it. No gloves here, no pencil stubs, no Patricia to hiss at him. Though it occurred to him, squinting across the large room at Anne—who was filing something in a cabinet and occasionally glancing in his direction—that Anne might be a nascent Patricia, given enough years.

And, he thought with a pang, enough men with attitudes like his own.

Columns of names, dates, deaths and births and marriages, all reasonably legible if you were used to the ornate curves of secretary hand.

In the second book of records, he found the name HaLevy.

September 4, 1666. Married. Manuel HaLevy of Richmond, to Ester Velasquez of Amsterdam.

He sat back in the wooden chair.

So she'd lived. And married.

He ought to be delighted. Delighted for Ester that she'd survived the plague; and for himself—because now he knew how the documents had come to be deposited in Richmond. Ester, obviously, had brought them with her when she'd married ... though in truth Aaron could hardly imagine what value a dowry of inked paper might hold for a man like Manuel HaLevy. The single reference to HaLevy in Ester's writing had made clear the man's disdain for learning. Was that why Ester had locked the papers away—to hide them from a husband who'd gladly have disposed of them in one of those broad stone hearths?

She'd refused Manuel HaLevy vehemently, or so the cross-written letter implied. She'd seemed to find him or his views repugnant. But then she'd married him anyway.

He tried to imagine Aleph leaving behind plague-stricken London to come here. He tried to imagine her being married in this village—married, in fact, while London burned behind her . . . because if he was remembering correctly, September 4th of 1666 was smack in the middle of the Great Fire of London. He tried to picture a festive occasion regardless—guests resigned or indifferent to the destruction happening just scant miles away. And Ester Velasquez under the marriage canopy, freed at last from the burden of all she'd once attempted. Had it been a relief?

During the months he'd labored over her handwriting, he'd gradually formed a mental image of Ester Velasquez: petite, large-eyed, too skinny, pale with dark hair. Emily Dickinson, he realized with a jolt—with a slightly Jewish nose. Had she truly become mistress of the once-grand house on the rise above the river? He imagined her, her spidery letter aleph retired for good, making her rounds supervising the servants' labors. Walking dozens of times each day past the expensively carved stairwell in which she'd entombed the brief budding of her intellectual and personal freedom. Perhaps she'd found moments here and there to unlock the cupboard and reread the papers, mementos of her lost liberty. Though perhaps she hadn't—perhaps she'd found the record of her bygone opportunities too painful to visit.

He shook off the thought. It was unlikely, wasn't it, that he'd ever fathom the mindset of an obscure seventeenth-century English Jew. Ester Velasquez had lived, scribed a while—then, in the wake of the rabbi's death, been saved by Manuel HaLevy's offer of marriage. Perhaps she'd been content here in Richmond, perhaps not. No one would ever know. And in any event, it had nothing to do with him.

He sat in the airless records room, a 334-year-old roster in his hands. It dawned on him that he'd been counting on Ester's story not to fizzle out in some trivial, humdrum ending. Alongside Helen, he'd ignored the unpleasant fact that Wilton's vision of Ester's aptitude and temperament was the most likely one. Instead, he'd wanted Ester's story to serve up something staggering: some triumphal parade showcasing the very qualities Aaron wished to see in his own reflection. He'd wished Ester to be independent, clever, indomitable, rebellious. He'd expected her story to serve as something unseemly: his own coronation. But in fact history was indifferent to him. It didn't matter what he wanted.

The world had simply closed over Ester Velasquez's head. And it could just as easily close over Aaron's.

This should not have been news to him.

In a rush of obscure panic, he searched the records for further news of Ester. Childbirth or death, perhaps both at once? He slid his finger down the lines, searching for her name, now wanting only the ending to the goddamn story that had gripped him all these months. Across the room, Anne was glancing reluctantly at the clock. He knew she was trying to delay, until the last possible moment, telling him he needed to leave. He turned pages; he'd made it through 1667, then 1668, 1669 . . . but the records were growing longer with every year, the population of the area apparently rising. Thus far he'd found no further mention of Ester HaLevy, though one Benjamin HaLevy, presumably Ester's father-in-law, had died in 1667. There seemed to be no children so far, though perhaps in the 1670s?

"I'm afraid it's time," Anne said. She was standing beside his table, one hand, with its trimmed-to-the-quick nails, resting tentatively on the back of an empty chair.

He offered her a humble smile. "I wonder if I couldn't go through just a few more pages?"

"No," she said simply. "Sorry."

Small wonder he couldn't get anywhere with the Patricias; even in their youth they respected the importance of limits. He packed up his notes. Preceding Anne down the series of corridors and stairs, her quiet tread trailing him, he wanted to turn and compliment her—yet though he meant it sincerely, he could think of no way to say it without sounding sarcastic: *you'll go far.*

On the street he hesitated. He wasn't ready to return to the bus station, but didn't know where else to go. Anne, who had locked and tested the main door, now descended the building's stone steps and started for the main street—but seemed to hesitate as well.

"If there's any other way I can help?" she said.

Her blue eyes were clear and lovely. He paused to curse a world that might never offer such a girl romance, or whatever it was she dreamt of. And he had a sudden, intolerable feeling that the shape of that world just might be his fault.

"Thanks anyway," he said. "It's just—I'm trying to find out when someone died."

She waited.

"It's 1670 or later," he said. "Ester HaLevy."

Nodding, she took out a notepad and wrote down the name. Then, with a slight flush, Aaron's mobile number. "I'll have a look for you."

"Thanks," he said. "Truly."

She turned and disappeared into the steady foot traffic.

The afternoon had turned to evening. All around him, English people were returning to their homes. But in an instant the foreignness of living abroad, which had sustained Aaron all these months, had lost its magic—and he saw how his new, exotic existence had allowed him to ignore the isolation that was the bedrock of his life, whether in England or in the United States. He, unlike these strangers striding with their briefcases and packages up the long, curving hill, had no one to go home to.

Some candle inside him was dangerously close to guttering. A definition of loneliness surfaced in his mind: when you suddenly understand that the story of your life isn't what you thought it was.

He fought back. So what if Ester had married Manuel HaLevy? It wasn't necessarily a defeat. At least she'd escaped the plague. And who knew that she didn't eventually fall in love with HaLevy, however much of a cretin the guy initially seemed? *That*, he resolved, was what he'd tell Helen Watt—for suddenly, maddening though Helen could be, he wanted to give her the gift of a gentle ending. *Look*, he'd tell her. *Puppy love blossoming out of disdain. Ester decided to marry the guy she once despised.*

Helen wouldn't be fooled for an instant. Ester—Aleph—could not have wished to marry a man with no patience for learning.

Through a break in the trees he stared down miserably at the mute river. Then, to his own surprise, he turned uphill rather than back down toward the station. He'd buy himself a beer at Prospero's.

But he didn't.

Bridgette answered the door. It seemed to take her a moment to place him. A small, wry smile formed on her face. She stood there for a long time, smiling. So long, he began to feel foolish.

"Hi," he said.

"Still curious?" she said.

He said, "A bit." Then added—a beat too late—"About the house."

That was what he meant. It was what he thought he meant. He'd turned off the street and walked up the narrow path across the Eastons' newly manicured front garden because he thought, somehow, that seeing the house once more might help him gain some still-elusive understanding of Ester Velasquez's choice.

"By all means, then," she said, "come see the *house*."

He wasn't sure whether to join her laughter.

Inside, all was quiet. He understood immediately that Ian wasn't at home. The high ceiling was lost in the dim evening light, and there was a smell of recent construction—plaster and paint. Bridgette flipped a wall switch as she passed him, and tiny spotlights illuminated the canvases lining the walls: abstract images lurid against the dark-stained, elaborately carved paneling. Through a doorway to the right, a smaller room featured a menagerie of torqued still lifes—flowers and fruits distorted in some unsettling way Aaron couldn't have named. Carved on the lintel over the doorway between the two rooms, like sentinels of the seventeenth century watching over what the Eastons had wrought, were two cherubs Aaron hadn't noticed before: expressive creatures of dark polished wood, their heads inclined as though regarding with curiosity all who passed below them. Their faces were lit with a conspiratorial amusement recognizable despite the centuries since it had been carved there.

The elaborate woodwork, the unsettling art, the high ceilings, the stark light from the mullioned windows ... Aaron had to admit that the *juxtaposition* (he could almost hear the word in Helen's flinty voice) was effective. The whole thing felt jarring in a way that wasn't necessarily bad, though he didn't know if it was good either. If viewers wanted visual tension, here it was. Speaking personally, it made his teeth hurt.

"Do you like it?" Bridgette said. "We open next week. Working to square renovation priorities has been a bit"—her face took on a hard expression, and he understood that Bridgette was in a dangerous mood—"intense."

He moved through the hall, pretending to look at the paintings and nodding with what he hoped was a thoughtful, approving mien. But all the while he was working his way toward the shadowed stairwell.

"We closed it up," she said flatly.

Dropping pretense and crossing directly to the base of the stairs, he saw that indeed the stairwell had been closed, the dark panel with the keyhole patched. The carpenter had done a good job. From a distance, the repair was undetectable.

Bridgette was watching. Had she noticed the sharp sting he felt at seeing the now-empty staircase so readily resealed? For it seemed to him that the staircase had itself become an exhibit in the Eastons' gallery: one demonstrating how inconsequential, finally, were someone else's passion and defeat.

"A drink?" Bridgette said.

He nodded vaguely, which seemed to amuse her. She turned, opened a pocket door between two paintings—Aaron noted that the narrow door bore a small, elegant sign that read *Private Area*—and disappeared through it. He could hear her moving away along what must have been an old servant's passage. Her footsteps faded; there was a distant sound like a heavy door closing.

Minutes passed. He stood beside the stairwell, the stilled heart of the house. The building echoed with silence; he could hear it breathing, moving, coursing from room to room like oxygen through a body. A three-hundred-year-old silence.

Sermon-quiet, he thought—but before he could traverse the worn mental path toward ruing the self-importance of his father's profession, he made himself admit it: he'd never gotten the rabbi thing out of his system. All his life he'd wanted to be what his father was—a devotee venerated for his humble devotion; a man standing in the middle, in thrall to something larger while others were in thrall to him.

That he'd failed to measure up to even his father's standard now seemed patently obvious. Aaron Levy lacked the gravitas to be a conduit for the wisdom of history. He'd thought he loved history; in truth, he couldn't even *see* history.

An uncomfortable question floated back to him. What *was* that story Marisa had told about her gay brother? He'd paid little attention at the time, focusing instead on calibrating the impression he was making on Marisa. But now the conversation returned to him like a thread unspooling. The brother was a jock, girls followed him everywhere; the brother never told anyone except Marisa, who would do reconnaissance for him, spying on boys he liked so he might run into them by accident, get a chance to at least talk. Later some asshole outed him and his life turned to shit in a couple weeks; he barely survived the depression. *Even our grandmother, who'd lived through Bergen-Belsen, just pretended it wasn't happening.* Marisa had spoken levelly, slowly. *It almost killed my brother. And I kept saying: Danny, why don't you let yourself be free? But he was too ashamed. So I decided I had to be free.* Despite the beer in her hand, Marisa's eyes had rested steadily on Aaron's. *People go through life trying to please some audience. But once you realize there's no audience, life is simple. It's just doing what you know in your gut is right.*

She'd said it, and she'd looked at him just so, hadn't she? And then she'd lofted her beer, and moved on to the subject of American Jews. And, foolishly, *that* was the part of the conversation Aaron had seized on. As if a little intellectual banter about history were his golden opportunity to prove his mettle to Marisa.

They don't want memory, she'd said, *or history that might make them uncomfortable. They just want to be liked. Being liked is their . . . sugar rush.* She'd been talking about American Jews . . . but she could have been talking about Aaron.

The silence of the house reproached him. With a jolt, Aaron understood. Marisa *had* been talking about him.

Closing his eyes now, he saw her. The warm, bold light in her gaze. The invitation and the dare. Rodney Keller had seen perfectly what made Marisa unlike anyone Aaron had ever met: her unsettling directness.

It made him think of Ester Velasquez. Or rather—he schooled himself—the Ester Velasquez he'd chosen to believe in.

He had no idea, really, why Marisa had decided to sleep with him that day five months ago. But he had an inkling why she wanted nothing to do with him now.

He didn't know what he was doing here in this house. He didn't know what he was doing in England.

With an echoing bang, Bridgette emerged from a door on the other side of him. Seeing Aaron's startled expression, she laughed. "This house is full of surprises, isn't it?"

"Well," he said. "You are, at any rate."

This pleased her. She gave him his glass, and drank from hers, and pulled over two sleek metal folding chairs. "So," she said. "What sort of discoveries have you made with those papers you're so mad about? Have you learned who invented the wheel? Or was the first to discover *fire*?" She waved her manicured fingernails.

"Yes. In fact, it all happened right here in your house."

She tapped her glass with a fingernail. "As I suspected."

A moment's silence. Slowly, then, Bridgette shook her head. Her face had tightened. "This goddamn house."

"What about it?"

She sniffed. "Nothing." She raised her glass, inspected it. "Tell me, has your lovely boss grown any cheerier? I thought she was going to burn a hole in Ian with her eyes." She stiffened in her seat. "*The papers are mine!*"

He couldn't help chuckling—he had to admit Bridgette did a good imitation, chin lifted and cheeks drawn, a wintry stare pinioning Aaron. "Not bad," he said.

"Well, your boss reminds me a bit of my aunt—another scold totally convinced of her own view of things. Except my aunt fancied herself a bit of a mystic. Always said she had *feelings* about people. She used to read me fairy tales when they'd send me here to visit her, but the only one I remember is 'The Little Match Girl.' You know the one? The freezing girl in the snow? Peeping through windows at people basking at their fires, only she can't feel the warmth of those fires one bit." Something unidentifiable flitted across Bridgette's face. "That's just how I always felt listening to her. I used to try so hard to be wise and worthy of her standards, only half the time I didn't know what the hell she was talking about. She knew it too. Do you know what the last thing was she said to me before she died? She was lying in the bloody hospital after they'd finally persuaded her to leave her precious house, but she squeezed my hand like I was the sick one. She said, *It's a shame, I'd hoped we could be good friends.*"

They drank.

"Hey," said Bridgette. "This is what you Americans do all day, is it? Sit about confessing things. What a rotten influence you are!" She leveled a long finger at his chest. "Yes," she said. "You."

Above him, the empty house towered. Windows with their black levers. Thick, age-distorted panes.

He answered Bridgette with a laugh, and drank again.

The moments of flirtation were ticking away. The angle of Bridgette's head; the way she cast her body sideways in her narrow chair; the lengthening pauses between her wry questions about *the solemn university life* and his parries: every cue followed a script Aaron knew. This was the instant when he was supposed to make a move. And this. *Now.* He felt each opportunity pass, felt Bridgette register his immobility. In fact Bridgette was undeniably attractive. Nor was Aaron too scrupulous to say yes when a married woman made herself available; he'd slept with a married woman in college, in her own house no less, with children at school and husband at work. Still, the time was passing and Bridgette was waiting and it hadn't escaped even Aaron's notice that he was failing to play his part. The silence of the house pressed on him intolerably. He wanted to stand, to shout: *Explain!*

But the house had explained the best it could. He simply wanted more than it had to give him.

Bridgette made another show of checking on his drink. As she leaned over him, he raised a hand—an almost automatic motion—and parted the swinging curtain of her hair. It was only a small gesture—but it was all that was needed. Her face flashed with a hopefulness that made no sense to him—then, smiling softly, she ran the tips of her fingernails across the leg of his jeans. The touch was electric, and he felt his body answer without consulting him: a bolt of clarity amid his confusion.

It happened shockingly fast. She had his hand, she laid it on her breast, and the thin silk of her blouse seemed to dissolve so he could feel the hard nipple beneath, and he rose to his feet with a feeling like floating. And there they were, ascending a 350-year-old staircase, with windows looking in on them at every turn and treads that creaked taking their weight—and as they rose up into the dark, Bridgette tugging his hand, they could have been levitating, so swiftly and smoothly did they arrive at the topmost landing, at a half-closed door, and onto Bridgette's cool sheets. Aaron had gone to bed with a woman on a whim before, but this blinded him with its suddenness. Bridgette smelled like lavender, like something at once spiced and anesthetizing, and it dizzied him, but that didn't matter, she knew what she wanted him to do and it was easy for him to do it, to move with her, roll in a rush of sheets, of breath and pleasure. He caught her eyes once and laughed, delight rising suddenly in him—but Bridgette didn't laugh, her face was fierce and focused—and he was swept away from this observation by an ingathering, down and down, the best of him concentrated in a single moment of such sweetness that distance disappeared, and he was flush with the world.

He came back to himself slowly. There was something sounding in his body . . . something steady, quiet as a voice whispering.

The ceiling above the bed was a clean eggshell white, an elaborate rosette in its exact center. Slowly his eyes slid down the far wall: the white trim; the paneled, white-painted walls.

At length he recognized it: the sound of his own heart.

He did not want to think of Marisa.

"Mmmm." He could hear Bridgette smiling. She splayed a hand on his chest. Sliding up, she kissed his jaw.

He tightened his arms around her reflexively, but didn't look at her.

"Don't tell me that wasn't good." She was whispering directly into his ear.

"It was."

There was a silence, enough time for him to hear how unpersuasive his own words sounded.

"Then," she said, "what is it?"

He glanced at Bridgette—and saw on her face the last thing he expected: yearning. A heartbeat later he realized that his own face wore a similar expression—and that he and Bridgette Easton were looking at each other with a mutual desperation he didn't understand.

He broke the gaze. When she spoke an instant later, she was once more the Bridgette he knew.

"*Noooo!*" she crooned. She pulled back as though to get a better look at him. "You feel *guilty?*"

He didn't. What he felt, to his surprise, was old. And as stilled and powerless as the witnessing walls around him. Somehow, though, he'd stepped into some drama of Bridgette's, some blunt-edged argument that she was carrying out with her husband or her life.

She'd propped herself on one elbow. "You do! You . . . feel . . . guilty." With each word, a jab of her finger in his chest. "But you're not even married, are you? How can you feel guilty," she said, "if *I* don't?"

It wasn't clear to him that Bridgette didn't feel guilty—only that this was the conversation she was willing to have. He opened his mouth and spoke his part. "Ian seems like a nice guy."

"He is." A small furrow appeared between her perfectly shaped eyebrows. "He is," she spoke slowly, "a very nice guy." It was clear this wasn't a compliment.

He was aware, suddenly, that they were both naked. He drew a sheet over himself.

"Listen," she said, looking away. "You know as well as I do that these things don't mean anything. We were both just curious."

Reflexively, so as not to appear prudish, he tossed back, "And are you still curious?"

But the flirtation was hollow.

She let the question hang. She'd registered that he was no longer enchanted with her. Her blue-gray gaze was bright and hard, and it told him that she saw through him too; and she had no use for a forlorn American in her bed.

"No," she said.

Dressing silently beside the bedstead, he looked out the window at the view it framed: the long slope down to the river. From this height, in the falling darkness, the water looked deceptively still. Zipping his jeans, he moved closer to the window, and he was seized by the feeling that she—Ester—had stood here at this very spot, in this very room, staring out just as he was at the last of the light on the slow-moving water, its current mesmerizing and out of reach.

Only when he was out on the street, Bridgette's ironic farewell kisses lingering on each of his cheeks, did Marisa's voice sound clearly in his mind.

Aaron, he heard her say.

That was all. In his head, he heard her calling his name. A simple, one-word reminder, like a conscience.

He wished then, wholeheartedly, that he hadn't had sex with Bridgette Easton. It wasn't that he thought there was anything so disturbing about a spontaneous hook-up—one whose implications were Bridgette's to sort out, not his. It was simply that a spontaneous hookup was no longer right for him, Aaron Levy. He'd changed enough in these past months to know that his old life was hollow.

Yet not enough to see a clear path toward anything he desired.

He passed Prospero's, his collar turned up against the dark and chill. Prospero's. He still didn't fucking understand *The Tempest*.

I loved. The words followed him through the darkness, down the long hill all the way to the station, and—as he could not leave them behind—he acknowledged them his.

Part 4

22

June 28, 1665
15 Tamuz, 5425
London

THE MESSAGE BOY, HAVING DELIVERED the pouch, tipped his hat and readied to flee.

"A moment's help?" Rivka gestured toward a poorly sewn sack of coal resting just inside the door, where a different delivery boy had dropped it earlier that week, refusing to cross the threshold to deposit it in the storage bin.

From her writing table, Ester watched this one, a tall blond youth with paltry whiskers, shake his head swiftly. So it was in London now, every soul afraid of every other.

The coal was packed heavy and required two to lift—a feat that had proved too much for Ester, who this morning had dropped her end and nearly split the sack, prompting Rivka to dismiss her without a word. With a sigh, Rivka said to the boy, "For pay."

The message boy—who himself looked in need of a good meal —hesitated. Then, peering at Rivka more closely, as though checking for signs of ill health, he stepped over the threshold with the shrug of one casting his lot. He hoisted the sack with Rivka and together they stepped it across the room and down a few creaking stairs to the storage bin. Then he followed Rivka back to the door, brushing his sooty palms. The coin she offered appeared to please him.

"'Tis a prayer and fasting day again, you know," he said, cheerfully pocketing the coin, "on account of the plague." He leaned back against the wall, supporting himself with his palms against the plaster, and bounced contentedly there, proud at being the bearer of important information. "The preachers agree 'tis God's punishment, of course—the warning's in the comet we see each night over London. The preachers say the plague is fire sent to purge us." His eyes turned briefly, dutifully, to heaven. Then searched beyond Ester and Rivka for the kitchen door. "Though in a house of Jews perhaps there's food on offer?"

"No food," said Rivka.

"See my rotten fortune?" he cried. "Even in a Jew house I'm too lump-headed to find food. So my mother would say." He shrugged, then —bouncing slow against their wall—spoke on. "But 'tis an unlucky day to be about in the street for such as you. You ought not be found, or they may say it's you that brought the sickness. You seem good sorts, if you don't mind I say so. Best to stay quiet and use your Jewish fortunes to buy anti-pestilence pills." He turned and gazed out at the street a moment, then nodded with an air of great wisdom. "Me, I believe it's the Papists, with their rotted ideas, as bring this judgment on our city."

When he at last departed, Rivka turned heavily to Ester. "Neither of us must venture out until the fast day's past."

Only at her words did Ester feel how rare speech had become between them, as though the dying of foot traffic outside their window had commanded them lately to hush their own voices as well. In truth Ester needed no admonition to remain indoors; only yesterday she'd been nearing home when she'd encountered a group of flagellants, a dozen men marching solemnly down the center of the narrow street toward the river, silent but for a low periodic chant and the sickening sound of whips on their bare backs. Ester had pressed herself against a shopfront to let them pass. The sight had stayed with her: men stumbling within reach of her; men walking stolidly on with the blood running wet down their naked torsos, the muscles of their low backs sheeted in red.

Rivka shut the door behind the message boy. Leaning against it, she opened the purse and counted the coins. From her expression of relief, Ester guessed the money Manuel HaLevy had sent would suffice not only for the week's necessities, but for laudanum. The illnesses that had for years pursued Rabbi HaCoen Mendes had taken renewed grip these past weeks, and now brought unremitting pain. Laudanum and willow bark were the only palliatives that relieved him.

The physician had come twice, on the second visit pressing the rabbi's belly and declaring that this great disturbance of the humors must soon prove fatal. Ignoring Rivka's soft moan at this pronouncement, the physician had knelt his substantial bulk with difficulty at the rabbi's bedside and, looking without flinching into his patient's face as though he could penetrate the rabbi's blindness to show his respect, said, "A man understands the span of his life is limited, and a man deserves to know of his dwindling days so that he may speak of them with dignity to his God, whether he be Christian or Jew." The rabbi, raising himself in his bed then, had clenched the physician's thick hand with a grimace of gratitude. Leaving, the physician accepted his payment and told Rivka and Ester that he'd come no more, for he could see money was too scarce to spend on fruitless treatment . . . and as for himself, he'd hardly slept in days for doctoring the ill and the merely frightened, and he feared the new contagion himself if he allowed his humors to unbalance through overexertion. He'd sprinkled their doorstep with vinegar to ward off the plague, and left in haste.

Since then, the rabbi's nights had grown fitful, punctured by pain from some unknown source that made him cry out in a thin, nearly unrecognizable voice. Waking at the sound of the cry, Ester would descend the stairs to find Rivka already at his side — for it seemed Rivka's ears could hear the cry even as it formed in the rabbi's throat: *"Me esta tuyendo, Mãe."* Sometimes thrice in a night they stood together beside his bed or outside his door, Ester and Rivka, waiting in silence to hear his breathing settle. Only once, her gaze touching Ester's shyly in the low light of the banked fire, did Rivka speak. "Who does he ask for?" Her voice was hoarse.

The fire flickered, for an instant revealing the longing on Rivka's worn, pocked face.

Ester answered as truly as she could. She said, "He calls for comfort. I believe he calls for his mother."

Rivka's eyes shone with brief disappointment, then relief — then she wiped them with a quick, dismissive hand. And Ester rued her own blindness: so firmly had she believed she alone longed for what was out of reach, she'd admired Rivka's wordless devotion to the rabbi without ever considering what Rivka's heart might wish.

With each day of the rabbi's labored breath, the solitude of their household seemed to deepen. A woman had knocked at the door on

Sabbath and, in low tones, urged flight to the countryside—but before Ester could rise to see which of the congregation's matrons it was, she'd heard Rivka tell the woman that the rabbi was ill, though not of plague, and couldn't withstand the journey. By the time Ester had reached the door the woman had hurried away, as though Rivka's answer were a pestilence in itself. Indeed Ester could no longer be certain which of the congregation were still in London and which had fled. The press of whispering women trading information outside the synagogue—who was leaving, who remaining in the city?—had vanished when the synagogue itself was shuttered. London seemed redrawn: the invisible borders between parishes, once unnoticed, now were gulfs to be crossed at one's peril—for the death-roll of each was attended to widely, and no matter how the dead's kin might lie to mask the cause of death, the numbers spoke plainly. The rising toll had spread these weeks from parish to parish like a tide—or rather, like a fire, for its advance was uneven, as though a quixotic wind carried sparks that might set one patch of forest ablaze while leaving another, for now, untouched. Fear now infected every human transaction.

What little income Rivka had once earned was gone: no mending or laundering had been sent to their household in a fortnight at least—attending to a torn seam or soiled shift was no longer worth the risk of contact with another household. London mended its own seams now; lived in soiled clothing; baked its own bread or bought it in a furtive rush, as though the disease might spy the transaction and pounce. Even Mary had sent no word to Ester in weeks—not since their day on the river. Nor had she answered the three notes Ester had left for her at her door—for the servant, arms outstretched, had barred Ester from entering, as though suspecting Ester herself of carrying the plague, and had said, with an asperity Ester disliked, that Mistress da Costa Mendes was not seeing company.

Shut in the house for long quiet hours, Ester read and reread the letters John had sent from his travels in the countryside, until their phrases made a strange poetry in her mind.

My heart is eager to return to you in London after I complete this brief business I do for my father.

I hear rumor of terrible things in the city, and hope not half of
them be true. Are you well, my dear Ester?

She'd not have known how to answer, even if his travels had allowed
him to receive a reply.

Only Manuel HaLevy seemed to intuit the privations that now
pressed their household—and, unasked for, supplied what was needed.
The pouch Rivka held was the third he had sent in as many weeks. The
first two had been accompanied by letters requesting Ester's company
in the countryside. In each, Manuel's hand was clean and decisive on
the page.

My father has completed building and appointing his new house.
Its grandeur might amuse you, Ester. Abundant carvings of wood
and stone, and a brick front to make the Jew-haters forget they
hate us and come polish our boots instead. My father looks out
from his window like a pontiff of the Thames . . . making me that
most common (though but little acknowledged) phenomenon of
the Catholic church: a pontiff's son. And when you are the pontiff's
daughter-in-law you may conduct the household's supper in the
manner of a church service or a synagogue, or perhaps after the
manner of the pasha of the Barbary Coast—if it pleases you, it's
equal to me.

Ester had sat long over each of Manuel HaLevy's letters, yet in the
end answered them simply, sending back his servant with the written
words *I thank you for your kind invitation, but it is not necessary.*

Rivka had finished counting the money in the third pouch. She
looked up. "No letter for you with this week's coins," she said. Ester
couldn't read her expression.

A fleeting disturbance seemed to wring the rabbi now in his sleep.
His mild face tightened—then, for the moment, the pain seemed to
let go its grip. As his face eased, Ester saw plainly the purity that shone
there. The last words he'd had her write had dried on the page before
her: *For I speak to you as a father to a son, and though your endeavor be beyond my reach, still I wish to gird you with all the understanding and love of*

*God that I harbor in my heart. It is for this that I labor, for I believe it will
be my last good deed in this world.*

If only she merited such words of trust and guidance as the rabbi
addressed to his pupil in Florence.

She stood. Rivka would need help in the kitchen. But as she stepped
away from his desk, the rabbi raised his head and spoke clearly, as
though he'd been thinking all these hours rather than sleeping.

"You must leave this city," he said. "And take Rivka with you. The
physician said the disease is spreading."

"I'd no more leave you than my own father," she said.

He spoke softly. "But I ask you to do so. Preserve yourself. You and
I have studied the four duties for which tradition commands one to
sacrifice one's own life. You know well that staying with the dying is not
among them."

"It wastes your strength to argue for it." Her words were more
clipped than she'd intended. She returned to the table, picked up a volume. "Shall I read to you from *Consolação*?"

He turned back to the fire.

At the sight of his tilted posture—his frame unable to support itself
upright even when seated—a fierceness rose in her. She knew she'd no
right to call this feeling love, when she betrayed the rabbi daily. Yet even
in her own writing, when she posed questions he'd regard as blasphemy,
she carried the rabbi ever in her mind, and his goodness remained the
standard against which she tested her understanding of the world. It
was the highest love she was capable of: respect. Yet respect also demanded that when the very tools of logic that he'd given her argued
against his beloved tradition, she must follow them toward conclusions
he'd abhor. The greatest act of love—indeed, the only religion she could
comprehend—was to speak the truth about the world. Love must be,
then, an act of truth-telling, a baring of mind and spirit just as ardent as
the baring of the body. Truth and passion were one, and each impossible
without the other.

Yet a love as would willingly bring the roof tumbling?

Such was thought cold-hearted in a man, and in a woman, abhorrent. Still, in her abhorrent, obstinate heart she called the ferocity she
felt for her teacher *love*.

The rabbi spoke so suddenly she started. "Did you write," he said, "while I slept?" There was something in his voice.

Softly she answered, "I wrote your words, I merely—"

"No," he said. He drew a long breath, and released it. When he continued it was not in Portuguese, but in Castilian. "I ask you now, did you write your own words?"

She sat perfectly motionless.

His countenance, lifted now to the blank ceiling, trembled, but he pressed his fingertips together and spoke. "You've been false." He struggled in silence to master his face. "To whom do you write," he said, "when you sit at that table?"

She'd no answer that wouldn't wound him.

"Ester."

There was a long silence.

"It's for you that I've composed my letters to Florence," he said. "It's for you that I've shaped my interpretation of the verses concerning the Messiah, that you might clad yourself in their warmth and remember the God of Israel." He breathed. "Since you were a girl, your mind has been restless not only for the truth of holy texts, but for forbidden questions beyond. I know not how you act on this ungodly hunger you were born with, yet I've felt the honesty in your spirit despite this error and I've wished, despite your actions, to remain your teacher. For this reason alone have I dared to argue boldly, challenging even those with greater authority than I . . . so as to illuminate for a mind such as yours the beauty of our tradition." Slowly, slowly, he shook his head. "Already," he said, "I have failed one of my keenest, most able pupils. I have done all in my power, Ester, not to lose the other."

She saw. She'd no words for the gift he'd given her, and no words for the shame she felt at his generosity. It struck her that he addressed her in Castilian not only because he was speaking to her of solemn things, but because—even now—he did not wish to shame Ester by allowing Rivka to learn what she'd done.

"I must know now," he said, "what you've wrought in my name."

"Please believe that I've never done it under your name, but under another."

After a moment he nodded. "I'm glad," he said.

"As to what I've written, and to whom, I beg you not to ask me, for I know my way of thinking is abhorrent to you."

He was quiet a long moment before speaking. "I will not ask. Yet let the blame for your errors, whatever they are, be put on me. It is I who shaped you amiss."

"No," she insisted. "The fault is mine alone. I deceived you."

But he shook his head—then held up a finger to stay her from speaking further. He'd another matter to address. "You had a chance, once, to marry Manuel HaLevy. Rivka tells me you may still."

"No, I—"

"Do it, Ester. If you must, then deceive your husband just as you deceived me—but you'll do it with a full belly and a house with children. I wish"—his mouth worked—"I wish you not to die, Ester. And not to know hunger. I wish that more fervently, God forgive me, than I wish for you to change your conduct. I know your obstinacy. My words won't keep you from using the mind God gave you, even if you forget it's God that gave it you. But allow me to be your teacher one last time. Marry, and have bread. And let your husband be more blind to your doings than was I."

She shook her head, hard. Of one thing she was certain. "Manuel HaLevy won't be deceived," she said. "He's told me himself that as his wife I would write only to teach his children their letters. He . . ." She hesitated. "He's a better man than I once thought. He's generous and honest when he wishes to be. But he turns all his force and intelligence to building an edifice for his heirs. There's much to celebrate in that life. But I fear it more than I rejoice in it. I'm not a woman who can be content where other women are." She closed her eyes, wishing now to see no more than the rabbi did. "So God made me." Behind her closed eyelids, the fire made small undulating patterns—an ocean of warmth and light dancing. And she saw that even as she'd tried to speak the truth, she'd fallen short of the mark. For were it John the rabbi was urging her to marry, she'd not claim herself incapable of joying in things other women wished for. And if it was so, that God had made her as she was, then whence this wild desire rising in her to entrust herself, soul and body, to an Englishman whose intentions she knew less than she knew Manuel HaLevy's? How difficult it was to grasp even a single truth of her own spirit.

"Now," said the rabbi, his voice weak, "you will write for me a letter to the Dotar, in Amsterdam. If you won't marry Manuel HaLevy, then perhaps a dowry from them will raise your prospect of another marriage. Ester. You must think of your future."

She said nothing.

"Write it," the rabbi said. "I believe, Ester, that obedience is due me now."

AT DAWN SHE ROSE, heavy with sleep. Through the night she'd fetched blankets and water at Rivka's request, venturing no closer—though the rabbi's shallow breaths sounded everywhere in the quiet house, measuring the passing hours. In the pale morning light, she read John's letters yet again.

> I think of you in that meadow, and the deer that allowed us so close.
> I think of your fist clenched so tight in the carriage after that foolish
> play, and the slow labor of unclenching your fingers. How I long to
> see you unclench your spirit until the full weight of your trust rests
> with me. For I see life has been hard with you and your trust is a
> thing not readily given.
>
> My business here finished, I return to London now with appre-
> hension of the pestilence but full of joy at the prospect of seeing you.

All morning, her thoughts bounded with confusion and hope, shielding her from her surroundings. At the apothecary's shop, ringed by grim-faced women trading advice about anti-pestilential herbs, Ester closed her ears to tales of children risen from their churchyard graves to comfort grieving mothers. When one woman raised a finger and pronounced that she could hear the comet in its dreadful passage through the heavy skies, its roar the voice of God's vengeance, Ester tightened her grip on the coins in her pocket and fixed her eyes on the apothecary's table. And carried the small vial of laudanum home, where she let Rivka administer it to the rabbi, herself staying at a distance. So it was Ester who stood close to the door when a messenger knocked, delivered a letter, and fled.

I stay with Thomas on Downgate Street, for he is in need of company as well as counsel. But I see London's sickness all about, and I would not linger. I have papers to travel, dear Ester, and wish to leave this city with all haste. Come with me. I'll take you to see green such as you've not guessed at in your life.

Ester, my father will wish your conversion. I cannot but say that such a choice would ease your life, though I won't press you for it. Even should you do this, whatsoever affections you hold for the beliefs of your people remain a matter of your own conscience, and I will cherish your conscience.

At noon she slipped from the house. Crossing Gracechurch Street, hurrying along Lombard, she opened her eyes as she had not in days, and saw London as John now must, having been absent during the weeks of its swift transformation. On Candlewick Street, a man had taken off his clothing and was waving it above his head, his ribs a piteous ladder, his private parts a dark smudge, shouting something Ester couldn't make out as she hurried by. Down a narrow alley she glimpsed a cross painted in rough white strokes on the wooden door of a house, warning all away. The plague had extended its fingers everywhere now, and grasped the city whole. Two men strode quickly past her, wearing nose cones of herbs and walking in the center of the streets so as to avoid coming near to any residence. They stepped aside only when a cart passed, bearing two bodies on the way to burial, one a man and one a small girl who seemed to rest her head on his chest. Ester glimpsed the dead girl's face, beautiful in its slumber despite the sores that marked it, as she slept alongside her father.

John answered Thomas's door.

Before she could greet him, he set a hand on her elbow and pulled her close. His kiss was light and questioning, then glad. He held her about the waist.

"Where's Thomas?" she said.

"Gone to see Mary. She begged him to visit, which he hadn't done these weeks. Is Mary well?"

"I wish I knew. She hasn't responded to my letters, nor would she come to the door when I visited."

John shook his head slowly. "It's not Thomas's first such trouble, I'm afraid. He dances away from it."

"Yes," Ester said. "We all understood that, save Mary."

John pursed his lips. "Perhaps one never can foresee what one hopes not to see."

"Perhaps not," she said.

There was no more to say on the matter. They stood together in the entry. After a moment John laughed, dispelling the silence. "You'll come with me, then? I wish to leave in the morning, no later."

They were near the same height, and she held his eyes. "I came to tell you why I cannot. Not yet."

He gave a slight, disbelieving laugh.

"The rabbi is too ill to travel," she said. "He's dying. I have to stay with him."

"You'll not get a travel permit if you wait, Ester. Already petitioners are waiting days, some only to be denied. The disease spreads too rapidly, hardly a parish is felt safe any longer."

"I know this," she said. "And if he should die tonight I'll be with you tomorrow. But understand, I can't leave him while he lives."

He hesitated, then shook his head. "In fact, Ester, I don't understand. If what you feel for me is love"—he laughed again, as though countering a child's foolish logic, and spoke to her slowly. "Your loyalty to the rabbi is an honorable thing. I respect it. But Ester, London is shuttering to burn itself to embers in this sickness. This is love, Ester, and it wishes to save you." He regarded her with an intensity she'd not seen in him before. "If you refuse, we might not see one another again. Does love matter so little to you?"

Words caught in her throat. "You misunderstand," she began. But how to explain what she felt, the absurd hopes he raised in her? She couldn't fathom a happy fate for herself—yet the very thought of him was a seed germinating, threatening to crack stone. The hour they'd spent beside the river had offered such a shock of beauty, she couldn't choose whether to banish it from her mind or think of nothing else. His quiet riveted her in a way all the proud promises of Manuel HaLevy could not. She wished to say even some small piece of this, but the words terrified her, like a prayer so full of hubris it might invite a curse.

She said, "I've done a wrong to the rabbi. I'll tell you of it one day. I cannot set it right, but I can accompany him now in his final days. If I fail to do that, I'll never be a spirit you wish to stand beside."

He nodded—a nod that gave away nothing. His face had altered. Something was awry.

Please, she thought.

But he was looking at her as though she'd beckoned him far, far out onto a narrow ledge and then, as his own balance trembled at the awesome height, excused herself from daring it. "I told Bescós he was wrong," he said. How ready to tumble he seemed, his expression pitching between ardor and sickness. "He said a Jewess will always pick her tribe over any other loyalty, and I said he was wrong."

"No," she said. "No, it's not that way. I choose with my heart, and my heart is for you." As she said it she felt her heart insisting within her ribs —indeed, for the first time in her life she almost could see her heart, and to her astonishment it seemed a brave and hopeful thing: a small wooden cup of some golden liquid, brimming until it spilled over all— the rabbi breathing in his bed, the dim candlelight by which Ester had so long strained at words on the page, the dead girl with her father in the cart. All that was beautiful and all that was precious, all of it streaming with sudden purpose here—to this place where they now stood.

John.

She laid her hands on his chest, his heartbeat rapid as her own. "The rabbi has been my father since my own died. I owe him comfort in his final hour."

"I understand," he said.

But she saw that he didn't. She saw that his own ability to save her had taken root in his mind; that it meant something prodigious to him; that this was the beacon he'd chosen to follow. He'd determined to be a pure and simple thing to her—her savior.

For the first time, she understood that words and logic could not convey all. They could not make John understand what she was willing to pledge to him, even as she refused his offer.

The image came to her of her grandmother's hands, delicate and sure on the spinet. She lifted her own hands from his chest. She set one on his shoulder. Then the other, and, stepping forward, she pressed against him as though walking through a door. Shocked by her boldness, he rocked back—then, tentatively, forward. The kiss he pressed on her lips was firmer—a test of something new—and she showed him in answer that she'd speak plainly to him with all she had. Swiftly, blindly, she led him to a side door, then another, behind which they found a bed, and there she lay him down beside her—and she chose not to think of Mary's fate, but helped John to unlace and unpin, her fingers atop his trembling ones, guiding them until she was bare beside him and he —realizing with absurd gentlemanly embarrassment that he alone wore clothing—hastened to join her, both of them laughing at the comedy of his shirt and breeches confounding him as he tried to slip them off in too much haste.

His skin was pink and pale, warm against the gold of hers, his body thin as she'd imagined, and she closed her eyes and found once more the green daylight she'd remembered from that day beside the river, and of which she'd dreamt since. But not even in her dreams had she unfurled herself so alongside him, the two of them in silent tandem using every sense but sight. His touch on her skin like spider's silk, so delicate a mere breeze could tear it beyond repair—for they were choosing not merely to love, but to love *thus,* and as he entered her the words were a piercing brightness in her mind: *we two invented this.* She opened her eyes to tell him, and his face was strange to her—wild and alive and beautiful as a storm crashing against every lit windowpane. John's dear face, quickened with such sacred clarity that she thought: so would be the angels, fierce with desire and understanding.

This love has no endpoint, she wished to say. See how we're borne within it, on and on and on? She called his name, and as she did she laughed aloud.

Yet even as she laughed, she saw his delight falter. She saw some stray thought tug at him, as though a voice had, for just an instant, called him—a tiny, flickering herald from a place beyond this bed: a world of iron-cast virtue and vice, where his own heart had never dared utter a sound, so its beating now was thunder and calamity. Unease fell over his eyes.

She lost his face, then. His body was flush with hers; he gripped her hard in his arms and his face burrowed into the cloud of her hair on the pillow. A hopeful confusion, his breath fast in her ear.

A wince of pleasure.

He lay quietly atop her. Then he separated from her. She felt his eyes on her, but when she looked at him he glanced at the window. They lay breathing on the bed. She tried again to meet his gaze; again it fled hers. As though she'd led him too far, too fast—as though a force had summoned him back from himself, and he'd fain be any other man now, so frightened was he to be John. The room was silent.

"You were a virgin?" he said.

The words were discordant, a script for the wrong play. Didn't he understand what she'd just said to him—what she'd offered—with her body? What had her virginity, or his, to do with what had just taken place?

Yet the question demanded an answer, in the same foreign tongue he'd spoken. Reluctant, she nodded. *Yes.* Seeing that words were still required, she said, "I trust myself in your hands."

She felt him nod. But something in his body had solidified. When he looked at her a moment later, it was as if from a distance—as if he feared something in himself, and her.

There was a bang—a door slamming in its frame. Thomas. At the sound John jumped to his feet and dressed, passing her things to her courteously but without looking at her. A moment later she was dressed —and John squeezed her shoulder with forced warmth, murmured something with a slight apologetic laugh, and then she was in the parlor and on her way to the door, with John out of sight behind her, Thomas greeting her with a bleary smirk as she passed.

She could not regret what she'd done. She could not.

SHE REACHED HOME WITH NO recollection of what she'd passed on the street, or whether she'd encountered any, living or dead. She shut the door behind her, turned, and the sight of Manuel HaLevy, seated at her writing table with a cup of ale, stilled her.

Rivka was perched uneasily on the rabbi's chair. It was plain she was restless to turn to her chores—yet the rabbi was asleep in his bedroom, and some unaccustomed impulse toward politeness seemed to have seized Rivka, preventing her from abandoning their visitor. As soon as Ester entered the room, Rivka turned to Manuel HaLevy, murmured

"By your leave" in thickly accented English, and left with a quick curtsy—a gesture so foreign to Rivka's usual demeanor that Ester simply stared.

Moving as in a dream, Ester turned to Manuel HaLevy. She saw, with a dull, distant shock, that she hadn't put away her writing from yesterday. So distracted had she been by her conversation with the rabbi that she'd let the page she'd written for him remain in broad view on the table. But Manuel had pushed it aside, and did not seem interested in reading. He looked in good spirits, his robust figure fit, his color high.

"I came to check on my investment," he said.

Her eyes could not seem to contract. There was too much light; the window was a white blur and his face hazed in her vision.

"My father sent me to attend to some small affairs of his here in London and make sure his servants take no advantage of his absence. But of course I was glad of the reason to visit—even with London in this state." He looked closely at her. Concern furrowed his broad brow. "You're not ill?"

Resisting the impulse to raise a hand to her flushed cheek, she shook her head.

He looked glad, then amused. "Has the pestilence tamed your famous tongue?"

She formed a small smile. "No," she said.

He drank from his ale, set the cup on the table. "Did you note that Sasportas has gone—and not just to the countryside, but out of England altogether? Our esteemed new rabbi, it seems, chooses not to shepherd his congregation through such a visitation. The plague offers him divine signal to flee, as he's wished to since first he arrived here. The man was too godly for a congregation of merchants." Manuel's full lips formed a wry rose. Then he turned serious. "There's no plague in Richmond, Ester. Come there with me."

She spoke flatly, with a mute gesture toward the rabbi's room. "I won't leave him now."

He nodded. "I understand."

She didn't know whether to feel grateful or bitter.

"I wish you'd come with me," he said, "but I respect you for the choice. When we marry, you'll show me the same devotion."

He leaned across the table and picked up the page he'd pushed aside. Quickly he read it. She knew what was there: the rabbi's dictation — words she'd committed to paper without ever understanding they were addressed to her. *For I speak to you as a father to a son, and though your endeavor be beyond my reach, still I wish to gird you with all the understanding and love of God that I harbor in my heart. It is for this that I labor, for I believe it will be my last good deed in this world.*

With a tolerant smile, Manuel HaLevy set down the page, patted it, and set his used cup atop it. "Remember the choice that's offered you," he said.

A NIGHT TORQUED BY DREAMS. In long wakeful hours, in a black silence broken only by the rabbi's faint moans, she rehearsed the day's events, as though trying to solve an equation with aching heart and flesh for its components.

Near dawn, carriage wheels below her window.

She descended the stair and opened the door before John had lifted his hand to knock. She stood, one hand on the doorknob for strength.

Behind John, set against the dark street and white sky, was a coach piled with baggage. The coachman hunched in his seat, his face shuttered against the city; framed in the half-closed window, silently facing forward, was Thomas. Before addressing her John glanced back at them, as though drawing strength from their impatience.

When he turned to her, she saw that he looked diminished, apprehensive.

Something had gone wrong, something whose name was still just outside her reach. All the world would have told her that her error had been in giving herself to him — that he abhorred her now because she'd so easily surrendered her virtue — yet she felt certain that wasn't right. Something had slipped between them, and in slipping had started a dreadful wordless tumble she didn't know how to stop. She'd given her body because it was the only way she knew to speak the truth — to make John understand what she pledged, lay it out plainly alongside the love he'd offered. Yet their joining had carried him too far, to a territory where he didn't recognize himself, or her.

If she could have curled herself up in his pocket as he stood there on the street, she'd have done it. She would even, in that instant, have abandoned the rabbi. She'd have forsaken her writing as a barren folly, climbed shivering into the carriage to warm herself beside him. *Take me with you.*

But it was too late. His face bore the marks of his own suffering. She read there his struggle to think well of himself, and his panic to flee all the sudden scourges of this city, herself among them.

"You'll come to join me," he said. "Perhaps. After." He essayed each word carefully.

She forced herself to walk the steps of his logic. "After the rabbi's death?"

He offered an uncertain nod.

She opened her mouth to insist: *But what of our love? What of all you swore?* And as John glanced yet again toward the safety of the coach, another, more desperate impulse rose in her: to speak words she knew would corral him in an instant. *I gave you my honor; now you know your duty to me.*

But she could not comprehend a love that must be purchased with pity. Nor would she force John to her side through a language of honor in which she did not believe. Honor and love were no kin — all who claimed so did ill in the world. At last, now, she understood her own grandmother's pained choice. *A heart is a free thing,* Lizabeta had said, *and once enslaved will mutiny.*

She thought, *Let me not enslave that heart that so wishes for liberty. Let him come to me in freedom, or not at all.*

She said to John, "I'll await word from you, then."

He appeared relieved. Then, as all she'd left unspoken rang in the silence, unhappy.

He mustered himself. Then looked directly at her. "I haven't your strength of heart," he said.

You would, she thought, if you had my life.

"I shall see you, then." A halting kiss on her cheek.

In her confusion she allowed it. Piercing words rose to her lips — but speaking them would squander a silence she needed, now, to absorb every detail of him. Had Ester once thought it frivolous for a woman to don breeches in order to learn the mind of her lover? She'd have done far more now, as John turned for his carriage. She'd have bent herself wholly to a new shape, if only she might understand. Enchant. Be other than what she was.

He'd loved her. To doubt this would be to doubt her very sanity.

His carriage receded down the street.

THE DAYS NARROWED, DIMMED, PILED one upon the next. They muffled one another, indistinguishable—save for the brief leap and tremble of shadows on Sabbath as Rivka lit the candles, then placed a drop of wine on the rabbi's pale tongue. Ester and Rivka waited, together, as he labored to swallow it. Outside the windows, London had reshaped itself. The sound of hooves had all but left the streets and what remained of all London's throngs was a populace of extremes: those too poor to flee, and those whose love of their possessions made them unwilling to leave them; those too ill for the journey, and those who trusted firmly in their good health; those who would plunder, and those few unselfish souls who still wished to tend the sick, in the watchful hush that had overtaken the city.

In the distance Ester at times heard bells, strange poundings, flurries of noise followed by dreadful quiet. Now and then, muted cries from beyond their door broke the silence. Ester ventured out when they needed supplies, offering herself for their errands and household labors so Rivka could remain at the rabbi's side. There was no more laudanum to be had in the city, and the apothecary had doubled the price for willow bark. The man would no longer take the coin from her hand, but with a wordless shake of his head bade her set it on his table—as though not only touch but even speech might prove deadly.

One evening near dusk, returning from the apothecary, she strayed to the park where she'd once encountered Catherine. A foolish thing to do, yet she no longer feared for her own safety. Grass had overgrown the paths, and the dim air was rich with birdcalls—for by the mayor's authority all London's cats, blamed for spreading the pestilence, had been killed. She stood beneath the fresh rills of song, amid cool waves of grass, until stars pricked overhead. From a deserted street nearby came the dim light of a single lantern, carried by an invisible stranger hastening through the streets toward home, its faint, aching glow careening from window to window.

Words she'd once read in another world, in a lamp-lit bookbinder's shop, floated through her mind: *What's gone and what's past help should be past grief.*

The soft English sod beneath her shoes.

She found Rivka red-eyed. Setting her cloak on the peg, she heard the rabbi breathing shallowly on the bed Rivka had made for him by the fire. His voice was a dry whisper. Hesitant, she stepped closer to hear. She hadn't allowed herself to be so near to him in weeks, choosing instead to make herself useful from a distance, for she felt certain her presence must burden him.

"Vidui," he said.

Were the world not so altered, Sasportas or some other respected man of the synagogue would receive the rabbi's confession. And wouldn't it be better for the rabbi not to confess at all, rather than have one who had betrayed him hear his *vidui*?

Yet the communication he must make now was with heaven—and she, with prayer book in hand, would be his necessary conduit. Closing her eyes, she pledged to purge all other thoughts from her mind, so that she might do at least this one task for him without fault.

She found the worn volume and read out the words slowly, allowing each phrase time to reach him. *Modeh ani lefanecha.* He repeated some of the words after her, and let others fall unvoiced from his moving lips. *Te'he mitati kapara.*

Some time after she'd finished, a parched sound came from his throat. With effort, he spoke again. "I speak now my own confession."

He swallowed, a long and labored process.

"The distances between things," he whispered, "are vast."

His hand rose, wavered in the air, then settled on the blanket covering his chest. "It is my consolation," he said, "to come safe to death, without being tested a second time. For I've known I would fail. Just as I failed in boyhood, when my soul was tested by the inquisitors.

"I have little memory of how I answered their terrible questions, though they asked again and again. I recall only trying to erase from my mind names I knew, names that would cause other Jews to suffer. Yet this I confess: had they asked me to deny my God, I would have done so—for in that dreadful place, my body felt only its own pain, and my weak spirit could not believe the suffering I witnessed to be the birth pangs of the Messiah."

He'd spent his strength. He rested, then gathered himself once more.

"After my eyes were taken, I felt my way through each room, each passageway and alley of Lisbon, and then Amsterdam, with my fingers outstretched. And do you know what I felt, Ester?"

She swallowed.

"That the distances between things were vast, vaster than I had known when I had sight. Everywhere I felt a void. Everywhere was hollow, God's presence withdrawn. I walked with fingers outstretched and felt the brokenness of God's world.

"God blesses me now," he whispered, "and spares me a second torment. It is the only thing I have feared in this world . . . that should the Inquisition take me once more, my soul would fail a second time. I have feared, Ester, to die without a psalm on my tongue." He raised a quaking hand and slowly, lightly, touched his sealed eyelids, first one and then the other. "As was Zedekiah punished," he said, "so have I been. For all my life, all these weary years, the last vision I saw has remained before me. My mother," he whispered, his hand hovering before his eyelids. "Upon the rack. Her body broken, but her eyes yet open, shining as the life drained from her. She had asserted her faith. She could not raise a hand to cover her nakedness." There was a long silence. He lowered his hand. "She has remained before my sightless eyes, every morning, every day and night, as I saw her then. I have walked through a hollow world, carrying her."

His breath was uneven, coming soft and then loud.

"I have worked to restore some of God's presence to the hollowness. For repairing the world through His words is the work for which God has intended us." He paused a long while. "Only," he said, "I have wished each day that I could stop seeing her. Even if it meant forgetting her beloved face forever."

After a moment he continued, his voice strengthened. "My sin that I confess now is to have wanted death. In secret I have longed for it, for blindness can never suffice to extinguish the sight of the terrors of this broken world."

Once more he fell silent. A moment later, he nodded slowly, his thin, stained beard rising and falling on the blanket that covered his concave chest. He said, "This I confess."

He said no more to her. Gradually he fell into some sort of sleep.

Rivka, bringing a chair, sat beside Ester and commenced whispering psalms from memory. Some time in the night, Ester joined Rivka in her recitations. Their words flowed in the silence. Beneath the current of whispers, by the light of the fire, Ester watched the transformation as the rabbi sank into himself. And as though he were even now continuing his gentle tutelage—instructing her, even as he slipped beyond her reach, to study him as carefully and minutely as any phrase they'd learned together—she felt that she saw a circlet surrounding his head and then his laboring chest, made wholly of pain. Yet the circlet, even as it was his torment, shed a soft reminder of something he'd known all his life—as though a voice within it or above it whispered: *you always knew so, did you not?* And she saw the rabbi heed it, and she saw him agree at last. For death—so it seemed to Ester now—awaits agreement, even where it must persuade and threaten and insist without mercy until agreement is granted.

She watched, then, as life trailed ragged from the rabbi like a ship's wake.

The fire, no longer needed to warm him, burned down to its last embers.

The sounds of Rivka's grief roused Ester.

Thus was the world altered. With a dull concussion in the chest.

THERE WERE NO MORE INDIVIDUAL graves nor headstones in London, the capacity of gravediggers and stone carvers being long outmatched by the pace the city now required. The earth of St. Peter upon Cornhill's churchyard, they said, had been raised to waist height with the coffins stacked one atop another, then abandoned in favor of mass graves. The dead were sent sliding now into pits, raising clouds of lime dust, hastily prayed over by clusters of the living who didn't dare approach one another. It made no difference that the rabbi had not died of plague, for all claims of other causes of death were now scoffed at, so often did families seek to mask the cause of death in order to make pretense that their home was not gripped by the pestilence. So Ester and Rivka hired a wagon and brought the rabbi themselves to the pit at Stepney Mount, and averted their eyes from what seemed a hundred bodies, many not even wrapped—limbs and sore-encrusted faces dusted with lime. They said what prayers seemed proper, then slid his frail body, in the shroud Rivka had stitched for him, into the silent, thronged gully.

They returned together to the house.

There, slipped through the crevice at the door's base, Ester found a note from Mary.

Please come, it said, in a hand too rounded and girlish for one her age and in her state.

The house, without the rabbi's labored breathing, stood in powerful silence. Following Rivka, Ester washed her hands and face in the kitchen basin; then lingered, strangely idle, in the front room. She allowed the thought: even should she and Rivka survive the plague, this household would soon be dissolved.

With a small scissor taken from her pocket, Rivka cut the cloth of her own collar to signify mourning; then Ester's. In the hollow house, the slow rasp of scissor biting cloth was alarmingly loud. But the quiet in its wake was worse. As Rivka lowered the scissor, Ester saw the realization reflected on her face: they were alone.

She said to Rivka, "I'm going to the da Costa Mendes house. I'll return. Before dark."

Rivka nodded, lips pressed tight.

SHE HURRIED THROUGH THE DESERTED STREETS. The Jewish houses around Creechurch Lane were abandoned or silent. If any remained behind those windows who might care that the rabbi had died or that Ester and Rivka still lived, they hadn't shown themselves in weeks. Still Ester couldn't help gaze into each, as if some familiar soul might peer back through the dark mullioned panes as though from underwater or from beyond this world.

She entered the gate of the da Costa Mendes house, shut it carefully behind her, and only then looked up to see the white cross painted on the door.

She hesitated. Then stepped up to it and knocked, avoiding touching the cross as though it were cursed.

Mary opened the door just wide enough for Ester to see her face. "I'm not sick," she said. Swinging the door wider, she grabbed Ester's forearm hard. "The cross is a lie."

Ester let herself be pulled through the familiar entryway, and Mary shut the door behind her and locked it.

It took Ester just one step inside the parlor to know that no one else was present. The fine furnishings were askew, pillows lay in piles on the floor, blankets were heaped on a divan, and used dishes were scattered here and there. Mary had never kept house for herself. Now it appeared she had been sleeping and eating here in the parlor, where the window looked out onto the deserted street. Mary herself was dressed in a stained blue dress that gaped at the placket. Her belly was swollen past the point where it could be contained in her usual bodices and stays. It was clear she'd had none to teach her how to dress in the manner of a woman expecting a child. Without her customary makeup and jewelry she looked like a child herself, settling now cross-legged on a cushioned chair and pulling Ester to the seat beside her.

"The servants left over a week ago," she said, still gripping Ester's arm. "They helped themselves to some of my father's things along the way." She shrugged, as though she didn't begrudge them what they'd taken. Then, releasing Ester at last, she said more quietly, "Thomas left."

"I know," Ester said, sitting. "I saw him go. With John." She looked up into Mary's wide, shadowed eyes—and could easily guess the terror of Mary's nights alone in the deserted house, the city's anguish sounding unseen all around.

"Did John ask you to accompany him?"

Ester began to answer, then faltered. At length she said, "At first. But I fear he wouldn't wish it now, even had I a travel permit."

In the silence that followed, an agreement passed between them: neither would make the other name what she'd lost.

"Why is there a cross on your door?" Ester asked. "Isn't it the mark of a plague house?"

Mary shook her head hard. "No one's died here, Ester, not yet. But Bescós came." Mary's soft face registered fear now, and she hesitated before continuing in a lower voice, as though they might be overheard. "Thomas told Bescós everything. He told him I'd stayed. That I was with child." Mary began rocking herself gently, forward and back, arms about her belly. "And Bescós guessed that the servants would leave me. He says that now that I'm the sole guardian of my father's wealth, it will be his."

Ester absorbed this. She believed Mary—yet something here fit amiss with her notion of Bescós. She'd taken Bescós for a hateful man, yes . . . even a dangerous one. But she hadn't thought him a petty thief. There had always been something haughty about the man. Wouldn't Bescós consider himself above threatening a frightened girl for petty gain?

"He sent someone to paint the cross, Ester," Mary said. "I didn't know it was there until I tried to go out, and a man on the street shouted me back indoors as though I were a rat trying to escape its trap." Her voice caught. "No one will come," she said. "All the congregation are gone from London—and they'd stopped wanting to speak to me even before the plague. When I stole out my door to try to find you this morning, the woman who saw me screamed and screamed for help, and said she'd set a mob on me, and I had to run past her—like *this*, Ester." She gestured at her belly, at the gaping fabric at her waist. "Bescós said if I don't start paying him from my father's silver, he'll simply wait until I die of plague or hunger, and he'll come get my father's wealth then."

Ester turned to the window. Through its panes she surveyed the empty street that had been Mary's solitary view day and night. "Leave your father's fortune," she said. "Let Bescós claim it, let your father mourn it. Manuel HaLevy will take us in. You and I, and Rivka, I'm sure of it." And she was.

And if Manuel asked her to pledge him something in return? Perhaps she ought. If she couldn't love Manuel—if she forever mourned John—what of it? For reasons she could not comprehend, John had turned away. All else she'd cherished—her carefully built edifices and spires of thought—had brought pain to the rabbi and benefited none but herself. But a choice to marry could save them.

Manuel HaLevy had been correct: in the end, life would force her hand, and she'd greet his offer with gratitude.

Mary stared. Then something akin to a laugh rose in her throat. "Manuel HaLevy is dead. He died over a week ago, of plague. The servants told me, before they left. He fell ill the day he was to leave London. He never passed the city walls."

The parlor was too dim. She could see nothing in the shadowed room. She stood.

Mary took her sleeve. "Stay with me, Ester."

Slowly she shook her head, not in answer but simply for the sensation of motion.

"I can't live alone," Mary insisted. "I don't know how. There are some foods still in the pantry and I don't know even how to cook them. I'll either die of plague or I'll starve, or else I'll live to birth the baby and I'm afraid to do that alone. I'm not brave like you." She stopped herself. "I'm sorry I didn't answer those letters you sent me. I thought . . . I thought perhaps you wanted to see me only because I paid you to look after me. I thought: first Thomas, then Bescós, all wanting only my father's money —maybe you were the same. I thought, I don't have a true friend. And then . . ." She looked up. "I thought you'd gone with John. And even if you hadn't, I didn't want any to see me like *this*." She gestured at her belly without touching it, as though it were a thing entirely separate from her. Then, a moment later, she wrapped her arms protectively about it once more. "I'm sorry," she said, her voice taking on a solemn hush, "about the rabbi. Is that where you were this morning?"

Ester nodded.

Mary hesitated. *"May the Holy One comfort you,"* she began uncomfortably, *"among the—"* She stopped, unable to recall the remainder. With a small, helpless giggle she subsided.

The world had reshaped so quickly, there was no room left—so it seemed to Ester—to do anything but act. In the rabbi's household there remained perhaps a few days' food and fuel, and after that nothing— no income, no salvation in the form of a purse from Manuel HaLevy. She thought with apprehension of the cross on Mary's door. Yet in this house there was also food, and silver and fine furnishings that might yet be traded for some means of escape. If they were careful, they might come and go as they needed.

"Rivka as well?" she said.

Mary nodded, relief suffusing her face so that for a fleeting instant she resembled paintings such as Ester had sometimes seen in rich homes in Amsterdam—of a young woman dreamy and ripe, anticipating the birth of her babe.

Mary stood, the pale skin of her belly bulging through the gap in her skirt. "Come today," she said. "This evening, before the curfew."

BY SUNSET IT WAS ACCOMPLISHED. Rivka, who'd replied to Ester's explanation of Mary's predicament with naught but pragmatic questions, set immediately to gathering her few necessities, then followed Ester—locking the door of the rabbi's house behind them and departing without backward glance, as though she couldn't bear to stay another moment within those walls without the sound of his frail breathing.

Rather than find a cart whose very wood might be permeated with plague seeds, Ester brought her possessions by hand, taking care to avoid being seen coming and going from the da Costa Mendeses' door. Her own belongings, bundled beneath her arms, required only one passage between the da Costa Mendes house and the rabbi's. Returning alone for the rabbi's books, Ester carried his library two stacks at a time.

Over and again she passed through the hushed streets, the tender pages and worn covers marking the exposed skin of her forearms with deep red grooves and slashes—like a mute alphabet spelling accusations she couldn't refute. Finally, on her sixth and final passage, she brought the papers. The rabbi's body lay in a pit, yet she could still preserve his writings. Unable to bear sorting the pages she pulled from drawers and shelves, she swept all together: household accounts, notices from the book bindery, the rabbi's sermons, all in a jumble. And somewhere among them, the rabbi's letters to his pupil in Florence—letters she now understood were intended for her, to pull her back from the folly of her own notions. She brought, too, her own writings. Yet it seemed to her now, as she hurried down long alleys in the fading light, that her very questions and propositions were themselves written in an alphabet of scored flesh and damaged spirit. Such cruel wounds, from such small markings of her quill on the page.

That night, Ester lay awake on one of the fine mattresses of the da Costa Mendes house. In a bed beside hers, Rivka lay quiet—whether asleep or not Ester couldn't say. In a nearby room, Mary tossed noisily in her bed.

She could not yet grieve the rabbi's death. Her mind failed, somehow, to comprehend it. Beneath the mattress where she lay, stowed there hastily this evening, were his papers and her own—a mute presence whose demands on her she couldn't fathom. Her spirit shrank, too, from the scalding thought of John.

Yet she circled back again and again, without understanding why, to one single comprehensible fact: Manuel HaLevy was dead. She could not break away from the thought of him. She could almost feel his astonishment at his first moment of faltering . . . his great body suddenly weak, hot with fever, not responding to his command that it rise, stride, shake off what dogged it. She could see his pale eyes, understanding at last that he too would yield. And although she hadn't loved him, that first night in her new lodgings she cried hot tears for his robust body, racked and stilled. And for the protection he had so long offered her. And for that protection which he had so fervently, even courteously, requested from her in exchange: the surety of a wife who would not succumb.

23

April 9, 2001
London

H E LINGERED IN THE SHOWER, took his time over coffee in the dining hall. He ran an errand he'd meant to run for weeks—stopping at the supply store near the Tube entrance to buy new toner for Helen's printer. Waiting to pay, he even let a mother, jabbering on her mobile while her toddler poked at a pen display with the sticky end of a lollipop, into the queue ahead of him.

But delay though he did, by late morning he found himself at the usual long table in the rare manuscripts room, facing the final batch of documents.

Grimly then, notched pencil digging into his knuckles, he worked his way down the evenly inked lines. He understood, of course, why he hated to finish the cache: like a gambler spinning the roulette wheel, he'd come to rely on the eternal promise of the next round of letters.

But as he made his way down the lines of the fourth-to-last document—and then the third-to-last—he acknowledged the folly of the trust he'd placed in these papers. There would be no grand revelation, no smoking gun, no hidden three-century-old wisdom to galvanize his drifting life. Ester Velasquez was not going to pop out from behind the curtains and save him from himself. Even if she'd actually written under the name of Thomas Farrow, they'd never be able to prove it. Not if the rest of the documents were like this.

The sole labor that remained for Aaron then, in these dwindling hours of reading, was to listen. No more, and no less. Which was, as he should have known all along, a historian's only true charge.

He tried now to listen to what Ester was actually saying, rather than what he wanted her to say.

There wasn't much of it. In silence, he translated another list of household expenses, this one without any extraneous doodles in the margins. He read a missive from the rabbi to his student in Florence, but it was brief and mainly repeated the rabbi's earlier opinions about Sabbatai Zevi and the dangers of misplaced fervor.

When Patricia lay the second-to-last document on the wedge before him, he realized he was clenching his fists.

It was a single sheet of paper, and the writing covered only half the page.

> June 28, 1665
> 15 Tamuz, 5425
> With the help of G-d
>
>
> To the Esteemed Rabbi Isaac Aboab da Fonseca,
> From my sickbed I send to the honorable kehillah of Amsterdam my greetings. Each hour now brings me closer to my end. The angels who escort the sun on its passage across the sky do not slow to lengthen my final days, nor do I ask this. Such work as I have had sufficient merit to do in this world is now ended, whether or not I have succeeded in it.
> My household here in London sees to my needs and reads psalms for me, and I am blessed to lack neither comfort nor a soul to whom to make my confession.
> I have a request of you. It is my hope that you will find merit in me to grant it. It is my wish that you should prevail upon the Dotar to provide a dowry for Ester Velasquez, should the day come for her to wed. Little has been given her and much ripped from her in her life. When she has attained the honor and stability of the marriage canopy I believe she will prove herself a woman of valor. Should there be questions about the girl's mother, I ask that the Dotar grant this wish nonetheless, as a duty to the dead. In this broken world, I request that you escort and comfort my departing soul through this good deed, which will bring you merit in the world to come.
> For my sins I beg G-d's forgiveness.

In faith in the coming of the Messiah and the merciful reign of
G-d, which will break on us like a dawn, illuminating every mystery
that now confounds our sightless souls.

Rabbi Moseh HaCoen Mendes

א

He sat back.

The quiet in the hall was absolute. A faint shaft of light rested on the
wooden floor beside his feet. His eyes stung.

After a moment he stood. It was two o'clock. Just another twenty
minutes until he'd have to leave to meet Helen in her office. In truth
she seemed to have lost her taste for the rare manuscripts room this past
week. He wondered if she, too, was dragging her feet about reaching
the end of the cache. She hadn't looked quite her usual fierce self lately
—and the rabbi's deathbed letter was unlikely to cheer her.

On with it, then. Librarian Patricia watched him approach.

"I'll take the last in the series." He tried to sound jauntier than he
felt.

She wasn't fooled. The look she gave him was almost, but not quite,
sympathetic. "The ivy letter isn't ready."

"Which letter?"

"The final document. It's a folded letter, with an unbroken wax seal."
She pursed her lips. "The seal is an ornate image of climbing ivy. Quite
lovely, in fact." Her eyebrows lifted just a millimeter; her smile this time
was faint but real.

"When will it be ready?" he said.

"My colleague upstairs has removed the seal and is preserving it for
display. The letter itself is now in the humidifying chamber. She expects
it will be ready in another week."

"That long?"

Librarian Patricia lowered her glasses.

He persisted. "I don't suppose you have any idea what's actually in
the letter?"

She closed her mouth, breathed out slowly through her nose. "You
don't understand the English at all," she said, "do you?"

"Nope," he said. "Not a bit."

She gave a short hum, then surveyed him in silence. "Let me help you, then." Slowly she leaned forward at her desk. "We're very patient people."

"It's getting old"—he said—"your stoic-Britons-confront-the-impatient-American thing. Thought I'd just let you know."

"Is it?" she said evenly.

"Yes. Also, it's nonsense. Professor Helen Watt, who's so English her resting pulse is a negative number, is at this moment putting on pompoms in anticipation of celebrating the last document's release. She's making a human pyramid, in fact, all by herself."

Patricia didn't blink.

"But if you get something out of the impregnable English thing," he said, "I'll go with it."

"Awfully game of you," she said.

"Quite," he said.

Neither of them had budged an inch from the desk. They stared at each other.

"Did we just make friends?" he said.

From the tables of laboring students around them, he heard a few snickers.

"I mean, is that how you people do it?" he continued. "Bully each other to a standstill—then buy each other a pint? Is *that* what I've been missing all this time in England?"

She raised her glasses again, and looked out at him from beneath them.

"Silly me," he said. "I've been skipping the bullying part."

She considered. "Try it without shortcuts next time," she said.

"I don't think I will," he said. "I'm not a very patient person. Besides," he added, "I rather enjoy how unnerved English people get when you tell them you like them."

Like a drop of soap in oily water, the words scattered gazes in all directions—Patricia's fled back to her computer, and the students on either side of him who had been surreptitiously staring a moment earlier now studied their manuscripts with renewed fervor.

"Well," he said to the silent room. "I'm glad we had this heart-to-heart."

BACK IN HELEN'S OFFICE HE set down his bags. Without a word he pulled the new toner cartridge from his bag and replaced Helen's old one.

"Thank you," she said faintly.

With a nod of acknowledgment, he took out his laptop and printed his transcript of the rabbi's letter. He set it on her desk. "Here's a tear-jerker for you."

She took the paper in a wavering hand and studied it a moment. Then she set it down beside her computer—carelessly, he thought, as though she weren't much concerned about its contents. Her gaze returned to her window.

Now that he looked at her properly, he saw she sat stiffly, and was wearing a heavy sweater despite the warm April afternoon. Briefly it occurred to him to be worried about her. Then again, how many times had he sat in her office, searching her distant expression for signs that she appreciated or even recognized a gift he'd just brought her? It had always been this way with Helen, and always would be. This, evidently, was the full extent of the friendship she cared to offer.

"Can you find the e-mail address of the Amsterdam Jewish archive?" Helen's voice sounded thin, though whether from disappointment or fatigue he couldn't tell.

"Sure, why?"

"Let's see if they have the final copy of this." She spoke almost gingerly, as though trying not to bite down on something sour in her mouth. "They've got the best-documented seventeenth-century Jewish community in Europe, and this letter is addressed to one of its prominent rabbis." She swallowed. It took a long time. "For once," she said, "we might be able to track down the second copy of one of HaCoen Mendes's letters."

He searched for the address and spelled it out for her; laboriously she typed it. Twice she had to backtrack and begin again, her index finger heavy on the delete key. Without meaning to, he drifted behind her to watch. The process was mesmerizing: words struggling to take shape on the screen. With effort, Helen moved past the salutation.

Then, backtracking once more, she accidentally deleted all she'd written.

She rose silently from her chair, stepped to the side. With one hand she gave him a vague wave. Swiftly, he took her place. Using the sort of formal phrases she might, he composed a query to the Amsterdam Jewish archives, signed with Helen's name. As he worked she breathed softly over his shoulder. "Yes," she said. "That will do."

The chime of the departing mail sounded in the office. He stood.

"Well," she said, resuming her seat. "The last letters." Then, surprising him, she added, "I'd hoped for more proof."

He nodded. Without more evidence, their conjectures about Farrow were fool's gold.

She was staring at him.

"What?" he said.

She shook her head, as though to rid herself of a fly.

Christ. "Helen Watt," he said, enunciating like a schoolteacher.

Reluctantly, as though confessing an intimacy she wasn't sure she wanted to part with, she said, "There's something about the Florence letters."

"Meaning what?"

"Why," she said, "is there no other record of the Sabbatean crisis in Florence?"

"Because most records don't survive 350 years," he said. "It's more surprising when we *do* have evidence of something than when it's missing."

"Yes," said Helen, "but why don't we have any of the letters from the rabbi's student in Florence, whereas we have other letters the rabbi received?"

"I'm not following you," he said.

"At one point, after the rabbi has come under pressure to stop using her as a scribe, the letters stop for a while. Then, a while later, they start again with these missives to Florence. Perhaps, don't you think, she was invited to scribe for the rabbi again only because the Sabbatean crisis in Florence demanded it?"

"It's possible," he began. "But there could be a hundred reasons for that gap in the letters. Ill health, documents lost in a fire, a voyage to—"

"And don't you think," she interrupted—and there was now something explosive in her manner, "that being barred from learning might give a young woman with enough hunger for education—enough love of the work of *thought* itself—sufficient incentive to *invent* a Sabbatean crisis?"

Now he knew she wasn't well. Helen Watt, in full possession of her faculties, would have torn this logical leap to shreds, and sought a more likely explanation. Something was wrong with her today. Or maybe it had been for a long while.

And she hadn't finished. "You know the Masada story, of course," she said. Slowly she pointed. Her finger, half bent at each knuckle as if she were unable to straighten it, hovered; then aimed itself, trembling, at the picture above the mantle.

"I know the story." As did anyone who ever attended a synagogue Hebrew school.

"How do we know what happened up there?" said Helen. Her finger still wavered in the direction of the sketch.

"You mean on Masada?" Aaron blinked. "It's in Josephus. *The Jewish War.*" But as he spoke, he realized for the first time what a foolish answer this was.

"Yes, and how did Josephus know?" continued Helen. "*He* wasn't on Masada, he was with the Roman army. When he arrived, the Jews had already committed"—she pursed her lips—"glorious martyrdom. Or, as the Jews' leader described it, a final act of *kindness.*"

He dug in his memory. "Something about women who hid?"

"Two women, yes. They hid in a cave with some children. It seems they disagreed with their leader's notion that kindness meant self-murder for a noble cause. It seems they were of the opinion that kindness meant something quite different." Helen's finger was now wavering so widely he wanted to grab and steady it. "Everyone looks at that silhouette," she said, "and thinks of people who chose to do the so-called honorable thing even though it meant death for themselves, their wives, and children. And that's the only story of Masada anyone talks about. No one ever mentions those two women who decided to live and be captured, and find a way in the world whether or not it was honorable or free. No one ever mentions that they might have been something other than weak-hearted—that they might in fact have disbelieved the worldview that required their murder. But they stayed alive—and Aaron, *they* were the ones who told the story to Josephus—they're the only reason we know what happened up there."

It was true. All those times he'd heard the Masada story, no one had ever troubled to linger on the question of how the details of the story were known—nor had he wondered. It was as though the story had been received from the ether. The one teacher who had mentioned the women hiding in caves, Aaron now remembered, had referred to them as cowards.

"Right there," Helen said. "There's the watermark of a different choice."

She lowered her hand.

She was asking him to connect dots across millennia, as though Ester Velasquez were part of the same invisible chain that included two women's refusal to martyr themselves on Masada. "You're proposing," he said slowly, "that a seventeenth-century woman would go so far as to fake a Sabbatean crisis, just so she could write a few letters to philosophers." He hesitated, feeling himself in an untoward position: he needed to impress upon a historian decades his senior the rashness of chasing grand, unsupported visions. "Don't you think we need to be a bit cautious about superimposing some template of modern feminist rebellion onto people we know almost nothing about?"

"I think, young man, that the time for caution has passed."

There was a long pause.

"You're not well," he said.

She didn't bother answering. But he saw. She'd been in some obscure decline since he'd known her, but something had changed. Something in her was pitching toward a destination that he didn't want to consider —that made him feel sick himself.

But now she was speaking firmly, as though to erase the sound of his words. "I contacted your Derek Godwin. Through the Internet. I trust you won't object. I told him I was fortunate to be working with you, you should know. And I kindly asked him for a sample of Farrow's handwriting—promising, of course, not to publish about Farrow until after Godwin's own article is in print. He was cagey, but he sent me a photo—a close-up of just a single sentence fragment. Aaron, it's the same hand. Ester Velasquez wrote under the name of Thomas Farrow. And if we know Ester Velasquez lied about one thing, then why should lying about a Sabbatean crisis in Florence be any more surprising?" In her excitement, she half stood. "It was *all* made up, do you see?"

His skepticism must have been written on his face.

"Are you shocked, Aaron Levy, by the cold-bloodedness of the woman?"

The words disoriented him. For an instant he was uncertain to whom she was referring.

"If it seems unlikely, just think—*think*, Aaron, of when Ester Velasquez lived, and what kind of person she'd have to be to write the heretical things she appears to have written under Farrow's name. Religious persecution, you'll remember, was everywhere. The tortures were grotesque. Even Jews who chose to *repent* to the Inquisition were killed— in exchange for confession they were just offered the supposedly merciful death of the garrote, rather than being burnt at the stake, though after the garrote their bodies were burnt at the stake anyway for good measure. Life was strewn with terrors, and the worst were reserved for atheists. Imagine the kind of person it took to defy all that, and question religious belief altogether—in writing, on paper. She could not, you understand, have been *nice*."

He'd no answer for this. Helen had always been a stickler for proof. Yet somewhere in the past few days—or maybe gradually, during the weeks since she'd learned of their defeat at Wilton's hands—she'd abandoned proof. He noticed, now, that her cardigan was buttoned askew.

Intolerably, now, Helen was resting her gaze on his, trusting.

A ping from Helen's computer. He turned gratefully to the screen.

To his surprise, there was already a reply to the e-mail they'd sent. At Helen's terse nod, he opened it.

From: Jewish Archives of Amsterdam
Subject: Letter

Professor Watt,
      You find me on a quiet day, and I'm glad to help with your inquiry. We do indeed have the letter you describe, and I've scanned it, see attachment. Please let me know if I can be of further assistance.
      Dina Jacobowicz

Fourteen minutes since they'd made the request. May the Patricias of the world be blessed, he thought distractedly—may they sleep well at night, their desks clear and consciences clean. Helen beside him, he clicked the document open.

There it was, Ester's familiar writing. But seeing it on a screen rather than under his hands on textured paper made him feel tender and apologetic, as though he were suddenly seeing a woman he'd cared for in a museum display, anesthetized and out of reach.

In the screen's glow, Ester's inked letters were a deadened, blanched brown. She'd copied the opening lines of the rabbi's letter to Aboab exactly, he saw. Yet in the third paragraph, she'd omitted the sentences that extended sympathy to her and vouched for her as a woman of valor. She'd omitted, too, the rabbi's request for God's forgiveness for his sins.

Aaron read the words she'd substituted.

I have kept to my path though surrounded by waywardness.

The rest of the letter Ester had copied faithfully.

So the rabbi had tried to provide a dowry for Ester—and she'd refused the benefit of his praise.

Hadn't he just been faulting Helen for unproven conjecture? But now Aaron couldn't resist picturing Ester Velasquez as he'd wished her to be all along—fierce, principled, determined.

Helen was squinting at the screen, the miniaturized image of Ester's script apparently defeating her. Without asking, Aaron leaned over and clicked Print.

As Helen lifted the page off the printer, Aaron thought, improbably, of the only morsel he remembered from high school physics: the story of Ludwig Boltzmann, a man derided in his lifetime for his theories. So adamant had Boltzmann been that he'd ordered his repudiated entropy equation carved onto his tombstone. And there the equation remained to this day—right there on Boltzmann's tombstone . . . and also in every physics textbook in the world, because Boltzmann, as he'd known, had been right, and had let nothing deter him.

Ester too must have possessed that sort of stubbornness. Aaron respected her for it—yet he also wanted to curse her stupidity. Why suddenly become a stickler for integrity, just in time to cost herself some measure of stability? Maybe if she'd actually tried for that dowry from the Dotar, she wouldn't have had to marry a wealthy man who wouldn't let her write.

Well. Not that any seventeenth-century husband would have let her write.

His mobile rang. Turning his back on Helen, he dug it out of his bag, answered. The voice of the English girl on the line disoriented him.

"Anne Fielding," she repeated. "From Richmond Local Studies."

"Of course," he said, but too late. The shy, hopeful voice with which she'd greeted him retreated immediately. In a tone of swift efficiency, she proceeded. "Ester HaLevy died in 1691. The records have it as June 13, of a fever."

"Thank you," he said slowly.

"You're quite welcome."

"Any mention of children?" he thought to ask.

"None we've record of."

He'd no justification for the disappointment he felt.

Helen had stopped reading to listen. He mustered another "Thank you."

Catching wind of his mood, Anne spoke in respectful tones. "I assume her husband outlived her. But so far I haven't found the date of Manuel HaLevy's death. We're missing three and a half years of records, though, from 1694 to 1697, due to some water damage that happened in the 1920s in the building where these records were housed. So I can't guess at what might have happened in those years. But as far as I can tell there were no heirs. The house was sold in 1698."

"Thanks," Aaron said. "You've been tremendous. Truly. I'm . . ." He didn't know how to say what he was. "You've been tremendous," he finished.

He could hear the intake of Anne's breath, then a brief hesitation. "Would you like me to search a few more years of records?" she said. "I can see if I can find anything else about the HaLevys . . . or perhaps the house's subsequent owners."

He pressed his palm onto the top of Helen's desk, watching his fingers splay. He was beginning to suspect that he, Aaron Levy, was many wretched things, and that some of that wretchedness was indelible. But he suddenly had a wish to be, at the least, a man who didn't lead Anne

Fielding on. "Yes, I'd be grateful for that," he said, in as indifferent a tone as he could summon. "I'll call you next week to follow up. My girlfriend is visiting right now."

His heart hurt just a little for Anne as she drew in breath—and said, with the impressive dignity of a girl practiced at recovering from such disappointment, "I'll hear from you, then."

He hung up and turned to find Helen regarding him skeptically.

He answered her silent query with a moody shrug. "No, I don't have a girlfriend." To prevent Helen from asking more, he said, "Ester died in 1691. No children on the record. So then, that's it. She lived twenty-six years after writing the last documents that were under the stair." He scratched at a nick on Helen's wooden desk. "No mystery as to why she stopped writing, is there? With Manuel HaLevy for a husband. What was Ester's phrase? *A man of a temperament to use a folio of verse to wipe his boots.*"

"Yes," said Helen softly. "The marriage would have brought the end of her writing. I'm guessing she didn't change her mind and fall in love with him, either. I'm guessing she married him to survive, after the rabbi died and she had no livelihood."

"Well, we'll never have the chance to know, will we?" He turned to the window. "Even assuming we can get a professional handwriting analysis to confirm that 'Thomas Farrow' was Ester Velasquez, I saw in the précis of Godwin's paper that he doesn't have anything from Farrow after 1666."

A brief bloom of intellectual freedom, a spasm of conscience, a quiet death. That was Ester's story in its entirety. It aroused in him both pity and a prickling sense of failure.

Still standing, he let his fingers stray to his laptop, which rested open on the edge of Helen's desk. A gambler uselessly spinning his roulette wheel—yes, that was him. Restlessly, reflexively, he toggled to his e-mail. There, like a bad joke played at his expense, was a single new message. As he stared at his screen, it struck him that the news of Ester Velasquez's death had summoned this too, out of the void of all that had once flourished but now was lost. It had floated back to him, heralded by two young Patricias like figureheads on a prow: the flotsam of all he'd once confidently pursued.

From: Marisa Herz
Subject: Sit down

He obeyed, sinking into the chair opposite Helen's desk, taking the laptop with him.

Aaron,

First, my apologies for my abrupt cut-off earlier this year. I can only assume it was confusing.

I know this is a shock, but I didn't want to involve you until I knew for certain what my decision was. I'm having a baby. Yes, you're the father.

So much for the reliability of birth control.

I've been through all the panic and denial and I've made my choice. Really it was clear to me from the start, but I figured I ought to give myself a little time to be sure of the decision, in case I was going through a hormonal thing.

I'm going to live here and figure out a way to have the baby. I'm going to do it by myself. I'm sorting out the practical pieces — money, job, childcare. It's going to work. And even if it doesn't work, it will anyway, if you know what I mean.

You'll need to do some thinking of your own now. I'm not getting married, to you or anyone. I'm not inviting you to live with us, either. But if you want to meet your daughter you can. Let me know what you plan to do. If you don't want to be involved with her, then let's keep it clean and cut off contact for good. This is my choice and I take responsibility for it. Just send me a little medical history or something in case she grows up and develops bizarre traits — that way I can tell her they're your fault.

Sorry if the jokes seem inappropriate. I've been at this for a while now. You're just at the beginning of taking this in, and I'm probably being too sharp. Sometimes I can be. I know myself, though, and I know I can't take care of your feelings while I'm taking care of myself and building a life to support the little one. So let me know what you decide, but please also understand that I can't hold your hand through your deliberations.

You're a good guy, Aaron Levy, despite all your attempts to
convince the world you're an arrogant bastard. Don't think I don't see
through you. This little gal and I have a long road ahead of us. I'm
not sorry you're her father.

Marisa

His eyes reached the end of her message. Somewhere in his reading,
he realized only now, a sound had escaped him. A single, winded *Oh*. It
lingered in Helen's quiet office.

At first Helen didn't seem to have heard. She was at her computer
again, murmuring. "The Amsterdam archivist is sending a few other
things, every document she found pertaining to HaCoen Mendes or
Ester Velasquez—" She stopped.

"I'll just print it all to read later, shall I?"

He didn't take his eyes off his screen.

He heard pages emerge from the printer, but Helen didn't reach for
them.

"Are you all right?" she said.

He didn't look at her.

"You're not all right."

He managed an unconvincing shrug. Slowly he turned. He tried to
focus on her face, but the effort was too great. His gaze settled somewhere near her chin.

"Do you need a moment?" She spoke briskly—but even through the
veil that seemed to have shrouded his senses, he sensed that she wanted
to ask what was wrong, and didn't know how to do it.

Slowly she stood. "I'll leave you, then?"

"Don't go," he said.

She didn't. She stood leaning on her cane. He saw she had no inkling
what to do with herself. He'd asked her to stay. Stay and sit? Stay and
murmur words of comfort? Twice she opened her mouth as though to
speak, but thought better of it. After a time, she sat.

He said nothing.

She played with the handle of her cane, fitting it into her palm over
and again as though measuring the heft of a suddenly unfamiliar object.
Aaron, gazing emptily at her, caught his pale reflection on the glass face
of the clock on the side of her desk. Even blurred, there was no masking

the truth written in that reflection. He saw his face, for just an instant, as others might. And tried to imagine himself, instead, as he wanted to be: a man who moved cleanly through life, because he understood some essential, elemental thing. A man irreducible, undivided, inseparable from himself. A man who deserved a baby.

The distance between himself and that man was so great as to be uncrossable.

He breathed evenly, and watched the golden second hand traverse the clock's face and his own. Needle-thin, alive with its own infinitesimal pulse, it passed through Aaron's reflection once more, then again, like some innocent and prophetic creature aware of what Aaron was capable of, yet keeping its own counsel.

24

July 25, 1665
13 Av, 5425
London

T HE RINGING OF THE BELLS. Day and night, the churches marked the departure of each perished congregant, every peal thickening the blood of the city. Sometimes half a night passed without a single tolling. Then a first heavy clang followed by a silence, long enough to draw breath in, as the bell swung back to speak again. Sometimes one tolling came on the heels of another—then the unseen hands working the belfry's rope abandoned their efforts quickly, letting each clanging dull and subside. Six times in an hour. More.

In the heat of day, the da Costa Mendeses' windowpanes fogged. Mary, jumping up from an hour-long torpor by the front window, stumbled through the house flinging windows open—her sudden rage like a tide sweeping along all the members of the household. Ester trailed mutely behind, and Rivka as well—Rivka's heels striking hard on the wooden floors as she grimly slammed each window shut—one, another, a third. *Bang.* "Plague seeds float in air!" Rivka cried after Mary—but Mary had already gained the second floor, where she threw herself sidelong onto her unmade bed and cursed Rivka viciously in Castilian terms that made even Ester call Mary's name in protest. Ignoring Ester, rolling onto her back and slapping her belly with a storm of blows, Mary cursed it in English: "Foul lump."

Was it a fortnight since Ester had spoken to any others? More? Those few who passed their door saw the painted cross there, and walked faster. Bescós's cross had hidden them from London—yet it remained unknown whether this made them safer or less so.

With each passing day of silence Mary's vexation seemed to sharpen.

Once, washing at her basin—a feat she accomplished with umbrage, for her belly now impeded her—she turned on Ester: "How can you bear to stay in this cage?" she cried, her face dripping with water she didn't bother to wipe. "Don't you want *air*?"

Ester blinked at her. How to explain that this reverie was all she wanted—that it was the world outside that had turned vertiginous? The pestilence, the bells, the rabbi. John. Unbearable, sickening thoughts.

Mary shook her head hard, droplets flying, her hair fanning about her like a wild creature's. Then she stopped and leaned forward, propping herself on her hands at the dressing table. In the mirror she looked at Ester, the tender hairs on her temples clinging to her pale skin. "You're glad to hide here," she accused.

It was true. Ester had lain awake that morning, her thoughts making a wide wary arc as though skirting a precipice. With her head heavy on the pillow, she'd endeavored to trace a logical argument. It began: Love causes pain.

Why does it cause pain?

Because it depends on another. Because it is not self-complete and therefore cannot be contained within one spirit.

She hadn't been able to follow the logic further. That part of her that had known how to inscribe clear lines of argument on the lurching world had fallen mute.

"Ester, if John spurned you"—Mary was searching Ester's face in the mirror—"well, then." She struggled visibly for unfamiliar words of consolation. "He was never so lively, was he? In truth, I thought him a bore! You can find another." Mary's expression darkened a moment. "Not like me." She stared long into the mirror. "But," she murmured, letting go of the dressing table to press palms to her belly, "Thomas will want *us*." Before Ester could answer, Mary fled the room, in her haste nearly knocking into Rivka, who was climbing to the second floor with a stack of pressed linens.

Sealed away though they were from the city's soot and dirt, Rivka had asserted a strict routine of housework to which she held herself and Ester, ignoring Mary as hopeless. In truth the fine things of the da Costa Mendes house seemed to exert on Rivka a kind of enchantment. Ester would come across Rivka running a hand over linens trimmed with point; sanding the iron clean yet again; adding indigo to the white starch to produce a still finer white for the linens of a household whose owners she neither liked nor respected—yet Rivka seemed to hold the possessions of the da Costa Mendes family blameless for their owners' sins. And while Mary paced about the house, sometimes muttering prettily to herself and sometimes snorting fragments of an argument—"I'll not be your doxy"—or with tearful disdain—"He's something like!" —Ester drifted down the stairs to labor alongside Rivka. For once Ester was grateful for the trance of work—her body pounding and wringing in a rhythm that obliterated thought. The very drudgery she'd hated for tearing her from her beloved studies was now salvation—and what was it, after all, that she had so treasured about her ability to think? What desire could she have had for the open landscape of her mind, when it harbored fearful things or—worse, now—a vast, featureless stillness? The papers she'd carried with such care from the rabbi's lay untouched beneath the mattress of her bed. She feared to look at them, as though they accused her of crimes she couldn't deny.

Rivka insisted that only she herself go abroad in the city, claiming she could not fall ill of the plague—for, she said, she'd suffered many girlhood illnesses in her Galician village and these strengthened her humors against disease. Mary scoffed at this reasoning, griping to Ester that Rivka only wanted all the freedom for herself. But Rivka seemed to trust in it, and often during their confinement Rivka slipped out late in the day to purchase provisions, returning just before curfew.

One evening, shortly after Rivka's return, a man's voice on the street roused Ester. She'd been sewing in the fading light from the downstairs window, mending a small tear in a seam of a sheet, her fingers stiff from working the needle. The bell had signaled three deaths already that hour.

"See here, the wily Jewesses!"

It was Bescós's voice. She rose, dropping her mending to the table. "You've multiplied."

He stood on the street outside the window, too close. His face, intent, peered at the pane. Then his eyes fastened on hers.

His face was thinner, and something about it was changed. Even in her fear, a strange thought occurred to her: he's in danger.

But the thought was banished by the sharp rasp of Mary flinging open an upstairs window. "It's true!" she shouted. "I've friends with me now."

Stepping back to squint up at her, Bescós shielded his eyes. Then he laughed. It was a long laugh, with time in it for him to decide what sort of man he wanted to be. After a moment, Ester saw him decide.

There were no other passersby. The shutters had now been drawn in every visible dwelling along the street—every house's eyes sealed by plague.

"So this is your new family?" Bescós called to Mary.

"Why, does it concern you that I'm no longer alone?" her voice sailed back.

"I'm only curious," he said. "Which of you is the mistress of this brothel? I'd have guessed the silver-headed one"—his eyes still fixed on Mary, he gestured at the window behind which Ester stood. "Yet judging by what Thomas was able to get out of John, she's taken to selling her own wares." He wagged his head, disappointed. "Or offering them without pay."

Abruptly, he turned and banged a palm, hard, on the wall of the house. Ester started, her heart thumping in her chest. From behind her, she heard Rivka's low gasp. Bescós was laughing—he'd guessed, even from the outside, how hollow the rooms must echo.

"The idiocy of some women," he mused, speaking slowly once more, "to give freely the only salable asset they possess. But unless you've some spare Jewesses I haven't yet seen, then the bald one must be the mistress?"

Ester turned at a quiet intake of breath behind her. Rivka stood, a half-unwrapped parcel in one hand.

"You might have found a better advertisement," Bescós continued. "The doxies are tolerable pretty, but their keeper needs a wig."

If ever Ester had thought Rivka beyond hurt, she was corrected by the sound of Rivka's treads fading to the pantry. A moment later, the soft pounding of a pestle.

Now Bescós neared Ester's window. She shrank back—two steps, three, deeper into the dim room. But he addressed her calmly through the glass panes, as though confiding some casual bit of information. His voice was low, the words for her alone. "Mary thinks she'll sit on her father's fortune like a bird," he said, "and lay her brat in a nest of silver. But you don't care about the money, do you?"

She didn't speak.

"Tell me, are there enough books for you here? Enough heresies of mind and body? An unnatural girl needs not only a man's *stuff*, but an entire library to appease her wild appetites." His voice rose. "Whereas a true maiden—"

He stopped.

For an instant he looked dizzy, uncertain of himself.

Then he continued as though there had been no interruption. "—needs only to trust. And remain pure."

A strange certainty pierced Ester: *she's* dead. Bescós's hoped-for love, his *maiden of fine quality*—their union blocked for a time by her father . . . and now, Ester thought, forever.

Through the mullioned panes, Bescós looked like a man assembled out of tiles, each laid alongside the next to form the semblance of a man. She thought: he's partitioned himself like this city—one portion shuttered from another. As Ester watched, he closed his eyes as if in fatigue, held them shut. Then opened them onto the street. It was like witnessing someone waking from a dream to a pitiless landscape, and swiftly calculating an acceptable path through it. *So if this is the world . . .*

With a jolt, she thought: it was like witnessing herself waking from a dream.

Looming closer, Bescós braced one arm at the top of the window, and spoke slowly through the glass. "According to Thomas's telling," he said, "John looked sick at the mere mention of you. Your appetites got the best of poor John, did they? Yet even as you try to prove your worth, you disprove it. For only one sort of woman is true, and all others repellent."

Her limbs had gone leaden. A line from a sonnet, read in a volume she'd paged at a bookseller's table, floated dimly to her. *Enjoyed no sooner but despised straight.*

From above, a slow scrape of wood on metal, then a foul splash on the pavestones beside Bescós. Mary had emptied a bucket from her window—urine or slops, or perhaps only dirty wash water. It missed Bescós narrowly, but some of the splash hit his boot and lower leg.

He jumped, cried out, and for a long minute shook his leg as though terrorized by the filth. In his struggle he appeared on the verge of weeping. It would have been comical, yet it seemed to Ester that she'd never seen a thing more dangerous, and she cringed at the sound of Mary's loud laughter from above.

Then all was still. The arch smile Bescós had worn earlier did not reassert itself. He leaned into Ester's window again, and his expression was wholly somber. Sharply, just once, he knocked on the glass with his signet ring, so hard she thought it would shatter.

He departed.

From behind Ester came Rivka's voice, low and quiet as breathing. "He's going to bring a mob on us," she said.

Ester turned.

"With someone tired of waiting for what he wants," Rivka said. "That's how it starts. That's how every evil in the world starts." She gestured, cloth in hand, at the da Costa Mendeses' silver, their tapestries. "He wants this."

Slowly Ester shook her head. "I think what Esteban Bescós wants is dead."

But Rivka only closed her own eyes and tapped her eyelids gently, almost caressingly, with two thick fingers. "I've seen." She opened her eyes. "I know."

Ester picked up her mending. What difference if he was driven by love of silver or his lost maiden?

But a wish for silver could be appeased.

IT WAS SEVERAL DAYS BEFORE Rivka ventured out again, and she was gone hours before she returned. She'd searched out three bakeries before finding one that hadn't been closed, if not by deaths then by rats —for since the cats had been killed, the rats had multiplied a thousandfold, the storerooms were plundered nightly, and there was no traffic into the city to restock London's shelves. Rivka didn't describe what she'd witnessed trawling the city's streets for bread—but as she stacked six loaves on the shelf, she said softly, "Now this city understands."

Ester, glancing up from rinsing butter, saw a look of sorrowful recognition on Rivka's face, and realized that at last Rivka had forgiven London, and made the city her own.

They sliced bread and spread it with a thick layer of butter—their new custom for the noon meal, for even Rivka could no longer bear to light a cooking fire in the day's heat. But when they called Mary to eat, she was nowhere to be found.

They searched the house, their voices calling her name plaintively into the cellar, the attic, the garden. She had disappeared.

Hour by hour, without Mary's fretful presence, the silence seemed to expand, until the house brimmed with a dreadful quiet that Ester and Rivka could break only in whispers.

At dusk, the front door slipped open. Rivka, waiting beside Ester on the stiff parlor cushions Rivka rarely permitted herself, sprang from her seat and grabbed Mary's arm, shoving the door closed behind her. "Where were you?"

"No business of yours!" Mary cried, wresting free with a furious gesture. In order to cover her growing belly for her outing, Ester saw, Mary had altered a skirt using extra fabric snipped clumsily from her bedclothes. Mary was flushed, her eyes bright—a marked contrast to her dull expression of these past weeks. The excursion, Ester saw, had done her good.

"The house's errands are *mine* to do!" Rivka's accent had thickened with emotion, her words barely intelligible. "Not yours. You should have sent *me*."

Mary, struggling in vain to release her arm, spoke with a repugnance long repressed. "You're a liar! A greedy . . . *thing!* Just"—she gestured at Rivka—"look at you!" Carved on Mary's face was a truth Ester hadn't before guessed: that what Mary feared most was ugliness. All her life, prettiness had ever been her polestar and her safety. Now all protection was gone. She stood, belly jutting, forgotten. Facing Rivka like a creature from a nightmare.

But Rivka laughed, and Ester was glad to see that Mary couldn't hurt her.

"You take all the freedom for yourself!" Mary pressed. "Or, no"—Mary pointed wildly—"you just want to escape this hell. *That's* why you want to go into the city! It's because you want to die."

Without warning Rivka seized Mary's other shoulder and shook her, hard, so that Mary lost balance and was kept on her feet only by Rivka's grip.

For a moment the room was hushed, Mary's face loose with disbelief.

Rivka released her. "Stay in the house," she said. "If you can't be sensible for yourself, do it for that baby."

Mary snatched her arm away and, rubbing it with her opposite hand, cursed Rivka in nearly incoherent temper. But Rivka had turned for the stair.

Minutes later, standing in the kitchen stuffing buttered bread into her mouth, Mary addressed Ester as if nothing had happened. "It's all filth and horror in the streets, Ester. There are people wailing like—like ghosts, but more. Like they've lost their minds." She stopped chewing suddenly, as though gripped by a pungent memory. Then she started chewing again, and Ester could almost see the energy surging up from her belly—an unthinking hunger for bread, drink, life. "I had to run past a dozen carts with bodies so I wouldn't have to see—the first one I saw was vile enough. It took me hours to find someone who would send my letter to Thomas. And then the knave ruined my letter by spraying it with vinegar so it wouldn't carry the distemper. I swore to him I'm not sick, but he wouldn't heed. Now Thomas is going to think I stink to the heavens."

Lovely tears welled in her eyes. Ester watched, riveted. Could Mary still care about such a thing? "Why were you writing to him?" she asked.

"I want him to know," said Mary haughtily, wiping her eyes, "that I'm alive. And I'm going to come to him, once I acquire a permit to travel. Even if he despises me. He *won't* despise me when I birth his baby." She looked at Ester as though daring her to argue.

The silence was broken by the distant clanging of a church bell. Mary bit her thumb at it. When the reverberations had ceased she drank again from her ale. "Do you remember," she said to Ester, "that day at the dressmaker, when you asked whether our will alters anything?" She wiped her mouth with the back of her hand. "And I told you," Mary's voice rose, "that I *choose* what I am?"

Hesitant, Ester nodded.

Mary's fingertips circled: a gesture encompassing the deserted house, her own swelling body. She spoke at an unnatural pitch. "Yet I chose this." Her face wrung with emotion. "So I *was* a fool."

"No," Ester said slowly. "*I* was the fool. I tried to tell you that love could be refused. That one might live untouched by it."

But Mary shook her head. Tears coursed freely. "Did I ruin all, Ester? Tell me."

Ester hesitated. What words of consolation had she to offer, when even this instant she stood yet again in memory upon the rabbi's threshold—watching John's carriage depart, the sound of the wheels fading down the street?

Closing her eyes, she imagined tapered fingers gently pressing keys on the spinet, dark hair turned silver—and heard the words of her own grandmother. She whispered them now to Mary. "It was the very shape of the world that made it so." Then, as though gentling an animal, she set a tentative hand on Mary's hair and stroked.

When Mary at last pulled away, the bell had tolled twice more. She wiped her face. Then rose briskly. Her expression had righted itself. "Thomas *will* take me," she declared. She turned on her heel and departed the kitchen, carrying with her a hunk of buttered bread.

Alone in the kitchen, Ester listened to Mary move about upstairs. There was a current of life in Mary that Ester could no longer locate in herself. She thought: of all of us, Mary will be the one to live.

But two days later, sweat ran in thin rivulets on Mary's cheeks as she combed her hair, and she snapped angrily at Ester and Rivka when they called her for her supper, until at last she lay abed, panting. The fever she'd brought with her from her escape into the city shook her and drenched her pallet and she threw off her underclothes and shift and lay moaning in her nakedness, unwilling to tolerate a stitch of cloth upon her. She spread her hands on her taut belly as though consulting it, touching now and then the soft dark wool beneath, which stood out on her pale skin like the brush stroke of some forgotten tenderness. Ester, forbidden by Rivka in harshest terms to go nearer, stood at the foot of the bed and brought what necessities Rivka dictated—while Rivka herself washed Mary's body and changed the soaked linens, and laid cool cloths on the small, secret hairs at the base of her neck, and all the while Mary cried and swam in the bed. She swore vengeance on Thomas, cursing his body's parts with such epithets as Ester had never heard—and then spoke of those same parts again in terms of such endearment that Ester blushed and Rivka closed her eyes and fled to the garden to bow the flowering bushes with bucketfuls of Mary's vomit. With her pretty face blooming in red patches where the blood spidered beneath her skin, Mary called first in English and then in Portuguese upon Thomas's love for his son in her belly, and once she called, in a sweet and remorseful voice, "*Mamãe*."

She was certain, now, that the baby in her womb was a son. She knew that the boy had dark brown eyes. Then she knew he had a merry laugh and a fine voice for singing. Lying alone in her bed, hands locked on her belly or clutching the bed sheets, she could hear him singing, *durme, durme,* and she called for her father, for she was certain he'd be amazed at how high and sweet was the voice of his grandson. "Listen," she called to him. "Only listen." Then she fell silent herself, to hear.

OUTSIDE, THE SKY WAS HOODED and silent. A bell somewhere in the city rang for someone else's death as they wheeled Mary's body, on a cart for which they'd paid a sum that might have sustained a household for a week, to the mass grave at Hand Alley. As they dropped the cart's railing to slide her down, Ester withheld her gaze from the other bodies. She kept her eyes instead on the pale moon of Mary's face. On Mary's lustrous black curls, as they slipped into the lime dust and were dulled.

Later, when they were locked back inside the house, the bell rang on, ceaseless this time, and all day and night they listened as a steady trickle of deaths became a clanging stream. A torrent. The bell rang that day until it broke and the city's deaths poured into the earth unheralded.

Three days later, Ester was slicing bread for their midday meal, the day's heat making her fretful. The knife felt heavy, but she pressed on, thinking perhaps the blade was growing dull. Still the thick-crusted bread seemed to resist, the blade slipped, and she felt herself stumble. She caught herself on the table, and when she raised a hand to her neck, it rested on a single aching lump.

Rivka was grimly ironing sheets in the parlor. As Ester left the kitchen to tell her, Mary was with her, and Manuel HaLevy too—and it was in their company that, obedient to Rivka's furious commands, she climbed the stairs and lowered herself onto the mattress where Mary had died, to take her own turn.

Why must man struggle to live, when he inevitably dies?

Rivka's hand on her forehead.

Why is it a sin against God to wish for death—yet a virtue to choose to die in defense of God's word? Is life a token, valued only for the thing it's sacrificed for?

Broth sliding down her chin, and a warm cloth at the back of her neck—she flung it across the room to be rid of it, for heat like this had never gripped her before. The evening slid and blurred. Night and then day, and then something that was neither.

Yet the body insists on the struggle for life. Why?

The world stretched wide about her. She could feel the spaces between things—the vast arching of infinity away from her lips, her brow, her breath . . . the distance separating her from the pinprick stars that must even now be shining somewhere far above London. She must tell the rabbi. But even as she merged into that great distance, she felt too the infinite smallness of every organ and vein—and every blood vessel in her, pulsing. She thought: Every living soul came into the world in infancy with wet bright eyes, blinking at motes. Every soul exited this same way. It was the damage that they wrought in between that she regretted. Her head shook slowly with regret. She stood lightly in John's arms. Either of them could have pivoted away, but neither did. The lightest brush of his hand on her breast. With one hand she braced herself against his chest, and leaned, and then she fell—but there was none to catch her, and the long, sickening tumble was stopped only by Rivka's rough hands on her bare body, rolling her back onto the mattress.

She was once a tender girl. She is almost certain she remembers it.

The circle is complete. In all the universe, she found one bright-seeming thing, and now she has lost it. *Love didn't fail, only one love did.* But there can be no others. Has she tried too hard to remake the world? Her mind stumbles, it lacks the nimbleness to understand. And death shakes the ground like a heavy cart nearing, long overdue in its arrival, and her emptied heart brims suddenly with a wish to lie down beneath its wheels. She has fought to stay in the world until fate took life from her with a heavy hand. And only now that the time has come for her to die does she confess, weeping, how she's longed for this release.

She can believe, now, that some of the martyrs sang on the pyre.

The thought confuses her. Is she permitted, at last, to wish for death? Permitted or not, she does.

But as the cart nears, and its thunder overwhelms her senses and shakes the earth with her every heartbeat, her body wakes—and without her willing it, rolls itself just clear of the oncoming wheels.

The thinning din of the receding cart leaves her grieving.

SHE OPENED HER EYES. A dim evening, the air inexplicably cool. A rough rime of salt on her face. She blinked into the lightless room, a first recognizable thought taking form. It hovered like a small nesting bird uncertain of its safety. Then, finally, it roosted: she understood that Rivka's hands had gone. Rivka's figure, hunched in a hard-backed chair in the shadowed corner opposite the bed, was motionless. Only when she spoke did Ester realize she was drunk. "You lived," she said. "Most don't."

Ester listened, as though the echo of these words might tell whether this was good or ill. Slowly, she raised herself to sitting. Then, when Rivka didn't chide her, let her feet slide to the floor, the skin prickling with the touch of the wood.

"How long?"

"A week," said Rivka. "More, maybe." She waved the fingers of one hand toward the window. "Ask him. He knows, for he counts each day and each night he sleeps on our doorstep."

Holding to the edge of the bed, then to the wall, she stood. Her body felt too light—a stick bobbing in an eddy. She felt her way to the window.

Below, seated on the broad stone in front of the door and leaning against it, was an unfamiliar figure in a broad-brimmed hat. The stranger appeared to be dozing.

"He came a few days after we buried Mary," said Rivka, who hadn't moved from her seat. "We're a registered plague house now, and not just because Mary's *friend* painted our door. The city sends guards."

"How long?" Ester repeated stupidly, her tongue thick.

"Forty days in all until a house can be reopened. He shouted his purpose up to the window the day he came, and they're the only words he's said all this time, except to tell me he wears that broad hat so we can't drop a noose from our window and quietly hang him by his neck to make an escape. *Into what?* I asked him." Her voice was loose, swimming with drink. Amid the vials and cloths arranged neatly on a side table was a dusty bottle with an ornate label—Ester guessed Rivka had pulled it from the da Costa Mendeses' cellar at the breaking of Ester's fever. "I told him"—Rivka continued, with a rough gesture toward the window—"the city is a worse demon now than the plague, and as far as I care he can guard us from it until the world turns to dust."

The journey from the bed had exhausted Ester. She grasped the windowsill.

Lifting a glass to her lips, Rivka said, "And it has."

Ester raised her hand feebly to her brow. She could feel no trace of fever—only the salt from her fever sweats, which coated her body as though she were some new-birthed thing. "I lived," she said.

Rivka swallowed her drink, then closed her eyes. She sat, palms open on her knees, cheeks flushed, her face strangely animated.

Slowly, as though thoughts might enter her mind only single file, Ester became aware that she'd never before seen Rivka rest. The endless labors of nursing had surely staved off Rivka's grief for the rabbi. Now there was no one left to nurse.

She didn't know how to say to Rivka: I understand you've no home anymore. So she said only, "Better souls than I were taken."

Rivka inhaled steeply. "Death," she said, "doesn't take the ones who want it." She opened her eyes and looked at Ester without accusation. "*You* wanted to die. I saw it."

In the dusky room she looked like something ancient and ponderous, a statue carved roughly out of a boulder.

"I was young," Rivka said quietly, "when the men came through my village. I was a girl." And by the way she spoke the final word, Ester understood what had been done to her.

Ester found the edge of the bed, and sat.

"If I'd been offered the choice to die," Rivka said, "my name would be among those of the martyrs."

Did Rivka still want to die? Then had Mary guessed aright, after all?

"*Did* you know you were safe from the pestilence?" Ester asked.

Rivka let out something like a laugh. She shook her head.

Yet the very Polish village that had burned behind her seemed in truth to have offered her some protection that Ester and Mary had lacked. Rivka's body alone had refused to sicken, though she'd offered it up at every chance.

The room darkened with the oncoming dusk. Rivka's close-set eyes were nearly lost to shadows when she spoke again. "Now you'll be able to go on with those letters you write," she said. And continued, more sharply. "About *truth* and *thought*. About whatever all of it meant."

"You—"

"I can read," Rivka said.

Over the rush of blood in her head, Ester could hear bitter amusement in Rivka's voice. "You're shocked."

The dim room swung about her and refused to steady.

"I learned when I was young. Not much, not like you. But some."

"If you knew—"

"I didn't try to stop you, Ester, because he"—her voice softened, caressing the word—"*he* needed learning. It was the only light he had. And you were the only one with enough learning to bring him that light. Something in those letters made him muster his strength and sit upright. If I'd had enough learning, *I* would have done it. And without lies." Briefly her voice rose. "I'd have lighted his vision. I'd—" She stopped.

When she spoke again, her voice slid with drink and feeling. "And you sat there writing down his words only for your own purposes, caging his thoughts in a drawer to send to no one. An unfeeling creature."

"Not unfeeling," Ester managed.

"You believe you're the only one who knows what it is to lose everything?" For a moment Ester entertained the notion that Rivka might stand and turn on her, strike down the very life she'd sustained through the fever. "Still," said Rivka, "I didn't stop you from doing it. And do you know why, Ester?" She wagged her head, then pronounced quietly, "He lived longer than he would have, because he thought someone in Florence needed his help."

"But he knew," Ester said. "He told me, near the end. In all those letters he had me write, he was trying to correct my thinking, in his own way. Only"—she drew breath—"I wouldn't be corrected."

Rivka absorbed this.

Slowly the room settled into darkness.

"He was the purest soul on this earth," Rivka said.

No candle, no light from the street. Ester had the sensation that neither she nor Rivka was real—that were she to try to locate her own body in the room, try to touch her own arm or leg or shoulder, she'd touch nothing.

There was a creak from the wooden chair: Rivka had stirred. "I didn't understand most of what you wrote," Rivka said. "But enough. I knew the words hurt him. And I also saw"—her voice arched, incredulous—"that you loved him. I saw that his letters to Florence hurt you."

Ester bowed her head.

"Even knowing you deceived him, he poured the last of his energies into your deception. Why, Ester? What was so important in your letters?"

Ester had no answer. She sat a long while in the dark. Then she said, "I don't believe I'll be writing anymore."

ONLY RELUCTANTLY DID STRENGTH RETURN to her body. Dizziness forced her readily back to bed. Five days after her fever had broken, she was able at last to stand without support and, gathering herself at a window overlooking the garden, unlatch and push open the heavy frame. The sunlight blazed in her eyes, the world swam. She knew the day was warm, yet her body seemed to have forgotten how to absorb warmth.

In the garden below, Rivka set down a full washtub, rested a moment, then upended it and stood watching a moment as the dark rivulets sank into the soil. *She can read,* Ester thought. In her pride, she'd been blinder than the rabbi—and now she saw how thin a divide had separated her from Rivka's fate. Had Rivka had the gift of just a few years' more education—had she been tutored in the necessary languages—then she, rather than Ester, might have scribed for the rabbi. Rivka would have sat in the warm front room, at the rabbi's table—doing his bidding without wronging him. And Ester would have labored at running the household, until a marriage to Manuel HaLevy would have seemed a very heaven.

And yet how strange it now seemed, her fervent pursuit of study against all obstacles, as though she couldn't live without the ability to write. Illness had proved more persuasive than any teacher; her old ideas, if she could recall them, seemed paltry, hollow things. She dozed and woke atop her mattress with hardly a thought of the papers lying untouched beneath.

How wrong she'd been, to believe a mind could reign over anything. For it did not reign even over itself . . . and despite all the arguments of all the philosophers, Ester now saw that thought proved nothing. Had Descartes, near his own death, come at last to see his folly? The mind was only an apparatus within the mechanism of the body—and it took little more than a fever to jostle a cog, so that the gear of thought could no longer turn. Philosophy could be severed from life. Blood overmastered ink. And every thin breath she drew told her which ruled her.

25

April 11, 2001
London

IN THE AIRLESS CONFINES OF the parish records office, Helen inched the cotton gloves back onto her hands. The fact that the records room was now requiring gloves had proved an unpleasant surprise. The gloves thickened her fingers hopelessly, so that every page turn required multiple attempts; worse, they rendered her unable to grip a pencil, so each note she jotted in her notebook meant long wasted minutes as she labored to remove her right glove, then put it on once more. The exertion worsened her tremor; at times, fearful of damaging the paper, she forced herself to suspend her work until it eased.

She'd woken that morning disoriented from a night of dreams piled one upon the other: a glimmering black well that repelled and drew her; the sensation of relinquishing some precious burden she'd carried; a crushing, absolute silence, in which not even her own racing heart was audible. Rising with a start after oversleeping, she'd skipped breakfast, telling herself she'd go directly to the parish records office, then drive to the university and eat in her office, away from prying eyes.

A thoughtless plan, and unlike her.

Her stomach growled again, loud and low. The middle-aged man working at the other end of the long table issued a reprimand in the form of a small, dry cough.

She squared herself, and faced off once more with the record book. Names and dates of decease blurred before her eyes. *John Williamson, dead of plague 5th July, 1665.* Below John Williamson's name were dozens of others from the same day, all meticulously noted in the careful slanted hand of some anonymous parish clerk. With difficulty, she turned another page. No trace yet of Rabbi HaCoen Mendes, but she knew she'd find him here. She could simply have taken Wilton's word for the rabbi's death date, of course; yet she'd felt she owed it to Rabbi HaCoen Mendes to do this herself, accompanying him to the very final words of his story: a single line of ink hidden somewhere here, amid this infinite roster of expired souls.

When she thought about Rabbi HaCoen Mendes's life, she felt at peace. It was the absence of a single written word in the wake of Ester Velasquez's marriage that refused, somehow, to nest peaceably in Helen's mind. She'd counted on Ester's obstinacy to vanquish all: loss, terror, death. She'd *needed* Ester's voice to endure.

In order to believe that she herself could.

With a shudder now, Helen recalled the abrupt, unanswerable silence that had haunted last night's dreams.

How great a weight she'd rested on what had never been more than an instinct.

Back in November on that last afternoon in Richmond, with Aaron vanished on one of his breaks and the snow falling thinly on the path outside, and the hours winding down to the moment when the Sotheby's assessor would arrive, Helen had stood from her seat and—following a feeling as steady and sure as the beam of a torch—climbed quietly and with effort up the great staircase. Treading softly, she'd surveyed the second floor—a scattering of small rooms, jib doors leading to servant staircases; and then, on opposite sides of the central gallery, two full sets of rooms in grand seventeenth-century style. The first set, closer to the staircase, was clearly in use by the Eastons—the faint sound of running water told her the original seventeenth-century closet had been turned into a bath. Farther along the upstairs gallery was the second set —a large chamber leading into a second, smaller one, and the second into the third: anteroom to bedchamber to closet, like nested boxes. The last and smallest room—the wood-paneled closet—was cluttered with the Eastons' boxes. Still obeying that same wordless feeling, Helen had picked her way past these to the single window, with its blackened metal lever jutting like a crowbar. Through the narrow panes, which had surely once offered a view of orderly gardens, she could see tangled vines, the neighbors' rooftops, and a patch of slow-winding river. Helen lingered here a while, for no reason she could explain to herself, watching the river through the uneven glass.

She'd just retreated to the central gallery when she heard a tread on the stair. She should've guessed, of course, that Aaron Levy would be unable to resist the lure of defying Helen's explicit orders. Stepping behind a column, she watched him crest the landing, stop in the upper gallery, and stare: at the carvings on the lintels, the shadowed heights of the ceiling. With a jolt she'd realized that Aaron Levy's face held the same reverence as had her own only moments earlier—the same astonishment at the simple fact that this was *here* . . . that a place like this should have survived . . . and that he, Aaron Levy, had the great good fortune to stand in its cavernous embrace.

A strange fascination overtook Helen, then, as she watched Aaron Levy try, one after another, the doors Helen herself had already opened. A moment later she'd been startled to hear Bridgette's voice, and then, Aaron's parry. Even from where Helen stood, around the corner and unable to see into the room where Bridgette was, the electricity between Aaron and Bridgette had been unmistakable.

Her own quiet tread, as she retreated to a jib door, didn't break the spell of their mutual enticement. She'd half-stumbled down the twisting staircase, a dreadful, chastened feeling in the pit of her stomach, her bony hands gripping the rail to prevent her fall. And some voice telling her she'd failed to understand something about life. Only her immersion in the documents had saved her from her confusion, and she'd returned to them with a ferocity that almost comforted her.

She roused herself: her watch read twelve-forty. Her hunger was nearly intolerable, her innards protesting at increasing volume. She was due in Jonathan Martin's office at two o'clock for what Penelope Babcock had referred to as *the standard pre-retirement sendoff.* Personally, Helen would have liked nothing more than to conclude her decades of service without Jonathan Martin's fare-thee-well. But even at this late date, she wouldn't do anything to jeopardize her or Aaron's access to the documents for the remainder of the term. She'd go to Martin's bloody patronizing sendoff, stopping first in her office to fortify herself with the crackers and soda water she kept there.

Her gloved finger juddering down the column of names, she scanned for HaCoen Mendes. And her finger stopped at a name that had no business being there.

Manuel HaLevy, of plague, July 6, 1665.

"Pardon me." It was the archivist. Helen's gaze swam upward. At length her eyes found him, haloed against the fluorescent bulbs. "It's been brought to my attention," he said—she noted he did not lower his voice to protect her privacy—"that your handling of the documents is inconsistent with our standards. I need to ask you to leave, and return when you've found someone to assist you in handling these records."

She looked away from the blinding light, down at the inked pages before her. She nodded into the list of deaths.

On the steps to the street she withdrew her mobile from her bag with shaking hands and, with difficulty, dialed Aaron's number. Ignoring the hesitant note in his greeting, she said, "I need you to check something for me."

"I'm at home," Aaron said.

It hadn't occurred to her that he could be at home. "Why aren't you at the manuscripts room?"

"I needed a day off." There was something strange in his manner. He didn't seem to care what she thought of his answer.

"I've just found a death record for Manuel HaLevy," she said. "And it's in the summer of 1665."

He seemed to wake slowly to this information. "But they were married in 1666."

"Yes," she said. "Exactly. How long will it take you to get to the rare manuscripts room?"

There was a long silence.

What on earth was preventing Aaron Levy from jumping to the chase? It occurred to her to ask just what had happened to him the other day in her office. But she was familiar enough with her own shortcomings to guess that her words would be too blunt, likely to slam a door rather than open it.

Aaron, for his part, seemed to feel no obligation to fill the silence on the phone line.

Never mind: there was just enough time, if Helen omitted the stop at her office, to do it herself. "I'll go to the rare manuscripts room and recheck Ester's references to him," she said. "Perhaps there's some other detail there—something to differentiate the Manuel HaLevy she married from the one who died. I've a meeting with Martin at two o'clock. Can you meet me in my office at three?"

"All right." He seemed to be processing information very slowly. "I can call Richmond Local Studies, to verify the marriage date." Another long pause. "Do *you* think there might have been more than one Manuel HaLevy?"

"No," she said. "Though we need to consider it a possibility. Also, the death record might be an error. One-fifth of the population of London died in that year. Surely mistakes happened." Only she didn't believe this was a mistake. She believed she and Aaron had gone wrong somewhere farther back up the trail.

She hardly was aware of getting into her car, driving, parking. In her absorption she noted only that the city seemed unaccountably miniaturized. She parked her car and locked it, and walked toward the library building with her head strangely abuzz, a smell like ammonia in her nostrils rendering her light and lofty.

Only when she'd entered the building, and the doors of the lift had enclosed her, did she note how her body was quaking. Not only her hands, this time, but her legs as well. She gripped the handrail, but it felt flimsy. The walls of the lift slid up and up around her, slow but unstoppable, then—abruptly—twisted as though readying to drop down on her for good. Standing was out of the question. Her knees hit the floor of the lift hard, and she let out a cry in a voice that wasn't her own. She'd dropped her cane—it lay out of reach—and still the walls seemed to rise and turn, stretching dangerously. So swiftly did the world upend, with no time for appeal. The floor of the lift was her god, and she clung to it as though she might fall off, for although it was bearing her higher, she herself was sinking. She was aware vaguely that her need to use the loo couldn't be delayed, and like a little girl she looked into the veil of dim air above her for permission. A warm stain and then cold, blooming on her skirt and stockings, leaking into her shoes.

The doors of the lift slid apart.

Ahead of her, in the amber light of the atrium, the student manning the security desk was intent on his computer screen.

The lift stood open.

She steadied the sole of one shoe on the floor, then the other. With her outstretched fingertips she found her cane. She reached into the infinity above her for the handrail, and grasped it. Slowly she stood, one shoe plashing in a small puddle of urine on the lift's floor.

The student at the security desk looked up. For a moment he looked uncertainly at her. Then he turned back to his screen.

With shaking hands, she pulled her card from her wallet, presented it to him, and swept through the turnstile without looking to either side, not allowing herself to see whether or not he noticed the dark stains on her clothing. Stiffly she made her way into the rare manuscripts room, the fabric of her skirt and stockings soaked. She shut the door silently behind her, and walked as straight-backed as she could past the students bent over their work, to the circulation desk.

"Patricia," she said.

Patricia Starling-Haight looked up. "Yes?" she said after a moment.

Helen closed her eyes. She stood mute before the desk, her head impossibly high.

Seconds passed. Then Patricia was standing beside her, her librarian's voice a crisp whisper. "Do you need to go to the hospital?"

"No," Helen said. "I need . . ." She gestured; she couldn't bring herself to open her eyes. "To clean up. And . . ." She licked her cracked lips. "I believe I need something to eat."

Only when she felt Patricia's arm tuck securely under hers did Helen open her eyes, and let herself be led. Turning their backs to the reading room, Patricia Starling-Haight steered Helen swiftly out a wooden door behind her desk. The narrow hall they entered was congested with laden carts. A pale young woman sorting binders looked up curiously. "Is there a problem, Elizabeth?" Patricia snapped, and the woman's face pinked as she returned to her appointed tasks. Patricia stopped them at a small cabinet, in which she rummaged a moment before pressing something to Helen's hand: a nut bar. "Open it in here," Patricia instructed, and guided Helen into a cavernous freight lift: a great, hollow, weather-beaten box. The doors closed on them.

With a soft, wordless sound, Helen handed the bar to Patricia, who unwrapped it briskly and put it back in Helen's palm.

Helen ate. Patricia watched in silence as crumbs rained to the metal floor.

When she was able to speak, Helen said, "What time is it?"

"A quarter past one."

"I have a meeting," Helen managed, "at two o'clock."

Patricia's face was somewhere above Helen, hidden from view. "And precisely what," she snapped, "do you find more important than minding your health?"

Helen straightened and looked into Patricia's face. "My last meeting with Jonathan Martin before I retire," she said.

Patricia's expression darkened. But her hand, which had been hovering over a button for a lower floor, hesitated—then swept decisively upward. The lift lurched and began to rise.

In the enclosed space, Helen was aware of the odor of urine emanating from her, filling the lift. If it offended Patricia, though, she didn't permit it to show.

"Where do you live?" Patricia said.

Helen told her the address.

"Give me the keys to your flat."

She did so, fumbling, keeping her eyes fixed on Patricia. It was impossible to speak her gratitude as Patricia pocketed the keys. But Patricia Starling-Haight only glanced at her watch, and Helen saw that the librarian was going to do her the dignity of not allowing Helen's predicament to make a ripple in her impatience.

The doors opened into a space as brightly lit as heaven—so bright Helen nearly fell back. But Patricia ushered her forward. The conservation lab was spacious and clean—the sort of stark, white-on-white workroom where technicians might assemble a spacecraft. Patricia Starling-Haight steered Helen toward a table in the far corner where Patricia Smith perched on a stool, tweezers in hand—her spare frame bent over a tray beneath the glare of a goose-necked lamp, her red-brown hair tied back as severely as ever. The tray, Helen saw, contained small fragments of paper. Beside it on the table, arrayed like a surgeon's tools, were labeled dropper-bottles and a variety of needles and fine threads; on a nearby table was a glass chamber that reminded Helen of old fairy-tale-book pictures of Snow White's coffin: a well-lit transparent bubble.

From Helen's elbow, Patricia Starling-Haight said, "Jonathan Martin is expecting Professor Watt at two o'clock for an exit interview."

Patricia Smith, confused, glanced up at the clock; then at Helen.

Patricia Starling-Haight continued, slowing her words for emphasis. "I have always believed that one deals with such men only, and always, with one's dignity intact."

The two Patricias looked at each other. Then Patricia Smith nudged restlessly at the goose-necked lamp and, with barely a glance at Helen, gestured her toward a stool. "Professor Watt," she said. "Make yourself comfortable." To Patricia Starling-Haight she said only, "I'll mind the rare manuscripts room for you."

Patricia Starling-Haight called the lift and was gone.

Patricia Smith turned back to her table. She tugged close a soup-bowl-sized magnifying glass mounted on its own goose-necked stand. Peering through it, she tweezed nearly invisible fibers from a fragment of paper with precise flicks of her latex-gloved hands.

Minutes passed. The nut bar had restored Helen enough that she was increasingly conscious of the cold press of her damp stockings. As she sat watching Patricia work, her relief silted away, replaced by the beginnings of shame.

Without warning, Patricia Smith pushed back from her table. "Water?" she said, her blue eyes naked and blinking.

Helen nodded.

Patricia disappeared into a narrow hall, then returned with a glass. As Helen gulped the water, Patricia Smith resumed her work—a show of unconcern that Helen knew was meant to offer privacy as she struggled fruitlessly to quell the waving of the glass. By the time Helen had finished drinking, the front of her blouse was soaked.

Patricia Smith, standing now, poured a clear chemical from a large white bottle into a second tray, then, with tweezers, dropped several of the fragments in. A taut, disciplined woman whose labor was the stuff of sorcery: to undo the wreckage of neglect and time.

After a moment Patricia rose, shed her gloves, and disappeared into the lift.

For a long time, Helen sat in the silent laboratory. All around her, on shelves and tables, on metal trays and in glass chambers, lay a silent company of paper: centuries old, leaf after leaf, torn or faded or brittle. Pages inked by long-dead hands. Pages damaged by time and worse. But they—the pages—would live again.

And Helen would die.

These fragments I have shored against my ruins.

The wet front of her blouse clung to her chest.

She'd spent the last of her energies trying to redeem Ester Velasquez's fate—believing fervently in some hidden truth that would upend the story of another woman's life. But all the while, it seemed, she'd failed to look for the same in her own.

Memory, spiraling down and down until bedrock. She sat among shards. Once she'd felt the terror of love in her body. Once she'd loved Dror amid his losses, and fled him. She'd spent the decades barricading herself from life, setting the conditions for love so high no one else could ever meet them. Few, in fact, had made any effort. It was a simple thing, in the end, to hide in plain sight. The world did not prevent you from becoming what you were determined to become.

For far too long, she'd failed to understand this.

She'd loved only one man. Year after year, studying the news in her quiet flat, she'd reached for him in the spaces between every article about Israel, felt for his presence in the most mundane details. And, sipping tea as she turned the pages of newsprint, she'd understood she'd been saved from it all: from the murderous traps Dror had warned against, from the bruising bewilderment she'd have felt with such a man, from his protectiveness—so fierce it terrified her. And she'd understood too that she was damned.

All too willingly had she let herself be fooled by Dror's severity. She'd told herself: my world and his are opposite and cannot coexist. But she was older now—and, looking back at that young man, she saw that all his warnings about the harshness of his history had been nothing but his fear that she'd step blithely into his world, then later feel its confines and flee. Of course he'd needed Helen to be certain: he'd loved her. And he'd understood, better than she, what love required.

Over the decades, she'd imagined him unchanged. Perhaps graying, perhaps sun-weathered, even stooped—but with his fist still raised, his anger intact, his heart still brimming with his dead. She saw now that she'd held to this image for her own comfort. She'd placed the portrait of Masada on her mantle to remind her of a man who hadn't existed—a rigid man she could justify having left.

To imagine that he might have softened was unbearable. But she'd been wrong. There were men who put ideology above gentleness. Dror —who had followed her from his quarters, who had called her name despite the stares—had never been one of them.

The thought of herself as a mother in Israel—carrying bright plastic baskets at the market, calling for a child amid holiday bonfires in a smoky valley—was a torture she now forced herself to. Sounds and smells and colors assaulted her senses: the hush of palm fronds in a breeze. The brash laughter of university colleagues she might have taught alongside in Jerusalem or Tel Aviv. Cucumbers and tomatoes in the bins of the market vendors, guava and hyssop and cumin, and the sharp whistles of parents as distant singing rippled and bonfires burned like fuses across the darkened valley. And the sound of the bus drivers' radios and the report of the bomb squad exploding something in the distance, and the sound of telephones ringing and ringing as women checked on husbands and daughters and sons. And the sound of her own voice, her own accented Hebrew, laboring to protect all that she could never fully protect—arguing, chuckling, weeping, soothing. Living.

And Dror's eyes, dark and bright, were even now fastened on her. Asking her to stay even as she slipped from him. Raising panic in her chest.

How fearsome a thing was love. She'd wasted her life fleeing it.

The fluorescent light vibrated quietly, flickering against Helen's eyelids like a summons. She opened her eyes and slowly, carefully, stood. There, a few paces from where she'd been sitting, encased in its humidity chamber, was a document. Even as she took her first step toward it, she knew what it was.

The lift dinged and opened, and Patricia Smith emerged. "Oh," she said, seeing Helen at the glass case—and it was the first time Helen had heard pleasure in her voice. "The ivy letter. I managed to remove the seal without so much as a hairline crack." She gestured proudly toward a separate teacup-sized case on a side table, where a small circle of intricately patterned brown wax lay on a square of white cloth. "Would you like to see? The integrity of the wax is quite remarkable."

Helen met her eyes and didn't answer. Then she completed her final swaying steps toward the large case where the ivy letter lay.

"Perhaps later," said Patricia, her irony tempered by something like respect.

She could not have stopped her hands had she wished to. Behind her, Patricia let out a sound of disapproval but restrained herself as Helen's palms rose and settled on the glass, and rested there. A tentative, fluttering embrace, like a lover made shy by years of rejection.

The handwriting was unmistakably different—rounder and less cramped, unrushed. Innocent. And when she reached the signature she understood at last.

"That's how you did it," she said aloud.

She read, and she reread, and the history that had refused for so long to speak to her now greeted her clearly. She listened with the flooding gratitude of a wanderer at last called home—her name sounding through the dusk in a voice raised up to remind her, finally, that she had been its child all along.

The lift doors pinged open once more, and Patricia Starling-Haight was back, bearing clothing from Helen's apartment. And like two sisters in a fairy tale, the Patricias flanked her in silence, outspread arms laden, to gird her for her final battle.

26

September 7, 1665
27 Elul, 5425
London

FORTY DAYS AND NIGHTS: a number even the Christians respected. Forty days and nights of flood to drown every stirring thing and wash the earth clean. Forty days and nights of Moses pleading forgiveness on the sun-beaten mountain; of Goliath's thundering challenges in the valley, met only with terrified silence.

Their pantry ran low. Only due to the da Costa Mendeses' servants' practice of stocking quantities of firewood and oil, and the fact that Rivka had for some time made a habit of purchasing extra flour, were they able to sustain themselves. Some time during Ester's sickness, Rivka had divided their stores into daily portions to last until their release from quarantine. Now every day she baked bread, which they dipped in oil with thyme from the garden and ate for each meal.

Just once, when but a week remained until the guard would leave his post at their door, did Bescós appear. Standing beside the bedchamber's window, Ester saw him enter the street. He walked like a man much aged. When he reached their house, he conferred with the guard in low tones. Straightening to squint upward, he saw her.

"You're alive," he said. Then he added, "Today."

Shadows under his pale eyes, under his cheekbones. His face was cavernous. She'd never thought of Bescós as a hopeful man, but she understood that the thing that had been burned out of his face was hope. Something keen and unbending had taken its place.

"You Jewesses make it tiresome to get my money," he said.

She stood rooted at the window.

On the street, Bescós made show of pausing a moment in thought.

"I wonder much," he called scornfully, "at the strange fate of the Jews. Always pouring out your lifeblood. You have an affinity for it."

The guard let out an uncertain laugh.

"Every moral error in Christianity," Bescós said, "can be traced—" But he stopped, then waved his hand dismissively—the recitation too tiresome to continue with only the guard for audience. He stepped back a few paces, and seemed to survey the entirety of the da Costa Mendes house with care. Then he nodded to the guard, and departed.

Avidly, the guard watched Bescós's retreat—the only sport to come his way in weeks. Ester too watched him go, her knuckles striated white where they gripped the windowsill, her heart banging. The temerity of her body stunned her: no matter how she counseled it to accept its own inevitable defeat, it refused, insisting on each next breath, and the next.

And didn't an equally insistent force animate Bescós? Dread shadowed him—yet stubbornly he refused dread's claim. He would hack at it with all he possessed, she saw, until it was eviscerated.

So when the fortieth day dawned and their doorstep at last was vacant, she wasn't surprised to see Esteban Bescós on the street. But he stood with his back to their house, as though awaiting someone.

Rivka joined Ester at the upstairs window. For a long time they watched Bescós. As though he might possibly overhear through the closed window, Rivka spoke in a whisper. "If he wants us out so he can have Mary's things, we'll go." There was a note in her voice Ester hadn't heard before. She turned. Rivka's eyes were intent on the street, her nostrils wide, her breaths now coming rapid and suppressed. "I won't," Rivka murmured, as though counseling herself. "I won't step out the door until he assures safe passage."

Voices in the street. Below, three men had joined Bescós. They were followed by two women entering from the direction of Bury Street, one stooped, the other young. The group stood in conversation. Then, at some remark from Bescós, they looked up in unison, at the window where Ester and Rivka stood.

Bescós's words were louder than necessary, meant for Ester's and Rivka's ears too. "Two Jewesses hiding behind a painted cross. Why didn't they die, if the sickness was here? If you wish to see sorcery, look in that window."

The ring of faces peered anxiously. Rivka stepped back swiftly from the window; Ester shrouded herself in a curtain, hoping to see without being seen.

"The younger one," Bescós continued with a gallant gesture, "believes herself to have powers of *thought*. She reads books that in the hands of a woman—let alone a Jewess—lead to heresy and worse."

The men and women blinked in the bright daylight. They looked, at present, too sleepy to be moved by Bescós's words. But the ugliness of their upturned countenances told Ester what she needed to know of Bescós's purpose in summoning them. Squinting to catch a glimpse of Ester were faces that told of poverty and ill health steadier and more clawing than the plague. One of the men had an inflammation of the skin that gave his nose the appearance of raw flesh. The young woman had one good eye, its companion so grossly swollen and crusted with pus that Ester's mind at first couldn't properly make sense of the woman's distorted features. Ester knew she herself must look unearthly as well: her complexion hollowed to ash by the distemper, her eyes emptied by all they'd witnessed—this much she'd glimpsed on the one occasion when she'd been tempted to lift a corner of one of the cloths with which Rivka had covered the house's mirrors. But the condition of those below her window was of a different order.

The woman with the diseased eye addressed Bescós quietly, her soft smile revealing broken teeth. As she spoke she lifted a hand toward him in emphasis—and he stepped back from her hand so swiftly he lost his footing and stumbled, catching himself on the low masonry wall. A slight stumble, surely not enough to hurt him—yet it was a moment before he stirred again. As he leaned on the wall, his face turned away from the others, Ester glimpsed his turbid expression. He seemed near weeping.

He righted himself slowly; when he straightened, his face bore only a trace of distaste. He resumed speaking with the woman, as though her near-touch hadn't undone him. But the woman had stiffened. When they'd finished speaking she turned away, her shoulders bunched.

"Jewish sorcery," one of the men called—the words still tentative.

Bescós wore a look of exasperation. "Jewish sorcery," he affirmed, impatient. "Yes. There they stand."

"The vicar's spoken of that," said the older woman.

Church of England, then. Bescós didn't even share their faith.

Now three more joined the group, most strikingly a young able-bodied man with a close-shaven head and puglike features. His gait was stiff, as though his very limbs were tight with rage. Ester watched him traverse the short space of cobblestones. Looking to the window the gazes of the others were trained on, he gave an impatient shudder that made her belly tighten. He barked something to Bescós.

How improbable it seemed—even tawdry—that a mob should gather. That she, along with Rivka, would die this way. Yet she was no better, and surely worse, than many who had died at the hands of mobs.

"Ester," Rivka said.

A thump on the upper window. Ester looked in time to see the manure sliding down the pane. Another thump—two streaks on the glass. Her body clenched, but she couldn't keep from staring down through the streaks at the pug-faced man, whose eyes were squeezed nearly shut with a wild hunger. He bent to scoop more from the street, took aim at the window, missed; she heard the muck hit the wall of the house.

The others watched, shifting uneasily, as though awaiting some decision. There ought to be more noise, Ester thought. *Why isn't there more noise?* But there was only the man's hard grunts as he worked, hurling one clod after another; now and again a sharp shout of encouragement from those watching.

Then with a nauseated, heartsick glance at Bescós, the woman with the diseased eye pierced the quiet with a scream. "Heralds of sickness!" And she lurched forward, bent to take up a rock, and hurled it with a cry.

Commotion. Bodies stooping, rising, jolting. Rocks against the edifice. Wild hoots, a cry of rage, the slam of something heavy—stone on wood. The air above the street seemed to shudder—Ester stared, but Rivka was pulling on Ester's sleeve, forcing her away from the sight. Something hard hit the window, leaving a long crack in a pane. Outside, an old woman's desiccated voice: "Shake the Jews loose from this house in the name of the Lord." And Bescós calling, in a voice too calm for the thought to be spontaneous: "They'll leave or be burned out."

A moment later, an insistent rapping below, on the front door.

Pushing past Rivka, Ester descended the stairs so fast it felt like tumbling. At the bottom she caught her balance on a wooden post.

Trying to quiet her own breathing, she stood listening in the shadowed entryway, poised between the front door and the kitchen, from which she could flee to the walled garden—and then where?

"You might save everyone the trouble of a fire." Bescós's voice was intimate even through the window, rich with astonishment at his own easy success.

"You'd burn this house for its silver?" she said.

"Even melted, the silver will satisfy me," said Bescós. "But perhaps not these good neighbors of yours, whom I found begging on the streets of their parish. Perhaps you ought to save them the exertion and do the knifework yourself, as your people did at York." He laughed. "None will mourn two Jewesses dead in a house they stole from a dead girl's family."

Beside Ester, Rivka's soft breathing.

"Take the house," Ester called to the door. "And the silver. Give us safe passage."

A low laugh. "That might or might not be mine to give."

One of her sleeves was pushed up past the elbow—she touched the soft skin at the crease of her arm, the faint blue trail of her own vein, pulsing.

"Ester." A plea like a child's.

She turned. Rivka's cheeks shone with tears, a thin line of mucus from each nostril. Her head wagged slowly, side to side. "They'll do it," she whispered. "Before they kill us."

"Rivka—"

"Or worse"—Rivka squeezed her eyes shut—"they'll do it and leave us alive." She wrenched back from Ester's outstretched hand and brushed roughly past, knocking Ester off balance. Stumbling, Ester followed, the sudden exertion dimming her vision, so she had to cling to the wall all the way to the kitchen.

When her sight cleared, she could not at first comprehend what she saw. Rivka, whispering psalms with her back to the oven. Rivka with a knife, its tip to her bosom—the metal piercing the fabric between her breasts. The look on Rivka's face had narrowed, as though she were peering down a tunnel to glimpse some invisible horizon. Her lips moved in recitation and her cheeks were flushed pink as with shame. She wore a strange expression of submission, like a child asking forgiveness. Ester cried out and threw herself forward—but the lunge she made for the knife was feeble, and Rivka knocked her back easily with one arm. Ester fell hard to the floor, where she struggled to catch her breath.

Rivka, looming above her, continued a broken recitation: "*Shfoch levavi—al mnat kedoshecha.*" Now she closed her eyes, her lips moving ceaselessly—and even as Ester cried out for her to stop, Ester recalled helplessly how often she'd heard Rivka speak of holy martyrdom and the kindness of a death that did not compromise the soul. And it seemed to Ester that Rivka had been rehearsing for her own death since she'd first been cursed with survival.

But the stream of Rivka's prayer seemed to have snagged on some detail. She squeezed her closed eyes, struggling to resume her concentration. She shook her head—once, twice—like a merchant ready to sign an agreement, but for one minor point. And for all she wished to, she could not let this point rest.

The tip of the knife quivered at Rivka's bosom. It writhed, burrowed, and then was still. Ester saw a small spot of blood flower on the front of Rivka's dress. But the knife pierced no farther.

Rivka opened her eyes. Gently she laid the knife down atop the stove, caressing its handle once, as though the instrument of her failure must not be blamed for her cowardice. She turned, and set her hands on the stout table where she'd labored to produce bread to keep them alive all these weeks.

Slowly, as Ester raised herself from the floor, Rivka bent forward in grief, giving the weight of her body to the floured wooden surface. Her flurrying prayer had ceased. Rivka would throw herself on the mercy of the world, Ester saw, and would wait for it to do the violence she herself had failed to do.

And how strange, when Ester's hands were hot and shaking, and her own pulse—*danger danger*—was thick in her ears . . . how strange that the words that floated into her mind should be words of reason. In silence she mouthed them: *life being the ultimate morality, so it must savage all.*

It took long minutes to coax Rivka into motion. When Rivka turned at last, she seemed uncertain, weak as though she herself had just risen from a sickbed. But at length Ester ushered her, with a hand on Rivka's back, up to the room where Rivka had nursed Ester through her fever.

There, Ester took Rivka's rough hand and squeezed—Rivka, her gaze downcast, let out a murmur—and Ester left her standing beside the bed.

Ester opened a window. The din outside had grown. A man now threw himself bodily against the door below, to cheers. There were several more men now, sour-faced and ill-favored—and more women too, and a few children on the edges of the crowd, one girl with a collection of small stones in her bunched apron.

A sharper shout—she'd been spied. A bit of refuse pelted the wall to her left.

She cried down to them—she had to call the words three times to be heard. "We give it to your church!"

There was a single shout, then a confused murmur.

A rock hit the brickwork above the window.

"We give all this house to your church." Ester drew another breath and trained her attention on the woman with the swollen eye. "We deed it, every bit of silver and furnishing and the very bricks and timbers, to your vicar. Let him come and accept our tribute."

The woman was about Ester's age and, Ester saw, must once have been pretty. Her brown hair, though dull, framed a heart-shaped face whose soft outline was still discernible despite the distorting eye. As Ester spoke, the woman fell silent. She turned to some nearby women who were whispering, and waved them quiet. As Ester repeated her message, one of those women turned to two men jostling beside her and laid a hand on one's shoulder. "The vicar!" she reprimanded him.

The men hesitated.

From below Ester's window, the dull noise of the man hammering his shoulder against the door continued, but fewer voices cheered each blow. From near the door, a harsh cry. Bescós. "It's a devil's trick," he shouted.

But Ester spoke above him, her voice thin and high. "We trust in *your* church, not this man's." Without looking at Bescós, she pointed a trembling hand in his direction. "Let your vicar use our wealth to expunge our sins. We'll give this household and all it contains to him and to him alone. This man here—he's called Esteban Bescós—he wishes to take it for himself. Don't let him withhold the fortune from your church."

Beside Ester, Rivka drew a jagged breath, as though she'd only now woken from a dream. She was staring as if Ester were the vilest of all traitors. Then she turned away, as though she'd discovered the same of her own self.

Below the window, the woman with the swollen eye was raising her voice to override the pug-faced man beside her. "Then go to the church and *find* him," she said.

A brief hesitation. Then the pug-faced man nodded and departed.

A rigid smile remained on Bescós's face. "It's a trick!" he shouted. And he gestured broadly toward the da Costa Mendes house, as though welcoming friends to a feast. But the woman with the swollen eye answered without turning to him. "We'll let the vicar say so, won't we?"

The man thudding against the front door made two last efforts, accompanied by a few companions' laughter, then staggered back into the crowd, calling for ale.

Ester shut the window. "We have to gather our things," she said.

For a minute Rivka didn't move.

Ester spoke softly. "Do you know what the rabbi said to me, before he died?"

Rivka looked up.

"He said he'd failed to be brave enough to be a martyr when he was young. And he was afraid he'd fail again, were he tested. Imagine" —Ester was shocked by the quaking of her own voice—"such a man believing he failed God. Rivka, I disbelieve this notion of God. A God who would ask this of us can't be the same as gave us our wish to live. If I'm wrong, then the sin be on me."

Rivka shook her head hard. "Don't speak these things to me."

Ester swallowed. "Then listen to the rabbi's words, not mine. He would wish you consolation. He taught the verse, *God is near to the broken-hearted.*"

Rivka said nothing, only turned for the stair.

AN HOUR, MORE. IT WAS afternoon, the air thick with heat. Ester watched from the window, clenching and unclenching in her hand the heavy key to the da Costa Mendes house.

Below, the crowd grew steadily, passersby trickling in from either end of the street as they happened upon the day's sport. Shouts and laughter surged. Several women walked the edge of the gathering—the one with the swollen eye and her companion with the babe on her hip and others—and with almost lascivious eagerness they appeared to be telling the story to all who entered. Two sharp cracks from the house's attic, loud as gunshots—Ester and Rivka cried out—then scattered shouts from below as shards fell to the cobblestones. A few youths stood on the street, picking up more rocks, taking lazy aim at the panes of the attic windows. Nearby, a small number of men stood stolid, paternal, their backs to the house as if to guard it from premature trespass; or perhaps merely to ensure their place in line to loot it. Almost furtively, they watched the women on the perimeter of the crowd. Something in their posture was wolfish and apprehensive—and Ester saw that they hungered for an enemy against which they might yet be capable of protecting someone. Then they'd fight it with a fury like none they'd mustered before—pound and pound until the fibers of its flesh loosened, and lost hold.

She couldn't see Bescós.

The vicar's arrival spread a simmering hush along the street.

Ester opened the window to its fullest and stood in plain view.

Could it be that a man so frail still walked? He was wrinkled, his form bent with age, his eyelids red and puffed. Perhaps, Ester thought, he was simply the only vicar left in the city.

But as he drew near, she saw that his pale face bore the fury of a man spurned. He spread his arms wide, and his voice had a shocking strength. "Do you give this house to the church?" As he cried out the question, the vicar glanced upward at the window only briefly. His glare slid from Ester's face to those congregated about him—as though he'd at last corralled his flock and this time meant to brand them. Those nearest stepped back from his fury. Ester saw a few bow their heads, though most of the crowd appeared unmoved. But the old vicar advanced on those around him, turning to one and then another. Still louder, he cried, "The devil must be driven out without mercy!"

Straining to be heard, Ester shouted from the window. "I give this!" She held out the thick key. "It opens every door. All will belong to the church, the house and all its wealth."

But the vicar still did not look at her. "The Lord does not accept empty riches," he screamed to those standing about him. "Not without the lone tribute that is eternal."

His words held the street in thrall.

He turned his withered face to Ester so suddenly, she stepped back from the window. "Do the Jewesses," he enunciated, "give their souls?"

She'd known it would be necessary. Yet the words were dreadful. She held herself upright. "I do," she said.

Behind her, a small sound escaped Rivka.

"This sin is mine, not yours," Ester whispered.

"They offer their souls," the vicar announced majestically to his congregation. Yet he raised a hand, delaying absolution. "Will God accept such an offering?"

Swiftly Ester opened a drawer of the dressing table that had been Mary's. "We have to gather what we can," she said to Rivka. With a whispered *discúlpame,* she slid Mary's necklaces and rings aside and, closing her spirit to all that the delicate, familiar baubles threatened to raise in her, she found a few coins—enough, perhaps, to pay for passage out of London, if they lived. Then, without a glance at Rivka—for it seemed to her that the slightest provocation might prompt Rivka to balk—she fled downstairs.

Moments later she heard Rivka thumping clumsily about the bedchambers as though blind. When they met at the foot of the stair, Rivka had donned a voluminous cloak, and her figure was thickened by bundles she'd stowed within her clothing.

Her brown eyes rested for a long moment on Ester's. Then she set a hand on Ester's arm, and gripped.

The sun was sectioning the floor of the front room, each wedge of yellow light a threshold. Together they crossed one after another, until they reached the shadowed entryway. For the first time in forty days, Ester set her hand on the lock, then turned to Rivka for permission.

Rivka drew a long breath through her nostrils, then nodded.

She unlatched the heavy door and swung it open.

An assault of sunlight. The strangers stepped back.

Ester opened her mouth to speak—but the words never sounded. Bodies shoving. Rough hands, grabbing. A face, too close to Ester's—a scabbed sore on a stubbled cheek. Shouts, open mouths, an elbow knocking her forehead, hard. A hand snaking into Ester's hair, twisting, wrenching—fiery pain, she heard the hank rip from her scalp. She gasped, but didn't let out a scream, nor did Rivka, whose grip was iron on her arm. A press of bodies pushed them forward, hands hard on Ester's shoulders, on her waist, feeling for her breast through the fabric of her dress, one unseen hand rummaging her skirt to squeeze sharply at her sex. She could feel Rivka struggling beside her, heard a man grunt as Rivka did something to make him twist away. And then before them the vicar stood waiting.

As they neared he spread his arms above them, a look of satisfaction on his fallen face. And the hands, one by one, released them.

The vicar regarded them. The scent emanating from him—incense and damp stone—pinioned Ester. How many had stood as she and Rivka did now, waiting to die for what they were, blood singing in their temples?

For a moment, as the vicar held them in his frail, vengeful shelter, the throng stood riveted. Then, as his silence lengthened, the crowd faltered—and in the next heartbeat, in some swift and mute decision, it broke, tempted beyond endurance by the open house and the shouts of those who had already ventured in.

Distracted by the dispersal of his congregation, the vicar cried, "He who takes for himself robs the church!" But it was plain that the house the vicar claimed would be a plundered one. By opening the door to the da Costa Mendes house, Ester had flayed open a body; now scavengers rushed to pick the meat from the bones.

She watched it happen. Beside her, equally fixed by the sight, stood Rivka and the vicar. Strangers emerged with arms full of valuables—Mary's father's silver plate and vases. A silk skirt of Catherine's. Mary's necklaces draped over the ten outspread fingers of the pug-faced man. A woman was busying herself nearby with a box of intricate velvet patches, running her thumb across the bristles of a brush Mary had used to glue them to her skin. Something—grief—seized at Ester's throat, but there was no time for it, and the vicar was shouting. What did he want? She couldn't make out his words at first, but saw that he, like she, was gauging the mood of the crowd. The house would yet be a fine shell, even if looted: a treasure for a church and its vicar to use in the world after the plague, if such a world even existed—and if the force of the

law didn't suffice to wrench it back to any surviving remnant of the da
Costa Mendes family.

"These souls cannot wait," the vicar cried abruptly, his voice at once
bitter and glad, as though he'd expected no better and it satisfied him
to know he'd been correct. "They must purge themselves now before
the Lord!" He turned away from Ester and Rivka and began to walk.
As Ester turned to follow, she spied Bescós framed for a moment in
an upstairs window of the house. His arms, she could see, were laden
with silver—yet his face bore a sickened expression as though they
were empty.

The vicar's calls had drawn half a score away from the spectacle of
the house, and this diminished escort moved Ester and Rivka along
in his wake. As they reached the end of the street, Ester wrenched a
last look at the house that had been their prison and shelter. Its façade
stood violated, filth-splashed, the mullioned windows missing panes. As
she watched, one of Rivka's reverently whitened bed sheets sailed down
from an upper window, forming a perfect bell of air as it fell—then,
with astonishing gentleness, collapsed on the street.

A boy had joined them, bearing a censer that gave off scented smoke.
He swung it hard, the chain jerking at the crest of every swing, and
positioned himself at the head of the procession—Ester couldn't guess
whether this was some part of a ritual or whether he simply meant to
drive off the plague, but the drifting smoke laid their path through a city
unrecognizable. Door after door with painted crosses. People with faces
pinched and ravaged walking singly on the street. A few hungry-looking
children joined the procession, but others shrank away, as though they'd
long since learned that death was in other people. Hands were upon
Ester and Rivka once more—fewer this time, exploring at their leisure,
more curious. Hands on Ester's back, her hair, her ears, fondling her
neck. Rivka, her grip dire on Ester's arm, shuffled amid the press with
head bowed and eyes half closed—a dreadful expression on her face.
Raising her head to avoid the scratch of fingernails on her cheek, Ester
glimpsed, for just an instant, something unexpected: high and sweet
above the city, visible between the overarching roofs, was a sky the like
of which she'd not seen since coming to England—a thread of thin
blue, stretching to infinity. The proprietors of the tanneries and lime
kilns that had fouled the city were dead or departed, leaving a clean-

washed sky like a new truth stretched above all the city's suffering, just out of reach.

Then it was gone. They'd come to an archway, and beyond it a court-yard boxed by high walls, each topped by stone-carved skulls. And then the church—how many times, in another London, had she hurried past these buildings? Now, prodded from behind, they entered the dim in-terior, the vicar barely visible ahead. Vaulted stone encased them; flick-ering candle-shadows, echoes, a dizzying smell like a hundred years' incense lingering in the air. Ester leaned into Rivka. Words from child-hood sprang to her mind—an incantation she hadn't known she re-membered, taught to Ester by a girl whose own mother had made her memorize it. "There's something you can say," she whispered to Rivka. "I learned it when I was a girl. It's Spanish. It means *Everything I'm about to say is null and void.* You say, *Todo lo que voy a decir es nulo*—"

"No," Rivka whispered. Her eyes were wide, fixed on the spot near the front of the church toward which they were being led. With her free arm she clutched her chest, as though cradling a baby. "God sees. I accept His judgment."

They were at the front of the sanctuary—pushed up a set of steps by the curious hands that still surrounded them—and as they approached the altar someone spat, and the spittle landed on Rivka's cheek, but though she flinched she didn't wipe it off.

"So come they to Christ," the vicar called in a high, thin voice.

There was a sudden hush, the nave echoing.

"So shall we," he said. "Our land is desolate, our city in ruins. God has shown these lost ones the way, and our forbearance toward them redeems all of us. For enough have died, and it is now in our hands to save."

His brittle mercy sank into the silence. In the expression of a white-haired woman standing near Ester, something dormant awoke. She nodded slowly at the vicar, and her eyes welled with a purity like love.

Entranced by the otherworldly peace on the vicar's face and the growing strength of his voice, Ester failed to comprehend his instruc-tions, even when he repeated them. But hands pushed her from behind so she fell into a kneel, and her head was pushed forward until her chin touched her chest, and the vicar spoke, and his hands, cold but efficient, worked some unfamiliar task. The vicar's fingers dripping oil, marking a swift cross between her eyebrows. Water splashing the crown of her head, running warm down the bridge of her nose. Then she lifted her face and looked not at the people about the altar, but beyond them to the stone walls and roof. The church bent and swam, glazed with what she realized were her own tears—though how could the vicar's gestures of conversion undo one such as she, who did not believe there could be a god who cared about such things? Still, she couldn't deny the feeling she had now, as though she'd been dirtied beyond the possibility of ever being clean. Gazing across the nave, she saw a statue carved in pale stone: a woman—one of the Christian saints—beseeching the heavens with raised arms, her body racked with suffering. And lowering her gaze at last, at the smallest sound of protest beside her, she saw Rivka kneeling: the vicar's cross oiled on her head, her weathered face lifted in supplication.

DUSK. THE RIVER WIDENED AND curved before them in a great gray arc. Overhead, a first prickle of stars—faint, sickly. The veiled smudge of the comet.

The boatman was bent to his task, his good hand grasping one oar, his claw-hand strapped with a leather thong to the other oar. Above the frayed nose cone of herbs that he wore against the distemper, his blue eyes rested now and again on Ester and Rivka—asking no questions, wanting no answers beyond the coins Ester had handed him, with the promise of the other half upon arrival.

Not a single craft approached them on the water. How sparse was the river's traffic now, compared to that spring day not four months earlier—Ester closed her mind against the memory.

The boatman had warned, as he'd tucked her money into a pocket with his good hand, that if they were hailed and their papers demanded, he'd put them ashore and be gone. He'd insisted too on delaying departure until the afternoon sun had begun its descent. But they hadn't been stopped—they hadn't seen more than a few solitary oarsmen, greeting one another with low calls as they passed at a distance. London, it seemed, had finally grown porous from the death or defection of its guards; few were left to keep the sick in their pen.

The river bent on ahead of them, broad and impassive, its destination hidden. Rivka sat in the stern of the small boat, her gaze fixed back at the water they'd traveled. They'd barely spoken since the church. When the ragged singing of hymns had ceased and the church had begun to empty of its small sated congregation, they'd made as one for the river, fleeing before some second thought of the vicar's could recall them. How strange it was, having been carried to the church by a crowd, to emerge from it to an empty city—and how easy it seemed now to pass unseen. If London had once been a city of a thousand eyes, now those eyes had been all but extinguished, and two women could wend their way down street after street, past a hundred shuttered windows, without a single greeting or jeer.

Here, Ester had murmured to Rivka, steering them down a narrow byway. *Here.* Down to the river she'd guided them with neither thought nor plan, pausing only briefly now and again to catch her breath— then leading on—*here*—*here*—to places where she'd once sought her brother. To a quay that had once shuddered with the sounds of men loading cargo—now forlorn, the tang of the tide heavy in the air. Down and down, to the shadowed lee of the bridge, Rivka following like a child. A moment's rest against a stack of splintered crates; then she ducked behind a wooden shed and fell upon a dozing boatman—who woke with a gasp to a ghostly apparition, silver coins in her outstretched fist.

Even in the fading light, the banks on either side were still verdant. The city's glut of death hadn't harmed a blade of their grasses. Ester watched them slip past. A soft breeze rose. The thought sounded in her like a single struck chime: if someone were to sing her a song, she would weep.

Rivka was struggling in her low seat—only now did Ester note that something prevented her from sitting properly. Her chin tucked, her body angled carefully away from the boatman, she was working at the fastenings of her cloak, then her dress. For a moment Ester thought she'd resolved to disrobe and plunge into the deep waters, embracing at last a death she'd only deferred. Yet Ester was too numbed to do more than stare as, with effort and evident relief, Rivka worked a thick sheaf of papers from deep within her broad bodice. These were bent from the curve of her body—scores of pages, hundreds. Ester watched, uncomprehending. The innermost page bore a small dark stain on its upper edge. Blood, from the knife that had pierced Rivka's skin.

She gave the papers to Ester.

For a moment Ester didn't recognize the hand—slanted, flowing, precise. Then she saw it was her own. Rivka had salvaged everything —all the papers Ester had left beneath her mattress at the da Costa Mendes house. And only now did Ester look down and see a few slim books beside Rivka's feet in the boat's stern, already deposited there while Ester had been in her own reverie—just a small portion of the rabbi's library, but more than Ester would have imagined Rivka could carry.

All about them the green, living countryside slipped by. For some time Ester watched it. "Why?" she said at last.

With her face still turned toward the water, Rivka shrugged.

In the silence, the soft, deep pull of the oars was audible, and their quiet drip as they floated above the water. The boatman had lowered his nose cone, closed his eyes in the fresh evening air, and bent his head to the task, and his breathing rose and fell in rhythm with his motions.

Abruptly Rivka turned, and the expression on her face was avid. "I needed him with me," she said. "There." In the church. Rivka had held the rabbi's words to her heart. *"God is near to the broken-hearted,"* Rivka recited—and in Ester's memory, the rabbi's voice quietly finished the verse . . . *those who are anguished in spirit.*

"I couldn't carry the rest of his books," Rivka said, "so I hid them. Behind bedsteads, behind a jib door. Perhaps some won't be ruined by the thieves. But his own words are here, safe." Rivka gestured at the papers in Ester's hands. Then added, haltingly, "And yours, Ester. I may never understand what drove you to disagree with him, but if those letters were important enough that you'd lie to such a man, and he'd permit it . . ." Rivka stopped. The gaze she leveled at Ester was naked. "Something had to be saved. Those papers are yours."

A soft wind pressed the river, weighting the heavy tops of low trees on the banks, then releasing them. From either side came the calls of unfamiliar birds, their whistles sounding clearly across the water. Overhead the stars were clarifying, the comet growing more vivid. Ester looked at the sheaf in her hands. The ink that had shone blue-black when she first touched it to the page was now a dull, senselessly unfurling ribbon. How had its twists and turns so excited her—as though thought could possibly reshape the world?

She held the sheaf above the dark, moving waters. It would take but an instant for the river to bleed the pages clean of the vanity with which she'd stained them.

Without meaning to, she rested her eyes on the top page in her hands: a half-finished letter.

The notion of God, then, may be simply another name for Universe, and it be a cold universe in which there is no preference for love over hatred, comfort over harm.

The folly of her own words astonished her. She pulled the papers back from over the water, and read more, and as she read she saw the enormity of her blindness. In her arrogance and loneliness she'd thought she understood the world—yet its very essence had been missing from her own philosophy.

The imperative—she whispered it to herself—*to live.* The universe was ruled by a force, and the force was life, and life, and life—a pulsing, commanding law of its own. The comet making its fiery passage across their sky didn't signify divine displeasure, nor did it have anything to say of London's sin; the comet's light existed for the mere purpose of shining. It hurtled because the cosmos demanded it to hurtle. Just as the grass grew in order to grow. Just as the disfigured woman must defy Bescós, who'd consider her unfit for love; just as Ester herself had once, long ago, written because she had to write.

She'd been wrong to think the universe cold, and only the human heart driven by desire. The universe itself was built of naught but desire, and desire was its sole living god.

And desire itself, now, was what detained her from throwing the spent, misguided papers into the water: she simply wished—for one stubborn instant, and then another—to hold them. She sat in the belly of the boat with the pages held fast to her chest, while the boatman pulled his oars through the water's sweet resistance, and birds she'd never heard before sang in bright piercing tones. She thought: I ought at least tell him. De Spinoza. A fish or tree was no god; yet the craving that flickered or surged or pulsed within it was.

A simple letter. Perhaps she'd write one last, simple letter.

It was nearly dark when they stepped out at the small splintered dock.

As Rivka surveyed the dim meadows about them, Ester paid the rest of her money into the boatman's good hand and watched him pocket it and push off from shore without a word. For a moment he seemed to hesitate midcurrent: the free night air filling his nostrils, or the city and his livelihood? He dipped an oar and turned his boat for London.

Above them, on a ridge of land a short distance from the river, the great house. There could be no mistaking it, even in this light. It rose formidable, walled and ornamented. *A brick front,* Manuel HaLevy had written, *to make the Jew-haters forget they hate us and come polish our boots instead.*

They walked blindly through the meadow for a few moments before their feet found a winding path. It climbed gently through a stone gateway before branching, one part proceeding to the house, the other disappearing between two arches of pleached branches to gardens beyond. The grand house itself was a pale orange, with light stone carvings, three stories high; in the dark Ester made out deep eaves and soaring windows, a few of which glowed with the light of some lamp or hearth within. A house of unguessable depths and dimensions, whose proper upkeep would require a fleet of servants. Manuel HaLevy had been right: his father had issued a challenge made of brick and mortar, so solid none could deny its claim to a piece of England's map.

In the growing darkness, Rivka's monumental figure—once more padded with the few books she'd salvaged—faltered.

Stepping into the boat in London, Ester had told Rivka only that they were going to Manuel HaLevy's estate. Rivka hadn't questioned the plan, nor had she asked who at the estate might receive them or what Ester might do, should they be refused. Now, though, as Rivka registered the scale of the great house, she stopped walking.

"Rivka," Ester urged.

In the dim light, defeat showed plainly on Rivka's face. She gestured at herself: too ugly, too poor, too tarnished.

Yet a moment later she resumed walking with the air of someone too depleted for skepticism—her defeat displaced, unaccountably, by trust.

They climbed the remainder of the hill.

She'd thought no further, in truth, than the grassy bank: stepping out of the boat, standing on a bed of green so soft it made her throat ache.

But now a plan formed in Ester's mind, and she steeled herself to follow it whether or not it had hope of success.

It took both her bony hands to lift the knocker from the carved oak door. It bounced heavily on its metal plate: a dry, solemn sound.

A shadow at a nearby window hesitated, then vanished. There was a long silence.

At length, a servant carrying a candle opened the door. His silhouette was framed by the firelit hall behind him. His grayed head and sloped shoulders reminded Ester of a stuffed hawk she'd once seen in a shop: frayed and molting, its scowl undiminished.

The man raised his candle toward Rivka, then Ester, not bothering to disguise his scrutiny. "From the city?" he said.

Too late Ester realized she must wear the catastrophe on her very skin. She resisted the urge to raise a hand to her face to touch the scars left by her illness.

"Papers of good health?" he said.

"We've none," said Ester.

He stiffened and stepped back from the door, closing it further before speaking again through an opening no wider than his narrow face. "You're not welcome."

She was about to insist that she knew his master, when from within the dim house came an indistinct call. Without another word the servant closed the door.

A low rumble of voices. Then the door swung open, wider this time, and peering at them alongside the servant was Benjamin HaLevy himself.

She'd long since grown accustomed to faces carved by grief. Still, the change in HaLevy was startling. Gone was the haughty merchant who'd stood in finery outside the synagogue, speaking with Mary's father of tides and profits. Benjamin HaLevy wore the dark colors and torn collar of mourning, and though he stood in silence as he regarded them, his breaths were dreadful to behold: each a silent indictment. He had the look of a man in a labyrinth who has just tried the only remaining exit and found it blocked; she saw that the very walls of his house, indeed his very breathing body, were prison.

A flinch of recognition. "You're the one he wanted. Aren't you? From the house of the rabbi."

She saw he could not speak Manuel's name. "Yes," she said.

"Where is your rabbi?"

"Dead, though not of plague."

He received this information without remark. His gaze on her face was pitiless. "Yet *you're* scarred."

She allowed his gaze without turning away—knowing as she did so that she gambled. He might recoil from the marks of her suffering, or see them as cousin to his own.

After a moment he turned from her to Rivka. Then, as though unable to resist staring at her scars, back again to Ester. "So," he said at length. "You come here bringing the city's pestilential air, to finish off what remains of the HaLevy name? You can't wait for it to die of its own decay?" For a moment his voice rose as if with anger. But almost at the same instant something in him gave way; he no longer had enough faith in anger's utility to pursue its course. He'd been defeated—not by her, but by his own impatience for this hour, this day, to be extinguished. Abruptly he motioned to his servant, murmuring, "Tonight they stay."

She'd always thought Benjamin HaLevy and Manuel alike in appearance—their stocky bodies and square-set faces, their green-brown eyes coolly evaluating the world. And now it seemed to her that in the father's grief-stilled countenance she saw both faces, Benjamin's and Manuel's—twinned in their comprehension of death, as they once had been in their determination to take firm hold of life.

"In the morning you go," said HaLevy. Turning from them, he added, "Don't eat from my plates." To his servant he said, "Burn the sheets they sleep on."

The servant cast his eyes once more over Ester and Rivka—then glared at his master's back.

HaLevy disappeared from the doorway. Ester heard his tread ascending a stair.

The servant stood with his arms folded. Rivka made a small, deliberate sound in her throat. Ester saw the two lock eyes. It would have been hard to say which looked at the other with greater haughtiness. Then, stepping aside to allow them entry, the servant called a maid to prepare their meal. He led them swiftly to the back of the house, bypassing a grand wooden staircase and rooms whose doorways offered glimpses of opulent furnishings. They followed, hurrying to match his pace, through a jib door and up one flight of a dim, twisting stair, into a maze of narrow passages—the hidden arteries through which the house's servants circulated.

The servant showed them to a windowless room with one narrow bed, upon which lay a pile of neatly folded bedding. He indicated a candle and striker, waited for Rivka to kindle a flame, then left, shutting the door behind him.

The water basin was empty and layered with dust, the bed sheets clean but patched, the bedding thin. A metal chamber pot adorned a corner. There was no hearth.

They sat side by side, listening to the house around them—its silence punctuated only by occasional footsteps that drew tantalizingly near before fading in distant passages. Some time later—a quarter hour? an hour?—Rivka opened the door to find food, left there unannounced: a basket of cold meats and dry bread, a small pail of water. There were no utensils or plates. They ate hungrily with their hands, then drank from the water and splashed their faces with what remained, and went to bed shoulder-to-shoulder on the hard cold bed, still dressed in the only clothing they had. Ester shivered, grateful for Rivka's warmth beside her and her cloak thrown over both of them.

She waited until Rivka was asleep and the house's quiet had reached a deeper register. Then she stood, found the candle and striker, and lit the wick.

The narrow passageway outside their door let into another longer hall, then a stair. She climbed, shadows stretching and looming at every turn. At the landing she hesitated, then made her way along another hall and turned again, the logic of the servants' passageways leading her to a jib door she felt certain let out onto the balcony overlooking the entrance hall two flights below.

Swinging the jib door open, she let herself into a cavernous space. She could sense the high ceilings above her, the grand entry below swathed in a darkness upon which her candle made no impression. The air of the house felt immense and foreign.

She stepped onto the balcony and touched the cool wooden rail. Making her way along it, she walked soundlessly to its end, then ventured a step into the blackness beyond. Another. And then a third, into a hall as broad as a thoroughfare, dimly illuminated at one end by rush-lights. Turning toward these, she moved down the hall, past carved furnishings and heavy-framed artwork whose bulk she felt more than saw. She found herself before a wide carved door, its wood so dark it was nearly black.

An instant; a last, shuddering thought of the path she'd walked to this moment.

She knocked on the door, quietly—she trusted that he slept lightly, if at all.

A moment. Then a slow tread—from his closet, through his bed-chamber, to his sitting room. His voice was hoarse. "Who goes?"

She didn't speak.

She could feel HaLevy straining to hear on the other side of the door. "Barton? Some trouble?"

She knocked again, softly.

He opened the door. The light of his candle fell on her—he registered her pale face—and he startled as though the apparition he saw were the very angel of death, come on silent feet to seize what little remained him. He shied from her, his candle raised as though it might protect him.

"*Por favor*," she said. He retreated farther—for a moment she thought he would close the door. Yet when she reached for him, he seemed unable to move. With the tips of her fingers she brushed, just barely, the weathered back of his once-powerful hand.

The candle in his hand wavered. A drop of wax fell to the floor between them. Slowly he nodded her in.

In the hearth in his sitting room, the coals of the evening's fire still glowed. She sat where he directed her to, on one of the silk-cushioned seats beside the hearth. He settled opposite her.

She waited, letting his agitation subside. Despite the rich fabrics of his dressing gown, the same chill that had gripped her in her mean quarters seemed also to possess him here at his hearth, and he huddled close to the coals. Seeing, she took a poker and knelt. He watched as she added some bits of wood, and the room brightened with their small flare. At length he reached for a flagon, and poured himself a glass of port, and then one for her. They drank. When he'd finished, he lit his pipe.

Only when he was wreathed in smoke did she judge it safe to speak.

From inside the heavy, sweet smoke, he heard out her proposition like a merchant weighing every nuance — his ear attuned to the balance of profit and loss, shame and the slim chance of comfort. Twice he interrupted with questions and weighed her answers. She finished. For a long while the room was silent save the occasional shifting of the low coals, and the sound of his slow breathing as he considered.

Part 5

27

April 11, 2001
London

Two days, and he'd told no one. This morning he'd managed to shower, but midway through dressing he stopped in his boxers and socks and slumped back in bed. The slow drift of his thoughts drowned him. What kind of man, he thought, gets a girl pregnant, then doesn't have a friend he trusts enough to tell about it?

The phone rang again. He didn't answer. Helen had already roused him once, something about Manuel HaLevy's death date. He hadn't pretended to care. Sorry, Helen. Sorry, world.

The phone stopped ringing. Then, after a few seconds' silence, it began again. The third time, he found himself standing, picking up his mobile off the table.

Helen, of course. Her voice prodding him in the depths. "Don't trouble calling Local Studies," she said. "Meet me at the bus station in Richmond."

He exhaled, letting it take a long time. "Can you tell me what this is about?" In fact he didn't imagine what in the 1665 death records could conceivably entice him to reenter the bright world of fact and consequence, in which dates had to be reconciled, dissertations had to be written, and a small floating fetus in the belly of a woman who didn't love him or even particularly want to see him was likely to be the sole viable product of Aaron's twenty-six years on the planet.

"It'll wait," Helen said. "I'll find you in Richmond, at three-thirty, at the bus stop. Then I'll drive us up the hill. Call the Eastons to tell them we're coming. Say whatever you need, but get us into the house. Please."

Please. That was unusual, from Helen. But nothing in the world could motivate him to call Bridgette right now. She was only going to make him feel worse—not to mention that giving Bridgette Easton notice that he was about to show up on her doorstep might be the best way to guarantee they'd be barred entry. Helen didn't know, nor did she need to, that Aaron had already burnt that particular bridge. Their best chance was probably just showing up unannounced. Better still, he'd claim a stomach virus a block shy of the Eastons' house and let Helen go in alone.

He put on his right shoe. Then, some time later, his left.

After a long blank space, he was seated on the bus to Richmond upon Thames, with no memory of standing in the queue or buying a ticket. Traffic slid past the window, nauseating. Had he ever loved Marisa? Or had he just been aiming himself at her because she was unattainable —didn't he want, in fact, a softer, easier woman?

Marisa was offering him the chance to quietly duck away, from her and from the baby. And it seemed to him that he ought to take it.

At the bus station Helen stood by the sign like a lollipop lady waiting for her charges. She was wearing a scarf, knotted at her throat, and a blazer considerably more elegant than her usual. He detached himself from the small stream of disembarking passengers.

"Why so formal?" he said.

For a moment she looked disoriented by the question. Something about her looked wrong—she was pale, and her features seemed somehow disconnected from one another, as though they no longer belonged to the same face.

Then the familiar world reasserted itself: Helen Watt's manner turned crisp. "I just had my final audience with Jonathan Martin." She offered a wan smile.

As he returned her smile, Aaron felt himself rising to the surface as well. There was something right, wasn't there, about the two of them braving it out, as though nothing were wrong. Something not false, but admirable.

It occurred to him that he might just have understood the English for the first time in his life.

"Was it a tearful farewell with Martin?" he said.

She gave him a look.

He said, "That look doesn't scare me anymore."

Her smile gained heft. "It never did, young man. That's been the trouble with you."

"Thank you."

She bowed her head in acknowledgment. "A satisfying meeting, I'll say. I told Jonathan Martin I never liked him."

"You told him *what*?"

She raised her eyebrows.

To hell with politics. To hell with access to the documents. He and Helen seemed to have chosen, at the same moment, to jettison everything. "Did Martin reciprocate?" he said.

"Of course not," said Helen. "He paid me an insulting compliment —offering the appearance of preserving my dignity while in fact assaulting it." She turned a ferocious, professorial mien on Aaron. "Remember, Mr. Levy, to recognize those compliments for what they are."

"Yes, ma'am."

"*Nothing you ever say could offend me, that's how much I respect you.* That's what Jonathan Martin said to me." A satisfied expression crossed her face. "So I told him that's precisely how I feel about him. And then he congratulated me on my *notable career.* And I did the same for him. And then"—Helen's words slowed—"he said what a pity it was that I wouldn't be able to work on the Richmond documents through the completion of the project, given my retirement and my health issues, which, if I didn't mind him saying so, seemed to dictate that I'd be slowing down altogether from here forward." For a moment Helen was silent. Then, shrugging, she let out a little laugh. Her face looked thinner, older, yet somehow lighter. Washed clean of something. "He'll be chuckling about it over cognac with his mistress by now, I'm sure."

"His mistress?"

"Yes," Helen said simply. "Penelope Babcock is Jonathan Martin's mistress. There, now you know a faculty secret."

"Well, he's a little bastard," shot Aaron.

"Stop being protective of me, Mr. Levy. Jonathan Martin might or might not be a little bastard."

"You'd actually *defend* him?"

"I care neither to defend nor attack him. Much as I detest the man, I'll never know the full circumstances behind his choices. Life is muddy.

Denying that—thinking there's only one noble path above the fray—can be a poisonous approach to life."

She'd spoken vehemently; now she stared at him as though insisting that he grant her point. She'd gone somewhere he didn't understand. He gave her a moment, then reeled them back to daylight. "He's still a little bastard."

She nodded, conceding.

"Now will you please tell me why we're here?"

Helen set her briefcase on the sidewalk and carefully extracted three pages of notebook paper. They were covered with penciled script, the writing tremulous and hurried.

"What is this?" he said.

"What we've been missing." She raised a shaking finger—and for an irrational moment, he felt certain she was pointing in accusation at his heart, rather than at the page in his hand. But Helen wasn't accusing; she was smiling—a smile of such simple elation he felt he was looking at the girl she might once have been. "This is the last document from underneath the Eastons' staircase. The ivy letter—the one that was sealed and positioned at the end of the shelf. I copied out the text this afternoon in the conservation lab."

She was looking straight into his eyes, still smiling. He had no idea how to respond to such an expression coming from Helen Watt.

She continued, her voice hoarse. "Read it, and you'll understand. We haven't been wrong about her, Aaron."

With difficulty, he began reading the shakily penciled lines—the text of a poem. After the second couplet, he looked up. "There's no way Ester wrote this clumsy stuff."

"She didn't," Helen said. "But don't sound so indignant. Read it all, Aaron. It improves as it goes."

May 26, 1691

An Apologie for That Denied the Fyre

A thief I never once have been
In all the days I e'er have seen
Yet from the flames I have purloin'd

That given by she to whom I'm join'd
One mayde I've loved and one alone
To she I'm wed and to she alone
She's fathomed my heart all my days
I've trembled e'er before her gaze
Though worship I with holy love
He who set the cherubim above
Still with sacred joy I call her wife
Who lent to me renewed life

I've made no impress on her heart
Which loves none yet loved me from my start
If read you this and think me horn'd
I say my heart has not been scorned
And though she fathomed not my desire
She blessed it with her spirit's fire
And so I bless hers ever.

Now each one of her pained breaths
Does hasten the hour of her death
Yet whilst that mayd lyes on her bed
Her illness heavy and her dread
In one thing does she rest content
For she her husband has sent
To set these pages to the pyre
And damn her secret to the fyre

I ne'er will her thoughts divine
Her understanding passes mine
It pains my soul to disobey
To deny her aught is my dismay
Her merest shadow I adore
Yet this I shall not do.

She bore no child, did not her duty
Kept house for none, tended not her beauty
Yet I her very soul do cherish

And will not suffer her word to perish
Let others mock my love for she
That gave not of her heart to me
For love be not a jeweler's pans
Gems' worth is oft misread by man

Now Death to that same mayde draws near
And in her eyes uncustom'd fear
Her soul's accounting now she does attend
Yet I, wretch, refuse to so embrace her end
For her to linger I do plead
For God to spare her! Physick bleed!
Yet even as death's tread does tremble the path
And she, content, believes these pages ash
She jealous guards with life's last sparks
The trace of treasured hands' marks
And for her pleasure does secretly preserve
Some letters to comfort as she does deserve
When sleep eludes and falters health
Her rest be eased by her inked wealth
Which she still reads and to them doth still reply
With quill and ink her sex she yet defies.
Though I fear she'll burn her treasures at the last
Till Death call her she will yet hold them fast
And through habits long of secrecy
She hydes this work from even I
And thinks I do not see.

Dare not condemn her, you who read
This trail of these, her fiercest deeds
And should you she past mercy deem
Her every thought a heresy seem
Recall she saved this poor wretch
From life of blackest dreams.

But seal I now these words. I've overstay'd
And dry my eyes, for weeping's debt's past paid

I would she'd know that by her side I stay'd
As I hold fast to her, my only mayde
And set her harvest 'neath ever-rising stair
And keep her spirit safe from all life's care
For never in her life could it exult
Redeemed at last from all the world's tumult
As did mine on that morn my Blessed Love
Arrayed the wise-eyed cherubim above.

At the bottom of the final page, Helen had copied the writer's signature in wide, loose letters: *Alvaro HaLevy.*

Aaron lowered the pages. "She—"

A high, glad laugh escaped Helen. She almost sang the words. "She married him."

"I thought he . . ."

"Apparently he didn't. Apparently he made it home to England. And they lived a long life together, they did."

The Richmond traffic furled around the curb where they stood. He reread the ungainly lines, the signature. The answer had been awaiting all along. He'd been outsmarted by a three-hundred-year-old woman and her homosexual husband. "I don't understand half of what he says here." His voice was ranging wide with incredulity and he didn't care. "I don't get the last bit at all. But I get enough."

The foolish wonder on her face mirrored his. He was certain her voice quaked as she said, "I'm glad for them."

A strange gladness ballooned in him. He'd never in his life felt this way: as though the safe landing of another human being could substitute for his own. "Do you think the other papers he refers to are still in the house?"

"If they are, they're going to be upstairs. Did you reach Bridgette to tell her we're coming?"

Aaron hesitated. "I need to tell you something," he said.

She looked at him. "No," she said. "You don't." She let out a slow breath. "I'm not blind, you know. Though I do wonder about your judgment. Let me manage her."

"Yes," he said. "I think that would be best. Do you want me to stay away?"

She snorted. "Are you mad? This is yours too, Aaron Levy."

THE NEW GRASS WAS MANICURED, the re-graveled path leading visitors past a small tasteful plaque on one of the stone gateposts: Prospect House, the Eastons had named it. He'd missed that in the dusk on his last visit here. He had to admit, the Eastons were doing well by the place. He paused to take in the de-grimed windows, the newly cleaned stonework.

The front door was propped open. Inside, a pretty but painfully thin girl sat behind a small table, beyond which a few visitors drifted between the entryway's brightly colored canvases.

"They'll be back shortly," the girl was saying to Helen when Aaron entered.

"Do you know when?" pressed Helen, leaning on her cane.

The girl's smooth brow furrowed, the clash between her natural politeness and the need for discretion clearly painful for her. "Do you have an appointment?" she said.

"No," said Helen, "but we've worked together before."

"I see," said the girl, looking from Helen to Aaron, and back to Helen's cane. "Would you like to see the gallery while you wait? I can set up a chair for you wherever you like."

"We'll wait outside, thank you."

He trailed Helen out of the vestibule, resisting the urge to suggest to her that they go upstairs to begin exploration without the Eastons' permission.

Outside, by the pebbled path, there was a low stone bench beneath a tidily pruned tree. He waited for Helen to sit first, her cane wobbling as she lowered her weight.

They watched the street, where a single car was parked. Nothing moved. After several minutes, a second car trundled by. The street returned to silence.

"What?" she said.

"What do you mean?"

"I mean, what's *this*?" she waved her hand, a gesture encompassing his slouched posture.

Nearby, a pigeon promenaded slowly across the lawn. It reached the edge of the grass, then flapped away abruptly.

"So no," he said, "I don't have a girlfriend. But I do have a problem." He rubbed his hand hard at the top of his head, as if doing so might judder something loose. "Or maybe it's not a problem. It depends what you think of babies." He puffed his cheeks, then blew out air. "Impending babies."

"Where?" she said.

He smirked at the dark pub barely visible across the street. "The usual place where they grow."

She waited.

"Israel," he said.

She let out a sound like some inner strut collapsing.

They watched the empty lawn.

"Go. You can't sort this out from here."

"She doesn't want me."

"Do you want her?"

"I don't know. I mean—maybe I do, but I've never spent even a full day with her. And honestly, I'm not sure a kid would want"—he gave a short laugh—"this." His gesture, following the same path as Helen's, traced his posture head to toe.

The pub across the street was opening. The proprietor unlocked the door, flipped the sign.

"Don't"—she bit her lip and held it. "Don't turn your back just because it terrifies you."

A long string of dim yellow lights flickered on behind the pub's windows. The windows to one side blossomed suddenly with steam, as though some unseen kitchen door had swung briefly open.

"I don't think I'm strong enough," Aaron said.

Slowly the steam faded from the pub's windows.

Helen was staring across the street as well. She said, "How do you think people get strong?"

A small silver car pulled up. Ian and Bridgette Easton got out—Ian first, with his blond hair and lightly lined, cheerful face, then Bridgette. A picture out of a magazine. Helen had risen and was making her way up the path when Ian saw her. His surprise turned quickly to an expression of dutiful solemnity—an overgrown schoolboy still endeavoring to prove himself worthy of a passing grade. At the sight of Helen, Bridgette's posture tightened. She turned instinctively to find Aaron, registered his presence, then let her gaze pass him over as though he were part of the bench he sat on.

The car door snapped shut and Bridgette strode over to Ian, who had bent to hear Helen's request. Hesitantly, Aaron joined them.

"Of course," Ian was saying. "But Bridgette will have to be the one to answer your questions, as I'm only stopping home for a moment. I'm eager to hear what you find, of course." He paused before continuing, apologetic. "The gallery *is* open to visitors. I know you'll understand about respecting the atmosphere of the place. Should any moving of furnishings be required, I'd ask that you wait."

"Naturally," Helen said. With a grateful nod, Ian gestured them through the door.

Bridgette passed Aaron with a quick step. She said something inaudible to the girl at the front table, who sat up straighter in her seat—then disappeared into a doorway. Indicating with a wave that Helen and Aaron were to make themselves at home, Ian followed.

Inside the large entryway, two women were making a slow circuit of the paintings lining the walls. Glancing at the nearest canvas—an abstraction in shades of red—Helen made a small, disapproving noise, then led Aaron to the staircase, which she began laboriously to climb.

He didn't think he could force himself to take the staircase at Helen's pace. Hanging back to allow her to proceed unrushed, he trained his gaze on the artwork, pretending to take it in.

From a room to the left of the stairs, voices.

"All they need is access to the junk rooms and possibly one or two others," Ian was saying.

"Yes, and to make a wreck of the day for me, and—"

Ian's voice rose. "I can't discuss this further now. I have to be to my meeting in fifteen minutes." There was the briefest of pauses, as though Ian's own words were a surprise to him. "But given how persuasively you argued for putting our resources into hosting the public, rather than prioritizing any real private space in this house, I trust you can manage to be hospitable to my former professor."

Bridgette let out a huff of indignation. Then, without warning, she strode out the doorway, stopping short at the sight of Aaron. He forced his expression blank, but there was no denying he'd heard. For an instant, Bridgette teetered before him, as though unsure what role she wanted him to play in her drama. A startling melancholy flitted on her face. Then she swept past Aaron and disappeared through a doorway on the far side of the entry.

Helen had reached the upper gallery. Aaron followed, climbing the shallow steps as though into a thinner atmosphere, his heart accelerating. A guard of carved angels lined his ascent; he reached here and there to touch their faces.

The air on the third floor felt cool and sharp. On the balcony to Aaron's left stood an old man staring at a painting of an enormous tilted apple, and a white-haired woman nodding her head in front of a small brown landscape. Choosing the balcony on the right, Aaron joined Helen near the end of the gallery. "Those will have been her rooms," she whispered, pointing to a closed door bearing another discreet sign: *Private Area*. "The other suite is even bigger, and would have belonged to the man of the house."

"Wait—*you've* been upstairs?"

A look of dark amusement crossed her face; but she dismissed the question with a shrug. She led him to the door, opened it, and entered. Glancing back, Aaron saw that the gallery visitors looked unperturbed, as if they assumed Helen and Aaron were part of the staff.

He followed her and shut the door behind him. Picking their way between boxes to cross the large, bright room, Helen's cane thudding unevenly, they made their way to a second door and into the bedchamber. Across that room, then, and through a third door into the closet.

A small, wood-paneled space with a single bright mullioned window in the far wall. Aaron joined Helen there. A tangle of vines shaded the window, but through them he could see, over neighboring rooftops, the slow gray shimmer of the Thames.

"Help me," said Helen. And she lowered her cane to the floor, braced herself with surreal slowness against one of the boxes, and began to push.

He caught her just as she lost balance. Her weight was less than he expected, her body somehow hollow under the padded shoulders of her blazer.

He helped her to a crate, where she sat beneath the patterned light from the window and wordlessly waved him on. Then he knelt and put his shoulder to the boxes, sliding them easily away from the wall. Two boxes, three, four.

There, set in the lowest row of panels, was a small round keyhole.

Helen's heavy breath came from right behind his ear.

"Open it," she said.

He cast about for a moment, hoping for a tool better suited to the task, but when nothing offered itself he pulled his army knife from his pocket, and unfolded it. "This'll splinter the wood," he whispered. "Shouldn't we ask Bridgette's permission?"

"Are you joking?" Helen shot back. "We'll ask her forgiveness. Ian's, actually."

He jimmied the narrowest blade into the hole, gingerly at first. No luck. It would require force. He could feel Helen watching him. As he worked, small chips spat from the brittle wood. The panel splintered loudly once, then again, a visible crack opening this time; two small spars broke from the surface, one piercing the skin of Aaron's wrist. But he'd gotten the blade through to some inner mechanism, and he worked it blindly until the hidden catch gave.

It took a few tries to slide the panel—it kept sticking; the wooden groove it was meant to slide on was either obstructed or warped. Finally the opening was wide enough. Aaron reached blindly into the space.

His palm swept a dry wooden floor about eighteen inches deep— then his fingers jammed against the cupboard's back panel. Seated on the floor with his body turned sideways, he plunged shoulder-deep into the narrow opening so as to reach the far corners. Carefully he slid his hand around the space.

The floor was bare. Had this panel, unlike the other, been discovered and emptied some time during the house's long history? But wouldn't there have been a record of the documents' discovery?

Not if they'd been found by the 1698 owners. A stranger's three-centuries-old leavings might be expected to have value, yes—but ten-year-old documents were mere trash.

He swept the space again, this time climbing the panel's back wall with his hand. His fingertips found an edge. Pressing himself as deeply into the space as he could, he felt its outlines. His fingers traced a rectangle—a thin item laid flush against the far panel, made of some material more resilient than the wood. Leather? He pulled at the upper edge, expecting it to refuse him: the wrong knight attempting to pull the sword from the stone. But it tipped forward easily into his hand.

He angled it out of the compartment—a slim, stiff leather folio, brown and dry and finely cracked in places. Cradling it carefully, he slumped back against a box, his body quaking as though he'd just run a marathon.

Helen was at his shoulder. He stood, then settled beside her on a box so their shoulders touched. Laying the folio gently across his knees and hers, he opened it. Inside, forty or more loose sheets of unmatched paper. The handwriting varied, as did the languages. English and Latin, one in French, the next in Dutch. Carefully Aaron turned the sheets. There was some ghosting where one document had lain against another, and one of the letters had halos of rich brown burn-through, but the paper was intact.

With a wavering hand, Helen took a page of Latin. Slowly she turned it over, adjusted her glasses, and brought it to her eyes. After a moment Aaron laid a hand on hers to steady it. She started at the touch, then nodded. They held the page together as she read, and after a moment he heard her breathe a faint, stunned "Oh." But before he could ask why, a sound that had registered only on the periphery of his senses cohered into the approaching rap of heels on the floor, and Bridgette was swinging wide the door of the closet.

In one triumphant glance she took in the army knife lying on the floor, the splintered wall panel, the dark gaping space behind it. Moving between boxes with shocking speed, she seized the folio from their knees, whipping the page from between Helen's fingers with a flick of her wrist.

"That's fragile!" Aaron said.

Ignoring him, she slapped the loose page back into the folio and turned on Helen. "What the hell do you think you're doing?"

"I understand your concern," said Helen. She spoke in the steady tones of a professor calming an overwrought student—but Aaron felt her knee tremble against his. "Our plan," continued Helen, "has been to come find you to discuss these documents once we retrieved them. But I'll confess I don't move as quickly as I once did. And, naturally, we needed to check the documents so as to be able to tell you whether what we'd found was more seventeenth-century paper, or simply a cache of fifty-year-old Vespa Girl calendars."

"That"—Bridgette pointed at the wall—"is destruction of property, do you realize that? That's in fact a crime."

He couldn't but admire Helen's outward calm as she continued speaking. "Our visit here is purely scholarly. If, in our enthusiasm, we've misstepped, you have my apology. And I can assure you that Mr. Levy is acting here only upon my direction, and the responsibility for our doings here lies with me." Helen raised her head to look directly at Bridgette, and the shadows from the mullioned window sectioned the weathered planes of her face. "As you can see," she said quietly, spreading both hands before her and raising them toward Bridgette, "I require some assistance."

For an instant, Bridgette looked mesmerized. But Aaron wrenched his gaze from Helen's quaking hands to her face. Some safety catch within her had been released. He no longer felt certain of what she would or wouldn't do.

Bridgette blinked. "Get out," she said.

Slowly, Helen stood. Aaron resisted the urge to help her. He could see that Helen wanted Bridgette to notice her frailty. "I do apologize for disturbing you," she said. "I'll certainly pay to repair the panel. And" —casually, as though it were an afterthought—"I'd like to offer to buy that folio of papers from you."

"No, thank you," Bridgette enunciated. "I understand Sotheby's is paying rather well these days."

"Of course. Only, as you know now through exasperating experience, that brings in unnecessary formalities and delays. Perhaps we shan't need to involve Sotheby's this time, or the university. I can certainly imagine you'd be out of patience with our prolonged scholarly processes."

"I'll tolerate scholarly processes for ten thousand pounds."

Aaron knew he should remain silent, but couldn't help himself. "Ten thousand for just a few pages? The other collection was one hundred and seventy-three separate documents. This might be forty."

But Helen was speaking over him. "*I'll* pay you ten thousand."

Bridgette laughed aloud. "You mean your department will? But this time I've a mind to double the fee. I didn't much like how your Jonathan Martin treated us last time. He's a smarmy bastard, that one."

Leaning heavily on her cane, Helen raised her head. "All right. Double it. I'll pay it myself. We're not going to involve the department this time."

Until this moment, he'd assumed Helen was bluffing.

"You'll pay me twenty thousand for a few dozen sheets of paper?" Bridgette weighed the folio in her hands. "What is this, original Shakespeare?"

"Hardly," said Helen coolly. "But it happens to fit within my area of expertise. I am about to retire, and I've no children and no heirs, and so I can do whatever rot I wish with my hard-earned money. And as my parting shot, I would like to publish something about those documents you're currently holding in your hands. It so happens that I've been treated with somewhat less respect by my colleagues than I feel my talents merit, and I would very much like to right that impression." She leveled a stare at Bridgette. "Given your own experience of Jonathan Martin, I imagine you can understand my wish to go out, as they say, with a bang?"

Bridgette snorted, but Aaron saw that she'd softened her grip on the folder.

"I'll go to get a bank check, then." Helen started for the door.

"What, right this minute?"

Bridgette stood in the only clear path across the closet, blocking Helen's way. Slowly Helen walked forward, leaning hard on her cane. She didn't stop until the two women stood mere inches apart. "Yes," Helen said quietly. "I'm not getting any younger. Are you?"

Bridgette flinched.

"There's a branch of Barclays down the hill," she said drily. She stepped backward a few paces, and watched Helen make her way out of the room.

For an instant Bridgette didn't seem to have registered that she was alone in the room with Aaron. But when she did, he knew he'd catch it for witnessing her knocked off balance. He stood. "Excuse me," he said.

She looked at him, suddenly ferocious. "With pleasure."

Helen was moving with more speed than he'd thought her capable of. Calling her name, he caught up with her in the outer chamber, and when she didn't slow he grabbed her bony elbow.

She turned on him. "This is not the time, Aaron Levy."

"Stop," he said. "Just stop a second. That's a huge amount of money."

"It's a bargain, for those documents."

"Why?"

She shook her head. "Stay with Bridgette. Don't let her make any phone calls. Try not to let her look at the documents."

"If they're that valuable, don't you think the university might buy them for us?"

She tried to shake her elbow free, but he gripped tighter, and wrapped her forearm under his. An unreasoning panic was rising in him—it was becoming a part of his life, this inability to control anything he cared about. "Where's that money coming from?" he asked her.

She spoke as though addressing a half-wit. "My retirement savings."

"I hardly think that's a sound choice," he said. "You're going to need that money to live on."

She seemed on the verge of laughter. "Don't think I'm not touched by your protectiveness, Mr. Levy. But do you know whose signature was on that letter in the folio?"

He shook his head.

She let out a long breath before saying, weakly, "Spinoza."

His grip softened. "Holy shit."

"Spinoza might disagree with the holiness part." An expression of barely contained incredulity had bloomed on her face. "But yes, Aaron. Ester Velasquez got him to answer." She shook her arm free, and this time he let her. "Stay with Bridgette."

He watched her disappear down the staircase.

Across the gallery, on the wall opposite him, hung a painting of a phallic tower thrusting out of what looked like a field of cotton-candy trees. A young couple stood before it, nodding approval—so eager, Aaron thought, to be shocked. Even as the house around them vibrated with a secret far more radical than any painting on its walls.

He'd once believed in a plain, patent world, in which whatever was noteworthy cried out proudly for attention. Now he saw how readily the most essential things went unseen.

He found Bridgette in the bedchamber, shuffling the pages. Seeing him, she snapped the folio shut. "I can't make out this bloody writing," she said.

"The style is called secretary hand," he offered.

"I don't give fuck-all what it's called, what the hell is in here that's so important to her?"

Her vulgarity told him that whatever veneer of polish she'd worn would now be dropped. He saw too that Bridgette was nearing the crest of some long-brewing storm that, he suddenly felt, had little to do with him . . . or with Helen, or even the documents, but rather with whatever private world Bridgette inhabited: a separate universe brushing his, but with the power to rip apart the culmination of all he'd labored for these past months.

And all that Helen had left.

He couldn't have said who deserved those papers Bridgette was holding, except that he knew it wasn't him. But he wanted them for Helen, because she wanted them.

"Who the *fuck* is Thomas Farrow?" Bridgette spat.

How much had she seen?

He spoke carefully: he'd tell the truth—just not all of it. "Farrow was an out-of-work actor. He wrote letters to philosophers. Mostly he ticked them off."

"Letters worth twenty thousand quid?"

"I have no idea what they're worth," he said. "The only way to know is to have them evaluated. But that brings in outsiders. And"—he added honestly—"I don't think Professor Watt's offer will stick around if you do that."

"Well," said Bridgette, "as for that, isn't there someone at the bank whose role is to prevent old bats from taking out all their savings at one grab, because some guru has offered them a séance with their dead Pekingese"—she chuckled—"or maybe because they're bitter and want to get revenge on people they've worked with?"

He knew better than to respond to Bridgette's jeering. Instead he formed a smile. "A banker might not dare stand in Helen's way," he said. "She can be a bit intimidating, if you hadn't noticed. I suspect you're in luck, if the twenty thousand appeals to you. I don't think anything short of a patrimony law will stop her from buying those documents if you're willing—and patrimony laws take years to enforce."

"I don't imagine she cares much what happens next year. Frankly, she doesn't look as though she's got too many more *hours* in her."

He heard his voice rise. "That's not true."

"You ought to call your Jonathan Martin. He'll love you forever for helping him snatch these papers from Helen. And so long as they pay me twenty-*one* thousand or so, I don't mind waiting a few days. Keeping this just a bit longer isn't going to cause me any trouble."

She patted the folio, snugged now against her slender waist—and with a pang Aaron thought of Marisa. In his utter stupidity, he realized, he hadn't yet changed the picture of her he held in his mind. It came to him now how Marisa must look: the curve of her belly like a taut half-moon, her keen gray-green eyes crinkled at the edges with laughter and strain, her strong back bowed against the weight. Her feet, shoeless, resting on a pillow at day's end. He imagined her like a goddess of certainty, and his own unchanged body seemed pitiful in comparison. He was grateful she couldn't see him here, obfuscating, in a building whose very walls were more soulful than he'd ever be.

Even as he thought this, Bridgette let out a soft laugh. Startled, he looked up to find her eyeing him with an unmistakably flirtatious expression. "Or maybe," she said, "that's going about it all wrong. Maybe *we* should evaluate the documents."

The wind had shifted, and he had no idea why. She raised the folio, weighed it softly in the air, as though daring him.

He was at a loss as to what kind of game Bridgette was playing.

"You and I don't have to be cowed by Helen's type, do we?" she said.

His mouth was dry. But this was no time for him to forget how to play the game. "Careful, now," he said lightly.

"Why?" Bridgette countered coyly, but she stopped waving the folio. "You're afraid I'll damage *Helen Watt's* papers?"

It was the way she pronounced the name—each syllable a slash of fury. Aaron understood that he wasn't the focus of Bridgette's interest after all. Something about *Helen* had stung Bridgette—and Bridgette wasn't going to rest until she'd repudiated it. Flirting was merely Bridgette's way of getting things done.

Opening the folio, Bridgette made a show of choosing between several pages, peeled out one with a flourish, and passed it to him.

He accepted it casually, with a smile that hurt.

The letter was addressed to Thomas Farrow, and signed Isaac Vossius. A man, if Aaron was remembering right, known in Europe for his large personal library. Vossius seemed to be responding to a query about several texts — the letter was written in Latin in a cramped hand, and Aaron struggled to make out the titles. A find, yes, but nothing on the level of Spinoza. It might show some later development of Ester's interests, though.

"So was she right?" Bridgette prompted. "Is this some rare discovery?" She leaned over Aaron's shoulder, her bright hair brushing the side of his neck.

He shrugged. "It's a note from a man with a famous library, answering a question about some books."

"Fascinating," said Bridgette drily. She pulled another sheet from the folio and dangled it before him. "Bet you can't resist one more."

He produced an unconcerned laugh. "How about if we leave the research work for Helen?"

"Don't think you fool me," she lilted. "You know you want it." She tilted her head at him. "I'm referring to the papers, of course."

How had it ever felt natural, to dance this dance with this woman?

"You were all right, you know," she said.

"You were more than all right," he countered.

A brief, grateful smile broke on Bridgette's face — a smile that seemed, for an instant, genuine. He hated himself then as he'd never hated himself. Whatever sort of person Bridgette was, he was doing wrong against her right now by flirting to gain time.

She handed him the paper, but held on a moment before letting go. "You're sure you don't only think of me as *provenance*?"

He didn't answer. He dipped his eyes and scanned the Latin.

There, at the base of the letter, in the thick defiant script of a man whose beliefs had damned and sustained him, was the signature. *Benedictus de Spinoza.*

What he did next, he did for Helen. Because what did it matter if he no longer liked himself, if he could save this one thing for her? With difficulty he raised his heavy head, looked at Bridgette, and forced a shrug. He handed the paper back to her as if it were nothing. Letting his voice convey all the irritability he could muster, he said, "Let Helen spend her retirement money on these. I don't care anymore. She's been a regal bitch to me."

Bridgette took the page, but instead of looking at it, she gazed in the direction of the balcony. She seemed to be thinking.

"Are you going to leave Ian?" he said, surprising himself.

She turned. "What's it to you?"

"Nothing," he said simply. Only for some reason he couldn't explain, he wanted them to be truthful with each other. "I'm spoken for. I was just wondering."

She cut her eyes at him. "What makes you wonder?"

"Well, you taking me up to your bedroom, for one."

She laughed but said nothing.

"Should I assume you do that sort of thing often?"

"You certainly should not," she shot back. "Just because I flirt doesn't mean I go further."

He didn't believe her. Then, a heartbeat later, he did. "Sorry," he said.

"I made an exception for you." Her voice was fierce—but it was something in herself, not in him, that she was trying to govern.

"Why?"

"I was curious."

"Bullshit," he said.

"What, you don't think there's anything intriguing about a stranger who comes to my house to exhume some history no one else cares about?"

"No, actually I don't."

"Well," she said, "you're right. There's nothing so special about you."

He let his gaze fall on several canvases propped against a wall—more of Bridgette's art, wrapped in a clear plastic packing material thick enough to render the bold images impressionistic. He stared at the vague forms: hints and evocations, shimmering with the possibility of some elusive wisdom beyond what might be visible in the ordinary light of day. He liked them that way. "You know," he said quietly, "pissed-off women have been telling me that for a long time. It's finally sunk in."

When he looked up, Bridgette's face wore a scrim of confusion, as though she'd been counting on him to be someone more mockable.

"The thing about you," she said, "is that you're so damned focused on history." She toed a box. "You love it." It was an accusation.

"So what if I do? I mean . . . you love art, right?"

"No," Bridgette said. "I like art."

She set her foot on a wooden crate in front of her. Slowly, she leaned forward. The crate slid against the floor with a scraping sound, which seemed to satisfy her.

"I took a drawing class, once. And some art history classes. And I have *taste*," she said. "Which mainly means I'm good at figuring what will sell. And I have some money too, don't I? But it's rather disappointing, isn't it, not to be more impassioned than that?" She'd tried for irony, but her voice was hoarse. "You should be proud, you know. My ridiculous aunt would have approved of the way you and Helen Watt are about history."

He watched Bridgette lift her foot off the crate, then set it on another — then hesitate.

"Ian and I don't love anything that way," she said. "Or at least I don't. Ian might love *me* that way." She grimaced, then added, "At least, he used to."

This time she shoved the crate long and loud. Then she squared herself, and faced him.

"If everybody thinks I'm soulless, then I might as well act the part, shouldn't I? Sell the documents to the most craven collector I can find, one who'll lock the papers away from historians. And then I'll use the windfall to fund my fondest wishes."

"Like what?" Aaron asked.

"Like," she said, "a new bloody kitchen." She laughed sharply — then rested the weight of her gaze on Aaron. "That's what Ian wanted. But I said we had to use the full renovation budget for the gallery's public spaces. I won the argument, as usual."

From beyond the door, the sound of visitors shuffling patiently along the balcony.

"I'm going to be a father," Aaron said.

Bridgette let out a hoot. For a moment, she stared. On her face a faint, wistful glimmer. "The poor kid."

He nodded.

After a moment, she hooted again.

It was clear to him, suddenly, that he wanted no power over Bridgette Easton. Over anyone. He no longer trusted himself with it.

I'm sorry. He sent the words silently to Helen, whom he'd failed.

"Bridgette," he said. "These letters? They aren't like the—"

"Of course they're not like the other ones," she snapped. "I'm not stupid, you know. And you're a terrible actor. If she wants them that badly, there's something different about them."

"Different," he said, "is possibly an understatement. I have to tell you something. There's at least one piece of paper in there signed by Spinoza."

Bridgette's brows rose. Then he watched her pretend not to be impressed. "Well," she said, studying her nails. "Twenty is enough for Ian's kitchen."

"That folio you're holding," Aaron felt compelled to press on, "might well be worth more than that."

Bridgette raised her chin. "Don't discuss money with the English. It's uncouth."

Aaron shook his head. Then shook it again.

Bridgette was enjoying his incredulity. He let her stare him down.

"Is there anything I can do for you?" he said after a moment.

"Other than getting the hell out of my house?"

"Other than that."

He waited for her parting shot. But her expression had turned contemplative.

They walked out of the antechamber. The landing was filigreed, the sunset stretching from the windows in diamonds and rhombuses. Gold on the shoes of the elderly couple lingering over the artwork—gold on the backs of their shoulders, on their hair, gentling the blatant braying art.

Surely the gallery had lights meant for this hour of the day, but Bridgette didn't move to turn them on. She stood beside Aaron on the landing while the art turned pale in the dusk, and together they watched Helen return: one hand clutching her cane, and in the other a trembling white envelope, her figure completing its slow ascent beneath the patient gaze of the cherubs.

THE DOOR OF PROSPERO'S SWUNG open to admit them, its smells of ale and pie crust and oiled wood filling Aaron's nose, and at just that moment the rain started: a swift hail of droplets like a hand at their backs, ushering them inside. The pub was snug and dry, their table warmly lit and bare as though prepared just for their purposes—and as Helen painstakingly wiped dust motes from the table, then removed each document from the folio and set it down with care, Aaron felt as though he were in some dream more real than reality, in which sounds were strangely magnified and every object backlit. The chairs creaked but held, and the amber pint cradled by the single customer at the bar was a chalice meant for some rite of solemn beauty, and the fact of Helen's quaking hands laying out documents before him one after another had been ordained before he was born—just as this impossibly perfect place had been waiting here for them all along, hidden across the road from the Eastons' gallery. The wizened bartender rubbing glasses peaceably with a white towel—the bartender with his impartial, half-shuttered eyes—was ancient Tiresias, who had foresuffered all; the bartender was Prospero himself—he'd broken his staff and relinquished his powers in order to make his peace with the ravishing world. And if only Aaron could understand how a man could live at peace with such a choice, or what it might wreak on him, then he too would have earned his place in this blessed circle that had sprung up so swiftly and magically around them.

Having arranged the first dozen letters on the thick wooden table beneath the mellow lamplight, Helen leaned back—and in an instant Aaron could see what she'd understood from the start. This folio held Ester's jewels. The other documents, the ones Alvaro HaLevy had hidden under the stair rather than burn, were the detritus—the long, arduous account of the road to these final ink-and-paper treasures. He and Helen had mistaken the earlier find for the real prize. But all along Ester had held back the best.

He read standing beside Helen's chair, beginning with the document farthest from them, making his way down each row. Ester's hand he read fluently; letters penned by unfamiliar hands required more care, yet each gave up its secrets. He read, in succession, letters from Thomas Farrow to a half dozen correspondents, each followed by the reply it had received and then Farrow's response—sometimes accepting his correspondent's arguments with brisk praise, sometimes rebutting, refining, challenging. *Yet how do you propose to reconcile such opposing views? Of this your reader remains in ignorance.* Sometimes Farrow's correspondent wrote back with his own rebuttal or clarification, and then more letters would be exchanged before the discussion was closed. Van den Enden. Adriaan Koerbagh. Thomas Browne. Aaron knew some of the names and others were unfamiliar, but in each case the precision and ferocity of Thomas Farrow's replies—sometimes through three or four exchanges —was breathtaking. He understood why Ester's correspondents were often prickly in their defense of their arguments—she gave no quarter to sloppy thinking, and mercilessly cut away false logic. But there were those whose replies indicated they'd recognized Farrow as a rare kind of friend. From Van den Enden:

> Your reasoning, which you build cunningly upon my own definition
> of piety, forces that definition to rebuke me, firming my resolve on
> a course I'd only half completed, this being the fullest incorporation
> of women in the citizenry of the ideal polity. Perhaps you know I've
> educated my daughters, though this be not greatly in fashion. Your
> proposal that I consider in theory the notion of a woman as a leader
> in a democratic body is a natural development of my own thoughts
> regarding universal education . . . one that would have presented itself
> in time but revealed itself more swiftly through your questioning, for
> which I offer my gratitude.

And, from one Jonathan Pierce,

> It pains me to understand from your last letter that your
> circumstances do not permit travel. May I suggest, honored friend,
> that it is to the benefit of a scholar to shake off other cares now and
> then to seek the company of like minds, and the solace this provides
> is also of benefit to the constitution. Should your health improve
> sufficiently to permit you to escape your seclusion, I promise the

fellowship of like minds will heal you further. Friendship is a physick all its own, and most especially to those such as we, who through the peculiar paths of our thinking must ever be lonely men. You would be welcomed here in London at the Royal Society, where I should be glad to acquaint you with many whose company fortifies mind and spirit.

And then—at Helen's direction Aaron carefully stacked these pages and laid out a second set on the table—the correspondence was no longer addressed to Thomas Farrow, but to one Bertram Clarke. And then, as the correspondence progressed through the 1670s and the 1680s, the letter writer was a William Harrington, and then an Owen Richards, and then, from 1688 to 1691, one James Goddard. But always the hand was Ester's, and the reasoning. *The highest principle is life, and this principle must therefore serve as the basis for all morality.* Aaron turned from one letter to another. Three exchanges with Pierre Bayle. *But can you be sincere in this elevation of faith,* Ester had written, *even as you declare it incompatible with reason? Or is it your aim to leave a trail you wish other thinkers to follow?* A letter to John Wilson that seemed to go unanswered: *I maintain that logic demands you reconsider your assault on* Philosophia S. Scripturae Interpres, *for the reasons I have here described.* And, to Aaron's astonishment, two exchanges with Thomas Hobbes. *If there exist no incorporeal substances, then this must unmake the world as it has been described to us. It is then the obligation of the philosophe to declare the world's true properties, for which reason I pose the following questions.*

The final set of letters Helen laid down was between Thomas Farrow and Benedict Spinoza. Scanning the pages, Aaron saw it had taken two letters from Thomas Farrow to goad Spinoza from hiding, and another three to elicit a first substantive response. The correspondence spanned years, starting and stopping for reasons that surely included the Anglo-Dutch and Franco-Dutch wars—yet whatever difficulties each had surmounted to send these pages of Latin between London and Voorburg were not belabored—as though the arduousness of life required no explanation, nor would it be permitted to further impinge on the urgent business of argument. Starting in the sixth letter, Farrow had pressed hard on a point of disagreement:

Yet despite your urging of the love of God you disdain the sensual.
You argue that man must attain equanimity and calmness. Yet a true
system of thought must not exclude passion but rather account for it
as the mathematician accounts for each component of his equation.
You argue as though human desire were error or blindness, rather
than an essential element within *Deus sive Natura:* a force always
in motion and questing. Without acknowledgment of this, your
universe lacks animating fire, therefore admire as I do the beauty of
your edifice I do not believe it.

Spinoza's reply to this was piercing. There were none of the niceties
of the other philosophers' letters, no *I have read your missive with interest.*

This argument is folly. You admix desire and passion in your reasoning as though these were the same, whereas passion is passive and
desire is merely the being's awareness of Conatus, a finite thing's
striving on behalf of its own existence. As for the passions, they are
a bog that snares the philosophical mind. Unless you would have a
morality rooted in baseness these must be subdued by reason, and
unless you would animate the universe with rageful trees or lusting
clouds and call yourself a pagan, you must concede that passion cannot be the essence of the universe.
      As for desire, it cannot be the essence of the universe because it is
bound to the consciousness of a finite being.

Yet Farrow, in a letter that likewise indulged in no niceties, was not
dissuaded.

I propose no dramas of tree and cloud or any such childish mysteries,
rather I speak of the impulse behind all life. Let us leave off discussion of passion, for there I accept your argument. Yet I must differ
regarding desire. There is nothing inert or impartial in the universe.
I mean by this not that rocks possess consciousness or that the earth
that opens and swallows a city is a ravening deity, or any such super-
stitious folly — rather that the impulse that acts through them is that
which I call God.

Spinoza's reply was still sharper:

What you speak of here is no more and no less than Conatus, which
already holds a place in my reasoning. Yet your arguments are ill
advised and I am not persuaded to carry the point to the regions to
which you take it.

Aaron read, and felt as though he were standing in a scouring wind,
two great forces buffeting each other over logical points he barely understood. He read, in Ester's hand,

Yet I maintain that while God cannot be attached to desire, God is
the storm that is the sum of all desires. Substance, in all its infinite
variety, is a manifestation of that storm, rather than the reverse.

The notion that man's actions might incur God's wrath or pleasure we both know to be absurd. A correct morality merely guides
desire toward that which does not violate the desires and needs of
others. When I speak of desire, further, I speak of much that is not
finite but infinite — or, to adopt the language of the theologians, holy.
I speak not of mere fleeting urges of the senses, but of deeper desire,
desire not only of body but of spirit. I speak of your love, and mine,
for truth. I speak of the impulse that bids us risk danger to pen these
letters. We do this not because we are rational seekers after our own
well-being — for we are not driven merely by Conatus. We do this
because we are creatures of desire.

You relate in your letter that in your labors on a compendium of
Hebrew grammar, you find that all Hebrew words have the force and
properties of nouns. Perhaps you will no longer be surprised to learn
that I myself know something of the Hebrew language. Yet it seems
to me, in truth, that it is the verb rather than the noun that commands the language.

In this perhaps lies the difference in our thinking.

To separate substance from impulse, our reasoned life from our
desires, is an error — one I regret though at times I have been forced
to it. Your reasoning being the purest and most capacious I have
encountered, surely you will not wish to allow such an error to taint
your philosophy.

And here, mid-paragraph, Thomas Farrow's letter switched from Latin to Portuguese.

You and I agree on much, I believe, despite our differences. And I feel we are in accord that, as Nature is one with God, the impulse toward life be of surpassing value. Therefore all imperatives that oppose it, chief among them martyrdom, are in error.

The teachers of the Amsterdam of your youth feared a God of scouring demands. Yet even should I shed my own name and existence, I shall not forget what I learned from those whose sacrifices I witnessed, and all the more strongly will I follow the sole God I know: a vast, blooming thing.

I have come now to understand that all that you have proposed, and perhaps all I believe as well, is not in fact atheism. It is, rather, something for which I do not yet have a word.

Spinoza's reply—the final letter in his hand—was addressed *To the Estimable and Insistent Mister Farrow.*

Like a child, Aaron had listened to them battle, and demur, demand clarification, and now, at last, settle into a spent silence. Reaching the final lines above Spinoza's last signature, Aaron was startled to see that these, too, were in Portuguese.

Therefore, although you and I do not and shall not agree, I will expand my language to address this argument, for which I send my appreciation. I will add that words you penned in your letter regarding the notion of kindness have returned to me of late, and I find much to recommend your thinking on this matter, which I hope to return to at some future time.

The ability to shed one's existence, Mister Farrow, is indeed a manner of freedom, and may bring comfort, in particular for those who have seen much. You are correct that the teachers of my Amsterdam knew a scouring God. This was true of even Rabbi HaCoen Mendes, for whom you and I share a regard, and whose test at the hands of the Inquisition was one of many stains upon humanity. I learned only lately of his death in London after years confined to his household. You, it seems, were one of few to converse with him in that span.

There were some fatal fires in Amsterdam, I recall. It is a consolation to imagine the survivors have found safe haven.

My text of *Tractatus Theologico-Politicus* now concluded, I labor in some whimsy on a treatise concerning the optics of rainbows. Yet it eludes me. Perhaps we who struggle much in darkness, as all thinkers must, may be forgiven for faltering at the contemplation of such a wondrous and unbounded thing as freeborn light.

Benedictus de Spinoza

Aaron looked up from the pages. Silently he took in the pub. The low scraping of a barstool; the rough grain of the tabletop under his palm. Each detail etched itself on his senses as though he'd never heard or felt such things in all his life, and every glint of glass from the barman's rack struck his eyes like glory. He understood why Helen sat with eyes closed, as though in meditation or prayer. On page after ink-damaged page, in documents meticulously restored and borne down to them by the Patricias, they'd witnessed Ester Velasquez starving in plain sight. Yet here, in the pages laid out on this wooden tabletop, that wild, insistent loneliness had at last been sated. Aaron could feel it in the thick ink of Ester's final letter to Spinoza, in Portuguese: *We understand one another well, and I shall now be content.* The words had been inked slowly, the quill shaping unusually broad lines on the page, as though each motion of the writer's hand had laid something to rest ... and all that remained in the wake of that final *now* was a satisfaction as heavy as sleep.

And though he knew it was folly to presume, it seemed to Aaron there was a fainter sigh of relief audible beneath the words of the famed philosopher. Spinoza: a man who'd tried, armed with only a placard and his outrage, to confront the mob that had ripped a tolerant leader limb from limb; a man well persuaded of the barbarism of humanity, yet still insisting, despite exile and already failing health, on the sanctity of the mind's cool reasoning ... Aaron couldn't escape the feeling that this man had, in these few pages of logical clashing, met something like a friend.

There was no further correspondence between them.

Standing in the soft light of the pub, Aaron murmured, "He figured it out."

Beside him, Helen nodded silently.

The letters he'd just read were an act of intimacy, and Aaron—in his cowardice, in his inability to make even the simplest answer to Marisa's e-mail—knew himself unworthy to have witnessed it. Yet it wasn't Ester, or even Spinoza, who now raised tears of gratitude in his eyes. It was Helen Watt. Her quaking hands, resting lightly on the tabletop, were the tenderest of sculptures, things of almost unendurable beauty. And he knew that he would never be able to tell her that he loved her as a foundering ship loves a lighthouse, even though the lighthouse is powerless to save it.

She opened her eyes and they looked at each other, and she offered him a weary smile. Then she turned back to the papers on the table.

It was as she leaned forward to reread that he saw there were a few pages still in the folio she held against her chest.

"What's that?" he said.

For just an instant, her eyes seemed to telegraph some sort of apology. She uttered an unintelligible syllable. She cleared her throat, then repeated the word. "Ash," she said.

"What do you mean?"

She spoke crisply now. "Iron gall ink." She drew herself back from the table, the folio to her breastbone. "Severe damage. These will need to go to the conservation lab before they're handled."

"Okay." He squinted at her, the bar's warm light suddenly inadequate for the task of interpreting the strange guardedness on her face. She hadn't been herself all day, he reminded himself. She was unwell. "Do you want me to take them to the Patricias for you? Maybe they'd agree to—you know—fix the pages up a bit, even if the university hasn't purchased them?"

She didn't speak.

"You look—" He hesitated. He said, "You look spent."

She smiled then, a small and rueful smile. "I'll see to it," she said. "Why don't you go home and get some rest."

He suspected it wasn't only pride that made Helen refuse his help. He'd never been able to fool Helen Watt, and no amount of bravado could now hide how utterly he'd lost himself. Surely Helen could see it —surely she could see he was too weak to shepherd even these papers back to wholeness. And suddenly, as though her words had the power of a spell, he felt how very tired he was. How heavily the air weighed on his shoulders. His head.

He didn't thank Helen, he didn't say *I'm grateful to you* or *You were right all along.* He gathered the documents one by one, and passed them to her, and with the bartender ushering them courteously to the door he accompanied Helen to the lamp-lit street and into the night, where they parted.

28

August 12, 1667
22 Av, 5427
Richmond, Surrey

A SOUND BEYOND THE WINDOW. A sharp, thin knocking. And again.

She looked up, noting as she did that the candle's light was unnecessary, for while she was reading the morning sun had strengthened, and now daylight flooded the panes and blanched half her writing table. Though such wastefulness would once have been unthinkable, she allowed herself a moment to enjoy the candle's wavering flame, pallid in the white sunlight—the waxy heat kissing the skin on the inside of her wrist as she reached past it and rested her palm on the cool lever of the window.

The knocking stopped, then resumed: a bird of some kind, one of the many river birds whose calls she woke to, mornings in her sun-struck chamber with her head on soft white linen. She'd lived in this house, in these rooms with their windows overlooking the slow bend of the Thames, almost two years, without knowing the names of those birds. Perhaps, she thought with a laugh, she would ask her husband. Yes. He'd know.

Yesterday's rain had passed, the mist had lifted off the hills, and something in their green had intensified in earnest. Even now, she thought, Richmond's seasons had the power to bewilder her. London had been no preparation for the English countryside—in that matter, John had been correct.

She raised the lever and pushed. The window swung open onto a day so vivid it scuttled thought. The sky was a vibrating blue she'd only recently have believed impossible. The brightness was almost more than her eyes could bear.

What a fool she was, to cry at a sky.

And how different from the sky beneath which she'd married—and how fitting, that they'd wed under an obscuring haze. But Benjamin HaLevy hadn't wished to delay the wedding a single day, despite the magistrate's insistence that the smoke was an ill portent to wed beneath. HaLevy had waited long enough, he said—for it had taken months for his letter to reach the ship in its port in the New World, and months to receive the captain's answer, and after that certain sums had to be paid in order to procure an impressed ship-hand's release. Indeed, each delay in the plan had seemed to raise in the old man a silent vexation, so Ester feared he might change his mind. But when at last the ocean had returned what he'd long ago tossed to it, Benjamin HaLevy insisted that the wedding proceed the very next afternoon. And so the preparations were made despite the dreadful smoke, and despite the grim faces of the London boatmen and their fleeing passengers—people who'd only recently reconciled with their city as the coals of its plague burned low, only to see the fates smite it with a conflagration such as none had ever seen. London was in cinders. The dome of St. Paul's had melted, people said; the lead ran streaming in the streets.

Yet in Richmond, the old man had presided over wedding preparations with a fury that cowed the household. The seamstress had pressed on with final adjustments on the silk wedding dress Benjamin HaLevy insisted upon, and throughout the morning the old man had checked on the progress of the work with an air of furious tension, as though each piercing of the woman's needle into the layers of fabric must now, after a long and unjust delay, piece together all that had been rent.

They faced each other for the first time in the great atrium of the house, beneath a canopy made of Benjamin HaLevy's prayer shawl and held aloft by HaLevy himself, his manservant, and two men mustered from the stables. The magistrate had been summoned to preside, though he spent most of the ceremony glancing anxiously back through a window toward the smoke slowly rolling from London. The ceremony was pronounced in Hebrew by a Jew even older than the master of the house, an ancient Italian, the sole learned Jew Benjamin HaLevy had been able to procure on short notice—for the letter announcing Alvaro

HaLevy's return had been delayed. In the end, the paper bearing the disembarkation date reached the doorstep only hours before the son himself: a lithe, nearly unrecognizable man with unruly dark curls, a weather-beaten face with a scar at the chin, a sun-kissed brow from his service aboard merchant vessels in far reaches of the sea, and fine lines of sorrow at the corners of his eyes.

A rim of fire stood on the dull horizon. Black smoke drifted amid the mossy trees beyond the windows, and the tinge of fire entered through the cracks of the closed windows. Any chink in the house, any door or window swung open for even a moment, seemed to admit ash, so that Ester's cream-colored dress was grayed by the time she finished making the seven circles around Alvaro HaLevy and stood opposite him beneath the canopy. She could feel the silt in her own hair—but it was the ash on Alvaro HaLevy's head that sowed the first bubble of laughter in her. Beneath his ash-grayed curls, his face took on a strange gravity, and it was a simple matter to imagine him in his dotage: the aged master of this manor ... with his devoted wife by his side? A joke to crown all jokes. The bubble rose in her chest, in her throat. She fought to quell it. Beneath the wedding canopy, Alvaro HaLevy was gazing at her with an uncomfortable, apologetic solemnity, which—to his own evident shock —cracked. Their laughter, escaping their closed lips, twice interrupted the old Jew from his recitation of the necessary words. Benjamin HaLevy shut his eyes as though in pain and did not open them until he had a daughter-in-law.

At last the old Jew closed his prayer book and coughed his disapproval in the thick air; the magistrate peered yet again out the window and then with an impatient gesture dipped quill in ink, and had Benjamin HaLevy spell for him the names of the groom and bride. Rivka, who'd stood shadowed at the side of the hall with a curious expression, as though she were watching the doings of animals in some exotic menagerie, now seemed to wake to something familiar. Swiftly she gestured Ester toward her new father-in-law. With a last glance to Alvaro, with his ashy hair and his eyes shining from their laughter, Ester formed her face into a more solemn expression and stepped toward Benjamin HaLevy. Was she to kiss him on his withered cheek? She did it, a quick deed with dry lips, and he appeared shocked, then grateful.

Only then did she glance down at the page where the magistrate had entered the marriage in the register—but where Alvaro's name should have been, the father had given the name *Manuel HaLevy*.

Benjamin HaLevy followed her gaze. Then his eyes rose to hers—a long stare that aimed for defiance but fell short; and she saw that the fire inside him had died with his elder son, and that he himself would soon follow.

"It should have been," he said, in a voice so quiet she almost pitied him.

She turned her body so that Alvaro wouldn't see the page on which his name had not been inked, and stepped back toward him. He smiled at her, hesitant again. More than a year at sea had trained the clumsiness out of him, but he still had the liquid gaze of a boy. How ancient she felt in comparison.

The thought must have flickered on her face, because Alvaro tilted his head. "You're not troubled by our arrangement?" he said.

She shook her head, incredulous.

"Is it him?" he whispered, indicating his father. His face tightened; the shadow of his long anguish passed over him. He did not attempt to hide it. But there was something else in him, too—she saw it—something that had formed in him during his exile, shaped out of the terror and wonder of his new life, nights watching the brave emptiness of the sea. "All the same," he said, "I think we can weather him. I'll help you if I can." He hesitated. "But there's something else troubling you. I see it."

How could one answer such a man, who said what he saw and didn't pretend the world was other than it was? She couldn't work out whether Alvaro was foolish or wise; whether she despised his innocence or admired it; whether she thought him the most soft-minded boy, or whether he'd grown into something different and altogether alien—a man unlike any she'd encountered. But at that moment she decided she would be as truthful with him as he was with her. "You," she said. And seeing her stern perplexity, he laughed.

Together they turned to Benjamin HaLevy: husband and wife. With a small sniff, HaLevy led the way to the meal he'd had the cooks prepare. It was a shadow of a real wedding feast, their forks clinking in the cavernous dining room, the magistrate working away dutifully at his plate, and only the old Italian Jew eating with zeal, consuming a startling quantity of food and drink. Benjamin HaLevy, for his part, set down his fork midway through the meal and stared at Ester, as though for a moment regretting the bargain he'd struck: that while he lived, he'd be seen after by a son and a daughter-in-law. She'd promised no heir to inherit the grand HaLevy house—she'd made clear that point. But there would be no shame on the HaLevy name while the old man lived. And he would die accompanied by kin, not only servants.

So he had. That winter following the marriage, the life had drained from the old man like water from a fissured vessel. He'd wanted death, Ester had known it, but now it came too fast, and daily she saw the dread on his face. One morning, finding him stilled beside the window at the turn of the grand stair, as though its vista of budding trees barred him from proceeding down to his meal, she'd said to him, "Death tarries and tarries, then speeds when we'd beg just another hour." And he'd turned his baleful wintry face on her as though he reviled her—then, something giving within him, nodded.

She read to him on his sickbed those final weeks from the only book he would hear—Usque's *Consolação às Tribulações de Israel*—its pages bright by the light of a fire he gazed at with a feverish hunger. "*Choradas que auemos jaa estas chagas . . . tempo he que busquemos o remedio e consolo pera todas ellos pois somos aquí vinos a ese fim o qual . . .*" She could not forgive the man, but she herself had been nursed back to health by Rivka when Rivka had reason to spurn her, and she knew now what it was to be tended by patient hands. She turned his bony body in bed when he could not turn himself, she moistened his lips with a wet cloth when he could not drink. She read to him, in a steady voice, words she did not believe. And on the day when she came to his rooms and found him staring mute at the frost on the panes of the window above his bed, tears threading slowly along the wrinkles on his pale cheeks, she summoned his son. Alvaro, who could no more withhold love than he could resist taking in each next breath, forgave his father in a rush of words the old man could only bat away with a circling, trembling hand—a veined, papery hand that pushed away and beckoned, pushed away and beckoned.

Alvaro stood over his father's bedside as the hand turned feeble and subsided.

So the house fell silent with mourning, and in that hush Alvaro at length turned from his father's deathbed, his face wet with tears he didn't bother to wipe away before the servants, his footsteps sounding thin on the polished floor as he passed from his father's bedchamber through the quiet rooms and halls of the great house, and became its master.

A knocking, a vibrating blue. Tears on her own cheeks.

The bird. She was crying because of a knocking bird. And a sky. And a feathery softness the bird and the sky made together in her chest —as if she might, with an effort no more arduous than a sigh, rise and reshape herself into something altogether new. Hadn't Rivka said as much this morning? She'd paused at the door, holding a stack of pressed and folded linens against her ample waist, and chided Ester. "You're not old enough to huddle here in the dark." Irritably, Ester had gestured in explanation at the thick book before her—though in truth, she'd been struggling to keep her mind on it. But Rivka continued. "London is past. You bargained for a different life. Why don't you live it?"

"Why don't *you*, then?" she'd retorted, heat spreading in her cheeks. She hadn't meant to speak sharply, but her heart had jumped in her chest at Rivka's question, her hands clenching the book as though her life depended on not easing her grip on it.

Rivka drew herself up with that pride she'd had about her lately, as she quietly but emphatically gave instructions to the household staff that was now hers to order. She said, "I am."

"As am I," retorted Ester, regretting her brusqueness even as she spoke. How strong, how admirable Rivka seemed to her now, as the older woman ticked her tongue against her teeth, then moved off on her rounds. All the sufferings they'd endured had left Rivka purified: a priestess of the house. Whereas even now, almost two years after their safe arrival, Ester felt as though she herself were poised midstep—one foot raised, uncertain, weary with the wish to set it down.

Pushing aside the book, she opened a drawer and retrieved the letter she'd begun writing. She hadn't yet decided to whom she'd send it. Perhaps this time she'd write a page that was only for herself. Perhaps, she thought restlessly, she'd write something unspeakable, and burn it in the fire.

She read what she'd inked earlier in the morning: *The universe is shaped by the desire for life. This is its only morality.*

She believed it, but something now troubled her.

She'd desired John, hadn't she? She'd gambled for his love. Yet in that first stunned season after the plague, when each passing day's silence affirmed that John had forgotten her, she hadn't pursued him. Perhaps if she had—if she'd shed pride, jettisoned all notion of the heart's freedom and reminded John of his debt to her—she might yet have persuaded him, roused his pity, sued for his reluctant love and won it. And if she had?

Had John asked aught of her, through words or simply through silence, she could no longer have refused him—even had he required her to extinguish her learning for the tending of house and children; even at the cost of becoming a spirit shuttered from thought. She'd never learned to measure out love: give so much, withhold so much. She'd known it even in London, when she threw down the gauntlet of her own body: *come with me in love*.

How bold she'd been. She could not regret it.

Nowhere in the known world, it seemed to her, could she live as she'd been created: at once a creature of body and of mind. It was a precept so universal as to seem a law of nature: one aspect of a woman's existence must dominate the other. And a woman like Ester must choose, always, between desires: between fealty to her own self, or to the lives she might bring forth and nurture.

Some months ago, she'd written to him at last. Alvaro, knowing nothing of what the name John Tilman might mean to her, had repeated to her a tale of a well-liked magistrate, married and settled in Coventry, to whom petitioners now flocked instead of to the father, for the son was the more merciful, even tolerating views that elsewhere incurred harsh punishments.

Her own letter had said but little: she hoped John was well. She wished him health and peace.

Ester, his reply had begun.

I am much gladdened to know you're well, for your wellness in this world matters greatly. I live now as a magistrate in Coventry. My father grows old and I ease his burdens from him, as is his due. My wife, Isabelle, is a good woman and much patient with the demands of my profession. We are blessed now with a child, a girl named Judith.

During my years in London I leaned as far as a man may lean

into a void of newness before he recalls his obligation to remain who
he is. I am not a bold man, Ester, except in my own wish to be so.

I do not forget my failures, or your courage that teaches me still,
and remains a standard against which I judge much, not least myself.

She'd read the letter until she knew it by heart, before setting it aside.
How fearsome a thing was love. She'd welcomed it, all the same.

She stared now at the words she'd already set to paper. Yes, the universe was driven by the desire for life. But the question remained . . .
whose?

Perhaps, it seemed now to Ester, the forcing of a woman's choice was
itself against nature.

She lifted her quill and wrote.

Yet sacrifice of the self is everywhere viewed as the highest calling,
and the more so for a woman, who must give every element of her
life to others. Kindness is at all times counseled to women, who are
called unnatural if not kind.

Yet how can a kindness that blights the life of even one—though
it benefit others—be called good? Is it in fact kindness to sever one-
self from one's own desires? Mustn't the imperative to protect all life
encompass—even for a woman—her own?

Then must we abandon our accustomed notion of a woman's
kindness, and forge a new one.

A light breeze from the window, and the candle's flame shrank to a
tiny globe, then vanished. A thin line of smoke rose, a perfectly straight
line. She watched it waver and break, and the sorrow of its dissipation
so gripped her that at the creak of a nearby floorboard she let out a cry.

Alvaro stood in the doorway, laughing. "Rebuke me then, will you?
When I've come to set you free?"

She said nothing, only crossed her hands primly over the even lines
of her writing. An old habit: hiding the page before her.

"Today," he sang softly.

"You've gone mad," she said, thinking as she said it that she almost
believed it.

"Please," he said. But seeing he wouldn't extract her so easily, he stepped deeper into the room to address her. "Tell me, what new invisible guests are we housing within these walls now? Thomas Farrow philosophizes no more, you've at last let the poor man die a decent death. Now who takes his place? Which of your invisible minions will be issuing letters from the HaLevy household this season?"

She couldn't help a small smile. "Bertram Clarke."

Alvaro, his white shirt open at the neck and tucked loosely into his breeches, was nearing her writing table, his amused expression deepening. Instinctively, she pulled the book over her half-written page. Her hand closed, protective, on the ink bottle.

He sat on her writing table. "Shan't we make him Sir Bertram?" he whispered, looking grave. "He might secure a more rapid reply."

She moved as though to shoo him off—but Alvaro's eyes were, ever, a pup's. "Perhaps," she whispered. "If he earns it."

Alvaro laughed. Then his gaze rose to her window: a reflex. She knew who he looked for, of course—she was as familiar with the comings and goings of his visitor as he was with the phantom philosophers under whose names she wrote—her *spirits of the air*, as Alvaro called them.

How painful it had been to begin telling the truth. The morning when she'd first confessed to Alvaro, her jaw had clenched so she could barely speak. Lying had become her clothing—without it she'd freeze.

Yet she'd decided that this new life must be birthed without lies. Rivka knew the truth—and Alvaro must as well. Nakedness was the least of all she owed him.

He'd surprised her with the delight with which he'd received her confession—his bemused *This explains matters!* so genuine she'd let go her grip on the armrest of her chair and breathed what felt like the first breath she'd drawn in years. Indeed, he'd so startled her with his happy exclamations over her halting account of her correspondences that she didn't know whether to disapprove—for didn't he understand the wrong she'd done to the rabbi? Shouldn't he despise her?

Yet though he turned obediently solemn at her insistence that he see what she was, he neither condemned her nor made any suggestion that she cease her writing. The possibility did not seem to occur to him.

It took her months after their wedding to understand what so captivated her about Alvaro: she felt unafraid of him. It was such an unaccustomed feeling that for a time she wondered whether this lack of fear might be love. She doubted that her heart was capable of new love. Yet in the absence of any demand that she be other than what she was, something small and insistent flowered within her—so that once, in a feverish hunger in the first spring of their marriage, she touched his sleeve, then led him to his rooms. It was their sole experiment with being man and wife: an awkwardness of laces and buttons, a rushed disrobing as though they both feared losing nerve, a wave that washed them onto his bed and left them marooned there . . . at length dissolving into fits of laughter that shook first his frame, then hers, then the bed they lay upon, so that a servant called from outside the door in a voice taut with concern, which quickly turned surly when the master of the house refused to open the door. This was their love: her naked chest shaking with laughter until tears slid down her temples, and then —as she lay beneath his bright window with his arm across her belly —into her ears, so the sounds of her heartbeat, and his, and the quiet household shifting all around them, made a sunwashed, underwater blur. For a moment, lying absurdly with her husband, the light and the tears making diamonds across her vision, it seemed to her these must be the sounds heard by a babe carried by its mother.

It was Alvaro who made arrangements for the printing of Rabbi Moseh HaCoen Mendes's *Seven Arguments Against a False Messiah,* and who himself went to London to carry the manuscript to the printer. She'd spent weeks redacting the rabbi's letters to his pupil in Florence into a single condensed argument. Where she'd thought the rabbi's arguments weak, she'd subtly strengthened and clarified them, so that when she finally ordered the pages and sent them with Alvaro, it seemed to her that no other denunciation of Sabbatai Zevi and the Sabbateans had so rigorously pointed out the follies of their arguments. The recent news of Sabbatai Zevi's arrest and conversion to Islam had not yet dissuaded his followers. The rabbi's words, she was certain, were still needed. It seemed to her that, were he able to overlook the identity of their editor, he might have been pleased.

She'd hesitated over the dedication, but on this matter alone Alvaro had been insistent. "Make it for my father," he'd said firmly. So she had inked the name onto the front page, followed by the words Alvaro dictated to her: *Benjamin HaLevy, a man with a heart heavy and brimming with love for his people.* She thought the words a desecration. But Alvaro had taken the manuscript from her hands with a determined nod. "This book is your atonement to someone you had to wound," he said. His gaze slid to one side of her. "The dedication is mine."

She wished to tell him there was no comparison between her need to atone and his, nor between the gentleness of Rabbi HaCoen Mendes and the stone-heartedness of Benjamin HaLevy. Hadn't HaLevy sent his son to be entombed in the sea? Hadn't all expected rosy-cheeked, faltering Alvaro to die the very week he sailed—impressed to a ship at the hand of his own father?

Unlike Alvaro, Ester had wronged a flawless man—and the wrong she'd done was of the deepest nature. For much though her deceit haunted her, there was a far greater sin she'd committed against the rabbi. She, Ester Velasquez, had taken the rabbi's teachings and his trust —she'd taken all his labors to show her how to use her own intelligence —and she'd employed these to prove that there could be no God who would prize martyrdom. The meaning of this was inescapable—and she knew the rabbi had understood it all too well. For when she proved that there was no God who could treasure martyrdom, then she proved, too, that Moseh HaCoen Mendes had walked through the world sightless, and his mother had offered up her body to be broken, for naught.

It was this that she could never forgive herself.

But she saw that Alvaro understood none of this—and that he was set on paying tribute to a noble father who had never existed, and that guilt still weighted him. So she allowed him to go to London and hand the pages to the printer with an inscription that was a lie, that it might lessen that weight. And they'd spoken of the matter no further.

She'd learned of Thomas Farrow's death in a riding accident a half year after it had occurred. Though she'd been writing under his name for months without knowing he was dead, once aware of his death Ester found herself unwilling to sign his name, using it only wincingly to an-swer those correspondences already set in motion. Her own fastidious-ness stymied her—she'd thought herself heartless when seated at her desk, long since numbed to sentiment.

Yet now London was in ruins. The synagogue, located in that sliver of city spared the flames, had survived. So too had the da Costa Mendes home, only recently reappointed by Mary's father and his heavily pregnant wife—a lady described by Rivka as young, and lovely, and unafraid to weep openly over Mary's fate while, with her very own hands, she helped Rivka retrieve those books left unmolested by plunderers. But the rest of the city that Ester had known—narrow Milk Street, Gracechurch and Thames Streets, Fishmongers' Hall, the binderies and the booksellers' tables outside Saint Paul's, and the thatch-roofed warren tipping down toward the bridge ... ash.

Some things deserved entombment. So she'd laid Thomas Farrow to rest—and after sitting at her table a long time, the ink drying on her suspended quill, she had dipped it again, and conceived Bertram Clarke.

These past months, Clarke had written a series of letters to Johannes Koerbagh, and he would author the next missive she was planning, to one Matthew Collins, whose recent essay on theology and social order had troubled her. After Clarke had lived his useful life, there would perhaps be another. A small school of philosophers, all claiming to be temporary guests at this address in Richmond, their views all cohering around the same beliefs ... their reasoned arguments floating ownerless from her window like the seeds of dandelions, journeying she knew not how far.

Alvaro had wished, of course, that she break her isolation. He'd taken her once to a London coffeehouse famed for attracting philosophes. There she'd cradled her cold tankard of bitter liquid for hours, listening to the small sparks of light generated by some speakers, and to the foolery of others. But the few women who essayed to enter the conversation pained her, for they spoke rarely, and seemed so conscious of their own figures and attire that they arrayed themselves artfully in their seats as they spoke, mingling coquetry with hurried bursts of talk—and she saw, for all this, that they were not heeded as the men were, and that their ideas ventured only into the terrain of women's concerns, and even there were diffident. Nonetheless she rose twice, leaving Alvaro dozing gently against the wall, to attempt speech with these other women. Yet she was not dressed in fashion as they were, and they seemed to think her strange. She could not fault them; had a creature ever approached her in such hunger as she approached them, she too might have balked. Finally, leaning forward in her seat and straining to be heard above the men's joustings, she herself essayed to enter her voice into a debate about the ideal political order—but when she'd finished her short speech, her lingering *Yet is that not the sum and purpose of man?* was answered with a gaping silence, and then a few uneasy laughs.

When she'd woken Alvaro to go, she'd thanked him. *Did you learn anything?* he'd asked as they stepped from the overheated coffeehouse into the cool, enveloping evening. *Yes,* she'd said, *I heard some new thinking and will consider it. Yet I learned too that I'm an ivy twined so long against a tower of strange design that I cannot now assume any other shape.* And Alvaro had taken her arm and said, *I understand.*

Yet now here he stood before her, insisting.

"Today!" Alvaro repeated. "I won't be put off anymore."

Again, that soft, lit-from-the-inside smile. He was the most maddening of men—or perhaps it was she who was maddening, for she could not hold steady in her estimation of him. He was a fool and she wanted him to leave her be. He was her friend, and she wanted him to stay in her room, with his smell of fresh air and his grass-stained shoes, and his collar loose at his throat—a brother who could be counted on to tease and forgive.

She spoke, her face stern. "Your cherub maker comes today?"

Alvaro's brows rose high and stayed there. "He's a master carver!"

She laughed in his face. "Who carved every last cherub in Petersham and Richmond."

Alvaro blushed. "His carvings are incomparable," he said. "Admit it."

She pretended to consider.

He pressed his case earnestly. "The king's residence at Windsor has invited him to carve three lintels. He's been asked to carve for the *French*. My father was fortunate to have him make the cherubs on our stair before his work was in so great demand as it is today."

She bit her lower lip, conquering a smile. "They're ..." She paused, watching him await her verdict. "They're agreeable."

Alvaro was still waiting.

And suddenly she could no longer be stern. "Yes, all right. *He's* agreeable as well," she said. "I'm sure."

His face broke into a broad smile.

"His name is Richard. And we've agreed there's no need to keep such

discreet distance when he visits. I've told him you understand." Alvaro
looked at her now, a request in his eyes. "Richard hopes to make the
acquaintance of the noble lady of the house."

She could not help the dark mood that enveloped her at these words.
Her eyes returned to the table before her. "This house has no noble lady,"
she said.

He said nothing for a moment, obedient to her mood. "Perhaps he'll
meet you another day, then?"

She lifted her head. She was too moved by his hopeful face to be
jealous of the earnest love written there. "Yes," she said. "Of course I'll
meet him."

He was smiling with such gratitude that she had to smile as well. His
eyes were bright. "No one but you knows of our love," he said.

She very much doubted if half the countryside around Richmond
and Petersham didn't know of their love—even Rivka couldn't quell
the servants' talk.

"To the river, then?" he said.

But she shook her head. Some obstinacy was pulling her back to
their earlier conversation. "You've a promise to make to me first."

"What promise?" His brow furrowed. Then he remembered. "Still
that?" he said, his surprise genuine. "But it's absurd."

She pressed her lips.

"No," he said. "I'd no more do it than break your arm. I'd no more do
it than"—he gestured, words failing. "I simply won't."

She couldn't allow his affection, or hers, to rule this moment. She
gave him her most severe look. "Promise."

He shook his head, stubborn.

His betrayal blinded her—what a fool she'd been to trust him. And
yet how could he not understand? She half stood from her desk, the
anger breaking in her voice. "Have I asked anything else of you?"

He shook his head, more slowly.

She steadied herself. She'd mulled the matter, and though she couldn't
separate the strands of her fears, she'd declared them sound nonetheless. She was a woman, and she'd written heresies. Even Spinoza and
Hobbes feared to make direct statement of their disbelief in God.

Yet after her death, as Alvaro argued, she'd have nothing to fear. Why
not allow him to preserve her papers, then?

Because her writings made a mockery of the rabbi's suffering.

But though she'd never forgive herself this, shouldn't she leave her writings intact so others might consider them? Wasn't the cruelty in the world, and not in her words?

She couldn't explain her choice, even to herself—no more than she could explain the terror she still felt at the most unexpected of moments: hands grabbing and tearing at her hair, her sex; diseased faces straining to spit in hers. She pressed on, speaking steadily as though the words cost her nothing. "I want you to burn my papers when I die. That's my request, and it's a simple one, and I won't rest until I've secured your promise."

He rose from her table. "Burn them yourself!" He strode toward the door.

A single thought took her: *Don't leave me alone in this room.*

As though hearing, he slowed, and stopped halfway through her bedchamber. After a moment, he returned to stand before her.

"I can't do it myself," she said. She gestured at the hearth. "I can't bear to. Not while I can still read and think and write."

He opened his palms, showing her he meant no harm. "I know you're"—he hesitated. Then continued firmly, "You've had to hide so very long."

Her anger had vanished, leaving her confused. She wagged her head slowly in apology, before realizing she ought to say it aloud. "I'm sorry."

"Ester," he said. "There's none left alive to be hurt by what you've done. Not the rabbi, not your family. *I* won't be unhappy if your work comes to light and stirs trouble. What might anyone do to harm you after your death?"

What, indeed? She was concentrating with all her strength on his words.

"What might they do?" he repeated.

She couldn't control her voice. "*Not listen,*" she said. "Because of what I am."

His hand was on her shoulder. He persisted. "So you'd have me burn your papers, and in doing so *ensure* they'll never listen?"

She hated to cry before him. Yet he, who idolized her strength, should see the truth: the small, weeping creature she was, beneath all.

He paused to let her gather herself. "You say it's enough that your ideas will be visible in the writings of others," he said softly. "But Ester, none will know they're *yours*." He waited a moment, then continued. "At the right time, the truth ought be known."

Slowly, she shook her head. "Let the truth be ash."

He stood for a moment. Then his long fingers loosened on her shoulder. After a moment, he nodded in something like defeat.

Yet when he raised his head and nodded again, squeezing her shoulder gently before letting go, there was something else in his manner. She wasn't certain it had been defeat, after all.

He'd reached the door between her closet and her bedchamber. With one hand he gripped the doorframe as though to swing himself through. "The river is calling," he said.

She stared at him. *Had* it been defeat? At length she nodded. "Thank you," she said.

He left. She settled back at her desk. The page before her was only just begun.

She'd finish it later. She stood now and, after a moment's uncertainty, opened the window wide to admit the fresh sounds of the river. Birdcalls, the hush of the moving current. The sun was stronger than she'd expected and she leaned out to feel it on her face, its warmth as shocking as laughter. Blue and blue and blue swam in her vision. A bright bewildering sky: a riddle she couldn't guess how to solve.

29

April 11, 2001
London

S HE'D KNOWN IMMEDIATELY THAT SHE needed to read it
alone. So she'd lied. When, laying out Ester's precious letters one
by one in that pub in Richmond, she'd reached the final pages in
the folio, her eyes had fallen on the date—*June 8, 1691. 11 Sivan of the
Hebrew year 5451*. The week before Ester's death. The writing was Ester's.
But even in the dim light of the pub, she'd been able to see that the familiar hand had been shaking.

Let me begin afresh. Perhaps, this time, to tell the truth.

Without a word to Aaron, she'd tucked the pages back into the folio. She'd told him, when he asked, that the paper was too damaged
—knowing even as she said the words that she ought to tell the truth
and permit him to make this last discovery with her. But wresting these
treasures from Bridgette, all the while knowing she herself no longer
possessed the stamina to study them in earnest—it had depleted her.
To read this final document with anyone else—even Aaron Levy—required more steel than she possessed.

So she was alone in her flat when she read it—first carefully setting
on the sideboard the letters they'd already studied together, then laying
out the remaining sheets one by one upon her small kitchen table. The
pages would not lie down peaceably, but rasped and buckled like living
things, several dropping to the floor. As she labored to pick them up,
they bent in her clumsy, pinching fingers, and she knew that in her refusal to accept help she was doing unforgivable damage. As she fought

to control the papers with her hopeless hands, the verse came to her. *Im eshkaheh Yerushalayim, eshkah yemini.*

If I forget thee, O Jerusalem, let my right hand lose its cunning.

She had devoted her life to remembering. And yet she'd failed. She had, somewhere across the years, forgotten what she'd once understood. What Ester Velasquez had understood. That desire was the only truth worth following.

She'd arrived at the end of her own life too stunned to make her own confession. Was it wrong to want Ester Velasquez's to speak for her?

She set the final piece of paper on her kitchen table and lowered herself into a chair. Whatever her flaws, she reminded herself, she was a woman without illusions, who faced what needed to be faced.

She sat under the steady light of the lamp, her feet in their bedroom slippers perched on the chair's rungs like a schoolgirl's. She traced an unsteady hand along the wavering lines, dropping caution and touching each word reverently, as though wet ink might yet rub off on the pads of her fingers.

She read.

> June 8, 1691
> 11 Sivan of the Hebrew year 5451
> Richmond, Surrey

Let me begin afresh. Perhaps, this time, to tell the truth. For in the biting hush of ink on paper, where truth ought raise its head and speak without fear, I have long lied.

I have naught to defend my actions. Yet though my heart feels no remorse, my deeds would confess themselves to paper now, as the least of tributes to him whom I once betrayed.

In this silenced house, quill and ink do not resist the press of my hand, and paper does not flinch. Let these pages compass, at last, the truth, though none read them.

My name is Ester Velasquez. I have lived fifty-four years and linger now at death's threshold, life being tethered to body now by mere filaments. My death calls and I answer, and through pain make confession, though it shall not satisfy the formula prescribed by my people. Yet I wish now to shed the secrecy that has been salvation and millstone.

Let each forbidden truth speak once its own name.

My husband and his beloved are silver-haired with the long years of their love—the love of two men which I have witnessed with envy and wonder, for love is not my fate. Of them I ask forgiveness for only the daily unthinking sins of life, for they and I have not wronged but saved one another, and with them my conscience is easiest.

Seeing the depth of my illness, this household has silenced itself. All about me it braces to mourn, though my hand moves on the page still.

In the autumn of the year 1657 I arrived in London, being brought to that city by Rabbi Moseh HaCoen Mendes in order to support his labors to bring knowledge to the Jews of London. That I did not do so, that I eroded the very foundation of his scholarship and peace—that I stood opposite him whose dearness was my world's greatest solace and allowed him to give his thoughts into my hands under the illusion that I was true—this I here confess. Yet I would choose again my very same sin, though it would mean my compunction should wrack me another lifetime and beyond. And so I die confessed but unrepentant, and if all my thinking be in error and there be wages to pay in some world beyond this one, though they be fierce I shall pay without murmur. Nor do I fault my father nor the rabbi for permitting me acquisition of learning deemed unnatural for the female sex, for they did not foresee the creature I would become, the greed that would grow in me to learn and question and crack the foundations of the world I perceived. Yet though I saw myself straying ever farther from the path laid before me, I cried out then and still: why say woman may not follow her nature if it lead her to think, for must not even the meanest beast follow its nature? And why forbid woman or man from questioning what we are taught, for is not intelligence holy?

The world and I have sinned against each other.

Here I might end my own confession, for though there be other sins upon my conscience, my condemnation is accomplished in this one stroke. Yet a few lines more remain for the writing. For confession is a gift permitted to those with days or hours in which to foresee their own deaths. There are those I loved who were denied it.

The servants have shed shoes and muffle their steps, for they have been ordered not to disturb me. In this hushed house a dread settles on me—I fear it makes my reasoning waver.

I believe in no heaven or hell, nor any world to come, yet I know not whether life be snuffed wholly by death or merely assume some unknown form. It is perhaps vain to hope that some essence of what yet beats within me, though in a torment of pain, might endure past death. Yet I love it. I love the sweet labor of this heart in my chest.

Even the birds are silent today.

I do not believe my soul as I know it will be allowed a single footfall beyond the threshold of death. Yet for the sake of others who did so believe and could not confess, I endeavor now to lay down their burdens here beside my own. My father's spirit I believe was at peace, for he was ever a man whose words and deeds were aligned with what he in his heart felt right and good. My brother, in turn, needs none to confess for him, for he repented unto giving his very life for a sin that was never his own. Dear Isaac. It was never yours. The deed was that of sparks and flame fighting for their own freedom, as do all things. My grief all these years has been that their will to leap and live robbed you of yours. Yet I wish you could know that you did not fail in your dream of saving another by your death. For though I would it were otherwise, your death paved the sole path my strange spirit could walk. I wish only, Isaac, that the one you saved had been more worthy than your sister.

It is my mother, Constantina Velasquez, whose regrets lay heaviest upon her heart. The unease of her spirit visits now and again in my dreams. Sometimes on the verge of sleep I hear her voice, though I've confessed this to none. It calls so simply, only one word: my name.

I write of her now to answer that call, though I know not of any help it be to any who exist today. Yet the unspooling of ink has brought me much comfort always, and often have I written what I would not speak.

I was ever ill-suited for this world and could not bend my nature to it. So, in her own manner, was my mother. Constantina de
Almanza Velasquez had a nature that might have flowered in other
climes, yet she was neither born nor constituted to be a matron of
the Amsterdam synagogue.

The writing, shaky but insistent, proceeded down the remainder of
the page, and filled two more as well. There were places where the ink
seemed darker or the quill tip thicker—here Ester had rested and returned to the text, perhaps an hour later, perhaps on a different day.
Helen's eyes slid down the lines, and with each she felt a lightening, as
though it were she disburdening sentence by sentence. *Her spirit could
not be bent, yet her rage found little purchase* . . . Helen read on, realizing
now and again that she was dragging her heavy finger down the paper,
heedless of the damage it might do. It was all here—Ester's family, her
mother, the pinched morality of Amsterdam's frightened Portuguese
refugees. And one detail—one absurd, audacious detail—Helen had
not at all expected. Rising with difficulty, she made her way to the cabinet and searched out what she'd pulled off her printer only two days
earlier: the final document e-mailed by the Amsterdam archivist. The
Dotar's self-righteous reply to the rabbi's final letter, dated weeks after
his death. The phrase that corresponded, word for word, with one of
Ester's.

Her head listing with fatigue, she closed her eyes and worked out the
dates twice, three times. Ester's year of birth; her mother's; her grandmother's.

A gossamer-thin connection. But if there was one thing she'd no
longer do, it was fight intuition.

Yes. It was indeed all of our history. No people's thread was separate
from any other's, but everyone's fate was woven together in this illuminated, love-stricken world. There could be no standing apart. She'd
known that always, hadn't she?

Long after midnight, she rose. Her legs wavered under her. Had she
eaten today? Patricia had fed her something, she was nearly certain of
it. Near the bottom of a drawer in her bedroom, sifting papers under a
bright light as though she were hunting for evidence at a crime scene,

she at last found the page. She unfolded it, clumsily tearing the brittle paper, and carried it to her kitchen table where she smoothed it atop Ester Velasquez's pages.

She reread the single dense, ruined page of notes. Had her own handwriting ever been this tiny, this precise, this bloodlessly certain of itself? Blue script covered the page: first her name in sharp, angry letters—*Helen Ann Watt.* She remembered how restlessly she'd penned it, planning to show her notes to Dror when he returned to the room where he'd left her to read his precious history book. She'd burned to mock this primary-school exercise he was forcing her into—as though reading his history could ever persuade her to leave him! Then, below this, scattered names of city-states, dates. Here and there, lower down on the page, a question: *Inquisition laid the ground for 19th century?* She saw where her fury had faded—where the history she was reading had caught her and her fury had given way to fascination. She saw where she'd run out of space at the bottom of the page, where she'd filled the back of it, turned the page upside down and written another full page between the lines of each side. Inverted words, observations, exclamations, all swarming up between the enraged logic of her earlier notes. And half of it ruined—blurred where she'd spilled the coffee Dror had brought her and the bright ink had bled freely, mixing lines penned in outrage with those written in growing understanding—a page poised between love and fear.

When she'd finished reading she closed her eyes, and only then became aware of a strange sensation, as though something cold and smooth were wrapping her left arm and leg, numbing them, gently separating them from her senses. A moment later, the feeling passed. But in its wake she at last permitted Dr. Hammond's somber predictions to nest in her mind.

Dread washed her. This time she didn't hide from it. What she'd experienced earlier today on her way to the rare manuscripts room was only the start.

The strange, numbing sensation grew again; then receded. It was different from anything she'd experienced with the Parkinson's—different in fact from anything even Dr. Hammond had warned about, in all his detailing of the protracted decline she must prepare for.

Yet illness had taught her already that the body was bound by no rules but its own.

A sense of imminence took her. Now, she thought. *Now.* For wasn't Ester Velasquez showing her, in thick lines of tremulous ink, that the time had come for Helen to say the things she needed to say—while she still could?

She felt for the paper, and slid it to one side. When she opened her eyes, she was looking at Ester's final page.

Here, at the last of her confession, Ester's hand had wavered more widely.

I have long lived alone in my mind, and would die alone—but my husband, fond man that he is, insists he shall attend my final hour and I cannot deter him. Yet to die alone would be honest. For is not life solitary, and every thinker lonely? The hand pushes on, cramping, laboring in the hope of a friend who might one day receive the ink's imprint. The friend, the dream of the friend, the wish that some welcome for one's spirit might yet exist . . . My hand makes its slow progress across the skin of the paper in candlelight, though my eyes close with weariness, fueled by this eternal hope: the mirrored image of my thoughts etched, if only for a moment, into another's.

I wish the servants would make a noise upon the stair.

Heaviness comes. If death muddies my thinking then death take me now, for I grow weak. This morn I cried tears such as never marred my vision when I had far greater cause to cry. My thoughts blur and I can no longer survey them.

When my husband comes, I shall ask him to douse the light.

It was Alvaro who counseled I write these words to relieve my spirit, and his physick was correct. I am relieved. I have given him my papers to burn, now—all but the last of my treasures. To my shame, I have not yet submitted these for the fire: letters exchanged with souls who feel and think as I. Still I cherish them, and still I steal hours to read and think upon them in my solitude. Yet I shall fortify myself before the end and give these greatest of my treasures into the flames. Those thinkers whose words are found in my prized pages have elsewhere printed their works for the world to see, speak-

ing more decorously than ever I was able; and such words of mine
as may be worth preserving have been sent ere now to others, who
may one day make use of them. It is not for me to determine which
of the seeds I scatter will blossom, nor have I the vanity to think I
ought leave greater mark upon the world that has so marked me. The
world too much hates a freed thought or heart. Let the pages burn,
for such be the fate of the soul, that all our striving be dust, and none
in the bright living world ever know truly what once lived and died
in another heart. And let me dispense with my foolish dream of leaving the tracery of my thought whole, perhaps to be read in an age in
which there is greater kindness.

It is not such an age.

Let the truth be ash.

Yet Helen held it in her two hands.

She set it down. Then, moving gingerly, stepped to her desk for paper.

IN THE MORNING HELEN ROSE, her hand still cramped from the
effort of writing. Standing from her bed, she was greeted by a chorus of
lights that she thought of, without alarm, as brain-lightning. A strange
calm took her as she made her way to the kitchen, and abided with her
even as she reached for her second shoe, and felt a ripping inside her
mind. A sudden, violent tearing of seams. It didn't feel at all like the Parkinson's; in the quiet lucidity that suddenly brimmed in her, it seemed to
her instead that this was something altogether new—something free-
ing—a thunderbolt, a stroke, a mercy. Saving her from the grinding fate
she'd most dreaded, even as it schooled her in disappointment. *It's all
right*, she told it. *I've known for a long time.*

Still wearing the rumpled suit in which Patricia Starling-Haight
and Patricia Smith had dressed her, she carried a slim envelope to the
post office half a block from her flat. The wait was long, and the low-
ceilinged room tilted and slewed about her. She shuffled forward in the
queue, holding to the wall.

The clerk behind the counter was sallow, lightly pimpled, too thin for
his clothing. She handed him the envelope.

He studied it, then held it up before her, pointing to the stamp she'd attached.

"This isn't enough postage to get to Israel," he said.

She smiled thinly. Then, to appease him, she fished her coin purse from her satchel. She opened it and set it on the counter.

He looked affronted. "I'm not going to search about in there for your money."

She waited, swaying slightly at the counter.

He squinted, perplexed—and then, when seconds had passed and still she hadn't spoken, as though he wanted to ask whether she was all right, but couldn't find the words in which to do it. She saw that he needed forgiveness for his failure to inquire after her well-being, and for all the things he'd failed to say in his slim but mounting years. And so, toppling the open purse with the tips of her fingers until it had disgorged a small pile of coins—enough, surely, to purchase postage for a letter that bore no signature and would not reach its destination because it had none—she answered him with a small smile that held the world's mercy.

30

August 12, 1667
22 Av, 5427
Richmond, Surrey

BIRDCALLS. THE HUSH OF THE moving current. The sounds of the river, fresh and expectant.

A bright, bewildering blue.

The large white sheet Alvaro had laid on the grassy bank was dazzling in the sun. She took the final steps of the dirt path toward the bank. Then, hesitating an instant, stepped onto the grass, her shoes slipping on the gentle pitch.

From the water's edge, he looked at her and smiled. His breeches were rolled above the knee.

"If I die of a chill," she said.

"At last," he said. "I knew I'd persuade you."

The grass smelled intoxicating. "You haven't," she warned.

"If you die of a chill," he said, as though he hadn't heard, "I shall publish your writings under my name, and become famous throughout the world for my thoughts, until some king removes my head to prevent it from producing them."

She refused to laugh. "Promise," she said severely. "Say you'll burn them."

Skimming the water's surface with one foot, he sent a splash just shy of her feet. "Shall I teach you to swim, now?"

"Not until"—she began again—but was stilled, unexpectedly, by a thought: how Mary would laugh at the two of them, and tut at the bargain that had bought this life, and laugh again.

"Watch now, Ester!" He stood, aligned his feet on the verge of the bank, and pushed off. His thin form dove arrow-straight into the water.

She watched his body shoot under the brown surface, a strange species not dreamt of in all her days.

He stroked back to her, his arms scattering brilliant droplets.

How, in the exile that ought to have killed him, had he learned this?

Pulling himself from the water, his white shirt clinging so she could see every rib, he squinted up the path—up the hill whence the cherub carver would come, once the servants directed him from the house. A glad anticipation lit his face.

"Promise!" she said weakly.

A bright, bewildering blue.

31

April 13, 2001
London

H E REACHED FOR HIS PHONE, the fourth time today. He dialed Helen's number—he'd learned it by heart since Wednesday—and spoke to her answering machine.

"Helen, it's Aaron again. I swear I'm not stalking you. Just let me know you're all right, will you? I promise I won't come steal the documents, despite being a marauding American." He hesitated. "Listen, this isn't a threat, but if I don't hear from you today I'm going to have to sound the alarm at the university." The silence on the line felt endless. "I promise not to tell Martin how much you've always admired him." While he was weighing how much further to carry the joke, the machine cut him off.

He turned back to the computer screen. The blinking cursor reproached him. Without the new set of Richmond documents in hand, and in the absence of any word from Helen for the second day running, he'd found himself at such a loss that, sometime around noon, he'd made himself open his dissertation. What he'd found there: pedantic analyses; notes for an argument he'd never succeeded in building. He'd read and read—walking circuits around his dissertation as though it were a walled city—unable to find a point of entry.

What was he waiting for? Something had happened to Helen; he needed to act. Yes, logic said she might just have retreated to work on the papers all by her prickly English self. But he didn't believe it. Something was wrong: she wasn't well, she'd fallen, she needed help. Or so it seemed to him—that is, if he could trust his instincts about anything anymore?

His own impotence shocked him. Four days had passed since Marisa's e-mail, and he still hadn't replied. Marisa would assume, correctly, that his silence meant cowardice. She'd sniffed him out from the start: Aaron Levy was half real, half façade . . . and by now it must be clear to her, as it was to Aaron, which half would prevail. This—his deadening failure, his inability to even approach the subject without an obliterating panic rising in his chest—was the measure of the man he would always be.

And now Helen had disappeared, and he couldn't even think what to do. How had he never bothered finding out where she lived?

Slowly he rose and forced himself to change out of his sweatpants —realizing only as he did so that he hadn't left his flat since the day before yesterday. He made it to the door and was blinded by the pollen-laden afternoon. The fact of spring seemed incongruous. But once out in the fresh air, he revived. Shaking off his torpor, he set off for the Tube.

He arrived at the rare manuscripts room only to find it closed. A sign indicated that a bookcase was being installed, and the room would reopen at three-thirty. It was three-fifteen, and he slumped against the glass wall to wait. He hadn't been there two minutes, though, when footsteps sounded on the floor, and he was joined by none other than Brian Wilton—who balked at the sight of Aaron but clearly could think of no plausible excuse to retreat. Wilton read the sign—then, with a polite nod, took up a station near Aaron.

They stood side by side, backs to the glass wall.

"Bloody bookcases," Wilton said.

"Bloody bookcases," Aaron echoed.

Wilton nodded agreement.

They stood.

Wilton's brown hair was thick and wavy; his clothing was rumpled but well-kept; everything about him was affable. Aaron had never disliked Wilton personally the way Helen did, but now it seemed to him that he might be able to muster the emotion. It was unnatural, Aaron thought, for a historian and an Englishman to be so polished. To have such an innocent face. Wilton would be the hands-down winner of the all-England charming historian competition. The all-England bodacious hair competition.

"You haven't seen Helen Watt lately," said Aaron, aware of a faint churlishness in his tone, "have you?"

"No," Wilton said immediately, as though he'd been thinking about Helen too. "Not for a couple of days." Something played on his face. Slowly it dawned on Aaron that it was guilt.

Speaking cautiously, Wilton continued. "I hear she's retiring."

"In word only," Aaron countered—too fast to mask his defensiveness.

Wilton smiled tightly and looked away.

What he wouldn't give right now to tell Wilton about the documents Helen had bought off Bridgette. Or see Wilton's face when Aaron and Helen published *their* article. If, that was, Helen hadn't decided to cut Aaron loose and go it alone. Or if she and the documents hadn't fallen into a rabbit hole. Or if she wasn't in a hospital somewhere in this crowded, lonely city—which he was determined to find out by the end of today.

Aaron looked at his watch. Five minutes to go.

Wilton exhaled, then spoke without looking at Aaron. "I've never forgotten the time I offended her." He shook his glossy head slowly. "It was years ago. I made a rude joke, and I turned around and she was there, and the look she gave me nearly turned me to stone."

At Wilton's admission, Aaron felt his lips curl into a smirk—but as Wilton continued speaking, the feeling of superiority faded and was replaced with a suspicion that, in fact, Aaron might like Wilton more than he liked himself.

"She's the kind of person whose good opinion matters, you know?" Wilton said. "Because it's not easily earned."

Aaron nodded.

"I've never earned it," said Wilton.

Behind the thick glass, Librarian Patricia materialized. A brief rasp of metal and she'd unlocked the door from the inside, and Wilton was off into the room before Aaron could find words for what he wanted to say: I could use a friend like you.

Patricia was staring at him. He realized he was standing in the entry, blocking the door from closing. "Listen," he said to her. "I can't reach Helen. She was going to bring in some documents, maybe you've seen her?"

Before he'd finished speaking, Patricia's expression had thickened into a scowl. She shook her head once, hard. It struck Aaron that she too had been worried—and that she was among those whose worry took the form of anger at the world for its failure to remain safe. "I haven't seen her since Wednesday," Patricia said—and as if his own troubles had given him new ears, Aaron understood that her terseness was love —that all of it was love: the Patricias' world of meticulous conservation and whispering vigilance and endless policing over fucking pencils.

"I'll call her myself," Patricia said. "If she doesn't answer I'll go to her home after the carpenter comes to finish the installation. That's in two hours."

Using the grooved pencil Patricia procured from a pocket, Aaron wrote his mobile number on a white slip of paper from the circulation desk, and accepted the one she gave him.

And then he was free. He couldn't believe how easily Patricia had slipped the responsibility out of his hands and into her own. He wanted to kiss her withered cheek in gratitude.

But a minute later, adrift in the atrium outside the rare manuscripts room, it occurred to him that she'd lifted responsibility from him the way one takes an injured animal out of the hands of a small child.

Was there no point when Aaron Levy would rise to the occasion —no *Thank you, ma'am, but I'll handle this one myself*? Wasn't that part of Aaron's definition of a man . . . or didn't he have one any longer?

The thought made him do something so illogical, only an idiot would call it courage. He made his way out of the building at a clip, across the courtyard, and to the History Department. Yes, he'd do it: announce his failure, fall on his own sword to prove (to whom?) he'd some grain of integrity left. For months he'd imagined rebooting his academic career with the work he'd done with Helen—he'd pictured marching into Darcy's office and informing him that while Shakespeare was no longer a going concern, Aaron had a brighter, shinier dissertation topic. Except now, since Marisa's news, he couldn't credibly argue that he was capable of writing anything. And without Helen's austere judgments echoing in his ear, it appeared he was capable of nothing. Hours at his desk producing no words, until the computer threatened to swallow him whole. Even the new documents now seemed a mirage, Spinoza's signature a fantasy of Aaron's own desperate ego. And here he was, knocking on Darcy's office door—not in the tweed jacket he usually wore to meetings, but in—what? He looked down and saw blue jeans and a blue T-shirt—both rumpled, as Wilton's attire had been, only Wilton's disarray had been fashionable and this was the real thing. As he heard Darcy's footsteps approach the door, he realized he'd worn this T-shirt three days already this week.

Darcy opened the door. "Hello," he said, looking surprised. "Had we scheduled a meeting?"

The mere sight of Darcy gave Aaron comfort: the square, metal-framed glasses, the thinning brown-gray hair, the tall but slightly stooped figure. Darcy had the mildly preoccupied air of a man steeped in the slow labors of history, whose confidence that the details of the rest of life could be entrusted to someone else—presumably a wife hovering just offstage—had largely been borne out.

Darcy still had a hand on the doorknob, and Aaron could see he was ruing the interruption. "Or did you want to schedule something?" he said.

His voice was reasonable, even fatherly, and it steadied Aaron. Still, he found himself unable to answer.

"Well," Darcy said after a moment. "Do come and sit."

Aaron stepped into Darcy's office, but instead of sitting in his usual seat beneath Darcy's towering bookshelves, he stood, his hands on the wooden back of the chair. "I'm having," he said, "a bit of a hard time."

His voice cracked on the final word. He felt himself on the cusp of a fatal error—yet unlike all the other times Aaron Levy had lost control, this time it wasn't his temper that had driven him here, but a sense that he was made of something so brittle the slightest breeze could turn him to ash and it was essential that someone see before it was too late.

Sitting very still at his desk, Darcy offered a cautious smile. "Shakespeare treating you poorly?"

Aaron shook his head. It was a moment before he trusted himself to speak. "I seem to have made a mess of my life."

A lone set of footsteps passed and faded in the hall outside Darcy's office. "How irretrievable?" Darcy said.

He felt feverish; his throat was impossible. "I don't know yet. I might need to take some time off. I think I'd like to write a dissertation with certain materials Helen Watt has found. Only I'm having trouble focusing, because of some personal things, and now . . ." He struggled. "Now

I can't find her," he finished, knowing he wasn't making sense, knowing he sounded like a boy who'd lost his mother in a department store.

"What do you mean, you can't find her?" Darcy spoke sharply.

Aaron recalled, suddenly, that they were friends. "She hasn't answered my calls."

Darcy frowned and glanced at the clock. Then, pocketing his worry for later, he leaned forward. Forearms resting on the desk, hands steepled, he addressed Aaron. "I never advise making sudden changes," he said slowly, "while one's life is"—he gestured with one hand—"in flux." The hand returned to its side of the steeple. He fell silent again, and Aaron saw he was trying to leave Aaron room to recover—backtrack, minimize what he'd said. But Aaron was silent.

"Perhaps," said Darcy—and he looked up at Aaron from beneath a furrowed brow, as though he were struggling to communicate in an utterly foreign language—"you might consult with your rabbi?"

Aaron blinked—did Darcy know Aaron's father was a rabbi? But of course Darcy didn't know—Darcy was simply assuming, as the English did, that a Jew, no matter how secular, would naturally solve his problems through a Jewish solution, rather than see a psychologist like anyone else. Aaron could have been offended—but who was he to be offended at anyone else's blind spots? He nodded—then nearly laughed as he realized, with a start, that it was Friday. And when he said to Darcy, who was looking alarmed, "Yes, I think I will," attending Sabbath services seemed such a logical choice that he hesitated only a moment more . . . then rose, offered his thanks, and, to Darcy's clear relief, made for the door.

The platform was already packed when he arrived. Some problem on the line had stalled the early evening commute. He waited amid a crush of Londoners of all shades and shapes—business-suited, turbaned, dyed, and pierced—packed together in restless silence.

It took nearly a half-hour for service to resume; once it had, six crammed trains passed before Aaron succeeded in boarding one. As his train started, he held to a pole, closed his eyes. For a moment, he imagined that Helen was somewhere on this car. She would make her way to him, size him up. Demand to know what he was doing outside the rare manuscripts room, when there was so much yet to be done.

The train lurched and rocked and reached its terrible speed—the tunnel blurring through the greasy window, each station a bright gift given, only to be wrested away. In the flickering light the strangers around Aaron were sculpted and beautiful, and in each face he read the reflection of all his own questions: Was Helen still alive? Was he, himself? Was there a world left, outside this tunnel, any longer? It was with unexpected relief that he gave himself over, hurtling amid strangers —palms bracing walls and poles and one another, the crowd rocking against his shoulders and back and arms—a hundred hands, living and dead.

When at last he stepped out onto Bayswater Road, he saw that it was evening, and that the afternoon's thick clouds had made good on their promise. The streets were wet, the light fading; by now, surely a Reform synagogue would have concluded its services. Still, he made for the address he'd written on his notepad.

In all his time in London, Aaron had never so much as tried to visit the synagogue, though of course his parents had recommended it; but he'd had no interest in English Reform Judaism, an even stuffier variant of what he'd left behind at home. And now that Aaron was looking for the synagogue, he couldn't find it. Three times he walked past the large yellow awning before he realized this was it. There was no sign labeling it as a synagogue, and in fact the burly security guards had at first appeared to be bouncers; he'd assumed the building was a club of some sort. It was the well-dressed middle-aged Jews exiting in twos and threes that made him stop and squint at the small sign inside the glass doors. Hebrew lettering. Three hundred and fifty years after Ester's time, he thought numbly, and London's Jews were still being careful not to stand out—though now the threat was not the garrote or the pyre, but bombs; and the grist wasn't heresy, but Israel.

The security guards eyed Aaron, then nodded him in. Inside, a jowly man regarded him. "You've missed the service," he said.

Aaron forced a smile. "May I at least look around?" he said, simply because it didn't seem right to let the man dismiss him so readily.

A shrug: it was all the same to the man what Aaron did.

Aaron walked through the foyer and deeper into the building, pausing outside the wooden doors of the sanctuary to read a small plaque. *This congregation was established in 1840, drawing its original membership*

from two sources: the Great Synagogue of London, an Ashkenazic congrega-
tion established in 1690 at Dukes Place; and the Bevis Marks synagogue,
which was itself built in 1701 to house the growing congregation of Spanish
and Portuguese Jews who had worshiped for much of the seventeenth century
on Creechurch Lane.

Inside the doors, the sanctuary was large and surprisingly ornate. Colorful designs capped the ceiling; an organ was set into the back wall; a dome overshadowed the bima, where a few people were gathered— stragglers from the evening's service, Aaron presumed. One of the side walls of the platform was a screen, behind which the synagogue choir surely stood unseen during the service: voices emanating from nowhere in anesthetized four-part harmony. He'd heard about English Reform congregations—Jewish services as High Victorian undertaking. In addition to a beadle, this congregation would have three top-hat-wearing wardens—he could see, at the front side of the sanctuary, the wooden box in which they must have been stationed during the service that had just ended, standing and sitting at the right moments in the prayers, the congregation following their lead.

Aaron walked halfway down an aisle, then settled into a seat on the end of a row: he'd sit just a moment, then leave. What better place for a rabbi's son—one, he admitted, with *father issues*—to contemplate fatherhood? But one of the people at the bima—a young woman who wore a green headband and long skirt and looked like a university student—had turned and was beckoning him. "Don't be shy," she called.

She was too cheerful and informally dressed to fit with Aaron's notion of English Reform services. In fact, most of those standing with her were young, and wore loose flowing skirts, casual slacks, even jeans. Some of them looked American.

"Just here to see the sanctuary," he called.

"Join us for a bit, anyway," the girl insisted with a summoning wave. "We're an alternate service, we meet monthly. You'll like it, we're a bit more fun than the regular services here."

Unable to think of an excuse not to, he stood. Shunning the upholstered pews, the group had arranged folding chairs in a circle near the bima, and as he settled into one near the girl with the headband, he saw that another member of the group—a bearded young man—was pulling a drum out of a cloth bag. A middle-aged man had a violin, and a woman with wild curly hair soon produced both a guitar and a flute. She—the woman with the guitar and flute—seemed to be the leader of this service. But so did the drummer, and so did the violinist, and so did the girl in the headband and two freckled teenage boys. With no fanfare beyond a round of smiles, they sang "Shalom Aleichem," then a psalm in Hebrew, set to a tune Aaron vaguely recognized—the flute sounding the melody simply under the ornate dome. The whole service, it soon became clear, was to be sung. No sermon would be delivered in sermon-voice; no freighted pauses would be sculpted before each next solemn declaration. In the seats around him, some people swayed or sat with their eyes shut; some tapped rhythm with their hands on their metal seats. Aaron nearly laughed aloud. No wonder the wary fellow in the vestibule hadn't thought this service worth mentioning—among the more old-school American Reform congregations this sort of service was still viewed askance; doubtless it went against the very DNA of the English Reform. The people on either side of Aaron seemed determined to wind as many harmonies around each melody as it could carry —or perhaps the harmonies were the main show and the melody was just along for the ride, but either way the sound was beautiful. Aaron himself had never believed in God. But whether or not these bright-faced people did, it was clear they believed in something they liked to sing about. Maybe they believed in singing. To Aaron, closing his eyes for a long moment amid the bed of voices, it seemed worth believing in.

Abruptly, the music stopped. Announcements. The woman with the curly hair gave the particulars of an upcoming dialogue about the Israeli-Palestinian situation. "Wherever you stand on Israel today," the woman was saying, "whether you're right or left or confused, we want to come together to grapple with these dilemmas." Nods around the circle; someone spoke up to clarify the location of the event. Then the singing resumed. And it struck Aaron: history, the god he'd worshiped all his adult life, was the wrong god.

He'd always pitied those ensnared in the time periods he studied —people captured in resin, their fates sealed by their inability to see what was coming. The greatest curse, he'd thought, was to be stuck in one's own time—and the greatest power was to see beyond its horizons. Studying history had given him the illusion of observing safely from outside the trap. Only that's what the world *was:* a trap. The circumstances you were born to, the situations you found yourself in — to dodge that fray was impossible. And what you did within it was your life.

Hadn't Helen tried to tell him so?

The singing ended. He watched the service-goers pack up their instruments under the absurdly ornamented dome and gather in clusters to share wine and challah. Neither synagogue nor prayer would ever be his thing. But it seemed to him nonetheless that the god these people had just prayed to was the present: a world in which they felt compelled to act, stepping into the history flowing right in front of their feet; making choices in the knowledge that they might fail.

Outside the synagogue, he dialed Librarian Patricia.

WHEN HE REACHED THE STOOP on Cranley Place, Patricia was fumbling with the key. She turned at his step, and let out a sigh of relief. "Thank you," she said.

Inside the tidy, shadowed flat, a single softly glowing lamp.

Patricia called Helen's name once, and then again.

Silence.

As they made their way through the rooms, Aaron touched each object he passed: the modest sofa and armchair, the low coffee table with its neat stack of journals, the wooden frame of Helen's bedroom door. And he touched Patricia's elbow to steady her as she swayed at the foot of the bed, in which Helen lay beneath her covers as though asleep.

When it was time to speak, he said to Patricia, "What do we need to do for her?"

IT WAS LATE WHEN HE left Helen's flat. He'd followed Patricia's directives, obtained phone numbers, unlocked the door for the man from the funeral home. And while Patricia made calls he'd lingered over Helen: slight as a child under her plain white coverlet, her pale face eased into an expression of girlish peace. He'd pulled over a chair and sat by her bed, and with both hands had grasped and held, through the covers, the curve of her right foot, as though the touch might at last tell her what he wanted her to know: *you're not alone.*

He'd lingered even after the man from the funeral home had taken over—but finally there was nothing left to do. Nowhere to go, it seemed, but home. It occurred to him that at an appropriate moment—perhaps tomorrow—he ought to tell Patricia Starling-Haight that Helen might have left valuable papers with Patricia Smith in the conservation lab.

In truth, with Helen gone Aaron found the existence of those last Richmond letters implausible. So desperately had Helen traded for that last folio that its contents now seemed synonymous with her life, and just as ephemeral.

But wherever the letters were, they now belonged to some unknown relatives of Helen's. At the right time, Aaron would need to reach out to those relatives—or, better, have Darcy do it. With luck, Darcy might dissuade them from selling to a private collector who would restrict scholarly access. Regardless, Aaron knew better than to hope he'd ever get his hands on those letters again, except perhaps as a peripheral member of Wilton's group. Maybe not even that. A postgraduate undone by his own dissertation could hardly expect to be trusted with such significant documents. He wasn't sure he'd hire himself for the job.

As he zipped his jacket beside Helen's front door, though, Patricia called his name. "This was on her kitchen table," she said.

Into his hands she placed a thick folder. Taped to it, slightly askew, was a small white square of paper that said, in Helen's shaky handwriting, *For Aaron Levy.*

Seeing he'd no words with which to respond, Patricia opened the door gently and let him out into the night.

He did not open the folder then, or on the train, or on the walk home, but held it to his chest until he'd reached his doorstep. He opened it there, his hands unsteady. Inside, a single sheet of lined paper was laid atop a folio he recognized instantly.

He read.

Dear Mr. Levy,

 If you're holding these pages, it's because I'm no longer able to.

 I'm not a sentimental person—a statement you'll surely find unsurprising. Yet you should know that I did wish very much to work with you on these documents. Your receipt of this file, however, means that that could not happen. Nonetheless, I've made my decision about the fate of the documents in my absence.

Here is your dissertation.

These papers are yours now. I lied when I said the last were damaged. It seemed to me important to read them alone. When you arrive at the next-to-final page of Ester's confession, please set it beside the letter from the Amsterdam Dotar. I've little doubt, Aaron, that you will recognize the repeated words. When you read them, think of our argument, please, concerning to whom this story belonged. You were very angry, and perhaps I returned your feelings in equal measure.

You were correct, Aaron, about who owns Ester's history. But so was I, though I never dreamt of this possibility. Perhaps you'll think the possibility remote. Certainly it is. But I feel I've earned the right, at this hour, to assert without proof that I believe it.

From the first, you recognized what a museum I'd made of my life. It would seem I found that insupportable. My apologies for my poor behavior.

Do what's right with these papers. I trust you.

Helen

He entered his apartment. He turned on the lights, unsteadily prepared tea. He read Helen's letter thrice more before opening the folio and beginning.

There you are, he said to Ester.

There you are.

Yet though I saw myself straying ever farther from the path laid before me, I cried out then and still: why say woman may not follow her nature if it lead her to think, for must not even the meanest beast follow its nature? And why forbid woman or man from questioning what we are taught, for is not intelligence holy?

The world and I have sinned against each other.

He read each section slowly, and reread before moving on. He took notes, reflexively, on the single paper within reach—a grocery list he'd

begun halfheartedly the night before, and abandoned after only three
items. Below *cereal* and *coffee* and *bread* he filled the page with notes
—transcribing phrases and even whole sentences, as though he didn't
trust these pages not to dissolve once he'd read them. He wrote blindly,
barely lifting his eyes from Ester's words.

Reaching the second-to-final page, he set his pen down, lifted Ester's thick paper, and held it in his hands.

Constantina de Almanza Velasquez had a nature that might have
flowered in other climes, yet she was neither born nor constituted to
be a matron of the Amsterdam synagogue. She escaped the terrors of
the Inquisition and came as a young bride to live amid Amsterdam's
Portuguese Jews, who feared nothing so much as outspokenness, or
any infraction that might visit upon them once more the troubles
they'd fled in Portugal, a vale of blood and sorrow. My mother, who
could not countenance being that thing she was to the priests of Lisbon, spent her days defying the elders of the Amsterdam community,
her husband among them. Her spirit could not be bent, yet her rage
found little purchase—and whilst I shall not enumerate her quar-
rels against her life, I witnessed much, and more did she confess to
me. I chose never to reveal to my brother that one of her rebellions,
unknown to any, led to his birth.

My mother's nature was jailed in Amsterdam, and all her attempts at escape failed to free her. Had I the mercy of the world at
my command, I would command it forgive her.

Though born in Lisbon in the house of her own mother and the
man she called father, my mother did confide in me that she herself
was conceived here in this England, in the city of London. Her true
father, she did aver, was not her mother's husband, nor any other
Jew of Lisbon, but one Englishman of fine letters—a man bound
in wedlock to another. My mother believed, or in her confusion and
spite wished to believe, that the Englishman's heart later misgave
him and he spurned the woman he had loved and the child she bore.
My mother averred that her own mother was a beauty to tempt away
a man's better angel, corrupting his saint to be a very devil, and she
swore she herself would do the same when provoked, for men were

faithless ever. The tale she told was mudded by time and drink and grievance. Yet despite all her fury, I heard in my mother's words a different truth: that my grandmother and her beloved feared the wrath and reprisal of a world that forbade them from joining hands. That they bore this fate with dignity merely added to my mother's rage. When my mother was but ten years of age, her own true father died without spurning all else to reunite with his beloved. This sin my mother never pardoned. For their love, my mother believed, was so great and capable of mending the broken world that its loss sundered all and could never be forgiven.

I know not whether to credit the drunken words of a spirit tormented by its own loneliness, yet my mother's ragged tale seared in me the knowledge that the power of desire is sufficient to shake the roots of the world. I have recalled this ever, though love has proven not to be my own fate.

I will not indulge the gentle lie of claiming I have not grieved its loss. A woman such as I is a rocky cliff against which a man tests himself before retreating to safer pasture. I cannot fault any such man as takes what ease the world offers him. Nor shall I blame those who disdain the life I choose, and think it misbegotten. Yet this life I have conceived and have sworn to nourish. The choice is mine, and I have borne its burdens.

He read to the end, through Ester's repeated avowals of her intent to burn her papers, the writing growing increasingly shaky.

Let the truth be ash.

He sat for a moment, Ester's final page framed between his hands. Then he lifted it. Beneath it were two sheets of crisp modern paper. The first bore a half page of sharp black ink—the issue, Aaron realized, of the toner cartridge he'd installed in Helen's printer. An e-mail from Dina Jacobowicz, in Amsterdam.

Dear Professor Watt,
      Here is a reply addressed to Rabbi HaCoen Mendes by the

Amsterdam Dotar. It was sent to London, but was returned unde-
livered to the Dotar, as neither the recipient nor any members of his
household were any longer to be found at the London address.

I hope this proves helpful. Best of luck.

Aaron turned the page.

> August 11, 1665
> 30 Av, 5425
> Amsterdam

To the Honored Rabbi HaCoen Mendes,

It is with regret for the lateness of this reply that we pen it. It
was some time before we ventured to open your missive, as there
are those who say that any communication from London may bear
the pestilence. We write in hope that this reply finds you recovered
through a miracle of G-d, and that your welcome in the world to
come has been delayed, that this world's pupils might yet reap the
fruits of your wisdom.

It is to our further regret that we inform you we are not able to
provide a dowry for the Velasquez girl. This matter was discussed in
the Mahamad with vehemence, for many recall the girl's father and
wish to honor his name. Yet to our great sorrow, the girl's mother
carried a wildness stamped deeply in the memory of this kahal. We
wish you to understand this matter, distressing though it may be.
The woman Constantina Velasquez, the mother of Ester, refused
to circumcise her son, fighting with spirit and body until the child
was wrested from her. Upon her comprehension that she could not
prevent the community from fulfilling this duty, she wrote to this
Mahamad a missive full of such spite as had never been heard in the
walls of a synagogue, calling us cowards and mice, and informing us
of her power to tempt the better angel of the most righteous among
us, and corrupt his soul to be a devil — a witchcraft she claimed to
learn from her own mother. She boasted, further, of her own mother's adultery with an Englishman she claimed illumined all England with his merest words — she claimed that her own blood was
admixed with such as made our community seem a laughingstock.

It was only in respect for the husband that the Mahamad issued no rebuke to her outrages, choosing instead merely to declare her madness a residue of the distresses of childbirth. Some members of this council who disputed that decision remain among our assembly, even these years later. It is therefore our opinion now that the community cannot support the marriage of a daughter of Israel who bears the stain of such a mother. Nor shall it be said that there is no consequence to insulting the authority of the Mahamad in Amsterdam.

On behalf of the Dotar, with prayers for your recovery and hearts eager for the coming redemption,

Efraim Toledano

Aaron sat for a long while, his face to the ceiling, trying to ford the sensation flooding him. The outrageous irony. History, coming back to him now like a torchlight procession—bearing a trick, a joke, a gift.

There was nothing more important right now than thinking clearly —and his mind, for the first time in what felt like months, was clear. As deliberately as he could, he worked his way through all he knew of Ester's story, and her mother's. Then, without warning, he found himself thinking, for a long and motionless time, about Marisa.

And then Helen's voice returned to him, snapping with conviction as it had that day they'd fought in her airless office. *This story, whatever it proves to be, belongs to all of us.*

No one would believe it. A fresh bit of potential evidence in one of historians' favorite head-scratchers, provided through a Portuguese refugee's aggrieved, possibly self-aggrandizing tale?

Slowly he reread Ester's lines. *A beauty to tempt away a man's better angel, corrupting his saint to be a very devil.* Then, the final lines of the letter from the Dotar. *Her power to tempt the better angel of the most righteous among us, and corrupt his soul to be a devil.* Even in the Portuguese, the reference was plain: a phrasing coined by William Shakespeare, presumably to describe the woman he loved against his better judgment. Sonnet 144.

Of course he could dismiss it as a coincidence—Ester's memory of her mother's story so closely echoing the Dotar's account of the same woman's screed. So what if both used the same peculiar, signature wording? So what if Constantina Velasquez had repeatedly insisted on expressing her fury through these specific phrases? Perhaps she was an avid reader of English verse. Perhaps she was delusional and had fabricated her mother's story. Perhaps Aaron was somehow misunderstanding the Portuguese.

And yes, so what that Constantina Velasquez, based on the records Aaron had long ago gathered for Helen, would have been ten years old in 1616?

He could publish a rich dissertation — *ten* rich dissertations — using the rest of the letters in this folio, without chasing after coincidences. He could bury this last coda to Ester's tale . . . let it, as Ester said, be ash.

But the thumping of his heart said he wouldn't. Once he'd feared his own clumsy weight could damage the fragile documents arrayed beneath the stair. Now he was their steward, protector of the life they contained.

And as such, he would before all else give Ester Velasquez her due. Ester's life and her letters required no embellishment, nor extra revelation of connections to another of history's marquee names, to make them important. It would take months, if not years, to track down any surviving letters she'd sent to her correspondents . . . and simply corroborating Ester's story in itself — verifying the origins of the letter from Spinoza, countering inevitable accusations of fraud — would be a great labor.

Only after Ester had had her day and he'd published her annotated correspondence would Aaron explore this final possibility. He'd need to be careful; Brian Wilton's haste to publish a false report of a Florentine crisis — a misstep for which Wilton would surely pay a price for years to come — was a cautionary tale. And amid the eternal flurry of cherished certainties and crackpot theories surrounding Shakespeare studies, would anyone be willing to entertain the notion that Ester's grandmother, a Portuguese Jewess, might have been Shakespeare's conjectural Dark Lady — his *woman color'd ill* with eyes *raven black*?

Aaron himself didn't know whether to entertain it.

But Helen had thought it possible. And one thing the past months had taught Aaron was that he understood less about secrets, or love, or regret, than he once thought he did.

He imagined an atlas of seventeenth-century history, its pages inked with a tangle of dangers—and all Ester's labors forming only the faintest watermark. But the mark was visible to those who knew to look. And whether or not any kinship through blood existed with Shakespeare—or for that matter with any other thinker of the time—one existed in spirit: Ester Velasquez was a link in the ongoing conversation that wove through Shakespeare's revolutionary humanism and on through Spinoza's wrenching, liberating depersonalization—and on beyond them, to all that roiled and consoled spirits even now. All that roiled and consoled Aaron Levy, as he sat, this very minute, at his kitchen table.

His mind was a lit corridor, each step before him clear.

In the morning he'd bring the documents to Darcy—Darcy, who could be counted on to graciously overlook Aaron's temporary breakdown. It was true that Wilton might be an ideal scholarly partner in this area, and perhaps Aaron would work with Wilton in the near future. But Darcy was the one who would help Aaron ensure that Helen's name would appear as first author on an initial paper that laid out Ester's story for the world to evaluate. Aaron would write that paper before anything else—*Helen's* paper, his name trailing hers on the byline.

And when he'd finished all his work on the documents, assuming patrimony laws hadn't taken them out of his hands before then, he'd sell them to the university. He wouldn't profiteer, but neither would he be a fool about the price. He wanted Marisa and the baby to be comfortable . . . and the salary of a historian, whether he spent his career in England or in Israel, wasn't lordly.

Marisa.

He didn't have her phone number. How could he not have the phone number of the woman he'd be connected to for life, whether she wanted him or not? He'd worry about airline tickets later. For now he stood, turned his back on the documents arrayed on his small kitchen table, clicked on his desk lamp, and opened his laptop, his fingers moving quickly on the keys.

Dear Marisa,

There's no point trying to find a good place to begin. What I have to say is complicated but really very simple, and it's true whether or not you decide you want me.

32

P ULLING HIMSELF FROM THE WATER, his white shirt clinging so she could see every rib, he squinted up the path.

"Promise!" she said. But the sunshine had turned delicious
on her face.

A high, clear birdcall sounded from a nearby tree.

Alvaro wrung his blouse at his narrow waist and watched her. "Richard says it's a linnet that makes that call."

The river flowed thickly before her, and she shielded her eyes to
watch it. Upriver, a few men fished off boats, their voices coming thin
across the water. Nearer to Ester, three boys were towing a small raft
against the current, laboring on the path on the river's far side. In a
brightly painted skiff, traveling more swiftly and in the opposite direction, a portly boatman rowed a bored-looking couple toward the city.
The young man stared unseeing at the riverbank, but the young woman,
fair-haired and expensively dressed with a trail of small black patches
just visible on her throat and bosom, leaned in the direction of the city
as though this might encourage the boat to travel faster—past this relentless greenery to London's enclosing walls, its parlors that cradled
and amplified laughter, its rebuilt theaters and newly widened streets.

The more Ester looked, the less tame the river appeared: the calling
birds unperturbed by the receding skiff; the high, ragged grasses along
the banks, bristling with hidden life. The wildness of things came back
to her.

Turning to Alvaro, she let him see she was afraid.

On the grassy hill above them, Rivka was laying blinding white linen to dry on the grass. They squinted up at her, and for a moment she paused to look down at them, shaking her head absently as though at two children. Then they made their way under a tangle of tree branches to the small inlet where, Alvaro said, she'd be shaded and safe from the current.

In the shelter of the tree, her back to him, she disrobed to her shift. When she turned, her arms crossed on her chest, shivering and regretful already, he was in the water, swimming a brisk loop across the current and calling back instructions. Yet, strange though it was, just then she did not comprehend his words, but only the confident voice in which he spoke them. Her husband: a propertied man, keeper of the ninety-nine-year lease inherited from his father that would outlast their lifetimes. Standing on the shore, she stared. Something was lodged in her throat, aching to come loose.

She stepped in, ginger, the muddy rocks shifting under her tender feet. One step; a second; she stood and dipped her hand into the edge of the current. Thick, cold water streamed between her fingers, gently at first — then more strongly as she stepped deeper, the water now forcing her palm open and her fingers wide as the current found its way between them.

How bitterly she'd been brought to understand — through fire and fever, through deaths and her own failure to die — that life fought for its own continuance.

But she realized now that she'd never thought to ask why.

This, she saw, was the reason. Water forcing her palm open, the current kissing her fingers. This. This shock of pleasure.

33

April 11, 2001

My dearest Dror,

How many years have passed since you stood that way, holding your broken arm in the base's dark kitchen? I never told you how you appeared to me that night. For all your severity, you were like a gazelle caught on that cement floor. How breathtaking it was, to see you uncertain.

And when you danced. Your steps brushing the ground in the middle of that desert, the cast on your arm. I fell in love with you then, too. But in my blindness, I saw only what frightened me. I never understood how truly a wounded heart could love.

Let there be one place where I exist, unsundered. This page.

When I heard you'd died, I couldn't understand it. I'd thought you invincible, it's true. But I'd also been waiting, although I surely knew better, for a day when some debt— How to say it? How did I conceive of it in those times, how would I have put words to what I hardly knew I felt?

I was waiting for a day when some debt of devastation and sorrow and vigilance would be paid, and my own petty fear would be spent, and we'd return to each other.

It took a long time for me to understand that you were dead.

But now that it's my turn, Dror, I see it clearly. Your car, the car you were driving for whatever mission they sent you on—whatever mission you undertook with a heavy heart, yet with the certainty (were you still certain, Dror? I hope so, I hope that you were)—the certainty that you were keeping them all safe, your loved ones, past and present and future. (I know you loved your wife and family. I know you did. I'd expect no less of you.) And I see clearly the car following yours. In my mind, it's black and featureless. And then the acceleration, and the impact that's no accident, your car bucking off the road and into the air. Your face turns grave as the tires leave the road. I see your car soar, I see how it spins. I see you, Dror, wrenched in the air. A calamity of sound, then. A heartbeat. An explosion. And then, a grieving quiet. I grieve when I hear it. The hollow rush of flames, sparks touching the heavy green treetops. There is smoke, Dror, impossible smoke, and heat.

Yet somehow you walk out of it, unscathed. A whole and beautiful man.

There is a hole where my heart once was. In its place, your history.

34

WATER FORCING HER PALM OPEN, the current kissing her fingers. And swimming to the place where she stood waist-deep, her husband: master of the great house commanding the hill. She couldn't keep from laughing in his face. He laughed with her — then, with a soft tug, pulled her off balance. The current tipped her forward and her husband led her, and the surface of the water was velvet and foam, and her legs and feet were absurd and she had no notion what to do with them — until the water lifted her limbs and made them glad and foolish. She settled her eyes on his, brown and sun-flecked as the water.

"Here," he said, guiding her wrists to his slim, sturdy shoulders. "Rest your arms here."

The characters and events of *The Weight of Ink* are entirely imagined; the novel's seventeenth-century backdrop, however, is real. The Sabbatean movement mentioned in the novel had a long-lasting impact on a large swath of the seventeenth-century Jewish community. The philosophers mentioned in this book are also real, as are the central figures from the Jewish community of Amsterdam; and while Rabbi Moseh HaCoen Mendes is imagined, his counsel to Rabbi Menasseh ben Israel about the latter's journey to England and its aftermath are based in the documented facts of Menasseh ben Israel's life.

The play Ester and Mary attend is invented; however, I based some of its details on Sir George Etherege's 1664 *The Comical Revenge: or, Love in a Tub,* and the song the players sing (*If she be not as kind as fair . . .*) is from that play. Ester's fictitious warnings to Mary about love likewise contain an allusion to Mary Astell's 1666 remarks about marriage. Several Shakespeare quotes also appear in the text (*The death of each day's life . . .* from *Macbeth; My love is as a fever . . .* from Sonnet 147; *What's gone and what's past help . . .* from *The Winter's Tale*). The line of poetry that Helen recalls in the conservation lab (*These fragments I have shored against my ruins*) is from T. S. Eliot's *The Waste Land.*

For the sake of clarity I chose to simplify certain references; for example, the area now known as Richmond upon Thames was called Petersham in the seventeenth century. Rather than refer to the same area by two names, I used the modern name throughout. And my depiction of the program through which Helen and other foreigners volunteer in Israel is based on programs that were developed several years after Helen would have been in Israel.

A list of the works I found helpful while researching this book could fill pages. I'd like to give particular mention, though, to Rebecca Newberger Goldstein's *Betraying Spinoza: The Renegade Jew Who Gave Us Modernity;* Steven Nadler's *Spinoza: A Life* and *Spinoza's Heresy;* David S. Katz's *The Jews in the History of England, 1485–1850;* Miriam Bodian's *Hebrews of the Portuguese Nation: Conversos and Community in Early Modern Amsterdam;* Julia R. Lieberman's *Sephardi Family Life in the Early Modern Diaspora;* Jonathan I. Israel's *Radical Enlightenment: Philosophy and the Making of Modernity, 1650–1750;* Kristin Waters's *Women & Men Political Theorists: Enlightened Conversations;* and Liza Picard's *Restoration London,* which I returned to again and again for the details of Ester's surroundings.

A master cherub carver worked in Richmond/Petersham in the seventeenth century; his work can still be seen in grand houses of the era, though his name has been lost to history.

ACKNOWLEDGMENTS

I'm deeply grateful to the historians, conservators, archivists, and others I consulted in the process of researching this novel. Among them: Amy Armstrong, Gloria Ascher, Zachary Baker, Rachel Brody, David De-Graaf, Frank Garcia, Jane Gerber, Dominic Green, Rachel Greenblatt, Joshua Jacobson, Paul Jankowski, Camille Kotton, David Liss, Sharon Musher, Nell Painter, Jonathan Schneer, Kathrin Seidl-Gomez, Stephanie Shirilan, Skye Shirley, Malcolm Singer, and Simon Wartnaby. My gratitude also to the staff and volunteers at the Northeast Document Conservation Center, the Jewish Historical Society of England, the Richmond upon Thames Local Studies Collection, and English Heritage, for their assistance and their patience.

I'm indebted to the Massachusetts Cultural Council, which offered crucial support in the early stages of this project, and to the Koret Foundation for the happy months I spent as writer-in-residence at Stanford University; my thanks especially to Steven Zipperstein for his vision, for his friendship, and for permission to sit in on history classes of my choosing. The MacDowell Colony and the Corporation of Yaddo provided me with precious time and space—opportunities I couldn't have made use of without the loving support of Ashley Fuller and Gabrielle Asgarian. Laura Kolbe's diligent assistance was essential as I conducted early research; and the Brandeis Women's Studies Research Center and the Hadassah–Brandeis Institute provided encouragement, community, and all-important library access. I'm indebted to Shulamit Reinharz, to Debby Olins, and to the wonderful Hilda Poulson for her invaluable and skilled assistance.

I'm grateful beyond measure for the thoughtful input of some of the scholars and artists whose books were most helpful in my research. For conversations that helped me situate this story on the map of Shake-spearean studies and attendant controversies, I'm indebted to Tina Packer and to James Shapiro. David S. Katz did me the prodigious favor of reading the manuscript for historical accuracy, as did Julia Lieber-man; I could not have found better guides to the seventeenth-century communities depicted in this novel. Steven Nadler, whose own works about Spinoza were essential guides, was generous with his time and expertise. My thanks to Kristin Waters not only for her own writings about political theorists, but for the humor and grace with which she helped me find my way into seventeenth-century philosophy. And I cannot sufficiently thank Rebecca Newberger Goldstein for her illu-minating writings on Spinoza; for her care in helping me ensure that the philosophical component of this story was accurate; and for dem-onstrating just how capaciously a philosopher engages with the world.

I could not have been more fortunate than to have Martha Collins, Tony Eprile, and Kim Garcia as readers and friends. During the years I worked on this book, many were generous with their time and help in ways large and small. I'm especially grateful to Howie Axelrod, Laurel Chiten, Sue Fendrick, Kerry Folkman, Laurie Foos, Rochelle Fried-man, Yaron and Tali Galai, Sarah Kilgallon, Lori Leif, Melanie Leitner, Sheryl Levy, Michael Lowenthal, Adrian Matejka, Lisa Mayer, Kiran Milunsky, Brian Morton, Lena Parvex, Heidi Schwartz, Susan Silver-man, Sharon Stampfer, Douglas Stone, Ellen Wittlin, and Heather Zacker. For their humor, advice, and excellent company I thank Emily Franklin, Heidi Pitlor, Joanna Rakoff, and Jessica Shattuck. I'm grate-ful beyond what I can express here to Tova Mirvis for her thoughtful input on the manuscript, and for her extraordinary talent for intelligent friendship. And Carol Gilligan made a home for this book on every level; her insight and her ability to hear fathoms below the surface made all the difference, as did the hospitality she and Jim Gilligan provided.

Sarah Burnes, aided by Logan Garrison and the rest of the crew at Gernert Company, were everything a writer could hope for. Thank you, Sarah, for your faith in this book. And Lauren Wein was the dream editor for this novel; enormous thanks to her, to Pilar Garcia-Brown for all her good-humored help, and to the rest of the wonderful team at Houghton Mifflin Harcourt.

A special mention to Adam Rivkin, for whose keen eye and quiet sense of humor I'm grateful. And to Anna and Larry Kadish, Lilly Singer, Joan Sherman, to my siblings Debbie and Jan and Sam and Ali, and all the nephews and the whole glorious extended tangle of family near and far, my abundant thanks for your warmth and support during the years I spent working on this book.

Finally, my gratitude to Talia and Jacob, whose love and enthusiasm are everything.

1. Describing the impact of his blindness, the rabbi says to Ester, "I came to understand how much of the world was now banned from me — for my hands would never again turn the pages of a book, nor be stained with the sweet, grave weight of ink, a thing I had loved since first memory" (page 196).

   For the rabbi and for Ester, ink means many things — among them freedom, community, power, and danger. What does the written word mean to you? Is it as powerful today, amid all our forms of media, as it was to the rabbi and to Ester?

2. The novel opens with a quote from Shakespeare's Sonnet 71: "Nay, if you read this line, remember not / The hand that writ it."

   Which characters in the novel choose to give anonymously, or without receiving any credit?

   Would you be willing to have your most meaningful accomplishments remain anonymous or even be attributed to others? In today's interconnected world, with privacy so hard to achieve, is there anything you would write or say if you knew your words would be anonymous?

3. In order to write, Ester betrays the rabbi's trust. Yet in her final confession Ester says, "Yet I would choose again my very same sin, though it would mean my compunction should wrack me another lifetime and beyond" (page 529).

   Is Ester's betrayal of the rabbi's trust forgivable? When freedom of thought and loyalty argue against each other, which should a person choose?

4. John, Manuel, and Alvaro offer Ester very different sorts of love. What does each offer her, and what sacrifice does each require?

How might you answer this question for the love between Dror and Helen?

5. Both Helen and Ester fear love. How do they wrestle with this fear? Could they have made choices other than the ones they made?

6. In what ways does Aaron mature over the course of the book?

7. Do the motivations of Ester, Helen, and Aaron change as the story progresses?

8. Ester's life is shaped by wrenching choices between the life of the mind and the life of the body. Can a woman today freely choose to combine love, motherhood, and the life of the mind, without unacceptable sacrifices?

9. What story do you imagine Dror would tell about his experience with Helen?

10. Ester grows up in a community of Portuguese Inquisition refugees who are fiercely focused on ensuring their safety in the "New Jerusalem" of Amsterdam; they place great importance on reviving Jewish learning and they give their harshest punishment to Spinoza for his heretical pronouncements. When Helen goes to Israel, she encounters Holocaust survivors struggling with the legacy of their losses and the need to establish safety in their new home.

    In what ways are these communities similar, and in what ways are they different?

11. What clues does the author include as to the identity of the true grandfather of the female scribe? Did Lizabeta (Constantina's mother) make the right choice in refusing to play on his pity and beg him to keep her and her daughter in London?

12. After months of chafing at the Patricias' strict stewardship of the rare manuscript room, Aaron has this epiphany: "And as if his own troubles had given him new ears, Aaron understood that her terseness was love — that all of it was love: the Patricias' world of meticulous conservation and whispering vigilance and endless policing over fucking pencils" (page 541).

    What sorts of love are on display in unexpected ways in *The Weight of Ink*? In what unexpected ways does love show itself in your own world?

How did the idea for The Weight of Ink *come about?*

In *A Room of One's Own,* Virginia Woolf posed this question: if William Shakespeare had had an equally talented sister, what would her fate have been?

Woolf's answer was succinct: *She died young—alas, she never wrote a word.*

Woolf was right, of course—that was the likeliest fate for a woman of that era with a capacious mind. The realities of women's lives made artistic and intellectual expression virtually impossible.

Yet I couldn't help asking, *What if . . . ?* What would it have taken for a woman like that not to die without writing a word?

For one thing, she'd have to be a genius at breaking rules. She'd have to flout conventions of womanly behavior, resign herself to being labeled unnatural—and perhaps lie, deceive, disguise her identity.

I became fascinated by the thought of how far a woman might go for freedom of spirit and mind, and at what cost. So I started writing . . . and writing . . . and Ester Velasquez surprised me at every step. Given the steep odds against a woman of that time making her voice heard, and given the subterfuge required, maybe it's inevitable that a story about a woman like Ester would unspool like a mystery.

What drew you to writing a historical novel?

As a child, I thought that an accent was something a person acquired with age. Growing up listening to my grandparents (Polish Holocaust survivors who escaped Europe via Japan, then Mexico, before reaching the United States), I just assumed that when I was older I'd develop some softened consonants and torqued vowels of my own.

While I soon realized that reaching middle age didn't make people turn Polish, I've never lost my fascination with the way history shapes how we experience the world. In my upbringing, history wasn't an abstract fact in a textbook. It was something personal and urgent: the earring lost in the snow that meant an official couldn't be bribed; the empty coffins my family slept in when a funeral home was the only shelter they could find; the border guards who might or might not be drunk enough on New Year's Eve to let a handful of people slip past in the snowy dark.

It makes intuitive sense to me that the past sometimes shows up when we least expect it, upending our assumptions and maybe even our lives. That kind of unexpected appearance is the starting point for *The Weight of Ink*.

How did you research the book?

I didn't know what I was getting into when I undertook the research for this book—and that's a good thing! But I also loved doing it.

I knew early on what sort of story I wanted to tell, but I needed to find the right historical setting—so during a stint as a writer-in-residence at Stanford University, I requested permission to sit in on history classes . . . which is how I first learned about the Portuguese Inquisition refugees in Amsterdam and London. Though I started out knowing nothing about those communities, they fascinated me. I read and read. I listened to music of the era, researched seventeenth-century architecture and clothing and food and sewage systems. I learned how people did their laundry. I visited London; consulted with experts in seventeenth-century Jewish history and in Judeo-Portuguese and Ladino dialects; learned how to write with a quill pen. I visited conservation laboratories, where I fell in love with the texture of seventeenth-century paper and the quirks of seventeenth-century ink—specifically, iron gall ink. Certain forms of iron gall ink dissolve paper fiber over centuries, so that the letters and words eventually burn their way through the page on which they're written. The results of iron gall ink damage can be hauntingly beautiful: sheets of seventeenth-century paper like lattices, with holes in the shape of the words an unknown hand once inked onto the page.

Since I don't have any background in philosophy, I had to work very hard to learn enough about Spinoza and metaphysics to write the book. Early in the writing process, I spent plenty of late nights struggling to get a toehold in Enlightenment philosophy, trying to make my way through a pile of books on the topic and fighting the worry that the best I'd be able to do was lip-synch seventeenth-century philosophy. I told my agent in despair that I felt like the Milli Vanilli of metaphysics. But finally, after a lot of reading and re-reading, books and articles that had seemed impenetrable started to make sense, and I was able to begin to understand where Ester's own thoughts and questions might fit into—and sometimes depart from—the philosophical conversation taking place around her.

I worked very hard to get the novel's factual details right. I was writing about a little-known history, and it felt important to represent it correctly. At times that meant going to somewhat ridiculous lengths. Here's one my kids still tease me about: at one point I turned to the collections of Harvard's Widener Library for a copy of *Consolação às Tribulações de Israel,* a book beloved by Portuguese Inquisition refugees. I was writing a deathbed scene in which a character reads aloud from *Consolação,* and I wanted to have the character speak a few words of the text aloud. All I needed, really, was a single sentence-fragment, but I wanted to quote it in the original sixteenth-century Portuguese. So I made an appointment to view the manuscript.

I don't read Portuguese, though I know enough French that I can often guess the general topic of a Portuguese text. So I sat in the rare books room at Widener with this beautiful old book, and I photographed sections of the sixteenth-century text that seemed promising, and then I emailed the images to a scholar of Portuguese-Jewish history who had agreed to translate for me.

She very gently informed me that I'd photographed the table of contents.

Back to Widener again, until I got it right.

Was it hard to figure out what kind of language to use for a seventeenth-century story?

That was a real challenge. There's a reason most people don't read Samuel Pepys's diary for fun, though it's completely salacious stuff; that seventeenth-century sentence structure is a fair bit of work for the modern reader. Yet when I started the book, I assumed that I needed to write in absolutely accurate seventeenth-century prose—which meant adopting that convoluted sentence structure. But that just didn't feel right for my story. So I struggled ... until an acquaintance referred me to an interview by David Mitchell.

Mitchell has this wonderful notion that the author of a historical novel needs to create a hybrid language—he refers to this language as *Bygonese*. The language has to sound old—and it certainly can't be anachronistic—but it also has to be modern enough that the contemporary reader feels at ease in it.

Reading that interview encouraged me to experiment. After a lot of trial and error, I settled on combining a somewhat modern sentence structure with strictly period-accurate vocabulary. My rule was that in the seventeenth-century sections of my book, I could use only words that were in circulation during that time. If Merriam-Webster kept track of this sort of thing, I'm certain they'd find that I hold the world record for using a little-known feature of their dictionary entries—the date of a word's "first known use." When writing the seventeenth-century sections of the novel, I made a practice of looking up any word I wasn't certain was old enough ... and if the word's first known use wasn't early enough, I didn't let myself use it. That meant, for example, that I couldn't refer to Ester as Mary's *chaperone* (a word that didn't exist until the eighteenth century) but rather as her *companion* or *duenna*. My hope was that somehow all of these small language choices would add up—and that by being vigilant about using seventeenth-century vocabulary within a more modern sentence structure, I'd end up with a kind of language that carried the depth of age while still welcoming the modern reader.

The storyline of the novel has unexpected twists and turns. Did you plan them before you started writing?

Not at all. The way I see it, I can't possibly know a story's plot until I figure out who my characters are and what pressures they're under. I never want to use my characters as marionettes, manipulating them through a predetermined plot—I think stories like that can feel forced. Instead I try to put in the work to get to know my characters. That's a process that can only happen one sentence at a time, one scene at a time. If a character is in a room, I ask myself: *what is she noticing? What does it feel like to be in her shoes? What does this situation remind her of . . . what hopes or fears does it invoke . . . how is all of that influencing her right now—and how will it color the words she speaks next, when someone asks her an unexpected question?* Once I've spent enough time with my characters, I'm able to begin to guess how they might respond to their circumstances. And that's when the novel's storyline begins to emerge. Which is to say: this novel was an act of improvisation. I got to know Ester and Helen and Aaron and the others . . . and the more I understood them, the more I understood what they might do next. That meant that I was on the edge of my seat for much of the time, and I wrote the first draft with very little idea where I was heading. Each of the major characters surprised me at one point or another—and some of the more minor characters, like Rivka, took on unexpected emotional weight and led the story in directions I never anticipated. For me, that's the fun of it. If I don't let my characters surprise me, I'm probably doing this wrong.